REIGN

OF

BLOOD AND POISON

THE AERMIAN FUEDS
5 & 6

FROST KAY

REIGN OF BLOOD AND POISON

Cover by Covers by Combs
Interior formatting by We Got You Covered Book Design
Copy Editing by Madeline Dyer
Proofreading by Holmes Edits

ALSO BY FROST KAY

TWISTED KINGDOMS
FAIRYTALE RETELLING

The Hunt

The Rook

The Heir

The Beast

DRAGON ISLE WARS
FANTASY ROMANCE

Court of Dragons

DOMINION OF ASH
POST APOCALYPTIC FANTASY ROMANCE

The Stain

The Tainted

The Exiled

The Fallout

The Chosen

To the man who made me believe in true love.
You are the treasure I never expected to find.

THANK YOU FOR SUPPORTING
AND INSPIRING ME.

THE
Five Kingdoms

Rooi

NAGALI

Janem

the Mort Walls

CASPERNE OCEAN

the Mort Walls

AERMIA

SCYTHIA

the Dregs   Salvren

Sanee

the Blessed Beach

THALASSIAN SEA

PART ONE

THE SPY'S MASK

PR⊙L⊙GUE

>•⟨◯◯⟩•◄————

MONSTERS.

Hell.

The myths and legends she'd once been told in the dead of night as a prank by friends weren't supposed to be real. It was all fun and games, a thrill. But what those innocents didn't understand was there were things in life, real things that rivaled any scary story. Hell and demons of their own making.

Sage wished what had befallen those around her was just a story, a fable to dismiss from her mind. But life was a cruel, fickle, and beautiful being that had no rhyme or reason. One never knew when whims would bless or curse you. Just the smallest detail could tip the scale.

From the beginning, life seemed to rage against Sage, a constant force that wore her down to her very bones. There were many paths for the rebel princess to travel, and they all led to one outcome:

Blood.

War.

ONE

THE WARLORD

ZANE SMILED AS HE WATCHED the Aermian army scurry about like ants as they built their camps. They had thought they were so clever. But they were just children really, playing at being warriors. They had no idea what the future held.

Ignorant.

They were ignorant of his spies. Ignorant that their greatest enemy walked among them. A leren among babes.

He stilled and glanced over his shoulder as awareness tingled over his skin. His sixth sense. She was near. He narrowed his eyes at the approaching royal party. The crown prince led the group, but Zane didn't care. He only had eyes for one person: the goddess in armor and war paint.

"Sage," he whispered, his tone thick with covetousness. His consort stole his breath away, her beauty so bright it felt like it burned him where he stood. A spark of pride lit inside his chest at the Tia paint that adorned her face in savage strokes that he couldn't help but find lovely. He never imagined he'd see her in his people's war paint. Possession and something darker wriggled in his chest.

Ours, the voices in his head whispered.

Fierce. Bold. Deadly. A dark queen he couldn't wait to get his hands on.

Zane kept his head bowed as the group passed him. His fingers brushed her cloak for one second before he receded into the bustling camp, just another

Aermian soldier following his orders. He could steal her away now, but that would be too easy.

His consort had challenged him, and Zane loved a good fight. No, he wouldn't take her this day. He'd wait for her to surrender, and it would be all the sweeter.

Zane adjusted his cloak and grinned.

Soon enough, she'd bow to him. All he needed was a little patience. His consort would grace him with her presence soon enough.

Then, he'd destroy her world.

TWO⊙

SAGE

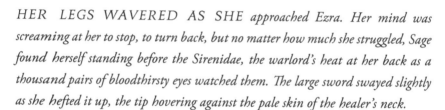

HER LEGS WAVERED AS SHE *approached Ezra. Her mind was screaming at her to stop, to turn back, but no matter how much she struggled, Sage found herself standing before the Sirenidae, the warlord's heat at her back as a thousand pairs of bloodthirsty eyes watched them. The large sword swayed slightly as she hefted it up, the tip hovering against the pale skin of the healer's neck.*

Ezra smiled at her, his mouth twisting in a way that seemed like he was laughing at her, before he began to weep at her feet.

"I'm sorry," she choked out, hating that her fingers wouldn't release the blade. "This is not how it's supposed to be."

His cries cut off as he looked up, his eyes changing from magenta to black. "Murderer," he hissed.

Sage jerked as if he'd slapped her. "I don't want to do this. I can't do this," she pleaded.

"You have to," the warlord whispered in her ear, his warm breath tickling her neck.

The hair on her arms rose, and her stomach rolled as she cringed away from the body leaning over her from behind. "Leave me alone!"

"If I can't escape you, how is it fair that you escape me?"

She stumbled a step closer to Ezra, her blade slicing dangerously close to his neck. Tears burned the back of her eyes, but she wouldn't let them fall. How could she cry for herself when she was the one committing the crime?

"It's okay, Sage," Ezra whispered, his voice strangely hollow. He leaned closer to the blade, the sword biting into the delicate skin, just below his hammering pulse. "I knew what you were when I saw you."

She cried out as he impaled himself on her sword. "No, no, no, no," she screamed, releasing the sword and falling to her knees. Ezra's mouth pursed as his blood pooled and spilled over his lips.

"He's not the only monster," Ezra whispered as he fell to the ground, his white hair turning red as it splayed around him.

Sage held up her shaking hands and stared at the blood that coated her palms. She was a killer.

A hand cupped her chin and forced her to stare at the warlord.

He smiled, flashing sharp fangs as he brushed a bloodstained finger along her bottom lip. "You're perfect for me."

"I'm nothing to you."

He tsked and knelt so they were at the same eye level. "On the contrary. Like calls to like." He jerked his chin to the right. "Look at the ruin you've caused."

Sage turned and screamed as bodies upon bodies lay in heaps around her.

She jerked awake and sat up, her heart racing. Her nightgown clung to her body, soaked with sweat. Her own breaths were heavy in her ears as she tried to orientate herself. A lantern hung from the ceiling of her sprawling tent, giving off just enough light for her to see Tehl's still form next to her.

Sage placed a hand over her pounding heart and tried to calm it down. *You're not there. You're safe.* It had been two weeks since she'd arrived at the camp, and each night, her nightmares had escalated.

Throwing back the blankets, she rolled out of the makeshift bed, quickly donned her leather breeches and boots, and tucked her nightgown into her pants.

"Are you all right?" Tehl asked, his voice rough with sleep.

Sage peered over her shoulder at her husband who stared at her with concern. "I'm fine."

"You were talking in your sleep. I don't think you're fine at all. Plus, Sam says when women use the word 'fine,' it means the exact opposite."

She turned fully and crawled across their pallets to peck him on the lips. "Well, your brother doesn't usually give the best advice," she joked. She cursed internally at how, even to her own ears, her tone was off.

Tehl cupped her left cheek with his right hand and smoothed his thumb along her cheekbone. "I'm worried for you, love."

"I'll be all right." She had to be. There wasn't another choice.

"Is there anything I can do?"

"Hold me when I get back?"

He stretched and kissed her softly. "I'll be waiting."

Sage reached up and squeezed his hand before crawling out of the bed and moving through the tent in the direction of the door. She retrieved her discarded cloak from the simple wooden chair in the corner and threw it on to ward off the night's chill.

Tehl's voice caused her to pause as she lifted the tent flap.

"Be safe."

"Always."

Guilt assaulted her as she stepped into the crisp night air. Puffs of white steam escaped from her mouth. Damn. It was getting colder every night, and the weather in the plains was more frigid than anything she'd ever experienced in her life.

Sage stomped her feet a few times and lifted the cloak's hood to protect her neck from the chilly air, nodding at the two guards stationed outside their tent. Garreth whispered something softly to the other guard and stepped away from them, moving to Sage's side—her silent sentinel.

Without one word, they began their walk through the camp, and her protection detail melted from the shadows and fanned out to circle her. Fires burned low, softly crackling—the only sound except for the occasional snore and the rustle of her cloak in the breeze.

"Rough night?" Garreth asked, his voice no louder than a whisper.

Sage nodded, her chest tight. She couldn't get Ezra's hate-filled face out of her mind. Reaching the edge of the camp, she acknowledged the guards on the perimeter patrol with a tip of her chin and continued her walk. By now, the men were used to her unusual nightly routine.

They paced around the enormous camp until they reached their destination. A huge rock sat at the forefront of the camp, an old relic of the Mort Wall that was never used. She clambered up the side and plopped down. Garreth followed suit, only pausing to make some sort of signal to her protection detail.

At one time, she would have begrudged the extra men, but now she appreciated their protection and Garreth's discretion. She understood their necessity. Sometimes one had to give up a little freedom to stay safe. Plus, she rarely spotted the men that trailed her everywhere she went.

Seemingly satisfied, he sat beside her and loosely clasped his fingers between his legs.

A black shadow solidified below the rock and blinked reflective golden eyes. Sage smiled at Nali. The leren had made friends with the men easily. At first, they'd been wary of her, but after they'd been introduced to the fiilee, the maneater was considered the lesser of evils.

Nali chuffed and then slunk into the meadow, disappearing like a ghost.

"Still unnerves me," her guard muttered.

"Mistress of the night," Sage said.

"What I wouldn't give to have stalking skills like that."

A smile touched her lips. The man already did. "Your skills are nothing to snub your nose at. If I didn't know any better, I would say you're akin to Nali."

Garreth snorted. "What gave it away? Our temperament?"

She laughed, the sound surprising her, but, almost immediately, she sobered as she stared at the far-away lights of the Scythian camp. The fires burned brightly just beyond the Mort Wall, casting ghoulish shadows into the night.

He was there.

A shiver worked down her spine. He'd be watching her as surely as she was watching him.

"Do you want to talk about it?"

No, she didn't, but when she opened her mouth to say just that, something else came out instead. "I murdered someone."

The silence hung between them. She continued to stare blankly at the Scythian camp, waiting for Garreth's judgement.

"War is a nasty thing. We're all capable of things we never thought possible."

True, but not applicable to her situation. "He was my friend." Her whispered confession tore her heart.

"May I speak plainly?"

"Always," she answered.

"I have known you for some time now and spent numerous hours in your company. I'd like to say I know a bit about you. From my time spent with you, I know two facts: you love as hard as you fight, and you have more honor than a thousand men. I'm sure you blame yourself for your friend's death, but that doesn't make it true." A pause. "Nightmares aren't truth. They are all of our fears and insecurities twisted into something no one should suffer."

Sage blinked. "Astute." He wasn't wrong. "They're getting worse."

"Why do you think that is?"

"Because he's haunting me."

"There's no such thing. It's in the mind."

"Mine is broken," she blurted.

"Whose isn't?" Garreth shrugged. "We all have regrets and demons that won't leave us alone. It's what we do to get past them that shows what kind of person we are."

"Again, very wise. How did you get so smart?"

His face creased into an expression of despair and regret. "Trial and error." He inhaled deeply, then pulled his sword from his scabbard and held it out to her. Sage's brows knitted in confusion.

"What's this?" she asked, not taking the blade.

"I must atone for my sins."

She shook her head. "I'm not a confessor."

Garreth shifted onto his knees and lay the blade across both his palms, holding it out to her once again, his gaze glued to the rock beneath his knees. "I've done something horrible, and I can't continue on." He lifted his eyes and met her stare. "The guilt is crushing me. Every day I see you fight and struggle, I blame myself."

Sage whistled softly and stood, looking down upon Garreth. Nali launched herself onto the boulder and crouched near her side, looking for the threat.

"What have you done?" Sage asked.

"I betrayed you."

She pulled her gaze from her guard and scanned the area around them. They were on the edge of the camp, and warriors surrounded them. She wasn't alone, so it couldn't necessarily be an ambush. "Speak your piece before I set Nali on you, Garreth. You're scaring me, and she doesn't like it."

Nali snarled in agreement.

"Did you know I had a daughter?"

"I did not."

Garreth hung his head, the picture of dejection. "I was married young, and my wife became pregnant almost immediately. We hadn't been married a year when my wee one was born. But as my daughter took her first breath, my wife breathed her last."

"I'm so sorry." She couldn't imagine the pain he must have suffered.

He nodded but continued. "I raised her the best I could. She was a little wild, but I loved her." Pride colored his tone. "A year ago, she disappeared."

Chills erupted along Sage's arms. She knew how this story ended. "Scythia."

"That's what we thought. The spymaster sent spies into Scythia to find any information about my child, but nothing came back. She was just *gone*." He finally glanced up, tears in his eyes. "I never gave up hope, and one day, I received a message that she was alive."

Sage's heart stopped.

Garreth's expression morphed into one of pure hatred. "A man held her for ransom. I offered him money, my service, anything that he desired, if only he would release my little one. But he wanted none of those things."

"What did he want?"

"He wanted a way to access the tunnels."

Eight words. Eight words explained something she'd wondered about so often when in Scythia. How had Rhys known where to find her? She knew there had to be a traitor, but she had never guessed it was Garreth. Emotion after emotion slammed into her—betrayal, hurt, anger, hate, sorrow—but she kept silent, as did the disloyal guard.

"What happened to the child?" Sage bit out, finally able to speak without screaming.

A shudder worked through him. "I found her body in a shanty near the fishing quarter. From what I could discern, she'd been badly abused."

Garreth's voice broke on a sob.

Her heart clenched. She couldn't imagine finding a child in such a state, let alone your *own* one.

"I don't deserve to live." He held the sword up higher. "My life is to be forfeit for my wrongdoing."

Sage carefully took the sword, and he hung his head, almost like he expected her to execute him on the spot. The moment he spoke his story, she knew what she was going to do, but there was one thing Sage needed to know. She placed the tip of the blade underneath his chin and pressed upward so he looked her in the eye.

"You betrayed me?"

"I did."

"And you make no excuses?"

"No. I knew the penalty when I made my choice."

"Do you regret your actions?"

"I regret hurting you when the Crown and you have been so good to me."

She nodded and cocked her head. Even though his revelation pierced her to her inner core, she knew Rhys would have used someone else if Garreth hadn't agreed. "Rhys would have found a way in no matter what. It wasn't your fault I was taken."

"I had a part in it. I'm not blameless."

"True, but you're not to be held accountable for everything that has befallen me since that moment. The warlord and his monsters are to blame." She sucked in an icy breath as the wind whipped her cloak around her body. "And I know what I've done for my friends would pale in comparison to what I would do for a child—my child. You erred badly, but I don't blame you for trying to protect your child, and, for that, you won't die." Sage lowered her sword.

Garreth shook his head. "I deserve death."

She shrugged. "All of us make mistakes." A wobbly smile touched her lips. "I'm a murderer. Surely, I deserve death as well?"

"Don't forgive so lightly. Treason is not something to be swept under the rug."

Sage scowled at her guard and friend. He'd hurt her, but she could at least understand the motive behind his actions. "Stop trying to goad me into killing you. I can't imagine the pain you must suffer because of what happened to your daughter, but I'm not going to allow Rhys to take another good person from this earth."

"I'm not good."

"No one is wholly good. But one bad decision shouldn't ruin a lifetime of good decisions." She stared him down. "Will you ever betray me again?"

"Never," he breathed.

"Swear yourself to me, and we shall stay as we were."

"I give my life in service to you."

"Good enough."

Sage placed the sword on the stone and hugged Garreth.

He stiffened. "How can you even stand the sight of me?"

She squeezed him tighter. "Because I understand grief and guilt."

His arms tentatively wrapped around her as he hugged her back. "Thank you. You'll make a wonderful queen."

She pulled back and met his watery gaze. "Don't thank me just yet. You still have to tell the crown prince."

He nodded and re-sheathed his sword into his scabbard. "Now?"

Sage shook her head and gestured for him to sit with her. Nali wedged herself between the two and laid her head on her paws, big golden eyes closing. Sage stroked the feline along her spine and peered at the meadow.

"We'll let him rest a bit. First, tell me about your daughter."

THREE

DOR

DORCUS WAS GOING TO BE late, and that was the last thing she needed.

She rushed down the rough, stone hallway and joined the other stragglers rushing toward their respective jobs. Their faces were masks of strain that surely mirrored her own. Her pulse picked up as she turned right and entered the main cavern of the Pit. Even though she'd lived in the Pit her whole life, it still managed to take her breath away with its beauty and simultaneously terrify her. The giant, hive-shaped cavern soared above her and plunged below. Wide, sloping trails curved around its edges in endless circles, only illuminated by the soft lantern light.

Her eyes sought the top of the cavern where one lone shaft of sunlight pierced the domed ceiling, the light harsh and bright. She squinted as her eyes began to water. Every day, she stared at that one little bit of sunlight. What would it be like to feel it on her skin? To live in a world of night and day, not just one of eternal darkness and slavery?

Dor stumbled and cursed as she scraped her left toe on the black, porous stone beneath her feet. She placed a hand against the wall and lifted her foot to check the wound. Just a scratch. Good. She couldn't afford to catch an infection.

An older woman hustled by her and glanced over her stooped shoulder to frown at Dor.

"You best be hurrying up, or you're going to be late, little miss. I heard the warriors are in a mood today."

A shiver ran down Dor's spine as she scurried forward. She glanced to her right, eyeing the edge of the walkway. The last time the warriors were in a bad mood, they'd shoved a worker over the edge. Dor swallowed thickly and moved farther to the left. Even though her mother and father had taught her how to climb as a wee one, the immense drop still frightened her. She couldn't imagine a worse death.

Dor burst into a sprint as she neared her assignment and ignored the pain as she forced her burning legs to move faster. Her back gave a twinge that caused her to gasp, but she didn't slow. She couldn't afford a beating today. Her lashings from the week prior were finally scabbing over and healing.

A bell rang.

"Damn it," she muttered. She'd have to take the shortcut to make it. Her assignment was still another rotation down.

She moved to the brink and sat, hanging her legs over the edge, before rolling onto her belly and shimmying backward. Her stomach dropped just as her toes found the first crevice. Making sure she was secure, Dor began to climb down. A sigh of relief escaped her as her feet finally reached the next landing, but there wasn't time to dawdle. She darted into a rough stone corridor, sweat dampening her brow. Just a little bit farther.

As she swung around a corner, her foot slipped in a puddle of water and her arms pinwheeled. She barely managed not to fall. Dor gagged as something squished between her toes. She huffed out a small breath, her lungs aching as she ran. Mercy, she hated the slime that liked to grow on the damp stone. The texture made her skin crawl. It was in times like this that she wished she had a nice pair of leather shoes. But that was a fanciful idea. Shoes were dangerous in the Pit. If someone didn't kill you for them, then they'd be the end of you anyway. Dor had managed to escape too many life-threatening situations by climbing the stone walls to safety. No shoes were as good as her toes.

Dor darted into the mine and rushed to the tools, snatching up a pickaxe. Spinning on her heel, she almost stumbled into an older woman who scowled at her with narrowed brown eyes.

"Sorry," Dor mumbled and raced to her spot.

Harsh, lofty voices echoed in the space around her as the warriors commanded that they start their work. Her breath came in gasps, and her heart pounded as she heaved her ax up and began her task, adrenaline running through her veins.

"That was close," her best friend muttered from Dor's left.

Dor glanced at Ada and smiled. "Nothing like a rejuvenating jaunt in the morning."

Ada rolled her eyes as she worked, her dirty arms flexing as she swung the ax. "You take too many chances. One of these days, your luck is going to run out."

Dor rolled her shoulder to dislodge the itchy feeling creeping up her back. "I wouldn't call the beating I received last week *lucky*," she said lightly.

Ada paused in her work and glanced up from underneath her lashes, her expression unreadable. "That's not what I meant," she said softly, her moss-green eyes honest. "I don't want to see you hurt again." She touched her heart. "It pains me when you have a punishment, and with the way they've been acting lately..."

Dor's eyes darted to the warriors who scrutinized the miners. Their body language screamed aggression. She nodded. The warriors *had* been more agitated of late.

"I'll be more careful."

Ada gave her a weak smile and returned to work. The two fell into a comfortable silence as they mined. Dor's muscles tensed as the warriors passed them. A warrior's gaze lingered on Dor for longer than necessary, causing the hair at the nape of her neck to rise, spreading a prickling sensation across her body. She released a breath through her teeth as they moved on, thankful they hadn't demanded her to stop and provide them with entertainment.

Dor glanced at her friend who astutely focused on her work, although Dor could tell Ada was tracking the movements of the warriors as they finished their rounds and passed by once again. The stiffness in her friend's shoulders melted away as the warriors rounded the corner and disappeared from sight.

Ada did have a reason to be on alert. Even beneath the dirt and grime, she was a beautiful girl. Her ragged dress and dirt couldn't conceal it. Dor glared at the rock and struck hard with the ax. Her mother spoke of how beauty was revered up on the surface, but in the Pit, it was a curse. Beauty drew attention. Attention that no one wanted.

Attention meant death.

Fatigue weighed down on Dor. Their short break at the middle of the day had come and gone, and her back screamed, but she continued to swing her pickaxe even though she was sure blisters were forming on her hands and sweat had clearly soaked everything she wore. Her upper lip curled. That was something she'd come to loathe about the damp pit. It made it impossible to keep the calluses she tried to build up each day. No matter how many days she worked, her hands stayed soft and formed blisters.

"Move faster," an angry voice demanded.

"I'm sorry," a little voice replied.

Dor peeked over her shoulder toward the sound of a tiny, placating voice. A guard hovered over a small boy and pointed toward the cavern wall. Her heart sank as the little boy, who couldn't have been more than eight, hefted up a large pickaxe and swung it, his thin arms shaking. She winced as he lost his balance and fell to his knees. The pickaxe was too big for the boy. She wasn't sure how he'd been swinging it all day.

The warrior stepped closer, his expression promising something terrible. "I *said* pick up your ax and work."

She willed the little boy to get up. "You can do this," she murmured under her breath.

Ada reached out and clutched Dor's arm, her small, dirt-streaked face holding fear for the boy.

The boy dragged himself from the ground, knees bleeding, and tried to pick up his ax. Tears trekked down his face as he barely managed to lift the tool from the floor. He attempted to swing the ax but lost his balance again and ended up back where he started. On his knees before the warrior.

Dor's stomach dropped as the boy stayed on the ground. He didn't cower or beg for mercy. He knew what was coming next. He was the picture of defeat. The warrior yanked the whip from his belt and reached for the boy.

Before she knew what she was doing, Dor tore away from Ada's grasp, dropped her pickaxe, and placed herself between the boy and the warrior.

"Get out of the way," the warrior snarled.

Heart in her throat, she forced herself to answer in a soft, mild way she hoped would calm him, and held up her hands in supplication. "My lord, he's tired and the ax is too big for him. He also hasn't had any food today. If you give him a moment, I'm sure he can finish his shift since it is almost over." She inhaled. "Or I can help him finish it after I complete my assignment."

She trapped a scream inside her mouth as he grabbed her by the throat and roughly dragged her forward.

"You think he should be rewarded for his laziness?"

"No, my lord," she said, her words wheezing out of her as she clawed at his hand. "I think he's worked very diligently today, and it would cost you nothing to show the poor child some mercy as a reward for working so hard."

The guard glared into her face. "You presume to tell me what I should do?"

"I presume nothing," she whispered.

"You presume much," he bit out, spittle spraying her nose and cheeks. "You'll be punished for your insolence once I'm through with the boy."

She closed her eyes so the warrior wouldn't see the hate she felt for the wretched creature holding her. That's what he was: a creature, a beast with no humanity left.

Dor forced back her revulsion and hatred, wrangling her temper. She couldn't lash out. If she did, she wouldn't be able to help the boy. Having been a recipient of lashings for many years now, she knew the boy wouldn't survive what the warrior planned. They were often careless with male children, because they were easier to come by than females.

Dor's mouth dried as she forced her eyes open to stare evenly at the warrior, her decision made. "I'll take his punishment."

He sneered. "You will be receiving a punishment of your own for being insolent."

She nodded, even as a trickle of fear slithered down her spine. "I know, but I'll take his as well."

The other warrior approached, taking in the scene with a smile. "What do we have here?"

"A bit of fun," the warrior holding her said, his expression melting into one of delight. "Michelle, you're going to be able to try out your new whip."

Dor kept her expression blank, letting none of her fear show. The warriors were deadly when they smelled even a trace of fear. Dor sucked in a deep breath as the first warrior released her. He rubbed his hands together in glee, and her stomach rolled.

"Come along," he commanded as he moved toward the whipping post.

She spun and helped the little boy to his feet. Dor handed him to the nearest slave, not even registering the person's face as she whispered to the boy, "Go find your mama."

The boy melted into the cavern's swarm of people amid the darkness.

"Come!"

Dor bit back her snarl and forced her legs to walk toward the whipping post. She glared at the metal ring set high in the stone wall. Why they called it a whipping post, she had no idea. The warriors smirked at her, which caused her to straighten her spine and lift her chin, despite her fear.

She didn't tremble when they tied wide, leather bands around her wrists, nor when they yanked her arms high above her head, causing her to lift onto the tips of her abused toes. Dor pulled in a deep breath and glanced in Ada's direction. Her friend's pale face had lost what little color it had possessed and now looked positively green beneath the layer of grime. Their eyes met, and Ada dipped her chin once in acknowledgment; Dor wasn't alone.

Turning to face the wall, Dor lowered her chin, biting her roughly woven dress and twisting her hands so she could hold on to the leather straps securing her wrists. She inhaled deeply and focused on the stone in front of her as they ripped open the back panel of her dress, exposing the skin of her back to the cool, wet air.

The first lash always surprised her. Her body tensed and jerked as pain radiated from her spine. Even though she expected the pain, it was always worse than she remembered. When the second lash struck, her teeth snapped together, and she pulled in a deep breath through her nose. Tears pricked her eyes. The pain never got easier. After receiving so many punishments, she would have thought it would get easier, but it never did. It was always like the first time.

Tears began to fall down her face, and whimpers slipped from her lips as the warrior continued to lash her, splitting open old wounds and scars on her back. Liquid ran down the back of her legs and pooled on the ground beneath her. Her body sagged as the punishment continued, the warriors laughing. The leather straps bit harshly into her wrists, but she didn't feel them. All she could feel was the fire trying to burn her alive.

Spots dotted her vision, and she smiled as darkness came to claim her. A large paw sank into her hair and yanked back. Her eyes flew open as the guard peered down into her face and licked his lips.

Bile burned her throat.

"Thank you for the pleasure of letting me beat you today. I've always wanted to do that. I had an itch I needed to scratch," he said, his hot, rancid breath wafting across her face. He pressed closer. "I have another itch I'd also like to scratch," he drawled.

Despite the immense pain, the threat of what he was implying had her forcing her legs to stand underneath her. She shifted toward him with a snarl on her face.

"Try it," she whispered, soft and deadly. Many a man had tried it before, but they never survived the encounter.

He stared at her, his smirk faltering briefly before he sneered and yanked her head back to the point she thought he might snap her neck.

"You're not worth it," he spat. "Too disgusting and grimy." A malicious smile. "I don't want used goods anyhow." He released her head and then slapped a hand against her back.

Dor screamed and swung forward into the stone wall. The pain was too much. Darkness blanketed her as the warrior snapped at someone next to her.

"Don't let her down until everyone is finished. Then, she completes her task and the boy's."

FOUR

DOR

———⟶∘⟨◯⟩∘⟵———

"DOR."

Dorcus moaned and tried to hold on to the warm darkness that caressed her senses and washed out the world around her.

"Dorcus, you need to wake up."

No. She didn't want to deal with the pain. Something sharp stung her cheek.

"You need to wake up now!"

Dor moaned but forced her eyelids open, water leaking from their corners as she squinted at her best friend. "Why?" she croaked.

Ada pressed closer and scanned Dor's face in concern. "How's your head?"

"Better than my back."

"That's good. Your skull took a bashing."

"My head?" Dor whispered, trying to keep the pain out of her voice. Ada was her closest friend, but growing up in the Pit had taught her many things, one of those being that you should never show weakness. "What's wrong with my head?"

"Many things." Ada quirked a half-hearted smile. "Don't you remember?"

She shook her head, triggering dizziness that caused the room to spin. The last thing Dor recalled was pain. Damned, incessant pain.

Ada slipped in front of her and reached up to untie Dor's hands from above

19

her head.

"The guard slammed you into the wall before he left. You hit your head pretty hard," her friend reiterated.

"I didn't feel a thing. I'm pretty hard-headed."

"That you are. Prepare yourself."

Ada released the rope and caught Dor underneath her arms to avoid touching her back. It was a small mercy, but it didn't stop the pain from ravaging Dor's back. The movement alone agitated her wounds something fierce.

"Devil, take me," Dor growled as the floor seemed to buck and roll beneath her feet.

"Watch your mouth," Ada hissed, dragging Dor farther into the cave. "Words like that have power. You never know who'll appear."

"So superstitious," Dor panted, trying to keep herself from vomiting all over her friend.

"*He* has eyes everywhere."

Dor sobered, if only for a moment. What Ada spoke was true. The warlord had powers beyond anything she could comprehend. The man was a legend. A god. The devil.

Ada accidentally pressed her hand against Dor's left shoulder, causing a searing agony. Dor whined and tried to breathe through the misery.

"I'm sorry," Ada grunted as she moved even deeper into the cave. She carefully deposited Dor on her belly so her back was exposed to the chilly cavern air, then squatted next to her. "You're going to be okay." Ada's gaze drifted to Dor's back, and the skin around her eyes tightened as she frowned.

"That bad?" Dor didn't need to ask. She'd taken beatings before, but this one she felt in her bones.

"It looks worse than it is."

Dor doubted it.

Ada bit her bottom lip. "You need to be more careful."

"A little boy, Ada. What was I supposed to do?" she asked, more tears coursing down her face and collecting in a small hollow of the porous rock beneath her right cheek. "I couldn't leave him to that fate. I couldn't."

"I know," Ada said softly. "They would've killed him. I'm so—" She began to shake as she curled her hands into fists. She stared at them for a beat, then looked at Dor. "Everything about this situation is wrong." She bent and pressed a kiss against Dor's temple. "I'm going to finish up your work and the boy's. Just try to relax, and then I'll get you home."

"Thank you."

"You'd do it for me."

Dor watched Ada heft up the pickaxe and begin to work. Everyone helped each other as much as possible in the Pit. They formed bonds and families, but the help only extended as far as not putting another in danger. Ada was a gem of a friend whom Dor could never repay.

Dor clenched her teeth as the muscles in her back spasmed, and her body throbbed in horrendous pain with every beat of her heart. As Ada worked, the earsplitting sound of metal on stone melted into the background, forming the beat of a melody her mum used to sing to her as a child. Dor began to hum to focus on something other than the pain and drifted off into the music around her.

"Swamp apples," Ada cursed.

Dor blinked slowly and focused on the blurry outline of her friend. "I thought we said no cursing," she slurred.

"We've got to get you to your mum. You've lost too much blood."

Dor's eyelids began to droop, and she knew somewhere in her mind that this was a bad thing, but she was just so exhausted.

Ada slipped her hands underneath her armpits once again and panted next to her ear. "This is going to hurt. Help me as much as you can."

Dor keened as her friend hauled her to her feet. Colorful dots expanded across her vision as Ada began to trek from the cave.

"It hurts so much. Just leave me."

Ada growled. "I won't do that. Your mum would have my head. Plus, we can't afford for you to get an infection. You and I both know what happens when someone visits the healers."

Dor winced and forced her shaking legs to bear some of her weight at the word 'healer.' The warlord's healers were the scourge of Scythia. Razor-like smiles and false intentions. Her mum had taught her to fear little in the world, but the healers were one of those terrors to be feared. They were the devils who pretended they were saints. Their elixirs were the bane of many a woman's existence. Yes, they could heal any affliction, but, with that, came a heavy price. A woman either gained the attention of a warrior, or she became an experiment.

Dor fought a shudder as her stomach rolled. Many girls had been exploited since they'd blossomed into womanhood, and Dor didn't want to be next. Bile burned the back of her throat as she thought of what befell Odia, one of her former friends. They'd taken her, bred her, and when the monster of a child was born, they'd ripped the babe from Odia, like she was rubbish, and left her for the dragons.

"Monsters," Dor breathed.

Ada glanced sharply at her as they hobbled toward the entrance of the cavern. "Hush. You're speaking nonsense that will get us both killed. Try to keep silent so we can get you to your mum. We can't afford to attract attention." She glanced pointedly at the guards patrolling a nearby corridor.

Dor forced herself to stand taller, despite her injuries, and hobbled with Ada toward their home. She eyed the guards from beneath the mop of hair that hung over her face. The warriors seemed to be able to sense weakness, so she kept her chin up and lengthened her stride. Once out of sight from the guards, she groaned and leaned heavily on Ada as they followed the circling corridors and stairwells.

The walk seemed to take forever; the hallway began to move.

"I don't think I can make it much further."

Ada glanced at Dor. "I don't know what to do. You can't climb, and I can't carry you, which means we have to walk."

"How much further?" she wheezed.

"One more level."

There was no way she could make it. "We need to take the shortcut."

Ada's eyes rounded. "You can't do it."

"I have to," Dor ground out.

Her friend studied her and blew a piece of hair from her freckle-covered face. "You better not fall."

Dor pressed a smacking kiss against her cheek. "I'll try not to."

They wove through a few more tunnels and finally arrived at the last little lip to reach their home. Dor almost broke down in tears as she stared at the six feet of stone that kept her from her bed. It seemed like thousands of feet when her back was shredded into ribbons.

"You can do this," Ada encouraged. "I'll go first and help you up."

Ada scampered up the side of the rock like a monkey and disappeared from sight within a couple of seconds. Ada's face popped back over the edge, her brown braid dangling as she lay on her stomach and reached for Dor with both hands. "Use your feet as much as you can. I'll do the rest."

Dor nodded and slowly lifted her arms above her head, tears rushing to her eyes as her back pulled and throbbed. She slipped her sweaty hands into Ada's.

"You're almost there," her friend crooned.

Dor pressed her head against the wet, stone wall and took a couple of breaths before tucking her toes into a crevice and pushing her body upward. A shout of pain exploded out of her when Ada tugged her higher. Dor snapped her teeth together, blood filling her mouth as she bit her cheek.

"Just a little further, Dor," Ada grunted.

Cool stone scraped her arms, belly, and shins, but it barely registered with her compared to the searing white-hot pain that burned her back.

"What happened?" a male voice demanded.

Dor glanced up as Jadim leaned over Ada. Sweet, sweet Jadim. If anyone could get her home safe, it would be him. A sloppy smile tugged one side of her lips up. If they had lived in another world, she might have married him.

"I've got you," Jadim crooned as he placed his hands beneath Dor's arms and pulled.

Dor wailed when her agony doubled and an inhuman sound escaped her mouth as he pulled her closer, his fingers pressing into her mutilated skin. *Just kill me.*

"No! Her back!" Ada yelled.

Dor flopped limply in Jadim's grasp, crying.

"I'm so sorry," he mumbled. He pressed her close to his body and sprinted toward her home.

She gagged and then promptly threw up. "Sorry," she bawled as she watched her vomit slide down his chest in revolting rivulets.

"It's nothing, Dor."

The smell of incense surrounded them and overpowered the putrid stench of her vomit. Home. The knot of fear in Dor's chest loosened. She was home. She would be safe.

"What the hell?" her mum shouted. "What happened, Jadim?"

Dor forced her eyes opened as Ada moved around Jadim's tall frame. "She took a beating."

"Place her on the bed, Jadim. Ada, I need you to fetch a numbing cream from the herbalist."

"What should I pay her with?" her friend asked, wringing her hands.

Dor's pregnant mum rummaged in a small, decorated box on the nightstand and pulled out two dainty, black pearl earrings.

"Mum, no," Dor whimpered as Jadim placed her as gently as he could on the bed. Her mother treasured those earrings. They were a gift from Dor's father, Blair.

Her mum placed them in Ada's hands before turning to Dor. She smiled and brushed a strand of hair from Dor's face. "They're just things. My family is *always* the most important thing to me. Do you understand?"

She nodded and focused on her mum's soothing touch.

"If you don't need me, I'm going to follow Ada and make sure she gets to the herbalist. The warriors are in a foul mood today."

"Thank you, Jadim."

A large hand touched the back of her head, and Jadim kissed Dor's hair. "I'll be back."

Her mum watched Jadim leave before heaving herself from the bed, her huge belly straining against the too-small dress. She poured water in a bowl and grabbed clean rags from the table, then returned to the bed, setting the bowl and rags down with care. "How did this happen?"

"There was a little boy," Dor whispered between clenched teeth. "He was so skinny, and he didn't have the right tool. It was made for someone twice his size. He couldn't work anymore." She drew in a slow, shallow breath before continuing. "It was the end of the day, and they wouldn't show one shred of humanity." More tears fell down her cheeks, but, this time, for a different reason. "They would've killed him."

Her mum placed a soft hand on her cheek and wiped away the tears. "You've done a good thing, love. You should be proud."

"I'm not proud. I'm angry. I want them to die." Shame washed over her. Such thoughts were ugly and led down a road she didn't want to travel. Silence hung between them at her voiced treason.

"The right way to live is not always an easy choice, but just remember those who commit atrocities against others will suffer. Such is the way of the world. Injustices will be righted. We just have to be patient."

Her mother's words seemed like a dream. They didn't live in the same world as the other kingdoms. They lived in darkness. In the Pit.

The only things that bred there were rage, pain, and bitterness.

They lived in hell, and the devil ruled them all.

FÍVE

SAGE

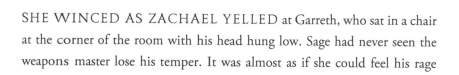

SHE WINCED AS ZACHAEL YELLED at Garreth, who sat in a chair at the corner of the room with his head hung low. Sage had never seen the weapons master lose his temper. It was almost as if she could feel his rage pouring from his person, the air heating around them.

"I can't even look at you." Zachael's voice turned ragged. "I helped raise you, boy. How could you do such a thing?"

"I have no excuse for my actions. I accept the consequences."

Hayjen scoffed and crossed his arms, glaring at Garreth. "Well, thank the stars for that. I'd hate to have to hunt your sorry arse down."

Sage pulled her attention from Garreth and eyed her husband. The man hadn't said one word since his Elite had begun his confession. She studied his stony face, looking for one hint of his thoughts.

Nothing.

He shifted slightly and startled her. Tehl hadn't moved from his spot in the opposite corner across from Garreth.

"Your life is – " William bit off his words as Tehl uncoiled himself from his wooden chair and stood to his full imposing height.

Sage shivered, and Zachael's anger paled in comparison to the ice-like rage that overcame her husband's face.

The prince took three steps closer and paused to stare at Garreth, his eyes like chips of frigid blue glass.

"You hurt Sage." A wintery-like chill seemed to whip through the room at his words. "*My* wife. *Your* princess. You deserve death, but that would be too easy." He paused, working his jaw. "She was your friend."

"I'm so sorry," Garreth said. He lifted his head and blinked back tears. "I never meant for anyone to be hurt, but that doesn't change my actions." He swallowed. "All I can do is try to make amends."

Tehl took a step closer. "You think you can make amends for the horrors she suffered? Because from where I am standing, there is *nothing* you could possibly do to make things better. I am tempted to just kill you. Our laws demand your blood for your betrayal, but it doesn't seem right that you'll be free from the sting and rot of guilt, and yet your princess will fight monsters for the rest of her life." His hands curled into massive fists by his side, and a slight tremor moved through his body. "She could have died there!" he thundered.

Sage stepped to his side and hugged his arm, stroking her hands soothingly along his skin. She'd never seen him this worked up before. He turned to look down at her, and she stiffened; his eyes were so cold, it was like falling through a frozen pool. She swallowed down her trepidation. Tehl would never hurt her, and he was hurting himself. He'd been raised with Garreth. His betrayal had cut him deeply.

"I am here. I am alive."

"No thanks to his actions," Tehl growled.

She bit her bottom lip, not agreeing or disagreeing with him. "Rhys was a wicked, vile creature that had no conscience. Garreth made a mistake, but he's not a bad man."

"You're sticking up for him?" her husband snarled. "The man who put you in that hellhole?"

Sage lifted his fist and ran her fingers over his knuckles. "If it hadn't been Garreth, it would have been someone else. Maybe someone with less of a moral code than your Elite. Rhys was determined to get to me, and he had ways to get what he wanted. Don't forget that he worked for you at one time," she said softly.

Tehl's lips thinned at the reminder. "Garreth is a traitor."

"Not by choice."

"He made his choices."

"You're right," she agreed. "But think about the circumstances. If your child had been the one threatened, how would you have reacted?" Sage pointed at Garreth's dejected form. "Look at him. Doesn't it seem like he's suffered enough? I know self-hate when I see it. I'm sure he hates himself more than you ever could."

"That's debatable," Tehl muttered, eyeing the Elite. "So, you would just let him go without any repercussions? A traitor? What's stopping him from doing it again?"

Sage dropped her husband's hand and faced her former friend. "Do you plan on betraying us again?"

"No," Garreth said, his voice ringing with certainty.

Tehl scoffed. "And you believe we can trust his word?"

"I do," she said, staring at the Elite. "He has nothing left that can be taken from him, but his own life. The Scythians have stolen his future from him. I believe he'll serve us quite diligently."

Zachael scowled and crossed his arms, mirroring her uncle's position. "Once a traitor, always a traitor."

"Since when did you start dealing in absolutes?" Sage demanded, arching a brow at the weapons master. "Your thoughts and speech are cloudy with betrayal, anger, and hurt. Have some bloody compassion and look at the whole situation."

Zachael pursed his lips. "I will try, my lady."

"Good." Her eyes snapped to her brooding uncle. "Do you have anything else to say on the matter, Hayjen?"

He shook his head. "No, I've said my piece."

She finally turned to her silent husband. "And what of you? Will you demand his life?"

"I am a keeper of the law, and the law states that he should hang."

Sage nodded, expecting that reaction. "But you have the capacity to show exceptions when there are extenuating circumstances?"

"Yes," he said tightly.

"He committed his crime against me. Then legally, I am to have a say in his punishment."

"That is accurate," Tehl bit out.

"Will you allow me to sentence this man, as is my right by law?"

Tehl flashed her a glare, but jerkily nodded.

Sage once again lifted his clenched hand and kissed his knuckles. "Thank you, my lord." She squeezed his hand once and addressed Garreth. "Are you ready for your sentence?"

"I am, my lady."

"You have admitted guilt of treason. The laws states that you must hang for such a crime, but as one of your sovereigns, I find this too harsh of a punishment. Therefore, I strip you of your Elite status. You will serve in the second battalion, and your holdings and monies will be distributed to those who are in need."

She turned her attention to Hayjen and Zachael. "Please direct this soldier to his new battalion."

Garreth stood and followed both men from the command tent.

Sage sighed and rubbed at her forehead. It was a just punishment, but she still felt guilty. She couldn't imagine the horror of losing a child.

Her skin prickled at the continued silence, and she faced the brooding man at her back. "Love?"

Tehl held up a hand. "I don't know if I can speak right now. I'm too angry."

"Thank you for letting me decide."

He flashed her a disgusted look. "He deserves so much worse."

"Perhaps, or perhaps not. But what is done is done. We can't go back, as much as we wish we could."

"I can't believe I ever trusted that lying, deceitful – "

"One mistake shouldn't be enough to ruin a lifetime of good deeds and service."

"You're too soft, love."

Sage shrugged. "Maybe, but I refuse to rule with a black and white attitude."

She squeaked when he wrapped her up into a tight hug, his breath ruffling her hair. Sage wrapped her arms around him and held him back.

"Stars, I love you."

Her body froze and the words seemed to echo in her mind. *I love you.* He loved her. He showed her this by his actions daily, but he'd yet to actually say it. Her eyes welled up.

"Do you realize that's the first time you've ever said you love me? And it's because I punished a man. That's twisted."

Tehl pulled back, his brows slanting together. "This isn't the first time."

"I assure you, it is," she whispered. "And I love you, too."

"I tell you I love you all the time," he argued. "I just said it moments ago when I said, 'You're too soft, love'."

Now, it was her turn to frown. "What?"

Her husband cocked his head, his black hair hanging around his face. "When you call someone love, it's because you love them," he said simply.

Sage blinked stupidly at him. "That's just an endearment or pet name."

"No," he murmured softly. "Endearment literally means a word or phrase expressing love or affection."

Warmth bubbled from her chest. He'd been calling her love since before they were married. A tear slipped down her cheek, and she smiled. "You've loved me for that long?"

He clasped her cheeks in his hands. "I think I loved you as soon as I saw you. Well, at least, once I discovered you were a woman."

Laughter bubbled out of her.

Her prince loved her.

All was right in that moment.

Until the warlord ruined it.

Again.

"No. We will not meet. It's too dangerous." Tehl commanded.

Sage stared numbly at the piece of parchment lying in the center of the table. It looked so innocent, not like the insidious poison it was.

"Does the warlord always send letters in the middle of the night?" Gav asked, his purple eyes filled with distain.

"This is the first," Lilja answered, leaning on the table.

Sage spared a glance at her aunt. The Sirenidae looked tired, but still beautiful. *It was unfair.* "All he wants is a meeting?" she asked.

"He supposedly wants to discuss peace terms to avoid a war that will bring about a devasting loss of life," William said.

Rafe scoffed as he stepped next to the round table. "If he wanted peace, then he could have fought for it when we were in his own kingdom. No, he doesn't want a peaceful solution. He wants something else."

His amber eyes locked on Sage from across the table and stayed.

She blanched but held his gaze. She knew as well as he what the warlord wanted.

"It's a trick," Raziel, the crown prince of Methi, muttered darkly from beside his brother, "or a trap. He would *never* compromise or retreat. The monster doesn't care about death. He's after something."

Her. He was after her.

Sage tried to speak, but her mouth wouldn't obey her mind.

Her aunt's gaze traveled from the map to Sage's stricken face. "My spies tell me that he is aware that the Methians have allied with us, but he is not afraid of their numbers. He still believes he has the advantage." Her lips pursed. "But he loves to play mind games. We have our Crown Prince and Princess – the Crown's Shield and Rebel's Blade – fighting with us. Our men have a mental advantage of their sovereigns riding into battle with them."

"This isn't about a trap," William said from her right. He reached across the table and lifted the letter toward the lantern light. "This is about unnerving those who are leading." He set the parchment down with a heavy sigh.

A nervous chuckle slipped out of Sage. All of their advisors turned toward her. She stood from her chair and reached for the letter. Her hand shook, and she gritted her teeth.

It was only a piece of paper. She could do this.

Tehl, who'd been pacing behind her, pressed against her left side. She smiled at him gratefully and read out loud a part of the message.

"It is in our best interests that we meet to find a solution that is advantageous for both our peoples. I look forward to meeting with your delegation. It's been far too long." Her throat constricted.

The last sentence was for her.

Sage placed the message back on the table. "I'll say what you all won't. He wants to see me."

"We won't give him the satisfaction," Lilja snarled.

"It's too dangerous," Gav said softly. "He's not capable of rational thought when it comes to Sage."

"In his twisted mind, our refusal will signal that we want war as badly as he does. He doesn't like to be ignored." She blinked repeatedly as a memory resurfaced of the warlord holding her face tight so she couldn't look away from his face. "We need to choose wisely."

"We can't risk it," William added.

Raziel and Rafe both nodded. "We agree."

"It's a mistake to refuse him," Sage whispered, then turned to her aunt. "Lilja?"

The Sirenidae massaged her temples and then straightened. "Sage isn't wrong. There will be consequences for our refusal, but we can't negotiate with a monstrous warlord. His motives are too murky."

"Then it's agreed," Tehl rumbled from her right. "We send a refusal."

"It will be done," Gav replied.

Sage's stomach bottomed out.

She wanted nothing to do with the warlord, but she couldn't help but feel like she'd just failed some sort of test, and that they'd just doomed themselves.

SIX

JASMINE

—◦◦◦—

SHE'D DREAMED ABOUT COURT WHEN she was a young girl.

She'd imagined there'd be decadent dishes of all her favorite things, including chocolate pudding, tartlets that melted on her tongue, and, of course, cake. One could not forget about the cake. She'd dreamed of sparkling crystal, fine young ladies draped in shimmering gowns, and young men in pressed breeches, velvet waistcoats, and boots so shiny she could see her reflection in them. Laughter would tease the air like soft musical bells while elegant couples whirled around the dance floor in a kaleidoscope of silken color.

But that was pure fiction, the dreams of a little forest girl who spent too much time with bows, hunting rabbits in the wild.

Jasmine shifted on her aching feet and glared down at the pale blue slippers pinching her toes. They were beautiful, finer than anything she'd ever worn before, but bloody uncomfortable. All she wanted were her sturdy boots. Well, at the moment, she also wanted to escape the drudgery of court and snuggle with the twins.

"Are you all right, my lady?"

She pasted a smile on her face and glanced to the left, meeting pretty brown eyes. "I'm fine, Gem, thank you."

Gem—Lady Hollisa—frowned at her but nodded slowly. "I don't believe you, but I'll let it drop." Gem took a delicate sip from her glass of wine and fell quiet as she scanned the room.

Jasmine eyed the lady. Gem was her only friend in court since Sage had left to wage war. She was just as much of an outcast as Jas. Gem's family held a modest demesne, but her father had gambled most of their wealth away, and her mother had caused one too many scandals. Gem and Jasmine had bonded over the twins. Gem happened to love children, and Jas loved anyone who loved the twins. Not much was said between the two of them, but it was a relief to have someone guarding her back. And she needed it.

Jasmine glanced around the room, still musing over her childhood dreams. She had it partly right. There were women in shimmering gowns, dashing men, and dancing, but that was where all similarities ended. Court wasn't a fairytale. It was a nightmare.

Women smiled prettily but spoke venom behind each other's backs. Beneath the handsome façade of many men lurked ravenous predators. And if those weren't obstacles in and of themselves, then there was the meticulous etiquette that was imposed on everyone. One wrong action could ruin everything.

But the joke was on everyone. Jasmine was already ruined.

Her eyes connected with Joshua, the foppish blond. He smiled at her from over the rim of his cup. He winked, and it was all she could do not to roll her eyes. Despite her newly announced marriage, he kept on persuing her. His cronies smirked in her direction before laughing among themselves. Shame washed over her as she glanced away. It was her fault. She'd made a name for herself since arriving at the palace, and not a good one. *Whore* was quietly whispered in every circle she came upon. She didn't feel much these days, but she carried the shame, guilt, and anger with her everywhere.

"Out of all the women he could've chosen, he chose *her*?" a soft whisper reached her ears.

"Rumor has it, they were found in a very compromising position before they wed," another voice whispered.

"I see. The poor man. At least a beautiful wife isn't necessary for an heir."

Gem had frozen at her side and now flicked a worried glance in her direction, but Jas ignored it.

The gossipers behind them weren't wrong. No matter how the maids dressed her, she still stuck out among her peers like coal among diamonds.

She was rough while they were class.

"No matter." The second voice giggled. "His marriage hasn't seemed to slow him down one bit."

That wasn't far from the truth, either. Her gaze sought her husband among the gallantry, and it was easy to spot him. His gilded curls were barely tamed back from his face, which was lit like a beacon. Men and women alike surrounded him like bees to honey. Jas eyed the beautiful brunette hanging off his arm, soaking up his every word. The prince smiled down at the lady, his lips turning up in a wicked grin that could charm the pants off a nun. The brunette simpered at him and batted her lashes.

Jasmine watched it all without one ounce of jealousy. Their marriage was one of convenience. Even though she abhorred unfaithfulness with every bone in her body, she didn't care what he did as long as he kept away from her and the twins.

The whispering started up behind her again.

"He even took in her two prior children." A pause. "She's not a widower."

Small gasps exploded, followed by titterings that had her fingers curling into the skirts of her dress. *Vicious vipers.*

"What a gem he is to take in the bastards of a whore."

Gem's eyes widened, and her hand touched Jasmine's bare arm. "Their words mean nothing."

She was right, but a line had been crossed when they started talking about her family. No one attacked the twins and got away with it.

"Don't let your temper get the best of you," Gem cautioned.

Jas smiled and patted her friend's hand as her anger melted some of the ice that encased her. "I suggest you leave so you won't be lumped into what's about to happen." She pulled away from Gem and spun on her heel, moving toward the group of whispering ladies with the grace she usually reserved for hunting.

Rose, the redheaded demon, lifted her head and smiled sharply at Jasmine as she neared the group. Jas returned the smile and paused by one of Rose's lickspittles.

"My lady," Rose murmured, "to what do we owe this pleasure?"

So that's how they were going to play it.

"You looked so entranced by your conversation, I just had to join the fun."

"We were speaking of the weather," a short ginger-haired girl blurted from her right.

Jasmine scoffed. "Come now, please tell me you can lie better than that?"

The ladies around her blanched, all but Rose who tilted her chin up. "Whatever could you mean?"

Jas leaned in close, like she was going to tell them a secret. "I heard mention of bastards, and I love a good story. Please continue on."

Silence met her statement, along with the shifting of feet and rustles of expensive crinoline.

"How disappointing you all are. I thought one of you would have the guts to say it to my face."

"You're making a scene," Rose murmured. "You should calm yourself. It's not good for someone in your condition, so I've heard."

She barely managed to contain her flinch. No one knew she was with child except for a select few. The harpy was trying to goad her into giving out information. Jas blinked owlishly and scrunched up her brows. "Condition? What ever could you mean?"

Rose smiled thinly. "I must be mistaken."

"That is the least of your mistakes." The twit never should have said something about the twins.

"I beg your pardon?" Rose said.

Jas tsked. "Your mistake was to speak badly of my family." She eyed the women around her – who dropped their eyes to the floor – before settling back on Rose. "You tread on dangerous ground."

"Are you threatening me?" Rose hissed.

"More like a promise. Keep your schemes and games to yourself."

Rose laughed. "There's nothing you can do to touch me, forest trash."

Several startled gasps escaped the ladies in the circle.

Jasmine grinned. "We can take this outside if you'd like."

More gasps.

The redhead tossed a curl over her snowy shoulder, sneering. "So barbaric."

"That's right," Jas purred. "I am a barbaric hunter. Let me tell you a little story about this forest trash. I spent most of my life hunting and tracking.

I rarely lost any prey I set my sights on, even if it took days. That sort of dedication takes commitment and patience. You think about that when you are falling asleep tonight, when you enter a dark passage, or when you hear the scuff of a foot upon stone behind you." She smiled; the sight was positively evil if the paling expressions of the women around her were anything to go by. "Harm my family by word or deed, and I will find you. There's nothing that could keep you from me."

A sliver of satisfaction curled in Jas's gut at how Rose's eyes had grown considerably wider.

"I—I'll out you. I outrank you. We'll receive protection."

"Do you think they'll believe you?" Jas asked curiously. "The matrons think I'm a delight, and then there's the matter of my marriage. I may just be forest trash, but I did marry a prince."

The redhead opened her mouth and promptly shut it. Large hands settled on Jasmine's shoulders, surprising her. She kept her expression pleasant and didn't shrug off his hands like she wanted to. Instead, she leaned back against his strong frame, making a point.

"Dear wife, I believe it's time for us to retire for the night."

She nodded and faked a yawn as she spun to face her husband. "I'm absolutely exhausted, my dear. Take me to bed."

Sam's brows rose in surprise, and then he smiled devilishly at the women behind her. "I can't possibly refuse such a wonderful evening."

The ladies curtsied to him as he drew Jas's hand into the crook of his arm. Attention followed them as they exited the dining room. She glanced over her shoulder and caught the nasty sneer on Rose's face. Jas was under no illusion that there wouldn't be consequences. But it felt good to finally push back against the harpies that had made her their target.

War was raging in Aermia, and now she'd started one of her own.

Sam led her down the arching hallways that echoed with their footsteps and up two flights of stairs to the royal suites.

"What was that about?" he asked, his tone casual.

Jas pulled her hand from his arm and opened the door to their suites. "Nothing." They'd only been married a grand two weeks, but she'd learned a few things about the man. He was an expert at wiggling information out of people.

"It didn't look like nothing," he said. "It looked like you were about to rip out their throats. It was a little sexy."

Jasmine froze and glared over her shoulder at the insolent man who was leaning against the wall, grinning at her. "I haven't the energy to slap you for all of your innuendos tonight, my lord. Take your presence elsewhere."

"I wasn't the one who announced that we were going to bed."

Her lips twitched. He had her there. "Nonetheless, I'd appreciate it if you'd leave me in peace." She stretched and winced as something pinched in her back. It had been getting worse and worse of late. At times, she'd cramp all day long.

His smile faded, and his gaze dropped to her belly for a moment. "Is it the babe?"

The babe.

Her stomach rebelled, and she dashed for the bathing room, barely making it to the privy. She heaved, careless of her honey curls tumbling onto her face. Hair could be washed, but no one wanted to clean up vomit.

A cool hand pulled her hair from her face and the other rubbed small circles on her lower back. Again, she heaved, the rest of her dinner making another appearance. Tears dripped from the corners of her eyes and snot from her nose.

She wanted to throw off the prince's hand, but it felt too nice against her heated, aching body. Every day, there were new aches and pains as her body stretched to make room for the babe. She'd never hated being a petite woman more in her entire life.

The babe.

A life was growing inside her. One she had no knowledge of creating. She heaved again as more tears began to flow down her cheeks. Mira said it was a blessing that she didn't have any memories of the begetting, but part of her felt empty, robbed, blank. A shudder worked through her.

Ruined.

She wiped at her mouth and panted. Sickness was expected with pregnancy, but this was something more. It was like she was trying to vomit up all her feelings, everything she tried to keep suppressed.

"Are you well?"

No. "I'm fine." Jas batted his hands from her person. "You don't have to stay here."

"You're right, I don't have to." But he made no move to leave. "You need to talk about it."

Jas glared up at the gorgeous man staring down at her with concern. "Because we're so close?"

His lips pressed together as his blue eyes narrowed. "We could be if you let me."

"Along with all the hordes of other women? No, thank you."

"You want to know about—"

She held up a hand. "I don't want to know. It's not my place."

"You're my wife."

"In name only." She stood on shaking legs and waved away the prince as he tried to help her. "I'm fine."

"Your color and retching tell me otherwise. Plus, I know when a woman uses the word 'fine,' she's clearly not."

Jasmine staggered to the huge vanity and eyed her pale complexion in the tall, gilded mirror. She used a deep purple towel to wipe her face. "What a joke," she said. "Those with child are supposed to be radiant. If I'm glowing, it's because I'm green."

She pushed from the vanity and left the room, the prince following on her heels as she bustled into their suite. Well, technically, it was *theirs*, but only Sam slept in the large royal chambers. She slept with the twins in a much more modest room adjacent to the opulent suite.

"You're sure you're all right?" he asked as he hefted a plain-looking, black, wool cloak from a plush, striped chair near the fireplace to her right.

"Definitely." Jasmine eyed the cloak but said nothing. He was probably up to more shenanigans. She didn't ask, and he didn't offer.

"I'll be back to wake the twins."

She pursed her lips, not wanting to agree, but nodded anyway.

"Good. Rest well, Jasmine."

"Happy hunting," she responded.

Sam paused with his hand on the door and studied her over his shoulder. An eternity passed as they stared at one another. It seemed like he was searching for something, but she wasn't sure what. One thing she did notice was that the man was unfairly handsome, beautiful even. Every morning, she woke feeling like death warmed up, but he never looked the worse for wear, despite his late nights out.

He winked at her, pulling Jasmine from her thoughts. "I'll see you in the morning, beautiful. Give both twins a kiss from me."

She opened her mouth to retort, but he'd already disappeared through the door.

That was the worst part of the whole arrangement—his involvement with the twins. Jasmine worried her lip as she stared at the closed door to her left. He seemed like a good enough person as a whole, but there was a darker side she'd caught glimpses of that she wasn't so sure about. It was like he had many versions of himself.

Then there were his escapades. The twins wouldn't understand now, but they would in the future and it would undoubtedly hurt them.

But those were troubles for another day. Carefully, she turned to the door directly behind her and twisted the knob slowly so it wouldn't wake the sleepy little monsters in the other room.

Today, being married to the prince proved useful in protecting her family, and she couldn't find a fault in that.

SEVEN

DOR

———◦◦〰◦◦———

DORCUS CRACKED OPEN HER EYES and squinted into the softly lit room. The piddly candle on the old table flickered and cast shadows on the walls of their home as it threatened to sputter out. Guilt washed over her. They could only afford so many candles a month, and they couldn't afford to burn them just because Dor was hurt.

She shifted on her bed and inhaled deeply as pain pulsed through her. Sacred darkness, she hurt. Once settled, she glanced at her mum's slumped form. Her mother slept near the bed in a rickety, old chair that looked like it would collapse at any second, her head hanging so her chin rested on her chest. Dark bruises marred the delicate skin beneath her closed eyes, and a soft snore wheezed from her nose. Dor's eyes dropped to her mum's arms which rested on top of her giant protruding belly. The pose was restful, yet protective. Even in sleep, her mum safeguarded her children.

Dor glanced back at her mum's freckle-covered face and luscious fiery-red hair. Her mum always claimed her hair was what had caught her father's attention, but Dor knew better. Her sire had fallen in love with her mum's fiery disposition. She was what had woken him up after Dor's birth mum died, or so he claimed.

Stars above, she wished he was here. He hadn't visited them in a while, and it pained all of them. She glanced at the carved doorway toward the small room her sisters slept in. It hurt the little ones the most. They didn't understand why their sire didn't live with them. Other slave men had offered to live with them as protection and support, but her mum wouldn't hear any of it, despite their eunuch statuses. She clearly still felt it would be a betrayal to her warrior, even if there wasn't a physical attraction between the slave men and herself.

Dor understood her mum's decision to an extent, but part of her wished there was another adult living with them, especially a male. Their sire's name was a curse and a blessing. Sometimes it brought safety, other times danger. But they did the best they could and kept their heads down.

Her mum's head dipped farther, and her red hair hung around her plump face. Dor smiled. Toward the end of the gestation cycle, her mother's face always rounded out, but even so, she was beautiful. The woman seemed to glow every time a child began growing in her womb. Dor hated to wake her up, but if her mum slid any farther down in her chair, she'd fall right onto the floor.

"Mum," Dor whispered, keeping her voice low so as to not wake her younger sisters.

Her mum jerked and sat up. Her green eyes scanned the room before landing on Dor, then filled with worry as she hefted herself from the chair. She knelt on the bed and brushed a piece of long, dark hair from Dor's face.

"How are you feeling, love?" she asked.

"Okay enough," Dor said softly. "I hurt."

"I know. Let me get you something for the pain."

Dor's back seemed to burn hotter at the mention of pain. "I can get through it."

Her mum ignored her and stood. "It was a blessing you passed out. There was so much blood, and we had to cut away some of the flesh." She shuffled to the side, so Dor stared at her profile.

Her stomach rolled, and saliva flooded her mouth.

Her mother glanced toward where her sisters slept soundly, and Dor followed her gaze. A small flicker of warmth entered her chest as she watched her sisters sleeping, how they wrapped around each other, clutching a roughly woven blanket.

"Ada and Jadim stayed to help. Ada kept the little ones occupied while Jadim and I cleaned you up the best we could."

"Thank you." She swallowed hard. She didn't deserve such a wonderful family. "How are the girls?"

"Scared, but they know how strong you are."

Dor didn't feel strong. She felt weak and stupid. "I'm so sorry for worrying you."

Her mum blanched and clenched her jaw. "It's never easy to watch one's child in pain or to see one's child hurt." She pressed a hand to her chest, just below her collarbone. "It hurts my heart that you've been abused, and it makes me want to rage."

"But you mustn't."

A bitter laugh spilled from her mum's lips. "I know better than most. I wish your father was here. He'd know how to proceed and protect you. I don't know what to do, Dor. How are you supposed to work tomorrow? How can we hide this from the warriors? We don't want to draw more attention."

They couldn't. If she didn't appear for work, the warriors would hunt her down and take her to the healers. A chill ran down Dor's spine. She'd never visit the healers unless dragged there by her hair.

"There isn't a choice," Dor said steadily. "I have to work."

Her mum's eyes glassed over, and she scrubbed at her tears, anger clear in the motion. "Damn hormones. I hate this. No one should live like this. If you can't complete your work tomorrow, they'll kill you."

The words didn't scare Dor. They should have, but when you live with death always hovering in the corner like an unwanted spider, it ceases to inspire proper fear.

Dor glanced toward the girls. But leaving her family *did* frighten her. They needed her, especially with another little one on the way.

"I'll get my work done. I have to. There isn't another option." She inhaled shallowly as another wave of pain crashed over her. "I can do it," she forced out while reaching her hand to her mum.

Her mother clasped her hand and gave it a squeeze. "I love you, sweetness. You're one of the best things this life has blessed me with."

Tears pricked Dor's eyes. It was she who was beyond lucky. Dor's birth mother had died while in labor, but the first person she could remember seeing was Bel, the woman who had raised her as her own. She stared at their clasped hands, hers a deep olive, her mum's creamy. It didn't matter what blood ran through a person's veins, only that love ran through their heart. And Bel loved Dor like a daughter. Dor *was* Bel's daughter.

"Love you, Mum." She blew her mum a kiss. "We'll get through this."

Her mum nodded and stared blindly at the floor. "I don't know how long I can keep living like this," she said under her breath. "But we have to keep moving forward. It's all we can do."

She patted Dor's hand and sat on the edge of the bed, her expression blank as she stroked her belly.

Dor watched the familiar movement and thought about what it would be like to be in her place. It would be lucky to be chosen as a breeder and be able to provide for your family, but that was the only part that appealed. Dor glanced away from her mother's belly to stare at the wall, fighting the nausea which rose at the idea of warriors touching her. The idea of submitting to one or several of the warriors chilled her to the very bone.

She frowned. Her father wasn't like one of the feral creatures that ruled over them, but he was the exception to the rule. He'd already warned Dor that the relationship between himself and her mum wasn't normal. In fact, in public, they never showed affection for each other since her mum was considered an imperfect. Her lip curled. Dor hated the word, but a very small part of her was thankful she wasn't the Scythian standard of perfect. If she or her sisters had been considered perfect, they wouldn't have been allowed to live with their mum. That thought terrified Dor the most. What if she *did* become a breeder and they stole her child? She knew how she'd feel about that, and she'd die before she'd let a child go.

But that was life in the Pit. Dor was destined to become a broodmare for the monsters that lorded above them. But at least she would be able to bear it because she had her family. Her mind wandered to Jadim. When the time came, she was sure he'd offer his protection and home for her. They could never be anything more than companions because of him being a eunuch, but at least she'd have someone to help raise any children she was allowed to keep.

"Have you any news of Father?" Dor asked, pushing aside her disturbing thoughts.

"He's been busy."

In other words, he'd been causing mischief for the warlord. Dor scowled. Everything wrong in the world was that monster's fault. "It's not supposed to be like this."

Her mum glanced sharply at her before her gaze darted to the doorway covered only by a threadbare blanket. "You need to watch your tongue. Such things have a way of being heard."

Wise advice. "I'm sorry. I just wish things were better."

"They will be." Her mother glanced at Dor's back and then glared at the doorway. "Your father wouldn't have allowed that to happen, and the warriors wouldn't think twice about hurting the commander's daughters."

Dor didn't argue with her. More often than not, it put a target on her back. Warriors seeking to hurt her father went after the imperfect children he'd been known to visit. Or because of her sire's position, the slaves around her looked at her with suspicion, like she was the reason they were languishing in the Pit, like she wasn't one of them when she suffered as they suffered. She wasn't quite a slave and she wasn't quite a Scythian either. She was something in between that had no place in her world. And if that wasn't enough, it was easy to set off the berserker side of the warriors guarding them. The newest warriors were sent into the Pit to learn control. Rage ignited in her gut. It wouldn't do for a warrior to lose control among the court of vipers that lived above them. Oh no, they were sent down to train among the unarmed masses. No matter where Dor turned, danger awaited her.

Her mum sniffed and waddled toward the table in the corner to retrieve a little jar filled with green paste. Once again, Dor brushed her morose thoughts away and focused on her mum's swaying gait.

"I think we've talked enough about my health for one night," Dor said. "How are you feeling?"

"Little bit is going to be in my belly for a while yet," she said, patting her stomach and then lifting the jar from the table. "She'll be here soon enough."

"You think it is a girl?"

"I know it is," her mum answered as she waddled to Dor, and huffed as she sat in the wobbly chair next to the bed that groaned as it bore her weight. "How is your pain?"

Dor swallowed, trying not to think about her mutilated back. "It's as fine as can be."

Her mother clucked and opened the jar. A pungent scent filled the air that Dor wasn't sure she liked.

"I know you, Dorcus. You have a high tolerance for pain and a penchant for ignoring what's best for yourself. You need this to sleep tonight if you're to work tomorrow."

"Did you really sell your earrings?"

Her mum leaned forward and pressed a kiss on her temple. "I did, and it was worth it. Things come and go, sweetness, but the people in our lives are always the most important."

"I hate being unaware of what's going on." Dor rarely took anything for the pain when she was beaten. It was better to be in pain and cognizant of one's surroundings than drugged and vulnerable. Her mind flashed to when she had passed out earlier that day. She was lucky Ada had been there or Dor could've found herself in a whole different position.

"I know, but I'll protect you. Nothing will come through that door without my say so."

Some of the tension in Dor's body released at that. She trusted her mum to protect her. She'd done the best she could all of Dor's life.

"Let's get you to sleep."

Her mum reached for a wooden spoon and placed it between Dor's lips. Dor bit down on the wood and then pressed her chin against the slightly damp bedding. Her mother's first dab on her back caused stars to burst across her vision and her hands to curl into the blanket beneath her.

"I'll be quick. Be strong, Dorcus."

Snot and tears dripped down her face as she hissed curses to keep from wailing and waking the little ones. Her body broke out in sweat, and she began to lose touch with the world around her as her back began to tingle and numb. A sigh of relief gusted from her lungs as her mum finished, and the medicine began to work its magic. Dor spat out the spoon and leaned her salty cheek against the cool bedding.

"Thank you, Mum," she whispered as her eyes slowly closed.

"You're welcome. Sleep well, precious."

"I don't know how I will survive tomorrow," Dor mumbled as sleep tugged at her.

"We will figure it out in the morning. Each day has its own worries."

Her mum capped the jar, stood, and blew out the candle. The bed dipped as her mum crawled in next to her and began playing with her hair, humming a lullaby about love, dragon songs, and a flying girl. Dor tucked her hands beneath her head and let herself drift into oblivion.

EİGHT

SAM

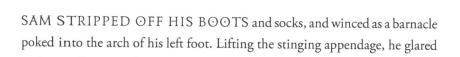

SAM STRIPPED OFF HIS BOOTS and socks, and winced as a barnacle poked into the arch of his left foot. Lifting the stinging appendage, he glared at the small cut as it began to leak blood.

No matter how careful he was when visiting his spy, he always managed to hurt himself.

He pulled off his jacket, vest and shirt, goosebumps running up and down his bare skin. Sam rubbed his arms and eyed the narrow entrance to the underwater cave in the stone floor. His nose wrinkled as he approached the dark, watery hole. His heart picked up as he strained to see what lay beneath the still surface.

"Wicked hell," he muttered, his whispered curse echoing around the stone cavern.

He hated this part. There weren't many things that scared him, but being trapped in an underwater coffin was one of them.

"Stupid Sirenidae." *Of all the places to meet.*

Granted, the risk of discovery was low, but it was a bloody nightmare getting to the rendezvous. At least, it was for him.

Inhaling deeply, he sat on the stone edge and swung his legs into the chilly water. He hissed. Damn, it was cold. Steeling his nerves, Sam sucked in a huge breath and shuffled off the ledge.

Darkness engulfed him, and he reached forward to grasp the rough, rock wall and push himself downward. His ears popped, and his lungs burned uncomfortably as the soles of his feet touched the sand. He squinted into the darkness and ran his hand around the tunnel wall ahead of him.

Some of his panic drained away as the plants on the walls began to glow; neon pinks, blues, and greens radiated light into the watery corridor. Sam pushed off the wall behind him and swam ahead, his legs propelling him through the space in a span of four heartbeats. The mouth of the tunnel widened, and Sam swam toward the dancing surface.

As his head broke the pool's surface, he sucked in a huge breath, his lungs bellowing like he'd just trained for hours.

"Running from something?" a sensuous female asked, her voice full of amusement.

Sam treaded water and spun in a circle until he located the source of the voice. His eyes narrowed on the Sirenidae, who was lounging on the smooth rock near the pool, like a lady presiding over her court.

"What are you doing here, Mer? I was expecting Oria." He pulled himself to the edge of the pool, which resembled a sparkling jewel due to all the bioluminescent plants. Water spilled from his body, and he plopped down on the rock next to her as he blinked saltwater from his irritated eyes. They never hurt while he was swimming, but once he left the water, they burned like the devil.

Mer straightened, her long, flowing, silver hair slithering around her like silk. "Not even a proper hello?"

Sam smiled at her and leaned closer to kiss her cool, pale cheek, thankful she was dry. The first time they'd met, he almost accosted her because of the Lure. He shook his head to dispel the sweet scent that haunted his memories. "I'm sorry. I'm a bit out of sorts after my swim."

The Sirenidae nodded in sympathy. "I live in the sea, and swimming through the tunnels still unnerves me sometimes."

He shook his head, displacing some of the water from his hair, and then slicked several golden strands from his face. "I'm surprised to see you, Mer. I honestly didn't expect to meet with you for at least another week. I thought we had agreed not to meet often because of the danger?"

The smile on her full, pink lips slid away as she turned to face him fully, crossing her long, pale legs. Her magenta eyes, so similar to Lilja's, locked on him. "I had no other choice."

His stomach soured. He had a feeling she wouldn't have good news to share with him. "What's happened?"

"Oria is dead."

"How?" he asked, shocked.

She pursed her lips and glanced away. "They spotted her before she could retreat from the cove. They hunted her down like an animal." Her voice wavered. "She barely made it back to me before she passed." Mer cleared her throat and turned back to him, tears shimmering in her eyes. One lone tear slipped free, and she touched the droplet as it moved down her cheek. She stared at her damp fingers for a second. "When we weep in the sea, the ocean sweeps away our pains like they were never there—I like that I can see the evidence of my pain."

Sam stared at her but kept silent, knowing it was better to let her get it all out.

Her jaw tightened, and she met his gaze, her eyes like hardened jewels. "She died in my arms."

"I know it's not enough, but I'm sorry for your loss." And he was. He liked Oria. She was quiet, to the point, and brilliant. Once she'd seen something, she could remember the details perfectly.

"She knew the risks of her journey."

"It doesn't make it any easier," Sam said softly.

Mer sucked in her lips and nodded. "True."

He watched the Sirenidae slowly compose herself as she tipped her head back to stare at the blue glowworms that shone like stars in the ceiling of her wet cave. Sam hated that she was in pain, and it bothered him that he still had to ask her questions after she'd lost a friend, but information was of the utmost importance. Without it, thousands would die.

"Mer…" he said carefully.

She held her hand up. "I didn't come here to cry on you." She swallowed and dropped her head to clash gazes with him. "Oria reported to me what she'd seen."

The bleak expression on her face chilled Sam more than the water he'd just exited. "And?"

"The Scythians are getting ready to deploy their fleet of warships."

"How soon?"

"Three weeks."

"Bloody hell," he barked, standing. The seaweed on the rocks squished between his toes. Three weeks. Twenty-one days. Stars above. So little time. His mind spun as he paced. They needed to have their fleet of ships sent out immediately. He turned to face Mer. "I need to get back to Sanee, so I can pass this on. Is there anything else you need to tell me?"

"The sea is restless."

Code for the Sirenidae people. "Do you fear an uprising?" Sam asked frankly.

"No." Mer shook her head. "But there are those who will stand with you when the time comes."

Sam froze, shock temporarily locking his muscles. "Has the king changed his mind?"

"No."

Worry wormed its way into his chest. "Are you in danger?"

The Sirenidae chuckled darkly. "The *world* is in danger. None of the four kingdoms, nor the sea, is safe from war now. If we do not fight, then we've already lost."

"Are you being careful?" His one meeting with the Sirenidae king hadn't painted the man as the most forgiving person he'd ever met.

"As careful as I can be." Mer's smile was sad as she gazed at him. "I refuse to stand by and let the world burn. My aunt was right in leaving. There will be consequences for my actions, no doubt, but it's not a sacrifice unless it's a sacrifice."

"I'm not asking this of you," Sam whispered. The Sirenidae assistance would make a difference, but he knew what she was planning was betrayal. "You'll be branded a traitor."

She shrugged. "It's possible, and I'm prepared for that outcome. No one really wins in war."

Truer words were never spoken.

Sam took two steps forward and wrapped his arms around Mer, hugging her. "If you need me for anything, just send word, and I'll come."

She eased back out of his embrace. "I'll hold you to that. Who knows? Maybe I'll end up at your doorstep asking for shelter when this is all through."

"I hope not," he said softly, stepping back and easing himself into the pool once again. "Be careful. Lilja would have my head if she knew you were coming to meet me."

A smirk touched Mer's mouth. "My aunt has eyes everywhere. I wouldn't be surprised if she already knows about this meeting." Her expression melted into seriousness. "I'll have my warriors scout the waters. As soon as the Scythians set sail, you shall know about it."

"Thank you." He wished he had better words to express his sincere appreciation. "I'll see you soon."

"Until then," she whispered.

Sam offered her one more smile before he dove beneath the surface.

The tide of the war might have changed.

NINE

DOR

DEVIL TAKE, BUT DOR HATED mornings. The cave's lighting never seemed to change, making it even more difficult to rise at the dawn of a new day.

Dor laid her head on the table and stared absently at the measly blanket that served as the curtain for their door while she waited for her back to stop throbbing. Her eyes were puffy from crying and lack of sleep, but at least her mum had cleaned the wounds and given her something for the pain before her sisters had awoken. She didn't want them to see how much pain she was in.

She closed her eyes and tried to imagine what it would be like to experience the warmth of the sun on her skin, to see trees towering over her, to feel the wind on her face. As little feet padded from the other small room, she cracked a smile and opened one eye.

"Trying to sneak up on me again, Lailana?"

Lailana squeaked and stomped around Dor. The four-year-old pushed back her black curls and squinted up at Dor with huge green eyes.

"How did you hear me?" she demanded, her chubby cheeks flushing.

Dor touched her ears. "I have powerful hearing."

Lailana sucked on her bottom lip, her gaze sliding to Dor's bare back. She winced and pointed. "That owie must hurt a lot."

"Not as much as it did before Mum cared for me," Dor answered truthfully.

"Did the mean man hurt you?"

Dor sucked in her cheeks, trying to figure out how to explain what happened. It did no good to lie to any of her sisters about the circumstances in which they lived, but she also didn't want Lailana to lose all of her innocence so young.

"I wasn't as obedient yesterday as I should have been."

"But Mum says you're a good girl who helps others."

"Even good girls make mistakes, and this is what happens when I don't do what I'm supposed to. There are consequences to every decision we make, wee one."

"That's not fair."

"Life isn't always fair, you're right, but we do the best we can."

Lailana stared at Dor's back for a few more seconds, her forehead wrinkling, brows slashing together. "I don't want an owie like that."

"Hopefully you won't ever have to experience it."

Her sister nodded and then glanced at the empty table. "Breakfast?"

Dor pulled her sister into a loose hug and kissed the unruly curls on the top of her head. "Is food all you think about?"

Lailana's stomach growled in answer to Dor's question. Lailana giggled, and, to Dor, it was the best sound in the world.

"I don't only think about food, sissy," Lailana protested.

"What else do you think about?" Dor asked with a smile.

"Dragons and sweeties."

"You would," she laughed.

"Father always brings me a treat." Her little face clouded over. "Where is Papa? I miss him."

Dor's stomach sank, but she was saved from answering as their mum pushed through the cloth door.

"This little one is hungry," Dor said, stroking her sister's curls. "Her belly won't stop shouting at me."

Her mum smiled and opened her arms as Lailana skipped over, gave her a hug, and then plopped a kiss on her belly.

"Ez?" her mum called. "Time to get up, love, or you're going to miss breakfast."

"I'm up," Ez mumbled, as she stumbled out of their darkened room.

Even at the age of ten, Dor's middle sister was a beauty. Short, dark wine-colored hair, green-hazel eyes, and pale skin. A year earlier, a warrior had taken a particular interest in Ez, and Dor and her mother had taken to cutting the girl's hair to avoid wandering, perverted eyes. The only thing that made Dor feel better about the whole situation was that her sire had made that warrior disappear permanently.

"How'd you sleep?" Dor asked.

"Just lovely," her sister replied, her tone tired and bitter. Ez stopped to Dor's right and winced as she took in the nightmare that was Dor's back. "That's going to take a while to heal. Do you need anything, sissy?"

Her middle sister had a prickly temperament, but she was more caring than many people Dor knew. "Mum took care of me. Why don't all of you go and get breakfast?"

"Are you coming?" Ez asked.

Dor placed a hand on her upset stomach, pain and anxiety causing it to roll. "No, I don't think I could eat a bite." With the work she had to accomplish today and the pain she was in, she would likely throw up anything she ate. "I'll be sure to eat dinner tonight."

"Jadim will be here in a bit to help you get to your assignment." Her mum placed her hands on her lower back and stretched, her face a mask of discomfort.

"How are you doing today?" Dor asked, eyeing her mum.

Her mum made a silly face that caused Lailana to giggle and everyone's countenance to brighten. "As good as expected. Now let's go and eat."

Her sisters followed their mum and blew Dor a series of kisses as they disappeared out of the door. Dor slowly straightened and glanced at her feet, wiggling her toes. Once again, she was thankful for not having shoes. She couldn't imagine the pain and effort it would've taken to get them on. She sighed, and forced herself to stand in their quiet home. There wasn't much in the room. A bed stood to the right of the entrance, a small nightstand next to it. There were three wooden chairs that circled the beat-up table and a rocking chair in the corner that had seen better days. It may have looked like meager lodgings, but it was still Dor's home, and the little sketches on the walls brought a smile to her face.

Dor slipped out of their cave and slowly began the trek down to her assignment, her muscles and back stiff. Pulling in a deep breath, she sighed. Not many people scurried about the Pit—a rarity—but that would change in a matter of minutes. No one missed breakfast. It was the one meal they were guaranteed. Dor took her time enjoying the quiet reprieve that she normally wasn't afforded. She loved her family dearly, but sometimes she longed to sneak away to a quiet cave just to be able to hear her own thoughts.

A hand wrapped around her elbow as she moved around a corner, causing her to stumble. She hissed as the wounds in her back pulled, then glared at the person who'd grabbed her. Ada frowned and squeezed Dor's elbow once before stepping back.

"I'm sorry, I didn't mean to scare you. You looked as if you were about to keel over."

"I'm fine," Dor replied.

Ada blinked and leaned comically to the side. "You were almost walking sideways." She straightened, pulled a piece of meat from her pocket, and slipped it into Dor's hand. "For your friend."

Dor tucked the meat away and glanced around the empty hallway before whispering a soft, "Thank you."

"Are you slipping to your spot?"

"Not until I've finished my assignment."

Ada nodded. "Can you even work?"

Dor smiled and strode toward her destination. "Mum numbed my back pretty well. I'm almost as good as new."

Her friend snorted. "I'll believe that when I see it." A pause. "I'll help you as much as I can."

Dor's heart warmed, and she carefully threw an arm around Ada and hugged her. "I love you."

"The same," Ada said, keeping her eyes down as they moved past stoic warriors who surveyed the area dispassionately.

They made their way into a smaller, stone corridor that smelled of damp rock, decaying leaves, and mold. Dor's nose wrinkled, and she breathed through her mouth to try to avoid the scent. She'd grown up in the Pit, yet, she'd never gotten used to the stench in certain areas.

"Don't be such a baby," Ada remarked as they arrived at their cave.

Dor pulled a face and glanced toward the whipping post. Dried blood covered the floor and the leather straps that had held her up. She blanched and hustled past the post to keep from heaving. Sweat broke out on her body as she retreated farther into the cavern and leaned her face against the cool rock.

Ada moved next to her and placed two sets of tools on the ground. "I retrieved yours."

Dor swallowed hard and used her open-backed shirt to wipe her face. "Thank you."

Workers filed in and moved to their designated work stations, all of them eyeing Dor's back as they set up. Dor scratched her arms and tried to ignore the feeling of many eyes on her. She held her breath as a mean-looking set of warriors moved through the group and signaled for them to start work. Thankfully, they paid her no attention, and her breath whooshed out. Thank the stars it wasn't the warriors from the prior day. At least, in this way, she was lucky.

Dor's arms shook, and her whole body broke out in a cold sweat. She'd only been working for a few hours and yet it felt like days had passed. Her back screamed with every movement she made, and wetness she suspected was blood trickled down her back.

"You need to take a break," Ada huffed as she swung her pickaxe.

"If I slow down any more, I won't be able to pick it up again."

"You'll kill yourself."

"Many things could kill me, but this isn't one of them."

"What if—"

Ada cut off abruptly and looked behind Dor. Dor forced herself to work harder and peeked out of the corners of her eyes to see what her friend was staring at. A man had materialized beside Dor and stared at her.

"Are you Dorcus?" he asked, his voice as quiet as the night.

Chills ran up and down Dor's spine as she forced herself to work harder. "I am."

He stepped closer and tugged the pickaxe from her hand.

Dor gaped at him and then glared at the man. "There are many tools. I'm sure you can find your own. Please kindly return mine so I can get back to work before either of us gets in trouble."

He flicked a glance around the cavern and then stepped closer to whisper in her ear. "You helped a little boy yesterday?"

Dor nodded and tipped her head back so she could meet his gaze. "Anyone would have."

He shook his head, his long hair falling into his eyes. "Not everyone." His gaze slid to her shoulder. "That was my little brother you saved yesterday. My family and I would like to pay back our debt. I shall work in your place today."

"I can't let you do that. There's no debt to pay. He is just a child, and children need protection."

The tall, young man nodded and squared his shoulders. "I understand, but I've heard eyewitness accounts of your beatings. If that warrior had touched my brother, he would have surely died. This is not something we can forget." His fingers curled possessively around the ax. "You're not well. Leave, and I'll finish this."

"And what of your own work?"

"I work during the night, so this is my resting time. No one is looking for me."

"And what of the other workers?" She glanced around the cave, noting the interested looks sent her way. Would they report her? It would be better to work in pain than receive another punishment. Surely, she wouldn't make it through another lashing.

"They won't say a word. They respect you for your sacrifice."

Her back spasmed, and pain lanced her spine. "I can't possibly accept your offer. It's too dangerous."

"I wouldn't put you in danger," Ada said softly to her left. "I spent most of the night making arrangements. You don't know him, but you can trust me."

Dor stared at her friend. "You helped arrange this?"

Ada nodded. "Let the man work, and you go to your spot for the rest of the day."

Dor glanced between the stranger and her friend, feeling like she would cry. "Thank you."

"It's the least we can do," the young man said. He lifted his chin. "Now leave before the guards return."

Dor kissed Ada on the cheek and crept to the end of the cavern to escape through the back passageway. Every step away from her post instilled more tension in her body as she waited for someone to call her out, but not a word was said.

Only the sound of metal striking stone accompanied her as she escaped working for the first time in her life.

TEN

THE WARLORD

HE WAVED AWAY THE MESSENGER and checked the seal for tampering.

Nothing. It was completely intact.

How boring.

He'd been suspicious of the messenger for some time now. He sighed. No executions today.

Zane slid a fine dagger across the seal and opened the letter hungrily. His expression hardened, and the voices inside him began to hiss their displeasure.

She's ours. They're keeping her from us. She should weep with gratitude and crawl to our feet begging for forgiveness.

He carefully placed the opened letter on his desk and inhaled deeply. The darker part of himself longed to crumple the letter or throw his desk through the wall of his tent. But those were baser feelings he'd mastered years ago, and he refused to lower himself to such beast-like behavior.

He pivoted on his heel and leaned a hip against his desk as he planned his next move. Their refusal didn't bother him. It was that she'd let them refuse him.

His jaw clenched.

His consort knew how much he hated to be ignored. A thought occurred to him. She knew him and understood him better than anyone other than his sister. Maybe this was a game?

A wicked smile curled his lips.

Zane loved games, always had. If she wanted to play, who was he to say no? It would make his victory all the more sweet.

"Blair!" he commanded.

Soft steps approached, and his commander entered the tent, then bowed so deeply his braids almost touched the leren fur covering the floor. "Yes, my lord?"

Zane pushed off the desk and eyed the map of Aermia pinned to the wall of his tent. "Burn the first southern village."

"It will be done."

"Leave the people."

"Yes, my lord."

"Very good," Zane murmured. "Dismissed."

He watched as his second in command backed out of the tent. Blair had been very devoted over the years, but he had his flaws. Zane's lips pursed. It would be a shame when the time came to execute the man. But it had to be done. If a warrior was left in power too long, it led to two outcomes: they either became too familiar with him, or they began to have doubts. Both options were dangerous.

The warlord reached a finger out and touched the black crown piece that represented his consort and her army.

"Soon, fiery one."

Soon, the voices chanted.

Sage would come to them.

It was only a matter of time.

ELEVEN

DOR

DOR CAREFULLY MOVED DOWN THE corridor toward the dull light and peeked around the corner, her heart picking up speed as guards patrolled the area.

Just act normal, Dorcus. You can do this. Don't let them see your fear.

She heaved a relieved breath as she maneuvered into the main hallway that circled the Pit in an endless spiral and joined the few workers heading toward their destinations below. At the thought of climbing all the way back up to her home, her whole body ached. But there was nothing else for it. She couldn't rest at home, so downward into hell it was.

Sweat beaded on her brow, and her breathing became labored as the path turned into steep stairs. Descending them was the worst part. Fear zipped through her veins at the thought of falling. She'd seen it happen before. Once a person slipped, there was no stopping their momentum. It only led to death.

She jerked as the woman next to her wrapped a firm hand around her left elbow and pulled her toward the inner wall, away from the edge. Dor glanced at her, askance. The woman smiled tiredly, deep lines marring the skin of what once might have been a beautiful face.

"You're making me nervous with all of your shambling about. Can't have you dying."

Dor nodded. "Thank you."

"It's no place to be daydreaming."

Thoroughly chastised, Dor thanked the old woman and continued her descent in silence. She ignored the heavy breathing of the workers around her, and focused on putting one foot in front of the other. As the group approached another set of guards, Dor tried to walk as naturally as she could and kept her head down to avoid attracting attention. The back of her neck prickled, and she glanced over her shoulder and locked eyes with a young warrior who seemed to scrutinize her. She whipped around, her pulse galloping, and prayed he wouldn't stop her. Each step she descended seemed to take hours as she waited for the warrior to call out. It was only when she'd moved down three more levels that she relaxed a little, her back screaming at the abuse. One worker after another disappeared into caves and crevices until it was just Dor.

Chills ran up her arms as the air heated and the light darkened to almost nothing. Her nose wrinkled at the cloying odor of brimstone and musk, and something dead. She eyed the gloomy surroundings and ran her left hand along the wall until her fingers caught on a star-shaped groove at about hip height. Then, she began counting. Fifty stairs until she would reach her destination. Dor blinked repeatedly as if it would help her eyes adjust to the almost-darkness that cocooned her like a cloud of smoke.

Forty-eight, forty-nine, fifty.

Her left hand ran along the wall and into a crevice that was only a handspan taller than her. With care, she edged sideways into the crevice and squeezed through its tight opening while trying to avoid scraping her back. Dor counted six steps and then reached her hands above her head as she entered a cool open space. She held in a deep breath and then released it. There was something about small spaces that always terrified her, and the older she became, the tighter the entrance to her secret spot became. It was only with memorization and the special breathing techniques her mum had taught which allowed Dor to still visit.

She blinked in the darkness, knowing it wouldn't magically become brighter. She placed one foot in front of the other and ran her hands along the ceiling as she traveled deeper into the narrow cavern. Realistically, she could have closed her eyes for all the good they did her, but she couldn't quite do it. For some odd reason, it made her feel safer if her eyes were open.

Her fingers brushed along the downward-sloped cavern ceiling, and her breath hitched as the tunnel tapered into a tiny passageway made of stone. Her heart pounded when at last she dropped to her hands and knees and began crawling forward into the small space. Rock scraped her shoulders after several moments, and she paused, her whole frame quaking. The stone felt like it was closing in on all sides. A sob escaped her as she imagined the stone suffocating her.

Dor shook her head to dispel the image. "Just a little farther," she panted. "You can do this." But her body didn't want to move. "Move it, Dorcus."

She drew in a deep breath and closed her eyes, to count her breaths like her mum had taught her. Once she was sufficiently calm, she began moving again through the tunnel she knew by heart. Hands and knees soaked from the small puddles she crawled through, she picked up her pace as the oppressive stone threatened to swallow her.

"Thank the stars," she gasped as the tunnel abruptly opened up and she spilled from the narrow channel into a small, round cave.

Dor knelt on the ground and placed her hands on the tops of her thighs, head bowed, and pulled in deep breaths. No matter how many times she went through the tunnel, each time was just as hard as the first. She didn't mind being in the caverns, but there was something terrifying about being surrounded by unforgivable stone that could easily take her life.

Once she'd caught her breath, she glanced around the space, barely able to see the spherical outline of the cave. When she'd first discovered this cave, she was only six years of age. Even now, she didn't know what had scared her mum so badly, but when her mum told her to run and hide, she did. She'd run and stumbled blindly until she couldn't crawl anymore. That's when she'd met her scaly friend.

Dor scooted forward and squinted at the wall until she discovered the rock she was searching for. Soft light slipped around the cracks as she wedged her fingers around it and tugged. Stone grated against stone until the plate-sized rock pulled free. Weak light flooded the small cavern, and Dor held an arm up and blinked. Her breaths caught as they did every time.

The cave sparkled. Every inch reflected light in the dark stone like thousands of tiny stars. It was beautiful. It was a piece of magic she held close to her heart. Even in the Pit, there was beauty.

A soft click caused her to smile, and she bent forward to peek through the opening to the other side. She whistled a soft tune and waited with bated breath for her friend. Her smile grew as scales scraped against stone and heavy footsteps neared her spot. The first time she'd heard such a sound, she'd been terrified, but not now. Now, she couldn't wait for what stood on the other side.

Dor carefully pushed her arm through the opening, and held her hand out as an enormous, scaled muzzle gently pressed against her palm. Heat infused her hand as the dragon nuzzled her in a happy hello.

"Hello, Illya."

Dor giggled when the dragon clicked a familiar *hello,* and a dry, rough tongue licked her arm. She playfully shook her hand out and then stroked the dragon's snout, marveling at the experience. It had been twelve years since she'd first met Illya, and each time she was able to visit him was like something out of a storybook.

Dor pulled back and leaned down, placing her chin on the edge of the stone. "How has your week been?"

Illya pulled back and hunkered down so Dor could see one silver feline-looking eye that reflected like rainbows in just the right light. His black scales caught the faint light and reflected colors like slicked oil. Dor's breath caught. He was the most magnificent creature she'd ever beheld. A sense of awe settled over her as she stared at the little of him she could see.

"You are the most beautiful thing I've ever beheld."

The dragon huffed, seeming to understand her. Over the years, she'd come to know Illya well. His mannerisms, likes, and dislikes. Some days, she'd prefer his company over that of the other humans she lived with.

He turned his face, as if preening.

Dor rolled her eyes. "Don't think too much of yourself, you vain beast." She scanned what she could see of his face and frowned as she noticed a new wound on his neck. The scales had been torn from him and his flesh had been cut open. A small growl escaped her. It sickened her what the healers did to the dragons. Their endless experiments made her want to kick something. "What did they do to you this week?" she whispered.

Illya blinked at her slowly, like he could understand every word from her mouth, and leaned closer as she reached a hand out to trace the scales under his eye, as if needing the soothing touch as much as she did. It was uncanny at times how he understood her moods better than she did.

Nothing that you could prevent.

Her dragon's clicks, hisses, and soft purrs had seemed to form the words that had blossomed in her mind, and she shook her head at her active imagination. Dragons didn't talk, and prisoners didn't have dragons. She pulled her hand back, earning a hiss of displeasure.

"Just wait, you'll enjoy my surprise." Dor wriggled her eyebrows at Illya. "I've brought something special for you, but I'll only give it to you if you promise to sing for me."

Illya hissed and pressed his snout against the gap and puffed air into her cavern. Her hair blew back from her face in a rush, and she grinned at the mischievous dragon.

"Okay, okay," she laughed as she pulled the small treat from her pocket and held it out to him. "I'm sorry it's not much. Next time, I'll do better."

He gently took the dried meat from her hand, conscious of his huge, razor-sharp teeth. It amazed her how he could be so gentle with such massive teeth—teeth he could tear her arm off with should he want. He gobbled down the treat with an enthusiasm that both buoyed and broke Dor's heart. Part of her was happy she could bring him something he enjoyed; the other part of her was broken-hearted he was so hungry. Illya hummed a satisfied sound in the back of his throat, and then sniffed her hand for more treats.

She smiled sadly and shook her head. "I'm sorry I don't have more for you this week. It's been a nightmare. I'll do better next week, I promise."

Dor stroked his scales above his eye and traced the long, jagged scar that caused his scales to grow up like spikes. Her heart squeezed. She still remembered when he'd received that one. She had been only eleven years, and she'd cried, thinking her dragon was dying. Even then, when he was in so much pain, Illya had snuggled as close as he could to impart comfort to her.

"It's not right how they treat you," she murmured.

Dragons were the worst kept secret in the Pit. Everyone knew they existed, but no one dared approach one of the beasts lest they be eaten. The healers starved the beasts and gave them elixirs to keep them calm while they experimented on them.

Her jaw clenched.

One of the only meals the dragons received were human traitors. It sickened her, but she understood what hunger could do to a person, let alone an animal. She couldn't fault Illya for any meals he had eaten. If she could get him and her family out, she would. Sometimes, in her space, she'd imagine them flying away and never coming back. But those were just childish dreams. There wasn't any escape for any of them, despite how much she wished it.

"I turn eighteen years in six days," she said. The words tasted sour upon her tongue. "Only six days until they come for me."

Disgust and burning hatred lit and began to simmer in her belly. Dreams weren't the only thing she indulged in with her dragon. She also released words and feelings that would get her killed if she ever repeated them in the hearing distance of another person.

"I hate them," she hissed. "I hate them so much. Sometimes I think about doing terrible things. Like... rebelling." Her last word was so soft, it was almost as if she never said it. But as soon as the word was released, a well of feeling rushed forward in her. "Everything is wrong about this place. No one deserves to live as a prisoner just because of the kingdom they were born in. No woman deserves to be bred like an animal. I'm sick of being judged because of how I look." She cursed and glanced at her hands. "Just because we're different doesn't mean we're inferior." Her skin prickled as she spoke the treason that had rooted deeply in her heart. "Who gave the warlord the right to leash human beings and declare them disposable because of their genes?"

A tear dripped down her cheek. "I hate him." Her hand shook as she reached toward Illya and stroked his frill on the crown of his head as he pressed as close to her as possible. "I hate being forced to live here. I hate the injustice. I hate being powerless."

That's what bothered her the most. She was powerless to stop the pain and suffering around her. She was powerless to fight the fate that had been placed before her.

Another tear fell.

"I'll be a mother soon." Her dragon nuzzled her fist, and she forced herself to open her hand and keep stroking his scales. "Maybe you'll be able to get to know my children." She swiped at her watery eyes with her right forearm, hating that she didn't get a say in what happened to her own children. The unknown was the most frightening. Would the warrior let her keep the children and raise them? Would he take the child and discard her like rubbish?

I will love your young.

Dor froze and blinked, staring at the dragon who eyed her quietly. She barked out a laugh. "I'm hearing things and laughing at my mind. It must be all the stress." And the pain.

She winced and cautiously stretched her back, the healing wounds pulsing with heat. Swiping at her gritty eyes once more, she got comfortable, pillowing her head on her arm as she stroked Illya's muzzle. "If you don't mind, I might rest a little bit, and, when I wake, I'll tell you a story."

Her dragon hummed and rested his head on his claw-tipped paws.

When she'd first met Illya, she'd been terrified and had started spouting stories to keep the dragon from eating her. She wouldn't step that near to him, and neither would he, but after that first visit, she'd found herself coming back. It took many months for them to trust each other, but Dor won him over by telling him stories. Some true, some nonsensical.

Her eyes slowly closed, and, as she drifted off to sleep, a deep voice crooned. *I'll watch over you.*

TWELVE

TEHL

"BLOODY HELL!" WILLIAM GASPED, STARING at the immense fiilee to his right, causing Tehl to hide his smile.

The older man gaped, his long beard quivering as his mouth bobbed in awe—and a good dose of fright, Tehl suspected.

"That's Skye," Tehl said, as the fiilee crept closer, sniffing the ground beneath his paws. His lips twitched. Nali had no doubt relieved herself in the spot, marking her territory, and the immense creature was clearly not thrilled.

"She's beautiful, no?" Raziel, the crown prince of Methi, said as he strode into the meadow.

Tehl glanced behind the Methian prince, hoping to spot his wife. The troublesome woman could scarcely leave the beasts alone. Every time he turned his back, she'd disappear from their camp to go and train with the beasts.

The first time he'd caught her flying on the back of one, Tehl's heart had practically leapt out of his chest. Once he'd calmed himself down, he'd then noticed the man riding behind her, pressed fully against her. That had stirred up feelings he'd rarely experienced.

Jealousy.

He knew what curves and beauty lay beneath her clothes, and it rankled him that another man was wrapped around *his* wife and could obviously feel her shape. When they'd landed, Sage had a skip in her step as she rushed toward him. Her green eyes had sparkled like emeralds and color had turned her cheeks a pretty pink that he wanted to taste.

Tehl honestly couldn't remember what she'd said to him. For one thing, she was speaking faster than his mind could comprehend, and he was a bit distracted. She pecked him on his mouth and then ran down the path toward camp like a wild fae thing he had no chance of catching.

"She's fiery," Raziel had commented.

Turning back to face the Methian prince, he had been relieved to notice the man wasn't watching his wife, but had been attending to his beast.

"I have no designs on your wife." Raziel's golden eyes had met his for a moment. "I like mine a little less jaded."

Tehl's hackles had risen at the insult. Raziel had taken one look at his face and held his hands up in surrender.

"It's not meant as an insult." A shrug. "I like my friends jaded and sarcastic, so she's perfect for that role. And you, my friend, have it bad," Raziel goaded.

"Have what?"

"You love your mate, as you rightly should. One day, I hope to find the same thing. You are a lucky man. Any person can choose a spouse, but those who have a love match are to be envied." Raziel had blown some of his wine-colored hair from his face and smiled wolfishly. "Plus, they always produce the strongest kits."

Now, Tehl wasn't an ignorant man, nor was he overly shy, but something about the Methian prince's words had made him want to blush. Instead, he'd smiled in pride. He and Sage *would* have amazing children.

"Tehl?"

He blinked and stared at William's lined face. "Yes?"

"Daydreaming?"

"Something like that."

Raziel gave William a knowing smile and gestured toward Skye. "Would you like to meet her properly?"

A boyish smile illuminated the general's face as he stared in wonder at the fiilee. "I don't think there's anything I've ever wanted more, other than to bed my wife," William said with glee.

The Methian crown prince released a booming laugh and slapped William on the back. "Well, I can't grant your other wish, but this is, at least, in my power." He glanced at Tehl. "One of my men is bringing the spymaster for a visit. He should be here within the hour."

Sam. Well, that was a piece of good news. They'd been at the war camp for several weeks, and, so far, all of it had been for nothing. The Scythians hadn't crossed the border. They'd made their presence known by their massive fires at night and the war songs and drums that never ceased to stop. Tehl had yet to figure out their aim. His best guess was they were trying to manipulate their psyche and intimidate them.

A shadow passed over Tehl and swung around the meadow. He tipped his head back and watched a pure-white fiilee glide to the ground. His brother grinned and waved. Tehl had to smile back. He wasn't sure if the reason Sam was so giddy was because of the flight, or the extremely attractive Methian woman holding him.

She slid off the fiilee and offered a hand up to Sam like he was a lady. His brother was too far away for Tehl to hear the words, but whatever he had said to the normally stoic warrior had the woman blushing. He rolled his eyes at his brother's antics, knowing Sam just couldn't help himself.

Sam climbed down from the fiilee and took the woman's hand and kissed it, further turning the woman into another admirer, Tehl was sure. The bastard.

Sam abandoned his happy victim and almost pranced across the meadow, a wicked smile on his face.

Stars above, Tehl had missed his brother. Things had been much too serious without his sense of warped humor to break the ice. He took a few steps and embraced him.

Sam pulled back, grinning. "Missed me? I'm flattered. It's only been a few weeks."

"Not long enough," Tehl muttered with a straight face.

His brother snorted. "I see the dry humor is alive and well."

He shook his head at Sam. The man wasn't wrong. "What news do you have?"

Sam's face melted into an expression much too serious for Tehl's liking. "I think you'll need to sit down for this one."

His blasted brother was right. If he hadn't been sitting, he'd have fallen down.

"Do the punches ever stop coming?"

"Not with the warlord," Sage said darkly. She leaned heavily against the circular, wooden table that stood in the center of the room. His wife stared blankly at the massive leather map that lay on the tabletop.

Raziel paced behind Sage and Lilja along the tent wall, his hair almost brushing the ceiling. Tehl had thought he was tall, but the damn man was a bloody giant. Did they breed massive humans in Methi?

"Tehl?"

He blinked slowly and turned toward Lilja as she pointed at the map. "Yes?"

The Sirenidae stood from her chair, her burnt-orange dress whispering around her bare legs. Tehl wondered how she could stand the cold with so few garments on. He pulled his jacket closer and stood to get a better look at the spot she was pointing to on the map. She placed a small pin at the mouth of Sanee's bay.

"If the Scythians get anywhere near the bay, we'll lose Sanee," Lilja declared.

"We can't lose Sanee," Tehl muttered. It was unthinkable to lose the capital. "Do you think this is a ploy to get us to remove our army?"

Lilja shrugged a snowy shoulder. "I can't presume to know the mind of the warlord. This could be a trap, it could be a legitimate maneuver, or he could just be trying to bluff us. General?"

William's mustache moved from side to side as he wiggled his lips, his eyes glued to the map like it held the secrets to the world. "It would be smart to pin us in on both sides, but I don't think he has enough men to pull off such a venture. Sage?"

"I don't know." Frustration colored her tone as she glared down at the map. "I didn't exactly see much of his stronghold. We were led through the jungle and then down into a cave-like hole area."

"The Pit," Lilja supplied.

"The Pit," Sage continued, "was massive, but I think it only held laborers." She pushed back from the table and crossed her arms. "I wish I had more information, but that's all I know."

Tehl frowned. Sage wasn't the only one who'd been in Scythia. "Where's Blaise?"

"She's out on scouting duty. She'll return this evening," Raziel supplied.

"And how do you know that?" Lilja questioned.

The Methian prince smiled, his golden eyes dancing. "My brother is also on duty."

Tehl smothered his smile. Rafe had assigned himself to every one of Blaise's duties, and the Scythian woman hated it. Just a week ago, Tehl had watched Blaise pull a blade on Rafe and almost take off the tip of his nose. What had been even better was the look on Rafe's face once he realized she'd pulled one over on him. She'd held not one blade, but two, and had also cut a good chunk of hair from his head.

"She's our best bet." Tehl turned to Sam. "But Jasmine has invaluable information. You'll speak to her?"

Sam frowned, but quickly smoothed his expression. "I'll speak to her and pass on any prudent information." He turned his attention on Lilja. "What of Blair?"

"Blair's been silent."

That settled like a rock in Tehl's stomach. Blair was playing a dangerous game. He didn't exactly trust the Scythian, but Lilja did, and that was enough for him. Anyone Lilja held in esteem was an ally worth having.

"Any word from the rest of the Sirenidae?" Sage asked Lilja.

Lilja shook her head. "It's been quiet in the seas." She pinned Sam with her magenta gaze. "How did you come by this information?" she asked curiously.

Sam smiled casually. "Spies."

Lilja smirked, a picture of amusement and sexuality. "And who is your spy? Or better yet, *what* is your spy?"

Sam grinned. "You know I can't tell you."

She laughed. "I have my suspicions."

"And that's all they are. *Suspicions.*"

William rolled his eyes and clapped his hands. "You young'uns and your games," he said gruffly, but with affection.

Lilja glided to his side and pressed a kiss against his whiskered cheek. "You flatterer."

"Let's reconvene this evening," Tehl said. "We'll be able to get a better idea of our enemy's numbers then."

Raziel nodded and strode from the tent with a nod at Sage and Tehl. Lilja looped an arm through William's and strolled out of the tent, leaving Tehl with Sam and Sage.

"What a nightmare," Sage breathed.

Tehl watched her in concern. She'd lost some of her color at the news of the armada the Scythians were readying.

She ran her hands through her dark brown hair. "I hate surprises."

"I love a good surprise," his brother piped in. "Especially when it involves a naked female."

Sage rolled her eyes, but a small smile touched her mouth, removing some of the grim lines that were bracketing her lips. She'd been much too serious since arriving at the camp. The circumstances were glum, but, still, she'd lost a little bit of the sassiness Tehl loved.

She walked over to Sam and hugged him. "How's Jasmine?"

"She's doing well."

"That's all I get?" Sage asked, stepping back.

Tehl full-on grinned as he stepped closer and wrapped an arm around his wife's waist, content with how she leaned into him. Stars above, they were in the least romantic setting, but he still couldn't keep his hands off his wife.

Sam watched the two of them, a twinkle in his blue eyes. "She told me if I didn't tell you to visit soon, she'd track you down herself."

Sage smiled. "That sounds more like her." She squeezed Tehl and moved out of his arms toward the tent flap to their right. "I'll let you two catch up."

Both men watched her disappear outside and then faced each other. Sam shifted from foot to foot in an uncharacteristic show of unease and nervousness.

Tehl cocked his head and arched a brow. "I thought Zachael beat that out of you."

Sam shrugged. "It rarely happens."

Tehl brushed by his brother and snagged a canteen from atop his cloak. He pulled the stopper out and took a huge swig. If his brother was nervous, then he had truly awful news.

He held out the canteen to his brother and was shocked when Sam took two gulps. That wasn't a good sign. His brother rarely drank spirits, and when he did... it was always because something terrible had happened. Whatever his brother had to say now would likely be worse than what he'd already dropped on them.

"Don't keep me on my toes. Just give it to me straight," Tehl ordered. He hated the suspense. "Tell me what's wrong."

"Jasmine's pregnant." Sam winced at his blunt words.

Tehl blinked slowly, trying to comprehend the two small words. Jasmine was with child? His brows pulled together as he counted the days since Sam and Jasmine had wed. It had only been a few weeks – how could he possibly know that soon...

He glared at his brother. "You did not. Tell me you did not do something so dishonorable."

Sam glared back. "Thanks for not jumping to conclusions!"

"As if you gave me any other options! What am I supposed to think? You have a history that I've tried to ignore, but at least you've married the girl." If he hadn't... well, they'd be having a very different conversation at the moment.

"The child is not mine."

Swamp apples. He'd seen how Jasmine had been acting promiscuously after the woman had escaped, but he'd hoped she'd had more sense than that. He didn't think her the devious type to trap a man into marriage. "Did you know before you wed?" he outright asked. It was better to be blunt than to miscommunicate.

"I did."

Tehl studied his brother. "Would the man who ruined her not do the honorable thing?"

The muscle in Sam's jaw ticked as he swallowed. "Tehl, she's *well* along. It won't be much longer until the babe arrives."

The blood drained from Tehl's face as he realized what his brother was telling him. If she was that far along with child, that meant she was in Scythia when the babe was conceived. "Wicked hell, *no*." It couldn't be true.

Sam's hands clenched and unclenched. "It seems not all have the control of their master."

Tehl sat heavily on the chair behind him. That poor girl. What she must have suffered. Did Sage know? "Who else knows about this?"

"Both healers, myself, and now you."

So, Sage didn't know. The news would kill her. "Why tell me?"

"I don't know what to do for my wife. She's struggling. I think," Sam paused, "I think she needs Sage."

"You know what you're asking of me? This will be a great weight of guilt my wife will have to carry."

"She'll be angrier if you keep it from her," Sam pointed out.

True, but not the point.

Tehl scowled at his brother. "I wouldn't have to keep anything from her if you'd kept this to yourself." He stared at his calloused hands. How was he supposed to tell Sage? "Does Jasmine know you're here?"

"Yes, but she doesn't know I've spoken to you about this. If it were up to her, she'd keep pretending like nothing is wrong at all. But she can barely hide the swell of her belly now. Palace gossips say they think she's just fat." Sam grimaced. "If she won't speak to Mira or I about it, I think she'll speak to Sage."

"You think ambushing your wife is the answer?"

Sam threw his hands up. "I don't know what else to do. She's wrapped an impenetrable wall around herself that I can't get through. The only time I see her soften is with the twins," he growled, frustration clear in every word.

Tehl watched his brother closely. "Do you want to get close to her?"

"Well, I married her, didn't I?" he scoffed. "I was trying to do the right thing. She'd suffered much to help Sage, and she didn't deserve what would happen to her once it was known she was with child. At least this way, she'll have the protection of our name and the love of our family." A pause. "So will the child."

Pride and tenderness bloomed in Tehl's chest. His brother had his faults, but Tehl had always known he was a good man. "You're going to be a father," he whispered. He stood and embraced his brother. "Congrats."

Sam hugged him and slapped him on the back. "I don't know what I'm doing."

"No one does." Tehl pulled back, grinning. "Despite how the babe came about, it's still a blessing. I'll send Sage home for a visit shortly." He sobered.

"Maybe she'll actually sleep."

Sam stared at him, askance. "She's not sleeping?"

"The nightmares are getting worse. She actually handed me her weapons to keep me safe. One night, she almost slit my throat."

His brother's expression morphed into something deadly and blood thirsty. "The monsters that caused our women pain *will* suffer."

Tehl mirrored his brother's smile. "That they will."

THIRTEEN

SAM

HE ROUNDED THE LAST TENT and strode toward his horse. His white war horse gleamed in the darkness and didn't startle as he approached. There was something cozy about the night. Most were terrified of the darkness, of what it concealed, but Sam thought of it as more of a warm blanket of protection.

Sam brushed his hand along Moonlight's flank and checked his saddle. He could never be too careful. No one wanted to die because of negligence.

"Leaving so soon?" a husky, sensual voice called.

He straightened and craned his neck to smile over his shoulder. Lilja stepped from the forest that bordered the war camp and sauntered toward him, all grace.

"I was wondering when you would come find me."

She smiled coyly and brushed a silvery-white lock of hair from her shoulder. "And what gave you the impression that I wanted to speak with you?"

Sam laughed softly and turned to face Lilja. "Like calls to like, love."

"That it does."

She sat daintily on a tall round rock and crossed her long pale legs that the slitted skirt just couldn't keep contained.

Sam groaned and ran a hand down his face. In his mind, he knew she was old enough to be his mother, but damn him, if the woman wasn't alluring.

"Do you really run around the camp in that getup? It's amazing you haven't been accosted."

Lilja laughed. "They've all seen me spar."

"That makes sense."

He considered himself capable with many weapons, but in a fight with the Sirenidae? She'd win, hands down. The woman was death wrapped in a beautiful package.

"What do you want with me?" he said tiredly. "It's been a long day."

"I suspect it has," Lilja replied softly. "I'm intrigued as to how you obtained the information about the Scythian fleet."

Sam arched a brow. He wasn't going to give her information for free. "You're fishing and you know it."

"Fish. What an interesting word to use. I've been in the caves that house the Scythian ships, and it would be impossible for anyone to get inside conventionally. They would have to be excellent swimmers," she enunciated and pinned him with a look.

He kept his expression placid. How in the hell did she know? "What are you getting at?"

"Don't play coy. You have a Sirenidae spy."

"Anything is possible."

Lilja brushed imaginary lint off of her skirt. "You should know that keeping company with you is very dangerous for your spy, and I'm not speaking of their missions. I'm speaking of what will happen to them if the king finds out about their extracurricular activities. Death would be a kindness."

Sam held back a shiver at her somber warning. "I assure you that I care for all of my spies."

The Sirenidae stood and shook out her dress. "I'm aware, which is why I'm imparting this to you." She took a step closer, her magenta gaze intense. "I may not be permitted to permanently reside in the sea any longer, but it does not mean I am ignorant of what happens in its depths. Tell my niece I love her, and to be safe."

He kept his mask in place and marveled at the woman standing before him. He'd spoken to no one about his newest recruit, and yet, Lilja knew. "I'd very much like to spend a day in your mind," he murmured.

"I just bet you would." She stepped closer and adjusted his coat. "You should also know that rebellion is brewing in Scythia."

It was years of practice that kept him from jerking at her words. "You have proof?"

"Someone I trust very much. I suspect when the time comes, we may have more help than we anticipated from the enemy side."

His mind spun. That would change things. "Would you please keep me informed of the situation?"

She nodded. "If anything changes, you'll be one of the first to know."

"Aermia is lucky to have you," Sam said, meaning his words. Information could make or break a war. It was the difference between defeat and victory. "If you ever find you want a job…"

Lilja barked out a laugh and hugged him. "I'm much too old for spying and trickery."

Sam snorted. "Who's lying now?"

"When this is all over, I plan on growing fat on my ship with my delectable husband."

"Debauchery," Sam joked.

"Only if one is not married… speaking of which, how is your new wife?"

"As good as can be expected when married to a rake and scoundrel. She hates me."

"How delightfully honest," Lilja remarked. "Maybe give her a reason not to. Show her the real Sam."

It sounded easy. But in truth, it was impossible. His scandalous behavior perpetuated his world class reputation as a rake and flirt. While everyone focused on his perceived debauchery, they never looked any closer at what was really going on. And it worked for him. Well, up until now.

"I don't know if I can," he said honestly. "I feel like I don't know him anymore."

"That is something I understand. I've played many parts during my life. It was only once I met Hayjen that he helped me discover myself. Jasmine and her children could be that for you. Don't give up before you've even started. That's the coward's and fool's way out."

Sam pressed a kiss to Lilja's cheek and then stepped back. "I'll think about what you said." He slipped his foot into the stirrup and slung his right leg over his horse. "Take care."

Lilja waved and smiled, flashing her white teeth. "You do the same. You might want to have a conversation with Gem when you arrive home. I believe she has something she wants to tell you."

Sam opened his mouth to ask what she meant, but the Sirenidae melted back into the forest. He chuckled and shook his head.

"Bloody woman," he whispered and then pressed his heels into the sides of his horse. "Home!"

FOURTEEN

DOR

DOR WOKE WITH A START, sweat dripping down her back. Where was she?

She quickly blinked, trying to get her bearings. Her breath caught as she admired the gemstone-walls of the cave. Illya's cave. She was safe.

Dor relaxed and glanced toward the small opening. Her hand rested on Ilya's snout as the dragon slumbered. How much time had passed? She squinted into the dragon's room—though she could not decipher the time of day, the amount of pain plaguing her bare back that was currently plastered to the rough stone behind her told her much time had passed.

"This is going to hurt," she whispered to herself. Illya lazily cracked one silver eyelid and stared at her while she panted and prepared herself for the onslaught of pain. "If I pass out, wake me, Illya."

Her fingers clutched at the uneven stone to ground herself as she sat up. Her gasp echoed in her cave, and a growl escaped her as she sat up, her raw flesh clinging to the stone behind her. Water flooded her eyes, and white light flashed across her vision as she pulled away completely. Warm liquid dripped down her back as she gulped in the heated air her dragon blew into the small space. She was going to pass out.

A series of concerned clicks, growls, and hums rumbled from her dragon as he pressed closer to the wall between them.

"I'm okay," she puffed as she leaned forward with a groan. Dor lifted her hair to make sure no strands had pressed into any of her gashes. Sweat dotted her brow as agony pulsed through her injuries. Stars above, she hated lashings. It was one of the cruelest forms of punishment. If it were up to her, she'd burn every blasted whip in the Pit.

Illya whined, and Dor reached through the opening to run her hand along the length of his scarred, midnight snout. "It's just a little kink in my back. I shifted in my sleep and slept the wrong way."

He inhaled deeply. *I smell blood.*

She was going insane. Maybe from the blood loss. Dor rubbed the right side of her face. "I was whipped yesterday," she admitted. "A little boy's life was in danger. I couldn't stand by and do nothing."

A true leader.

She snorted at her active imagination. She was a leader of nothing and no one. The Pit didn't breed heroes and saviors. It bred monsters and madness – she just happened to be one of the lesser monsters.

Pushing onto her knees, Dor pressed her face into the small rock opening and waited for Illya to press closer. Her eyes watered as he exhaled hot air into her face. "That was not necessary," she muttered as she brushed a kiss against the tip of his snout. As if the dragon couldn't help himself, he breathed on her again. It seemed like he enjoyed marking her by whatever means possible.

Dor pulled back and caressed his face, feeling a sense of loss at the prospect of leaving. This was the worst part. It felt like she was abandoning him. Each time she visited, there was a possibility he wouldn't answer her call. She couldn't imagine life without him. He'd become the best part of her life.

"I wish I could free you." The words were fanciful, filled with longing, truth, and hopelessness. Freedom wasn't in their future, but at least they had this time together.

You will free us all.

She ignored the unbidden thought as Illya stared her down like he was trying to tell her something.

"I have to go," she said, forcing a smile. "Thank you for sharing this afternoon with me and letting me rest here, but I need to return to my family."

Her dragon pushed harder against her hand and briefly curled his tongue around her wrist in his goodbye. Absently, she wondered if Illya longed for her company like she did for his. Maybe he was just biding his time with her, but it felt like something more. Inside, she knew he was inexplicably hers and she was his.

Dor massaged underneath his chin and pulled away. If she didn't go now, she wouldn't leave. Glancing over her shoulder, the hair on her arms rose as she stared at the small black hole she'd have to crawl through. A shudder worked through her body as she turned back to Illya. "I'll come back and visit you tomorrow, if possible. I'll try to bring a bigger treat for you."

Illya sniffed and clicked a soft, crooning sound. *I'll await your visit, precious one.*

Her eyes widened as she swore the words formed in her mind. "Illya, there's something wrong with my mind," she whispered. Her mum had always encouraged imagination, but at the age of eighteen years it was time she grew up, and yet, every time she visited, she imagined her dragon spoke to her. Which was impossible. Animals didn't speak. She eyed the dragon. Well... dragons weren't really animals. They were myths.

She shook her head at her fantastical thoughts. "Until we meet again," she whispered as she heaved the huge rock from the floor and inhaled deeply before shoving it back into place. Her pulse pounded as the stars around her winked out and inky darkness cloaked the space with its smothering presence. She sucked in a steadying breath and forced her legs to move away from her dragon. Time seemed to stretch as she made her way out of the secret spot.

Dull light spilled through the narrow crevice as the tunnel widened, and she was able to climb onto her feet. Her back protested the movements, but she didn't stop as she kept focused on the light. Almost there. She rotated sideways and shuffled through the crack, biting her bottom lip to keep from crying out when a sharp stone jabbed her back.

She paused, holding her breath, and scanned the staircase. Nothing stirred, but her skin prickled nonetheless. It felt like a million insects were crawling over her body. It was almost impossible to see at this level, she reminded herself. No one was watching her. She slipped onto the smooth, dry pathway and began the long trek up the winding staircase. It was one of the few places in the Pit that stayed dry. Dor stared at the black stone beneath her feet. The only explanation for this that she could figure was that the dragons released so much heat in their breaths that the surrounding area stayed dry. Which meant—she scanned the area—Illya couldn't be the only one.

Her legs wobbled, and Dor stumbled. She latched onto the wall to her right as she caught her breath, staring at the drop. That was the second time today. She needed to be more careful. She heaved a breath and glanced above and immediately wished she hadn't. The pathway seemed to spiral on forever.

Her legs burned as she forced herself to start climbing. The longer she tarried here, the more worried her mum would be. Guilt pricked her. Worrying was the last thing her mum needed to be doing in her condition. The babe was due soon.

The steep stairway ended and melded with the sloping pathway that circled the Pit like a giant, coiled snake. The air cooled, as did Dor's sweat. Her stomach sank as she eyed the lanterns flickering around the Pit. They glowed a sickly green color. Night had officially come. Her mum would be worried.

Dor forced her legs to move faster and eyed the slaves that descended toward her. At least the night workers would cover her arrival. There was safety in numbers. She noted three guards loitering by an intersection of corridors to the main path. She tucked her chin and kept her head down as she approached them. They seemed too relaxed to be on duty. That always spelled trouble. It meant they were visiting for recreational purposes.

She held her breath as she passed the warriors, and thanked the stars that they were too occupied with bawdy jokes to notice her. That was until she caught a low whistle and murmured words.

"Long legs, but look at that back. That one screams trouble. Not worth it."

Her shoulders pulled up toward her ears as she hunched forward and practically ran away from the men. For once in her life, she was thankful for the beating if it meant it kept warriors from looking too closely at her.

She rounded a corner and plowed straight into a wide chest. A scream caught in her throat as two calloused hands wrapped around her biceps. Her gaze flew to the man holding her, and she almost sobbed in relief.

Jadim.

He stared down at her with arresting blue-green eyes, his lips pinched. He glanced over her shoulder and then directed her down a maze of hallways.

"Where have you been?" he hissed.

"Out." His jaw clenched in a familiar way. They'd been friends since childhood, and he'd always done that. She used to see how many times a day she could get him to clench his jaw. "Ada told you where I was?"

"She said you were safe, but that was hours ago. She's been so worried."

Dor shook his grip off and then placed her hand in his as they continued walking down the dark stone corridors. She shivered at the sickly green light that seemed to move and writhe around them. Devil, take it, but she hated the night lanterns.

"I didn't mean to worry anyone. I fell asleep." She straightened and winced as her back twinged. "My guess is that my body is trying to heal so I slept longer than I intended to."

Jadim's square jaw loosened, and he glanced at her through a thick fringe of lashes. Dor almost stumbled at the look. Sometimes she couldn't help but notice how devastatingly handsome he was. It was a shame what the healers had done to him.

"Don't look at me like that."

She forced her gaze away from his face, hating that she was mooning over a man she could never have. The healers had made sure of that, and her reactions only made it worse for him. Ashamed, she squeezed his hand once. "I'm sorry."

"It's not your fault," he said softly, squeezing her hand back. "In fact," he paused, glancing around before slowing to a stop.

Dor arched a brow in question.

He wet his plush lips and stared down at her, his expression serious. "In six days, the healers will come for you."

Her stomach dropped and rolled at the reminder. "What of it?" She glared at the ground, hating how her voice wobbled, how fear showed its ugly face. Only six days until the last of her freedom would be ripped away, and she'd become just another broodmare for the Scythian court.

He dropped her hand and crooked a finger under her chin, forcing her to look up at his handsome angular face. "It is what it is, but you're not alone."

"I know," she croaked.

"Chances for perfect offspring are low," he murmured, telling her what she already knew. "So you'll be raising babes in the Pit."

Dor shrugged a shoulder. "It's not much different than what I've done with both of my sisters." But her stomach quivered at the thought of having her own child. "Chances are it will take time for a babe to catch in my womb."

Jadim stepped closer and clasped her face between his hands. "It only takes once, Dor."

She shuddered at the possibility of a child within the next year. She wasn't ready for a child, but wouldn't it be better to be only taken once? She didn't know. "I'm scared," she admitted.

"I know, but you won't be alone." He leaned forward and kissed her forehead. "I'll help raise the babes, if you'll have me."

She froze and stared blankly at his chest. "You wish to bond with me?" Her voice cracked.

He pulled back and brushed his thumb along her left cheek. "I do. I'll care for you and any children of ours."

She swallowed her tears and stared up at the selfless man before her. He would care for them, and help raise children that weren't his own? "What could you possibly gain out of this union? How could I accept such a gift?"

He wiped away a tear that dripped down her cheek. "I would gain a wonderful, capable wife who happens to be one of my best friends." He glanced away, his throat working, before staring down at her. "You know how I long for children."

Dor swallowed back the ugly sobs that threatened to break free. What the healers had done to Jadim was possibly one of their most heinous crimes. In a bid to control the slave population and to ensure imperfection wasn't passed to other children, the healers sterilized all the males. None of the men could have children or even accomplish the act of love making. They'd turned every male slave into a eunuch, and it sickened her.

"I do."

He stared down at her and slowly leaned closer to press a soft kiss against her lips. Her skin tingled, and she wrapped her hands around his wrists and leaned against him. Slowly, Jadim pulled away and brushed his nose against hers.

"Will you accept me?"

Dor swallowed and stared at the wonderful man who held his breath while awaiting her answer. A small part of her didn't want to accept. It felt like she was taking advantage of someone she loved. But the reasonable part of her mind knew she couldn't raise wee ones on her own. Jadim would treat whatever babes she birthed as his own, and he would be a wonderful father. Plus, she loved him. He was one of her best friends, and she could see herself growing old with him. And there was the tiny part of her that she liked to pretend didn't exist which had loved the boy standing in front of her for years, despite knowing what their future could only hold.

"I accept you," she said reverently.

He smiled and pressed another kiss to her lips that was all too quick, but Dorcus knew it was for the best. It was better not to court disaster and disappointment, for both of them.

"Thank you," he breathed, his eyes sparkling. He hugged her close, mindful of her exposed back and then stepped backward, taking her hand in his. "We should speak to your mum."

Dor nodded, staring at the man who began to direct them both toward her home. She had a nagging feeling that what she had just agreed to would lead to heartache and pain for both of them, but she'd had no choice. And really, there wasn't anyone else she'd ever want to grow old with. She had loved Jadim for as long as she could remember. She squashed that thought and concentrated on the pain throbbing across her back. If she let herself dream of the impossible, the agony and disappointment for both of them would be unimaginable.

She was lucky, but she didn't feel it. It felt like she was being denied the most important relationship of her life. Their bond felt like a cheap imitation of what a marriage should be.

Stars above, she was ungrateful and greedy. She mentally slapped herself and thought about everything she was gaining, not what she would lose in six days.

Everything would turn out all right. She had to believe that, or she'd disappear down a black hole she'd never be able to crawl out from. She had an amazing family and now a mate who would support her despite how others would use her.

That had to be enough. If it wasn't, she wouldn't survive much longer.

FİFTEEN

SAM

———⊸∘⟅⟆∘⊹———

SOMETIMES HE WAS SO BLOODY tired.

Sitting on his desk was a never-ending stream of information to sift through, and women to calm. Most men thought women were irrational creatures prone to hysteria and bouts of fancy. But Sam knew better. They were smart, cunning, creative, and stealthy. If he had a choice in whether to remove the world of men or women, he would burn the male population. Plus, women were a delight to look upon. He was the first to admit he loved them. But at the moment, he wanted to tape one woman's mouth shut.

He set his documents aside and surveyed one of his lovely spies who was doing her best impression of sucking on a lemon. "Would you repeat that?"

Her nose crinkled as if she smelled something rotten. "You weren't listening?"

Of course, he was listening. It was his job to listen, but if she intended to irritate him with her petty complaints, then surely he'd needle her back just a bit. "I dropped off when you began to prattle on about hair colors, but I'm focused now. I had a bit of a busy night, so please forgive me."

Marilyn's expression softened a touch. "I heard what you did for those girls yesterday. That was well done."

Sam smiled weakly. He wished he could've done more. Hopefully, the mother and her young daughter would enjoy their simple life in the country, away from the monster who had made them his personal punching bags.

"As was the man's punishment," Marilyn said with a feral smile. "Maybe he'll see my brother in hell."

Sam's smile mirrored Marilyn's. There would be no tears for the man who'd suffer for the rest of his life in the mines or die, or for Marilyn's brother who'd taken it upon himself to hurt children. Sam was still unsure where that man's bones had ended up.

"I did my best. Now—" He rapped his knuckles on his desk, eyeing Marilyn's hair covering. "What's happened?"

His spy's right eye twitched as she pulled the veil and embroidered cloth band from her head. Her hair was not her normal blonde with silver streaks, but bright orange. "I believe some of the girls thought it would be amusing to pull a prank."

His lips twitched. "I see."

She puffed out an annoyed breath. "It seems I was not to be the original recipient, but I am the victim, nonetheless. How, my lord, am I supposed to serve my lady with hair the color of carrots?"

He coughed and kept his laughter held back, as he knew it would set her off in a fiery tirade. Marilyn may be an older woman, but, in all her years, she still hadn't learned to control her temper. It was ironic. Her hair now matched her temper.

"Is there a way to get it out?" he asked smoothly, not one tremor of humor in his voice.

"If there is, I don't know of it." She harrumphed.

"I'm sorry about your beautiful hair. I'll reach out discreetly to one of my contacts to see if they can find something to help. And, as for the girls, I will personally speak with them." He stood and walked around his desk, taking Marilyn's hands in his own. "For now, go to the garment room and pick a new fabric for a new veil."

She smiled at him, her wrinkles becoming more pronounced. "I thank you, my lord."

Sam patted the top of her right hand. A woman never complained about new clothes. Unless it was Sage, or his wife Jasmine, who refused to wear anything he put in her closet. It drove him crazy that she wouldn't accept his gifts. Even thinking about it now put him on edge. He hid his frown and smiled at one of his oldest spies. "My pleasure. I'll speak more with you at the end of the week."

She nodded and left the room, the door clicking shut quietly behind her. Sam shook his head and sat once again at his desk. Marilyn could be as mean as a dragon at times, but she was one of his most loyal and experienced spies, and tough as nails. His spies weren't machines; they were human beings. So, he did his best to be as understanding as he could.

He sorted all the documents on his desk and piled all the important ones in a stack in front of him. Sam began decoding each message. Absorbed in his work for hours, he didn't notice how the candle had burned low and how dark his hidden office had become until it was very late.

Sam straightened, rolled his shoulders, and stretched. Stars above, did he long for his bed.

Someone knocked timidly on his door. There were very few of his girls that knocked that way. "Come in," he called.

He set down his letter and smiled as Lady Hollisa, or Gem as her friends called her, stuck her head into the room, her large brown eyes blinking at him owlishly.

"May I come in?" she asked.

"You know the answer to that." But he stood and swept his hand out in an invitation. Gem was proper through and through, and skittish as hell, so he tried to make her feel as comfortable as he could.

She tiptoed in and hovered in front of the doorway, wringing her hands. "You've been missed during your absence," she said, her voice soft.

"Thank you, Gem. How are you?"

"I'm doing well."

"And your mother?"

Gem pulled a face. "Causing mischief as usual. I'm surprised my parents haven't killed each other yet."

Sam smiled. That was why he loved Gem. She was honest. She made a wonderful spy. Her title afforded her certain liberties and allowed her into social circles most of his spies could not gain access to. It helped that her mother was a bed-hopper and her father a gambler. It also made her invisible.

Sam knew most people ignored Gem because of her family's scandal, which clung to her like a foul odor, but they couldn't downright dismiss her because of her family's title. But Sam had noticed her. They'd even become friends before he'd offered her a position as one of his spies. She'd accepted, and, to his surprise, she'd admitted to having a perfect memory. If she saw or heard something, she was able to recall it perfectly. It was a bloody gift for them both. Sam was able to gather reliable information, and she was able to earn coin without her father's knowledge.

"You've been gone two weeks."

A statement. Very typical of Gem. She rarely asked a question outright. She skirted the issue until her converser revealed themselves without remembering what she'd primarily hinted at. It was brilliant.

"Yes?" He crossed his arms and arched a brow at her. "What do you want to know, Gem? You know, if it's within my power to tell you, I will."

"It's not that," she said softly, bunching her pale pink skirt in her hands.

"What is it, dear?"

A small blush touched her cheeks at his endearment. "I hate spying on Jasmine."

So that was what she was after. "You're not necessarily spying *on* her – you're protecting her."

Gem scowled. "Don't split hairs. I've lived in court for almost as long as you have. It feels wrong to report to you. She's my friend."

Sam pursed his lips. That was one of his biggest rules: you couldn't be friends with your mark. Once feelings were involved, it always became messy and dangerous. But, in the case of Jasmine, he knew his wife would need friends in court, ones that wouldn't stab her in the back. So, he'd assigned Gem to her, and it pleased him immensely that the two had got on as well as they did.

"You want her to be safe and successful here, right?" Sam drawled.

"I do, but I don't want to betray her confidence."

"I'm her husband. By law, I'm privy to everything that involves my wife. Legally, you're doing no wrong."

Gem glared at him, and placed her hands on her narrow hips. "I'm speaking morally. And, despite how you pretend, I know you understand my meaning." She straightened, looking as ferocious as a kitten. "I came here to tell you that I'll continue spying for you, but I refuse to give you any information as to her thoughts and feelings. Jasmine is broken enough, and I refuse to cause more harm."

He blinked. Gem had a spine of steel, but he rarely glimpsed it. Part of him was happy she loved his wife so much and was willing to stick up for her. The other part was irritated, because Jasmine was impossible to read most of the time. He had a talent for coaxing, charming, and soothing women, but everything he did seemed to push his wife farther away.

"I respect that," he forced himself to say.

"Good," Gem exhaled, relief clear upon her face.

"May I ask what brought about this change of heart?"

"Jasmine's a good person, and she's shouldering so much. I love children, but I couldn't imagine raising twins at my age."

"She's not alone," Sam said.

Gem raised both eyebrows. "And just when have *you* been around, my lord?"

Sam scowled. "When I'm here, I do my best."

"Well, I don't think it's helping."

"And why is that?"

"Because she believes you're out galivanting with half the female court, and she's planning on moving into the country with the children."

Sam kept his expression blank. Jasmine was leaving? "My wife is trying to escape me?" he asked calmly. His hands clenched, and, suddenly, he felt too hot under his collar. He wanted to throw something.

Gem blanched. "Damn, you just can't help yourself," she accused.

"What did I do?"

"You needled me, and I played right into your hands. You wanted information on Jasmine, and, like an idiot, I just handed it right over."

He had wanted information on his wife's activities, but he wasn't interrogating Gem. "It wasn't on purpose."

Gem studied him and shook her head. "I believe you, but—" She pointed a finger at him. "Keep your mouth shut." She scanned the room and met his gaze. "The only reason I'm telling you this is so you won't do something rash and muck up your marriage even more than it already is."

"How have I mucked it up already?" he cried. "I've done everything in my power to make sure she and the twins are cared for."

"Sure, you've cared for their physical needs, but what about their mental and emotional ones? Wicked hell, your wife is *happy* believing you're out with other women." Gem's gaze bored into his. "You need to be honest with her, Sam, before it's too late."

"When is she planning on leaving?" Saying the words aloud make him slightly ill.

"During your next trip to the war camp. She seems determined to leave within the next three weeks."

"So, I have three weeks to woo my wife. I can do that." He could. His parents fell in love in two. He'd spent his whole life around women.

"But that's not the reason for my visit."

"There's more?"

She sat daintily on the chair in front of his desk. "She's been disappearing for two hours every day."

Every muscle in his body locked up. "Have you tailed her?"

"She gives me the slip every time."

His brain scrambled for answers. How in the blazes did a pregnant woman give Gem the slip? His pursed his lips in thought. "And what does she look like when she returns?"

Gem swallowed. "Tumbled."

Sam slowly stood from his chair, placed his hands on his worn, wooden desk, and leaned forward. "Like the wind blew her around, or are you insinuating that *my* wife is unfaithful?"

"I would never insinuate anything like that."

He eyed her. "You're close with her, so you must know what condition she's in?"

Gem blinked. "Yes."

"You also know that she's been a target for some of the more vicious back-biters and that some of the men have set their eyes upon her?"

Gem nodded, her lips pressed firmly together.

"I want to protect her, and I can't do that if you're not honest with me."

She sucked her lip in and released it, scowling and stabbed a finger toward him. "I'm just sharing what I've seen, and don't think I don't know what you're doing. Stupid, manipulative man," she mumbled and then continued. "There are many explanations for what she might be doing. Don't jump to conclusions."

Sam scoffed as she repeated what he had taught her over three years ago. "But usually the most obvious conclusions are the right ones. Humans rarely change their habits." He hung his head. "I can't believe this."

"Can't you?"

He lifted his head to glare at Gem. "I'm sure you'd like to tell me."

She tilted her chin in a haughty way and stared down her button nose at him. "You've established an entire persona of being a world-class rake and scoundrel. Your wife believes you have multiple mistresses and visit different women every night. So, why are your delicate sensibilities so offended? This is of your own making."

Sam straightened. "That is too far."

"That is the truth of it, my lord," Gem said gently. "I don't believe it is of her character to do such a thing, if that helps."

It didn't. He knew the self-destructive path she'd been walking down before they married. He inhaled deeply and went to the calm, logical part of himself he liked to use when figuring out a problem. He'd been absent enough. It was high time he found out what Jasmine was up to.

He smiled at Gem. "You're right. I think I should pay my wife a visit."

His friend blinked at him and then pushed up from her chair. "Don't do anything you'll regret."

"I don't have regrets."

But he did have a wife to spy on.

Jasmine might have been able to give Gem the slip, but she'd never been stalked by the best.

Sam moved to the wall and lifted a worn black cloak from the hook and clasped it over his chest, before pulling the hood over his golden hair. Today, she'd have the pleasure of meeting the spymaster.

He moved to the door and opened it for Gem. She took his hint and scurried to the door, pausing in the threshold. She placed one hand over his, the other holding the door, and squeezed.

"I wish you luck."

"Thank you, but I don't need luck when I'm hunting."

SIXTEEN

JASMINE

STARS ABOVE, SHE HURT.

Jasmine glanced over her shoulder at the lush, dark-green woods with longing. This was always her least favorite part of the day. As she turned around to face Sanee and the massive hill that led to the castle, part of her soul shriveled inside her chest.

By all accounts, it was a beautiful sight to behold. Tiny, cobbled streets wound in curving paths that were lined with faded, quaint, but well-kept homes. Her gaze latched on to the great stone structure that was her new home. The sunset haloed the castle and washed the white stone with a pink so soft it looked like a maiden blushing. If it wasn't for the menacing wall that surrounded the palace, the castle would almost look harmless and welcoming.

Her jaw clenched as she hiked farther into town. Little did the dreamers like her former self know that the palace held vipers and intrigue that no one wanted to be part of. She stumbled as she stubbed her toe on a loose cobble, and barely caught herself against the plain wall of an apothecary. As her eyes watered with pain, she had to admit that living in the palace wasn't all doom and gloom. She'd met some amazing people, and Tehl and Sage were making changes for the better.

Jasmine turned left and opened the back door to the apothecary. Carefully, she clicked the door shut and set her belongings on the floor.

"Jas, is that you?" Vienna yelled.

She rolled her eyes. The old woman only had one volume. Loud.

"It's me," she called back while peeling her leather trousers down her legs that were loosely tied over her protruding belly. Quickly, she yanked her tunic off and pulled a simple muslin dress over her head. A small growl escaped her as she tried to lace the back herself.

"Why didn't you call for me?" Vienna demanded as she bustled into the room, her gray hair a fuzzy halo around her wrinkled face. She batted Jasmine's hands away and laced up her gown.

Jasmine placed her hands on her hips and scowled down at the bump that wasn't as easy to hide anymore. "Who invented dresses like these? It's ridiculous."

Vienna snorted, her scent of thyme and lilac swirling around Jasmine as the old woman released her and began rummaging around the room. "Men. I think they like us to be dependent on them. Aha!" She pulled a small bottle from a heavy wooden shelf and held it out to Jasmine. "For the marks."

"How did you know?" Jasmine asked, not hesitating to take the gift.

Vienna quirked a smile. "It is my occupation to help everyone I can, and if that wasn't enough, I've birthed six babes myself. You'd be shocked to see my skin. It looks like a leren took a liking to me."

Jasmine winced. Good hell, she hoped hers wasn't *that* bad. She wasn't a particularly vain creature, but she didn't want to look like something had mauled her. "Thank you. I appreciate it."

"It's nothing, my girl." Vienna waved her off and then gestured to the game bag. "It's nothing compared to what you bring me." She licked her lips. "What did you trap this time?"

Jasmine grinned. "I've brought you four nice-sized rabbits and a haunch of venison."

Vienna's beady eyes widened. "Tell me you did not drag a deer around in the woods?"

"No. I did not. Luckily, my aim was true and the beast didn't travel very far. As for this—" She pointed at the chunk of meat. "It wasn't too heavy for me to carry. I'm pregnant, not an invalid. Women have been caring for their families for ages while they've been with child."

The old woman harrumphed but took the meat. "Would you like to stay for dinner?"

Jasmine hid her look of pity for the woman. Vienna was as tough as nails, but she was lonely. She'd lost her entire family to the sickness that swept through the kingdom. "I would love to, but I must get back. But, if you're up for a visit, I'll bring the twins in two days. They've been dying to play with that green muck you've been experimenting with."

"Slime," Vienna said with a twinkle in her blue-grey eyes.

Jas shuddered, thinking of the wet sludgy texture. "Children find the oddest things to be interested in."

"You can't tell me you weren't enthused about mud, muck, and bugs when you were a child."

"Touché," Jasmine said with a smile. She placed her bow and quiver in the back corner of the room and wrapped her bloodied clothing in a sack. Skinning and cleaning meat was always a dirty job.

"Goodness me, child. You cannot take those back with you. Hand them over."

She rolled her eyes, but did as she was bade. They argued every night about this, but Vienna always won. "I feel like I am taking advantage."

"Nonsense. You provide me with food and good company. It is I who is in your debt. I'm the lucky one who gets to entertain royalty."

Jas snorted. "I'm not royalty, no more than you are."

Vienna tossed the soiled clothing on the square wooden table, and studied Jasmine in a way that was far too knowing. "I've been on this earth for a long time, my girl. Many things have come and gone, but there is one fact that is always true. We're only hindered by ourselves. You have more power than you believe. Open your eyes, and you might be surprised by the influence you have."

Jasmine kept her mouth shut and nodded. She didn't necessarily agree with the old woman, but Vienna had more experience than herself. "I will give it some thought."

"Good, now, get back home. I'll see you tomorrow."

Jasmine slipped on her boots once again and snatched up her other small game bag, tucked the bottle into a pouch at her waist, and retrieved her cane. She glanced longingly at her bow, hating that she had to leave it behind, but it was way too cumbersome and suspicious to lug around. "Goodnight, Vienna."

"Goodnight, child," the old women said, following her into the dark alley. "Be safe. There have been more crimes in this area since the army has moved out."

"I'll be cautious." The fingers of her right hand tightened around the cane. She may be without her bow, but she wasn't without a weapon. She waved goodbye and trotted onto the busier street ahead.

With care, she moved through several streets without so much as one person looking her way. But a scratchy feeling had begun spreading between her shoulder blades a few alleys back. Someone was following her.

Awareness crept along the nape of Jasmine's neck until the fine hairs stood on end. This was the part she hated the most. Lately, she had the feeling of being watched whenever she went on her weekly visit to the woods and then the apothecary. So far, there had been no evidence to justify her feelings—no glimpse of a person behind her, no sound of footsteps—but she knew what it was like to stalk prey. And, during these moments, she knew she'd become someone's target.

Carrying her leathered game bag in her left hand and her hickory cane in the other, Jasmine continued to walk at a brisk pace, her back and feet aching with every step. But she wouldn't let the pain distract her. Her gaze took in every detail of the buildings around her, and she cursed as she realized, in her haste, she'd taken a wrong turn toward the docks. That was not a place to be careless.

"Stupid," she breathed. Jasmine glanced at her belly and then scanned the area for familiar sights. She exhaled in relief as she figured out where she was—only two blocks away from the main road where there'd be more lanterns and guards. Chastising herself, she picked up her speed and veered left. She needed to pay more attention. Lapses in attention could mean the difference between life and death for a lone woman.

As she passed near a drainage ditch, noxious fumes wafted upward and made her eyes water. Swamp apples, that was disgusting. She instinctively covered her lips with the left sleeve of her dress, but it didn't help. She caught the gleam of a man's gaze and quickly dropped her arm to breathe out her mouth. Sticking out in this area of Sanee wasn't a good idea, and any resident who lived around here would be used to the God-awful stench. Why would anyone live here when they had the choice to live in the country? That was something she'd never understand.

A chill ran through her body that had nothing to do with the fall weather. The road was eerily quiet. Most of the dilapidated buildings had been abandoned, but held flickering lights of pickpockets, drunkards, and ladies of the night who were squatting in the buildings' entrances. The glow from the broken lamps on either end of the street scarcely cut through the fog that began to creep up from the bay, slinking over and around homes like an insidious nightmare.

We'll get through this little bit. Just a block more until we reach safety.

But her pace faltered as new figures emerged from the weak light. A momentary surge of relief washed over her as she identified the trio of off-duty soldiers. They laughed loudly as they advanced in her direction, clearly well into their spirits, on their way to being truly drunk. They wouldn't be any help to her

Jasmine crossed to the other side of the street, keeping to the shadows, hoping they were too inebriated to notice her. She glanced in their direction and caught the eye of the tallest soldier. *Damn it. Too late.*

The tall one smiled lazily and swerved in her direction.

"Here's a bit of luck," he exclaimed. He slapped hands with his companion to his right as they strode in her direction. "I've been hankering for a bit of sport."

Distaste threatened to wrinkle her nose, but she kept her expression cool and picked up her speed, her heart hammering in her chest. "I'm sure you'll find your amusement just down the road," she said stiffly, while her grip tightened on the crooked handle of her cane.

The men were obviously worse for the drink. Stars above, she hated drunks. Her uncle had a taste for spirits, and it never failed to bring out the worst in him. Even thinking about it, Jasmine could swear she could smell her uncle's foul whiskey breath. She didn't doubt that the soldiers had been loitering at the tavern all day. Everyone knew it was a death sentence to go into battle against Scythia, so the men were trying to soak up as many amusements as they could before they were called upon.

If only their tastes were a little less sinister.

Her heartbeat escalated as their long legs caught up with her. "Allow me to pass, gentlemen," she said crisply, crossing the street once again. She was thankful for the speech lessons she'd been given. Maybe if they realized she wasn't some light skirt, they'd leave her alone.

They moved to block her totally.

"Talks like a lady," observed the youngest of the trio. He was red-headed, his hair springing up in unkempt rusty coils.

"She *is* a lady," remarked the tallest, hulking, hatchet-faced man—the one she'd caught the attention of. "I've never had a lady before. I bet she's looking for some fun if she's out for a stroll on such a night." He regarded Jasmine with a yellow-toothed leer and waved his hand toward the moldy, wooden wall of a home that shouldn't have still been standing. "Go stand next to the wall and lift your skirts. I'm in the mood for a little play that's upright."

"You're mistaken," Jasmine said sharply, attempting to walk around them. They barred her way, and her pulse whooshed in her ears as she glared at the men. "I'm not a prostitute. However, there is a fine brothel just down the road where you can find such service from what I hear. Now, let me pass."

"But I don't want to pay for it," the large man said nastily. "I want it free with a pretty little thing, and I want it *now*."

For a brief moment, she thought about screaming. But what good would that do? It would probably just call more predators in. And it was hardly the first occasion Jasmine had been insulted or threatened. That was one of the reasons why her father had trained her with a bow and staff. Sometimes, men took it upon themselves to take what they wanted, despite the refusal. She didn't want to fight them. She was exhausted after her long hunt in the woods, and, frankly, she was hungry. A certain sort of numbness trickled through her veins as she decided on her next action. If she did nothing, chances were they'd be so rough they'd hurt her, but if she fought, she might be able to get away unscathed. The key word being *might*.

Her jaw set as her fingers curled even tighter around her cane. Men were such pigs. They thought they could take and take and take. Tonight, they would take nothing from her. They were bullies and nothing more. She'd looked into the black eyes of true evil. These men had nothing on the warlord.

"As soldiers in His Majesty's service," she said acidly, "has it occurred to you that your sacred duty is to protect a woman's honor instead of violating it?"

To her distaste, the question elicited hardy chuckles instead of shame.

"Needs to be taken down a peg, if you ask me," commented the third man, a stout coarse-looking fellow with a pockmarked face and dark eyes that robbed the words from her tongue.

He looked like... She shook her head. She couldn't think about him.

Jasmine blinked as the younger one rubbed the fabric of his crotch in a crude gesture.

"She can ride my peg."

Terror threatened to swamp her, but she shoved it down deep. Fear would get her hurt or killed. "I don't see much of anything."

The young one glared and crossed his arms as his two companions cackled.

The hatchet-faced man grinned at Jasmine with easy menace as he wiped the corners of his eyes. "Over to the wall, my fine lady. Don't be causing a scene." He pulled a serrated blade from his belt and held it up to display its wicked edge. "Just do as we say, and it'll be over before you know it."

Jasmine's stomach flipped unpleasantly, and her legs quivered. "Drawing a weapon while off-duty is against the law," she observed coldly. "Added to the offenses of public drunkenness and rape, you will earn yourselves a flogging you'll never forget and at least ten years in prison." She didn't know that for sure, but their punishment would be hell if Sage caught wind of it.

The hatchet-faced man bared his yellow teeth. "Maybe I'll cut out your tongue, so you won't tell anyone," he stated.

Jasmine didn't doubt for one second that he would. As the daughter of a former soldier, she knew that pulling out a knife meant he would most likely use it. Her mum had been a healer, and once she'd seen a woman who'd managed to get over the Scythian wall so cut up that Jas had barely been able to tell where one cut had ended and another began. When the woman had healed, she explained that a man had wanted to give her something to remember him by.

"Calm yourself," the young man said to the hatchet-faced man. He brushed his copper curls from his freckled face. "There's no need to terrify the poor girl." Turning to Jasmine, he added, "Let us do what we want." He paused. "It will be easier if you don't fight."

Bile burned the back of her throat. There was no way she wasn't fighting.

Taking hold of the strings of her surging fear and anger, Jasmine recalled her father's advice about distracting your opponent.

Keep your distance, and avoid being flanked. Use speech as a distraction.

"Why force an unwilling woman?" she asked carefully and set her game bag down on the dirty street. "If it's the lack of coin, I'll give you each enough to visit a brothel." Carefully, she slipped her hand into the outer back pocket of the bag and closed her fingers around her skinning blade. Deftly she concealed it from their view as she stood, the familiar elk-horn handle resting in her palm.

In her peripheral vision, Jasmine saw the hatchet-faced man with the bayonet knife circling around her. At the same time, the stout man began to close the distance between them.

"Thank you for the offer. I'm sure we will take your coin once we make use of you."

Jasmine adjusted her grip on the skinning blade, resting her thumb on the flat side of the handle. Gently, she applied the tip of her index finger along the blade. She may be little, but like Hell would she let them anywhere near herself or the babe.

Make use of this.

Drawing back her arm, she released the blade in a slinging motion, stabbing her wrist straight to ensure the wickedly sharp dagger aimed true. A feral grin curled her lips as the knife sunk into his cheek. He roared with astonished fury, stopping in his tracks. Jasmine pivoted around the soldier with the bayonet knife, whipping her cane in a horizontal hard strike. Then, she smashed it against his right wrist. Taken by surprise, he cried out in pain and dropped his knife.

Jasmine followed the blow with a backhand strike against his left side and heard a vomit-inducing crack, then jabbed the tip of the cane at his groin to make sure he wasn't getting up. He'd doubled over, and she used the handle to strike him over the head.

He crashed to the ground like a marionette with its strings cut. *Good riddance.*

Jasmine snatched up the bayonet knife and spun toward the other two soldiers.

In the next moment, she froze in surprise, her chest rising and falling rapidly, her heart threatening to explode.

The street was silent.

And both men were sprawled on the ground.

What in wicked hell?

Was this a trick? Were they playing dead to lure her in?

Her hands began to shake as quivery energy worked its way through her, and her body began to slow and recognize that the emergency was over. She bent over and puked, her body shaking, but she never took her gaze off the men.

Slowly, she stood and wiped her mouth with the back of her left hand. She ventured closer to look at the fallen men, taking care to stay out of arm's reach. Her skinning blade had left a bloody wound in the larger one's cheek, but that wouldn't have knocked him out. She eyed the red mark on his temple. That wasn't from her. Even if she'd jumped, she wouldn't have been able to hit him on the head.

Her attention darted to the younger soldier whose face was a swollen, bruised mess, and his nose was streaming. It looked broken to her.

"What the devil?" Jasmine murmured, looking up and down the silent, foggy street.

She had that feeling again, the prickly awareness that someone was there. She rolled her eyes and straightened, clasping her cane and bayonet knife in each hand. Obviously, there was someone else here. The other two soldiers hadn't knocked themselves out.

"Come out and show yourself," she said sharply. She clenched her jaw as her voice wobbled on the last word. Heat pressed against the back of her eyes.

Stupid hormones.

She cleared her throat and tried again. "There's no need to hide like a rat at the back of the pantry. I know you have been following me. Come out."

A masculine voice came from directly behind her, nearly causing her to jump out of her boots. "My, my, my, what kind of mischief have you been getting yourself into, my dear?"

Jasmine turned in a quick circle, her gaze chasing over a flicker of movement in one of the darkened doorways. It was unnerving how the tone dripped sin and depravity. Despite herself, she couldn't help but shiver. "Enough of the games."

A stranger emerged from the shadows, the darkness forming into the shape of a man in a fine but worn black hooded cloak. He paused a few feet away and lifted back his hood, revealing blond hair that fell in waves around his face and deep, piercing blue eyes she'd know anywhere.

Jasmine's jaw slackened. "It's you!" she exclaimed. This was not good.

Her husband, the prince of Aermia, smiled wickedly at her. "Hello, my love. Have you missed me?" he crooned at her.

SEVENTEEN

SAM

HIS WIFE WAS BLOODY INSANE.

Certifiably insane.

And it was quite possible he'd committed murder tonight, and that he'd now chain her to his bed.

Well, that was a little dark, but the circumstances warranted it. If he hadn't found her when he had, he dreaded to think what might've happened. Sam forced his hands to stay loose and relaxed, instead of curling into fists like he wanted to. He glared at the soldiers littered across the ground, and something feral threatened to break loose inside him. He might even reach out for Rafe's expertise in making vile men disappear...

The idea had merit.

If he hadn't found her in time... Hell, he knew exactly what those low-lives would have done. What really rankled him was that they were Aermia's own men.

Filthy garbage.

Sam pulled his eyes from the carnage sprawled across the darkened street to stare at the bane of his problems this evening.

Jasmine stood, gaping at him, her cane clutched tightly to her heavy chest, her pants the only sound to cut through the swirling fog. He scanned her from head to toe, looking for injuries. No blood. But that didn't mean there weren't injuries. She had wounds that she hid from the world, and this would just make them worse. With his spies, he'd seen what happened when one didn't face their trauma. And Jasmine? She was the queen of avoidance and ice.

"Are you all right?"

She blinked, and her whole demeanor changed. His scared wife melted away, and an imperious charlatan took her place. "What are *you* doing here?"

That was the question of the evening. What were either of them doing down here? What was his wife doing down in the dock district, attacking men with a skill he didn't know she possessed? His gaze moved a fraction to the hand she held against her belly, and his rage ignited once more. This time at Jasmine. How could she be so careless? He planned on asking her this, but what came out of his mouth was so much worse.

"Are you stupid?" The question hung in the air, and he wanted to scoop the words right back into his mouth. What did he think he was going to get out of her by being an arse?

Her lips thinned, and a storm began to brew in her ocean-blue eyes.

Devil take it, a storm of his own making was about to erupt.

EİGHTEEN

MIRA

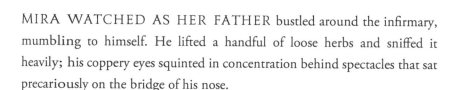

MIRA WATCHED AS HER FATHER bustled around the infirmary, mumbling to himself. He lifted a handful of loose herbs and sniffed it heavily; his coppery eyes squinted in concentration behind spectacles that sat precariously on the bridge of his nose.

"What is that?" she asked, folding a set of homespun sheets and setting them on the cot in front of her.

"Something special," he answered before carefully wrapping the plant in a leather square and then placing it gingerly in his travel bag.

Her lips pinched as she stared at his full pack, and the smallest bit of envy made her frown at the pile of sheets she still had to fold. Mira understood why Jacob was needed at the war camp: he was *the* Healer for the royal family, and most of the royal family was stationed around the battlefield. She loved the infirmary, she truly did, but she wanted to be able to help with more than scrapes and headaches. One of the only things that kept her sane was her work near the docks. Many people could not afford the services of a healer, so when she had spare time, she visited the poorer folk and did what she could to help.

"What are you thinking, my girl? Your silence unnerves me, and I can practically smell your anxiety and fear."

She peered up at him from beneath her lashes, another sheet clutched in her hands. She'd never thought of her father as being old. He had too much energy and never seemed to slow down, but, in the last few months, time and stress had taken a toll on him. Deep lines bracketed his eyes and mouth, his hair was almost snow-white, and his skin had taken on a translucent quality. He wasn't sick—she knew this, because she'd badgered him to allow her to check him once a week.

No, her papa was aging, and she *hated* it.

"I'm worried for you."

He nodded, his metallic eyes boring into her as if he could see all of the fears she tried to hide from him. "I'm not going to die, my girl. I'll be home soon."

Heat filled her eyes, and she turned her attention back to the crumpled sheets between her fingers. Jacob was all she had. They might not have shared blood, but he was her papa in every way. And a life without him? She couldn't imagine it.

A soft rustle filled her ears as he approached and lay a hand over hers. "Come here, darling."

Mira dropped the sheet and pivoted into her father's waiting arms. The tears she'd been holding back now ran down her cheeks as she cried her fear for him into his clean, linen shirt. Her papa hugged her close and pressed his cheek to the crown of her head, rocking her back and forth.

"It'll be all right. It's not like I'm going to be fighting. I'll be helping those who need it." He released her and cupped her damp cheeks. "I know you're worried, but I promise to be careful. I have many years left in me. I'm not dead yet," he said bluntly, his copper eyes twinkling.

She laughed, her smile watery. "I can't help but worry."

"I know, I know," he murmured and dropped a kiss onto her forehead. "I'll be back before you know it."

Nodding, she tilted her right cheek into his hand and then stepped back, wiping the tears from her face. Mira swallowed down her worries and put on a brave face. She didn't want him leaving with the memory of her weeping for him.

"So, what else do you have to pack?" she asked.

He waved a hand at the table covered in tinctures, herbs, and poultices. "I need all of that."

She huffed and affectionately kissed his whiskered cheek as she eyed the bag that looked like someone had thrown dirty laundry into it. "You may be a brilliant healer, but you don't know how to pack a damn thing."

He chuckled and followed Mira to the table as she began rearranging the mess that was his travel bag.

"That's what I have you for, my girl."

"I shall forever go down in history as the girl who could only pack a medicine bag," she said sarcastically, then smiled. She'd learned many skills from her papa over the years, but organization had not been one of them; that had come by naturally and out of necessity, since Jacob was horrible at organizing or labeling anything.

She peeked at him from the corner of her eye as he sniffed an unlabeled bottle, his copper eyes intent on the purple-pink flowers inside. For as long as she'd known him, he'd had an uncanny way with scents, more so than any other person she'd come across. Sometimes, it was like he truly could smell her emotions. As a child, it had driven her nuts, but now she was just curious. Jacob was an eccentric man, but how he reacted to certain situations in life wasn't what she would call normal.

Or even *human*.

The Healer had raised her to use her mind and the power of deduction, and every logical conclusion she came to said he wasn't like her. She didn't know exactly *what* he was or *where* he was from, but he wasn't Aermian. However, she kept her suspicions to herself. Her papa was a wonderful father, an amazing healer, and a devoted servant to the Crown. Nothing else really mattered.

She took the bottle of fully-submerged magenta flowers from her father's fingers and wrapped it, then carefully stowed the herbs in the bag.

"Done," she said as brightly as she could and closed the bag.

"Thank you, Mira."

She stared at the leather satchel as trepidation churned in her belly. "You'll be careful?"

"I will, darling. I promise."

Mira faced him and narrowed her eyes at her papa. He was an honest man, but sometimes his idea of being careful wasn't the same as hers. "You need to sleep."

"I will do my best."

"And you'll call for me if you need me?"

He watched her, his expression grave. "I will, but I hope that will not be the case. I want you as far away from the war as possible. It's no place for a lady."

She stiffened. "Many have said that being a healer with you is no place for a lady. Well, I was born in the streets, so I'm not a lady."

He smiled at her softly and took her left hand in his. "I didn't mean that you couldn't handle it. I just want to protect you from the ugliness of war. It changes a person, Mira. And you have an empathetic, kind heart. I don't want that to change."

Mira swallowed down her ire and pulled him into another hug, relishing his rosemary-and-smoke scent that was completely unique to him. "I love you, Papa. Be safe."

"I love you, too, darling." He kissed her on the cheek and grabbed his bag from the table. "Say a prayer for us, and don't get into too much mischief while I'm gone," her papa called as he shuffled from the infirmary.

"I'll try not to," she said.

Her papa barked out a chuckle as he waved one last time and disappeared through the infirmary door.

Her heart clenched, and Mira glanced around the room blankly. She rubbed at her arms as if the chamber had chilled slightly with the departure of her father. Stars above, she hated being alone.

"You're not alone," she muttered to herself. *Get to work and stop moping.*

Mira sighed and moved back to finish the laundry. As she was folding the last towel, a faint howl caught her attention. She frowned and looked toward the door as the wail grew louder. An old woman burst through the door, carrying a small, squalling child.

"Lady healer, please tell me you can help me with this child?" The old woman panted as she plopped down onto a cot. She brushed a lock of shockingly red hair from the child's face and crooned softly. "Isa, love, this healer is going to make it all better."

The little girl sniffed and clutched her hand to her chest. "It hurts, Nanny."

"I know, child."

"What happened?" Mira asked, abandoning her laundry and kneeling in front of the pair.

"A d-d-doggy bit me," the little one cried.

"I see," Mira said gravely. She held her hand out to the child. "May I see it? I promise to help make it better, but I can't do that until I look at it."

The little girl cautiously held out her bandaged hand.

"What's your name?" Mira asked as she unbound the bloody linen, hoping to ease the little one by means of conversation.

"Isa."

"What a lovely name. My name is Mira." She pursed her lips as she got an eyeful of the bite. There were several deep punctures and one tear, but none looked like she needed to stitch them. She sighed. Stitching children was the worst. It killed her to watch the little ones cry and wiggle away as she tried to help them.

"Do you like mint?" Mira questioned as she pushed from the ground and went to her workstation to wash her hands.

"Y-yes," Isa whimpered.

"Well," Mira said, grabbing a pot of hot water. She poured the steaming liquid into a bowl, then added lemon juice and basil oil into it. "You're in luck." She tossed a cloth into the bowl and snatched a sprig of mint from a jar. She strode back to Isa and knelt once again, holding out the mint. "Here you go, little one."

Isa loosened her hand from her nanny's blouse and took the mint with a small smile. "Thank you."

"You're welcome, but I need you to do something for me." Mira held Isa's unique purple gaze and blinked. She'd only seen eyes like that once before. Was this Gav's child? She brushed the thought away and focused on Isa. "I need you to be brave. This will hurt, but if I don't clean it properly, you can get very sick and even lose your hand."

The nanny glared down at Mira, disapproval dripping from her. Mira arched a brow at the elderly woman before meeting Isa's stunning gaze again. She wasn't going to lie to the child.

"Lose my hand?"

"Yes, Isa. Infection is very dangerous. A little pain is worth being able to do all the fun things we can with our hands, don't you think?"

Isa nodded, her wild hair bouncing around her face.

Mira reached for the cloth, and the child stiffened and bit her lower lip. "It's okay to cry, Isa," she said gently before beginning to wash her wound.

She went as quickly as she could, and, all the while, the little one wept, but Isa didn't scream or throw a fit. Only twice did Isa pull her hand away. The tension in Mira's shoulders melted away once it was done, and she rose to get the honey and bandages for the wound.

"I want my papa," Isa croaked.

"I know, love," the nanny murmured.

Mira faced the pair and smiled as the little girl's eyelids drooped and then closed.

"The mint always does wonders," she said as she moved back to Isa's side and dropped to her knees. "My father found a way to coat them in a honey and whiskey combination. Helps dull the pain."

"Thank you," the older woman said. She huffed as she adjusted Isa's body against her own frail one.

"It was no problem," Mira responded while slathering honey over the bite, and then wrapped the bandage around the wound. She tied the linen into a knot and stood, gathering her supplies from the floor. "I'm sure she'll be as right as rain in a few days, but visit me tomorrow just to make sure an infection hasn't set in. Dogs can be nasty carriers of disease."

The nanny frowned. "I can't keep her away from them. Any time there's a stray animal about, it finds its way into her arms."

Mira smiled as she dumped the tainted liquid into the large sink near her table. "Animals can sense kindness. She must have much of it in her heart." She dried her hands with a towel and then spun to face her guests.

"That she does. Just like her mother." The old woman groaned as she tried to stand, but didn't manage it.

Mira bustled to her side and placed her hand on the woman's elbow to help her up. The older woman smiled at her gratefully and strolled to the door, Isa limp in her arms.

"Thank you again, lady healer."

"It was nothing," Mira replied as they disappeared through the door. She smiled and turned back to what was left of the linens.

Perhaps she wouldn't be so lonely after all. Even though Isa was in pain, the little one had eyed the infirmary in wonder. Mira wouldn't be surprised if Isa visited her sooner than they'd planned.

NINETEEN

JASMINE

———⊸∘⟨⟩∘⊷———

THE JOINTS OF JASMINE'S FINGERS began to ache, and she forced herself to loosen her grip on the cane. Sam sauntered forward, his black cloak brushing worn, scuffed boots. She cocked her head. For someone who was royalty, he sure did dress drably. Odd. Maybe he was visiting a woman?

Jasmine shook her head and threw back her shoulders, trying to calm her inner panic.

Her husband paused and scowled at one of the soldiers. He slowly lifted his gaze, and what she saw made her want to run and hide.

Pure, unadulterated rage.

Her lips thinned as he stalked closer. Even in plain clothing and angry, he was an unfair specimen of beauty. Like an avenging angel.

"Are you stupid?"

His words lashed out like a whip, striking her. If she hadn't had her feet firmly planted, Jas was sure she would've stumbled back from the vehemence in his tone.

'Stupid' echoed in her mind. Stars above, she *hated* that word. It was a special sort of slur, one that men in her small village loved to burden their women with to make them feel small and worthless.

"Excuse me?" she hissed.

Sam paused and held up his hands. "That's not how I meant it."

"Then how did you mean it?" she spat. "Because, where I come from, those are fighting words."

"I was worried. The words just came out. I'm sorry."

Jasmine chuckled, the sound hollow in her own ears. He sounded apologetic, but living with the prince had taught her a few things. He was honey-tongued and could sway almost any woman. An expert performer. Others might not be able to see through his masks, but she saw him for what he was: a fraud. Which made it that much worse that he'd seen her at her worst, and the good times just kept coming. He always seemed to be there when her life was falling apart. Speaking of which…

"How did you find me?"

"I happened to be out for a nightly stroll."

Right. She glanced down the road. Faint, bawdy music floated through the dark of the night. Men only walked this path for two things: drink and wenches. She turned back to Sam, revolted by either diversion he might seeking.

"Are you following me?" she demanded.

Subtle amusement flickered across Sam's face, but his tone was serious. "I would never. In fact, I've just arrived from the battle front."

"Then why are you here?" She winced. Jasmine did not want to know. Why couldn't she keep her mouth shut?

"I happened to be passing nearby, and the sound of a scuffle piqued my interest. I'm sure you can imagine my shock when I discovered my wife, my very *pregnant* wife, in the center of a brawl with unsavory characters." His tone dripped disapproval and something else she couldn't quite put her finger on. "It would be a shame if anything happened to you," he whispered the last part.

Her gaze dropped to the men and she swallowed hard. The outcome could have been very different tonight, but on the other hand—she eyed her cane—she might have been able to care for herself.

"I need no protection," she informed him. "Furthermore, if I did, you're not the one I would come to for it." She owed him too much as it was.

Sam gave her an inscrutable glance before going to the soldier she had bashed with her cane. The unconscious man was sprawled on his side. After using his booted foot to roll him onto his belly, the prince pulled a length of cord from inside his cloak and bound the man's hands behind his back. "You do have skill."

She smashed the small flicker of pride that lit inside her chest. She didn't need a man to validate her worth.

"As you just saw," Jasmine continued, "I had no guilt or difficulty in taking out the bastard, and I would've defeated the other two on my own."

"No, you wouldn't have," he said flatly.

Jasmine felt the simmer of irritation. "My father was a soldier. I've been trained in the art of cane-fighting, as well as with a bow. I know how to take down multiple opponents, if need be." *Thank you, Papa.* His training had served her and her babe well.

"You made a mistake," Sam said, his blue eyes glittering as he stood from his crouch.

She'd made many mistakes, but Jasmine was curious as to which one he was referring to. "What mistake?"

As Sam held out his hand for the knife, Jasmine gave it to him reluctantly. He slid it into his leather sheath he'd taken from the soldier and hooked it on his own belt as he replied, "After you knocked the knife from his hand, you should have kicked it away. Instead, you bent to pick it up, turning your back on the others. They would've reached you if I hadn't intervened."

She shuddered, the scene playing out in her mind, and retreated a step back as the youngest man began to moan.

Sam glanced at the bloody soldier who'd continued to groan and stir. The prince stepped closer and smiled at the man. "If you move at all, I'll castrate you like a pig and throw your balls into the sea." His pleasant tone caused ripples of unease to skate along Jasmine's nerves. His tone of forced casualness was all the more chilling.

The soldier stilled, his breathing shallow and panicked.

Good. He deserved to be as frightened as he had made Jasmine.

Sam returned his attention to Jasmine. "Fighting with a retired man of arms isn't the same as fighting on the street."

Like he knew so much about being on the street. Just because he wore a pretender's clothes, it didn't mean he knew what it was like to live in an impoverished area. Jasmine knew. Just like she knew she should have paid better attention tonight. Vienna had warned her.

"Men like those," Sam continued, flicking a contemptuous glance at the soldiers, "don't wait politely for you to fight them in turn. They rush simultaneously, and, as soon as one of them came within reach, your cane would've been useless."

"Not exactly," Jasmine argued. "I would've jabbed him at that point and felled him with a hard strike." That's the way she imagined it anyway. When her child's life was on the line, she was fairly certain she could do almost anything.

Sam moved closer to her, stopping within an arm's length. His shrewd, blue gaze slid over her, and Jasmine held her ground and his gaze. Turbulence swirled in his eyes, and, for a brief second, his right eye twitched.

"Try it with me," he invited softly, his gaze locked on hers, vying for her to accept his challenge.

Jasmine blinked, momentarily surprised. "You want me to hit you with my cane, now?" She kept the excitement out of her voice. She'd wanted to smack him for quite some time.

Sam gave a slight nod.

"Isn't it a crime to strike royalty?" They couldn't send her to prison now that she was married to the man, could they?

"It is, and you won't."

So arrogant.

He grinned, and she scowled at his dimples. It was bloody unfair to flash those things. No wonder hordes of women followed him around like lost puppies or bitches in heat.

She eyed the way he stepped closer. He trained for hours a day and had a muscular, fluid, limber way of moving that, even when standing, conveyed a sense of explosive power. At least she wouldn't feel bad for striking him. He was trained, after all.

"I wouldn't want to hurt you," she said, prolonging her hesitation.

His grin melted into a sinful smirk. "Who knows? Maybe I'll like—" he whispered just as she surprised him with an aggressive thrust of the cane.

As fast as she was, however, Sam's reaction was lightning-swift. He dodged the cane, turning sideways so the tip barely grazed his ribs, grasped the length of the staff, and levered Jasmine forward. Her toe caught on a cobblestone as her momentum pulled her forward. She lost her footing and released the cane, wrapping her arms around her belly. A strong hand closed around her arm, and his free hand caught the staff easily, as if vesting people of their weapons was child's play.

Her hands trembled, and she stared blankly at the moss-covered stone wall ahead of her as she found herself firmly held against Sam's body, the knit of muscle and bone as unyielding as steel. A feeling of helplessness washed over her. She'd known he was battle-trained, but *that* was something else. He moved with feline grace. Like an assassin. Just who in Hell was the man she had married? Was there no escape from men with secrets? Phoenix's face flashed through her mind, and she shut her eyes to dispel his image and the knowledge of what they'd done.

No. She opened her eyes and forced herself to inhale deep breaths. It was unfair to compare Sam to the Scythian men who'd taken everything from her. The prince might keep things from her, but he'd never hurt her. *Yet.*

Fatigue crashed over her, and each of her limbs seemed impossibly heavy. Trying to piece together what happened in Scythia, combined with the attack and two hours of hunting, was catching up with her. Mira had warned her not to overdo it, but there was too much to be done to sit around. It was in the quiet stillness that the nightmares, guilt, and pain threatened to drown her.

Vaguely, she became aware of Sam's arm loosening and his hand slipping across the swell of her belly. She stared down at his tan hand, resting on her body like it belonged there. Tears threatened to fall, but she willed them back. When was the last time someone had held her? Perhaps it was the reckless velocity of her pulse that accounted for the strange feeling that came over her, but she found herself *leaning* into him until his warm chest was plastered against her back. What was wrong with her? She should move, but she didn't. In that moment, the world disappeared and she felt safe. Part of her realized this was ridiculous. They were in an unsafe part of Sanee, and yet... being held by Sam made her feel safer than she had in a long time.

"How's the wee one?" Sam asked, his voice soft and hypnotic.

Jasmine closed her eyes, conscious of only the faint scent of mint on his breath, and the measured rise and fall of his chest. It was bizarre to say the least, but she could have fallen asleep right there.

The spell was broken by his soft chuckle, the sound rippling gently along her spine. "Making yourself comfortable, are we?"

Mortification slammed into her. Jasmine's cheeks flushed, and her eyes began to pool. What in the blazes was she thinking? She tried to wrench free from him, but he kept his hand in place, holding her against him.

"Don't laugh at me," she said fiercely, hating that her emotions were so unpredictable because of the babe.

Astonishment washed over her when she felt him kiss the top of her head.

"I wasn't laughing at you. I only laughed because you caught me off guard. Not many have that ability." He squeezed her once and released her, handing Jasmine back her cane. His gaze was soft as he looked down at her and brushed a stray strand of hair from her cheek. "I don't wish to fight with you, and now is not the time." He glanced over his shoulder at the unconscious men and then back to her. "We can be friends, if you'll allow it. Life will be miserable if we don't come to some understanding."

Slowly, Jasmine lowered the cane and scrutinized his expression. He seemed sincere. "You'd like to be my friend?"

He flashed white teeth in a smile so bright and genuine, she was sure sugar was pouring from his veins. "I do."

"Why?" They didn't need to be friends.

He cocked his head. "We're bound for life. I don't want to spend our time together as enemies."

She pursed her lips, not convinced. If she had her way, she'd be in the country with the twins in just a few weeks. "You have many friends."

"Friends and confidants are two very different things. I've guarded your secrets, and I hope to trust you with mine." He sighed. "But if that doesn't convince you, think of the twins." A pause. "Think of the babe. Children thrive when they have a set of parents raising them. While it can be done alone, why should it be if there is a choice?"

Why, indeed? "So, we'll just be friends?" She had a feeling she would regret this.

"Friendship," Sam said with a smile.

It would be nice to have more friends. She'd been terribly lonely since Sage had left. The twins were Jasmine's heart and soul, but there were times the darkness seemed just a little too heavy to carry on her own.

"I'll be your friend, but nothing more," she warned.

"I'm asking nothing more from you."

There wasn't anything dangerous about a friend. "Okay," she said softly.

Her husband grinned, delight clear on his face. "Excellent. Well, the first order of business, dear wife, is to get you to bed."

Her eyes narrowed at him.

Sam waved her off and pulled a small whistle from the inside of his cloak. He blew three times and then put it away. He snatched her game bag up with what was left of her venison, tossed it over his shoulder, looped her arm through his, and began to lead her away from the soldiers.

"Aren't you going to do something about them?" she asked.

"Someone will pick them up shortly. Don't worry yourself."

"They'll be punished?"

Sam bared his teeth in a smile that was anything but nice. "They won't ever hurt anyone again."

TWENTY

DOR

DORCUS WIGGLED HER SHOULDER AND glanced quickly out of the side of her eyes at the warrior monitoring her end of the cave. Ten days had passed since her brutal beating, and her back still ached, but at least the pain had lessened. She rolled her neck and quickly hefted her pickaxe and swung it as the guard's attention turned her way. The resounding clang of metal against stone vibrated through her, and she clenched her teeth as it rattled her bones. The warriors had become more volatile in the last few days, and she would take blisters and sore muscles rather than gaining the attention of the men prowling the cave, looking for a fight.

Footsteps echoed and splashed through puddles, growing louder as they moved in her direction. Sweat beaded on her upper lip, and she swung even harder. Maybe if she focused harder on her work, they'd pass her by.

"You think with the warlord gone you can slack off?" a deep voice growled, causing the hair on her dirty, bruised arms to stand on end.

No. She shook her head but dared not answer or slow her work. Silence would be key. Let the warrior have his say, and then he'd leave her in peace. She smothered a gasp and flinched as a huge hand ran down her spine and hovered just above her butt before kneading the flesh.

"You'd be a pretty thing if you weren't such an abomination."

Humiliation washed over her as she did nothing to stop his groping. It was just a touch. She could bear it if it meant survival. And as for his words... well, she'd heard worse over the years. Living in the Pit had forced her to grow thick skin at a young age. If she objected, things would become infinitely worse.

Just breathe, Dor, breathe.

A gasp exploded from her as his hand roughly grabbed the back of her neck, fisting her hair. He yanked her backward, and her bare feet scraped against the porous rock floor as she stumbled, barely clinging to her tool. Panic rose up as she glanced at Ada who locked eyes with her. Dor lifted her chin toward the wall and mouthed *keep working.* She hissed as he yanked on her hair again, pulling her even closer to his massive frame.

"You'd be lucky to entertain someone like myself."

Tears burned in her eyes, and, with her left hand, she reached back and clung to his muscular arm as he lifted her higher, onto her toes. She choked back her cries, and tried to calm her panic. She couldn't panic. It was a rare thing, but every once in a long while, a warrior would lose control and go into a berserker rage. Fear and pain were almost aphrodisiacs to them. Her mum had warned her to hide if she ever noticed the signs. She'd only seen it twice in her lifetime, and she'd never forget the bellows of fury as the warriors destroyed the out-of-control monster.

She glanced from the corners of her eyes, looking for the other warrior, but he wasn't visible. Her stomach tumbled. If she roused his inner demon, there would be no savior for her. The other warrior wouldn't get to her in time before this warrior tore her apart and killed other innocent laborers. A spark of anger lit in her belly as the people around her kept working, all of them glancing at her from the corners of their eyes. She understood why they did nothing, but part of her wanted them to fight for her.

The warrior's other hand slipped around her body and groped roughly at her chest. She bit the inside of her cheeks as he grunted in surprise as he found the ample treasures he sought. Damned breasts.

"And what do we have here?" he purred as his hand roved down her belly, moving south.

"Stop!" she commanded, her words a snarl. As soon as the words escaped her, she wanted to pull them back inside her mouth. *Stupid! Stupid!*

He froze his assault, his hand tightening minutely. "You presume to give *me* orders?" the warrior whispered harshly, his hot breath fanning across her neck and right ear.

Dor winced and barely hung on to her pickaxe as he shook her roughly, her teeth rattling. She could get through the pain, but she needed to keep calm.

"I think you need a lesson in humility, and your sire won't be here to save you this time. Plus, from what I've heard, you're ripe for the picking."

She closed her eyes, fighting panic. Her sire. Blair. One of the warlord's favorites, and she'd come of age. No one would object to this warrior claiming her. Her vision swam.

"That's right, little bird. You're all mine."

He released her hair and slapped her on the arse so hard that she stumbled forward, left hand slamming into stone wall. The cave dipped, and the back of her scalp burned from where he had most likely yanked hair from her head. The bastard.

The warrior laughed, the sound sinister as it echoed around them, accompanied by the sharp tempo of the others working the stone. Dor cradled her right arm against her chest, the ax loosely clasped between her fingers as she hung her head to stare at the floor. Her tears dropped silently to the ground. It seemed wrong that her tears fell so quietly because each one was a cry for help.

Why me? Someone help me! Why can't I fight back? Stop crying. Fight back.

Dor sniffed and blinked away her tears. They would help nothing. She had known this day would come, but she'd hoped it wouldn't be so horrendous. She bit the inside of her cheek as the warrior kicked her legs apart and shoved her head down as he leaned over and whispered in her ear:

"I'll bet you'll be as good as your whore mother."

Ten words.

That's all it took to change her life.

Ten words.

Without a conscious thought, her hand clenched around the wooden handle of the pickaxe, and she swung it up over her shoulder. A sickening thud reached her ears, and the warrior slumped against her. Dor crashed into the wall, her breath exploding from her lungs as the warrior gurgled.

"Die for this..." the warrior slurred.

Dor wriggled out from under his weight, and twisted around to stare wide-eyed as he dropped to the floor face-first. She scrambled backward and gaped at the collapsed warrior, her pickaxe lodged in his back.

"Stars above," she whispered. What had she done? She was a dead woman now. There was nowhere she'd be able to hide to get away from this. The warrior knew who she was. Even Illya's cave wouldn't protect her. If they didn't punish her, they'd punish her family.

Trembles wracked her body as the workers stopped their mining to stare. She jumped when the warrior at her feet moaned, turned his face toward her, and opened his pain-filled eyes to glare at Dor.

"You're dead."

A shiver worked down her spine as she stepped away from him, trying to figure out where to go from there. Ada grabbed her hand and pulled Dor into a hug.

"Are you okay?" her friend asked.

"No. What have I done, Ada? What have I done?" Dor cried. "I'm dead."

Galen, a tall, thin slave, stepped from his post and paused at her side, others crowding closer. He stared silently at the bleeding warrior and then pinned Dor with his gaze. "You need to leave."

Dor shook her head but couldn't make her feet move. Her eyes were glued to the injured warrior trying to push himself onto his knees. Her breath whooshed out of her as another worker lifted his pickaxe. Horror washed over her as other laborers moved closer and fell on the warrior. Galen spun her around and wrapped his arm around her shoulder to move her away from the hideous murder scene.

"You can't be here. You need to run. Now."

"I don't know where to go," she murmured through numb lips.

"Find your mum."

"That's the first place they'll look for me." She squinted at the man she barely knew. "Why are you helping me?"

His dark gaze roved over her face. "Because it's the right thing to do."

She laughed, the sound hollow. Being born in the Pit gave one a sick sense of morality.

Galen nodded at Ada. "Get her out of here."

Ada clasped Dor's hand and tugged her toward the back entrance. Dor lurched after her, stumbling and tripping over her own normally graceful feet.

"We have to run, Dor," Ada whispered. "Don't look back."

Dor wiped the tears from her face and moved as quickly as she could, hardly noticing their surroundings as they raced toward her family's home. A shiver rocked her body as she clung to the shadows, saying little prayers each time they passed a warrior. She felt like she had her crime tattooed across her forehead. She'd sentenced a man to death. A dull ringing filled her ears as she replayed what had happened. It had all transpired so fast. She hadn't really understood what was happening until she'd been standing over the monster's bleeding body.

Bile burned the back of her throat. It was the silence that bothered her the most. There were always background noises of some sort, especially with violence. But, as a warrior was murdered in cold blood, no one had said a damn thing. There had been no screaming or sounds of a struggle, just absolute, suffocating silence. Another shiver worked through Dor, and she rubbed her arms to dispel the chills, coming to one conclusion: she'd rather hear her enemies coming for her. Dor could fight the enemies she knew were there. It was the silent ones that were the deadliest.

Silence was the sound of danger.

And of death.

Ada jerked her arm, yanking Dor into her home.

Dor's mum blinked at her and stood, holding her burgeoning belly. "What's wrong?" she asked, her tone sharp.

Dor tried to respond, but her numb lips wouldn't form the words. The confession caught in the back of her throat and she choked.

Ada squeezed her hand and spoke in a rush. "There was an accident today."

"What kind of accident?"

"A warrior is dead."

Her mum's expression eerily blanked. "How long ago did this happen?"

"Minutes ago."

"Witnesses?"

"Many, but they protected her."

"It won't be enough," her mum muttered, her face hardening.

"I killed him," Dor whispered, the words bitter on her tongue.

Her mum darted toward the bed and glanced at Ada. "Help me move this."

Ada released Dor's hand and helped move the bed. Her mum carefully dropped to her knees and pried a loose rock from the floor. "Watch the entrance, Ada."

Dor stood like a statue as her friend disappeared outside the front door, and she stared at her mum as she leaned down and lifted weapons out of the secret cache. What in the hell? Why did her mum have weapons? She blinked and forced herself to step toward her mum.

"Mum, what are you doing? We can't have those. They won't protect us, and, if the warriors discover those in our home, no one will survive." Other workers had died for less.

Her mum returned the rock to its place, collected the daggers, and deftly leapt to her feet despite her huge, pregnant belly. Swiftly, she tugged her skirt up and hid two daggers, before placing a sheathed blade between her ample breasts. She approached Dor and jerked her chin.

Dor placed a hand over the offered thigh holster and blade in her mother's pale hand. "We can't."

"Lift your skirt," her mum demanded.

"This will just put us in more danger." She met her mum's gaze. "This is my mess. I'll figure something out, but you can't put yourself in danger. Think of the girls and the babe."

Her mum cupped her cheek with her free hand. "Love, I *am* thinking of the girls, all my girls. Your sisters are safe, and it's time for us to leave. Put this on so we can leave. Everything will be okay, but you have to trust me. Can you do that? Even if there are things you don't understand?"

"Yes," Dor said immediately. Her mum had always taken care of them and kept her word.

"Do you remember how to put this on?"

Dor nodded as she took the dagger and sheath from her mother. Years before, her sire had shown her how to wield a dagger. It had always been so exciting when he visited and would train Dor and her sisters with his own weapons. "Did Father leave these for you?"

"He would never leave us unprotected in his absence."

So, in other words, yes.

Ada swung inside. "A commotion is starting up on the lower levels."

"We need to leave now," her mum said. She glanced around the room and shoved the mattress back in place, and then she swept away the evidence of their activities.

Dor blinked. "What about Jadim?" They'd been bound two days prior, and surely he'd be looking for her?

"He knows what to do in this instance. He'll be safe. He'll meet us." Turning in place, her mother held out her hands to both girls. Ada and Dor both stepped forward to take one of her mum's hands. Her mum's serious hazel eyes moved over both girls. "There will be violence, so stick close to my side. Don't stray for a moment."

The hair along Dor's arms rose. "What's happening?"

"The people are rebelling."

She sucked in a breath. Rebellion. She'd dreamed of that for years, but that was all they were. Dreams. The people couldn't possibly win, and everyone would suffer. The warlord's response would be swift and brutal.

"Both of you know how to protect yourselves. If it comes to it, you protect yourself at all costs and keep moving. You don't stop, no matter what you see. If you do, it could cost you your life."

Dor glanced at Ada in surprise. Dor had been trained by her father in secret, but she couldn't imagine her sweet friend fighting. Ada nodded, a feral glint in her eyes that Dor had never seen before.

Her mum pressed a kiss against her forehead and then on Ada's. "History will change today." She stepped back and tied part of her dress up so the skirts wouldn't trip her up, then tucked her braid into the back of her dress. Her mother lifted her chin, and power slid over her like a mask.

Dor stared at her mum. She'd always been a force to be reckoned with, but she hid behind a demure façade most of the time. Even with child, her mother looked like a dangerous warrior. A dragoness.

"Love you both. Keep close."

With those words, her mum strode for the door, not glancing behind her. Dor rolled her shoulders and followed with Ada hot on her heels. She shoved all her questions and feelings down deep and focused on the rising clamor of thousands of voices. Focus was key if she was going to survive what was waiting. She'd heard stories about the last revolt. It occurred ten years before her birth, and, still, the people whispered in fear of the atrocities committed.

Her mum glanced over her shoulder, her eyes turning more green than brown. "Not one sound," she whispered as they moved off the main path and into one of the darkened corridors.

Her mum ghosted down the hall silently, and both girls followed, Dor's gaze stuck on her mother. The woman moved like a wraith, her steps silent and fluid. She'd never seen this side of her mum. Who was she?

Dor shook her head and concentrated on slowing her breathing as they slipped past the junction of stone hallways. The curved ceiling dripped cool water on her head as they slunk down the hallway. A woman screamed, and the sound echoed around them. Down the right hallway, a warrior fell on a man and woman, his roar enough to terrify Dor into freezing. Dor's jaw clenched as she compelled her legs to move, leaving the couple to the violence of the raging warrior.

Her mum ran ahead and paused, holding her hand up. Ada stopped, and Dor followed suit, trying to blend in with the wall. Ada's muscles locked as someone sprinted down an adjacent hallway, their boots thumping against the stone. Her mum crouched and slid the dagger from her sheath.

The blood in Dor's veins froze as an immense warrior rounded the corner. His gaze narrowed on Ada, and that was his downfall. Dor's mum struck like a viper. She swung her leg, tripping the warrior. He stumbled as she leapt, and, in one smooth jump, she launched over his back, sank her hand into his hair, tipping his head back, and slid the dagger into the flesh of his neck. He collapsed on the ground, face-first, with Dor's mum perched on his back. She straightened and wiped her blade on his tunic, then tucked away her dagger.

"Let's move."

Dor stared at the dead warrior as she moved past the body. "Who the hell are you?" she whispered, staring at her mum's back.

The way she'd moved was unlike anything she'd ever seen. She'd never seen a warrior defeated that quickly. They had every advantage over the laborers. It dumbfounded her to see a petite, pregnant woman down a warrior in close quarters.

"Do you think your father would ever leave his girls without protection?"

her mum whispered as they wound through a labyrinth of tunnels.

Honestly, Dor had never given it much thought. Her sire had made sure to instruct his girls to defend themselves from the moment they could master a weapon, as he did with their mother, but he'd never taught Dor anything like that. Her mum had never given any indication that she could fight like a warrior. Hell, wasn't it just yesterday she was shuffling about their home like an invalid, complaining about her back?

Her mum peeked around a corner and waved them forward. They followed the hallway until it dead-ended.

"Dor," her mum called softly. "Open this door."

She squinted at the wall. There wasn't a door. "I don't see anything."

Her mum huffed a breath and jerked her chin toward a small crack in the stone. "Press your fingers in the crack, and then use your shoulder." Her face tightened, and she inhaled deeply, clenching her jaw.

Dor eyed her mum and gingerly slid her fingers into the crack, feeling around until they caught hold of something metal. Her brow furrowed as she pressed on the metal lip, and the stone wall groaned.

"Wicked hell," Dor breathed as she leaned all her weight against the stone. The stone groaned again and began to move inward, revealing a hidden stairway. Ada slipped through the hidden doorway and up a few steps to make room for Dor and her mum.

"Damnation," her mum cursed.

Dor turned toward her mum and swore a black oath. Translucent liquid gushed down her mum's leg and pooled on the ground. The women stared at each other, knowing what would come.

"Of all the blasted times," her mum growled.

"How long til the babe makes her presence known?" Ada asked.

"Each one comes faster than the last," her mum gritted out as she slipped into the passage, and Dor closed the stone door behind them, cutting them completely off from any light. Water dripped around them, and her mum's breathing deepened as her hand latched onto Dor's and squeezed.

"Can you make it?" Ada asked from the darkness.

"I have to," her mum grunted, her hand squeezing Dor's until she thought her fingers would fall off.

A match struck, and Ada's face became visible. "Lantern?"

Her mum grimaced and jerked her chin up the staircase. "It's about twenty paces up."

Ada spun on her heel and powered up the stairs, disappearing around the corner.

Dor sighed in relief as her mum's grip loosened, despite how her heart galloped in her chest. "I'll be here every moment. If you need to stop, tell me."

Her mum nodded and glared at the door behind them. "The timing couldn't be worse."

"We'll get through this." They had to.

Her mother smiled, dropped Dor's hand, and began trudging up the stairs. "We need to keep moving."

"Where does this lead?" Dor asked, brushing her hands along the walls, the stairway brightening as they joined Ada.

"The surface."

Dor almost stumbled. The *surface*. How long had she desired to see the world above? She shook her head. It was too good to be true. "That sounds deadly."

"It is, but we'll have help."

"Help?"

Her mum nodded. "Yes, there are people on our side."

Dor bristled. Other people? Could they be trusted? For so long, it had only been Dor and her family. And now she was to trust strangers?

Her mum glanced over her shoulder and stared down at Dor, half her face in shadow. "Change is part of life. Choices will have to be made, love. Don't shy away from the unknown. Trust me and your instincts."

That couldn't be any vaguer.

"Will they help protect us?"

"Yes, they will. To the best of their ability."

"Who? Will Father be among them?"

"No. One of his companions."

Another warrior was helping them? Apparently, miracles happened in the Pit.

A miracle in Hell? Dor snorted. It seemed too good to be true.

TWENTY-ONE

SAGE

"WHAT IS HE WAITING FOR?" William asked, his white brows furrowed. He shook his head and stared harder at the huge map dominating the table in the middle of the war tent.

"He's playing with us," Zachael growled, pushing away from the table, his steps agitated.

Sage eyed the group of weary men around her. They were tired already, and it had only been a month. Tehl had expected a proper war, but she'd known otherwise. The warlord had no honor, and he'd do whatever he had to. He could've marched in and met them head on, but he hadn't. He played with them, trying to entice them into entering his jungles, but no one was stupid enough to take his bait.

It was frustrating, yes, but it also worked in their favor.

It gave them more time to prepare. Every day they gained was to their advantage.

As soon as Tehl had sent warning, the Methian army had mobilized. But moving thousands of men took time, especially when they were traveling through the mountains. Their feline counterparts had made it much sooner with their riders, but their number was a drop in the ocean compared to the Methian army hiking their way through the mountain range that separated Aermia and Methi. But they did what they could.

They sent their men in waves to train with the Methi riders and fiilee in private, while the rest held the front line, not that there was much to hold. When they'd arrived the first day, Sage's breath had been knocked from her lungs at the sight of the Scythian warriors lined up along the Mort Wall. Chills had run up and down her arms, and a sense of numbness had settled over her when her eyes had landed on the warlord. His dark gaze had been pinned on her as he gave her a slow, intimate smile.

The pained, broken girl inside her wanted to run and hide, but she had forced that part down and drew on the rage that always teemed just beneath the surface and gave him her own cold smile in return. She wasn't the girl he knew. He'd created a dangerous creature when he'd kept her a prisoner. One he wasn't prepared for.

His smile had grown, and, without a sound, his warrior army had melted back into the jungle. One moment they were there, the next they were gone, vanished like smoke in the wind. That's what chilled her the most.

How could they fight an army they couldn't hear or see?

Sage blinked back the memory and leaned against the table, her leather breastplate creaking. She'd taken to wearing one at both Rafe's and Tehl's insistences. A volley of enemy arrows had almost ended her life. They hadn't been aiming at her, but if she hadn't been paying attention, that incident could've ended much differently.

Focusing back on the map, she squinted at the small pieces depicting the Aermian and Methian armies, as well as their enemy's movements. She reached out and brushed the black piece that represented the warlord. "There's a pattern, we just haven't found it."

"We've been looking for a month. If there is, I can't find it," Gav said, running a hand through his hair, his raven locks disheveled.

"It's here." She knew the warlord. Nothing was chance. Again, she scanned the worn, leather map. The clue was there, she just needed to find it.

"It's late," a deep voice rumbled, causing goosebumps to run up her arms.

She glanced at her husband. Tehl stood to her left, his legs braced apart, his powerful arms crossed. Dark stubble shadowed his square jawline, and the color of his sapphire eyes seemed to intensify as he stared at the map in concentration. It seemed wrong to call him beautiful, as he was too rugged for such a pretty word. There was a new edge to Tehl that he'd not had before she escaped Scythia. One that was wholly appealing in a dark, sinful way.

He sighed and straightened. "We all need sleep. We'll reconvene with the Methian queen tomorrow morning, as well as with Lilja. Hopefully, Lilja will have some news from her spy."

Sage hid her smile as he caught her interested, blatant stare, and his eyes widened just a fraction. It amused her that he was still a little uncomfortable with attention so publicly, and he acted surprised every time she showed any carnal interest in him whatsoever. Her smile deepened.

Not that he didn't like it.

He'd shown her how much he loved how she'd shed most of her modesty and reveled in it. Well, at least, in private, he did. That's where they differed. He kept his affections mostly private, and she... well, didn't. Some of her humor dropped away at the thought. It hadn't always been that way. Living in Scythia hadn't given her much of a choice in the matter.

A smile flavored with bitterness and irony tipped up the corners of her mouth.

If only the warlord knew what she was doing with the lack of modesty he'd forced upon her.

"Dismissed," Tehl commanded.

Sage barely noticed as their advisors filed out. Her eyes focused on the only black piece marring the map. It seemed, no matter what, she couldn't escape the warlord.

Heat suffused her back like a warm blanket, and Tehl leaned into her, his lips skating leisurely along the left side of her neck.

"What occupies your mind, wife?" he murmured against her skin, between kisses.

He tilted her head to the right to give him better access, her skin beginning to tingle as he grasped her hips with his rough hands.

"Madness," she whispered, the faint rhythm of drums reaching her ears. She wished the incessant drumming would stop. But it hadn't in all the time they'd been at the war camp.

Just another tactic the warlord was using to unnerve their men.

It bothered her. Sometimes, she'd disappear into the woods and place her hands over her ears, so all she could hear were her own breaths.

"Mad brilliance more like," Tehl said, smiling. His lips burned their impression into her skin.

She snorted and shook her head.

"Come to bed," he coaxed, his tone lowering.

The hair rose on her arms as he caressed her sides and pressed his hips against the back of hers in an unabashed invitation.

How she longed to accept, but how could she possibly accept when her mind was filled with the warlord? It would pervert what they had.

Sage captured his roving right hand and kissed his fingers before biting the fleshy pad of his thumb.

A groan rumbled against her back, and she smiled before tipping her head backward and staring up at Tehl. "I'd love to, but I need a little quiet moment to myself." His expression fell, and she was quick to continue. "A few minutes." She wrinkled her nose and sniffed loudly. "Plus, I believe you need to bathe. You smell like a wet, dirty horse."

A gleam entered his gaze, and, before she could protest, his arms wrapped around her, and he rubbed his sweaty self all over her.

"No," she screeched, trying to fend him off.

He laughed, and Sage stumbled forward and spun around, glaring at him. "What was that for?"

He grinned, the look utterly heart-melting and boyish. "Now I'm not the only one who needs to bathe."

That devil.

Tehl pecked her on the cheek, swept by her and out of the tent, issuing commands about a bathing tub for his wife.

She rolled her eyes and snatched her sword off the pale wooden chair near the entrance of the tent. If he was going to make the men haul pail after pail of water for a bath for her, she'd better train hard enough that she needed one. Sage chuckled. The sneak would blame it on her, but he was the one with a weakness for baths.

Sage nodded to the men as she strode through the camp and held her heavy braid off her neck as sweat dripped down her spine. Time at the camp had taught her one very important fact: she was out of shape.

Every day, she trained as hard if not harder than the men. She needed to make up for the time she'd lost in Scythia. It had been difficult; she'd practiced when she could, but it wasn't the same as being in the ring with an opponent, let alone with armor. That was what was the worst. The extra pounds of weight she was trying to work with.

Dropping her hair, she tossed back the tent flap, passed through the war room, and pushed aside the second flap leading to their personal quarters. Sage discovered her husband lounging in a large, crude metal tub. Scented oil perfumed the air, and her cooling skin warmed with the veil of aromatic steam. Her eyes rounded at the size and depth of the tub. It had to have taken forever to heat the water and laboriously fill it.

Tehl leaned back with one long leg propped up at the far end of the tub, a glass of spirits clasped lazily in one hand. His inky blue-black hair was handsomely swept back from his face. She blinked at all his exposed, tanned skin, a small flush touching her cheeks. Stars above, her husband was handsome.

His deep voice cut through the haze. "I was wondering when you were going to appear. I was waiting to let you get in first, but the water was beginning to cool, so I climbed in. How was your bout?"

Sage smiled and walked toward him while unbuckling her leather breastplate. "I did well. I'm sure I can do better." Carefully, she set the breastplate and her sword on the bed to her right before kneeling beside the tub so their faces were level. "How is your bath?

"Hot." His gaze caressed her face, while his forefinger traced the curve of her cheek. "Who did you spar with?"

She pursed her lips and answered honestly, even though she knew he wouldn't like the answer. "Garreth."

Tehl's gaze cooled, and his lips thinned. "With the traitor?"

She tilted her face into his hand. "No one is perfect. And he never meant me any harm."

"And yet you were hurt nonetheless." He glanced away, his chiseled jaw clenching. "By all accounts, he should be hung. His life is forfeit for his actions."

"True, and yet he still lives," she said softly. "Your mercy couldn't have been bestowed on someone worthier. He's served with you for a long time, Tehl. You grew up together, as children. If it had been someone else, the punishment would've come much easier. It always hurts more when betrayal comes from those we love, but at least we can forgive."

Tehl's sharp, blue eyes snapped back to her. "I haven't forgiven him. I just haven't killed him. Yet."

Sage closed her eyes briefly and reached for the glass in his other hand. She downed what little was left and set the cup on the floor. "Children change everything."

Tehl's gaze softened. "That is true, which is why he lives."

"I understand." And she did. If it had been for any other reason, she might have taken it upon herself to rid the world of him. But she understood sacrifice when it was done for loved ones.

A comfortable silence settled between them.

Two long, wet fingers hooked the top of her linen shirt and tugged her closer to the side of the bathtub. Tehl's eyes were a deep, velvety blue, like the sky in the darkest hours of night. "I find I am unable to properly clean myself, and I require your services."

A smile curved her lips. "What services?" she asked, playing along.

"I need a bath maid." He caught one of her hands and drew it down into the water. "For my hard-to-reach places."

Sage arched a brow at him and stifled a chuckle at his terrible flirting. She tugged at her wrist and feigned shock. "My lord, I'm sure you can reach *that* by yourself. You go too far!"

"My love," he said, nuzzling the crook of her neck. "Why do you think I married you?"

"For my excellent sword skills," she deadpanned.

Tehl released a huff of laughter against her skin. "That should have been my line."

She giggled, a happy buoyancy bubbling in her chest. She schooled her expression and tried to sound severe as his wet hands roved over her curves in lazy abandon. "You, sir, need to watch your hands or you're going to ruin my clothing."

"Not if you remove it." He gave her a positively wicked smile.

Smiling wryly, Sage pulled away and stood. There were many surprises being married to Tehl, but one of the most delightful of them was that he never held back his pleasure in her form. Every time she undressed for him, especially if clothing had many fastenings, he watched, completely riveted like she was the most gorgeous creature to ever be born. It made her feel like a goddess.

Her husband slid a little lower in the water, his gaze roving over her in a way that caused her belly to flip in anticipation and her skin to heat.

"Tell me about your day," he murmured.

"Well, I trained with another Methi warrior today." She smiled as she unlaced the top of her shirt, remembering the small fiilee and his mistress. "Nali seemed to take to the runt. She cuddled right up to him and played nice." Sage scowled at the row of tiny buttons running along the front of her shirt. Buttons were the worst. She stripped the shirt off and tossed it into the corner. One problem solved.

Tehl's gaze dipped to her steel corset, and a small smile touched his lush mouth. The blasted thing was uncomfortable, but it added more protection. It was miserable to wear, but the look on her husband's face when she took it off was worth it. She blinked as she realized Tehl had spoken.

"What did you say?" she asked, reaching back to loosen the laces.

"I asked if you could undress any faster."

Sage huffed in exasperation. "I challenge you to get out of a steel-and-leather corset faster than me." She stiffened and instantly wished she could retract her words. That hadn't sounded like a retort, but a challenge. And, if there was anything she'd learned, it was that Ramses men loved a good challenge.

"I'll give you thirty seconds before I cut it off of you."

She froze, her fingers tangling in the laces. "You wouldn't!"

The crown prince's eyes glinted with devilish mirth. "It's hiding your skin from me. No piece of clothing is more alluring than your naked skin," he said with a bald look. "I want to see what is mine."

"Yours? That's awfully presumptuous," she said as she picked up her speed.

"Fifteen seconds left, by the way."

"How can you even tell how much time has passed?" she huffed as she untied a stubborn knot.

"I'm counting by heartbeats."

Her stomach flipped. "Well, that's not a completely accurate form of time-keeping." She glanced down anxiously at her corset and threw her hands up in the air. The stupid thing was stuck. "The ties are knotted. There's no way I can get out of it without help," she mumbled with a sigh.

She heard his smoky laugh and a sluice of water. He stood, and streams of water ran over the sleek, muscled contours of his body. She stumbled when he pulled her into his steaming embrace. Sage placed her hand on his naked chest and shivered when he leaned down to whisper in her ear.

"My poor little wife. You misunderstand me. Let me be blunt. I have no plans of helping you out of it. Cutting it from your body will serve me just fine. If you'll recall, I'm excellent with my blade."

Laughter spilled from her lips. "How long have you waited to say that?"

"I've waited weeks for the perfect situation."

TWENTY-TWO

DOR

THE DARKENED STAIRWAY SEEMED NEVER-ENDING, and their journey was only broken up by the frequent stops her mum required in order to breathe through the birthing pains. The timing between pains and stretches of stairs began to shorten. Dor kept her gaze glued to her mum's back, afraid that she might stumble and fall. An image of her mum tumbling down the staircase flashed through Dor's mind, but she shoved the thought away. She didn't want to dwell on how long one would fall if they slipped.

Her mum wavered to the left and placed a hand against the wall, her groan barely audible. Dor had been present the last two times her mum had given birth and understood the kind of agony her brave mother must be battling. It was a marvel she could walk at all.

"Are you all right?" she couldn't help but ask. She'd uttered that question more than ten times already, but she had to ask it once more. Just watching her mum trudge up the stairs was causing Dor pain.

Her mum waved away her question, but Dor saw her jaw was clenched. "I'm fine," she gritted out through bared teeth.

"Like hell you are," Ada muttered from ahead, pausing for Dor and her mother to catch up.

"Don't curse," her mum bit out despite the labor pains. She pulled in one more deep breath and nodded for Ada to continue.

Ada turned back toward the stairs and lifted the lantern higher. Dor tipped her head back and wished she'd kept her gaze on her mum or the floor. The stairs above them spiraled into oblivion, like a gloomy, twisted version of inside a shell.

Her mind shifted to Illya. What would become of her dragon? The thought of him being caged in a stone hell for all of eternity made her step falter. How could she leave him?

You can't help him if you're dead.

"I'll come back for you," Dor promised with a whisper. She'd do everything within her power to free him.

Wicked hell.

Dor's legs seemed to quiver in rebellion as they continued to move up the stairs. Step after step was torture. She stopped counting the steps once they reached the seven-hundredth stair. A complaint was on the tip of her tongue, but she swallowed it back. If her pregnant and in-labor mum could make the horrendous journey, then she could, too. With renewed conviction, she forced her shaky legs up the steps ahead of her.

Dor jerked and glanced above when Ada yipped in happiness.

Thank the stars.

Ada cleared a platform that led to three different hallways and branched away from the staircase. Dor bent over to inhale deep breaths. Ada did the same but kept the lantern high enough that it still illuminated the stairway.

"Dragon's fire," her mum wheezed as she stumbled onto the platform and leaned against the wall. Her green eyes closed, and she clutched her belly, her face tightening with discomfort. "This babe will be the death of me."

Gooseflesh erupted up and down Dor's arms at her mum's grim words, made a little worse by a sudden slight breeze whistling through the hallways, causing a hollow, wailing screech to echo around them. It was something from a nightmare. Dor was sure the sound would haunt her for the rest of her nights. A tingle ran down her spine as she stared into the darkened hallway to her left. The jagged stone opening looked like a giant maw ready to devour them.

"Let's leave this place," Dor found herself saying as she wet her lips. "I feel this is a bad place down to the marrow of my bones." Dor glanced at her mum. "Which way do we travel?" Her eyes darted to the stairs and back to her mum. Stars help her if they had to continue up the devil stairs.

Her mum opened her eyes and held her hand up as Ada's lips parted like she had something to say. Her head tipped to the side as if she was listening for something, and then she glanced in each direction before settling on the left corridor. Her body stiffened, and something akin to horror contorted her face. "Dampen the light," she hissed, lunging from the wall.

Ada scrambled to obey as Dor's mum grabbed both of them by the arms and hauled them along the inky corridor that seemed to mock them as it swallowed them whole. The lantern light completely disappeared, and Dor kept close to her mum as she fought to swallow down the terror that was trying to spew itself from her mouth in noncoherent whimpers.

She stumbled along, stunned at how her mum moved through the darkness with complete ease, like she could see through the gloom. Dor reached her left hand out, touched dry stone, and skimmed her fingertips along the wall to try to orient herself in the debilitating gloom. As much as her body wanted to freeze in fear, her thoughts kept turning to what was coming for them. She fought the urge to look behind, knowing that it wouldn't reveal anything, but only serve to stumble her.

Her mum's hand tightened on her arm, signaling for Dor to stop. The hand on her arm tugged her to the right, and a door creaked. Her mum pulled them forward, and Dor could tell they had now moved into another section of the maze. She placed her left hand over her nose and pinched her nostrils shut as her mum closed the door softly. This room stank of dust and decay. When had the room last been used?

Her eyes watered from forcing back her sneeze. Her mum released her arm and moved farther into the room, her bare feet hardly making a sound on the stone floor. Dor inhaled through her mouth and grimaced when she could taste mildew and dust upon her tongue. *Disgusting.* The hair at the nape of her neck rose as tension seemed to detonate inside the room. Her mum sucked in a sharp breath.

"What can I do?" Ada asked softly from Dor's right.

"Prepare yourselves," her mum barely breathed, discomfort edging her tone. "I need a moment. The birth pains are coming more frequently. Dor, watch the entrance. We're being followed."

A cold sweat broke out between Dor's breasts as she spun and ran both hands along the craggy walls to the wooden door. She darted to the right when her hand touched metal hinges. If their adversaries came through the door, they'd receive a surprise. The silence in the room became deafening as her mum's birth pain passed. She pulled her dagger from her sheath and pressed her ear against the wood, listening. It was as if the room was holding its breath.

Tension bunched her shoulders as she strained to hear anything. Her heart stuttered when she caught a whisper of cloth against cloth from underneath the door. She squinted and waited for it again. A moment passed. Maybe she'd imagined it. Her eyes widened in the darkness though when steel against steel hissed as if a blade slowly slid from a sheath. That was a sound she'd never forget. She'd seen her father pull his daggers from his sheaths every time he'd visited, since Dor was a child. The sound was distinctive. Someone was definitely in the hallway. Just outside their hideout.

Dor held her breath and braced her shoulder against the wood, cursing the absence of locks on it that could barricade them inside and bar their enemy's entrance. Besides her weight, she had nothing but her teeth and nails. It wasn't like she even had time to search the room for any armor to help protect them. Determined to keep anyone from entering, she leaned further against the door. Perhaps, if they tried pressing on the door, they'd think it was locked.

But it wasn't meant to be.

Someone pushed on the door from the outside, and it edged open. Her pulse leapt, and she scrambled to find purchase on the floor with her bare feet without success and leaned into the door with all her weight, but it wasn't enough. The door slammed open, smashing her against the wall behind. Pain seared through her and white dots flashed across her vision. She groaned and pushed the door away from her and sunk to the floor, fighting to stay conscious.

A warrior covered in chainmail, sword in hand, pushed into the room, followed by a soft light that illuminated their haven. Dor swallowed the bile in the back of her throat as she stared at the corpses hanging from the walls. All these men had died long ago, but the corpses hanging from the walls by chains were a living nightmare she desperately wanted to escape.

Dor blinked as another man moved into the room. He carried a torch. She fought through the stars moving across her vision as Ada held her daggers tightly at each side, slipping into a defensive position in front of Dor's mum.

The warrior wearing the chainmail held up his hands. "There's no need for a fight. Clearly, you're with child. We'd never hurt the unborn."

Her mum's eyes narrowed as she took one step forward in challenge, putting herself in front of Ada. She casually removed a wicked blade from her hip and examined it as if she wasn't being threatened. "I will warn you once. You shall not take me or mine." A simple statement said softly, but it was as if she'd shouted a battle cry.

The warrior shook his head. "Swords don't have to come out and play. We can work this out. Isn't that right, Lazae?"

The warrior holding the torch nodded, but stayed mute.

"All you need to do is stand down," the warrior in the chainmail crooned.

But they all knew his words were false; the warlord never showed mercy. It was one reason he was so feared. If he let a threat go, that person became an enemy who might rise against him. Dor carefully tried to get her feet underneath her without drawing attention. The warriors had all but forgotten her.

She stilled as the second warrior moved farther into the room and angled himself toward her mum, exposing his back to Dor. That was his mistake. Her sire had always told her to never turn her back on the enemy. These weren't men trained by her sire, and that gave her an advantage.

She pulled in a deep breath and steeled her nerves. It was now or never. Dor leapt onto the back of the torch-holding warrior, cupping her right hand around his chin. She arched his head back and dragged her knife across his throat with her left hand. Disgust churned in her belly as he choked, staggered, and tumbled backward, crushing Dor against the floor under his body. Agony crashed into her, and she cried out as she was slammed against the stone. The torch tumbled to the floor and sputtered, casting ghoulish shapes across the room.

Darkness threatened to swamp her, but she forced herself to keep her eyes open. Dor squirmed, attempting to free herself. Ada's scream sent a shudder through her body, and she watched in horror as her mum launched herself at the warrior wearing chainmail, sword swinging to meet his with a mighty clash. Dor released a wheezed breath as another huge warrior moved into the room from the corridor. He stepped over his fallen comrade as if he was a bit of rubbish.

Dor's gaze darted back to her mum, just as the chainmail warrior pushed her mother's blade aside. Her mum twisted as he struck, leaning into her space. She surprised him and slashed across his belly with the blade in her opposite hand. He stumbled and clutched at his stomach for just a second before she swept the warrior's feet out from under him, dumping his body onto the mostly smothered flames.

The newest warrior released a war-cry that Dor swore she could feel in her bones and charged at her mum. Her ferocious mother sneered and stepped into his attack as Ada lunged forward and attacked in a series of parries that left Dor dizzy. As her mum and Ada both tried to take the warrior down, Dor cursed as she struggled to free herself from the corpse that weighed her down. Her breath stuck in her throat as her mother stumbled and clutched her stomach, sucking in a deep breath, her flowing movements halting. The warrior tossed Ada against the nearest wall, and didn't pause in his assault on Dor's mum as he went in for the kill.

Dor's pulse thundered in her ears, and she got her right hand free. Her sire had always told her to never throw her weapon, but his advice didn't matter now. She held her blade and clenched her teeth. Partly underneath the dead man's weight, she threw her blade. Her vision dipped as it struck true, right in the back of the shoulder of her mum's attacker. He bellowed and glanced over his shoulder, his eyes holding vengeance as he locked gazes with Dor.

The sounds in the room disappeared as she stared into the eyes of death. Her gaze moved to her mum's pain-filled face, and Dor smiled at her. It would be okay. By her estimations, the birth pains would subside and her mother would see justice done. She was the most formidable woman Dor had ever beheld. There was nothing that could conquer her.

Movements behind the warrior caused her to smile wider. His eyes narrowed as he took a step in the direction that would cost him his life. Ada launched at the warrior and slammed the butt of her dagger against his temple, her full weight crashing into him. The warrior's eyes blanked and rolled in his head. He fell forward and dropped onto his face.

Three bodies littered the floor, and only the sound of harsh panting could be heard. Ada groaned and sat up, rubbing her right shoulder, her nose wrinkled in distaste as she glared at the warrior she'd clouted, her face cast in shadow from the sputtering torches.

Dor glanced across the room and stared at her mum who looked no worse for wear, except for her torn skirt.

"Is everyone all right?" her mum asked.

"Fine," Ada muttered, wiping her dagger on her skirt.

"I'm okay," Dor said, finally wiggling out from beneath the warrior. Devil take it, the man was heavy. Wincing, she swayed on her feet, and the room spun as she pulled her dagger from the warrior's shoulder and stumbled over to her mum. "Are you sure you're okay?"

Her mum embraced her tightly and then pulled back, glaring. "Don't ever put yourself in danger like that again."

Dor touched the back of her head and winced as blood stained her fingers. "I could say the same thing to you."

"I'm your mother. It's my job to protect you." Her mum stepped to the side and hissed. She yanked her skirt up and revealed a blade wound high on her thigh that wept blood. "The bastard got me," she remarked, very put out.

Ada strode to her side and knelt, checking the wound on Dor's mum's thigh. "It's going to need stitches. You're losing too much blood. You should sit."

"I can't," her mum argued. "Another pain is coming. I need to be able to move through it."

"You'll faint long before the babe is born if you don't take care of that wound," a deep voice murmured from the darkness of the corridor.

Ada sprung to her feet, and both she and Dor stepped in front of her mum as she began to breathe through the waves of discomfort. Dor peered into the darkness, trying to see the newest threat.

A heavy sniff. "From the smell of this room, it'll need to be cleaned thoroughly or she'll breed infection."

Dor held her bloody dagger out in front of her defensively. "Show yourself."

A muscled warrior materialized from the darkness, stepping forward into the dim light. His dark eyes swept the room, taking in the scene. Dor steeled her nerves as she assessed the warrior. This one looked hard. The way he moved reminded her of the jungle cats that were the monsters every child was taught lurked in the dark.

His gaze settled on her mum, and an emotion flittered across his angular face. "Thank the stars, I found you alive."

Her mum placed a hand on Dor's left shoulder and limped in front of her. She placed her hands on her hips and glared at the man. "It took you long enough. My children could have died. Where the devil were you?"

He arched a midnight eyebrow and hooked a finger over his shoulder. "Do you really think they'd only send three men for the commander's property and daughter accused of murder?" He shook his head. "Some from above are foaming at the mouth to see your demise and the commander's reaction."

He took another step forward, and Dor matched his step, keeping pace with her mother. Anyone who spoke of another person as property wasn't any friend of hers.

"Not one step further," she growled, surprising even herself with the menace in her tone.

"Dor," her mum called softly. She placed a hand on Dor's fist clenched around the dagger's handle. "It's okay, love. This is your father's man, the one I spoke of."

The warrior met her gaze, and Dor stared him down, not wanting to move one inch. "You really expect us to believe you're helping my sire? You're the one hunting us down!"

He rolled his shoulders and sighed as if aggrieved to have to explain anything to a stupid worker. She bit the inside of her cheek to keep her teeth from lashing out at him. She loathed the man already.

"If there was someone hunting you, who better than me? I needed to find you." He kicked one of the warriors on the floor. "These monsters made it faster and easier."

"How convenient for you."

"Dor," her mother chastised.

The warrior held up a hand. "It's all right. She has every right to doubt me after what you all experienced." He nodded toward her mum's bleeding leg. "But we don't have time for your doubts at the moment. Your mum is losing blood, and she's exhausted herself before the most critical part of the birth.

She needs a healer's attention."

Dor's skin crawled at the mention of a healer, but she knew he was right. "I swear to all that is holy, if you make a wrong move, I will end you."

"Dark," he murmured, a strange twinkle entering his coffee-colored eyes. "I like it." Her mum cleared her throat and stared down the warrior, who pursed his lips like he'd tasted something sour. "Let's move before your mum births the babe in this hellhole," he said brusquely.

Dor nodded, slowly put away her blade, and took her mum's arm.

"That'll take too long," the warrior said, breaching the distance between them and gathering her mum in his arms as if she weighed nothing at all.

Her mum paled and sweat dotted her brow. "Hurry, girls. The babe will soon be here."

The warrior spun on his heel, stepped over the bodies of the fallen men, and strode out of the room. Ada kicked the chainmail warrior and followed. Dor blankly scanned the room, vaguely wondering whose family hung on the walls. She forced her legs to follow the others and glanced at the warriors she'd felled. The ugly red cut along the first one's neck looked like a demented smile. Her stomach rolled, and she stumbled against the door and puked on the stone floor.

She'd taken a man's life. *A life.* She heaved once more and wiped at her eyes and mouth. Not just one, but two. *She was a murderer.* There was no coming back from that.

Dor straightened and fled the room, but leaving the scene of the crime would not undo what had happened. She'd wear the stain of what she'd done on her soul for the rest of eternity.

TWENTY-THREE

TEHL

———⊶∘⟨⟩∘⊷———

MORNINGS HAD BECOME TEHL'S FAVORITE part of the day.

He stretched his back slightly and pulled Sage's warm, naked body more fully into the curve of his own. A smile tugged at his lips as she sighed and wiggled but didn't wake. Carefully, he propped himself up on one elbow and stared down at his beautiful wife. Every morning, it was a surreal experience to watch her slowly wake and sleepily smile at him, not even aware she was doing so.

His heart clenched as she snuggled closer, hugging his arm closer to her chest. In moments like this, he could almost forget the world around them. Tehl enjoyed the silence during the birth of a new day. In fact, silence had been his constant companion his entire life. Sharing it with someone else was an unexpected joy, especially seeing Sage without the constant weight she carried. In sleep, her hard edges fell away, leaving only the embodiment of warmth in its place.

"Are you going to keep staring?" Sage murmured, her lips barely moving, eyes still closed.

Tehl's mouth hitched up at the corner as he kissed her bare shoulder. Caught red-handed, and he wasn't the least bit sorry. "It's hard to look away."

His wife cracked one sleepy, green eye and arched a brow at him. "Compliments in the morning? Whatever could you be after, my prince?"

His smile widened. "Whatever indeed..." He pressed his face into the crook of her neck and bit down slightly before tightening his arm around her slim waist and rubbing his beard along her tender skin.

Sage squealed and writhed. "Noooooo," she laughed. "Make it stop."

Tehl rolled her toward him and onto her back. Her laughing, green eyes stared up at him, and he swept his gaze over her face and sent a silent *thank you* to whatever forces had sent this woman onto his path. Her mirth died away as she watched him.

"I've never had anyone look at me the way you do," she whispered into the chilly air.

He didn't know what to say to that, so he kissed her softly, hoping it conveyed his feelings. Actions meant more than words.

A cacophonous sound reached his ears, and he paused, staring down at his wife. Her brows slashed down, and a wrinkled formed between them.

"That's not good," Sage remarked.

Tehl kissed her once more, rolled off of her, and stood, the covers slipping from his body. His skin pebbled as the cold air rushed around him. He quickly slipped on his pants and groaned as Sage crawled from the bed, all bare skin and lush curves. Tehl eyed his wife and then the bed mournfully. What started out as a wonderful day was soon to turn sour, he was sure of it.

He yanked his shirt over his head, and grinned when Sage lifted her discarded corset from the floor and shook it at him.

"Look at what you did," she complained.

"You didn't mind so much last night," he countered.

She rolled her eyes, a small blush touching her cheeks, but smiled at him as she tugged her leather pants over her flared hips. "I won't argue that."

A touch of pride and possessiveness rolled through him at her statement. "You're going to be the end of me, woman."

She grinned impishly while pulling up her boots and then retrieved her leather breastplate. "I'm not sorry."

Tehl took the breastplate from her hands and slipped it over her head, careful to mind her long, loose hair. "Temptress," he said without heat as he tightened the armor to fit her figure.

"Beast," she replied.

He stepped back, and they stared at each other, acknowledging the playful moment before they settled into the roles they would both play when they left the comfort of their room.

Sage glanced toward the tent flap as the noise in the camp rose and seemed to move in their direction. "I fear what's coming."

So did he. Nothing was certain in war. "We'll do our best to get through it. Have no fear."

A small laugh fell from her lips. "There is much to fear."

Oh, how he knew. She'd shared some of her horrors from Scythia with him, but many others he'd experienced as she fought to escape them in her nightmares. Sometimes, he wished he could forget them, too. One too many times, he'd awoken with a racing heart, bitter fear coating his tongue, and his grip too tight around his wife.

He held his hand out. "We'll face this together."

Sage glanced down at his hand and slipped her small, calloused one into his and squeezed.

"To the end."

TWENTY-FOUR

SAGE

SAGE'S HEART THUNDERED AS LOUDLY as Peg's hooves beneath her as they approached the remote keep near the Nagalian border.

Smoke singed her nose when she inhaled sharply as their riding group crested the hill and slowed. Her mouth dried, and her eyes stung as they approached the wreckage below them.

It was as if fire had rained down from heaven and scorched every part of the earth.

What remained of the blackened stone keep stood like jagged, rotten teeth amongst the ravaged remains of the village.

Could anyone have survived?

Tehl steered his black beast of a horse to her left side as Zachael pressed closer to her right. Their men formed a loose circle around them.

"My men have searched the area for enemies. It seems they came in like shadows and left just as quietly," Zachael said, his normally warm voice harsh and biting.

Sage watched her husband's cold profile as he scanned the area, his expression chillingly blank.

"Any survivors?" Tehl demanded.

"None so far, my lord," Zachael answered. "They pillaged and took what they wanted before burning everything else."

Her stomach soured, and her husband pressed his heels into the flanks of his horse and began the descent to the decimated village. She urged Peg forward and ignored how sweaty her hands felt inside the leather gloves she wore.

No survivors.

"Did they take captives?" she asked softly.

"We believe so, my lady," Zachael answered.

Her hands tightened on Peg's reins, causing her horse to snort. Death seemed preferable to captivity.

Ash and smoke swirled around them, falling like snowflakes. Sage's eyes stung, her nose wrinkling from the smell, and she blinked several times to keep from rubbing them as they entered the village, the noise of the horses' hooves against the dirt the only sound.

The hair at the back of her neck prickled as the gray cloud that surrounded the village kept thickening. She urged Peg forward and almost jumped from the saddle when a soldier coughed behind her, shattering the solemn silence.

Tehl eyed her but said nothing as she stared impassively back, hoping to convey that she was strong enough to do this. He already worried about her too much as it was. He nodded and continued deeper into the smoldering ruins.

Sage glanced to the left, and paused as a shadow darted past the remnants of what looked to be some sort of shop and home. Peg skittered to the side when Sage clicked twice, her attention on the alley. A familiar shape slunk by but didn't move any closer.

She blew out a relived breath.

Nali.

Her feline companion disappeared into the gloom, and Sage steered her mare to the left, trailing the rest of the group. Three soldiers still accompanied her, but she barely noticed them as they moved through the destruction.

The road opened up to a stone courtyard that led to the entrance of the keep. The men ahead had stopped, forming a line to block whatever was ahead.

"My lady, I don't think you should see this," the soldier to her right murmured.

Sage glanced at him, meeting his pained eyes that were just a little too close together to be handsome. She nodded. "Thank you for your concern, but I'll see for myself."

The men moved aside as she approached, and what was revealed caused flashes of hot and cold to run through her body. She gagged as the stench of burnt meat overwhelmed her senses.

One immense pole had been erected in the center of the courtyard and attached to it were bodies.

"Stars above," a young soldier breathed.

"Were they burned alive?" Sage forced herself to ask.

"We found no evidence of prior executions," Zachael said heavily.

Tears pooled in her eyes at the thought of the excruciating pain the men must have faced.

"Am I correct in assuming it was just men?" Tehl asked, his voice like ice.

"Yes. The bodies are too large to be women or children."

Sage inhaled through her mouth and tried not to breathe too deeply. It sickened her to think what she was breathing in – or whom. The young soldier to her right heaved next to her, and she met his ashamed gaze as he wiped his mouth.

"There's no shame in being sickened by something so heinous," Sage said softly, her own stomach rolling.

The young man nodded, his eyes glassy.

"Cut them down," Tehl commanded. "And bury them properly. They deserve that."

"It will be done," Zachael said.

The weapons master uttered commands, but Sage barely heard them as she counted the bodies. A hand touched her arm, pulling her from her morbid task. Deep, somber, blue eyes stared up at her from a face that could've been made from stone. Tehl placed his hand over hers but said nothing.

"I'm so sorry," she whispered, knowing the words would neither help nor change anything. But they needed to be said, nonetheless.

Tehl's jaw clenched, and he swallowed once. "I'm going to help."

Sage nodded and moved to swing off her horse. It was a grisly task, but it had to be done. Tehl's hand on her thigh stopped her movement. She glanced askance at him.

"I would prefer it if you didn't help with this."

Her gloved hand touched his cheek. "I can do this."

"I know you can. I'm asking you not to."

She scanned his face and nodded. "Okay."

He pressed his cheek into her hand for an extra beat before straightening and striding into the fray of soldiers retrieving the bodies. The men made room for him and didn't comment as he began to work beside them. A surge of melancholy pride moved through her. He'd make a wonderful king someday.

The creak of a wagon alerted her to the soldiers moving in from behind. Sage nudged Peg to her left to move out of the lane so the soldiers could move the beaten-up wagon into the square. Sage longed to slap her hands over her ears as they began to cut down the corpses. Her nerves put Peg on edge, and, soon, she found herself near the keep.

She gazed up at the ominous soot-covered stones and almost wept. How long had this keep stood? How many lords and ladies, babies and grandchildren, weddings and funerals had it seen? So much was lost.

The ground groaned, and her brows pulled together. Sage glanced down as Peg shifted, and sand slipped through a few cracks beneath her mare's hooves, revealing rotted wooden slats.

Wicked Hell.

"It's okay, sweet girl," she murmured to Peg as she inspected the ground around them. One wrong move, and they'd fall right through. She forced the tension from her limbs, and urged Peg to take one step backward.

Another crack.

Sweat beaded on her forehead. There was less distance to travel if Peg moved backward, but she was slower. If they moved forward...

The ground groaned and shifted.

"Yaw!" she commanded, her heels and knees digging into Peg.

Her mare shot forward as the wood began to crumble. Shouts exploded from behind her, but Sage focused on making it to the other side. Only a few more paces. Wood splintered, cracked, and gave way behind them. Sage leaned forward as Peg launched over a hole in the ground and narrowly made it onto the dirt waiting on the other side.

Air rushed out of her lungs as she let Peg run off her nervous energy, and then she spun her horse back the way they'd come. They approached the collapsed ground, and Sage shakily swung her right leg off of Peg and dropped to the dirt, clutching her mare's reins, her legs trembling. She stroked her hand along Peg's quivering shoulder.

"That's a good girl," she soothed. "You're such a good girl. So fast."

"Sage!" Tehl barked.

She glanced across the gaping hole in the ground and met Tehl's frightened gaze. His hands opened and closed as he stared at her.

"I'm all right," she called back, gesturing to herself. "Not a scratch." Her gaze dropped to the collapse, noting all the broken wooden pieces that could've impaled Peg or herself. *We were lucky.* She released Peg's reins and crept toward the gaping maw in the ground.

"Don't get too close," her husband cautioned.

"I won't," she said as soldiers arrived on her side.

She waved away the ash floating in front of her face and knelt next to the edge. Dirt and ash obscured what was far below. She squinted at the length and width of the space. It looked like...

"An escape tunnel," she murmured, hope blossoming in her chest. "Tehl, it's an escape tunnel!" She eyed part of the road that collapsed, creating an angled wall that disappeared into the dark. All she would have to do was slide down to investigate it.

"Don't you dare," the crown prince threatened.

Sage studied him. In that moment, Tehl was a commanding royal, not her husband. He was giving her an order as her sovereign, but if he was willing to bury the dead, she could surely make sure there weren't any people down there.

"Follow me," she called to the soldiers who had surrounded her. She tipped her chin to Tehl and slid down the makeshift slide into the darkness. Her boots slammed against the ground, causing dirt, dust, and ash to stir around her. She smothered a cough, and held her arm across her nose and mouth as she tried to make out the area around her.

"Coming down," a deep voice warned.

She stepped out of the way as Zachael descended into the tunnel and landed much more gracefully than she had done. He glared at her and reached for a chunk of wood.

"You're going to be the death of him," the weapons master muttered as he wrapped a piece of cloth around the top half of it, ready to create a makeshift torch as soon as a flame caught on. "And I think you took ten years off my life. You need to be more careful. I'm already old."

Sage snorted. He may have had children her age, but there was nothing old about him. He was as fit as any young man and could out-spar anyone. "I'm sure you'll survive."

Flint struck steel, and Zachael's torch caught fire. She squinted at the sudden light. The weapons master lifted the torch and swung it to his right, illuminating a huge stone door that sealed the entrance into the stone tunnel from the keep. There clearly wasn't anything in that direction. Sage turned to her left and eyed the wide, dark tunnel that stretched on. She was studying its ceiling, which had collapsed in several places, when something smooth and pale caught her attention.

Her gaze narrowed, and a warning screamed in the back of her mind. "Zachael, would you hold the light higher?"

The weapons master stepped closer to her back and lifted the torch over his head, casting more light around the tunnel. Icy disbelief trickled down her spine as the soft firelight highlighted a small pale arm. Dread filled her belly, and she wanted nothing more than to run away, and, yet, she found herself scrambling over the debris.

"Sage!" Zachael yelled.

She hissed as she tripped and grabbed a particularly ragged piece of wood, but she barely felt the pain as she ignored the weapons master's calls. She couldn't distinguish his words over the beating of her own frantic heart. A hand wrapped around her arm, halting her movement. Sage glared over her shoulder at Zachael.

"Let me go," she said with venom.

He gazed at her impassively, and then his eyes shifted over her shoulder, and horror and anguish rippled across his face. "You can't help them."

Them?

Slowly, she turned her attention back to the arm, and the world dropped from beneath her feet. Her knees crashed to the stone floor, and an inarticulate sound escaped her mouth.

They'd found the elderly, the women, and the children.

Tears dripped down her face, and she crawled to the little girl sprawled face-first on the floor. Her hands shook as she turned over the toddler. She placed her hand around the little one's cool wrist, praying for a pulse.

Nothing.

She hiccupped and placed her ear over the little one's chest.

Nothing.

"No," she moaned. Her eyes roved over the girl's round petite face and rested on her blue lips. There weren't any injuries on the child that she could see, but... the blue lips, and ten blue little toes.

Sage pulled the little one's hand into her own. "She suffocated." Her words echoed around them. At Zachael's silence, she glanced up to see the weapon master's own stricken expression. Carefully, she placed the little one's arm across her still chest and stood, her knees almost buckling once again at the sight that greeted her.

The other side of the tunnel was sealed as well, and from the bodies littering the tunnel, it was clear someone had locked them inside and then slowly suffocated them.

Her gut clenched and she turned to the side to vomit out all the contents of her stomach. She heaved and heaved, her heart breaking. Wiping her mouth, she stooped and picked up the toddler with care. Her body hardly weighed anything. Sage's hands shook as she held the child close to her chest and passed by Zachael, who'd not moved but stared at the crime with the horror it deserved.

Sage clambered over the rubble and found an easier way to climb up. When the soldiers saw what she carried, they reached down and helped her leave the tomb behind. She took a few steps and fell to her knees with a soul-rendering cry.

"How could anyone do such a thing?" she whispered, her bottom lip trembling as she looked at the wee one in her arms. She brushed a finger along the child's cool, downy cheek and once again turned to the side to dry-heave.

Hands touched her shoulders as she straightened, and then massive arms wrapped around her from behind.

Sobs wracked her body as Tehl sank to his own knees and began to rock her and the child.

"Why?" she cried. "Why?"

"There's no reason for such wickedness."

There wasn't. How could a human being treat another person in such a manner?

"She's just a baby," Sage wailed, the image of the silent tomb seared in her mind. "What was the purpose of this? I can't understand it."

Nali prowled closer and bumped Sage in the arm with her head, her golden eyes seeming concerned. She wished she could assure the leren that she was okay, but she couldn't get any words past her sobs.

Tehl said nothing but continued to hold her as she mourned. Eventually, her tears dried, and a sense of numbness and fatigue settled over her. She adjusted the child in her arms and forced herself to get to her feet, Nali shadowing her. She swayed and turned to face Tehl. Heartache and grief were etched into his face.

"Fix this." She knew that he couldn't.

"She's gone, love. You need to put her down."

Sage clutched the child closer to her chest and took one step back. "And leave her for the predators?" She shook her head. "No. She deserves better." Her gaze strayed to the soldiers pulling the too small bodies from the debris of the tunnel. "They all deserve better."

Oh god, she was going to be sick again.

"We'll make sure they're buried, and we'll get vengeance."

"Vengeance?" she asked dully. She glanced at the toddler once again. There was nothing—*nothing*—that could make this better. "It's not supposed to be like this. War. Books speak of honor, courage, and glory," she stated. "This is none of those things. This is the ugliest kind of evil."

Sage swallowed down another cry that threatened to break free as Tehl picked up a shovel and met her gaze.

"Where do you want to lay her to rest?" he asked softly.

She peered around the ruins and paused, spotting a lilac bush up on the hill behind the keep. "There."

Tehl said nothing else but strode toward the spot she pointed to. He hefted his shovel and began to dig a rectangular plot.

One that was all too small.

Sage followed him and stood by his side, Nali their silent sentinel. Time passed, but she couldn't be sure how much.

Her husband touched her shoulder and held out his arms. She released the child, her arms feeling oddly empty as he stepped into the small grave and laid the child down, each movement mindful. He placed a lilac bloom across her little overlapped hands and pulled himself from the plot. His chest and shoulders heaved as he sucked in deep, pained breaths.

Sage slipped her right hand into his and sunk her fingers into Nali's soft midnight fur. They stood there, both silently crying for the cruel, heartbreaking loss of so many innocents. She released Tehl's hand and picked up the shovel, then scooped up some dirt. For a second, she hesitated.

"I'm sorry, wee one," she whispered, tears thick in her voice. "I promise you that I'll kill the man who did this and that you'll never be forgotten."

It took all her strength, but she sprinkled the dirt over the child's body. With each scoop, her resolve solidified, and she buried a piece of her heart.

The warlord had crossed a line she never thought he would. He was a monster.

But by his actions, he'd created something worse: a consort as deadly as he was.

TWENTY-FİVE

DOR

THE FLOOR LURCHED UNDER HER feet as she stepped into the hallway. Her breath hitched, and her throat dried at the sight of two warriors sprawled on the ground. Who had killed them? A chill ran down her arms as she hurriedly stepped over a motionless warrior, his sightless eyes blankly staring up at her. Her legs locked in place as she stared, stricken, at the warrior. He was dead. Death claimed him for following the orders of the warlord. It could have very well been herself lying in a pool of blood.

"Dorcus, come on," Ada pleaded.

As much as Dor wanted to follow her friend, she forced herself to stare at the warrior for a second longer. This was the price of rebellion. The consequences of fighting for one's life. The dark part of her knew that she'd exchanged the warrior's life for her mother's and Ada's, but even so, he was still a human being, and that deserved acknowledgement.

She knelt down and reached out with her right hand, ignoring how it shook when she gently closed his eyes. This man may have committed horrendous crimes for all she knew, but he could have hated the warlord as much as Dor. She didn't know his circumstances, and he deserved more than being left to rot in the godforsaken dark. She could do this much.

Dor straightened and glanced over her shoulder to find the warrior and Ada staring at her. A prickle of self-consciousness caused her cheeks to heat, which she ignored. She already knew she was particular, but she'd be damned if she let someone else's opinion of her determine her ideas on what was right and wrong.

She turned away from the fallen man, and scurried forward at the crumpled expression on her mum's face.

The warrior pulled her mum's face closer to his chest and lifted his chin at Dor. A clear command. "Follow me."

Dor's lips pressed together as she stared at his broad back as he stomped away, his steps quick and staccato-like. She didn't want to go after him. Every part of her screamed not to follow him or trust him. But he held her pregnant mother in his arms and was quickly disappearing down the hallway, so she didn't have much of a choice. Dor rushed to catch up, her skin tingling like a thousand spiders were running up and down her arms. When she'd awoken, it had been a normal day, but after this morning, she was sure she'd never have a normal day again.

"This way," he said gruffly, rounding the corner to the right.

The light from behind them slowly faded to a dull glow. She squinted into the dark and ran her hands along the wall, keeping her gaze on the warrior and Ada ahead of her.

"Grab the lantern," the warrior commanded, looking over his shoulder. His coffee-colored eyes flicked to Ada and then to the wall. Her friend scrambled to comply and quickly lit the lantern.

Their faces glowed eerily in the low light, and Dor blinked at how the light seemed to catch all the handsome angles of the warrior's face. Her lips curled as he faced forward and began moving without another word. *Rude.*

Her mum bit out a curse that had Dor speeding up and pressing closer to the warrior's right side. Her mother's face crumpled, and she hissed out a breath between her teeth, before panting and clutching at her belly. *Not a good sign.*

"Are you all right, Mum?" she asked, trying to keep panic from her voice. It wouldn't do to distress her mum even more.

Her mother nodded and gave a pained smile. "Women have been birthing babes since the beginning of time, love. I'll bear it as I have before."

Dor eyed her mum. They'd never had a babe come this early. It was happening a lot quicker than it should have been. But she kept her mouth firmly shut. It wasn't like *she'd* birthed babes before.

Her mum's expression cleared, and she opened her watery eyes and unclenched her hands. "I'll be fine, love. There's no need for so much concern. The babe will come, but I want to get to safety first."

Dor schooled her expression, smiled weakly, and jogged to keep up with the massive man carrying her mum, Ada keeping pace with her.

Safety. Was there even such a thing? In the world she was born into, there never had been.

Nothing was safe.

Ada squeezed in on her left side and looped her arm through Dor's. She clutched her friend's arm gently, and some of the panic loosened in her chest. None of them were in this situation alone. Ada scooted a little closer, as if seeking comfort, and lifted the lantern higher. A groan slipped from Dor's lips as they approached another staircase. Her legs were barely working as it was. It would be a bloody miracle if she got out of the maze of tunneled hallways alive.

The warrior cut her a look that spoke of irritation as he stomped up the stairs. Dor managed to keep from rolling her eyes, and swallowed back a sharp reply that would surely distress her mum and needle the warrior. Now wasn't the time. He was helping them and, even as tiny as her mum was, there was no way Ada or herself would have been able to carry her mum this far, let alone up the stairs. So, she swallowed back her complaints and trudged up the circling, black stone staircase. There were worse lots in life.

Thankfully, they only climbed a few more steps before they tapered off into a half-circle landing with tunnels leading in five directions. Ada set the lantern on the floor, pressed her hands to her knees, and panted while the rest of them caught their breaths.

Dor leaned against the wall and stared at the warrior. "So, since we're causing mischief and mayhem, are you going to share your name?"

"Names are a dangerous thing."

So, no. "I could easily identify your face," she argued.

He raised an imperious eyebrow. "Are you sure?"

He did look like most of the warriors, but there was something different about his eyes. She shrugged, neither confirming nor denying his words. If he wouldn't answer her, she wouldn't answer him. To some it may seem childish, but fair was fair.

"We need to move," he said, gently shifting her mum in his arms.

Ada snatched the lantern from the floor and rubbed at her back as she straightened. "Lead the way."

The nameless warrior dipped his chin and pressed into the far-right tunnel, disappearing into the darkness with her mother. Both girls locked arms once again and followed. The tunnel stretched on and on, curving left then right, up and down. It was disorienting, and goosebumps pebbled Dor's forearms as the temperature cooled. Her friend pulled the lantern closer as she practically plastered herself to Dor's right side.

"This tunnel creeps me out," Ada whispered, her words seeming to be absorbed by the inky darkness hovering just out of reach.

"I don't like it..." Dor trailed off as she caught sight of the end of the tunnel. It just *ended*. A flare of panic ignited in her gut. Had they made a wrong turn? Somehow, she doubted it.

Her heart began to pound in her chest as the man slowly lay her mother down on the floor and spun to face both Ada and her, his expression unreadable. Hell. She dropped Ada's left arm and palmed the blade at her hip. She knew they couldn't trust him.

Ada placed the lantern on the floor, stepped slightly in front of Dor, and effortlessly drew both daggers from her sheaths. No one spoke a word as tension filled the hallway.

"What do you want?" Ada asked, softly.

The warrior scrutinized both of them, letting no trace of his thoughts cross his face. Her mum moaned, momentarily pulling his attention from them, as she clutched her stomach and curled into herself, apparently oblivious to the situation around her.

Uneasiness coiled in Dor's belly. If they didn't get to a healer soon, the babe might not be born at all, or her mum could die.

The warrior's gaze narrowed and then moved to the wall behind his back. He heaved in a deep breath and then faced them once again, his expression cold as stone. "What is beyond this door will change your life."

"Hurry up," her mum grunted from the floor.

He glared at Dor's mother for a second and then focused back on Ada and Dor. "There will be no going back," he murmured quietly, his tone soft and low, carrying a deep warning. "This is permanent. Serious." A pause. "If you pass through this gateway, you must never speak of what you will see."

Dor's pulse accelerated even more. What could be so horrid that she must never utter a single word about it?

"Decide now."

Decide now? "You've told me nothing." Dor wasn't about to agree to something when she didn't know the particulars. That was stupid. And stupid in her world led to death.

"I'm bound by the same laws you are. Decide or walk away."

"Walk away?" Dor wet her lips, her gaze bouncing between her mum and Ada. "You would let us go?"

The muscle in his jaw twitched. "I would allow you to walk away, but not to live."

Ada gasped, and dread twisted in Dor's belly. Her feet wanted to turn and flee, but she knew from experience she couldn't outrun a warrior, and there was no way she could leave her mum or Ada behind. They were family, and family stuck together.

"You would kill us over nothing?" Dor said flatly.

"This is not nothing."

A flare of anger ignited in her chest, making her a little bit reckless. She waved a hand at the invisible door. "I didn't ask for any of this. I don't even know who you are," Dor reminded him, her brain scrambling to find a way out of the situation. "*You* have a choice. You don't have to kill us. We'll disappear. You'll never see us again."

He shook his head. "I'm sorry, but that's not the way this works. You need to make a choice, but know if you do choose to walk the path ahead and you ever speak about what you see, your life will be forfeit."

"It's not really a choice. You're saying you'll kill us if we don't like what's on the other side," she pointed out. "Or if we ever try to speak about what's behind the door, we'll die. Death is on every path!"

"Lives are at stake," he said woodenly.

"Yes," she bit out. "*Our* lives."

"We cannot risk a breach."

We. Who was the *we* the warrior was referring to?

"Dorcus," her mum whispered.

Dor tore her gaze from the warrior and knelt beside her mum, careful to keep the warrior within full view.

"What, Mum?"

Her mum reached out and squeezed her hand, her hazel eyes filled with pain. "Go through the gateway. This is your future, love. You've never shied away from doing what's right. Take the path."

Dor swallowed, her tongue sticking against the roof of her mouth. She didn't want to admit it, but she was scared, not of death, but of whatever was on the other side of the door. Terrified of the change that would surely wreak havoc on her life.

She glanced at the dark, stone wall. Her fear drove her to back away, but she wouldn't give in. Fear had never ruled her in the past, and it wouldn't now. Even when she felt cornered, she still knew she had a choice. There was nothing to go back to. The only way she could go was forward into the unknown.

"You can do this, Dor," her mum whispered.

Dor nodded, pushed herself to her feet, and stood on shaking legs, meeting the warrior dead in the eyes. "I understand and agree to move forward." She inhaled then exhaled shakily. "But I want something in exchange. Care for my family-"

"Done."

"I wasn't finished speaking."

His lips twitched. "By all means, continue."

"I want your name."

The warrior blinked, looking a bit shocked. "My name?"

"It's only fair. I want to know whom I should hold accountable if things don't go well."

He cocked his head. "Darius." His coffee gaze moved to Ada. "Do you accept the terms as well?"

"Yes," her friend answered without hesitation.

Darius turned from them and pressed a series of spots and hollows on the door. Stone groaned and shuddered, then the door swung open silently.

"Enter."

TWENTY-SİX

SAM

⟶◦⟨∞⟩◦⟵

SAM GHOSTED DOWN THE HALLWAY to his chambers, his footsteps muffled on the lush carpets running the length of the arching corridors. A faint peel of laughter reached his ears as he arrived at the ornate, wooden door that led to his rooms. With care, he rested his forehead against the smooth wood and listened to the twins' squeals of happiness.

He loved listening to them laugh. They'd been through so much at such a tender age. Ethan was the more wary of the two, but he'd been warming up to Sam since he'd been bringing treats and little trinkets every time he visited.

Bribery at its best.

Jas, of course, had tried to keep the children away from him as much as possible. Sam's lips turned up in a devious smile. She may be stubborn, but her stubbornness was no obstacle for his plotting. Every time she turned her back, he made sure to spend time with the twins. It hadn't taken him long to win them over.

He reached for the handle and pushed the door open. As Sam stepped inside, his breath was knocked from him at the picturesque scene taking place in his chambers. A fire crackled in the hearth, and curled up on his bed were Jasmine, Jade, and Ethan. Both children had their cheeks pressed against Jasmine's swollen belly as she read from a storybook.

It was the picture of domesticity.

His heart swelled, and he longed to join them, to wrap his arms around his family and kiss his wife on the top of her head, but they weren't there yet. The children had accepted him, but their aunt had yet to do so.

Her gaze flicked up to his above her book, and he held a finger to his lips. The children apparently hadn't noticed his entrance yet. Jasmine pressed her lips together, but she didn't out him, so that was progress. She dismissed him and began reading the story once again, her voice changing pitch for each character.

Sam stealthily snuck up on the twins, who were enraptured with the story, and then launched onto the bed, snagging each child by their waist. Jade and Ethan screamed, and began to wiggle and laugh as Sam tickled them.

"What miscreants have invaded my lair?" Sam demanded in a deep voice. "Do you seek to steal my treasures?"

Jade shook her head, her tawny hair flopping around her chubby face. "I would never steal, that's bad!"

Sam turned his attention to the little boy pummeling him with his fists. "And what about you?"

"Whatever does a dragon need treasure for?" Ethan retorted as he struggled not to laugh.

"Indeed," Sam whispered conspiratorially. "Dragons do like treasure, but do you know what they like better?"

"What?" the twins said in unison, their faces red from laughter and exertion.

"Dragons love maidens like your auntie. Maybe I shall keep her forever!"

Little war cries exploded out of the twins, and they began to attack him with fervor. Sam loosened his grasp on Jade and let her worm her way out of his hold. She hopped two steps and picked up a feather pillow, a wily gleam in her eye.

"No one takes my mama!"

Sam stilled as Jasmine's face paled and lost all expression at Jade's innocent words. It was like someone had punched Jas in the gut. He barely noticed as Ethan slipped from his fingers and launched the pillow-attack with his sister, the feathered blows skimming off of him.

"Are you all right?" he asked Jas.

Jasmine blinked and rolled from the bed, leaving the storybook forgotten on the brocade blanket covering the bed. She brushed the wrinkles from her dress and said softly, "It's time for bed, you two."

"Aw, come on," Ethan protested. "Sam just got here."

"I understand, but it's well past your bedtime as it is. I promised you could say goodnight and nothing more."

"But I want to—"

Sam placed a hand on Ethan's right arm, pulling the little boy's attention from Jasmine. "Don't argue with auntie. Do as she says."

His lip protruded as he stared imploringly at Sam. "I missed you."

Sam swallowed and pulled the little boy into his arms. "I promise to be here when you wake."

Jade sniffled, and he opened his other arm to the rambunctious little girl. She flung herself into him and wrapped her arms around his neck. Sam scooped the twins up and moved toward the door to their room. Jasmine bustled forward and opened the door for them.

Toys littered the room, along with books stacked haphazardly and drawings pinned to the walls. Leaning down, he placed Jade and Ethan onto each of their beds, and lit the lantern that stood on a small blue table between them. The soft glow warmed the dark room.

He leaned down and placed a kiss on the top of Jade's head as she snuggled into her covers. "Night, Sam," she said with a yawn.

"Goodnight, sweetheart," he replied, pushing the hair from her face.

Next, he moved to Ethan's side and sat on the edge of his bed as the little boy stared up at him, Ethan's expression grave. He latched on to Sam's hand with his little fingers.

"You promise to be here?"

"I promise," Sam said warmly.

"Not everyone comes back," Ethan whispered.

Sam swallowed hard and ignored Jasmine's sharp inhale at Ethan's remark. He squeezed the little one's hand. "You're right, not everyone comes back. That is a sad part of life. But there's nothing that would keep Jasmine or myself from you, if you needed us. That's what being a family means."

Ethan's eyes darted around the room before settling on Sam once again. "I see scary things in my dreams sometimes. It makes me scared."

"I'm sorry," Sam said gently. "That happens to me, too. Do you know what I do that helps?"

"What?"

"I say a prayer, and then I think about all the people who love me and will protect me."

"Do you love me?"

Sam's chest seemed to crack. "I do love you, Ethan. And I promise nothing can hurt you here. I'm a dragon, remember? Is there anything that can get through these stone walls and defeat a dragon?"

Ethan's brows furrowed as if he was in deep thought. "I suppose not."

"You'd be right. And not only do you have me, but you also have Tehl, Gav, Sage, Mira, Jasmine, and the king to look out for you."

"The king," Jade breathed from her bed. "Is he the king of dragons?"

"He is," Jasmine said, rounding Jade's bed and sitting down next to the child to play with her hair. Jas glanced at Sam before looking back at the wee one. "He's the fiercest man I've ever met, and, yet, there's nothing that compares to the danger a dragoness poses when her kits are threatened. Myself, Auntie Sage, Mira, we're all dragonesses. We'll protect you."

Jade's eyes shone in the lantern light. "Will *I* be a dragoness?"

"One day, sweet girl." Jasmine bent down and kissed Jade's cheek. "Now, sleep."

Ethan squeezed Sam's fingers, and Sam turned his attention back to the boy. "Can we fight in the morning? I saw soldiers training, and I want to be like them when I grow up."

"I'll see what I can do."

Ethan squeezed Sam's hand one more time and then burrowed into his covers. Sam kissed his forehead and stood, staring between the two beds at the precious people who had been dropped into his life.

He'd never felt so lucky.

However, he did frown as he noticed how small the beds were. Where, in the devil, was Jasmine sleeping? He opened his mouth to ask, when she shot him a look, clearly telling him to leave. Sam crept from the room, but left the door open, hoping she got the hint that he'd like to speak with her.

They needed to discuss some things.

TWENTY-SEVEN

SAM

QUIET FOOTSTEPS PADDED INTO THE room, and the door softly clicked shut. Sam didn't turn as Jasmine joined him, standing in front of the fire. She held her hands out to the flames but didn't face him. Regardless, he could still feel her appraising him.

"Do you want to talk about it?" he asked.

"Talk about what?"

"Whatever you're stewing about," Sam said, turning to face Jasmine.

The firelight played over her face, highlighting the spray of freckles across her sloping nose and sea-blue eyes. Eyes that were currently scrutinizing him.

"They're becoming too attached to you."

Not what he meant, but it was a start. "Should they not be? Am I not the man who will have a hand in raising them?"

Her rosebud lips pursed. "I don't expect *you* to parent them. They'll be fine without your meddling."

Meddling. He'd done a lot of meddling in his life, but this was *not* meddling. Every action he took regarding the twins and Jasmine served the greater purpose: building a family.

"You don't believe that they need two parents?"

She shook her head. "I've been doing fine on my own."

He nodded. "You've done an excellent job with the twins. They are remarkable."

A little color touched her cheeks. "Thank you."

"But—"

Jasmine groaned. "Must there always be a 'but?'"

"Yes."

She waved a hand at him. "Very well. I'm sure you'll tell me your opinion, even though I don't want to hear it."

Sam hid his smile. "I appreciate your never-ending suffering."

She snorted but said nothing else.

"I lost my mum well before I was raised," he said seriously. "Then, my father suffered greatly. It was like I lost both parents for years, and, even when my father was present, I longed for my mother. There's a reason the forces at will deem it best to have two parents. It helps the children thrive and gives each parent someone to lean on when things are difficult. Would you take that away from the twins?"

"So, you're saying I'm not enough?" she said flatly.

"No, I am saying that you're not alone. You don't have to be alone. You don't have to prove anything to the world. I am here." He stabbed a finger at the twins' door. "I love those wee ones already. I have not asked much from you, but I'm asking you now not to take them away and to let me in."

"Take them away?" She eyed him. "Who told you?"

"Told me what?"

"Don't play dumb. It's unbecoming, for you and I. How long have you known that we were planning on leaving?"

"For a little while," he admitted.

"And, yet, you've kept silent and not threatened me?"

Sam scoffed. "What did you expect me to do? Did you think I would chain you to my bed and keep you as my love-slave until you submitted to me?" Once the words passed his lips, the image flashed through his mind, and the darker part of him admitted he liked the idea of her as a love-slave, a willing one that desired him as much as he desired her.

Jasmine's eyes crinkled, and her lips twitched before her laughter spilled over. "Did you get that from a dark, romance novel or come up with that all on your own?"

He rolled his eyes but chuckled. "I made that up all by myself, thank you very much."

She wiped the corners of her eyes. "I'm sure your wicked mind has many such scenarios lurking in its depth."

Sam flashed her a devilish smile and inwardly purred as she blushed. He tried hard to make her like him, but so much stood between them. Her unwillingness to trust, and his secrets, but this was simple, easy. He imagined this was what it would be like if each of them leaned on one another.

Jasmine sobered and cast a searching glance at the fireplace. "You've done much for the twins and myself. I admit, I hate how it happened." She glared at him and he winced. "Having a choice is very important to me. I understand why you did what you did, but it must never happen again."

"I promise." And he meant it.

"I miss the country," she blurted.

Sam blinked. "I suspect living in the castle has been somewhat jarring."

"It feels like a cage," she said softly. She peeked up at him from under her lashes. "I wish to return to the country." Sam held his breath. "But you've given me much to think on. I promise not to steal away in the night."

"Thank you," he said wryly.

She took in his expression and laughed. "If our positions were somewhat reversed, I'm sure you're not the one who'd be left. If I was to stake gold on it, I'd say you're the one to steal away in the night."

He forced himself not to grimace at her observation. He was aware of the rumors that circled the court around his behavior concerning the fairer sex. He'd encouraged it before, as it just obscured his true motives and actions, but having a wife... Well, it made the gap between them wider, filled with all of his lies, spoken and unspoken.

"She called me Mama."

Sam blinked at the change of subject. Obviously, she didn't want to discuss that, either. "How do you feel about that?"

"Confused," Jasmine said. "And hurt." She placed a hand over her heart. "My brother and sister-in-law were amazing parents. I remember them. I remember how they cared for the twins, how the twins were the light of their lives. But the twins barely remember them. Ethan has a vague idea of my brother, and Jade? She's lost all touch with them." Jasmine sucked in a breath. "The only person who truly remembers is me," she whispered, her voice cracking.

"Don't feel guilty for that."

Jasmine met his gaze. "How can I not? I survived, and they did not. I've taken their place."

Sam leveled a stern look at her. "I'm sure your family would be eternally thankful that you're living, so that you can care for the twins. Who better to raise them in their absence?" He reached out and touched her slim shoulder. "The twins may not remember your brother and his wife, but you do. You can teach Ethan and Jade about their wonderful parents who doted on them, and entrusted you to care for them."

Jas bit her bottom lip when it wobbled. "Even now, I fear I'm forgetting things about them."

An idea struck Sam, and he moved around the bed to dig through the top drawer of his dresser until he found what he was searching for. His fingers wrapped around a leather notebook, and he pulled it from the drawer and strode back to Jasmine. He held the notebook out to her. "Here. Use this to write down what you remember. Then they will never be forgotten."

Jasmine reached out and took the notebook from him. Her hand shook as she brushed her fingers across the embossed cover. She glanced up at him, eyes glossy. "Thank you," she choked out. "This is such a thoughtful gift." But she held the notebook out to him. "But my writing and reading is poor."

Tenderness flooded Sam. He pressed the notebook back into her hands. "I'll help you. My handwriting is terrible, but we can work on this together."

Jas placed her hand over his and squeezed. "Thank you."

Warmth filled Sam at her sincerity.

She gasped and dropped the notebook, her face creasing in pain.

"What is it?" Sam barked.

She yanked him forward and placed his hand over her belly, her fingers splayed over his.

Sam's jaw dropped as something kicked his hand. His gaze flew to Jasmine's face, which was still creased in a grimace.

"She's a strong one," she breathed.

"She?" Sam echoed, his gaze dropping back to Jasmine's moving belly.

"It has to be a girl," Jas gritted. "Only a girl could be this vicious."

Sam beamed as the little one continued to move and roll beneath his hands. "It's a miracle," he breathed.

Until this moment, the babe hadn't felt real to him. He'd seen the changes to Jasmine's body, but feeling the child move? Well, it changed everything. Delight and joy filled him, along with a strong dose of protectiveness and possession.

That was *his* babe.

He peeked up at his wife who watched the little one move with wonder.

And she was *his* wife.

One day, she'd realize it, too.

All too soon, the babe settled down and Jasmine shifted on her feet, as if embarrassed. Sam reluctantly removed his hands and stepped away.

"It's amazing, isn't it?" she asked before yawning behind her right hand.

"There aren't words."

She smiled tiredly at him, which reminded him of something else he needed to speak with her about.

"Where have you been sleeping?"

"With the twins."

In the tiny beds. The beds designed for short, wee persons, not grown, pregnant women.

"I don't sleep much," he started.

Jasmine rolled her eyes. "I am aware."

He bit back his retort and gestured to the huge bed. "You're welcome to sleep in my bed."

"Your bed?"

"Yes, alone."

Her brows rose, and she eyed the bed.

"I guarantee you'll sleep better," he promised.

"And where will you sleep?"

"Somewhere else." Outside their door.

She glided to the side of the bed and ran her hand along the silky blanket before glancing over her shoulder at him. "The bed is enormous, and if I wasn't desperate to get away from the twins' kicks, I'd say no, but my back is killing me." She swung around to face him and crossed her arms. "I won't steal your bed. Our attractions both lie elsewhere, so we needn't worry about the other making advances. Do you agree?"

What devil had her attention? Sam fought to keep the scowl from his face. He'd had her followed since the night he found her by the docks. True to her word, she'd been careful. But it bothered him terribly to think she was seeking out another man.

"True enough," he admitted.

She didn't need to know how much her form appealed to him. The first time she'd scowled at him, all those months ago, it had been instant attraction for him, but her growing a child? He must have become some sort of deviant. He'd never found a pregnant woman attractive before, but, with Jasmine, he could scarcely keep his eyes off her.

"So, you're welcome to sleep in this bed with me as long as you stay on your side and don't kick me."

Sam nodded, keeping his glee at bay. "Agreed. But you need to promise not to steal my pillows. I tend to be territorial of them."

Sam was sure she didn't know it, but this was just the opening he needed. Close quarters usually bred intimacy, not always sex, but closeness, and that was what he wanted.

She rushed from the bed and flung her arms around him, hugging him tightly. Sam didn't hesitate in hugging her back and even dared to lie his cheek on the top of her head. Tonight had given him more gifts than he knew what to do with.

"Thank you," she whispered, her words heating his exposed skin at his collar. She inhaled and then pulled away, leaving Sam's arms feeling empty.

Her expression slowly cooled, and she bent to pick up the leather notebook, then trailed back to the bed and tugged back the covers, placing the notebook on the side table. "You might need a shower."

He barked out a laugh. This woman. She would drive him crazy with her mood changes. He strolled to the bathing room, deciding not to push his luck. "Your wish is my command."

It was a good thing she had no clue how true those words were.

TWENTY-EİGHT

JASMINE

SHE WATCHED HIM SAUNTER INTO the bathing room and pause in the doorway. Sam glanced over his shoulder and wiggled his eyebrows.

"You could join me?" he trailed off.

Jasmine narrowed her eyes and placed her hands on her hips. "Not on your life."

He laughed. "You don't know what you're missing." Sam winked at her and closed the door behind him.

She stood stiffly until she could hear the water running in the bathing room. Her shoulders slumped, and she practically collapsed against the bed. Jas ran a hand over her face. What in the blazes had she been thinking when she'd invited him to sleep in the same bed?

The notebook. That was why.

She glanced at the book on the side table, picked it up, and couldn't help but bring it to her nose and inhale deeply. There was nothing she loved more than the smell of leather. The damned man had found her weakness.

Carefully, she placed the notebook back on the nightstand, and stared idly at the fire burning low in the hearth. Her gaze unconsciously wandered back to the bathroom door as her ears picked up the sounds of splashing. What the hell was he doing? And why was she bothered?

"Get it together, Jas," she chastised herself.

He might be her friend, possibly her partner, but he wasn't her lover, and most definitely wasn't her husband in the true sense of the word. She couldn't let herself get carried away with romantic notions. His familiar touches and flirtatious behavior meant nothing. She knew what he was when she married him.

A rake. Scoundrel. Sin reincarnated.

Jasmine forced herself to look away from the door and squeezed her eyes shut. When he'd hugged her, she'd detected another woman's scent on him. He made her no promises. She didn't expect him to be faithful, and, if she let herself get caught up in him, it would only end with her having a broken heart and a strain on their friendship—if that was what she could call it.

Forcing herself to stand, she rearranged the pillows to form a border down the middle of the bed and tiptoed to the closet. Quickly, she stripped off her dress and tugged a nightgown over her head. The fabric fell to her toes. She scowled at the material.

Stars above, she hated sleeping in clothes, especially something so long. Every time she turned in her sleep, the garment would tangle around her legs. She sent a longing glance at one of Sam's lightweight linen shirts. What she wouldn't give to sleep in one of those.

Jasmine shook her head and hung up her day-dress. Her maid always got annoyed with her when she cleaned up after herself, but she couldn't help it. It bothered her to have someone clean up after her.

Jas poked her head out of the closet and tiptoed back to bed, sliding into the cool sheets. There was no better feeling than cool sheets. She snuggled into them, and peered drowsily at the fireplace. If she were smart, she'd stay awake until Sam came to bed, so she could keep an eye on him. A yawn snuck up on her, and she tugged the covers higher, her eyelids drooping.

Who was she kidding? She was pregnant with another man's child and getting fatter each day. She wasn't in any danger from the sultry prince. If anything, he should be worried about her mauling him in his sleep.

A smiled tugged up the corners of her mouth. He didn't have to worry about his pillows. Thank the stars he hadn't asked about snoring.

The feeling of being watched was what woke her. Jasmine blinked, disoriented. Where was she? She lifted her head to peek over the pillow and lay back down immediately.

Sam's bed.

A hand brushed her belly, and her eyes widened as she realized Sam's arm had pushed beneath the pillow-wall during the night, and she had curled herself around his arm.

One finger at a time, she released her death grip on his arm and slowly scooted backward, so he wasn't touching any part of her.

Two stifled giggles caught her attention.

Jasmine sat up and found the culprits crouching at the bottom of the bed like the early-rising monsters they were. She held a finger to her mouth, signaling the twins to be quiet, but the harder they tried, the louder they became, and pointing to the door to their room did nothing.

"Dear, I think we have an infestation of sniggering mice," Sam rumbled, startling her.

She glanced over at him and wished she had not.

His blond curls were mussed in a soft, sexy way, and he had a shadow of golden scruff growing along his jaw and cheeks. But that wasn't the worst of it. It was the way his blue eyes squinted as he beamed at her, like she was the reason he was so joyful to be on this earth.

Bastard. It wasn't right to look that perfect when one woke up.

She swiped at her face, hoping she didn't have dried drool around her mouth.

"Who could have snuck into our rooms?" Sam growled.

"We did!" Jade exclaimed as she clambered onto the tall bed, followed by Ethan.

The twins bounded across the blankets and pillows and settled themselves in between Sam and Jasmine.

"I'm hungry," Ethan proclaimed.

Jasmine blushed as her belly released a growl that could rival Nali's.

Sam grinned at Jade, and she snuggled closer to him, resting her head against his arm. "I'm hungry, too," she said.

"Well, that's settled. Let's get some breakfast!" Sam hoisted Jade onto his shoulders and plucked Ethan from the bed, setting him on the floor with care before taking the boy's hand.

Jasmine blinked as he started for the door. "They're in their nightclothes."

The impertinent man turned toward her with an impish grin. "And that is relevant, why?"

"It's not decent."

"There are many things in my life that are not decent, and this is the least of them. They're children. Now, get out of that bed before I decide to carry you, too."

Jasmine crossed her arms over her chest. "I need to change."

Sam rolled his eyes. "Please. I've seen what you wear to bed. It's more modest than most women's everyday gowns. Now, stop fighting me, and let's feed these children before they expire this very moment."

She tossed the covers away and slipped from the bed, her toes curling as they touched cold stone. He wasn't wrong, but she'd been given so many lessons on proper behavior since she'd become a prince's wife that she hardly dared doing anything she used to. She bustled into the closet, grabbing the first robe she spotted. She smiled as she pulled on the blue, silk dressing-gown with silver snowflakes embroidered along its hem and sleeves.

"We're positively wasting away," Sam moaned, and the twins giggled.

"I'm coming, you arse," she muttered as she secured the tie around her waist.

"I heard that."

Her lips twitched. She meant him to.

She exited the closet and moved toward the gaggle of starving individuals to open the door. "Let's be gone then. I can't have you starving to death."

The men stationed outside their room smiled and greeted them as the twins babbled and waved like they did each day.

"So, what would you like for breakfast?" Sam asked.

"Everything!" Jade exclaimed.

"Everything?"

"Yes. That's what Mama said yesterday. The baby was sooooooo hungry."

Jasmine shook her head at her niece. No one could keep a secret.

Sam cast a look her way, full of mirth. "Well, we'll see what we can do."

He was true to his word.

She didn't know how he managed it, but a feast arrived when they entered a cozy dining room Jasmine had never seen before. It was only after she'd gaped at the food, saliva pooling in her mouth, that she noticed there was one more occupant in the room. Her spine straightened as she realized he was looking at her over a sheaf of paper.

The king.

She pivoted and executed a curtsy. "My apologies, my lord."

He set his papers down and smiled, his arresting blue eyes, so similar to both of his sons, sparkling. "No need, my dear."

So that's where his son learned the endearment.

Her eyes widened as Ethan plopped himself in the chair next to the king and reached for the orange juice.

"Ethan, no—" she said, but it was too late.

The little one tipped the juice over, and it rushed over the king's papers and down onto his lap. Panic spurred her forward, and she snatched up napkins and began cleaning the table.

"I'm so sorry, my lord. Please forgive my son, he didn't mean any harm, he's only four…" She trailed off as a large hand settled over her trembling one.

She peered up at the king as he gently pulled the napkins from her fingers.

"There's nothing to forgive, my daughter. I raised wee ones myself. And, from experience, I know they make great messes that seem impossible for their size."

He lifted his papers from the table and shook them off before wiping himself down. He glanced at Ethan, who'd curled in his chair with wide eyes. The king held his hand out to Ethan. "Come here, little one."

Jasmine stepped back when Sam cupped her shoulder with his hand and squeezed gently.

Ethan slipped down from his chair and stood beside the hulking king.

"Are you still thirsty?" the king asked.

"Yes, I am."

"Do you know who I am?"

Ethan nodded. "My lord."

The king smiled, flashing straight white teeth. "To many, yes, but to you?

I am just Grandad."

Tears flooded her eyes. *Stupid hormones.*

"Grandad," Ethan parroted.

The king held his arms out, and Ethan moved into them without hesitation. Jasmine could only stare as he poured what was left of the juice into a glass for the boy and plopped some food onto a plate for him, too. Once Ethan was settled, the king cocked his head and wiggled his eyebrows at Jade who watched him shyly.

"Would you like something, too, sweet girl?"

Jade nodded and scampered over to him. He made another plate, and once both children were eating, he turned his attention to Jasmine. Her breath seized at the massive smile stretched across his face and the emotion gleaming in his eyes.

"Thank you," he said roughly. "Ivy and I always dreamed of grandchildren. I didn't think I'd live to see the day, and what a wonderful unexpected blessing it is." He gestured to the chair to his left. "Please sit and enjoy a meal with me."

Sam's hand moved to her lower back and nudged her forward. She bit the inside of her cheek at the intimate gesture that didn't seem to faze the prince.

On trembling legs, she shuffled to the chair and sat just like her instructors had taught her. Carefully, she chose dainty portions of food and placed them on her plate. Stars above, she was hungry. How she was going to make it through the meal without making herself look like a glutton, she didn't know.

A deep, male laugh rumbled from the king. She blinked at him.

He gestured to the food. "My Ivy was so sick for the first part of each of her pregnancies, she wouldn't touch a thing. But, near the end, she'd eat everything in sight. We don't stand on ceremony here, my daughter. Eat."

Jasmine smiled and tugged another hotcake onto her plate, as well as a few more slices of bacon. "Thank you, my lord."

"Marq," he said softly. "We are family now." His gaze narrowed on Sam who'd sat to her left. "Although, my son has kept you from me."

She shook her head. "The fault is mine. It's taken some adjustment, and I'm not overly fond of people I don't know. We've kept to ourselves, for the most part. I'm sorry if I've offended you, but it wasn't your son's doing." She snapped her mouth shut and shoveled a bite of buttery hotcake in her mouth so she wouldn't correct the bloody king again.

"And, now that you have met me, will you keep them from me?"

Swallowing slowly, she eyed the man who ruled their kingdom. "I would deny you nothing. You're the king."

"I'm giving you the choice, my dear. I won't force myself into your life."

Jasmine's attention drifted to the twins who were eating with gusto and getting syrup and God-knows-what-else all over the king, and he didn't even bat an eyelash. He seemed to be enjoying himself as much as the children.

"If you desire grandchildren, they are yours," she said softly. "My own grandparents passed when I was young, and I always wished I had more time with them. The twins have lost much in their life, and I think they deserve all the family and friends who will love them as much as I do."

"I am glad for it," Marq replied.

She watched the king as he returned her regard. In that moment, she felt like she'd found a kindred spirit. He'd suffered pain, and, yet, he'd found joy in life. She hoped she could do the same. Jasmine turned back to her food and continued eating, savoring every delicious bite. Time passed, and the king chatted with the wee ones until they finished their food and the twins began to get antsy.

Jasmine eyed the food on her plate, sad to leave it, but if she didn't let the twins burn off some of their wiggles, it would become a warzone. Sam placed his hand over hers and her heart jumped as she began to push her chair back, and then he stood.

"I promised to take them to the training grounds. Finish your meal, and then follow us at your leisure." He looked at the twins. "Let's go!"

Ethan hugged the king, and Jade pressed a sticky kiss to his white-whiskered cheek, and then they both bounded from the room before Jasmine could even protest. She gaped at the door.

"He moves all too quickly," she muttered.

"He's been that way since he was a babe."

She startled and glanced at the king in surprise. How had she forgotten he was still there? "I don't doubt it. I aspire to have his stamina. I find myself worn out by the end of day." Her stomach soured, and she stared blurrily at the food before her. Of course, he knew. Everyone could see she was pregnant, but she didn't doubt that the king knew the real details of her shame, especially since she was so far along.

"Don't hang your head, daughter. Creating life is a wonderous miracle and a show of immense sacrifice."

She slowly looked up at the king. "You are aware of the circumstances of this child?"

He met her gaze and nodded. "I am."

Shame caused her belly to roll. "And what do you say?"

"I'm excited to meet my next grandchild, and I thank you for bringing such a gift into my life."

She couldn't contain it. Ugly sobs exploded from her chest, and she covered her mouth to muffle the terrible sounds escaping her. Jasmine pushed to her feet, determined to find the door, when giant arms encircled her, pressing her face into a wide, muscular chest.

"Let it out, my dear. It's okay," the king soothed. "Let it all out."

It should've felt odd to have a man she didn't know holding her—let alone her sovereign—but it didn't. She experienced a sense of acceptance and belonging she hadn't felt in ages. She sobbed and sobbed, but Marq never released her, just crooned softly, rocking her back and forth.

"How could they do this?" she cried. How could the men who'd protected her, do this?

"I don't understand it. It wasn't right, no matter their reason. And it wasn't your fault."

"I hate not remembering. Mira says it's a blessing, but the blankness terrifies me. What else did they do when they drugged me? I'm sure my imagination is worse than anything they could've done."

The king didn't answer but held her as she lost the shame, tears, and pain that had gathered in her heart for months.

Her tears slowed, her face hot and swollen. She pulled back and winced at the mess that was the king's shirt. It was stained with orange juice, syrup, and now, her tears. "I'm sorry about your shirt." She hiccupped. "I'll replace it."

"The shirt means nothing." The king tipped her chin up and scanned her face. "Did you get it out?"

Jasmine heaved out a breath and nodded. "For now, at least." Embarrassment started to creep up on her, but she batted it away. She and the king were kindred spirits. "If *you* ever need a shoulder to cry on…"

He hugged her and then moved back to his chair and leftover breakfast. "You will be the first person I seek out." He smiled at her. "Just be prepared, my crying is ugly—nothing like yours."

She snorted. "That is a damn lie, my lord."

"Marq, if you please."

Jasmine resumed her seat. "Marq."

His smile grew. "Now, tell me about my grandchildren, please."

TWENTY-NINE

JASMINE

IT WAS TOO EASY, SLIPPING into her new life with Sam. Only ten days had passed, and the children were completely enamored with him.

The man was all too charming, and she couldn't help but love his father. The king was nothing like she'd expected and was everything she'd been missing from her life. Plus, the twins absolutely adored him. And for the past week, he'd visited the children every day, and Jasmine couldn't help but love someone who loved her twins.

She wound around the small tavern just outside the castle gate and entered into the palace courtyard, strolling toward the training yard, her homespun dress rustling with each step and her cane whistling as she twirled it through her fingers. Soldiers circled the fenced-in training area, shouting at the men who were fighting in the middle. She watched in interest as the smaller man twisted and rolled, out-maneuvering the large one with sinuous movements. Familiar sounds teased the air: the clashing of swords and canes, curses, and the ever-present commands of battle instructors advising their men to disengage, straighten the arms, and engage in cleaner footwork.

Jasmine's fingers curled around the top of the fence, and she rested her chin against the smooth wood to observe. Stars above, she missed bouts with her father. He'd never turned down a chance to spar and play with her. Her hand rubbed the exposed skin above her heart like she could get rid of the grief that struck her at the oddest moments.

The dark-haired soldier to her right straightened as he noticed her and cleared his throat. She ignored him—and hid a smile as the small man slipped beneath the larger man's guard and swept his opponent's feet out from underneath him. The smaller soldier pounced on the prone form of the other and wrenched his opponent's arm behind his back, holding him pinned to the ground.

Jasmine smiled, set her cane down, and began a slow clap. The small man's head snapped up, and he grinned back at her, his crooked, white teeth bright against his amber skin.

Kylir.

She'd been wandering around the palace nearly a month prior, completely lost, when she'd spotted him. Normally, she would've kept moving on, but the way he moved while training had caused her to halt in her tracks. It was like watching water flow over stones. The fighting style was so foreign and unique, and, yet, so familiar. She used to sit on the floor of her bedroom and, through the crack of her door late at night, with only a small candle for light, she'd watch her father practice. Every move was so precise, so smooth. It seemed magical.

That day, she'd found herself entering the small training room and settling into a place next to Kylir. If he'd noticed her, he hadn't shown it. She'd stretched and then begun to follow his steps. Her body had burned and stretched, and sweat had drenched her immediately. Her breath had been billowing from her lungs when he finished. Kylir had turned to her and smiled, his chocolate eyes so very warm. He'd said two words that day, and they'd changed everything: "Hello, sister."

From then on, she'd snuck away every day to stretch and train in companionable silence with Kylir. After they finished, sometimes they'd talk. She'd learned that he was Zachael's ward, and that he had a Nagalian ancestor somewhere in his bloodline. He was kind, quiet, and seemed to have more wisdom than most who were triple his age. She was so grateful she'd met him. It was luck that he was still training at the palace. Soon he'd be summoned to the war front. Her heart sank at the thought, but she shoved it down and focused back on the bout.

Jasmine whooped when the man beneath Kylir slapped his hand against the ground. Her spry friend sprung from the soldier's back and held his hand out. The larger man grinned and slapped his massive paw against Kylir's.

"I almost had you," the soldier said, his tone teasing and breathless.

Kylir nodded. "If you continue with those exercises, I have no doubt that you will next time." He patted the soldier on the shoulder and called, "Next."

Jasmine blinked but kept silent as another tall man entered the ring, his blond curls shining in the light like spun gold.

Sam.

Jasmine pressed a little closer to the fence as he pulled his sweaty, linen shirt over his head and tossed it over the fence, into the dirt. He took off his boots and stripped off his socks, so he was wearing nothing but his tan leather pants. Despite her husband's reputation of wickedness, she'd never seen any part of him bare. For a moment, she averted her eyes and blankly stared at a round pebble near her left toe.

No wonder women flocked to him.

His face wasn't the only thing that was attractive.

She couldn't unsee what he'd flashed to the world. Jasmine swallowed hard and shook her head at herself.

"Get it together," she whispered, startling the soldier to her right. She'd seen half-dressed men before. Sam was nothing new.

Lies. There wasn't *anyone* like her husband.

Steeling herself, she lifted her chin and pasted a bored expression on her face. Sam's back still faced her as he accepted a cane from a nearby soldier on his left. Kylir held his staff out, and both men tapped their canes against each other's.

Her eyes widened as Kylir attacked immediately in a sustained sequence of combination blows. She winced as their canes met in a series of harsh cracks. Her hands flexed on the fence as she imagined what the impact must have felt like. She could almost feel the vibrations moving through her arms.

Sam retreated, the muscles in his back straining as he met another of Kylir's blows. His legs flexed as he leaned into the smaller man and pressed forward, his feet digging into the soil of the training ring. He disengaged and spun, darting under Kylir's staff as it swung just above his head. Kylir adjusted his attack and struck again in flawless, easy movements.

To her surprise, Sam was just as precise as his opponent. However, his style of fighting was unlike anything she'd ever seen. He never allowed the match to settle into a familiar rhythm. He attacked unexpectedly and retreated before Kylir could strike. There was something catlike about his movements, a vicious grace that raised every hair on Jasmine's body.

Fascinated, she lifted a foot onto the bottom rung of the fence and stood to get a better look at the match.

The night Sam had found her near the docks came to her mind. She hadn't seen him attack those men. Hell, she hadn't even heard him attack. But, in a matter of seconds, those men had been taken out. The prince hid much from the world.

Or, is it, you don't really want to know him?

She ignored that thought and tried to memorize one of his more complex movements.

"My dear, it makes me very uncomfortable to have you leaning into the training ring," Sam grunted as he blocked another one of Kylir's strikes.

Jasmine narrowed her eyes on his back, and, for some reason, her heartbeats seemed to collide as his deep voice curled around her in a delicious way. What in the world was wrong with her? She lifted a hand to her forehead. She wasn't sick. Her lips pursed as she glared at his back. And how did he know she was leaning into the ring?

"It would soothe my frayed nerves if you would step back."

She didn't move.

"I've warned you. If you don't heed my warnings, you may need to call for the smelling salts."

The soldiers around her chuckled, and Jasmine smirked. "Certainly, not for me?"

"Of course not," Sam huffed. "I have a delicate constitution."

She snorted as the men guffawed, supremely amused with his antics.

Sam dropped low and attacked beneath Kylir's staff, tapping her friend on the ribs.

"Stop," Kylir said, his voice soft and melodic as usual, his accent lilting.

The two men disengaged.

Chocolate eyes moved from Sam and met her own. "Would you like to try next?"

Jasmine grinned and nodded, but she froze in place as Sam whirled and glared at her. It felt like he was trying to set her on fire.

"Train?" he asked, his voice deceptively soft.

Forcing herself to move, she loosened the ties at the front of her dress and tugged the garment over her head, exposing the pants and loose linen shirt she wore beneath. Some of the men clapped and whistled, but one glare caused the whoops to turn into coughs.

She rolled her eyes. *Men.*

Jas popped her neck and smiled brightly at Sam. "Good evening, my lord," she said cordially. "I train every day with Kylir. Now, if you'd be so kind as to exit the sparring ring..." she trailed off as she noticed where Sam's attention was pinned—on her shirt.

Well, technically it was his shirt, but she'd stolen it and claimed it as hers. It hid her bump well, and it kept her cool.

She cleared her throat, pulling his attention to her face. "If you'd please move."

Sam eyed her and leaned on his staff, the picture of laziness. "I had reservations about Kylir training you, so I figured I would test out his skills to judge his abilities."

"Are you serious?" The words popped out of her mouth, and indignation burned inside her chest for her friend. "Kylir is one of the best weapon-trainers I've ever had the pleasure of sparring with. And how did you know I was training with him?"

"You've never asked *me* to spar with you," Sam said with a chuckle, not answering her question.

She ignored his comment and gave Kylir a lopsided smile. "I'm sorry."

Her friend smiled back at her, and a playful gleam entered his gaze as he looked between Sam and herself. "Thank you for your kind words, but I have to tell you, your husband is a rake, and I cannot condone your association with him. He'll ruin every method you have ever learned."

"I hope so," Sam snorted. "Some ruffian from the street won't hold back for her, as she's well aware." He stared her down as if challenging her to remember the night by the docks that could have ended very differently than it had.

Jasmine pressed her lips together, and leaned against the post behind her, raising her brows. "Are you going to leave so I can have my turn? Or will I have to throw you out?"

Sam arched a haughtier brow at her and faced Kylir. "We weren't finished."

Kylir settled into place just as Sam uttered, "Go."

Her husband attacked, and another duel commenced so lightning fast the two men blazed and burned. A large hand helped her through the fence, and she glanced up, meeting identical eyes to her husband's.

She jabbed a finger at Sam and rolled her eyes, conveying to the king how much his son annoyed her. Marq smiled, his white mustache hitching up at one corner.

"Boys," he muttered.

It was just one word, but Jasmine felt like it summed up everything. She turned her attention back to the ring as Sam twisted out of Kylir's hold and deliberately shoved a shoulder against the other man to knock him off balance. After making a strike, Sam dropped to the ground in a roll, then sprang to his feet, and jabbed her friend a second time.

Her hands curled into fists. He'd cheated. "This isn't a tavern brawl!"

Jasmine yanked her incensed gaze from her poor sport of a husband and paused as Kylir beamed, his smile so big it seemed to take up his entire face. What the devil? What was he so bloody happy about?

Turning to face her, Sam lowered his staff. "Isn't trying to win the objective of a bout?" Sam said calmly.

"The goal is to train. There are some rules," she said.

"And who taught you that?"

"It's a well-known fact."

"Answer me this: have you ever seen a spontaneous fencing match break out in the slum, or a tavern, or on the battlefield?" Sam asked with blistering sarcasm. "The rules are just a courtesy for those we train with." He pointed his finger toward the castle wall. "You won't be fighting gentlemen outside this training yard. They won't wait for you to catch your breath, and they won't play by the rules. They're ruthless, and the best defense anyone has is to fight with everything they have."

Embarrassment colored her cheeks at his public chastising. Then anger rose swiftly behind it.

Sam cleared away the blond locks of hair that hung in front of his eyes with a quick shake of his head, the blond layers seeming to come alive before settling into place. He skewered her with a hard stare.

"You have no idea what to do when it comes to the scum that would harm you. You may have pretty little cane twirls, but they mean nothing when your life is on the line. Your ladies' parlor exercises are picturesque, but they won't help you fight for your life. One day, you might be doing just that, armed only with the skills and values you hold dear. If you cannot let go of your preconceived notions, you'll end up on the street with your throat slit."

Jasmine shivered at his gruesome words. The man didn't pull any punches.

Sam shot Kylir a dirty, angry look. "And you! You've been training her? In her condition?"

A deep-seated rage flamed in her belly. She was pregnant, not stupid, and no one—*no one*—attacked her friends.

Marq placed a hand on her arm, and she glanced up at him, not realizing she'd started to climb the fence.

"How dare he!" she whispered harshly to the king. "I am not an invalid."

The king smiled softly. "My son is worried about you. And he's not handling it well."

Jasmine patted his hand and pulled away. "I'm not going to let him carry on. I'm going to prove him wrong."

Worry lines creased Marq's forehead. "Be careful."

"I will."

She clambered over the fence and dropped into a crouch on the other side, dust puffing up into the air. Slowly, she straightened and stormed toward her husband who was threatening Kylir with passive-aggressive comments.

"Why have you been training her?" Sam barked.

Kylir blinked slowly but didn't react to the prince's hostile tone. "My lord, she has been trained well. I didn't realize that I needed your approval to train a willing soldier, or I would have come to you."

"She's not a soldier," Sam said, his tone cutting.

"Could have fooled me," Kylir said mildly. "She has advanced training that has nothing to do with my skill. She's been sparring lightly, which is good for a woman in her condition, from what I'm told. I visited Jacob."

Jasmine winced and scanned the ring, noting all the soldiers leaning closer to watch the maudlin scene unfolding. Stars above, this would be all over the court by morning. So much for keeping her pregnancy a secret. Her stomach rolled. The rumors were going to be worse than the actual truth.

The two men stared each other down, apparently having a silent conversation.

"I don't appreciate both of you speaking like I don't exist," Jasmine hissed.

Sam pivoted to watch her with blue eyes practically spitting flames.

"Did you forget our prior conversation?"

His lips thinned but he didn't answer.

"I informed you that my father was a retired soldier. He taught me how to wield the staff, cane, and bow. I'm not the most skilled, but my skills are not something to be tossed aside."

Sam's blue eyes narrowed. "I don't like it." His gaze dropped to her belly and then back to her face. "You need to be careful."

She huffed. "Believe me when I say I am. If you'd spoken to the healers, you would know they encourage physical exercise and stretching—which is what I have been doing." A nasty smile touched her mouth. "But I'm more than ready and able to show you what I've been doing with Kylir for the last month."

Enjoy that innuendo.

Her husband stilled. He slid his attention to Kylir and then back to Jasmine.

"Just what has he been teaching you?" he asked, his voice soft and savage.

One look at him told her he wouldn't hear anything she had to say. One could not reason with an unreasonable person, and until he calmed down, she wouldn't be speaking with him. Disappointment tugged at her, and she slowly roved her eyes up and down his form, making sure he saw that she found him lacking.

She spun on her heel and climbed over the fence, collecting her discarded dress and her cane. Jasmine pressed a kiss on Marq's cheek and walked away. She kept her chin up and shoulders back, trying to project a regal demeanor. She hated walking away from a fight, but, sometimes, walking away was the best thing. And, right now, she wanted to rip Sam's head from his shoulders and she was pretty sure that was against the law.

Insufferable lout.

"Jasmine!" Sam called, his tone sharp with a touch of darkness.

A shiver skated down her spine, but she ignored him and didn't look back.

Never had she been so mortified in her whole life! If he wanted to speak with her, he damn well better be on his knees, apologizing and bringing a honey cake with him.

Her stomach growled.

Honey cake first, then she'd deal with her irritating husband.

THİRTY

DOR

⟶◦⟨⟩◦⟵

EVERY INSTINCT DOR HAD HONED over the course of her entire life begged her to turn around and leave the dark, haunting place that seemed like it would gobble her up. What disturbed her the most wasn't the complete darkness lurking just past the dimly lit hallway. It was the way the wide, heavy stone door swung silently open as if it was holding its breath for what horrors were to come.

Ada lifted the lantern higher, the light stretching just a bit farther into what looked like a small room and highlighting the paleness of her friend's face. Dor wasn't the only one who was terrified. Her eyes moved to the warrior who once again watched her like she was his prey. There was something in his gaze she didn't like, no matter what her mum said. She needed to be careful of him. Dor knew when she'd discovered a predator.

She pulled her gaze from Darius and stared at the white stone floor. Then, she started abruptly, her attention on the floor by the entrance. Her eyes narrowed. She'd never seen a creation that was so smooth, so flawless, *perfect*. This time, she couldn't hide the shiver that raced down her spine. This wasn't the Pit any longer. They were entering the domain of the most sinister enemy she'd ever come across. The warlord. Only he'd have something so atrocious and unnatural gracing the rooms of his abode.

"Are you quite done gawking?" Darius said, sarcasm coloring his tone.

Dor pursed her lips to keep a nasty comment from bursting free and turned her attention to her mum, who shivered on the floor. "By all means, let's go."

The warrior glared at her and then addressed Ada by jerking his chin toward the wall. "Leave the lantern on the hook."

Ada glanced at Dor and reluctantly followed his command.

Darius bent at the knees, gently pulled Dor's mother into his arms, and walked past the threshold. Dor didn't move as she watched him step onto the alien, white-stone floor, his boots making not one mark on the ground. Frowning, she peeked at her dirty blood-spattered feet. They'd leave a mark for sure.

Dor, stop thinking about things that don't matter.

"Enter at your leisure," Darius snapped at her.

She clenched her jaw and bared her teeth at his back, hating how scared she was to follow him. Digging deep, she swallowed down her fear and followed the man into the darkened room. Her toes curled as they met the cold stone floor beneath her feet. It was so smooth, it almost felt wet. *Focus, Dor.*

Ada stepped closer and slipped her hand into Dor's. "We have each other."

Dor squeezed her friend's fingers, grateful to have her company. They'd known each other since they were young and had always had each other's backs, no matter what. It was fitting they were entering this together. Dor squinted as they moved farther into the dark.

Ada gasped, and Dor followed her line of sight, her own gasp falling from her lips as the stone behind them slammed shut. She lunged for the wall, releasing Ada's hand and scrabbling in the dark. The sound seemed to echo around her as she blinked repeatedly.

"Ada?"

"I'm here," her friend's soft voice trembled from Dor's left.

Swinging her arms toward the sound, she moved in Ada's direction. "Don't move," she barked. "I'm coming to you." Her left hand smacked into flesh, and she jerked back, fear thundering through her veins. That wasn't Ada.

She blindly scrambled away from the flesh she'd touched, her feet slipping on the floor, so disoriented. She yelped when a small hand grabbed her dress.

"Dor?"

Just Ada.

She spun toward Ada's voice and hugged her friend close, as her heart did its best to beat out of her chest. Her friend's slight frame trembled against her own as they clung to each other. Despite the utter darkness, Dor kept her head up, eyes open, and tried to see through the darkness. There were others with them, but how many? Were they in another torture chamber? Did the flesh she'd touched belong to someone alive or dead? And where in the hell was the warrior?

"Darius, so help me, you better light the lantern right this instant or I will reign Hell upon you." She just managed to keep the tremble from her voice in the silence. "Answer me."

Silence.

"Did he leave us?" Ada whispered, her voice seeming hollow in the room.

"He couldn't have," Dor reassured her. He couldn't have left without them. Or could he? What did he do with her mum?

The complete darkness surrounding them seemed to surge forward and slither around them. Her breaths became shallow, and her panic rose. They were trapped. Who knew how large the space was? Her breaths turned to pants as the suppressive panic began to scream at her. She was trapped. The nothingness around them was suffocating.

"Are you all right?"

Dor shook her head, then stopped, knowing the gesture was wasted in the dark. Her fingers dug into Ada's arms as she pulled away slightly and bowed her head. She couldn't let her panic get the best of her. She needed to use the breathing techniques her mum had taught her. She pulled in a slow deep breath and held it while counting to five, then repeated it again and again until she was breathing normally, and her pulse had slowed from a thundering of a hundred horses to a short, fast staccato. Not great, but better than passing out.

The deafening silence around them crept in once again, and she began to focus on what was most important. They needed to figure out where they were and where her mum was.

"Mum?" she called, hoping she would answer her.

Nothing, not even a whisper of sound. Surely if Darius was still in the room, she'd hear her mum breathing? If it hadn't been for Ada holding her, Dor would've thought she was the only one in the entire room.

Either the warrior was gone, or he was playing with them. Neither was a great option, but the latter made anger burn in her veins like fire.

"Mum, please answer me."

Nothing.

Dor inhaled deeply before speaking. "Darius, speak up now or face my wrath when I find you," she said a little bit louder, trying to hide her fear. *Still* nothing. "We need to move."

"Move? We can't see," Ada said, her voice trembling slightly.

"We can't stand here forever. Close your eyes and hold your hand out in front of you. It might not be so off-putting."

Dor couldn't tell if her friend would follow her advice, but Ada squeezed her hand once and Dor straightened and lifted her chin. From the echoing of their voices, the room was large. She wouldn't be hitting her head on the ceiling any time soon. She held her left hand out and shuffled forward, through the dark. Each step was terrifying, but at least they were moving. She blew out a breath when her hand touched stone. Her fingers explored its texture, and she determined it was a wall.

"Ada, let's move to our—" She paused, cutting off her words as a foot scuffed against stone. The hairs on her arms rose.

They weren't alone.

That was even worse to imagine. What sort of creature could stay that still for so long?

Dor slowly pivoted to face in the direction of a foot against stone and closed her left hand around her dagger at her waist. She didn't want to scare Ada, but she needed to know what was going on. "Ada?"

"I heard it," Ada said softly. "We're not alone, are we?"

"No."

Dor's softly exhaled word seemed to stir the tension in the room, and beads of sweat broke out along the back of her neck, despite the cold. Her feet slid apart as she braced herself for whatever nightmare stalked them. Carefully, she pulled her dagger from its sheath, with a soft hiss of leather against metal, and held it ready at her side. She strained to hear any new sounds, and her eyes frantically searched the dark, but she spotted nothing. In the back of her mind, she knew what it was.

A man-eater. A leren.

And, in all likelihood, she and Ada would end up dead.

"We don't taste that good," Dor crooned. "I promise, we'll make for a very nasty meal."

"Devil, take it," Ada cursed. "You think we crossed into a leren's territory?"

Dor listened harder for any clue as to where the large jungle cat lurked. "I don't think we crossed into anything. I think we were led here to die." Her tone was still lilting.

"An execution?"

Dor nodded and then spoke, knowing Ada couldn't see her. "Yes." She turned so the stone wall was to her back, tugging Ada along. This was so the leren couldn't sneak up on them. "I'm not one for games," she cooed. "I'd rather you just attack than lie in wait for us."

Ada snorted, and a nervous giggle escaped her. "Leave it up to you to bait the leren into killing us in a sing-song voice."

"If death comes for me, I'd rather face it head-on than have it catch me unaware and stab me in the back."

"Words spoken like a true warrior," a female voice said, her tone velvety soft and yet somehow as strong as steel.

Dor jerked. Not a leren. Something much more devious. With the jungle cat, she knew what it wanted. But a Scythian had motives she couldn't pretend to understand or guess.

"Show yourself," she barked, her voice echoing in the space around them.

Stone striking stone pierced the silence, and a small spot of light erupted directly across from them, illuminating the woman's face. Firelight played over the woman's formidable features that were much like her voice: feminine but sharp. Caramel-colored eyes seemed to glow like twin flames as she stared impassively at Dor. A small smile touched her full mouth and drew attention to her high cheekbones and straight nose. Feathers and beads adorned her coal-black hair and plinked together in a soft symphony as the woman tilted her head back, obviously studying Dor as well.

With care, the woman took the small flame in her hand and lit a lantern hanging from the wall behind her. Dor swallowed as she was able to see the woman fully. Her thick, black braid hung over her shoulder, and silky furs draped over her back in a becoming manner. Tight leather pants ran down long legs and into sturdy boots. But what alarmed her the most was the vast array of weapons the woman had strapped to her lithe body. Everything screamed danger with this woman. The woman smirked, and her gaze bored into Dor's like she could see the deepest parts of her soul. One thing was certain, the woman was not to be trifled with.

Most assumedly, this woman was every Scythian's dream of perfection, of purity. And while the woman was beautiful and terrifying to behold, there was something repugnant about her because of what she stood for. A deep-seated fear made Dor want to cower away from the woman and the warriors that melted from the shadows like wraiths and stood in a circle around the room. Perfection like the woman's came at a cost. Only those closest to the warlord could afford such perfection. Even the tilt of the woman's chin spoke of a regal bearing.

This woman wasn't just Scythian – she was something *more*. Dor wanted to cower against the wall, to seek a way of escape, but fear and stubbornness kept her feet rooted to the smooth floor beneath her toes. In that moment, Dor made a choice. She wouldn't be a coward. Chances were she'd end up dead by the end of the encounter, but she'd go out with integrity and honor.

Swallowing, she forced her tongue to work. "Where is my mother?" she asked in a careful tone.

The woman tilted her head to the side and scrutinized Dor. The woman's eyes scanned Dor from head to toe, and she pursed her lips in a way that betokened disapproval or deep thought.

Dor lifted her chin and threw back her shoulders, determined to hold the woman's gaze. She had nothing to be ashamed of. If anyone should be ashamed, it should be the creatures standing proudly before her. The perfection-seeking monsters from above the Pit were the ones that had caused the pain and the suffering she'd experienced her entire life. They were the blight on the world, not her or the laborers in the Pit.

She dared to smile at the woman and almost dropped into a mock bow. She wouldn't let a perfect intimidate her, not in this moment. Dor may be covered in dirt and grime, her hair matted, and her clothes old and worn, but she still had value, despite what she looked like. She would not feel shame for her poverty. In fact, the woman should feel shame just looking upon *her*. To see the wreckage their people had caused.

The woman spoke, breaking through her thoughts. "Your mother's fine."

A snort escaped her. She didn't believe her one bit. "I want to see her."

The woman smiled slightly and nodded.

Searing light exploded around the room, causing Ada to cry out and drop Dor's hand, and Dor squeezed her eyes shut and covered her face with her hands as colors flashed across her vision. Tears leaked from the corners of her eyes as she squinted and tried to get her bearings. Now was not the time to be blind.

"Not nice," she said, blinking repeatedly in an attempt to see the room. She vaguely detected that the woman had moved closer, and Dor lifted her blade higher despite her seared eyes. She held the blade defensively as she tried to get her damned eyes to stop watering.

"There's no need for that."

Dor laughed. "So says the woman who debilitated her prisoners."

"You're not prisoners."

She chose to stay quiet as she was able to finally get a good glimpse of the room. Terror was too small of a word to describe what sank down to her very bones. Immense warriors circled the oval-shaped room, silent sentinels whose attention was completely focused on them.

The woman had moved to the left and up a set of stairs that led to a dais. Dor's pulse kicked up as she noticed her mum's prone form laying near the woman's feet. Her red hair was strewn across her face and draped down the white stairs like dripping blood. Her face was completely blank of all expression, eyes closed as if she was asleep.

Dor rushed forward and sprinted up the stairs to her mum, dropping to her knees. She was highly aware of the warriors moving closer to her, but she ignored them as she checked her mum's pulse. It thrummed beneath her fingers as she clasped her hand around her mother's wrist.

Carefully, she laid her mum's arm across her swollen belly, and glared up at the woman only five paces away, barely managing to keep her tone civil. "What have you done to my mother?"

The woman stepped closer and Dor lifted her blade, her lip curling as Ada moved to her side. "Not one step closer, or you die," she threatened. She'd never been more serious about anything in her whole life. The woman shifted, cocking a hip, and Dor held her blade a little higher. *Try me, wench.*

The woman studied her for what seemed like hours. Dor's arm trembled as she fought to keep her blade held aloft. If they kept the staring contest going, Dor was going to lose in a spectacular fashion.

"Your mother is close to birthing the babe. I gave her a moment's reprieve from the pain, to rest before she begins her battle."

Everyone lied. Surely, this woman wasn't an exception.

"And you expect me to believe that?"

"You will have to trust me."

"I don't trust anyone." Trust meant betrayal. Betrayal meant death.

A throaty laugh spilled from the woman's red lips, the corners of her caramel eyes crinkling in mirth. "I see your sire didn't hesitate to train you well."

Dor stiffened at the mention of her father and stayed silent.

The woman held her hands up and slowly dropped to her haunches. Her liquid gaze held Dor's until she glanced at her mum's swollen belly. "Your mum trusted me and my men, and you would not be here unless she wished it. She's guarded you zealously all your life. So, it seems you have no choice in the matter."

Bitterness and fear left a bad taste at the back of Dor's mouth. The woman wasn't wrong, but hearing the words out loud made it that much more frightening. She was trapped, but all wasn't lost. The woman obviously held power. The question was what she wanted with Dor.

A clammy hand touched her arm, causing her to jerk and glance down. Her mum wetted her lips and gazed up at her, strain pulling the skin covering her cheekbones taut. "Love," she said, her tone soothing. "Listen to Maeve."

Maeve. So that was the woman's name. Dor squinted as she tried to remember why that name was so familiar. Where had she heard it before? It was uncommon. Her brow screwed up as she strained to place it. Nothing.

Dor met Maeve's direct stare and bluntly asked, "Who are you?" She swore every pair of eyes in the room seemed to focus on her at the moment.

The woman stood fluidly to her full height and smiled. "Now, that is an interesting question. Do you want an interesting answer?"

"I want the truth."

A feline smile graced Maeve's face, making her seem infinitely devious and cunning. "I am the warlord's right hand."

The air from the room was sucked away, leaving Dor gasping for breath in the silence. The warlord's sister. Death would surely come for all of them. What was her mum thinking, dealing with such a deadly predator?

"Leren got your tongue?" Maeve asked, her eyes sparkling. The woman was enjoying her discomfort. Dor forced herself to focus and glared at Maeve.

"What do you want?" Dor's tone was far from respectful, but she couldn't find it in herself to care. The monster before her was a mass murderer. The warlord's handmaiden.

"Everything."

"Sorry, not on the menu."

Maeve cocked her head and arched a brow. "We'll settle on one thing then."

She had a distinct feeling it would destroy her. "What is that?"

"You are the future."

"I don't follow," Dor said slowly.

"You, my dear one, are going to start a rebellion."

Dor's blood turned cold.

Maeve's lips hitched up in a sharp smile. "You will be the end of everything."

Dor didn't know about that. But one thing she knew for sure:

The warlord's handmaiden would be the end of her.

THIRTY-ONE

SAM

HE WAS AN IDIOT.

And his spies were turning against him.

Sam trudged up the hidden spiral staircase that led to the docks. Water dripped from his clothes as he wove his way through the long-forgotten passages deep in the bowels of the castle. Next time he visited Mer, he needed to leave a stash of clothing in the cave. He was sick and tired of moving around in cold, wet clothes.

He frowned as he thought of his meeting with Mer. She'd looked more haggard than usual. It seemed that war was being waged on all fronts. Tensions were at an all-time high below the surface of the sea. Mer had revealed that one of her generals had broken rank and challenged the king publicly, which had led to the Sirenidae's very humiliating execution.

Thank the stars Mer hadn't been exposed, but Sam worried it was only a matter of time until all was revealed. Mer's men had moved into place, shadowing the Aermian fleet as they created a blockade around Sanee's port. The Scythians had launched their armada and, all too soon, come to their capitol's door.

Sam turned to his left and sprinted up the next three flights of stairs. His heart pounded, and his breath came in short pants as he crested the stairs leading to his office and training room. He spied several of his girls, including Gem, peering into the training room. He crept closer and looked over Jacie's broad shoulder.

His lips thinned as he got an eyeful of what had captured their attention.

His wife.

Jasmine stood alone in the middle of the room, practicing hand-to-hand combat. Her eyes were closed, and her expression was one of complete peace as she flowed from one exercise to another.

"What are you all doing?" he asked softly.

Gem shrugged a shoulder but didn't glance in his direction. "Watching the show."

"It's like she's made from water. I wish I could move like that," Jacie whispered.

"You can," Sam said. "If only you practiced more."

The younger girl tipped her head back and smiled impishly, her crooked teeth somehow endearing and not appalling. "Perhaps."

He rolled his eyes at her sass.

Ruth, the redhead to his left, grinned at him. "You sure do take dangerous ones to bed." She flicked a finger toward Jasmine. "Your wifey could kill you in your sleep."

"As could any of you." He shook his head dramatically. "What have I done?"

A small smile flickered across Gem's mouth, and mirth entered her eyes. "Apparently, everything."

Sam scowled, his eyes narrowing on Gem. She definitely knew something. Jasmine had practically fled from him every time she was in his company for the last two days. The only time he'd actually spent time in her presence was when they put the twins to bed and when Jasmine shared his bed to sleep.

Thank the stars for small miracles.

She hadn't left his bed, and, every morning, he'd find her in his arms, her belly pressing against his stomach, or she'd wrap herself around him with her belly poking his back. It delighted him to have the wee one kick him until she woke. Still, each time, he'd pretend to be asleep when she woke, because, as soon as she realized what had happened, she'd wiggle to the other side of the pillow wall she built every night and pretend it never happened.

"Don't you girls have something better to do?" Sam whispered with fake exasperation.

"Better than spying? I think not," Jacie piped in. "We're just doing what you taught us to do."

"I didn't mean spying on my wife." He shooed them away from the door. "Unless you have something you need to discuss with me, get out of here, you wenches."

His girls rolled their eyes at him and reluctantly followed his orders. He watched them disperse between the tunnel that went to different parts of town until he was sure they were gone. Sam swiveled back to the doorway and crept a little closer to admire the way his wife moved.

He held his breath as she bent to pick up the staff lying at the edge of the mat, the image of her climbing into the training pit flashing through his mind. He knew now what possessed him to act like a total ass, but, at the time, he was too angry to understand what had spurred him into action: he'd been surprised when he'd noticed her lurking next to the soldier. His urge to impress her had been strong, so he'd fought harder than was necessary. What he didn't expect was for her to be absolutely furious with him and accuse him of being unsportsmanlike. It had rankled him, but not as much as her defending Kylir had.

His jaw clenched.

That damn traitor. Kylir had been training with her for a month and had never said one word about it.

Then she'd tossed her dress aside, showing off her curved thighs and small waist despite the babe. Everything about her looked tousled. She looked like a well-loved woman, and he knew all the other soldiers were imagining it, too. Then there was the matter of the babe. He couldn't believe she was being so careless with *his* child. He may not have been the one to put the babe in her belly, but, once he'd felt the wee one dancing beneath his palm, the babe had *become* his.

And that was what had turned him into an idiot.

He'd let jealousy and overprotectiveness override his common sense and vast knowledge of how to handle a woman. As the aggressive and chastising words had flown from his mouth, he'd wanted nothing more than to snatch them from the air, shove them back into his mouth, and swallow them down.

He knew better.

Then she'd walked away.

Panic had flared in his chest.

He'd planned to go after her, but his father had pulled him aside and given him a stern talking to. Feeling like a little boy, he'd stayed silent until his father had finished. A little raw from his father's words, Sam had exploded. His father had listened to his side of things, acknowledged his concerns, and given him wise advice. But as much as Sam had tried to put it into practice, the words stuck in his throat each night Jasmine had crawled into bed and turned her back on him. It was like she'd cut him off.

And he *hated* it.

He'd always understood the female sex. Hell, he even got along with them better than he did with men—but Jasmine? She confused him. She was unlike any woman he'd ever met before.

But enough was enough. His father said not to go to bed angry, and Sam had let it happen for two days. Two days for things to fester and stew.

He stepped through the doorway, and Jasmine faltered, her rhythm slowing as she noticed him. Immediately, she appeared to dismiss him and focused on a stone on the wall across from her.

Oh no, you don't. They were going to fix this now.

She spun her staff in an elaborate twirl.

"Those are a waste of motion," he murmured. "But very pleasing to the eye."

His wife slammed the tip of the staff against the floor and glanced at him. "I'm not sure if you're insulting me or trying to pay me a compliment. But, if it was the latter, you're doing a poor job."

He edged closer.

Prickly. That was how he'd describe her.

It was if she had invisible spines surrounding her, keeping anyone from getting too close.

Time for a different tactic.

"When did your father start training you?"

She squinted, and her jaw set. For a second, he thought she wouldn't answer him.

"I was young. Maybe three years? I remember going to the square, and two older boys picked on me. They knocked me down into a puddle, and

I skinned my palms. My father found me crying in the dirt. He didn't say anything as he'd picked me up, but he told me to dry my tears. After that, he began training me. It was games at first, but then they got consistently harder." She glanced away from him.

"Sounds like a good father."

Jasmine barked out a laugh. "He wasn't much of a father. He was my commander. The man was cold and distant and hardly showed any amount of affection." Her expression softened. "But I loved him anyway. He gave me the tools to protect myself. I've never been at the mercy of a man because of that."

Her fingers turned white as they tightened around the wooden staff, her lips thinning. He didn't think she'd noticed as her left hand moved to her belly.

"At least not the ones that I knew to be monsters."

"I'm sorry for what you suffered," he offered, knowing the words weren't enough.

Her brows furrowed, and her gaze blanked as if she'd gone to some distant place.

"Suffering," she whispered, her voice hollow. "I didn't suffer, not like Sage. I wasn't beaten, tortured, starved, forced to kill, or accept another's touch." Her eerily placid gaze disappeared as she blinked, her stormy eyes clashing with his. "My suffering is nothing compared to some."

Sam balked. "It's not fair to compare what you've been through to that of others. It's okay to mourn what you've lost. It's not something to be brushed aside."

"And how do I even know what I've suffered?" she challenged. "Let's be honest. I don't know what happened." Her eyes became glassy, filled with unshed tears. "I've seen how others act when they've been into their cups too much. Drunks are freer with their actions, and, sometimes, they don't remember their actions in the morning. How do I even know that I didn't ask for it?"

"No!" Sam said vehemently, slicing his hand through the air. "You aren't accountable for a man's perverted choices. You must never blame yourself. I know you. You wouldn't have done that."

"Don't you remember how you found me? Maybe that's who I am."

"No, that's not you," he said gently as he approached her and grasped her upper arms with care. "During the time we've spent together, I've been able to discern one of your driving factors. Do you know what it is?"

Jasmine shook her head.

"You are one of the most caring and compassionate people I've ever had the pleasure of knowing. You put others' needs above your own, and you go out of your way to help those in need. That is not someone who seeks pleasure above all at the expense of someone else."

"You can say it." A tear dripped down her cheek. "I was raped."

The ugly word rattled around in his head. He lifted his left hand and brushed a sweaty strand of hair from her face, while figuring out how to phrase his next words. "Yes," he murmured. "And that was not your fault. No one—no man, woman, or child—deserves to be abused in such a demonic way. The fault lies with the disgusting men who took advantage of you when you deserved their protection."

Her bottom lip quivered, and she leaned closer, placing her forehead against his chest. "It's so confusing," she confessed. "I keep going over everything I remember, and they were good to me. My warriors," she paused. "The warriors cared for me and protected me. How could they do this? I just can't understand. I don't understand. I thought they were my friends." Her voice dropped to a whisper. "I loved them a little bit."

Jasmine pulled away from him and dropped her staff, spearing her fingers through her tangled hair.

Sam kept his expression placid, even though he hated the thought of her caring at all for her abductors. He understood what captivity could do to a mind, but watching the aftermath of such a trauma? Well, it was heartbreaking.

"How can I still feel this way?" She dropped her hands and rubbed at her arms. "I want to scrub the shame from my skin. I want the ugly, disgusted feeling to go away."

Sam held his empty hands out. "What can I do to help?"

Her bleak gaze met his. "There's nothing you can do to remove this stain from me." She bent to pick up her staff. "But you can help me train. It quiets my mind, and I feel more in control."

"Okay." Now, he felt even more like an idiot. He'd been so angry two days ago that she'd put herself and the babe at risk, and all she was doing was trying to find a way to feel safe. "If you'd like, I'll show you a way to protect yourself in close quarters." He pointed at the staff. "You won't need that."

Jasmine wordlessly set the staff along the wall and turned toward him.

He smiled. "This will be easy for you. Hell, you might enjoy it after the last few days. In a few minutes, I'll let you throw me to the floor."

Her formerly haunted gaze narrowed, and a spark of interest lit in her eyes. "You're twice my size. How could I do that?"

"I'll show you. But, first, we'll start with something simple. Did your father ever teach you about the most common ways women are attacked?"

Her lips pursed. "They're choked from the front."

"Yes. Usually against a wall." Slowly, he stepped closer to Jasmine and placed his hands carefully on her shoulders. He waited for her to tense or step back, but she just looked up at him, waiting for the next instruction. Sam guided her backward until her spine was pressed against the stone wall. When her breathing didn't accelerate, he slid his calloused hands to her neck.

Jasmine stiffened.

Instantly, he let go, his brows drawing together in concern.

"No," Jasmine assured him. "I'm okay. I've just never had anyone wrap their hands around my throat before."

"You have nothing to fear from me. Ever."

Her expression softened. "I know."

Sam could tell she meant it. He edged closer and placed his fingers around her delicate neck. He focused on the front of her neck where his thumbs rested. "In this situation, you only have a few seconds to react after he takes hold."

"Breathing is important," Jasmine huffed, amusement lifting her lips into a dark smile.

Sam barked out a laugh. This woman. Her hands snaked up to grip his elbows.

"If I yanked down on his arms, like this, could I get out?"

He shook his head. "Not if he was my size. You wouldn't be able to budge him. So, tuck your chin down to protect your neck and then put your palms together like you're praying. Then push your hands through the circle of my arms."

She followed his instructions.

"Good," he murmured. "Now, push higher, until it forces my elbows to bend. Can you feel how it loosens my hold?"

She grinned, clearly pleased with herself. "Yes."

"Now, grab my head."

She cocked her head. "Do what?"

"Go on. You heard me."

Tentatively, she placed her hands on his head.

"Take hold of my face, so you can push your thumbs into my eyes."

"That's brilliant," she hummed, adjusting her grip so the pads of her thumbs rested at the outer corners of his eyes. "Show the bastard no mercy."

Sam grinned at his bloodthirsty little wife, but he quickly sobered as the image of three men attacking her near the docks rose in his mind. "That's right. As he will show you none," he continued. "As you apply pressure to the eyes, you'll be able to push the head back easily. Then jerk it down until the nose meets your forehead, thus breaking the nose." He cupped a hand over his nose. "But please show me mercy."

Jasmine rolled her eyes. "I'd hate to mar such beauty."

"You think I'm beautiful?" He winked at her.

"Oh hush, you vain creature. You and everyone else knows you're devilishly handsome."

She pulled his head down so his mouth and nose rested on her forehead. The contact only lasted an instant, but something powerful rocked through him. Her feminine scent teased him, and all he wanted to do was hunt for the source of it like a bloodhound. But he tugged on his self-control and drew back slowly.

"You could follow that with a knee to the groin if your skirts aren't too heavy." His gaze dropped to her leather pants. "But, as it seems, your choices in attire are as conducive to fighting as they are inappropriate."

His wife snorted. "As if you've ever acted appropriately or made apologies for it."

Here was his chance.

"Speaking of apologies. I owe you one."

Jasmine's mirth melted away, and she cocked her head, studying him. "For what?"

"I acted like an utter arse at the sparring ring." He sighed. "When I saw you climb over that fence intending to fight, I lost my mind. I was worried for the babe and for you. I didn't handle it well, and I embarrassed you. I'm sorry for it."

Sam held his breath when her expression revealed none of her feelings.

"I ought to let you suffer," she muttered. "I was so mad at you."

"I know. My reaction was out of line, but can you understand how it looked to me? Then there was Kylir." His brows lowered as he remembered the silent conversation that seemed to flow between Jasmine and one of his best spies. He wanted to gouge the man's eyes out for just staring at his wife. "And I allowed my jealousy to get the best of me," Sam admitted.

Jasmine surprised him by laughing. "*You* were jealous?"

"Out of all of that, that's what you focus on?" he demanded.

"I just find it ironic that you were jealous of me. You literally have hordes of women who follow you around and pant at your heels, and yet I have just one male friend, and you lost your temper?"

He shifted uncomfortably. Wicked hell, he hated feeling guilty. It was a feeling he rarely dealt with. "I sound very ridiculous when you say—"

"Utterly ridiculous," his wife cut in. "I'm a peasant woman carrying the bastard child of monsters. Believe me when I say your fantastical ideas have no basis in reality. I don't chastise you for your liaisons."

He winced. If only he could tell her the truth. There weren't any romps or rendezvous, but how his meetings appeared to others served his purposes in protecting his spy ring. He bit the inside of his cheek. It hadn't bothered him terribly before, but now it affected not just himself, but his entire family.

"But I can let that go. Men are volatile creatures with too many feelings that they're not willing to deal with. And, as for the training, well, I'm not going to stop. I feel better than I have in a long time."

"I don't expect you to stop," he spoke up. "I visited Mira."

Her brows rose almost to her hairline. "You did?"

"I did, and if you want to keep training with Kylir, I won't stop you. All I ask is that you be mindful of your limits. I don't want to see you in pain." He held his left hand out toward her belly. "May I?"

She nodded slowly.

Sam placed his calloused hand on the top of her belly and marveled at the life growing there. "I don't want anything to happen to this wee one."

Jasmine dropped her hands from his face and proceeded to stare so hard at him, he was surprised she didn't bore holes through his head.

"Is there something on my face?" he asked.

"Your nose."

He cracked a smile and pulled back. "You and that mouth."

She winked at him and brushed her hands over her shirt. "My father always said it would get me into trouble, and you know what?"

"What?"

"He was right."

Sam sniggered.

She smiled and then shifted her stance, her gaze flickering to his crotch and then back to his eyes. "So, back to our lesson, you want me to use my leg to…"

"Well, not to me, per se, but if you feel threatened by any man, you do it. It's the most impactful target on a man. The pain shoots through all of our innards."

"Hmmm… My brother was apprenticing as a healer before he died. We had many interesting conversations, including what he referred to as nerves that run from the groin and into the belly."

Sam blinked at her. She wasn't shy, that was for sure.

Jasmine smirked at him. "Have I made you uncomfortable?"

Rising to her challenge, he stepped closer, laughter glinting in his eyes. "Never. There isn't much in the world that can make me blush. I've just never met anyone like you, my lady-wife."

She threw her head back and laughed. "I'm no lady. The twins will be the first ones to tell you that."

THİRTY-TWO

JASMINE

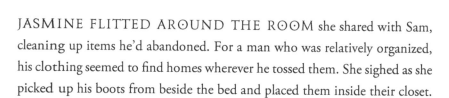

JASMINE FLITTED AROUND THE ROOM she shared with Sam, cleaning up items he'd abandoned. For a man who was relatively organized, his clothing seemed to find homes wherever he tossed them. She sighed as she picked up his boots from beside the bed and placed them inside their closet. Why he couldn't just walk the few extra paces to put away his boots, she would never understand.

Her silver, silk robe flared around her bare feet as she spun to survey the tidy room. There were a few things still lying on his side table, but she wasn't about to touch a man's weapons. Her father had been very particular about that when she was growing up. She rubbed at her eyes, weariness blanketing her. Blearily, she glanced at the doorway that led to the twins' room. Sam had disappeared to say goodnight to them, but he hadn't reappeared.

She crept toward the cracked door and listened. Nothing. Well, he wasn't telling them a story. Jasmine pressed against the wooden door and peeked into the darkened room. Moonlight streamed in from the window above the twins' beds, illuminating the room just enough for her to make out everything. Her breath caught as she tiptoed farther into the bedroom.

Sam sat in the chair between the twins' beds, each of his arms reaching out to hold Jade's and Ethan's hands. His head lolled to the side, and he released a deep snore. Jasmine's heart clenched at the precious picture they made. Her eyes watered. Somehow, they'd created a family. She wiped her cheeks and snuck around Jade's bed to place the soft blanket over her shoulder. Her niece snuggled deeper into the covers and sighed.

Jasmine glided around the bed and paused in front of Sam, admiring him. The moonlight transformed his golden locks into silver waves. His dark lashes swept downward and rested on his cheekbones. The man was stunning. She reached out and brushed a wayward curl from his forehead, tracing his dark-blond brow in the process.

Sam's eyes popped open, and awareness filled them immediately. Jasmine leaned over him, her fingers still on his skin. They watched each other in the silence, neither of them moving. She continued her exploration and skated her fingers down his face to cup his cheek.

In that moment, she made a decision. Jasmine bent down and pressed a kiss against his opposite cheek. Sam might have his flaws, ones she didn't care for, but, all in all, he was a good man.

One she loved.

She wasn't sure if she was *in love* with him, but she couldn't help but have love and affection for the man who was so good to the children.

Jas pulled back, her lips tingling as she met his deep, blue, fathomless eyes, almost silver in the moonlight. "Come to bed, love," she whispered and straightened.

She turned her head and looked over her shoulder to see if he was following her as she moved into their room. Nerves caused her belly to quiver as she edged around their bed. Sam closed the twins' door and quietly moved to his side of the mattress. He flicked back the covers and began constructing a pillow wall down the middle.

It took a great amount of effort for Jasmine to pull back her side of the covers. She watched Sam crawl into bed and yawn.

Be brave, Jas.

She fumbled as she untied the sash fastened below her breasts and shrugged off the robe, letting it slither to the ground. She hiked her nightgown up and clambered into the bed as awkwardly as a newborn foal.

Sam squinted and rolled to face her fully. "Something wrong?"

Jasmine blinked, realizing she was staring. Instead of answering, with trembling hands she grabbed the pillows that ran down the middle of the bed and tossed them onto the floor. Her breathing increased as Sam seemed to quit breathing entirely. Tension filled the space around them, and her doubts crept in.

What if he wanted the wall there? What if he didn't want her near him? What if—

Sam lifted the covers and extended his arm toward her, from beneath his pillow.

An invitation.

Relief swamped her, and she carefully scooted closer to snuggle into him. Her nose pressed against his chest, and her pulse pounded as his arms draped over her loosely. Yet, he still said nothing. Slowly, her tension melted away as his breathing deepened and the stiffness in his body disappeared. She wasn't sure how much time had drifted by, but she tipped her head back to peek at his sleeping face.

Her mouth parted as his blue eyes opened and looked over her head toward the fireplace heating her back. Then, his eyes dropped and locked on to hers.

"Thank you," she blurted.

"For what?" he asked, his tone like velvet.

She swallowed hard. "For taking care of the children and me. It means the world to us."

"I'm happy to do it." His jaw tightened, and his gaze bored into hers. "You know you don't owe me anything, right?" Sam's arm cinched on her waist. "This. You don't owe me this."

Jasmine snorted. "I know."

"So, you're not doing this out of a sense of obligation?" he asked cautiously.

Dumb man. She rolled her eyes but smiled at him. "I would never cuddle you because I felt obligated. I just wanted to cuddle because I like you." Her cheeks heated at her admission.

Her husband's face lost its edge, and something tender moved across his expression that made her palms sweat. His hand smoothed up her back and then down her braid. "I like you, too, Jasmine."

"Jas," she said.

"Jas," he rumbled and smiled.

Stars above. It was downright cruel that he possessed such a smile. Surely, the angels looked on with envy.

She bit her bottom lip as he leaned forward to kiss her forehead. Her eyes closed, and, in that moment, she'd never felt safer.

"Sleep, dearest," he breathed across her skin.

He turned onto his back and pulled Jasmine against him, tucking her into his side. Her head pillowed on his bicep, and he drew her left hand onto his chest to rest over his heart, where he tangled their fingers together. He squeezed her hand once and settled in the nest of blankets.

Each of her muscles slowly relaxed, and a contentedness she hadn't felt in forever seeped into her bones.

Home.

She finally felt like she was home.

Awareness crept in, in increments, along with a familiar feeling of being watched.

"Jade," Jas grumbled, not opening her eyes. "Must you stare?"

"I'm hungry."

"Me, too!" Ethan piped in.

A deep chuckle rumbled against her right cheek. "You beasts are always hungry."

Jasmine's eyes popped open, but she didn't move. It shouldn't have shocked her that she woke up snuggled with Sam. She'd woken up that way since they'd decided to share the bed. The only difference was that she had made the *conscious* choice to do so this time. She felt her cheeks scorch at how she'd thrown her leg over him.

She moved to pull her leg back but gasped when Sam's hand wrapped around the back of her knee and held her in place. He pushed up onto one elbow and peered down at her.

"Don't," he said in a hushed tone. "The babe has been saying good morning."

"What?"

He beamed down at her as the little one in her belly stretched and pressed into his side. "See?"

"How long have you been awake?"

Sam shrugged and lay back down. "A while."

She tilted her head back to admire his profile. He wasn't normally an early morning person. "Did the babe wake you?"

"Something like that," he said wryly.

"I'm sorry."

"Don't be. I liked it."

Her chest warmed.

"Mama?" Jade trilled.

Jasmine stiffened and lifted her head to look at the twins peeking over the bottom of the bed at them. "Yes, baby?" It still bothered her that Jade called her that. Even Ethan had called her "Mama" two days prior.

"I'm hungry."

She grinned. "Go and get dressed in proper clothes, and we'll go find something to eat."

"With Grandad?" Ethan said with excitement.

"He wouldn't miss it for the world," Sam said. "I'm sure he's waiting for you already."

The twins screeched and scrambled to their room, bickering with each other to move faster.

Jasmine reluctantly rolled away from Sam and sat up, swinging her legs over the side of the bed, the linen nightgown tickling her calves.

"It's okay, you know," Sam murmured.

"What?" she replied absentmindedly, rubbing at her temples.

"They're very young. You're the only mum they might remember."

Guilt and sadness warred with each other in the pit of her stomach. "It catches me off-guard every time it happens."

"That's understandable." Sam shifted in the bed behind her and rested his chin on her right shoulder. "But, it's okay if they do. You're the one raising them; it's only natural that they think of you as their mum."

His hand curled around Jasmine's right bicep, his thumb running back and forth over her skin. Absentmindedly, she placed her left hand over the top of his and squeezed, thankful for the comfort.

She turned her neck to thank him, but the words died on her tongue when her lips brushed his chin. When had he gotten that close? She pulled back, her eyes connecting with Sam's deep pools.

"What is it?" he asked, his deep voice sending a shiver of pleasure down her spine.

Jasmine had always liked kisses, and, in that moment, all she wanted to do was touch her lips to his. She wanted more from him, but those were thoughts for another day. She couldn't deal with that now, but a kiss she could handle.

Instead of answering, she twisted to fully face him and leaned forward, brushing her lips softly against his. Her belly quivered when he didn't move away and his hands lifted to cup her cheeks, seemingly content with her taking the lead.

A spark of excitement and something much deeper flamed in her chest. There wasn't guilt, self-loathing, or numbness, just a complete and utter sense of rightness. Her pulse picked up its pace, and she gathered her nightgown in her hands and slipped onto his lap, straddling his thighs, *needing* to be closer to him.

Sam's arms wrapped around her and pressed their bodies together. Jasmine paused to run a finger along the prince's face, admiring his high cheekbones, sharp jaw, and beautiful blue eyes that promised things Jas wasn't sure she was ready for.

Once more, she returned to his lips and sank into the kiss. There were many unknowns in her life, but Sam had been one of her constants. He never asked for anything from her, but she could give him this, give *them* this.

Jasmine ran her hands along the hard planes of his body that seemed to fit her just right and sighed against his lips. Sam froze and then groaned, the sound vibrating against her own chest.

She gasped as his hands wrapped around the backs of her bare thighs and he jerked her impossibly closer with a growl, her round belly pressing insistently into the firm muscles of his stomach. Her hands sank into his gilded waves as his lips trailed down her neck and stopped to lavish the spot above her collarbone.

Stars above. This man was going to wreck her.

Her skin prickled as he pushed her nightgown off her shoulder and brushed more kisses against her skin.

"So beautiful," he murmured, his hands clenching on the backs of her thighs, like he was holding himself back.

A wildness filled Jasmine, along with a sense of reckless urgency. She'd never done anything more before that she remembered. Jas pushed the thought away and focused on the man all but worshiping her.

But she wanted to. With this man. Only this man.

Jasmine yanked his head up and crushed her lips to his, her hands running along the bands of muscles hidden beneath his clothing. What would it be like to have his skin pressed to hers? Brazenly, she reached beneath his linen shirt and scoured her nails up his back.

Sam's breaths came faster, and he exploded into action.

His hands were everywhere, like he was trying to touch every part of her that he could. Gooseflesh rippled down her arms as he bit her bottom lip before soothing it with his tongue. He glanced up into her eyes, and what Jasmine saw caused her heart to accelerate.

Pure heat.

Raw want and rapture.

"I've wanted to be this close to you for so long, love," he whispered.

Love. That's what they had—love and companionship—everything.

Jasmine closed her eyes and pulled her hands from his tempting body to lift the edge of her nightgown. The choice had been taken from her the first time, but this time, she got to choose.

And her choice was Sam.

"No," Sam whispered, slightly breathless.

Jasmine stilled, her eyes snapping open. "W-what?" she stuttered.

Sam's hand slipped over her clenched fist, and he lowered her nightgown. A crushing sense of disappointment and embarrassment rushed over her at his gentle refusal.

Tears flooded her eyes, and she dropped her head, trying to hide them. What was she thinking? He may have enjoyed her company, but that didn't mean he *wanted* her. Stupid, she was so stupid. She tried to backpedal, but

Sam's left arm banded around her waist, holding her in place.

"I need to check on the twins," she said thickly. "Please let me go."

"No. Look at me, Jas."

She shook her head. If she looked at him, surely, she would sob all over the man. How embarrassing. "Let me go."

"No."

Her head snapped up, and she glared at him through her tears. "Let me go!"

"Not until you listen to me," Sam said, infuriatingly calm.

Jasmine threw her hands in the air. "I'm sorry I accosted you. Now, let me go."

"No."

He reached out and sank a hand into her hair before yanking her close, his mouth slamming against hers, his other arm crushing her against him. It was desperate, hot, and messy, like he was trying to imprint himself on her skin.

Sam pulled back, releasing a shuddering breath as Jasmine trembled from head to toe. She touched her swollen lips and stared at him in shock. The wicked man had the audacity to grin at her.

"What in the wicked hell was that for?" she demanded.

"To get you out of your head. I could see rejection and hurt dripping from you like you'd just taken a dip in the sea."

"I'm sorry if my feelings bothered you so," she sniped, wishing she could leave the room.

Sam rolled his hips, and her eyes widened in shock. He laughed. "You bothered me alright. You plague me every damn day."

"What a romantic way to be described. A bloody plague."

He narrowed his eyes at her. "You're not listening." He removed his arms from around her waist and clasped her face between his calloused palms. "I want you, dearest, I do," he ground out, "but we don't need to rush this. We have time. And that's what I want with you—time—not just a quick romp between the sheets." He tilted his head toward the twins' doorway. "It's lucky they haven't burst through the door already."

Her cheeks burned even hotter. "I'm an idiot."

"No, you're human." A slow smile spread across his face before it melted into something completely sinful. He leaned forward and pressed his lips against her ear. "Be thankful our children are in the other room. I don't think you're ready for what's in store for us."

A thrill went up her spine at his words. She jerked when he bit her ear and then pulled back, looking way too pleased with himself.

Bastard.

Two could play that game.

She arched her back and stretched, hiding her smile when he hissed and then cursed. His hands grabbed her hips as she crawled off of him, making sure to give an extra wiggle. He smirked at her.

"Wench."

"Rake," she retorted.

He winked at her and brushed a surprisingly sweet kiss along her brow before stiffly climbing from their bed. He strolled to the bathing room and glanced over his shoulder. "Just remember, love, I always give as good as I get."

A good kind of shiver trickled over Jasmine's skin.

She didn't doubt it for one second.

THIRTY-THREE

JASMINE

———⊷∘⟨≋⟩∘⊷———

SWEAT BEADED ON JASMINE'S FOREHEAD and slid down her hairline. "Don't go so fast!" she called to the twins. Ethan paused while Jade continued to scamper ahead. He held his hand out to Jasmine, and she took his little hand in hers as they clambered down the last of the porous sea rocks to get to the tide pools.

"Jade, you best turn around right now, young lady!"

Her niece paused in her explorations, then skipped back to them, her feet kicking up white sand as she crashed into Jasmine's legs and almost bowled her over.

"Good gracious, baby. You almost knocked me down." Jasmine laughed as she patted Jade's head.

"Don't go so far," Ethan chastised. "Jas is slow today."

Jasmine narrowed her eyes at her nephew. "I'm not that slow."

He smiled at her and nodded. "It took you *forever* to climb down the rocks."

"Well, I had to make sure I was careful. If I fell, it could hurt the babe."

His eyes rounded and dropped to her midriff. Her heart fluttered as he pressed his little hand against her belly.

"The baby is okay?" he asked, worried.

"The babe is happy," she said reassuringly. She released his fingers and dropped her slippers from her other hand into the sand. "I don't think I'm the only slow one." Jas lifted her skirts just a touch and glanced conspiratorially between the twins. "I think we need to have a race!"

The twins flashed her excited smiles. And Jade took off running.

That child.

"You have to wait for everyone else," Ethan shouted at his sister. "You're cheating!"

Jasmine waved Jade back. Again. "Okay, first, we need to make a starting line."

Ethan nodded, his brows furrowed. He bent down on his hands and knees and methodically began to draw a straight line to the left. Jade watched him for a moment and then dug her foot into the sand, dragging it behind her to create a line the other way. It never ceased to amaze Jas how different the twins were.

Once both children were satisfied with their lines, they tromped through the sand to get back to her. Jas hid her smile when Ethan caught sight of his sister's very crooked line and scowled. She ran her hand over the back of his head and smiled at him.

"It's okay. Your line looks very nice."

He stood a little taller at her praise.

"Are you ready?" Jas asked.

Both twins nodded and lined up.

Jasmine hitched her skirts up and looked from one twin to the next. "Get set." Both children tensed. "Go!" she shouted, and she burst forward. The twins screeched in joy and ran alongside her.

She laughed breathlessly and ran with the children until the docks disappeared and the castle loomed above them on the cliff. Jas hissed when a stitch formed in her side. She slowed and threw her hands up in the air.

"You both won," she huffed, collapsing into the sand. Ethan and Jade plopped down next to her.

Jade lay on her back and began to move her arms and legs like she was swimming. Jas groaned as sand collected in her niece's hair. *That will be a nightmare to get out.* But they'd worry about it later.

Jasmine ran her hand over the warm sand and wiggled her toes in deeper, sighing when the cooler earth touched her overheated skin. She always used to be cold, but something had changed once the babe had begun to grow. Now, Jas was perpetually hot.

A cool ocean breeze ruffled her hair, chilling the sweat on her face and arms.

Ethan stood and held a hand out to her. "Can I take you to see the tide pools now?"

What a little gentleman he was turning out to be. She grinned at him and placed her hand in his. "Why, thank you, kind sir."

Ethan kicked his foot in the sand, his cheeks pinking slightly as she pushed herself up and then offered her other hand to the sand mermaid who was attempting to bury herself alive.

"You ready?" Jas asked.

Jade scrambled out of the sand and placed her gritty fingers into Jasmine's. The three of them slowly weaved around the huge, white rocks that jutted out of the sand like giant broken teeth. She kept an eye on the surf as they attempted to find the perfect pool—it was still receding, so they had time.

Ethan jumped up and down as they rounded a particularly huge rock, and they discovered a beautiful cove. Rocks rose up on each side, protecting it from the wind. The water lapped gently on the shore, and little tide pools were scattered around the edges.

"We've found our own secret world," Jasmine said excitedly. "Let's see what treasures we can discover!"

Time passed as they moved from pool to pool. Ethan exclaimed over all the variations of crabs he found, and Jade had to touch every sea anemone she could get to. Jasmine smiled as she ran a hand over a rough pink starfish, marveling at the texture. She'd abandoned all attempts to keep the twins out of the water. They were happy, and that's all that mattered. One could always wash them later. A bit of sea water and sand never hurt anybody.

"Look at this shell!" Ethan exclaimed, holding up a huge fan shell.

"It's beautiful. Are you going to keep it for your collection?"

He nodded and placed it on her lap, along with other treasures the twins had collected.

"We needed that for our gate," Jade objected and gestured to the sand castle they were building.

"I've found something better." Ethan handed her a piece of curved driftwood.

Her niece eyed it and then nodded. "It'll do."

Jas stretched her back and slowly stood, making sure to keep the sea trinkets safe in the top layer of her skirt. "The sun is going down, loves. Only a few more minutes until we have to leave."

A chorus of groans reached her ears.

She took a step forward, and her eyes widened as her bladder protested the movement. Devil take it. She had to use the bathroom. *Right now.*

"Stay where you are," Jas called as she hustled to the edge of the cove. "I need to relieve myself."

Ethan's nose wrinkled. "Gross."

Jas ignored him and rounded the edge of the rock so that she could see the twins but they couldn't see her while she did her business. Jasmine finished up and sighed in relief. Every day, she learned something new about pregnancy. Women glamourized it, but from her experience, her body was falling apart.

She snorted and adjusted her dress. *If they actually told us what it was like, no one would have children.*

She'd taken one step toward the twins when hushed voices reached her ears from behind her. Jasmine frowned and backtracked, very aware of the dagger strapped to her thigh beneath her dress. She never went anywhere without it.

Carefully, she peeked around the huge boulder she'd relieved herself behind and frowned as the setting sun temporarily blinded her for a second. Jas held her hand up to shield her eyes and froze, her mind not able to comprehend what she was seeing.

She whipped back around the rock and squeezed her eyes shut. It couldn't have been…

Look again.

Jasmine glanced around the rock and swallowed hard as she got an eyeful of the lurid scene. A stone settled in the pit of her stomach as she watched Sam pick up a beautiful pale woman with scarcely a stitch of clothing on. Her mouth dried when he dropped to his knees, the goddess straddling him. The woman took his head in her hands and murmured something to him. Bile flooded Jasmine's mouth as his hands ran up the woman's back and tangled in her silver-white hair.

She couldn't watch anymore.

Jas stumbled back into their cove, her heart feeling like it was breaking into a thousand pieces. She closed her eyes to keep the tears from falling, the image of her prince and the flawless woman seared into her mind.

Jasmine gasped as pain washed over her and wrapped around her heart like thorns. How could she be so stupid? Her sight blurred as more tears filled her eyes. No wonder he didn't pursue what she'd offered two days before. A bitter laugh escaped her numb lips. Why in the blazes would he want a pregnant woman when he could have a goddess like that?

She knew better. He'd made her no promises, and yet she'd gone and let herself get attached to him. Hastily, she wiped her eyes and strode to the twins. She forced a wobbly smile onto her lips. They'd had a wonderful day, and she wasn't about to ruin it for them.

"Time to go, sweet ones," she rasped.

Jade moaned, but Ethan studied her in his quiet, contemplative way. He stood and walked to her and took his shells from her skirt and put them in his own pockets. She stared down at him, not even realizing she was still holding her skirt up.

"Let's go, Jade," Ethan said.

Her niece eyed Ethan and then acquiesced. "Could we see Vienna today?" She reached for Jasmine's other hand.

"That sounds like something we can do," Jasmine said and squeezed both of the children's hands as they walked back the way the, came.

The walk back was a quiet one. The sun continued to sink low in the sky, and Jasmine kept looking over her shoulder expecting to see Sam running after them. But the beach was empty of all life.

She bit her trembling lip and tried to get herself together as they neared their abandoned shoes they'd hid behind a rock, which was shaped like a heart.

"Hurry," she said, eyeing the sinking sun. She squinted as she noticed familiar shapes on the horizon. More scouting warships. The navy had spread out their ships in and around the port to protect Sanee from a sea attack. But there'd been no news about a sea attack, so she wasn't too worried. Maybe she should ask Sam. She sucked in a sharp breath like someone had thrown icy water over her.

Sam.

How in the world was she going to face him?

Mortification washed over her as she and the twins hiked back up to the marketplace that was on the edge of the docks. She'd made a fool out of herself. Why had she made the first move?

Because you're all alone and lonely.

Jas shook her head at her maudlin thoughts and pulled the twins closer to each of her sides, their tiny hands wrapped in hers.

No, she wasn't alone.

As much as she wanted to disappear and never face him again, she'd made him a promise. He may not love her, but he loved the twins, and they loved him. She couldn't do that to either of them.

Her throat tightened as they turned left and moved down another cobbled street toward the apothecary, sand chafing her toes in her tight slippers.

Sacrifice. That's what love demanded.

Even if it hurt her going back to him after what she'd seen, she'd do it for the children and, damn him, for Sam.

One lone tear escaped.

Because as much as she didn't want to, she loved him.

THIRTY-FOUR

SAGE

⟶∘⟨⟩∘⟶

"HE WON'T STOP UNTIL WE meet."

Sage rubbed at her burning eyes and coughed. She had scrubbed herself twice and yet the stench of smoke seemed to still cling to her.

"We've discussed this before," Zachael said. "It's too dangerous."

"You're right. It is too dangerous, but the longer we wait, the more people die!" Her voice rose. "More men, women, and children," she croaked. "We can't keep going on like this. People are suffering because of us."

Little blue toes flashed through her mind.

"Not because of us," Gav corrected gently. "Because of a mad man."

She nodded. Logically, Sage knew he was right, but all the deaths weighed heavily upon her, regardless. "Not because of us, but we can do something about it. We need to meet him."

On her left, Tehl hung his head and shifted from foot to foot. "I don't like it. I don't want to give in to his demands. It gives him power."

"No, we are taking the power back from him," Sage said. She had to make him see. "He wants to see me, and he will, but we won't give him the reaction he expects."

"And what does he expect?" William asked, running his fingers over his white beard, his expression shrewd.

"He thinks I will go crawling back to him with a bleeding heart. And while I am broken inside for what he's done –" she swallowed, "I will never cower before him or go back. He crossed a line I didn't know a human being could." Her smile was bitter. "He also changed me in ways I'm not sure he understands. He's the one who should be afraid."

Rafe pushed through the tent entrance with a missive in his hand, his hair rumpled from his flight with his fiilee. "I've just received word. Mother and the Methi army are a day's travel away. More soldiers will be arriving tomorrow."

A sigh of relief seemed to move through the entire group. They needed the soldiers badly.

Tehl eyed Sage and then the map spread out before them. "Sam says that the Scythian fleet approached Sanee. Soon we'll have war along the southern region of Aermia. If the Methian soldiers are arriving tomorrow, then I want the third battalion moved back to Sanee now. Gav, I want you to go with them."

"I will leave now and arrive before the army to inform Sam." Gav moved around the table to clasp forearms with Tehl, and then he scooped Sage into his arms. "Be strong and brave, sis."

She nodded as a lump lodged in her throat. What if this was the last time she saw him? "Take care. I'll see you soon."

"That you will."

Gav waved at the group and left the command tent.

Sage stared after him and said a little prayer. *Please keep safe.* She focused back on the conversation as Tehl gave William instructions.

The older commander nodded. "It'll be done, my lord." He bowed and left the tent, a gust of cool wind following his departure.

One by one, their people were disappearing, and it sent unease down her spine.

Her husband focused back on the map. "We will send a message to the warlord."

"He won't refuse us," Sage added, swallowing down her morbid thoughts. "This is what he's been waiting for."

"Zachael, we'll need protection."

The weapons master pushed his black hair streaked with white from his face. "I will arrange it."

Tehl turned to Raziel. "It would help if we had a view from the air."

The crown prince of Methi dipped his chin. "Our warriors, including myself, will protect you."

"Thank you," her husband whispered. "Is there anything else anyone can think of?"

"We all need sleep," Lilja muttered from the chair in the far corner. "Tomorrow will change everything." She stood with a stretch and wove around the table to pull Sage into her arms. "If you need me, all you have to do is send for me."

Sage nodded and hugged her aunt fiercely. She didn't know what it was, but it seemed like the air held a charge, like it was trying to tell her something. So, she held on to Lilja a little longer, and made sure to hug all of their friends and advisors as they left.

Rafe was the last to leave. He pulled her into a bear hug.

"We will win, little one. My people will protect you from the sky, and I will stand at your side. He will never touch you."

Sage squeezed him back as hard as she could. Sometimes, it felt like he could read her mind. It was one thing to imagine seeing the warlord, and another completely to be in his presence.

"Thank you," she whispered against his heavy fur jacket.

He dropped a kiss on top of her head and pulled Tehl into a hug before he left.

She gazed at her husband, feeling like she was about to fall apart.

Tehl said nothing, but approached her and swung her into his arms. He pushed through the rear flap that led to their sleeping quarters. Gently, he set her on the bed and pulled her boots from her feet. Next, he unbuckled her breastplate and set it next to the bed. Tehl dug around in the bag next to her side of the pallet and unearthed a brush.

"Turn around, love," he murmured.

Sage stared at him as love and affection for the amazing man before her threatened to drown her. She'd never been one for decorum, so she abandoned all pretense and launched herself at him, upsetting his balance. Tehl caught her and braced a hand on the bed as they toppled forward onto the blankets.

"I love you," she murmured.

"I love you more."

She arched against him and kissed him with everything she had. Sage twisted her fingers in his black hair and pulled him closer, needing his skin against hers, the assurance that he was with her.

"We're not going to die tomorrow," Tehl murmured against her lips. He didn't let go of her as he hauled her up the bed, and then with some finagling, he yanked the covers from beneath them with one hand and pulled the quilts over the top of them.

Sage tipped her head back and smiled at Tehl. He grinned at her, and her heart flipped.

"You and I 'til the end?" he murmured.

"'Til the end," she promised, snuggling into the cocoon of warmth he'd created.

She'd cling to life with everything she had.

The warlord would take nothing more from them.

THIRTY-FIVE

SAM

—⟶○◦⟨⟩◦○⟵—

"SAM, YOU NEED TO BREATHE through it."

He dropped to his knees and gazed up at Mer in awe. How could one woman be so heartbreakingly beautiful? He ran his hands up the sides of her bare thighs and onto her back, her skin as soft as silk.

"Stars, you're stunning," he whispered in awe. His eyes dropped to her pink lips, and he leaned closer, determined to find out what they tasted like.

Mer's hands cradled each side of his face and held him captive, her magenta eyes wide and her expression pinched. "It's the Lure, Sam. You don't want this."

Oh, he very much did. He wrapped his hand in her hair and pulled her closer to his chest, the saltwater from her skin seeping into his clothes. "I know exactly what I want."

"Do you?" she whispered, her voice somewhat painful. "Because I know you don't want me. You want your wife. Jasmine is who you want."

Sam blinked slowly, and a small voice in the back of his mind that he'd been ignoring grew a little louder.

You don't want Mer. What about Jasmine? What about the twins?

He shuddered and pressed his forehead to Mer's chest, his body trembling as rational thoughts began to filter back in. He'd just accosted his friend, a friend he wanted nothing to do with romantically—nor she him, she'd made that clear before.

"I'm sorry," he panted and released her hair, his arms still staying wrapped around her. He tried not to inhale her scent, but it curled around him like a lover, intoxicating him with each breath.

"It's okay," she whispered. "It's not your fault. You've done nothing wrong, but if you don't get yourself under control, I think we're going to have company."

"Company?" he said groggily like he'd just awoken from a deep sleep.

"I heard children laughing, and I'm pretty sure a woman saw us."

"Damn," he growled and forced himself to release Mer. When he'd received her urgent message, Sam had dropped everything and come running. Whatever she was here for, it wasn't good.

The Sirenidae scrambled back and clutched at her stomach, red liquid seeping through her fingers.

He cursed. "By the stars, what in the bloody hell happened?" he demanded. Disgust and horror rolled through him as he still felt a carnal pull toward Mer. He'd been so absorbed in his attraction to her, he hadn't even noticed her injury.

Damn Lure.

Mer threw a sealskin pouch at him. "I need you to help me and listen. There isn't much time."

He nodded and put all his attention into opening the pouch instead of staring at the woman he desperately wanted to kiss. Sam pinched the bridge of his nose. That wasn't right. He didn't *want* to kiss her. She was his friend. He was only reacting to her Lure, to the pheromones her body created when it came in contact with air and seawater.

His hands shook as he pulled out a vial that held pink flowers. "What do you want me to do with this?"

Mer coughed and pointed to the nearest tide pool. "Gather some algae and crush the flower into it. Please."

Sam forced himself away from her and followed her directions. He approached her and breathed through his mouth as he gently applied the paste to her pale skin. Paler than usual.

"What happened?"

Mer blanched as he pressed some of the paste deeper into the wound.

"Depths below, that hurts!" she snarled. She dropped her head back into the sand. "They're almost here."

He nodded, not surprised in the least. "How long do we have?"

"Hours," she whispered. "I came to warn you."

"Thank you," he said, brushing her silvery hair from her face. "I'll alert my captains immediately." He eyed her wound. "How did that happen?"

"A spear."

He winced. "What else can I do to help?"

Mer sat up and wrapped a hand over her wound, her face creased in pain. "You've done everything you can." She grabbed her sealskin pouch off of the sand and stood, swaying.

Launching to his feet, he steadied her. "Are you sure?"

"I need to get back to my people, and you need to prepare yours. War is upon us." Her mouth twisted into an angry, ugly line. "And they're just as barbaric and monstrous as we expected." Mer pressed a kiss to his cheek. "I'll see you on the battlefield."

She turned on her heel and strode straight into the water, disappearing from Sam's sight, just as the last vestige of the sun sank below the horizon.

Sam allowed himself one minute to calm his racing heart before he transformed into his role as spymaster and general. He spun toward the palace and then sprinted for the secret entrance.

The time for preparations was over.

War was here.

THIRTY-SIX

JASMINE

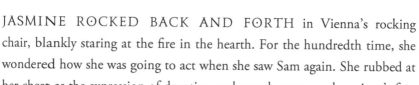

JASMINE ROCKED BACK AND FORTH in Vienna's rocking chair, blankly staring at the fire in the hearth. For the hundredth time, she wondered how she was going to act when she saw Sam again. She rubbed at her chest as the expression of devotion and pure hunger on the prince's face floated to the forefront of her mind. Her heart seemed to shrivel. He'd never looked at *her* that way.

She hung her head and covered her face with her hands. For the last four hours, Jas had been berating herself for getting attached, for letting him in, for trying to help Sage in the first place, for being a sad excuse of a mother. Basically, for breathing.

Vienna's rosemary scent teased her nose right before her old friend placed a hand on the back of Jasmine's neck and kneaded.

"It seems you have much on your mind tonight. You've not spoken more than ten words. What's on your mind?"

Jas dropped her hands and studied her palms while trying to come up with an answer that wouldn't make her look like she was a sniveling, lovesick pup. "I have decisions to make," she said slowly. "But I am not sure which course of action I should take."

"Well, you're not alone. Have you spoken to Sam about what's bothering you? He's known to be fair and levelheaded, which is rare in a husband," she said wryly.

Jasmine squeezed her eyes shut, and her hands curled into fists.

"So that's how it is," Vienna said with sympathy. "The prince is the problem."

"Vienna, I made vows," Jas choked out, her eyes unconsciously seeking out the twins who played quietly in the corners of the living room. "He loves the twins and is a good person, but there are other sides to him that I don't know I can live with. I thought I could, but things have changed. And it... it hurts *so* much."

"That's love, my girl. At times, you feel like you could float above the ground, and, at other times, all you want to do is bury yourself in a hole to escape the horror of it. You have to be willing to take the good with the bad. Real love is not all flowers and romance. It's gritty, and it's hard. Those that are brave enough to really see the flaws of another person, and then accept them for it, will suffer pain like they've never felt before—but they will also experience love, friendship, and laughter like nothing the world has seen. And I've never known you to be a coward, Jasmine."

Jas lifted her head and craned her neck to look up at the older woman. "I don't feel very brave right now. I feel broken."

Vienna dropped her hand from Jasmine's neck and pulled up another rocking chair next to hers. The healer groaned as she lowered herself into the wooden seat and took Jasmine's left hand in hers.

"You are one of the bravest women I've ever had the pleasure of meeting."

Jasmine scoffed.

"You've shared with me bits and pieces of your life, but don't forget, the whole kingdom has heard what you did for our princess."

"I'm sure what you've heard is greatly exaggerated," Jas said softly.

Vienna narrowed her sky-blue eyes at Jasmine. "I'm an old woman, Jasmine Ramses, and a healer at that. I know what you did for Sage, and I know what it cost you," she said gently.

What it cost her.

Everything.

"I wouldn't change it," Jasmine admitted. "I hate, *hate,* how everything's happened, but—" Her gaze slid to the twins. "They're happy and thriving.

Before, in the village, each day was just about surviving. But they're happy here, and I would give my own life for that."

"You're a good mother and friend."

"I don't feel like it," she muttered.

Vienna patted her hand. "And that is the curse of being a woman. We feel guilty about everything and rarely believe we are good enough for any task we complete, but that is just our skewed perception of ourselves. It's not the truth."

"What is the real truth?" Ethan said, abandoning his toy and crawling up into Vienna's lap.

The healer cuddled Jasmine's nephew close and kissed the top of his dark head.

"Listening in, again?" Vienna said with exasperation, but her smile betrayed her true feelings.

Ethan shrugged and squinted into the hearth. "I like your talks. They're interesting." He tipped his face back to stare up at Vienna. "So, what is the real truth?"

"The real truth is that—"

A screech followed by a bone-jarring boom rocked the room. Dirt from the thatched ceiling drifted down in puffs.

"What in the wicked hell?" Vienna blurted.

Another screech followed by an explosion set Jasmine's teeth on edge. She jumped out of the rocking chair and strode to the window. "Stars above," she whispered as a macabre scene played out before her eyes.

Flashes of light from cannon fire illuminated warring ships in their harbor. Her stomach bottomed out as a trebuchet released a huge, flaming rock toward Sanee. The ground seemed to roll beneath her feet as the stone crashed through a tavern five streets from Vienna's apothecary.

Good god, they needed to get farther into Sanee and away from the floating war machines.

She scanned the chaos in the streets. People had abandoned their homes and were screaming and stumbling away from the ensuing battle. Jasmine covered her mouth as a woman tripped and fell to the ground. The woman cried out as a man trampled over her.

Jasmine spun away from the window, panic starting to rise up. Vienna placed Ethan in her rocking chair and stormed toward the back room.

"Barricade the entrance, Jasmine!"

Jas hurried to the front door, slipped the heavy wooden slat into place, and stared at it as an ear-splitting scream pierced the air. Her pulse picked up, and she eyed the heavy trunk next to the door. She grabbed the handle and heaved, moving the blasted piece of furniture a few inches.

"What are you bloody doing?" Vienna barked, storming into the room.

"Helping," Jas gritted out, and she pulled again.

Vienna reached for the other side and helped move the enormous trunk. Once they'd managed to move it in front of the door, the older woman wiped the sweat from her brow and gestured at the windows. "We need to board them up."

Jasmine pulled herself to her knees and hugged each of the twins, who were watching with wide, fearful eyes.

"It'll be okay, loves," she whispered. "Vienna and I will keep you safe. Cover your ears, okay?"

The twins nodded, and Jas hurried to help Vienna lock the shutters over the large front window, then yanked the curtains closed. Jasmine moved to the children and stumbled as another explosion rocked the earth. She dropped to her knees and wrapped her arms around Ethan and Jade, their little bodies trembling against hers.

"We can't stay here, Vienna. It's not safe."

"We can't go out there, either," the older woman replied, peeking through her keyhole. "It's utter madness." She sucked in a sharp breath. "No."

The hair rose on Jasmine's arms, and a tingling sensation began at the base of her neck, a sixth sense of foreboding, and she knew what the healer was going to say.

"They're here." Vienna glanced at Jasmine with fear in her eyes. "We need to leave *now*."

A hysterical laugh threatened to escape Jasmine's mouth. "We've no place to go." The palace was the safest place to be, but... She peered down at the whimpering children in her arms. They couldn't drag the children through the nightmare outside the door. They'd never make it.

Vienna stood from her crouched position and gestured for Jasmine and the children to follow her.

"Come on, children," Jas urged.

The twins followed her, completely silent.

They entered the back room of the apothecary. The rows of tinctures, tonics, and salves rattled against each other due to the raging conflict outside.

"Help me move this table," Vienna barked.

Jasmine hurried to assist her, and her brow wrinkled in confusion as the older woman dropped to her knees, her fingers pressing along the grooves of the wooden floor.

"Come on," the healer breathed.

Vienna pressed harder, and a faint click sounded beneath the floor. She dug her fingernails in between the floorboards and pulled. A trapdoor lifted, revealing a pitch-black hole.

"An escape route?" Jasmine asked.

"My grandfather's father was a paranoid man." Vienna gestured to the children. "This will get us into the sewers and close to the palace. Once there, we can—" She snapped her mouth shut as gruff words spoken in a foreign accent echoed down the alleyway.

Scythians.

Jasmine began to tremble as the voices neared the back door to the apothecary. She held her finger to her lips. Ethan nodded and hugged Jade closer to his own body. The room seemed to hold its breath as the warriors paused, and then their footsteps faded away. They waited a minute before Vienna moved into action.

She snatched a small lantern off the shelf and gestured to the trapdoor.

"Down you go, my girl."

Jasmine eyed the escape route. If Jas went first, there was no possible way for Vienna to hide the trapdoor after her, but if Jasmine went last, she could probably shove the table over the trapdoor and squeeze into the escape route.

"You go first. I can move the table and hide our escape the best I can," she said in a hushed tone, too spooked to speak above a whisper. Scythians had uncanny hearing. Who knew what monsters might be listening in.

Vienna eyed her and then the table. "You're right. I wouldn't be able to move the table myself."

The older woman handed Jasmine the lantern. Jas held the light up, illuminating a short ladder that led to a tunnelway covered in cobwebs. Vienna didn't hesitate in lowering herself into the rickety-looking ladder. She reached the bottom and held her hands up. Jasmine lowered the lantern into the healer's waiting hands and turned to the twins.

"Come on, loves. It's time to go." Her heart picked up its pace as another explosion sliced through the air.

They scurried forward, but Jade clung to Jas's dress.

"There might be spiders down there," her niece cried.

Ethan hugged Jasmine but climbed down to Vienna.

Jas grabbed each side of Jade's precious face and stared into her eyes, so like her own. "I need you to be brave right now, baby." She swallowed down a sob. "Can you be brave for me?"

"Y-yes, Mama," Jade stuttered, before crawling into the tunnel.

Jasmine closed the trapdoor and pushed up from her knees, then yanked on the table with all her might. She gritted her teeth as the wooden legs scraped against the floor. Jas panted as she sprinted for the broom in the corner and swept away the evidence of her having moved the table.

She placed the broom against the wall and hustled back to the trapdoor. Carefully, she felt for the edge and lifted. Jas shifted to her side and slipped her legs down into the space. Her nerves were so shot that she almost screamed when a hand clasped her ankle and directed it to the ladder.

Her teeth chattered as she eased herself lightly onto her belly and wiggled backward, her flesh scraping against wood, Her muscles trembled and her jaw clenched as she managed to get her belly into the opening, her chest still pressed to the apothecary floor like she was prostrating herself before an altar.

Jas sucked in a deep breath and froze, her brows furrowing. Ripples of unease rolled through her. It was quiet—too quiet.

The back door to the apothecary exploded inward. Shards of wood flew across the room. A piece struck her in the forehead and cheek, but she barely felt the pain. Terror froze her screams of horror as a Scythian stepped into Vienna's home.

Recognition washed over her as she got a good look at the warrior's face.

Phoenix. One of *her* warriors.

She must have made a sound, because his chocolatey eyes dropped to hers, and a triumphant smile spread across his face.

It was the smile that had her scrambling back.

"Go!" she screamed, ripping her dress as she managed to get farther into the tunnel. Her foot slipped on the rung below her.

A roar of fury, followed by a crash and shattering glass, had her moving down faster, the trapdoor slamming above her.

"Run, Vienna, run!"

The trapdoor was flung open above her head, flooding the tunnel with light. She didn't look up but jumped. It may hurt to fall, but she didn't have time to climb all the way down.

Jas cried out as Scythian hands caught her hair and dress.

God, no.

She reached up and raked her hands along the arms pulling her upward, away from her family. But it was no use. They didn't release her.

With tears streaming down her face, she met Vienna's eyes. "Go," she mouthed. Her eyes moved to the twins. "I love you."

The arms jostled her and yanked her out of the tunnel. She gaped at the trapdoor that had been torn completely off its hinges. Jas squeezed her eyes shut and focused on slowing her breathing.

She couldn't escape monsters, but maybe she could divert their attention from her family. A strange calm settled over her as a large hand brushed the hair from her face and settled her on the floor of the back room.

Jas opened her eyes and shrank back from the men who surrounded her.

Phoenix's immense form stood in the entryway, eyeing the alleyway. Orion crouched next to her side, his raven-colored braids hanging around his face as he slipped a finger under her chin and lifted it, examining her face.

"She's bleeding," Orion growled.

Another Scythian pushed past Phoenix and stood before her, his expression one of relief and disgust.

Mekhl.

Her most volatile warrior.

Jasmine blinked and looked away toward the door. Not her *warrior*. Her *captor*.

"We need to move," Phoenix rumbled from the doorway. "Time is short." He glanced over his shoulder and pinned her to the spot with his gaze. "Hello, consort."

She bared her teeth at him. "I'm *not* your consort."

His gaze dropped to her pregnant belly, which was on display, because her dress was pulled taut against the bump.

A smile full of male satisfaction, and a touch of something else, transformed his serious face into something hauntingly beautiful.

"The babe says otherwise."

Bile flooded her mouth.

The babe.

Orion smiled and reached out to touch her belly. She slapped his hand away and curled her arms around her belly.

"Don't touch me."

Orion tucked a braid behind his ear and glared at the floor. "We're trying to help you," he whispered in his quiet way that was so familiar.

She touched her bleeding cheek where the wood had struck her. "This is not helping," she hissed.

"She's going to be a problem," Mekhl snarled. His brown eyes narrowed on her. "Orion?"

Jasmine scooted backward as Orion pulled a cloth from his leather trousers.

"Don't fight it," he said softly.

Jas scrambled backward and attempted to get away.

An arm wrapped around her, just below her breasts and above her belly.

"No!" she screamed. "Please, no."

"I'm sorry," Orion said, and he shoved the cloth over her face.

A sickeningly sweet scent invaded her nose and mouth. She kicked and screamed, but as her eyes drooped, she knew it was all for nothing.

Jasmine had always had a feeling they'd come for her.

Her last thought was of the twins as everything faded to darkness.

Sam would take care of the twins.

They'd be all right.

THIRTY-SEVEN

THE WARLORD

COMING, COMING, COMING, THE VOICES sang, completely satisfied.

Zane stood tall, his left hand resting on Nege's motionless black head. The feline's muscles were tense as he watched the party approach on horseback, their army standing guard in a solid wall of blue and white.

She comes.

Pride blossomed in his chest as his consort galloped toward him, her brunette hair shining like polished wood. Warpaint cut bold black lines down her eyes and high cheekbones. Her emerald eyes seemed to glow in her heart-shaped face and held him rooted to the spot. He tucked away the triumphant smile that threatened to break across his face as he studied the fine figure she cut in her armor and her silver breastplate that gleamed in the morning sun. The Aermian banner whipped in the air behind her, a great sapphire dragon.

She looked like a warrior angel, one he was happy to play the part of the devil with.

The warlord arched a brow at her as their party halted just over twenty paces away. Sage gazed at him as the rest of her warriors dismounted and circled her, her expression giving nothing away.

"Magnificent," he breathed, his praise lost in the bitter wind.

Something flashed across her face, and she blinked, breaking the spell that had been woven between the two of them.

His gaze dropped to the hands that circled *his* consort's waist, helping her from the spirited mare.

Ours, the voices snarled.

And he couldn't help but agree.

Nege growled lowly, and Zane ran a soothing hand over the maneater's head in an absent manner, letting none of his feelings leak out from the raging chaos that swirled inside his mind. He lazily observed the Aermian party as they arranged themselves into a barrier around *his* consort and the boy who thought himself a king.

This time, he did smile at the group of children playing at war. They were children in comparison to him, at least. His gaze snagged on a pair of cool magenta eyes that appraised him with indifference. Zane's smile deepened as he moved on, ignoring the reflective amber eyes that held hate.

So, they brought the Sirenidae and the Methian beasts. That was significant. They feared him.

As they should, the voices hissed.

Blair shifted closer to his right side.

"They reek of aggression," his commander spoke lowly, so only Zane could hear his words. "This will end in war."

"So be it," he whispered.

His heart picked up its speed as his consort stepped to the front of the group with the royal pup at her side. Zane appraised the Aermian prince and admitted that he was a handsome man, but too pretty and innocent for *his* Sage. He had an eye for those who knew true suffering, who were broken, but the man almost shone with wholesomeness.

Disgusting.

He dismissed the man who practically towered over his consort and let his gaze truly feast upon her figure. She was exactly as he remembered her. Although... his eyes narrowed slightly at the paleness of her complexion. His consort looked tired.

Pleasure unfurled in her chest when Nali sunk into place next to her mistress, her feline gaze alert. They were two parts of a whole, he and his consort, almost mirrors of each other. Nege huffed at his side but he ignored the beast, his eyes only for Sage.

A fissure of delight ran up his spine when she held his gaze, not cowering in his presence. For a long moment, they stared at each other, and the only sound was the wind whistling through the meadow and trees.

He took one casual step forward and grinned at how the warriors guarding his consort tensed. Zane wanted to scoff.

As if he'd hurt *his* woman.

"Consort," he murmured, practically purring.

Sage's eyes flashed, and an emotion broke free from her face for just one second before she tucked it away. But it was too late. He'd seen it.

Worry. Worry for *him*.

Try as she might, deny it all she could, but in the end, she was still his.

"Warlord," the prince muttered, his tone somewhat bored. "We've come as you've requested. You spoke of peace —" he cocked his head and looked past Zane, "—and yet you have an army that has encroached upon my land."

"My apologies, but it's been difficult to get your attention, my lord," Zane said.

The prince had held out longer than the warlord had expected. The young pup had a bit of backbone, which was as surprising as it was thrilling. There was nothing he loved more than a fierce opponent. Zane hadn't enjoyed burning the villages, but he gained a grain of respect for the man who wouldn't bend to him.

And yet, *she* was here.

"Another simple note would have sufficed," the Sirenidae said, her husky, sensual voice washing over him. He closed his eyes and savored it. There was something he loved about their rich musical voices. The Sirenidae voice was a thing of beauty.

It was too bad their kind were the children of beasts, whores, and cowards.

"The first wasn't taken too kindly." He opened his eyes and pursed his lips. "Decisions had to be made."

Pleasure swelled in his belly when his consort took one step forward and Nali appeared at her side. Sage braced her feet apart, one hand on the maneater's head, the other hanging loosely by her side.

A mirror of Zane's posture.

It was almost poetic.

Her green eyes glittered with rage and sorrow. She swept over him with her gaze, lips thinned like she found him distasteful. But he knew the truth. Sage was an excellent actress. Like called to like. With time, she might become as skilled as he. But that wasn't something he wanted for her. He wanted her just as she was.

"We're here. Will you consent to peace and retreat to your lands?" she asked, her voice sharp like a steel blade.

"I will consent to leave your lands under one condition." He held his hand toward her, palm up. "Come home and all shall be forgiven."

The warlord stilled, and the hairs on his arms rose as the prince pressed against Sage's back.

OURS! How dare he touch what is ours?

"You are a liar." Her voice rose and thundered in the space between them. "There will never be peace between us as long as you plague this earth."

"What an interesting term, plague," he replied. "Plagues have an essential use. They weed out the old and weak. They help control the population, so that people won't starve. Plagues have a purpose, and so do I. The world will be a better place, wild one. *We* can make it better."

"And what of the children?" she flung at him. "What did they ever do to deserve your wrath?"

Sorrow twisted his guts. War was ugly and violent, and sacrifices had to be made for the greater good. It didn't mean it was easy. "It pained me as much as it pains you."

A shudder worked through her body at his words. A guttural scream exploded from her chest, and the rest seemed to happen in slow motion.

One lone tear dripped onto her cheek.

His consort tore two daggers from the sheaths at her arms.

Her gaze latched onto his.

"Death comes for you," she shouted. "For Aermia!"

And then she attacked.

Like water bursting free from a dam, his warriors sprinted past him to meet the Aermian army that burst forward at their mistress's command, voices raised in battle cries.

One simple silver blade lodged in Zane's shoulder; the other he caught by the blade. His palm began to burn and dripped blood. He beamed at his consort as her warriors dragged her back from the bloody fray that had begun.

She had struck first blood. He was a lucky man to possess such a woman, such a champion.

Zane slipped her dagger into his belt and pulled the dagger from his shoulder with his cut hand, warm liquid leaking from the wound. He dipped his chin to her in respect.

The warlord of Scythia would only ever bleed for his consort.

And she for him.

Both broken but made whole together.

A deep chuckle passed his lips at the mayhem of clashing swords, grunts, horse screams, cries of terror, bellows of triumph, and the thunder of thousands of footsteps.

Beautiful.

An Aermian soldier broke through his guard. He knocked the sword from the man's hand, swept his feet out from underneath him, and clenched his head beneath his palms. One swift jerk and the man fell to his knees like a marionette with its strings cut.

Zane lifted his head and met his consort's tumultuous gaze. "I'll see you soon, wild one," he whispered.

Her eyes widened before a Methian beast yanked her back from the front line. Sage disappeared from view, but he didn't worry.

No one would hurt his consort.

She'd be back.

And he'd be waiting.

He lifted his hands to the heavens.

"Bring forth the fire! Let us scourge the earth of those who are not worthy!" the Warlord bellowed.

THİRTY-EİGHT

SAGE

ABSOLUTE CHAOS REIGNED AROUND THEM.

Her breaths seemed abnormally loud in her ears as men crashed together, screaming for blood. Bile burned her throat as a Scythian warrior cut down a young Aermian soldier with hardly a flick of his sword. He charged toward her, his war cry rattling her very soul.

She stared into his dark, bloodthirsty eyes as he closed the distance between them and pulled her sword from her scabbard. Her fingers wrapped around the metal hilt of her blade, her palm slipping from sweat.

The warrior bared his teeth at her, and she braced for the strike that never came. Rafe slammed into the warrior from the side, both men crashing to the ground in a heap of limbs, armor, and deadly weapons.

Her skin prickled, and sweat dripped down her spine as she watched them grapple. An inner bell went off inside her mind, telling Sage that she should be more aware of her surroundings, but she couldn't look away from the warrior who was howling for her death.

The Scythian spun and managed to slash his blade across Rafe's arm. He roared in pain and his attacks grew tighter, more focused. As if her body belonged to someone else, she pulled a dagger from her hip and crept forward, the anarchy around her fading into nothing. She focused on the vulnerable spot just below the warrior's ear.

He didn't notice her coming as he was so hellbent on killing Rafe.

Rafe met the enemy's downward strike and locked swords with him, a slow smile creeping up his face. Her friend never even looked at her, but he knew she was there. Sage jumped onto the warrior's back and struck true.

It was over in an instant.

She released the warrior and landed in a crouch as the Scythian crashed to the ground between her and Rafe. Sage lifted her dagger and stared at the scarlet tip.

She'd taken a life.

Someone she didn't even know.

Her gaze moved back to the felled warrior.

He was Scythian, by all accounts a soulless monster, and yet he bled the same color she did. A shiver worked through her and the dagger slipped from her shaking hands.

Murderer. A cold-blooded killer. Just like the Warlord.

Sage jerked as fingers lifted her chin and she met Rafe's burning amber eyes.

"This won't be the last life you take," he said gruffly. "This is war. If you don't get it together, you and I will both die on this field. Remember your training. Now is not the time to feel."

He stood abruptly and spun to meet another enemy, one who was clearly less experienced. She watched dispassionately as he dispatched the man, and once again knelt beside her, ignoring the bedlam around them.

Rafe leaned into her, his face mere inches from her own. "Snap out of it! I will drag you back to the war camp by your hair if I have to," he growled. He plucked her dagger from the ground and wrapped her bloodied fingers around the handle. "Can I trust you to protect yourself?"

She blinked slowly and nodded once, some of the fog around her mind dissipating. Her hand tightened around the blade while the other dug into the earth, grounding her. She bowed her head and inhaled deeply. This is what the Warlord had wanted. He'd forced her hand.

Sage stood and lifted her head, the cool numbness seeping through her veins, but not keeping her prisoner in her own body any longer. She scanned the immediate area, looking for potential dangers, but none approached her.

Rafe, Zachael, and a few guards had formed a loose ring around her as the battle surged like waves around them.

A screech cut through the air, followed by a bone-jarring boom. The ground rolled beneath her feet, and Sage stumbled. Her eyes watered as smoke filled the air. Slowly, Sage spun in a circle and scrutinized the mayhem. An unbidden chuckle burst from her lips at the indescribable horror unleashed upon their people.

Blood soaked into the ground, creating a garish, unholy painting. War machines lined the edge of the Mort wall, catapulting burning orbs that shot across the sky like hellish shooting stars, leaving destruction in their wake. Her breath seized as a rain of whistling fire descended from the sooty sky.

"Shields!" Zachael bellowed.

Sage yanked a discarded shield off the ground and held it above her head. Men cried out around her as fiery arrows pierced flesh, earth, and shield. She bit the inside of her cheek and fought not to cover her ears. A haunting melody of thwarted arrows clinked against metal like a chilling version of ice clinking against glass.

She hefted the shield back up until she formed a triangle of protection with Zachael and Rafe. "This is madness," she said woodenly, hardly able to comprehend the destruction around her. How had so much carnage happened in such little time? It was unthinkable.

Too much violence.

Too much death.

And it had only just begun.

"We need to fall back," Zachael muttered.

Sage's heart thumped painfully in her chest as she spotted Tehl and Lilja more than twenty paces away. "Not without them."

Rafe and Zachael exchanged a look but nodded.

"On my command," the weapons master said.

Another explosion rocked the earth.

"Now!"

THIRTY-NINE

TEHL

HE GRITTED HIS TEETH AS he slammed his sword against the wicked blade of the lanky Scythian warrior who seemed to appear out of thin air. His muscles trembled with strain as the warrior growled and pressed forward. Tehl's heels dug into the dirt beneath the soles of his boot as he leaned into his strike, trying to unbalance his opponent.

He gasped when the enemy spun away quickly and darted forward in a serpent-strike that had him on his toes. Lilja cried out from his left, but he didn't dare take his eyes off his opponent for one second. The Sirenidae could handle herself far better than he could.

"You're going to die today," the warrior snarled. His gaze slid over Tehl's shoulder. "And then, everything you hold dear will be ours."

"Over my dead body," Tehl gritted out, meeting each bone-jarring strike.

"Your wish is my command," the warrior whispered with glee.

Tehl gasped as the Scythian caught his thigh with the tip of his blade. He ignored the burning pain and lunged forward, pushing the Scythian backward. From the corner of his eye, Lilja emerged from the fray and attacked his opponent from the left side.

The warrior growled and disengaged, then spat on the ground as he got an eyeful of the Sirenidae.

"Disgusting," he hissed. "Unnatural."

Lilja arched a haughty white brow. "If anyone is unnatural here, it's you. You're a mongrel." She sidled farther from Tehl, keeping the Scythian's attention on her. "Who do you think your warlord experimented on to get your precious elixir, hmmm? He coveted us, our abilities. You're nothing but a poor replica."

The hair on the nape of Tehl's neck rose as the warrior began to tremble. His whole body seemed to vibrate, and his muscles bulged. Tehl moved cautiously to his right, searching for a way to attack the dangerous man who looked like he was one moment away from jumping out of his skin.

Lilja laughed, the sound condescending and sharp. "So, you're one of those? Are you going to let your berserker out? Come on, let him out to play with me," she taunted.

Tehl paused when the Scythian's head whipped in his direction, his braided hair slapping against his burnished skin. The warrior's wrathful gaze pinned him to the spot before moving back to Lilja. Tehl released his breath and shoved his terror down. There hadn't been anything human left in the warrior's face, only rage and hunger.

The Sirenidae shifted her stance and batted her lashes at the unraveling warrior. "It must gall you that you're so weak. What would your Warlord say? I bet he hasn't even gifted you with a woman yet." She let her sentence hang and then smirked. "I'm sure he never will. If I can see that you're lacking, I bet your leader can, too."

That was the final straw.

The Scythian bellowed and lunged. Lilja met him blow for blow. Her magenta eyes caught Tehl's for one moment, and he knew what he had to do. He attacked from behind. The warrior swung around and slammed his fist into Tehl's stomach. He wheezed and hunched over, knowing he'd suffered a few cracked ribs.

Quickly, he yanked his dagger from his bicep and swiped at the man's hamstrings. He rolled out of the way and hopped up onto his feet as the warrior spun with a cry. He took one limping step toward Tehl when Lilja swept under the Scythian guard and slammed her dagger into his neck. The warrior gurgled, clutched at his throat, and dropped to his knees. He gave them one more hate-filled glare before his eyes rolled into his head.

"Are you hurt?" Tehl panted as he scanned the pandemonium.

His guards had formed a barrier between him and his advisors. He exhaled and wiped the sweat from his forehead. The ground shuddered beneath his feet with an explosion. Smoke singed his nose.

"No."

A screech of pain caused him to glance upward. His stomach bottomed out as a fiilee and his rider plummeted from the sky in a ball of flame. "Hell." He prayed that it wasn't Raziel plunging from above.

"Remember this feeling," Lilja said in a hollow voice. "It will keep you from ever seeking war again."

Tehl nodded. He'd never forget the horrors of this day.

"How is your leg?" she asked, wiping her blades on her pants.

He glanced at the seeping wound. "It's nothing." Tehl lifted his head and scanned the fray, looking for his wife. Sage stood back-to-back with Rafe, fighting their way back from the front line. Somehow, they'd gotten separated. "We need to move." They needed to regroup and plan.

"I agree." Lilja straightened and lifted her chin toward Sage and the sea of warriors between them. "If you can, goad the warriors."

Tehl fought a shiver. "Into the rage?"

"Yes. They're less coordinated."

He nodded. That was something he'd noticed. "You lead, and I'll follow."

The Sirenidae flashed him a bitter smile from a dirt-smeared face. "Age before beauty?"

"More like experience before ignorance."

Lilja sobered. "I'll protect you with my life."

"As will I." He rolled his shoulders and hefted his sword higher as another warrior broke through the makeshift ring. "Let's be done with this."

FORTY

LILJA

SHE STEPPED OVER THE WARRIOR she'd dispatched and locked eyes on the Warlord.

His sword flashed as it reflected the liquid fire that the war machine catapulted through the sky. He looked exactly the same as when she'd met him years prior, before she knew the extent of his depravity, cruelty, and corruption.

Devastatingly handsome, even covered in blood and grime.

As if he heard her thoughts, his face turned toward her, and a handsome smile tipped up his lips. Everything began and ended with him. He curled a finger toward her in a "come closer" motion.

His words floated to the front of her mind like he'd just whispered them in her ear.

Animals deserve to be chained.

She smiled at him and began to carve a path in his direction. The only animal that needed to be put down was the Warlord. His brand of unhinged delusion could not be allowed to live any longer. He'd played god for long enough.

Her stride lengthened as she drew closer to the Warlord.

A warrior charged her but halted when the monstrous ruler of Scythia held his hand up. The warrior backtracked and entered gleefully into the battle.

She stared at him, an ax in one hand and a sword in the other.

He brushed his raven hair from his face and grinned impishly. "I was wondering when we'd speak again. It's been far too long."

"Indeed, it has," she murmured, eyeing her greatest enemy. "I was quite hoping you'd be dead by now."

The Warlord barked out a laugh. "I forgot how frank you are. I remember a time when you were quite innocent."

"Those days are long gone," she said honestly. The warlord and his men had made sure of that.

"I have to say, I like you this way better." His black gaze wandered down her figure. "Jaded vengeance looks good on you, Captain Femi."

She batted her lashes and moved to the right with slow, cautious steps. "You've heard of my antics?"

The Warlord mirrored her actions and shrugged a shoulder. "You've been plaguing my ships for years now. It's hard not to notice an irritation that won't dissipate. But I wonder... was it worth all of the lives you lost in the process? Do they weigh heavily upon you?"

"They lived their lives the way they desired. I miss them, but they ultimately chose their way of life," she replied evenly.

"What a refreshing answer. I can't tell you how tired I am of sniveling guilt mongers."

"I'm not sure you know what guilt is," she whispered, slinking closer to his right side. "You'd have to have a conscience."

She swung her ax, and he danced away, delight burning in his soulless eyes. Revulsion and rage filled her as she eyed the ancient creature masquerading as a man. Lilja had lived a very long time, but she was a pup compared to him.

Keep focused. Don't let your emotions get the best of you.

Her lips twitched with the smile that she smothered. He'd been stealing her people for as long as she could remember. To experiment on, to breed, to retrieve precious herbs from the sea. Even seemed appropriate that retribution come from the Sirenidae.

She eyed the vulnerable side he'd left open, but she didn't take the bait. He was an expert weapons master, and even if she was young compared to numerous years, she hadn't been born yesterday. She knew a trap when she saw one.

Lilja didn't delude herself into thinking it would be easy to vanquish her ancient enemy, but she'd be satisfied if she shed just a bit of his blood.

"I can see your mind working behind those ethereal eyes of yours. Will you not share your thoughts?"

"How I am going to rejoice over your dead carcass," she purred, her boots sinking in the mud beneath them.

He tsked and shook his head, the feathers in his hair quivering in the wind. "So violent and naughty. Come closer and put those hands to good use." He sank into a defensive crouch. "It's been so long since I killed a woman."

She bared her teeth. "I'll not die this day."

Then, she sprung.

FORTY-ONE

SAGE

STRAY HAIRS THAT HAD ESCAPED her braid were plastered against her face and neck.

Sage scrambled out of a warrior's path and attacked with everything she had.

Rafe had been the first one to notice the pattern.

The warriors never attacked to kill her. They were trying to capture her. And as terrifying as that idea was, it gave her an edge. There was no way she was going back to the Warlord.

She'd die first.

A roar pulled her attention to the right. Another Scythian cut his way toward her, atop an Aermian mount. Ice trickled down her spine at the expression on his face.

Pure loathing and hatred.

This man she wouldn't trust to capture her. He was out for blood.

And he had the high ground.

Her heart picked up its pace when she saw that she was alone. Rafe and Zachael were both locked in battles. She was on her own.

She braced her legs and readied herself.

Stars above, this would hurt.

He thundered closer, trampling all in his path, and her mind screamed at her to run, to find escape. But there was none.

Sage cursed when he dropped his sword right before he was upon her and grabbed at her breastplate. She sliced down with her own sword, only managing to scrape the bracer on his forearm. Her breath whooshed out of her as he yanked her off her feet and continued to ride. She dropped her sword and pried two of his fingers from her breastplate until they cracked.

The warrior yelled, but he didn't release her. Roughly, he tossed her over the saddle.

The horn of the saddle pressed relentlessly into her belly. Nausea rolled through her, but she managed to rip the necklace from her throat which hid a petite blade Lilja had gifted to her. Sage pressed a hand against the horse's sweat-streaked side and slammed the dagger into the warrior's calf.

The Scythian brute grabbed her by the hair and yanked her head up. She gritted her teeth and barely managed to keep ahold of her blade.

"Aermian whore!"

He lifted his hand as if to strike her, but she didn't care. Her eyes were focused on the soldier riding toward them like the devil was chasing him.

Garreth.

And he wasn't slowing as he approached.

Sage slid her hand back and sliced at the warrior's hand before pushing from the horse. Pain burned from her scalp as the Scythian tore hair from her head. She wrapped her arms around her head and crashed to the ground. Agony slammed into her as she tumbled, praying that she wouldn't be trampled by the beast.

She lifted her head, and the world blurred and tilted around her. Breathing seemed almost impossible. Through watering eyes, she forced herself to focus. It wasn't safe to lie about on the ground.

Garreth, wielding a long sword, had cut his way through the fight. Sage watched as the huge warrior closed in on her friend, hacking at him from horseback. She crawled to her knees and snatched a sword from a dead soldier.

Frantic to get to her friend, she used the sword as a cane and stood on wavering legs. The men crossed swords, and their mounts kicked at each other. Garreth slashed at the Scythian's saddle, and time held still for a second.

The warrior's saddle slipped, and for a moment, all she could see was

Garreth's intense expression before the brute tore her friend from the saddle with him. The warrior was on his back, his hand reaching for a dagger. Garreth lodged his blade through an opening in the warrior's armor and cut deep as the brute plunged his blade into her friend's chest.

Sage shrieked and clawed her way toward the two men who stared at each other, both in shock. Garreth glanced to her and gave her a small smile, a look of peace crossing his face.

"Everything is going to be okay," she chattered as she slid her way through the muck and mud to get to him. "We'll get you to Jacob, and you'll be healthy before you know it." Her voice wavered as she tried to keep her sobs at bay.

"I'm so sorry, Sage." He tipped his head back and roared in a voice that could be heard over the clash of weapons and shrieks of warriors. "For our future!" he bellowed.

Garreth wavered, his gaze blank, and his body tumbled onto his already slain enemy.

"No," she whispered. Sage didn't realize tears streamed down her cheeks as she stood on shaking legs. She swiped at her face and brandished her sword.

Zachael pressed past her and placed his fingers over Garreth's pulse. His grief-stricken face told her what she already knew.

Her friend was dead. Gone.

And he'd saved her life.

A broken sob tried to pass her lips, but she swallowed it back. If she started now, she wouldn't stop.

"We must move," she said dully, wrapping an arm around her bruised stomach. A brush of black fur tickled her cheek. She blinked into fierce feline eyes. "Where have you been?" she whispered.

Nali's ears twitched and she bumped Sage's chest with her head as if she was trying to offer comfort.

The weapons master closed Garreth's eyes and stood, tears tracking lines through his soot and dirt-covered face. They gazed at each other, not ashamed of their sadness, and then tucked it away.

Distractions would get them killed.

She studied the raging battle for allies. Fiilee and their riders soared through the sky, loosing arrows on the enemies below. Sage dropped her gaze and paused when wind whipped around her, clearing the smoke for one precious moment.

Her heart ceased to beat as she was given the perfect view of the Warlord and Lilja. Panic and terror washed away her pain and sadness, spurring her to pick up a shield and sprint farther into the battle. Zachael cursed and ran beside Sage, her constant protector and shield on her left, and Nali right side, snarling at any enemies that dared approach from the direction.

Lilja slammed sword to sword with the Warlord, her arms straining as he used his larger frame to upset her balance. Her braided white hair whipped around her in a silvery flash, much like lightning. Sage panted and pushed herself harder when he broke away and kicked her aunt in the knee. Lilja grunted but stayed upright, her face creasing in pain.

Sage stumbled but caught herself on shaking legs.

Only a little farther. You can make it.

The Warlord laughed and struck again. Her aunt held her own, but even Sage could see that her strength was waning. Sage slammed her shield against a warrior, and swung under his sword arm as she kept moving through the bedlam warring around her.

Lilja danced closer and slashed her sword toward the Warlord. He danced out of the way. The Warlord paused and touched a hand to his cheek. His smile turned dark as he held up his blood-covered hand.

Sage's stomach dropped. She'd seen that smile once before. When he slaughtered Rhys before her very eyes.

"No!" Sage screamed. *He wouldn't.*

The Warlord met her panicked gaze with devastation in his own. He was done playing with Lilja. The demon was about to make his appearance. He lifted his weapon and blurred into action. In the span of a heartbeat, he stepped behind her aunt.

"Please, Zane," Sage begged. "Don't!"

She tried to move faster, but it was like her feet were stuck in quicksand, each step too slow, too late.

Lilja thrashed, dropped her ax, and pulled a blade on the Warlord, but he was so much faster. Her aunt swung toward Sage, and her magenta eyes widened. Lilja gasped as a blossom of red bloomed across her chest. She coughed and shuddered. With care, the Warlord pulled Lilja into his chest and wrapped an arm around her, his lips resting near her ear as he observed Sage. For all intents and purposes, they looked to be two lovers.

"Please, no!" Sage screamed, plowing through the nightmare around her. A Scythian screamed as Nali pounced on the warrior creeping up on her, but Sage couldn't look away from Lilja.

Tears slid from her aunt's eyes, and she smiled softly at Sage. "It's alright," she mouthed. But Sage knew down to her very marrow that nothing would be okay.

Lilja's eyelids slid closed, and her body collapsed against the Warlord's form. Sage tore her eyes away from her aunt and regarded the devil himself. Her eyes filled with liquid heat, and the world turned to a haunting watercolor hue.

Lilja was gone.

Gone. Gone. Gone.

Sound faded like someone had shoved cotton into her ears. Her heart pounded in time with the war drums as she watched the monster who continued to destroy her, one broken piece at a time.

Time blurred as they studied each other, his gaze filled with remorse and triumph, hers with devastation and disbelief. She trembled as he lay Lilja gently on the ground and stood.

He lifted his arm and held his hand out to her.

Even though a battlefield still separated them, it felt like he stood just in front of her.

"Come to me," she read upon his lips. "End this."

End this.

A tremor worked through her body, and she took one choppy step forward. He would never stop. He'd burn the world around them to get to her. The longer she fought, the more deaths and blood would be on her hands.

A bellow broke through the fuzziness in her ears. She slowly turned to the left and gasped. Hayjen plowed through soldiers, Blair at his side, cutting a swath through the warriors. Her uncle's gaze was pinned to the Warlord.

The heartbreak on his face was enough for Sage's knees to weaken.

A hand curled around her arm. "That's far enough. It's time to retreat, Sage," Zachael said tightly.

She shook off his hand and turned back to the Warlord, then blinked at the distance she'd traveled toward him. It was if he had some sort of power that drew her to him. Sage straightened her spine and locked her knees.

He took one step closer and raised his hand higher. "Come to me," he commanded.

Nali hissed at her side and growled, the sound sinister enough to rise the hairs along Sage's arms.

Her fingers clenched around the sword in her right hand, and she stared blankly at his handsome face. There wasn't anything she could do to keep him from his ambitions. Even if she went to him, the bloodshed would continue. He was too broken, too warped.

Sacrificing herself would fix nothing.

It would only give him what he wanted.

She forced herself to remember the little one she'd buried. He would never stop. Sage lifted her chin and leveled her gaze at the demon destroying her kingdom and shoved the broken, abused little boy he used to be in a box deep inside her soul. Trauma didn't turn you into a monster, a person's choices did. He'd had ample opportunities to change, but he chose the dark path each time.

"Never," she said.

His eyes glittered in excitement. "Never is sooner than you think."

FORTY-TWO

SAGE

SHE CRASHED INTO THE TENT, her broken heart threatening to fall from her chest. She gasped, tears pouring down her filthy face.

Lilja.

Cut down in just a moment. There one second and gone the next.

Sage stumbled farther into the room, her blood-slicked boots catching on the rough-sewn rug. Pain bit into her hip as she bumped into the table holding the spirits. In a fit of rage, she swept her hands across the surface, scattering goblets and spirits across the dirt floor.

How could he take Lilja away from her?

Her fingers clutched at the heavy wooden table like the solid piece of furniture would keep her grounded. Salty tears burned down her wind-chapped face and lips, tasting like bitter loss and hopelessness.

"How could you?" she whispered brokenly.

Even after all this time, a small piece of her believed there was some part of him that wouldn't harm her so intentionally. But he proved her wrong once again.

Lilja's cry echoed in her mind, causing her to spin around and lean against the table for support. She slammed her eyes shut to keep the memory from replaying in her mind, but it stopped nothing.

A white braid.

A dark smile.

Blood.

Pained magenta eyes.

An ugly sob burst from her chest as the tent flap rustled. She opened her watery eyes and absorbed Tehl's shattered expression. He unlatched his dented chest plate and let it fall to the floor with a clatter. He brushed his sweaty hair from his face and opened his arms, striding toward her.

Sage pushed from the table and launched into his arms with a cry. He wrapped her in a crushing hug and sank to the ground, cradling her against his chest.

"I'm so sorry," he choked out.

Sage sobbed louder, her fingers clutching at his stained linen shirt.

"I'm so sorry, love," Tehl whispered, his voice hoarse. He swallowed hard. "I don't have any words."

Neither did she. There weren't words for the agony coursing through her veins. It felt like part of herself had been ripped apart.

"I hate him," she cried. "I hate him so much that I can't breathe."

"I know," Tehl crooned, running a hand down her tangled hair, and hugged her even closer, like he could keep all the cracking pieces of herself together by the ferocity of how he held her.

"He won't stop. He'll never stop," she wailed.

She pressed her face against his chest and held onto him with everything she possessed, her body trembling. How could she bear so much anguish?

Her husband pressed a kiss on the top of her head and rubbed his nose along her temple. "We'll find a way." His tone was so sure.

Sage shook her head, glanced up at his dear face, and released the shame she'd harbored.

"He beckoned me, and I almost went to him."

They were the softest words, but they felt like they rocked the room. Tehl's chest stilled under her hands as he held his breath, seeming momentarily stunned. His deep blue eyes scanned her tear-soaked face. He brushed the sweaty strands away from her wet cheeks.

"You didn't go to him."

"No," she stuttered. Had she made the right decision? Everything was so muddled.

Tenderness softened the sharp angles of his face as he leaned his dirt-smeared forehead against hers.

"You know I'm terrible with words." Frustration creased his brows, and his jaw clenched. "How I wish I wasn't. But know this, it's okay to break down. Just hold on to me, I'll be the light to guide you from the darkness, your sanctuary when it seems like you'll drown." He placed both of his hands on her cheeks. "Hold on to me, and I'll never let go."

Tears of gratefulness rushed from the corners of her eyes. How did she get so lucky? "I love you."

"I love you," Tehl said softly. "Always and forever."

For a man of few words, the ones he did express we're more than enough.

"Always and forever." She hiccupped. That was what Lilja and Hayden had. "How can she be gone? It's not right."

"Death is not something we can ever make sense of. Believe me, I've tried," he said solemnly.

She swiped at her face, hating her tears, but didn't try to stop them from flowing. Lilja deserved that. "I'm going to kill him." It was an oath.

Her husband said nothing but kissed each damp cheek.

She soaked in his support and wrapped his love around herself like a warm blanket on a winter day. She wasn't the only one suffering.

"How's Hayjen?" she questioned.

"I had him sedated."

Sage jolted and stared up at the prince in shock.

Tehl shrugged a shoulder, his eyes suspiciously shiny, before he glanced away. "He was going to get himself *killed*." His voice broke on the last word. "I couldn't lose two friends today."

Stars above, she was selfish and completely blind. She wiggled until she straddled his legs and wrapped her arms around his neck.

"I'm so sorry, Tehl."

He dropped his head and rested his face in the crook of her neck. Warm liquid dripped onto her throat and slid down her collarbone and into her shirt. Her husband's fingers knotted in her shirt and pulled her tighter against his body as he shook with silent tears.

They'd both lost someone they'd loved dearly today.

It was on the tip of her tongue to tell him what befell Garreth, but she couldn't. He protected her from so much, it was the least she could do. Tomorrow would come soon enough.

Sage sank her fingers into his hair, pressed her cheek against the side of his head, and cried with him.

At some point, they ended up cocooned in furs on their pallet. Tehl wrapped himself around her body, his lips resting against the back of her head.

She stared blankly at the side of the canvas tent as exhaustion threatened to swamp her.

"He's going to die."

"He is," Tehl answered simply.

She'd let herself mourn tonight, and tomorrow, she'd scheme to end the monster's life.

No one hurt her family and lived to tell the tale.

PART TWO
THE COURT'S FOOL

PROLOGUE

DARK PRINCES AND DEMON KINGS.

Lady Spies and Assassins.

Pirate Queens and Spymasters.

Beast Masters and Dragon Songs.

Freedom and Captivity.

Consorts and Warlords.

Pain and Pleasure.

Death and Life.

Fables and Myths.

Betrayal and Love.

Truths and Lies.

All belonged in fairytales.

All were Sage's reality.

ONE

MER

SIRENIDAE WEREN'T SUPPOSED TO DROWN.

Mer clutched at her throat, desperately trying to seal the wound that slashed through her gills. Blood leaked between her fingertips, creating a grisly halo of swirling water, debris, and blood.

She choked as warm liquid dripped down the back of her throat. Her stomach cramped and lurched as another casualty from above crashed through the surface of the unruly sea and began to sink.

A chill swept her as the faint notes of a haunting melody reached her ears. Mer cocked her head, and listened intently as the cacophony of the cannon fire and explosions of war raged above.

The hunt song.

Ice filled her veins at the clear words. Her magenta gaze darted to the soldier, struggling as he made his way back to the surface, his movements wild and unchecked. He was beckoning his own death.

Guilt pricked Mer as she pressed harder against her injury and kicked with all her strength toward the surface. The predators of the deep had no interest in the Sirenidae, but with copious amounts of blood, flesh, and prey struggling in the sea, it would be so easy for one of them to mistake her for something tasty.

Her legs ached as she fought her way toward the rippling surface. A deep-seated panic wrapped around her heart and squeezed when the muted, dull tones of death drew closer, and her waterlogged clothing began to drag her down once again.

Mer tore at her clothing, shedding the linen shirt, exposing her bare breasts and scratching herself in the process. Her feet tangled in her pants, and she found herself sinking deeper while she wrestled with the infernal garments.

Relief was a short-lived victory as she kicked free from her pants and caught a glimpse of a huge black fin.

Wicked hell. The leviathan. Time to move.

Abandoning her attempt to seal her gills, Mer clawed at the water and pushed toward the surface. She had to get out of the water. Now.

Her lungs burned and screamed for air. Motion flickered at the corner of her vision, and she locked gazes with the soldier just as a shape formed with oil-slicked skin from the inky darkness.

Don't show fear.

With the last of her strength, Mer smiled at the man and held her hand out, betraying none of the guilt she harbored for not warning him. Just as he reached a hand toward her, the leviathan struck. She pulled back her arm and slowly moved toward the surface as the predator tore apart his meal so not as to attract his attention. Her gaze never moved from the red haze.

Where there was one beastie, there were always others.

Mer gasped as her head broke through the barrier of one world and into another. Seawater spewed from her lungs as she coughed and hacked. Lightheaded, Mer tried to make sense of the anarchy lighting up the sky.

Cannons thundered, metal shrieked, and the cries of a thousand men pierced the air. Disoriented, she craned her neck, searching for her ship. Lightning cracked across the night sky, highlighting the skeletal forms of sinking ships, floating debris, and phantom-like fins slicing through the ocean. She sucked in a breath as she spotted her ship to the right.

The Dauntless.

She inhaled deeply and sank beneath the waves, fighting the urge to allow the change to overtake her body. With careful, steady strokes, she worked her way toward the Dauntless, very aware of the dangers lurking above and below.

Her strength lagged as the hull of the ship grew closer, and darkness hovered at the edge of her vision.

Only a few more paces.

Mer crashed through waves and into the open air, the frigid wind stabbing her skin like a thousand needles. It was on the tip of her tongue to call for help, but she caught herself. If by some miracle someone heard it, she would have put a target on them and herself.

The ladder is here somewhere. Don't be lazy.

She moved along the side of the shuddering ship and grinned when she spotted the ladder the pirates had left for her kind. With blood and saltwater slickening her hands, Mer attached herself to the ropes. Now for the hard part.

Between her silvery-white hair and unnaturally pale form, she'd become a target the moment she scaled the ship.

Be brave.

Mer inhaled deeply and sprang into action, pushing past the pain, nausea, and fear. Hand over hand, she hauled herself up the rope.

One, two, three, four—

Heat seared her bare back, and agony sliced through the back of her right thigh.

"Damn it," she yelled, clinging to the rope as cannons fired on the Dauntless. Her muscles trembled, and bile flooded her mouth. Mer panted and yanked herself a little higher. A high-pitched ringing filled her ears, then the world imploded.

Her body soared through the air, and she crashed into the midnight waves, knocking the breath from her lungs.

Like a falling leaf, her body began to sink. Mer blinked until her eyes adjusted to the sea. Stillness settled over her soul as she came face to face with a leviathan. This was how she'd die. A memory flashed through her mind.

"I will love you for as long as the tides rise and fall." Ream's magenta eyes filled with emotion.

Mer blinked tears back, feeling like she would burst with love. "I will love you and stand by your side as sure as the moon fills the night sky."

No one was present for their bonding ceremony. Her grandfather certainly wouldn't approve, but she didn't care. It was her life, and they'd waited long enough. War was on the horizon, and time was precious.

Seahorses and jellyfish danced around them in the current as Ream leaned close to place a sweet kiss on her lips.

"I love you."

Her fingers tangled in his loose, white hair. "As I love you." Would this be the last time they saw each other?

Ream cupped her cheeks and smiled at her. "This is our beginning, not our ending."

She nodded, fear flooding her for the first time. It was happening. The Scythians were really attacking, and she'd committed treason to give the people above support. There was no going back.

"You're everything to me." Mer leaned her forehead against his and stared into his eyes. "Once this is over…"

His soft smile grew. "We'll spend copious amounts of time lounging in bed and celebrating our marriage and victory."

Mer snapped out of the memory as the beast glided closer, rows of daggerlike teeth gleaming in the patches of moonlight that lit up what had become a watery grave. Mer gazed blankly at the monster and hummed a few notes of the kin song in a last-ditch attempt to dissuade him from eating her.

He paused and slowed his approach, circling to her left. Mer kicked her good arm and leg and kept him in her vision. If she was going to die, it wasn't going to be from a sneak attack.

Again, she hummed a few notes of the kin song, something she was taught as a child to help the beasts distinguish her as friend instead of food. Her heart galloped in her chest as he drifted closer.

I'm sorry, Ream. I love you.

The beast did not attack. He bumped her chest with his pointed snout. Mer blinked in shock. Her fear dissipated at the affectionate greeting.

With slow careful movements, she ran her hand along his snout and down his back to his dorsal fin. Mer slid her good leg over his spine and laid her cheek against his rubbery hide, her fingers curled around his fin. She clicked gently, using the last of her air to politely ask for a ride.

A smile touched her lips as the beast glided forward in response. Her eyes turned toward the writhing watercolor surface of the sea as dots crossed her vision and the world blurred around her.

Death wasn't beautiful, but at least she'd finally know peace from the weighty guilt she'd carried around for far too long.

"Breathe, damn it!"

Mer spewed seawater, her throat burning. She coughed, pain wracking her body as the change took over.

"That's it," Sam crooned. "You're alright."

It didn't feel like she was alright. It was as if someone ran a fire poker along her neck and then shoved it down her throat. "What?" she croaked, blurrily staring up at Sam's bruised face.

He held a finger to her lips and cradled her against his chest. "Don't speak. You have severe wounds to your gills and neck."

She swallowed, wincing at the pain, and the taste of metal coins in her mouth, even as her eyes drooped. Damnation, she was tired.

"Don't worry. Ream will be here soon. Just rest a little and you'll be able to fight another day."

Oblivion washed over her.

TWO ☉

SAGE

⇒○⟨⟨⟨⟨⟩○⟩⟨⟩⟩○⟨

BLOOD SPRAYED ACROSS HER FACE. Sage jerked her blade back as the warm, Scythian lifeblood ran down her hand and forearm. The warrior gurgled something unflattering and bared his scarlet-stained teeth before his lifeforce fled his body. His last breath froze in the winter wind for a moment before being swept away.

She stared at his body strewn across the first skiff of snow winter had to offer—his body an ugly reminder of what the days ahead of her held. Sage crouched and wiped her slick fingers on the warrior's leather jerkin, her eyes surveying the chaos and violence that rolled like the raging sea around her. She scarcely registered anything but her own heart beating frantically in her ears. Her lip curled as she spotted an Aermian soldier pinned down but fighting wildly.

Damn, Hayjen.

The frigid wind whipped across her face as she stood, and she caught Rafe's eye signaling her next move, then sprinted toward her uncle, leaving Rafe behind. He'd catch up soon enough.

A warrior spotted her and lunged into her path from the right, swinging a massive battle ax. Sage dropped onto one knee and slid in the muddy snow. Time seemed to slow as the ax cut through the space above her head, the slick soft sound of metal slicing the empty air. It was a sound she'd become familiar with; she'd managed to escape with her life for over three months, incurring more scars than she could count.

She twisted in the snow, then swung her sword backward, catching her enemy above his ankle, severing his Achilles tendon. The man bellowed and crashed to his knees. Pain echoed in every line of his face as promises of revenge fell from his chapped lips.

Sage pushed herself back to her feet and continued to run, the mud beneath her boots threatening her balance. She wobbled for a moment, then steeled herself, before she crashed into the melee surrounding Hayjen. Breaching the madness her uncle had waded into upped her chances of death—or worse, capture—a hundredfold. Her fingers squeezed the hilt of her sword, and she shoved the small prickle of terror away. It had been her constant companion for so long, her sense of fear had dwindled to almost nothing.

Except fear of the warlord, her mind whispered insidiously.

Her jaw clenched, and she narrowed her eyes on the Scythian about to cut Hayjen down from behind. The rush of her footsteps must have given her away, but not soon enough to change the outcome she had in mind for him. The warrior spun toward her, his black dreads flaring around him, as she sprinted up the remains of an old war machine and launched through the air. By the time she hit the ground, the warrior fell beside her. It wasn't guilt, or shame, or rage that fueled her—just a blank numbness and an animalistic need to save her family.

Hayjen was a madman. Scythian warriors came at him from every angle, but he never slowed, never faltered, even as some of their blows struck true.

A pair of hands seized Sage from behind and pulled her against an armored chest. "My lord will be so happy with my catch."

Doubtful. The Scythian warrior wouldn't take her anywhere.

He grabbed a fistful of her braid and yanked her head back. She hissed and spun toward the bulky warrior. He smiled at her, pulled her hair to his nose, and inhaled, his whole body shuddering in delight.

His mistake.

Sage lashed out with her dagger, cutting off six inches of her braid as well as two of his fingers. The warrior stared blankly at his bloody hand, then began to tremble. Now came the worst part: the berserker rage. It was a blessing and a curse. The rage made the warriors stupider, but they also became virtually unstoppable.

She geared up to take on the swelling monster of a man when Rafe attacked him from behind, dispatching the warrior without more than a flick of his wrist. He eyed Sage, seemingly scanning her for wounds, before slanting his gaze toward her uncle.

In unison, they attacked. It felt like coming home.

Every movement she made was calculated, and, no matter where she turned, Rafe was always at her back. Her arms shuddered with fatigue by the time they reached the center of the mayhem and closed ranks with Hayjen, who was covered in scarlet. His blood or their enemies', she didn't know.

"It's time to come in," she said, her voice rusty from disuse.

Hayjen shook his head, his ice-blue eyes searching the battlefield. No doubt for another hopeless fight. "I can fight."

"Just because you can, brother, doesn't mean you should. The next wave of soldiers are coming," Rafe rumbled softly.

Hayjen shook his head and took one step forward.

"You're done." Her whisper cut through the air like her blade, icy and hard as steel.

Hayjen froze and glanced over his shoulder, his face pinched in stubbornness. "No."

"No?" she repeated, some of her numbness burning away as her rage surfaced. "I will drag you back myself. Get your ass back to camp."

"Is that an order, my lady?" he sneered.

"It is."

Hayjen snarled but took no further steps to wage war.

Sage glanced at Rafe, palming her blades. "Are you ready?"

Rafe graced her with a chilling smile that set the hair at the nape of her neck on end. "Any time you are, little one."

White flurries dropped from the dark clouds above, swirling in a pagan dance as their trio finally set foot in their camp. Soldiers bustled from tent to tent or lounged in intimate groups. Pots and pans clanged together as the camp's cooks prepared dinner, while horses nickered in the background. It was almost cozy if one could blot out the sound of the Scythian war drums and stench of death that followed Sage wherever she went. Her right knee buckled, and she wobbled before regaining her balance. She'd pushed herself too hard during this last round, and that was dangerous.

"You need to rest," Rafe said softly. She lifted her eyes and followed his gaze to the fiilee mulling at the far edge of the camp.

Sage nodded and rolled her aching right shoulder. She wouldn't be surprised if her entire arm was one big, ugly bruise. The Scythians hit harder than anyone she'd ever sparred with before, with the exception of Rafe. But her friend never fought with the hatred and rage that the warlord's warriors were capable of. They were madmen on the battlefield.

Her mind flashed to the memory of Zachael cutting down a massive Scythian warrior. The weapons master kept on moving, so he didn't see the monster push his guts back into his belly and force himself to stand, his predatory gaze latching on to Zachael's back. Sage had, and she'd attacked. It took herself and three other men to bring him down.

A shiver worked through her, but she ignored it as Hayjen broke from their group. Her eyes narrowed on his back. *Oh no, he did not.*

"A word," she bit out.

Rafe's eyebrows rose, and he passed her a knowing look. "I'll meet with you and Tehl tonight."

Sage nodded curtly but never took her gaze from her uncle's stiff form. "Follow me if you'll please, Hayjen." The *or else* was implied.

She turned her back on him and stalked toward her tent. Soldiers scurried out of her way with polite nods or bows, and she swiped sweaty strands of hair from her face, not about to force a smile for the friendly faces she passed. Too much weighed on her shoulders. Too much anger teemed beneath the placid surface of her expression.

Her tent came into view, and she didn't slow as she pushed through the outer entrance flaps. It was blessedly empty for once. She stopped at the edge of the round table that dominated the space and studied the map and the small pieces representing their soldiers and the warlord's forces. Her chapped lips thinned at the sight.

Scythia was winning. Their own forces were like locusts. The enemy never faltered, but kept advancing.

Hayjen entered, his footsteps stopped behind her.

Sage closed her eyes and tried to grab the inner threads that barely leashed her temper. She faced Hayjen and leaned against the table, eyeing her uncle. He looked awful. His light blue eyes had sunken into his pale face that now had too many sharp angles. He'd lost weight. So much so, that, despite his burly build, he reminded her of a scarecrow. Ropy muscle wrapped around his bones in a grisly sight. For a moment, her anger dwindled, cooled by empathy.

"When was the last time you ate?" she asked.

Hayjen's brows wrinkled, confusion evident on his face. Clearly, he expected another line of conversation. She'd get to that.

He rubbed his bristly jaw, and her stomach lurched. He'd wiped his blood on the short strands in a macabre painting on his chin. It was enough to set her off. Bile flooded her mouth. She'd warred for hours today, and nothing made her want to heave more than seeing his blood smeared face.

"I can't remember."

His comment snapped her out of her thoughts, and she swallowed hard, her breathing shallow. "That's not good," she gasped.

Hayjen frowned. "Are you all right?"

Sage waved him away and shoved her nausea down. She wouldn't puke over something so stupid. "Funny, I was going to ask you that same question."

His lips firmed into a thin, white line. "Nothing to report."

She laughed, the sound sarcastic to her own ears. "Nothing to report. I find that interesting."

He shrugged. "It is what it is. Now, I'd like to take my leave."

Sage glared at him. "We haven't talked."

Another damn shrug from him. "Nothing to talk about."

Her eyes turned to slits, and she slapped a hand against the tabletop. The small figurines rattled. Then she stabbed a finger at her uncle. "This needs to stop," she growled. "You almost died today."

"Men are dying every day."

"But you're *trying* to die. That's different." Hayjen stiffened, and she took a closer step to him. "How do you think that would make Lilja feel?" Her aunt's name seemed heavy upon her tongue.

Her uncle jolted and glared at her. *"Don't."*

"Don't *what*? Say her name?"

"Just don't."

Sage forced herself to laugh. "You and I both know what she'd say if she saw the way you were fighting. You're being reckless. She'd hate that."

Hayjen trembled, and his fingers curled into fists. "Stop it."

"Stop telling the truth? Never, and neither would my aunt."

"Enough!" he bellowed.

Now they were getting somewhere. Anger, she could work with—numbness, not so much.

Sage circled closer to him. "What did you think you were doing out there? Other than courting a death wish? Did you think you could fight your way *through* the warriors?"

"No."

"Did you think you could reach the warlord on your own?"

His upper lip curled, and he bared his teeth. "You know nothing."

"You're wrong." Her throat tightened as the words tried to stick in her throat, but she forced them out anyway, despite how they tasted like ash. "I know pain. I know suffering. I know loss. And I miss her so damn much." Sage rubbed her chest, her gaze earnest. "I can't imagine what you are suffering—"

"No, you can't," he bit out.

"But I know she wouldn't want you to give up like this."

"How am I giving up?" Hayjen exploded, throwing his shaking hands in the air. "I am giving Aermia everything!"

"No, you're not! Aermia doesn't need soldiers who wade into the fray, heedless of their orders or the lives of the men around them."

"I've only risked myself."

"Wrong," Sage shouted. "You've left your battalion short a man and without the direction of someone who's skilled in battle. They're *boys* without experience, Hayjen, practically children."

"They'll die with or without me."

Sage jerked at his callous words. "Do you even hear yourself? She'd be so disappointed."

Holy rage lit in Hayjen's eyes, and he approached her quickly, stabbing a finger into her leather chest piece. "You're a child! How would you know what she wanted? You knew her for a year. I spent twenty years of my life with that woman. I knew her backward and forward, just as she knew me."

Sage slowly lifted her hands and clasped his fist between her fingers as he towered over her. "I know." He tried to pull away, but she tightened her grip. "I know you miss her."

Hayjen choked, a sob gurgling in the back of his throat. "There's not a word to express what I feel," he said raggedly.

Squeezing his hand, she let go and hugged him, her cheek flush with his metal chest piece. "When I came back from Scythia, I contemplated dying."

There they were. The ugly words that shamed her so much.

Sage continued on, "The pain seemed like too much, the emotions too bright and sharp, the nightmares too terrifying. What scared me the most was the isolation. I could be in a room full of people, and, yet, I'd feel alone, empty." She licked her dry lips. "I haven't suffered your tragedy, but I can recognize pain and self-destruction. You wear it like warpaint."

"He needs to die."

She pulled back and craned her neck to look her uncle square in the eye. "You and Lilja helped save my life when I couldn't even see why it was worth saving." Emotion swelled in her chest, and tears flooded her eyes. "You both gave me a life and showed me love that I could have never imagined, and I'll be damned if I don't fight for you like you fought for me."

Her words lingered between them, and a tear slipped down his cheek.

"You are not alone. You are loved." Her bottom lip wobbled. "I refuse to let him destroy your life. Don't let him win. Fight!"

Hayjen's whole body began to shake, and he snatched her up into a rib-crushing hug. She hugged him back fiercely, wishing she could imprint how much she cared for him into his skin. Hayjen silently wept, and Sage let her tears loose.

They grieved together.

Slowly, some of the tension in his body released, and he pulled back, his pale eyes overly bright in his haggard, dirty face.

"I don't feel alive," he whispered. "I feel like I died with her."

More tears flooded Sage's eyes. "You're not gone yet."

"I see so much of my sister in you." Hayjen smiled weakly and swiped at her cheek, her salty tears lingering on his fingertips. "And *Lilja*." Her name was said with reverence.

"We may not have shared blood, but she was blood. She changed my life."

"She *was* my life." Her uncle scraped a hand through his hair until the ends stood up, making him look so boyish, it caused her heart to clench. "I'll do better tomorrow."

"Tomorrow and all the other tomorrows after that."

"I'll try."

Sage knew he would. She had let him rampage for long enough. Today wasn't the end of his pain, not by any means, but it was a step in a healthier direction.

"Get some sleep."

Something haunted flashed through his eyes. "It's not so simple. The horror doesn't go away when sleeping."

Nightmares were miserable. "I'll have Mira mix something for you."

He nodded and lifted the tent flap, then glanced over his shoulder as he left. "Love you, baby girl."

Sage pinched the bridge of her nose to keep from crying. That was the first time he'd used the endearment since Lilja's death.

"I miss you," she whispered to the empty war chamber.

Wiping her face, she inhaled deeply to get ahold of herself, then latched onto her cold determination to destroy the warlord.

Sage flicked a glance at the map. Scythia might be winning, but the tide would turn.

If she had to cut every single warrior down herself to get to the bastard on the Scythian throne, she would. The warlord had claimed that he'd made her what she was today.

In that moment, he was right.

He'd twisted her into a killer.

In response, she'd forged herself into a weapon.

Sage pulled the necklace from her shirt and stared at the dainty poison ring hanging from the dull, silver chain. Lilja had given it to her before they rode out months ago. Sage toyed with it until the poisonous needle lunged from its hidden position, a translucent poison seeping from the tip.

It was only a matter of time until she destroyed the warlord.

THREE

TEHL

THE SCYTHIAN ARMY BUZZED WITH activity in the distance as the evening light waned. The clank of metal gears told Tehl his enemies were cranking the catapults. The warlord shouted orders to his men, and smaller machines rocketed forward as foreboding warriors rechecked their levers.

The first massive stone launched into the air from the distant war machines. The rock disappeared into the dark, swirling clouds and reappeared just before impact.

"Get down!" Tehl screamed as the crack of stone on stone filled his ears.

Another boulder launched into the air and came crashing down to the earth, the vibration under his feet causing him to stumble. The soldiers around him dove and created one massive shield to protect their battalion from the volley of arrows that followed in the wake of the stone.

Tehl lifted his head, ears ringing, and scanned the area around him. Soon, it would be too dark to see anything. They had to take out the war machines. Now.

Raziel crawled to his side, dirt smeared across his cheek. The Methian prince's amber eyes found the closest catapult. "Their machines are too powerful." He glanced at Tehl. "We need to take them out."

"My thoughts exactly." He pushed to his feet and eyed what was left of his battalion. "We're pressing forward. The goal is to destroy the closest ballista.

We'll have the cover of darkness."

Grave but determined expressions rippled through his battered battalion. His attention paused on a scrawny boy who didn't look to be over the age of fourteen. He was hardly a man. He shouldn't be on the battlefield. Damn Scythia. Damn the warlord. Aermian children were dying.

"What's your name?" he asked gruffly.

The boy's eyes widened, and he nervously shifted from foot to foot, his sword looking far too big in his small hands. "Benjamin, my lord."

"Benjamin, I need you to report to Lord Zachael and inform him of our movements. Can you do that?"

"Y-yes!"

"Get on with you and be aware of your surroundings."

The boy nodded and sprinted toward their camp in the distance, the bloody mayhem swallowing his small form. Tehl's heart squeezed. He prayed that the boy made it back safely.

"That was well done," Gav muttered from his right. "The boy wouldn't have survived. He would've only been another distraction for us."

"Heads up," Raziel bellowed.

They tightened their circle just as the machines flung burning, tar-coated stones into the teeming mass of soldiers. Several fell short, exploding into the ground in a spray of earth, carving craters into the wet dirt. The other stones bounced into the fray, the explosion sending men flying like sticks in a children's game.

Fire-covered stones arced through the air like shooting stars, then crashed back to the ground, flames licking over men before flickering out, leaving scorched earth and death in their path. The wind rose and cut across the chaos with a whistle in a swirl of dust, smoke, and debris.

"Let's move," Tehl commanded. "The smoke will give us cover." They only had a short window of time to reach the machine before the enemy saw them. "Pick up anything you think will make a good torch. We'll burn that monster to the ground."

He smiled darkly as he slipped his sword into his scabbard and plucked an abandoned Scythian spear from the ground. He ripped fabric from the nearby slain Scythian and wrapped it around the tip of the blade. The warlord had inadvertently given them the weapon they need to destroy his catapults.

Raziel growled and spat onto the dead warrior. "Unnatural trash."

Tehl ignored the prince's comment and cautiously made his way forward, his eyes watering from the grit. The sickly stench of smoke and death invaded his nostrils, and he tugged fabric up and over his nose and mouth. He never seemed to be able to wash the stench from his skin.

The rattle of chainmail caught his attention, and Gav lurched forward. Tehl clapped a hand on his cousin's shoulder and shook his head, even though his heart was heavy. They couldn't help the pinned down soldiers. "We cannot stop and fight every fight along the way," he told Gav softly, firmly keeping anger out of his voice and off his face. Not anger at his cousin, but at the fact they were leaving soldiers to their deaths as Scythian warriors cut a swathe through them like a plague of locusts.

Gav's jaw clenched, and he wrenched his shoulder out of Tehl's grip, but he kept silent.

"If you want to drop out and foolishly die, then do so without argument," Tehl said. "I will not stop you. The rest of us have a mission, a vital one. We cannot afford distractions, no matter how many dire circumstances we come across. The machines are the huge problem here. If we don't take them out, we can't win this war. Either leave or be silent."

No one moved. No one spoke. So be it.

Sweat dampened Tehl's palms as they crept closer to the huge catapult, fire raging across the dry meadow grasses. The beat of the Scythian war drums echoed in his ears, along with his racing pulse. With each step, they got closer to the ballista, and he expected a swarm of warriors to attack them. He searched the darkening night for any hint of threats. Tehl paused when a low shriek filled the air.

His eyes widened. "Arrows!"

The soldiers lifted their shields, once again creating a barrier from the threat in the sky. Tehl hefted his shield closer to his chest and clenched his right fingers tighter around his spear as they waited out the fall of armor piercing projectiles.

"Do you think they saw us?" a soldier grunted from behind as the barrage continued.

"No," Raziel muttered. "If they knew we were here, we'd be dead already."

Gav snickered, and Tehl shot an annoyed glance at him over his right shoulder.

His cousin sneered at him and held up his hands. "You know I can't help it."

Gav had always been prone to laughing when things got tense or awkward. It seemed, even in war, that hadn't changed.

The smoke cleared, just for a moment. Tehl turned back and strained to peer through the deepening evening light to get a clear look at their destination. All sound ceased, and his vision dipped. The warlord stood two hundred paces from the catapult, laughing like a madman as he slashed his way through Aermian soldiers.

Before he knew what he was doing, Tehl sprinted toward the devil.

FOUR

JASMINE

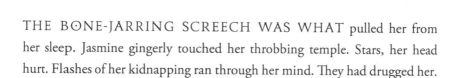

THE BONE-JARRING SCREECH WAS WHAT pulled her from her sleep. Jasmine gingerly touched her throbbing temple. Stars, her head hurt. Flashes of her kidnapping ran through her mind. They had drugged her. What else had they done?

She slowly blinked her eyes open and gritted her teeth as another explosion went off, rattling the window to her right and lighting up the curtain and the man currently staring outside.

Orion.

Her stomach bottomed out, and she jerked upright. The room seemed to roll, and Jas placed her left hand down to steady herself. The soft quilt and mattress beneath her palm caused panic to wrap around her chest. They'd placed her on a bed. Her hands shakily ran over her body. Her dress wasn't disturbed, and her body felt normal, but…nausea slammed into her, and she leaned over the bed to vomit.

Her eyes watered. Feeling fine didn't mean she was okay.

"Are you all right?" Orion asked, stepping toward her.

Jasmine thrust her hand out to stop him and scrambled backward until her spine met the corner. The leather of her thigh holster rubbed against her inner left leg. Sucking in a deep breath, she tried to calm herself. If they'd touched her, they would have discovered the blades and taken them from her. They'd left her unmolested, and she wasn't powerless.

Pain rippled across his handsome face, and he held his hands out in a placating manner. "I won't hurt you."

Traitorous tears sprang to her eyes. They already had. "Stay away from me," she whispered harshly.

Thunder rumbled, and a crack of lightning lit up the room, giving her a better sense of where she was. It was a small home with only one door and window. Across the room from where she sat held two chairs, a short table, and a screen which she assumed hid a chamber pot from the rest of the room. Her gaze darted back to the door. Only one escape, and Orion was guarding it.

He stared at her with remorse. "Do you need anything?"

Jasmine fought not to throw up again. He had always been the most caring and sensitive of her warriors. She froze. Not *her* warriors. Her *enemies*. Orion didn't get to care for her. "Where are we?" she croaked.

"Somewhere safe."

Safe. What a joke. Her arms curled around her belly as Orion dropped the curtain once again. His gaze paused on her bump, and a small smile lit up his face.

"You're a miracle." He said it with so much awe and what she refused to acknowledge as love.

Jas swallowed thickly, her throat aching and the cloying scent of the drug still stuck in her nose. "I need to go home." She scanned the simple room again. The daggers strapped to her thighs practically burned with the need to be used on the Scythian warrior. "Why am I here?"

"You know why," he whispered, his dark eyes soft. "We came for our family, for you and the babe."

Rage unlike anything she'd experienced burned through any residual fear she was harboring. *Family?* "I am nothing to you," she said coldly. "This babe is *mine*." And Sam's.

Orion winced and rubbed at his brow. "These aren't the best circumstances, but let me explain to you how much we—"

"No!" Jasmine sliced a hand through the air. "You get to say nothing to me. Let me go. I need to return to my children."

"They will join us soon."

Ice ran down her spine. "Excuse me?"

"We would never take you from your children, Jasmine. Mekhl and Phoenix are retrieving them."

Crippling horror settled over her. *No.* "Leave them alone! Don't you dare touch them!"

"We would never hurt you and yours." He moved back to the window and lifted the curtain, scanning whatever lay outside. "They'll be well protected."

Her plan of escape dissipated. There was no way she could leave without knowing if the warriors had Ethan and Jade.

Please, Vienna. Please have escaped. The older woman would take care of her children.

A tear dripped down her cheek. "You can't keep us. Please let us go."

"Jasmine," Orion whispered. "I cannot. You're breaking my heart."

"I'm begging you. I'm happy in Aermia. You need to let us go and forget this plan." She hiccupped and prayed he would falter. "Are you under command?" She edged toward him. "There's protection for you in Aermia. We can live there." A lie. "Please, don't take me back."

"You don't know what you're saying," Orion hissed, his gaze searching the room like there was someone listening to the conversation. "Be silent before we all die."

Jasmine placed her feet on the floor and began to tremble. "If you won't let me go, I promise I'll hurt myself and the babe." The words were a bitter lie on her tongue. She'd never hurt the babe, but he didn't know that. Orion faced her, his expression blank. "I know what you did," she choked out. "You know it was wrong."

He took a hesitant step in her direction. "You don't know what you're saying. I read books on breeding women. Your moods get out of control."

A bitter laugh escaped her, and she pinned him with a hard glare. "Try me. Do you really think I could ever love a child from a monster? A child of rape?" she shouted, shaking. The hateful words weren't true. She loved her babe without limit already. There was nothing she wouldn't do. But her words struck the intended chord. Orion looked like he was about to break into a thousand pieces.

"I wish you hadn't said that," he murmured, sorrow creeping into his expression.

That was her only warning before he attacked, pinning her to the bed. Jasmine screamed once before he placed a piece of sweet-scented linen over her nose and mouth. She bit his hand. Her struggles slowed, and her eyelids grew heavy, even as she begged her body not to give up the fight.

"I'm sorry," Orion whispered, his soft brown eyes watching her. "We can't take a chance of you hurting yourself or the babe. You're too precious." He drew a calloused finger softly down her cheek. "Sleep well, love."

That was the last she heard before darkness washed over her.

FÍVE

SAM

"I DON'T CARE HOW YOU do it, but get them out of the city with minimum losses," the king commanded.

Sam brushed his dirty hair from his face and added, "It's a ploy to draw our attention from the bay. We can't allow them to get any closer. Our port is everything."

The king nodded to the captains of his fleet. "Dismissed."

Their men filed out, and Sam ran a hand down his face.

"Son, you look tired. You should get some sleep."

Sam nodded, not really seeing anything. "It's just beginning, and I'm exhausted already." He cast a glance east. "And the sun will rise within the hour."

His father moved around the makeshift table in their training yard and slapped him on the back. "It will only get harder from here. Go and spend time with your family."

"My lord?"

Both royals turned to face the Elite striding their way. Xav sketched a short bow before stepping closer. "I have an old woman trying to enter the palace gate."

"The order has been given that no one but military personnel is to enter," Sam said slowly.

Xav nodded. "Yes. We've followed protocol, but she keeps insisting to see you."

"Me?" Sam asked, his mind whirling. Was it one of his spies? He'd sent Marilyn out this morning. Did she have news already? If so, why was she coming through the gate? "Take me to her."

Sam followed the Elite across the training yard and to the heavily-fortified stone wall surrounding the palace. Xav waved a hand at the guard stationed at the entrance. The portcullis rose, and they exited. Sam scanned the darkened streets, his attention landing on a stern-looking older woman speaking heatedly to two soldiers. Her curly gray hair was a fuzzy halo around her wrinkled face. He'd seen her before. A little face peeked around her dirt-streaked skirts, and the world disappeared from beneath him.

Ethan.

Terror rushed through his veins. He launched forward, startling Xav. The older woman met his gaze as he barreled down on the group. Ethan released the woman's skirts and launched into his arms. Sam clutched the little boy to his chest as Jade followed suit. He dropped to his knees, holding both children to his chest, his heart thundering.

"Mama's gone," Jade sobbed.

Sam held them close as the twins cried, their little faces pressed into his shirt. A stillness settled over him as Jade's words finally registered.

Mama's gone.

He pinned his icy gaze on the older woman. "Where is she?"

The older woman didn't flinch. "The apothecary was attacked. We almost made it, but Scythians broke in. Jasmine sent the children with me."

Their enemy took Jasmine. They took *his* wife and babe. For a moment, he thought he'd suffocate.

"Papa, you're crushing me," Ethan wheezed.

Sam forced himself to loosen his grip on the twins. Time was short. The longer they dallied, the less chance they had to find Jasmine. A hand settled on his shoulder, and he turned to meet his father's eyes.

The king held his arms out. "Let me take one of them."

Ethan went easily into his grandad's arms, and Sam stood, Jade clinging to him.

"You come with me," Sam barked at the old woman. "I need you to tell me everything you saw. Follow me."

For the first time in his life, he was on the edge of breaking apart. He wanted to destroy something and kill. Whoever had taken his wife would pay. A dark smile curled his lips.

Blood would spill.

SIX

SAGE

SAGE USED TO THINK THAT *bloodstained hands* was a metaphorical saying. War had taught her otherwise.

The water turned pink and cooled, but still she scrubbed on, determined to clean the blood from her hands. Her skin ached as she pressed the rough bristles of the crude brush deeper into the grooves of her fingers and palms. Sage hissed when the cuticle of her thumb ripped, and she slammed the brush down, panting heavily. Her chafed fingers flexed against the small table while her gaze locked on the soiled water.

If only it was that easy to wash away pain.

Her conversation with Hayjen had left her feeling dull and out of touch with the world. It was so tempting to sink into the little black box in the back of her mind that offered numbness and shelter from the pain and loss their camp suffered each day.

Soldiers were dragged into camp—some dead, some alive—and, statistically, it was only a matter of time before someone close to her died on the battlefield again. She hung her head as Garreth and Lilja flickered through her mind. Tehl could be dying among the fallen right now—

"Stop it," she whispered. "He's all right."

Sage squeezed her eyes shut and attempted to calm her racing pulse. There was no use borrowing trouble. If that scenario happened, she'd cross that bridge then.

Inhaling deeply, she opened her eyes and straightened, her blurry gaze resting on their unmade bed when she spun around. Crawling in the bed and passing out sounded wonderful, but Sage knew what would happen. Even if she got into bed, sleep wouldn't come until Tehl arrived. Staring at the ceiling, imagining every peril her husband could be going through, wouldn't help anyone.

Sage exited their quarters and passed through the war room area of the tent. She paused at the tent flap, and doubled back for her dark green cloak. The times for strolling outside without a fur or wool covering from head to toe were over.

Clasping the cloak around her throat, Sage lifted the hood and slipped through the tent flap. Stars above, it was bloody cold. Winters near the mountains and plains were harsher than she'd ever experienced. An Elite stood to her left, and a Methian warrior to her right—both silent, watchful.

A pang seized her chest. It was at times like this when she missed Garreth the most. He'd been with her since she'd entered the palace. Sage scarcely remembered a time when he wasn't quietly following her, his footsteps almost silent. Tehl didn't say much, but she knew he mourned his friend.

"A walk, my lady?" Domin, the Methian soldier, asked softly.

They'd learned her nocturnal habits pretty quickly, although her radius for travel now stayed firmly inside the camp due to a raid that had gotten too close for comfort one week prior.

"No, tonight I seek the infirmary."

Sage strode forward, this time more aware of her surroundings. Fires scattered throughout the camp, casting warm light against the canvas tents. She smiled and murmured words of encouragement as she weaved her way toward the sick tent. She paused just outside the infirmary, her nose wrinkling at the smell wafting from it.

The place reeked of despair and death.

Puffing out a breath, Sage forced a smile on her face and stepped inside. A wall of heat slammed into her, and sweat beaded on her forehead immediately. She pulled her hood from her head and moved to the first bed on her right. The soldier rolled his bandaged head to the side and smiled, revealing his missing teeth. Reslin.

"Back so soon, Princess?" Reslin asked and gestured with his burned stump of an arm.

"With company like yours, how could I keep away?" she joked, all the while feeling like she was going to throw up. It wasn't the injuries that bothered her non-existent sensibilities, but the fact that she couldn't fix them, she couldn't take away their pain, that they'd suffer for years after the war ended. Her smile waned, and she jerked her chin toward his arm. "How are you doing, really?"

Reslin teetered his head back and forth. "The pain is gruesome, but I'm one of the lucky ones." His expression cooled. "I couldn't keep count of how many they brought in today, but I know six were taken out."

Sage nodded, her heart turning to lead. Six more dead. Mira was probably destroyed. "How is Mira?"

Reslin shook his head. "She's pale, and I haven't seen her eat all day."

"Thank you."

Sage smiled at him one last time and scanned the gigantic tent for Mira. She caught a glimpse of the healer sponging the forehead of a Methian warrior. There wasn't any way Sage would be prying her away for a meal anytime soon.

"Will you have someone bring some bread, cheese, and wine in?" she whispered discreetly to the Elite on her left. He nodded and ducked out of the tent.

Sage continued down the line of beds, speaking with every soldier. She halted next to the last bed and scowled at its occupant.

Blaise.

The Scythian woman scowled back at her and leaned against the tent wall. "Don't give me that look."

"I'm allowed to glare at you if I want to. You should be resting." Sage waved a hand at the pile of weapons resting in the center of the cot.

"I *am* resting. You don't see me walking about." Blaise stabbed her blade at the cot. "Sit."

Sage rolled her eyes and sat, mindful of her friend's leg, and picked up a stone and blade. The Methian warrior took his place near her side. She flicked a glance in his direction and watched as he scanned the room for threats. Sage turned back to sharpening the blade and both women fell into a comfortable silence, the slick sound of metal being sharpened.

"You need to prepare yourself," Blaise said in a low voice.

Sage paused and glanced at her friend. "For what?"

The woman held her gaze. "For the next phase."

"We're prepared as much as we possibly can be."

"When's the last time you saw him?"

There wasn't any doubt who the *him* referred to. Sage wet the blade in the bucket near her feet and started working the blade over the stone once again. "It's been a while."

"He's planning something."

She scoffed. "He's always planning something. He's always three steps ahead of us."

"He's had centuries to plan this."

Sage shivered at the reminder of what kind of creature they were facing. "We'll handle whatever he throws at us." Little blue toes flashed through her mind, and her jaw set. "He's tried to break us before."

Blaise readjusted her leg and rubbed at her knee, her brow furrowed.

Sage watched her then asked, "How is it healing?"

Her friend shrugged. "It's almost there. I'll be able to go into battle on the morrow, I should think."

Sage jerked and narrowed her eyes at Blaise. "You're not going onto that battlefield tomorrow, even if you have the advantage of speedy healing."

"That's exactly *why* I should be out there. I can heal faster than everyone else."

Sage wiped the blade against the blanket and placed it next to the other finished blades. "Do you know how many times you've been hurt?"

"Only a handful of times."

She glared harder at Blaise and held up her right hand, fingers spread. "Five times. Five times you've almost died. As soon as you enter the battle, you become the target. I've seen the way the warriors go after you. They aren't just out for blood. They're out for your pain."

Blaise held her gaze. "I'm a traitor."

"So you deserve to be raped and killed?" she hissed. Her stomach turned as she remembered Blaise's torn clothing and the pattern that had been carved into her skin.

Her friend blinked and stared at her lap. "In our culture, betrayal is the ultimate sin." She lifted her dark brown eyes and squarely met Sage's gaze. "Betrayal is disgraceful and begets disgrace."

"What they've been attempting isn't disgrace, it's barbaric. Animals don't even treat each other in that way."

Blaise shrugged. "I knew what the consequences would be when I helped you escape. I don't regret my choices."

"I regret a lot of things," Sage admitted.

"Regret helps no one. Move forward."

"I'm trying." She sighed and stood, her body aching.

"You're pushing too hard," Blaise said, her gaze running over Sage's form. "You'll get yourself killed if you don't slow down."

A wry smile touched her mouth. "That's a little like the pot calling the kettle black, isn't it?"

Her friend arched a midnight brow. "I'm Scythian," she said haughtily, as if that explained everything.

Sage shook her head, muttering, "You can take the princess from the palace, but you can't take the—"

Blaise growled and stabbed a short sword toward Mira's bustling form. "Go check the healer. She's pushing herself as hard as you, I suspect. Every day, I'm amazed she's still standing."

Worry filled Sage as she approached Mira, who had moved to the center of the massive tent and washed her hands vigorously with a strong-smelling soap. Sage snatched the pitcher up before Mira could reach for it and poured the warm water over the healer's hands.

"Thank you," Mira mumbled.

"You're welcome." She eyed the tent, spotting only two other healers. "Where's Jacob?"

"He went home today. They need a healer of his talent in the capital."

The capital: Sanee. Stars above, she was so glad they hadn't pulled their soldiers from the fleet before war broke out. If they had left them... Sanee would have been captured.

"It's come to a standstill from what I've heard."

Mira wiped her wet hands on a clean towel, blew the loose blonde strands from her face, and then smiled weakly. "Father doesn't like to be far from the king."

"It's good that Sam and Marq have Jacob as a support." Sage gave her friend a concerned look. "You need a break."

Mira shook her head. "No time. Bandages need to be changed, wounds cleaned, poultices brewed, fevers managed, and then the surgeries…"

Sage shivered. She'd already assisted in two amputations, and the sounds the men made would forever haunt her.

One of the Elite entered the tent with a loaf of bread and a bottle of wine tucked under his arm and a hunk of cheese in his hand.

"At least eat," Sage implored.

"I'm not very hungry."

She wouldn't be either if she had been dealing with pus, blood, and bone all day. "If you don't care for yourself…" The Elite paused by their sides, and Sage took the cheese and wine from him. "You can't care for anyone else."

Mira eyed the cheese tiredly. Then, she plopped onto the dirt floor and held her hand out. "Hand it over."

Sage broke off a large hunk of cheese and passed the bottle down to Mira before gesturing for the bread. The healer took a bite of cheese and then drank straight from the bottle. After a few swallows, Sage tactfully stepped in and took the wine. She tore off a piece of the rough wheat bread and handed it to her friend. Mira ate mechanically, like she tasted nothing.

Handing the rest of the bread back to the Elite, Sage knelt and pulled Mira into a hug. Her friend pressed her forehead against Sage's shoulder and shuddered.

"Six today. Six."

"I know," she whispered.

"I thought I was prepared for this." Mira's voice hitched. "I wasn't, I'm not—*six!*"

"You did your best," Sage crooned softly.

The healer pulled back, her blue eyes sad. "But it wasn't enough."

"It's enough that you're here."

Mira pasted on a bright smile. "And I'm not going anywhere."

"I know." Sage squeezed her once more and then stood, taking the leftover food from the Elite. She placed it in a clean towel and set it on the counter near some lavender. "Eat this."

"I'll do my best." Mira stood and kissed her cheek. "Be safe."

Sage nodded, then continued her round along the next wall of soldiers. By the time she reached the exit to the camp infirmary, her eyes felt like they had sand in them, and her bones threatened to collapse.

Tehl had to be back by now.

Once again, she lifted her hood and strode out into the freezing night air, her cloak stirring a flurry of snowflakes around her boots. The walk back to their tent seemed to take no time at all. She stood outside the entrance and stared at the tent flap. Anxious voices murmured just inside.

Her heart clenched, and fear started to rise when she didn't hear her husband's voice among them.

Be brave.

Sage prepared herself for the worst and stepped inside.

SEVEN

SAGE

ALL VOICES CEASED AS SHE stepped into the tent. Four pairs of weary, concerned eyes stared at her with too much sympathy. Tehl wasn't among them.

The air was sucked from her lungs, and Sage couldn't get a decent breath. *No.*

She began to tremble but forced the words from between her numb lips. "Does the crown prince still live?" she rasped, her voice almost failing.

Queen Osir gasped and strode from the war table, her amber eyes wide. "He's fine, little one. A few small injuries but fine." Sage's whole body sagged, and the Methian queen pulled her into a hug. "You okay?"

Sage nodded and pulled back. She pushed the loose hair from her face with a shaky hand and smiled weakly. "How goes it?"

Zachael eyed her and then the war map. "We're just discussing the movements of the Scythian army."

She squeezed Queen Osir's arm and moved around her to get a better look at the map. The Aermian and Methian soldiers were slowly being pushed backward, and the Scythians were taking over the south and the north. They couldn't allow the warriors to gain any more ground. If they weren't careful, their enemies would have them back up against the mountains.

Her gaze was drawn to the river that cut across the plains to the south.

"They won't cross the river," she mused out loud. "They'd be bottled up."

Raziel hummed in agreement, the Methian prince looking more like a ragged pirate than royalty. "It would be the more difficult path. Logically, they should attack from the north."

Gav snorted, his lavender eyes filled with humor. "We all know how *logical* Scythia is."

Sage shot him a confused look. Why was he so chipper?

Raziel rolled his eyes. "More like crazy."

Zachael crossed his arms over his chest. "Crazy as the warlord might be, he's a tactical genius."

Gav's humor cooled, and something dark slithered through his eyes. "Some of our men were able to destroy one of his war machines today." A pause. "It wasn't easy."

Raziel scoffed. "It was a nightmare."

Sage leaned a hip on the table, her eyes feeling like they were filled with sand. Zachael squeezed her shoulder and moved to collect his cloak.

"Well done. The sooner we destroy every machine, the sooner the queen can launch the aerial attack and we can pull the fiilee from the coast." He tossed his cloak over his shoulders. "Our soldiers have their commands." He pulled his hood over his dark silver-streaked hair and held out his arm for the queen. "Tomorrow, we shall reconvene. My lady."

Sage nodded tiredly and didn't comment on how easily the queen took the weapons master's arm and disappeared out of the tent. Interesting. Maybe love had wiggled itself in, despite all the death they were exposed to.

Exhausted, Sage dragged her attention from the tent flap as Gav wove around the table and hugged her. She sank into his warmth and leaned her cheek against her friend's shoulder.

"I'll see you both in the morning," Raziel whispered before he slipped from the room.

She shuddered and hugged Gav tighter. "I thought Tehl had—"

Gav placed a hand on the back of her head and stroked what was left of her braid. "I know, I know. When I saw the look on your face..." He sucked in a sharp breath. "The fact is that he's okay."

"You were gone too long. How bad is it?" she murmured.

"A wound to the arm but not with a poisoned blade, thank the stars. He needs to be stitched."

"Thank you." She stepped back and studied her friend. His black hair had grown longer, and he'd taken to braiding the sides back in the Methian style. He used to carry an air of approachability. He was harder now. They all were, she supposed.

Gav kissed her forehead. "Get some sleep. Morning will be here soon."

"You too." She rubbed her forehead as he collected his brown cloak from the chair in the corner of the tent. If she wasn't mistaken, he smelled suspiciously like whiskey. Today must have been a close call. He rarely drank. Her mind wandered to the long list of things she needed to take care of tomorrow. "The messenger is leaving with info for Sam tomorrow. If you have a correspondence for Isa, leave it here. I'll make sure it gets to her."

He smiled and pulled a letter from the breast pocket of his cloak. "I'm one step ahead of you."

Sage padded over to him and took the letter from his calloused fingers. "I know you miss her."

Gav frowned. "It's bizarre not to have her underfoot." His expression cleared. "Thank you and goodnight."

She watched him exit and rubbed her thumb across the rough parchment of his letter, then turned for their chambers. Tehl would come back when he'd finished with the healers. Hopefully, she would be able to keep her eyes open until then.

She lifted the flap and jerked to a stop at the sight that greeted her. Tehl was sprawled across their bed in his armor, sound asleep. Nali had wedged herself against his side and draped over the foot of the bed and onto the roughly woven rug that protected them from some of the chill of the frozen ground. The feline cracked a golden eye and rumbled a lazy hello. The fist around Sage's lungs loosened at the cozy sight.

Tehl was okay. Not dead on the battlefield somewhere.

"I wondered where you got off to," she whispered to Nali as she stepped fully inside. The feline huffed a contented breath and nuzzled the side of Tehl's neck. The man didn't even stir. She probably didn't want to know what had put him in such a state.

Sage toed off her boots and skirted around the end of the bed. She eyed his filthy armor and the bedding. It would need to be shaken out before they actually went to bed for the night.

"Tehl," she murmured.

Nothing.

"Tehl." Still nothing.

Biting her lip, she stared at the pillow and then his face. All she wanted to do was lie by his side and wake him gently, but that wasn't in the cards for them. He'd almost strangled her three weeks prior when he came out of whatever horror had plagued him while he slept.

"You might want to move, Nali." The leren didn't budge. "Your mistake."

Sage plucked the pillow from the head of the bed and, before she could feel guilty about it, smacked Tehl in the face with the feather pillow and lunged backward. Tehl exploded from the bed, gasping, weapons in both hands. Nali growled at being disturbed and slinked off the bed and out of the room.

Tehl's sapphire gaze followed the feline and then scanned the tent, settling on her. Recognition dawned, and he lowered his blades.

"Sage," he said with a half-smile. "The pillow again, love?"

Her heart clenched at the devastating smile on his face, and she forced herself to shrug. "I couldn't wake you."

"You didn't take my weapons?"

"You always hide them. I never know what you have stashed away." Her voice cracked.

His smile melted, and he squinted. "What's wrong?"

She swallowed. "Nothing is wrong. I'm fine." She wasn't at all fine. He'd come close to death; she knew it in her heart.

Tehl scoffed and shook his head, his midnight hair whipping around his face. "Not that word. Tell me what has you so upset."

Her bottom lip trembled and betrayed her as heat filled her eyes. She launched herself across the bed and into his arms. He'd dropped his blades when he'd stood, and now his arms snaked around her as she trembled.

"I thought you died," she choked out.

Tehl leaned back and cupped her face between his palms. "Whatever gave you that idea?"

Tears blurred her eyes. "You were late in arriving and then, when I entered the war room, you weren't among the war council. They all looked at me with so much pity. I just assumed…" An embarrassing hiccup escaped her.

He yanked her back into his arms and squeezed her against his chest. The metal from his breastplate dug painfully into her ribs, but she didn't care. He was real, alive, and whole. Sage ran her hands down his biceps, and he inhaled sharply.

Sage jerked back and eyed him with irritation. "You haven't seen Mira?" she demanded.

"I intended to. But I sat down just for a moment to take off my armor. Nali was purring, and I guess I fell asleep." He smiled sheepishly.

Men.

Rolling her eyes, she lifted her arms to the latches of his chest piece and began to unbuckle the right side. "Blaming it on the cat?"

Tehl grinned in amusement. "The cat? If that man-eating nuisance was here, I'm sure she'd be highly offended."

"Hmmm."

She finished up with the right side and moved to the left, her adept fingers making quick work of it. Sage grunted as she pulled the heavy breastplate away and leaned it against the small stationary washtub to the left of the bed.

"I don't know how you lug that around all day." She thumped her molded leather chest piece. "This is so much lighter."

"True," he said, running a knuckle across her left cheek. "But you're also a much smaller target. Harder to hit. Chances of an arrow finding your chest are slim."

She scoffed, helping him out of his pauldrons and depositing them on the floor. "I could make one stronger that was half the weight. Weight makes you slower. Slower means death."

Blood soaked the sleeve of his left bicep, and she winced when she saw the angry cut peeking out. "Do you want to go to the infirmary?"

Tehl released her and reached for the small, wooden box they kept at the end of the bed for occasions such as this.

He lifted the lid and pulled whiskey, bandages, and a needle and thread from the box. "Too tired." He held out the needle and thread to her. "Will you do the honors, wife?"

Sage took the needle from his fingers and gestured to their bed. "You know my stitches aren't as straight as Mira's."

Tehl tossed the supplies onto the bed and sat so he faced her. "Don't I know it."

She hid her smile.

"Help me with my shirt?"

He bent forward so she could help him pull the soiled linen shirt over his head. Blood rushed to her cheeks as she got an eyeful of naked chest and the small trail of dark hair that disappeared beneath the edge of his leather trousers.

Dirty and bloody.

Still, he was one of the most attractive men she'd ever laid eyes upon.

A goofy grin lifted her husband's lips, and his hands crept to her hips as he scooted to the side of the bed and tugged her closer to the mattress.

Sage arched a brow at him, knowing exactly what his game was.

"Not the time. We need to clean and stitch your wound."

With gentle pressure, he guided her into the space between his parted legs and rested his cheek against her lower belly. "You never know when the last time could be."

True.

She ran her fingers through his inky hair, and he tipped his head back so he could meet her eyes. It was moments like these that affected her the most. Quiet, humble moments when they held each other with love and affection. No outside world to interrupt them. She bent and placed her lips against his in a sweet kiss. Tehl's eyes closed as she pulled away, and she sat next to him, eyeing his cut. It was around three inches long and not terribly deep. More of an irritation than anything.

"Pass me the whiskey," she said briskly. They might as well get the worst of it over.

Tehl uncorked the spirits and took a heavy swig before handing the bottle over to her.

"I love you."

Sage startled and looked at him with surprise. Tehl showed love, affection, and devotion in his everyday activities. Rarely did he utter them out loud.

Bloody hell, it must have been a really close call. Her pulse sped up, and she forced herself to take a calming breath. It wouldn't help anyone to think about what might have been.

"As I love you," she murmured back. Her gaze dropped to the whiskey. "But you might not by the time I'm finished with you."

EIGHT

TEHL

TEHL SHIFTED TO HIS SIDE so he could stare down at his wife's face, the lone flickering lantern highlighting the contours of her skin. Sage's eyes flickered behind her eyelids, but she didn't otherwise stir. Even with dirt smeared on her cheek and a bruise forming around her left eye from a fight two days prior, she was still the most beautiful thing he'd ever seen.

She whimpered softly, and he reached out his right hand, gently stroking the downy hair at her temple. The furrows between her brows softened and disappeared. She snuggled closer to him and sighed deeply, her breath heating the bare skin of his chest. It was moments like this that he cherished the most. The unguarded way she sought his comfort even in slumber gave him a deep sense of satisfaction.

He ran his hand down her arm and carefully slipped his arm around her waist, gently tugging her closer into the shelter of his body, his wound burning. It had taken a lot to get them to this point, but even love couldn't fix everything. There had been some nights her nightmares were so vivid she'd attacked him. Her eyes had been open, but her mind was lost to the horrors she'd suffered in Scythia. His jaw tightened. The warlord had damaged her in a way Tehl couldn't fix. An invisible wound buried so deep in her heart that he doubted it would ever fully heal.

Tehl had promised that he would never hurt Sage to the best of his ability.

Today, he broke that promise.

The look on her face when he'd woken had absolutely gutted him.

Being pinned down hadn't terrified him, nor had the close call with destroying the war machine. It wasn't until they'd escaped and made it back to camp when the terror had set in, almost knocking him to his knees.

If Gav and Raziel hadn't taken care of the situation, Aermia would be down a prince and his wife would be a widow.

Guilt churned in his gut. The thought of death didn't scare him as much as the idea of leaving his wife behind with no one to protect her.

His lips twitched into the ghost of a smile. She would probably stab him for even thinking she needed someone to protect her. He traced her left, arching eyebrow with his fingertip and then ran it down the smooth bridge of her nose. A small part of him missed the little bump she used to have—a training badge of honor—one that had been erased by the demon ruling Scythia.

His lip curled.

The rage he hid from Sage sparked, and he had to release a slow breath to contain the urge to scream. It was a difficult thing to control; one's emotions. Over the years, he'd thought he'd mastered the art.

Sage taught him differently.

He thought he'd known anger when she disappeared, when the warlord sent his letter, or at the mockery of a peace treaty. But it all paled in comparison to the fury he experienced when he'd watched Mira pry the metal thorns from his wife's neck. The devil had collared her—*collared her*—like an animal.

His gaze dropped to the silvery scars that circled her neck. She'd left Aermia bearing all the scars of her youth—accidents, fights, victories—only to return home with her past erased from her skin, and the warlord's actions imprinted there forever.

Tehl glared at the scars. Stars, he hated them. He'd die before he'd ever see her chained like that again. And he'd be damned before he let the warlord win the war and enslave the people of Aermia.

Sage shivered, and he pulled their covers over her bare shoulder.

He lay his head down and stared at the wall of their tent, his gaze blanking.

Today, he'd almost died.

Nothing in life was guaranteed, but today, he'd been too reckless. That recklessness had almost cost him his life.

He glanced back at Sage's face.

He'd let his emotions get the best of him. It was time to get them under control.

Tehl eased himself forward and pressed a soft kiss to Sage's forehead, his eyes drooping.

It was too late for midnight musings.

Tomorrow was coming all too soon, and, on the heels of it, more death.

NINE

SAGE

SAGE PUSHED HER LEGS HARDER, *her eyes locked on Lilja. Her aunt smiled sadly.*

"Finish this," she mouthed.

A horrified scream caught in Sage's throat as the warlord's blade plunged through the Sirenidae's chest. Lilja began to convulse, and all sadness was wiped from her expression, replaced with disgust and disappointment. Blood dropped down her pale chin as she glared at Sage.

"This is your fault," her aunt spat, spraying blood. "You failed."

"No!" Sage screamed.

"You're worthless."

"I'm sorry," she sobbed, stumbling closer. "I tried."

"Not good enough."

Lilja lunged forward with a snarl and stabbed Sage in the chest. She gasped and gaped at the Sirenidae in betrayal.

"Why?" she gurgled, pain cutting deeply until she couldn't breathe.

Her aunt's magenta eyes darkened until it was the warlord's eyes looking out at Sage from Lilja's face.

"Because you've been found unworthy." Lilja leaned closer, her black gaze holding glimmers of hate. "Because you're mine."

Her eyes flew open, and Sage gasped, clutching her chest, the phantom pain disappearing. Goosebumps ran along her arms and legs as she sat up and scanned their tent, the warlord's presence still lingering in her mind. Nali huffed and snuggled closer to her left side between the mattress and the canvas wall.

She placed a sweaty palm on the feline's head and stroked her soft ears with shaking fingers. That dream was a new one. In the weeks since her aunt's death, she'd relived Lilja's murder almost every night. But, tonight, it seemed, the warlord had deemed to visit her.

A shiver worked through her, and Sage clutched the blankets closer to her chest as she scanned their quarters once more for anything unusual. One chair in the left corner with their discarded armor. A small washtub to the right of the bed. Nothing else. No intruder.

Even though she could clearly see no one was there, it still felt as though she was being watched.

Tehl's rough hand moved beneath the covers and squeezed her thigh.

"Nightmare?" he mumbled, still half asleep.

She swallowed hard and forced the tremble out of her voice. "The usual. Go back to sleep, love."

He scooted closer and wrapped an arm behind her back, then one across her thighs, effectively hugging her. He pressed a kiss to the exposed skin at her hip.

"You first..." His words drifted off, and he released a snore.

A sleep-deprived giggle slipped from her, and Sage slapped a hand over her mouth. Tehl still never believed her when she told him that he snored. She pulled her hand from her mouth and gently combed the black hair from his handsome face. He looked tired. Dark smudges lingered beneath his eyes, and, even in sleep, his expression never slackened. It was as if he was still battling.

Her brow furrowed. She wasn't the only one who had nightmares. He didn't always thrash or call out like she did, but, in mornings, the haunted look in his face gave him away.

Nali plopped her head in Sage's lap and purred. She smiled at the leren. "Are you jealous?"

The feline butted her in the belly with her head, encouraging Sage to scratch her ears. Sage touched Tehl's whiskered cheek one last time before she wrapped both her hands around her companion's pointed ears and massaged them. Nali's purr rumbled louder in pleasure.

"Hush or you'll wake him up."

Nali and Tehl both had a way of calming her down and helping her fall back to sleep. In no time, Sage's eyelids were drooping, and she found herself snuggling back into the blankets and her husband's body, one hand idly running through her feline's coat.

She was almost asleep when Nali's purr cut off abruptly, and the fur beneath Sage's palm stood on end.

Sage stiffened and slowly sat up, her ears straining to hear what the leren's could. What was coming for them?

Her right hand squeezed Tehl's shoulder, and she shook him. He jackknifed upward and blinked at her, sleep fleeing his eyes when he got a look at her expression.

"Something's not right—" she began to say when the first explosion shattered the stillness of the night.

Tehl crashed into her as he threw his body over hers. Nali snarled and then whined.

Sage tampered down the scream caught in the back of her throat, her fingernails digging into his sides. She peeked around his shoulder as the second explosion went off. Immense light flared outside their tent, showing the shadows of soldiers running past.

"Get up!" Gav bellowed. "Fire!"

"Wicked hell," Tehl muttered.

He jumped up, pulled Sage with him, and tossed his shirt over his head, then threw Sage's leather chest piece at her. Hastily, she slipped her arms through the straps and scurried over the bed to haul Tehl's metal breastplate from the floor. He moved to her, and they made quick work of his armor.

She jammed her feet into her boots just as Tehl tossed her cloak over her head.

"Put it on," he said gruffly, already disappearing through the tent flap.

Sage hastily swung her cloak over her shoulders and bounded after him, her boots thumping against the hard ground. She burst from the tent and froze. The blaze raged in the not-so-far distance, flames dancing above the sea of tents in a pagan dance. The hair at the nape of her neck rose at the tormented screams that sliced through the air.

"Princess?" She slowly turned toward the speaker; Domin looked at her with concern. "What do you need?"

Her mouth bobbed and she scanned the pandemonium, her eyes snagging on Tehl's wide shoulders. She shook her head and sprinted after him. Two soldiers flanked her as she barreled toward the blaze, her eyes locked on the light.

What had the Scythians targeted?

Her brows furrowed. There wasn't anything on that side of the camp except... Her breath caught, and she stumbled a step before catching herself and speeding up, her heart in her throat.

The infirmary. Mira. Blaise. Her friends.

Her stomach twisted as the scent of charred flesh entered her nostrils. A flash of burned bodies and pale blue lips hovered in the forefront of her mind. Sage shoved the thoughts aside and pushed herself harder, thighs and calves burning. Sweat dampened her temples as the temperature increased. She swung around the last tent and skidded to a stop, a wall of heat and light slamming into her.

Sage raised her arm and squinted at the ball of fire, her clothes instantly sticking to her. Soldiers scrambled from the front part of the massive tent, carrying the wounded and sick. She frantically searched for a blonde braid or long, black hair. Her panic ratcheted up a notch when she didn't see either. She had to get to them. Had to help.

She took one step toward the infirmary when a hand wrapped around her bicep. She glared into Tehl's determined expression.

"You're not going in there."

Sage tugged her arm out of his grasp. "I won't stand on the sidelines. They need our help." They were wasting time. They didn't have time to argue.

His gaze darkened as he pulled a bandana over his mouth and nose. "I'm not asking you to stand aside. Help those who need it."

He swiftly kissed her on the forehead, tore his breastplate from his chest, and waded into the fray. The fire swallowed his form when he rushed into the blaze.

For one second, she pondered obeying him, but then the wooden support beams of the tent released a pained groan. The ground seemed to drop out from beneath her. It was only a matter of time before the whole thing collapsed.

Once again, she scanned the fallen. At least half the soldiers from the infirmary were still missing. Someone needed to start working from the rear before the entire thing burned. She ran around the side of the infirmary, and terror flooded her as she took in the mangled mess. The rear of the tent had been hit the hardest.

Oh god. Blaise.

Soldiers collected water from the nearby horse trough and stream and tossed bucketfuls on the inferno. Gav appeared at her side, sweaty and soot-smeared, his black hair singed at the front.

"It's going to go any second," he shouted over the cacophony.

Sage ignored him and climbed into the horse trough, cloak and all. Frigid water caused goosebumps to erupt over her skin as she leaned back to completely submerge herself. Her fingers curled around the trough's metal edges, and she hauled herself from the trough, water streaming from her clothes.

"Have you seen Mira or Blaise?" she demanded and blinked the water from her eyes. They had to be there somewhere. Time was being wasted. Every second her friends were in the tent, they were closer to death.

"No."

"They're in there. I know it. Mira would never leave her patients behind." She turned her eyes on her friend. "Help me."

Gav cursed. "I'll cut the canvas. You stand back." He wrapped a wet scarf around his head and over his nose, then pulled his sword from the scabbard at his hip and pushed past the soldiers fruitlessly tossing water onto the inferno.

Sage shivered and pulled her soaking cloak tighter around her. Domin wordlessly handed her a wet piece of fabric to tie over her nose and mouth before doing the same to himself. Not once had he questioned or slowed her down. Only offered his aid.

Her legs tensed as she switched her attention back to Gav. They had minutes, seconds to help those inside. He sliced at the canvas and lunged back as a burst of flames, heat, and smoke billowed from the tent.

"Quickly!" he screamed. "Follow me and don't touch anything."

A flicker of fear flashed through her as she dashed into the tent after Gav. Her eyes immediately watered and then dried. The skin on her face and hands felt like it was cooking. She scrambled to the left, toward where she'd left Blaise, her Methian protector hot on her heels.

"Blaise?" she screamed, eyes stinging.

Steam began to rise from her cloak. Bloody hell. It was way too hot.

Her heart bottomed out as she found a cot with a charred body lying upon it. As much as she wanted to look away, Sage forced herself to look closer. The physique was too masculine to be her friend.

She swung around and carefully maneuvered through the disaster zone as the flames hungrily licked at everything they could get to.

"Blaise!" Her eyes skipped over the still bodies that she couldn't help. *Please let Blaise or Mira not be among them.* "Mira!"

"Here," a strained voice called over the roar of the fire.

Sage spun, her damp cloak slapping her leather breeches. She squinted, desperately searching.

"Got 'em!" Gav bellowed.

She scrambled toward his voice and winced as she passed too many unfortunate souls.

Domin ghosted beside her, checking for pulses as they quickly moved deeper into the room. Sage skirted around a collapsed beam and coughed as the smoke thickened. Where in the hell were they?

"Don't step on me," a dark, rough voice rasped.

Sage dropped to her knees and reached through the swirling smoke toward the familiar voice. "Blaise?"

The Scythian woman lay across the floor, her leg pinned beneath the beam. The burning beam.

"Oh, god," Sage whispered as the Methian warrior knelt and began to pull fabric from his pockets and wrap them around his palms.

"When I lift, you pull her out," Domin commanded.

She crawled around him and grabbed Blaise beneath her armpits. "Gav?"

"Right here," Gav huffed from behind her. "Found Mira. She's not well."

"Get her out," she commanded, her attention focused on Domin.

"I can't leave you," Gav snarled.

"You can and you will. We'll be right behind you."

Gav rushed by their side, his clothes steaming. "I'll be back."

Domin braced his legs and cast a glance over his shoulder. "Ready?"

"Do it," she gritted out. She stared down at Blaise, determined to get them both out. "This is going to hurt."

"I can handle it," Blaise growled. "Get me out of here."

The warrior grasped the wood and heaved. Blaise screamed as Sage pulled as hard as she could, dragging her friend out from beneath the beam. The Scythian shuddered, and her eyes rolled into her head.

"Damn it."

Sage pulled Blaise a few more inches and lifted her head to check on the warrior. Domin set the beam back in place just as the room groaned and let out a horrific shudder.

Their eyes connected as the burning roof gave up the fight.

TEN

DOR

—◦⟨∼⟩◦—

HER LIFE SEEMED TO CHANGE by the hour.

A week prior, she'd decided that there was no chance in ever catching her breath. Dor had to run with it. But the dark, creepy tunnel was sending chills down her spine. She eyed the soaring ceiling that hosted a number of ominous webs. Wicked hell, she hated spiders.

"Are you coming?" a smoky, feminine voice asked. She turned her attention to Maeve, who hovered a few paces away. The woman's eyes danced in amusement.

Dor shot an annoyed glare in the woman's direction. They'd only spent a few weeks in each other's presence, but it felt like she'd actually known Maeve her entire life. Even so, Dor was still wary of the warlord's handmaiden. It was uncanny how the Scythian princess could go from laughter to bloodshed in the blink of an eye.

With that in mind, she slowly trailed behind Maeve. The tunnel sloped downward, and she cast surreptitious glances at the silent warriors who formed a loose circle around both women. They'd been trailing her since the day she'd stumbled into the stone room with Ada. She should feel safe, but they put her on edge. They were too silent, too big, and they'd always been her enemy.

Dor quietly followed Maeve deeper into the earth, the air cooling as they descended. It didn't bother her skin. After spending her whole life in the Pit, the cool, humid air felt like coming home. Her heart squeezed. The Pit. She'd unintentionally helped start a rebellion. In her mind, it had seemed glorious—romantic, even. In actuality, it was bloody. Blood was spilled on both sides daily, and while the Scythian society as a whole was corrupt, what went down in the Pit wasn't innocent. Every death weighed heavily on her conscience. How much blood would need to be paid for equality and freedom?

She shook her head and pulled herself from her morose thoughts. The silence stretched on, only broken up by the occasional water droplets falling from the craggy ceiling. Unable to stand it a moment longer, she asked, "Where are we going?"

Maeve smiled a secret smile but didn't answer. Dor rolled her eyes. That was nothing new. The woman collected secrets like her father collected blades. She huffed and continued the silent trek. The tunnel curved to the left and then to the right, sloping steeply downward. Her legs began to ache, and she gritted her teeth. It had only been a few weeks since she'd traipsed about the Pit's staircases, but she'd lost the muscle strength she'd gained, regardless of the relentless training the Scythian princess had thrown her into.

They swung around a curve, and her eyes widened when they approached a huge opening with enormous metal bars that ran from ceiling to floor like great, steel teeth.

Maeve halted and turned to face her, the dark maw behind the woman looking like it was about to swallow her. She gave Dor a piercing look that flayed her to the bone. It was uncanny. Maeve didn't look much older than herself, yet knowing Scythia's bloody history, she'd lived a long time.

Dor's skin prickled with unease. She crossed her arms to hide the goosebumps that had erupted along her forearms. It wasn't easy to trust the warlord's handmaiden. Well, work with her. She didn't really trust anyone.

The warlord's handmaiden tipped her head, her gaze intensifying.

Once again, Dor's skin crawled, and she shifted uncomfortably on her feet. Maeve had a way about her, like she could look inside your soul and delve into your deepest thoughts and feelings.

"What?" Dor barked, breaking the silence. "What are we doing here?" Was it another training exercise?

Maeve smiled and gestured toward the lever on the right-hand side of the bars. "Gentlemen, if you'd be so kind."

Three warriors broke off from their group, and each of them grabbed hold of the lever. They put all their weight into pulling the metal lever down. The stone around the opening groaned, and the giant bars began drawing upward.

Dor took a step backward, her instincts screaming for her to run. She'd never been a coward. She forced herself to stand her ground and face whatever was lurking in the darkness.

"Don't be afraid, Dorcus," Maeve soothed. "Your future awaits you if you're brave enough to face it." She stepped aside and held a hand toward the darkness. "Enter."

Her stomach bottomed out. "Weapons?" she croaked.

"You will need only what is strapped to your person."

Lovely. Whatever test this was, it would end up bloody. Although, they knew she couldn't outright die, so that was something. Dor cursed herself for not wearing better armor, or even bringing a sword. That was her father's number one rule: never go anywhere without a weapon. And while she harbored a few daggers, they wouldn't be enough if she went by the size of the bars. Whatever was hiding in the darkness wasn't an easy foe.

Woodenly, she took one step after another until she was standing in the immense doorway. "Light?"

Maeve gave her an amused smile. "In good time."

What the hell did that mean? "Am I to go in alone?"

"It's not my place to enter at your side."

Dor scoffed. Not the handmaiden's place? What rubbish. Maeve did what she wanted.

"You're hesitating."

"Wouldn't you?" Dor retorted, sarcastically.

She flinched in surprise when Maeve stepped close and cupped her left cheek. "Today is not a day of death, but of rejoicing. Step into the darkness like the warrior your sire raised you to be. Claim your birth right." With those cryptic words, Maeve stepped away and faced the darkness.

Dor scowled. The woman knew how to play on her pride. But pride never kept one alive. With careful, gliding steps, she moved past the entrance. She pursed her lips and whistled softly, the sound echoing around her.

A large cavernous space.

While stealth was usually the best form of attack, the creaking of the bars had already warned whatever was lying in wait for her that she was coming. The echoes at least gave an idea of what kind of room she was in.

It wasn't easy to put one foot in front of the other and stride toward the darkness. She paused and glanced over her shoulder as she hovered at the edge of the pool of lantern light, her ears alert to any sound.

At the entrance of the room, Maeve smiled, satisfaction clear on her symmetrical face. Dor stiffened and caught the slightest sound of something slithering against stone from her right. A snake? She squinted and searched the area around her for the threat. Was this an initiation? Her pulse thundered in her ears and a *shhhhh* sound came from the left. A second creature?

Precious one.

Dor froze at the familiar nickname running through her mind over and over. There was only one who referred to her in that way. Well, at least in her mind. She inhaled deeply, noting the metallic and musky smell she missed before. There was only one creature who smelled like that.

She stood taller and searched the darkness. "Illya?" she whispered.

A familiar click greeted her. *I am here.*

Dor gasped and stumbled into the darkness, holding her arms out in front of her, heedless of anything but reaching her dragon. It had been weeks since she'd seen him, and while she'd longed to visit, she didn't know Maeve's view on the creatures.

Her fingertips grazed warm scales, and a smile burst across her face. Carefully, she traced a scale, discovering the pointed edge that was razor sharp and tapered to his tail. Dor stumbled forward, determined to reach his face so she could give him a proper hug.

"I've missed you so much!"

Another series of clicks and hums greeted her. Some of her joy waned, and she paused, her left hand still on the dragon's side. She frowned. That didn't sound familiar. The scales seemed to expand and contract with the beast's breaths.

"Illya?"

Silence.

Real fear slammed into her, and she yanked her hand back. She'd imagined

Illya, but the dragon in the room was very real. Her heart flew to her throat, and she took measured steps backward, trying to make herself seem as harmless as a fly.

"I didn't mean to intrude in your home," she murmured. "I'll leave you alone." Dor stiffened when the light disappeared behind her, and warm air blew across the back of her neck, a dry tongue licking her from shoulder to the crown of her head. She knew that familiar hello.

Welcome, precious one.

Tears burned in her eyes, and she spun around, opening her arms wide. She didn't imagine him.

Welcome.

"I can't believe you're here," she choked out, voice thick with tears.

Illya hissed softly and blew another breath into her face. He lowered his face, which was barely visible in the low light, and pressed his muzzle into her chest. She wrapped her arms around his snout, her forearm brushing one of his long fangs that stuck out from his mouth. Dor squeezed him tightly and leaned her cheek against him, her eyes closing. The small scales that covered his nose scratched at her skin. It was the best feeling in the world. She was actually here with him, no stone wall to separate them.

"Dorcus," Maeve called.

She opened her eyes and squinted toward the entrance, where Maeve's body was haloed by the light.

"Please ask your dragon if we may enter. We bear no ill will, and no weapons shall enter this sanctuary."

Ask her dragon... That was a weird request. Dor rolled her eyes and hugged Illya again. "May they enter?"

The Dragon Song and her protectors may enter.

Dorcus stiffened and lifted her head. Lanterns along the walls began to light, one by one. She stared at Illya, her mouth hanging open. She had no clue what a Dragon Song was, but she hadn't made it up. It had come from him. The dragon.

She stumbled a step away. Animals couldn't speak.

As the cavern lightened, her breath caught. He was massive! His black scales caught the faint light and reflected it like slick oil. Illya arched his long, sinuous neck and blinked at her with a large feline silver eye, like liquid mercury.

"You're magnificent," she breathed. Awe settle over her as she noticed his leather-like wings settled against his back.

Precious one. Her attention was pulled back to his face. His clicks, hisses, hums, and soft purrs seemed to form the words in her mind. *It's time to speak and to plan.*

Dor blinked slowly, pressed her palms to each side of her head, and dropped to her haunches. Her eyes squeezed shut. What was happening to her? Before, she'd chalked it up to her overactive imagination and the need for friendship. Was she going insane?

"Dor," Maeve cooed. "It's all right. Take a deep breath." She inhaled slowly. "Now open your eyes."

The Scythian princess knelt a few paces away, not even glancing in Illya's direction. "I know you're overwhelmed, but it's going to be okay."

"Am I crazy?" she rasped.

Maeve smiled, and, for the first time since Dor met the woman, it seemed genuine. "No, you are not. You're a Dragon Song."

"A Dragon Song?"

"Yes." Maeve's smile grew bigger. "It's so very rare now, but once upon a time, dragons and Dragon Songs were very common."

"What are you saying? That I can speak to animals?"

"No, but you do understand the dragon language."

"Dragon language," Dor repeated, casting a glance at Illya.

Her dragon lowered his head to the obsidian stone floor.

Listen to the Dragon Song. She is wise.

Dor blinked. He spoke, and she understood him. Her legs turned to jelly beneath her, and she plopped onto her arse. "He speaks." With wide eyes, she turned to Maeve. "I understand him."

Warmth filled the Scythian woman's face. "You do. You are so very special, Dorcus. You will change the world."

"Me?"

"You." Maeve stared at Illya. "Your bond is strong. One of five Dragon Songs left."

There were four more dragons? "Why am I special?"

I am Alpha. Her dragon's rumble held satisfaction.

"Your dragon is the Alpha, and you are the heir."

"The heir to what?" Chills ran up and down her spine. Somehow, she knew what the warlord's handmaiden was going to say.

"You, dearest, are the last remaining descendent of the Nagali royal house."

The world tipped on its side. A million little things snapped into place. Why she'd always been treated differently. She'd always assumed it was the color of her skin.

"What do we do now?" she asked, overwhelmed and lost.

Maeve's smile turned dangerous. "We free the dragons and reclaim what was stolen."

ELEVEN

TEHL

TEHL'S LUNGS SCREAMED AS He carried a hacking soldier from
the burning infirmary. His legs almost buckled as he moved away from the
blaze, fatigue riding him hard. Soldiers rushed toward him and relieved him
of his moaning burden. He bent over and placed his hands on his knees as he
gulped huge lungfuls of air.

He flicked his eyes up when Zachael placed a steadying hand on Tehl's
shoulder, and he forced himself to straighten, his back complaining in the
process. Today, he felt old.

He yanked down the wet linen covering his nose and mouth. "Is that
everyone?" Tehl shouted over the noise.

The weapons master nodded, his expression grim. "We got out all who
were breathing."

The infirmary groaned, pulling Tehl's attention to what was left of the
heavy structure. It swayed and then crashed to the ground, belching flames
and smoke.

Tehl held his arm up to protect his face and tried to take small inhalations
as smoke and ash rushed back at him. His nose wrinkled at the bitter taste
of ash on his tongue, and his gaze locked on the inferno. They'd managed to
save a fair amount, but it still wasn't enough.

Clenching his jaw, he dropped his arm and raked his sweaty hair away from his face. He scanned the crying mass of the wounded. Guilt swam in his belly for all those who had died. How many women had lost their husbands, children their fathers, and mothers their sons? He scanned the chaos of soldiers and the wounded, his gaze snagging on a Methian woman with half her face burned. Tehl swallowed hard. How many had lost their wives or daughters or mothers?

Too many.

"What about the rear?" he asked woodenly.

Zachael's expression hardened. "The rear of the infirmary took the most damage. There wasn't much to salvage."

Tehl swallowed hard and forced his mind away from the gruesome deaths the men and women must have suffered. There wasn't anything he could do for them now. Their focus needed to be on those who lived. They needed immediate care. Burns were painful, but with burns came infection. That's where the true danger lurked.

"Our healers?"

"Queen Osir has opened her tent as the new infirmary. Everyone with herbal or healer training has been instructed to gather there and tend to the wounded. I've been told the queen is an excellent healer."

"Then we are fortunate to have her skills. Jacob departed for Sanee, leaving Mira with the bulk of the responsibilities. Another pair of skilled hands will lighten the load."

"She's a capable healer," Zachael commented, his eyes narrowing. "Speaking of which, have you seen her?"

Tehl frowned and groggily tried to remember if he saw her among the fray. He didn't recall seeing a blonde. He reached out to a young soldier. "Check the new infirmary for Healer Mira."

The boy scampered off into the sea of tents toward the new infirmary.

Once again, Tehl scoured the cluster of wounded. Mira wasn't someone to stand by. She never waited in the infirmary for the wounded to be brought to her. She waited on the edge of camp for them. Mira had to be somewhere close by.

Tehl's brows furrowed as he scanned the group again carefully, looking for a blonde head. Where was she?

The young soldier jogged up to them, an apologetic look on his face. "She's not with the healers." He wrung his hands. "I'm happy to keep looking, my lord."

"Search the wounded," Tehl commanded, his stomach twisting.

The boy burst into action.

"Where is the healer?" Tehl asked hoarsely, his gaze focusing back on the inferno. She couldn't be in there.

The weapons master studied the chaos around them. "I don't see her, but that doesn't mean anything."

A sick sense of foreboding settled on Tehl's shoulders as he realized his wife was nowhere in sight, either. Wicked hell. Where was Sage?

"Sage," he gasped. "Have you seen her?"

Zachael stiffened. "No."

Tehl's eyes darted back to the blaze. She wouldn't have gone in, would she? Surely, he would've seen her. He closed his stinging eyes and tried to remember anything from inside the infirmary. All he could remember was smoke, heat, and the scent of charred flesh. He opened his eyes, gazing blankly at the fire.

"Search for the princess," Zachael barked at the remaining Elite guarding them. The men immediately waded into the crowd.

Where the blazes was she? Sage was supposed to stay here. But if Mira was missing...

"She wouldn't have left her friends behind," he muttered to himself. His heart thundered in his chest. Stars, he was so stupid. He knew exactly where she went. "The rear side."

Zachael's lips thinned, and both men started running toward the rear of the enormous fire.

The flames seemed to rise up and touch the stars. Tehl's breath shortened as they rounded the back of the collapsed tent and spotted a group of soldiers yelling at each other.

Gav knelt in the middle of them, a lifeless female form lying on the ground.

Tehl stumbled a step.

No. Not Sage. Please God, no.

He barreled through the group and skidded to a stop. The men quieted as he inhaled sharply. Blonde hair, not brown. *Mira.*

Gavriel didn't take his eyes from Mira as he placed a wet rag over a nasty looking burn on the healer's right shoulder and she took a shallow breath.

She shivered and moaned, coughs rattling her abused body. Tehl knelt and stared at her dirty, bruised face, and then pinned his cousin with a fierce look.

"Where is Sage?"

Gav lifted his head, his eyes holding pity. "Tehl," he said softly.

There was too much emotion in his tone. Loss. Guilt. Sorrow.

No.

Tehl wouldn't believe it.

A tremor worked through him, and he glared at Gav. "Where is my wife? Where is she?"

Gav held his gaze, pain and guilt written all over his expression. "It happened so fast."

Zachael placed a hand on his shoulder, but Tehl shook it off.

"You left her inside?" he roared.

"She was right behind me," Gav whispered. "One moment there, the next gone."

Gone.

It echoed in his mind, a morbid chant that he couldn't quite comprehend. It wasn't possible. Sage couldn't just be *gone.*

Tehl shook his head and stormed away from the group, his eyes pinned to the fire as he moved around the far side of the infirmary. Maybe Sage had escaped and was on the other side.

But there was nothing there. No one.

His heart began to crack. She couldn't be inside. Surely, if she'd died, he would have felt it, felt something?

"Tehl..."

He shot a black look at Zachael. "Don't."

The weapons master snapped his mouth shut.

If Sage was inside, there was still a chance she lived. Tehl needed to get inside. Now.

He rushed to the horse trough, one thought in his mind: find her.

"I know what you're thinking, and I won't allow it," the older man said with determination.

"I'm the bloody crown prince. No one gives me orders," Tehl growled and dunked himself in the lukewarm water. He jumped from the trough and slicked his wet hair from his face.

Zachael placed himself between Tehl and the remnants of the infirmary. "You *are* the bloody crown prince, and as much as it pains me to say this— you're more important. You can't risk your life this way."

Tehl wanted to point out all the ways he risked his life every day, fighting monsters, but he didn't have time for that.

"Don't make me cut you down," he warned the weapons master. "Get out of the way!"

"She'll be long gone by now," Zachael said softly, pulling his blade from the scabbard at his hip. "I'm so sorry, but I can't allow it."

"Who's long gone?" a raspy voice coughed.

Tehl jerked around at the sound of Blaise's voice and scanned the bushes behind them. Blaise lay on her side just behind the trough, her muted clothing blending in with the blackened brush along the ground.

"My wife." He couldn't say her name.

The Scythian's forehead wrinkled, confusion twisted her face. "No, she's—" Blaise wheezed, her dark eyes closing as she struggled for breath.

Zachael moved to her side and slapped her on the back.

She gasped, a cry bursting from her mouth. "*Burns.*"

"Bloody hell," the weapons master hissed. He jerked his hand away.

Tehl rushed to her and knelt, his hands clasping either side of Blaise's face. "Where is she?"

Blaise opened her eyes, tears streaming down her face, and Tehl's heart cracked further open.

"Her guard took her to the creek."

He stiffened and blinked slowly, not able to understand her words. "She's alive?" he croaked, his hands trembling.

The Scythian studied him. "I can hear them coming."

Tehl's fingers tightened momentarily, and he forced himself to carefully release Blaise. It was too good to be true. Woodenly, he stood and took two halting steps toward the creek. Sage pushed through the brush, soot-streaked and soaking wet. Her gaze locked onto his, and she froze as if detecting a predator.

His mind screamed for him to rush to her side and scoop her into his arms. To reaffirm that she was whole and healthy. Yet, his body refused to obey him. All he could do was watch her as numbness crept through his limbs. She was alive, but from the state of her torched clothing, she had gone inside the infirmary.

She'd risked her life and his heart, and she'd ignored what he'd asked of her. Reckless and selfish.

Sage pressed her lips together and opened her mouth to speak.

He held up his hand. If she spoke, he would lose it.

Tehl ran his eyes all over her body one last time to affirm that she was okay before turning his attention to the Methian warrior standing by her side, his expression serene.

"Make sure she gets back to our quarters safely."

He spared his wife one last accusatory look and turned his back on her. He didn't feel the heat from the fire, nor did he take in the scenery around him. He only welcomed the numbness as he moved toward the chaos that awaited him.

She hadn't listened.

She'd almost died.

It broke something inside him.

TWELVE

SAGE

SHE'D MESSED UP.

The look on Tehl's face wasn't something Sage would soon forget. She glanced around the new, makeshift infirmary and took in a shallow breath through her mouth. Charred flesh and singed hair created a pungent odor that had her frequently retching.

A moan sounded from her left, but Sage forced herself to keep her eyes pinned to her mud-covered boots as she shuffled to sit on a stool placed between Mira's and Blaise's cots. It was cowardly of her, but the burned remains of the soldier two cots down were just too much. The pieces of flesh didn't even resemble a human being anymore, more like a melted candle.

Her stomach rolled, and saliva flooded her mouth a second before she heaved into the tin bucket firmly planted between her feet. Tears sprang to her eyes as the contents of her belly revolted against her.

"You should get some rest," Mira rasped. "Being here isn't good for you."

Sage wiped her mouth with her dirty, trembling hand. "The moment I leave, you'll get up." She lifted her head and glared at the cot to her left. Mira stared back placidly through bloodshot eyes. "That innocent gaze doesn't fool me."

Mira wasn't in good shape. She'd inhaled a lot of smoke. Her voice was so hoarse, she could have passed for a man. She had burns everywhere and, while it could have been worse, she still was a bloody mess. Sage's gaze wandered to Mira's bandaged palms. The worst was her right hand. Apparently, she'd tried to move a burning tent support that had fallen onto one of her patients. It had to hurt like hell, yet Mira hadn't uttered one complaint other than the fact that she hated being a patient.

"I'm no good to anyone, lying here," Mira had argued. "There aren't any other healers of my level of expertise here. I'm needed."

Blaise had released a smoky chuckle. "Don't let the Methi queen hear you say that."

Now, Sage craned her neck and peeked over her shoulder at Queen Osir. The woman was an army in her own right. In the hours that had passed since the Scythian attack, she'd not stopped moving. She'd marshaled a troop of healers to help those who'd suffered in the fire.

A sniff pulled Sage's attention back to Mira, and her heart clenched.

The healer released a hacking cough, and a tear dripped down her cheek and onto the cot as she stared at the ceiling.

"Is it the pain?" Sage asked in concern. "I can get something for you."

Mira shook her head and croaked, "I couldn't help them. I couldn't save them."

"Don't think like that," Sage crooned. She placed her hand gingerly on Mira's uninjured shoulder. "You did your best."

Mira twisted her neck and met Sage's gaze. "It wasn't good enough." More tears tracked down the healer's cheeks. "How could someone do such a thing?"

That was the very question Sage had been asking herself for hours. It was inhuman. Monstrous. Mira released a gurgling, hiccupping laugh. "I should have known when Tehl brought you to me. I'd never seen someone in such a state." Sage hid her flinch. Her friend wasn't trying to hurt her. "We're dealing with a demon and his monsters. No one with any shred of humanity would cause the suffering and torture he does."

Sage nodded. "You're right."

Her friend angrily wiped at her face and sat up, her face creased in a grimace.

"Whoa!" Sage said, holding her hands out. "Take it easy."

Mira gave her a withering glance. "Like you do?"

"She's got you there," Blaise piped in.

Sage rolled her eyes at the Scythian woman. "What would you know about it?"

Blaise snorted and then released a chest-rattling cough, her whole body convulsing with the movement. Once she'd gained control of herself, all humor fled from her expression.

"I've never seen you hold still for more than a few minutes of time. You've lost weight. When is the last time you had a full night of sleep?" the Scythian woman asked.

Sage pursed her lips.

Before the warlord.

Blaise nodded as if she could read her mind. "I lived with that monster my whole life. I know what effects he can have. You're working yourself to the bone and if you keep it up, you'll break before we've defeated him."

Sage's jaw clenched, and she had to look away. She knew Blaise was right, but it didn't mean it was easy to hear. The warlord was always one step ahead of them. No matter what it felt like, she was fighting against a raging storm.

"You need to set boundaries and keep them," Blaise suggested.

Sage bristled. "Aermia can't afford any." She didn't even want to think about what would happen if they failed. The world as they knew it would cease to be. The warlord's dark smile flashed through her mind, and she fought back a shiver. It would be a bleak world indeed.

"They can't afford a dead queen, either."

Her eyes widened. "I'm no queen."

Blaise gave her a bemused smile. "Crown or no crown, you are these men's queen. They look to you for guidance. You need to set the example. Even in war, there must be rest for healing of the mind and body."

"I will try harder," Sage gritted out. It seemed impossible, but she vowed she would *try*.

"Do so." Blaise's attention wandered to something over Sage's shoulder. "Your mate is waiting for you."

Now it was her turn to snort. "I doubt it. He hasn't looked at me all night." Ever since he'd walked away from her earlier, Tehl had completely ignored her. It was as if she had become a piece of furniture.

"Maybe not in the way you're accustomed to, but he's been tuned in to your every move," Blaise said.

"I don't know what to say to him." If Sage told him the truth, it would just upset him more. Her gaze moved between her two friends. Her risk was worth it because the three of them were whole and alive. That's what mattered. Sage couldn't lose either of them.

"Tell him you're sorry for being stupid," Mira wheezed. "And lay it on thick if need be."

"If I hadn't acted rashly, both of you would be dead," Sage pointed out.

Blaise reached out and squeezed her wrist. "Boundaries. Trust that others will take the training you've given them and be successful. Be humble. You can't do everything. When you make a mistake, even if the outcome is a positive one, apologize to the ones you've hurt. Your man is hurting, whether he's showing it or not."

That was true enough. Sage knew Tehl was the quiet sort who didn't show his feelings to hardly anyone. She'd also known, the moment he locked eyes on her near the forest, she'd angered him.

"Thank you," she said softly. "I'm blessed with wise friends."

"That's not the only thing you're blessed with," Blaise retorted, eyeing Tehl. "Make use of my advice."

Sage smiled. "Do either of you need anything before I go?"

Blaise quirked a half smile. "No, the healers will care for my burnt arse."

Mira inhaled sharply as she swung her legs off the cot. She patted Sage's knee and then leaned back, bracing her left hand against the cot. "Leave. We're well looked after, and you've done all you can. Stop putting off the inevitable."

She stood and glanced at her two friends. "I'll see you both once I get some proper rest."

"We'll be here," Blaise retorted, lacing her fingers together and then placing her head on them, the picture of relaxation.

Sage marshaled her thoughts and pasted a smile on her face. Blaise was right. She couldn't let the men see her down and beaten. It was bad for morale.

She turned on her heel, and kept the horror off her face as she passed the other fire survivors. The walk to the entrance of the tent seemed to go on forever as she passed cot after cot.

Queen Osir caught her eye and jerked her head toward the tent exit. Sage dutifully followed the Methian queen. Her breath came easier as she stepped from the cloying tent and into the fresh, early morning air. Her eyes lifted to the still-dark sky and part of her wanted to cry out to the stars.

Why? Why this?

"You did well," the queen said.

"Did I?" Sage frowned. "I puked."

"Lesser men would have never even stepped inside that hellhole." The queen narrowed her amber eyes and laid a hand on Sage's chest. "How is your breathing?"

She shrugged. "Fine."

The older woman gave her a skeptical look. "You need to rest. You're no good to us worn down."

"So I've been told," she muttered. Was she doing such a bad job?

"You'll be short of breath for several days. With luck, you won't get sick. I want you to stay off the battlefield."

Sage glanced at her sharply. "I won't agree to that." The Scythians were pressing forward every day. The Aermian army needed all the help they could get.

The queen's expression hardened. "What do you think will happen when you go out onto the field and your lungs seize? Your enemy won't wait for you to recover. You will be a danger to everyone around you—a distraction. My son fights with you every day. He tells me of your strength, but of your weakness, too. If you falter, he will fight to protect you." She stepped into Sage's space. "Rafe loves you. He will die for you. Are you really willing to risk my son's life for the sake of your pride?"

"There's no guarantee that would happen," Sage argued. "What if I'm not there to protect Rafe's back?"

The queen snorted. "My son can protect himself."

"Now who's prideful?" she said softly.

"It's not easy, is it?"

Sage frowned. "What?"

"Being a woman in power who is surrounded by men," the queen said. "We always feel the need to prove ourselves. It's never easy for us. Men often seek to dominate us or look for every flaw and weakness. I've learned over the years that a wise ruler needs to step back and take a look at the bigger picture." She touched Sage's cheek. "You are a fine warrior and will make a wonderful ruler, but only if you let yourself heal. I can hear how you're trying to cover the wheeze in your chest. Lying to yourself and to those around you about your health will help no one. It's okay to let others take care of you."

"It's not so easy," Sage whispered.

"No, it is not." The queen removed her hand from Sage's face. "Think about what I have said and take care of yourself, dear." She turned on her heel, her silver-and-black braid swinging behind her. She paused by the tent flap and turned, shooting Sage a menacing look. "If you decide to be stupid and my son is hurt, I will hold you responsible."

Sage eyed the Methian queen as she disappeared into the tent. She wouldn't want that woman as her enemy. She cleared her throat as the tickle became almost unbearable. How had the damn queen heard the wheeze in her lungs? Her lips pursed. While the Methian soldiers hadn't said anything outright, she had the sneaking suspicion they possessed remarkable senses. Rafe certainly possessed gifts she'd never seen in anyone—but the warlord—before. She swallowed, and her gaze drifted past their tents and the battlefield to the dark tents of the Scythians. What sort of secrets did the warlord have?

"I wish you could feel the hate I have for you," she whispered into the early morning air.

She jumped when the flap to the infirmary snapped open and Tehl's scent invaded her senses as he brushed by her without a word. Sage stared guiltily at his back and fell into step behind him as the Elite materialized from the dark and formed a loose circle around them.

Her lip curled in distaste. How much had they heard of her conversation with the queen? Nothing was private or sacred anymore. Her mind flashed back to her kidnapping. Even with the inconvenience of never being alone or having a private conversation, the protection was worth it. Never again did she want to be taken against her will.

Sage counted each step through the camp toward their chambers, feeling a prickling of doom along the bare skin of her arms. She shivered, and her brows furrowed. Where did she leave her cloak? In fact, when had she lost it?

But there were more pressing matters than her damn cloak. Raised voices pierced through the twilight air as they drew closer. Hayjen's voice was louder than the rest. Leave it to him to be the one shouting.

Her eyes burned, and her throat ached. She really wanted to go to bed.

Her gaze wandered to Tehl's back as they neared their own tent. She needed to make amends but now wasn't the time.

Aermia came first.

THIRTEEN

HAYJEN

———◦◦◦◦———

"WE NEED TO STRIKE NOW!" Why were they all dragging their feet? Hayjen glared at the men clustered around the circular table in the center of the room.

"They will expect us to retaliate," Zachael said calmly. "We need to proceed with caution."

Caution? Caution got them nowhere. Lilja's crumpled form was still seared into his mind. Caution led to more death. They had to fight. "If we do nothing, the warlord wins." Did no one understand that?

Hayjen's gaze snapped to the entrance of the tent as Tehl and Sage stepped inside. His attention homed in on the blank expression on the crown prince's face. War wasn't ever pretty, but the destruction tonight was something else entirely. It was enough to break a man. He studied Tehl and slid his gaze to his niece. Sage flicked questioning glances at her husband as they joined the small war council. She looked concerned but not terrified. The prince hadn't been broken; he was just processing.

"Tonight's attack is most troubling." William ran a hand along his white, pointed goatee, and his bushy brows furrowed. "The Scythians have disregarded all war etiquette. Things are about to get infinitely darker. We need to tread lightly, or we'll lose ourselves to this madness."

Rafe snorted, and his brother Raziel chuckled.

"We're dealing with animals. What makes you believe that they will act like civilized, human beings?" Raziel asked sarcastically. "Mark my words, it will only get bloodier from here. We will have to match their efforts if we want to win."

Bloodstained lips taunted Hayjen from a ghostly, pale face, Lilja's pained magenta eyes dulling. He pinched the bridge of his nose and tried to control his emotions. Over the last several weeks, he'd been either numb or burning with rage. There wasn't a middle ground. Even in sleep, he couldn't escape the horror of his soul-rendering loss.

"We must destroy the rest of his war machines," Tehl said, his tone flat. "Soon."

"At what cost?" Sage whispered. "You saw what he did in retaliation tonight. We've lost many in one fell swoop."

Hayjen lifted his head at her anguished tone and studied the young couple. The crown prince stood as stiff as a board. Shadows slithered through his eyes, but his expression never cracked.

"You believe I'm to blame for the attack?" Tehl asked, never taking his attention from the war map.

Sage's mouth opened and then snapped closed. The members of the council all found somewhere else to look, but Hayjen watched the drama, a pinprick of jealousy stabbing him. He missed arguing with his wife. Marriage to a Sirenidae wasn't easy—hell, no marriage was easy—but he'd kill to be able to fight with Lilja one last time.

"It's no one's fault but the warlord's," Sage said after a moment of uncomfortable silence.

She shifted from foot to foot, reaching a hand toward Tehl and then dropping it before she touched him. Definitely trouble in paradise.

"This is on him and no one else. We need to tread carefully," she reasoned. "He'll anticipate our moves. We need to act rationally and not in anger."

"That's my specialty," Tehl said woodenly. "Can you say the same?"

Heat rushed into Sage's cheeks, and she glanced at the group, clearly embarrassed. Raziel coughed into his fist and side-eyed the tent flap. Hayjen scowled at Tehl. There was no need to embarrass her in front of everyone, no matter how angry Tehl was. Hayjen almost stepped in, but then good old

William broke up the tension.

"Dawn is approaching, and we haven't had a full night's sleep in weeks. This needn't be decided right now. We will reconvene in a few hours when all our heads are clearer."

Sage smiled gratefully at the grizzled general while the Methian princes quietly departed. Tehl didn't say anything as he disappeared into the rear section of the tent where his chambers were.

Hayjen stayed put as William clasped Sage's shoulder in support, and Zachael offered a quick hug before both men left. Sage leaned a hip against the table and rubbed at her forehead, further smearing the spot of soot already lodged there.

She sighed. "Whatever you have to say, out with it. I'm exhausted and need to go to bed."

"I doubt you'll be asleep anytime soon," Hayjen murmured. Whatever was between the two of them, they'd work it out, but it would take time.

"What makes you say that?" Sage fiddled with a chain at her neck, avoiding his gaze.

Hayjen focused on the giant map and the small wooden carvings on it that marked the armies' locations. "I was married for a long time." He swallowed hard and soldiered on, despite how the words stuck in the back of his throat. "I can sense when a storm is brewing." He peeked at his niece from beneath his lashes. "And by the look of guilt upon your face, I suspect you have some apologizing to do, baby girl."

Sage darted a glance toward her chambers and then shot him a dirty look. "It's just a misunderstanding." She ran her finger along the dangling charm and flicked her finger against the clasp.

"Then why do you feel so horrid?" He straightened and crossed his arms, for some reason transfixed by her nervous movements. Something seemed so familiar about the necklace.

"He's angry because I disobeyed him," Sage hissed. "I never signed up to be his subordinate."

Hayjen squinted harder at her fingers. It wasn't a charm... Was it a ring? Damn, he'd soon need some spectacles. "What did he tell you not to do?"

His niece held the ring up and flipped open the lid. Recognition slammed into him, followed by fear. Sage inspected the needle of the poisonous ring and pulled it closer to her face to get a closer look.

Good god.

"Close the damn ring!" he barked, his voice louder than he intended. Sage startled but snapped the ring closed.

"You didn't have to yell," she said crossly.

Hayjen rushed around the table and snatched the ring from her fingers, pulling her along with the chain. He leaned closer and held the ring up to the lantern light. Stars above, how long had Sage had this jewelry? How many times had she opened the poison ring? "Do you know what this is?"

"A gift."

"Death," he whispered. How could she not know? "A horrid death. I assume Lilja—" he swallowed at the use of her name "—gave this to you?"

"She said to use it if I was ever captured again." A look of uncertainty crossed Sage's face. "It's my escape."

He nodded, his heart aching. "While that is true, she didn't explain how it works. The poison in this ring comes from some of the deepest trenches in the sea. It has been brewed to kill Scythian warriors. If even the smallest drop were to touch your skin, you'd die—no prick or cut necessary." Sage's eyes widened. "That's right. You were just playing with death." He carefully lowered the necklace and cupped her shoulders. "Never, ever do that again."

A tremble worked through Sage. "That would have been nice to know earlier," she croaked. "I've always liked dangerous things, but that's a little extreme. Even for me."

Hayjen huffed out a laugh. "Your aunt had an interesting idea of what was an appropriate gift."

"After my experiences, I welcomed her sort of gifts. Even if she didn't warn me that I was literally playing with death."

"Sometimes she forgot others around her weren't from the sea." He crooked a smile. "She never saw a difference between peoples. Everyone was the same to her."

"She was one of a kind," Sage whispered.

A pang of loss shot through him. He needed a drink, and some damn sleep before he went back to the battlefield. He leaned down and kissed Sage on her forehead. "Don't let the sun set on your anger. Fix what you need to before you sleep."

Sage sighed. "Mum used to say that all the time."

Hayjen pulled back and smiled softly. "That's because I taught her. Goodnight." He wove around her and lifted the flap.

"Hayjen?"

He paused and glanced over his shoulder at his niece, her face looking far too weighed down for someone so young. "Yeah?"

Something dark lingered in her gaze, but she blinked it away, and a small smile touched her mouth. "I love you."

He stiffened, and liquid heat burned at the back of his eyes. Hayjen nodded and gruffly choked out, "You too, *ma fille.*"

He ducked out of the tent before he could make an ass of himself. He needed some bloody sleep and a heavy dose of whiskey. The sun had already begun to lighten the sky to the east. Damn it. Sleep would be short. Maybe his wife wouldn't torment him while he snatched a few winks of sleep. A twisted smile lifted his lips. He'd rather have her haunt him than have her not grace his nightmares at all.

Or worse: forget her.

He made his way to his tent and plopped down on his bed roll. He glanced at his pillow in longing. Better not. He'd need to get to the battlefield within the hour.

Hayjen swiped the bottle of whiskey from the floor and uncorked the top. He took a heavy swig, barely tasting the bitter swill. A single tear rolled down his cheek. Most would scold him for drinking so early. Most wives would berate their husbands. But Lilja would have grabbed a glass and had a drink with him.

"I miss you," he said to the empty tent.

FOURTEEN

SAM

SAM PLACED HIS HANDS ATOP the huge vanity and eyed his pale complexion in the tall, gilded mirror. He looked like hell. He scoffed. He was pretty sure he'd been there and back in the weeks prior.

A soft knock at the door.

"Enter."

Marilyn, one of his oldest spies, entered his chamber. He lifted his head and smiled weakly at her. She didn't smile back, her frown causing the wrinkles around her mouth to deepen. His heart fell.

"Nothing?"

She shook her head. "We've searched high and low, my lord. There hasn't even been a whisper of a woman of her description anywhere. If she were in the city, we would have found her by now."

"A person can't just disappear. You're not looking hard enough." An unfair assessment, but he was so damn worried.

Marilyn didn't respond to his sharp tone—if anything, her expression softened. "We're doing our best."

"It's not good enough," he snapped. Sam immediately regretted his tone and closed his eyes, pinching the bridge of his nose. "I should not have spoken to you that way. Please accept my apology."

"There's nothing to be sorry about. These are trying times. I'm not sure how you handle everything without losing your bloody mind." Her gaze moved over his shoulder, toward the twins' room. "If you need someone to look after the wee ones again, I am happy to." The gruff older woman smiled, revealing crooked teeth. "Gems they are."

Sam nodded. His spies had been helping with the children more often than not. "I'll let you know if I need you. Keep your eyes and ears open. I'll send your next assignment on the morrow."

Marilyn nodded and left the room, the door clicking shut quietly behind her.

Sam stared blankly at the vanity. They had Jasmine. His wife. What was she going through? Bottles crashed to the floor, and he blinked at his hand. He'd just reacted. In *rage*. That hadn't happened before.

He laced his hands behind his head and stared at the ceiling. Losing his temper wouldn't help Jasmine. He had to do better.

"Papa?" a little voice murmured.

It was like someone had punched him in the gut. Sam turned toward Ethan, who stood in the entryway to the twins' room, sleepily rubbing his eyes. The little boy had called him *Papa*. His chest swelled with emotion, his throat clogged and heat built up behind his eyes. It wasn't the first time the children had used the endearment, but it floored him every time.

"Yeah, little man?" he choked out.

Ethan yawned. "I heard a loud noise. It scared me."

Sam swallowed and dropped to his knees in front of Ethan. He pulled his son into his arms and hugged him close. "I'm sorry. I promise to be more careful next time."

"S'okay, papa," Ethan whispered, wrapping his arms around Sam's neck.

Papa. "How about we get back to bed, huh?"

Ethan didn't say anything when Sam scooped him up and moved through the doorway to the twins' room. Toys littered the chamber, along with books stacked haphazardly and drawings pinned to the walls. His gaze snagged on one of Jas. *Where are you?*

Leaning down, he placed Ethan in his bed. He didn't let go.

"Stay?" his son whispered.

Sam sniffled and smiled. "Of course." He tucked Ethan in and then squeezed into the narrow bed, his hair no doubt tickling Sam's nose, but the child didn't move. The only time Sam had had even a modicum of peace since Jasmine's disappearance was when he was with the twins.

He pressed a kiss to the top of Ethan's head. "I love you."

"Love you too, Papa." A beat of silence. "I miss Mama."

"I know, Ethan. So do I."

"When will she come home?" Jade's high-pitched voice asked. Her covers rustled, and then she was clambering over Sam's side and wiggling in beside him.

"Soon, loves. Now go back to sleep."

Jade grinned and peppered his cheek with kisses. "All right, Papa."

The twins snuggled into the covers and quickly fell back asleep. Sam stared at their tiny faces.

"I promise to bring her back," he whispered.

Ethan huffed and tossed his arm over Jade, his pointer finger poking her in the nose. Sam chuckled and moved his son's hand. How did he get so damn lucky?

His arm went numb first, and a stitch cramped his side, but there wasn't a torture in the world that would move him from his spot.

For now.

Tomorrow, he'd once again board a ship and wage war.

FIFTEEN

SAGE

———⊸∘◦⟜∽◦∘⊷———

SAGE STARED AT THE EXIT to the tent long after Hayjen disappeared through the flap. It would be so easy to go back to the new infirmary. And do what? Stand around some more?

Stop being such a sissy, Sage.

She reluctantly turned toward her and Tehl's chambers and frowned. Maybe he would be asleep? Sage shook her head. Facing angry men had never scared her before; she wouldn't back down now.

With soft steps, she approached their section of the tent, her fingertips grazing the canvas flap. She hesitated. Sure, she and Tehl had disagreed many times before, but this time was different. The look of disappointment earlier that night had almost gutted her.

Get in there.

Squaring her shoulders, she pushed through the flap, her heart racing as she spotted Tehl across the room, washing his face. She paused but forced her legs to move to the right side of the bed. He didn't say anything or even acknowledge her presence as he used a rag to wash his bare chest and arms. It was like she was a doormat. Invisible and unimportant.

Slowly, Sage tugged off her boots and sodden wool socks. She wiggled her chilled toes and then tucked them under the edge of the bedcover to keep them warm. Her lips pursed as she stared at the rumpled bed. Under normal circumstances, she would have stripped and crawled right into bed, but that felt too much like giving in. The tension in the air was almost choking her. A fight was coming, and she needed to have the high ground, so to speak.

If Tehl would say anything.

She cleared her throat. He said nothing.

This was not the response she was expecting. Sage expected him to yell, curse, something. Maybe he hadn't been pushed to the brink yet? Perhaps he wasn't as angry as she suspected.

"Are you going to look at me?" she asked softly. There, that was nonconfrontational.

He ignored her and began cleaning the back of his neck.

Sage let him have his silence for a few moments and observed him struggling to clean his back. The stupid, stubborn man.

She rolled her eyes and crawled across the mattress. He said nothing as she took the lemon-and-pine smelling cloth from his hands and stood, then began to wash his back with tender strokes. His muscles twitched beneath her touch, but even as she kneaded his back, the tension never left his frame. He really wasn't happy with her.

Her gaze darted down to the bed. It would be so easy to just climb in, turn her back on him, and go to sleep. Maybe they would both be more reasonable after a few hours of rest. A little time to cool down never hurt anyone.

Don't let the sun set on your anger, her uncle had said.

Sage's lips thinned. As much as she wanted to avoid this conversation, it wasn't going away. It helped no one to go to bed angry. And it was a sure way to have a poor night of sleep and an even worse morning. If Tehl wouldn't speak, then she needed to say something for the both of them.

She let her fingers wander upward and combed his damp, black locks with care, mulling over what to say. Sorry should be in there somewhere… but the problem was, she wasn't very sorry. In fact, she felt irritated at his high-handedness. Tamping down her own feelings wasn't easy, but one of them needed to be rational.

"Do you want to talk about it?" she asked.

Again, he said nothing, but he didn't move away from her massaging hands. That was something, at least.

She pressed closer and leaned her chin on his shoulder. "I'm sorry for not obeying you."

Tehl stiffened and pulled away from her, his movements jerky. She wobbled as he slowly spun to face her, his expression like stone. "That's what you think this is about?"

His voice held the chill of a bitter, winter wind. Sage shifted uncomfortably and fiddled with the rag. She hadn't heard him use that tone since he'd threatened the rebels into giving her a choice in marrying him all those months ago. Unease skittered down her spine, not from fear, but because, for the first time, she couldn't get a read on him.

"You commanded me to stay put, and I disobeyed," she responded, hating that she felt like a child about to get reprimanded by a parent. "I'm sorry."

"Unreal," he breathed. His deep blue eyes narrowed as he studied her. "For someone so intelligent, you're acting pretty stupid, and your apology needs some work."

Sage bristled. If there was anything that could ignite her temper, it was the word *stupid*. Men liked to throw it around to make women feel inferior to them. The fact that he would use it now angered her to the point of wanting to slap him.

She forced herself to uncurl her fists, and exhaled slowly before answering him. She could do this. A little patience and understanding never hurt anyone. "I would appreciate it if you would refrain from using that derogatory word when speaking to me."

"And I would appreciate it if you listened for once." He said it without any inflection—like he wasn't spoiling for a fight.

Lies.

"I'm happy to listen," she gritted out, "if you actually deemed to speak to me. You've barely said a word." Sage eyed him. "Would you please accept my apology?"

He pinned his gaze over her shoulder and nodded once. "Fine." Dismissing her, he kicked off his boots and began to unlace his leather pants.

Sage peered at him in confusion. It couldn't have been that easy, *and* he'd used the F word. Every woman knew what the word *fine* meant in a fight. It meant everything was certainly *not* fine.

"You're lying to *me*," she accused.

Tehl stopped untying his pants and his gaze rose, meeting hers, a hint of blue fire heating his eyes. "You wish to speak to me about lying?"

She almost took a step back at the vehemence in his voice, but she stood her ground, despite the way her toes curled into the furs covering their bed. "I don't lie to you, Tehl." They'd promised to be honest to each other, and she kept her vow to the best of her ability.

His hands clenched into fists at his side, the first show of emotion. "You looked me in the face and smiled as if agreeing with me to help those who needed it and then, as soon as my back was turned, waded into the fray."

"I never said I wouldn't do that," she pointed out. He'd just assumed she would obey him.

"That's splitting hairs and you know it. You should have listened."

"I'm your wife and your partner. I'm not a subordinate to be ordered around."

"You are so blind!" he growled.

"Then tell me what I'm not seeing!" What was he getting at? She was trying to make things better.

"It's not about obedience," he said raggedly. "Do you know what I felt when I got out of the fire with the last living man? As I lay him on the ground, I was thankful none of my family had been in there. I felt guilty that I would get to sleep next to my wife while others would never know the love of their women again." His gaze darkened. "But then, I couldn't find you. No one knew where you were." He raked a hand through his hair and then stabbed an accusing finger at her. "When I rounded the burning infirmary and Gav told me you were still inside…" His voice broke. "I… I couldn't breathe, and I wanted to be inside the fire with you."

Sage's bottom lip trembled at the emotion pouring out of her husband. She *was* stupid.

It wasn't about her disobeying. It was about the danger. "I'm so sorry you had to go through that…"

"When you were taken into Scythia, that wasn't your fault. I managed, because I knew who to punish for my pain and anguish. It wasn't *your* choice to leave. But this time, you *chose* to go into that fire without any regard for my feelings."

A tear dropped onto her cheek. Was it just yesterday that she thought Tehl had died in battle? How could she forget how that felt? Inadvertently, she'd caused this pain for him.

"How would you feel if I disregarded your feelings and got myself killed? Do you know why I didn't want you to go into the fire, other than the obvious?"

She shook her head. It was only fair to let him have his say. It was better for her to stay silent and let him get it all out.

"Most of the wounded were men." He paced at the foot of the bed and shot her a glare. "Not that you can't hold your own in a fight, but do you think you could have slung a grown man over your shoulder and hauled him out? No, Sage. You couldn't have, not without endangering him, yourself, and everyone else around you because of your petite frame."

That rankled her, but she let it slide when he fully faced her, destruction and sorrow clear on his face.

"I thought you'd died. For five minutes, I believed I would have to walk this road alone, and I imagined every horror you would've suffered."

"I'm okay," she whispered and took a small step toward him.

He held up his hand and then dropped to his haunches, both of his hands pulling at his midnight waves, his gaze distant. "I can't bear this." His haunted eyes rose to her face. "I can't deal with the emotions. It's too much. I can't live like this. How am I to survive it?"

Her stomach flipped, and she dropped the rag, took three careful steps to the end of the bed, and knelt. She'd done this. Tehl allowed her to wrap her arms around his neck and pull him into a hug.

"I'm so, *so* sorry," she said, guilt churning in her belly. Tonight had been a close call. Death had crept too close. "I should have listened." She should have. But, even in her heart, she knew she'd do it again if it meant saving her friends.

He tipped his head back and scanned her face. "I know you're sorry, but we're going to be in this position again."

She wanted to deny it, but she couldn't. "It's possible."

Tehl cocked his head and brushed his thumb across her cheek, catching one loose tear. "I hate emotions. How am I to bear all of this without turning into a madman?" he asked hoarsely. "I don't know if I can do this. I'll turn into my father."

Sage wanted to cry, but she held herself together. "I guess you have to ask yourself if the good outweighs the bad?"

He pushed to his feet, slipped his hand behind her neck, and tipped her head back. She stood, ashamed tears streaming down her face.

"Love isn't easy," he rumbled.

"No, it isn't."

"There's no going back."

"Not for me," Sage whispered. "There's no one else but you for me."

"Until death do us part."

It was a grave, dark statement that resonated in her soul.

She wasn't sure who moved first, but all she knew was that she needed to be in his arms. Tehl's lips crushed hers, fierce and demanding. He wasn't gentle or careful. He kissed her like it was his last chance to ever touch her. Sage threw her arms around his neck and kissed him back with the same urgency. Who knew what tomorrow held?

Her hands fisted in his hair, and she parted her lips, inviting him in. Warmth swept through her middle as he deepened the kiss. His fingers slid down the sensitive skin of her neck, catching on her soiled linen shirt. He snarled and released her for a moment, then tore the worn shirt straight down the center. Sage jerked back and stared at him wide-eyed. That was new.

Cool air teased her belly, and a shiver worked through her at how his gaze burned through her. It was like he was devouring her with his eyes. Observing him closely, she shrugged her shoulders, and the tattered linen fluttered to the mattress along with her modesty.

"I'm sorry," she said genuinely. Tonight, she'd deeply hurt him. Sage shakily drew in a breath. "I'm so sorry." More tears blurred her vision. "I didn't mean to. I would never hurt you on purpose."

"No, no tears," he whispered.

His hand curled around the back of her neck, and he pulled her mouth to his once again. His lips trailed lower, nipping at her chin, then her neck, his tongue tracing the salt of her tears.

His fingers slid down the sides of her neck and over her shoulders, his mouth never leaving hers. She gasped when he pulled her hard against him, his hands finding the soft skin behind her knees. Wrapping her legs around his waist, he pushed her onto the bed. She squeaked as he came down on top of her, his weight pressing her into the furs. The rasp of his stubble against her neck arched her off the bed, and she dug her nails into his shoulders.

"Don't ever do this to me again," he said gruffly. Teeth grazed the twisted scars around her throat, a teasing bite that threatened and tempted. "Spare my soul the anguish."

How she wished she could give such a promise. "I'll do my damnedest to never hurt you."

He growled. "I guess that will do." His hands slid down her sides in feverish need and paused on her hips, ever the gentleman.

Sage clasped the sides of his face and forced him to look her squarely in the eye. "I love you."

His eyes burned like a blacksmith's forge, the heat blistering her scarred soul. "As I you, even when you tear my heart from my chest." He had the power to shatter her. "But it's worth the pain," he breathed. The power to make her whole once again, too.

Sage kissed him eagerly, her hands sliding up his chest where she could feel the frantic rhythm of his heart beneath her palms. Tehl shackled her wrists and pinned them above her head. A flicker of unease washed over her, but his hard lips were there, capturing hers, ravenous and brutal. He tasted divine—like sin and redemption rolled into one. His kiss didn't just steal her breath, for he owned, possessed, and punished her.

For once, there was nothing but Tehl and herself. Two halves that created a whole. All thoughts disappeared when his hand slid between the furs and the naked small of her back, pressing her harder against him, like he could imprint himself on her skin, like he was trying to make sure she was still with him.

Sage bit his bottom lip and his lips parted, his gaze becoming distant.

"Devilish woman," he hissed. "Don't tempt me."

"Beastly man," she taunted. "Don't think you can handle it?"

His lips curled away from his teeth in a dark smile, and something hard and predatory slid over his face. "Be careful what you ask for, love. The beast might eat you all up."

Her smile was devious as she crooked a finger at him. "I'll take that gamble."

SIXTEEN

MIRA

MIRA TUGGED THE BLANKET HIGHER over the shivering soldier and forced herself to walk away. He was lost to pain and a high fever. There wasn't anything more she could do for him.

Her feet dragged as she moved down the center aisle, scanning her patients as she drifted toward her herb station where the queen sat idly, brewing willow bark to help with the fevers. The Methian royal had been a godsend. Without her help, Mira doubted most of the men would have made it through the night. She rubbed at her eyes with her good hand and stumbled a step, her right hand knocking against the nearest tent support. Gasping, she clutched her right hand to her chest as colored spots splashed across her vision. The ground seemed to roll, and she lurched sideways as pain pulsed up her arms in waves. Her left foot caught on a worn rug, and Mira braced herself for the horrible fall. Huge hands curled around her biceps and steadied her. Dazedly, she looked up, way up into the face of Raziel, the Methian crown prince.

She opened her mouth to say thank you, but all that came out was a hoarse groan.

"Are you okay?" he asked in a deep timbre.

Was she? Nausea slammed into her, and she tried to jerk away as bile flooded her mouth. "Gonna be sick," she wheezed before puking. With every heave, jerk, and twitch, more pain flooded her body. By the time she came out of it, Raziel had placed her on a cot and had a bucket on her lap.

Mira leaned her cheek against the wooden edge of the bucket and took shallow breaths, the warrior's scent curling around her comfortingly. A large hand stroked her braid and rubbed small circles on her upper back. How embarrassing. Not the vomiting, because in truth, sickness was a part of life, but the fact she wasn't trying to get rid of Raziel. It was so bloody nice to have someone care for her, even if it was for five minutes.

She cracked one eye and gave the prince a silly smile. "Haven't run away screaming yet?"

He returned hers with a devastatingly handsome grin. "And miss the chance to hold your golden hair from your beautiful face? Never."

"You, good sir, are a pretty liar."

"And you, lovely healer, are too sick to be out of bed, let alone working." His expression turned serious. "You're to the point of collapse. When was the last time you slept?"

Sucking on her bottom lip, she debated lying to him, but the Methians had an uncanny way of knowing when a person lied. It was better to be truthful. "Since before the fire."

Raziel's eyes narrowed into golden slits that reminded her of the way Nali stared at rodents before she pounced on them. Thank the stars for the blessed feline. Mira hadn't spotted any mice at all.

"You mean to tell me you haven't slept in almost two days?" Raziel demanded.

She closed her eyes in an attempt to ignore the censure on his face. "What am I supposed to do? They need me." A calloused finger touched the delicate skin beneath her right eye. She flinched and opened her eyes.

"You're a healer, are you not?" he cajoled.

"A tired one," she said, trying to make a joke. He didn't crack a smile.

"So, you know how the body needs sleep to heal. You're doing yourself and these men a disservice when you don't care for yourself."

"Let me ask you a question," she said roughly, her voice still rusty from the smoke inhalation. "If they were your men, would you rest when you knew they needed you? When they suffered and you could alleviate that pain?" His silence answered her question. "I swore an oath when I took up this profession. I will do everything in my power to help them."

Raziel surprised her and brushed a stray hair from her cheek. Her chest warmed at the sweet gesture, but she shoved it down deep. He was just being nice. She'd seen how he acted with women in general. Plus, he was a prince and she a commoner.

"Beauty as well as intelligence, compassion, and loyalty. The day you were born must have been something special."

Heat filled her cheeks. "Save your sweet words for someone who will believe them," she retorted.

It was in moments like this that she loved and hated the most. Since she'd come to the battlefront as a healer, Raziel had slowly inserted himself in her life. It started out as little things, but now she looked forward to his visits and conversations every day. It was stupid of her, really. He meant nothing by it, but it was the first time a man had looked at her without the stain of her past or judged her for entering a predominantly male profession.

"You don't believe I think you're one of a kind?" he asked, his voice deceptively soft.

"I think you love women. With your charm, I'm sure you make all of us feel like royalty," she murmured, her pain slowly fading to a dull throb.

"You know, in my culture, you don't have to be royalty to be considered *royal*. It all comes down to your actions. Believe me when I say that you could be anyone's queen."

Such pretty words said in earnest. "You flatter me," she huffed. Mira slowly sat up and glanced over her shoulder to break the tension that was building between them. If she wasn't careful, he'd steal her heart before she knew it. "Your mother looks like she's almost finished. I should help her."

Raziel pulled the bucket from her lap and placed it on the floor, never flinching at the sloshing contents within it. He straightened and shocked her by cupping her right cheek. "You can pretend all you want, Mira, but you and I both know there is something here."

Her eyes widened. "You've known me for a handful of weeks."

"We don't court like you Aermians do. We judge a mate by their fortitude, loyalty, and caring nature. Spending time in your presence has taught me that you're by far one of the best people I've ever had the privilege of spending time with. Normally, courting couples come to an understanding and then one kidnaps the other."

"Kidnapping is *not* okay." All she could see were Sage's haunted eyes and the thorn-adorned collar around her bloody throat. His thumb brushed her cheekbone, pulling Mira back to the present.

"I understand your reservations, which is why I have moved slowly."

"Slowly?" she whispered. "Slowly is a six year courtship."

Raziel's nose wrinkled. "Why would anyone agree to that? Our time on this earth isn't guaranteed. Why waste time living it without those you love?"

"That's the point of courtship—it's to make sure you really love them. Marriage is forever."

He dropped his hand. "What you speak of is attraction and infatuation. Love grows over years of time spent together, or child rearing. Why would anyone base their relationship off infatuation? That's the perfect way to ensure an unhappy union."

She must have been more exhausted than she thought, because the damn Methian was starting to make sense. Perhaps she would take a bloody nap. It wouldn't be long until her body gave up on her.

"So, what are you really getting at?"

Raziel brushed a wine-colored braid from his face and leveled a determined look at her, filled with promise. "I am going to pursue you, my golden one."

A startled laugh escaped her. "Excuse me?"

"Don't pretend like you didn't understand my words. You know exactly what I mean." He leaned closer, his golden eyes twinkling. "I intend to make you my mate, Mira. Even if that means courting you the Aermian way."

"You're joking," she muttered.

"I am not. I wouldn't joke about mates."

"I'm not going to marry you," Mira said bluntly, even as her traitorous heart skipped a blasted beat.

"I'm not asking." A devilish look. "Yet."

Mira rolled her eyes. She had to be hallucinating. Maybe she had passed out and her overactive imagination had spun out of control. Raziel touched her chin and leaned so close that she held her breath. Stars, he better not try to kiss her. She'd just puked. He brushed his nose along hers.

"Seek your bed soon, or I will have to take measures into my own hands." With that last comment, he stood and strode out of the infirmary.

Mira stared after him in shock and confusion. Did that really just happen? She stood on wobbly legs and turned toward the herb table. The queen had a hip leaned against the table and her very familiar golden eyes focused on Mira.

"Run while you can, my dear. It's only a matter of time."

"Until what?" she found the courage to ask.

"Until he captures you."

SEVENTEEN

SAGE

THE BLASTED RAIN MADE EVERYTHING harder.

Sage shivered as cold droplets slipped down her neck, to her already soaked shirt. The linen chafed against her skin. She swiped the rain from her brow and blinked, searching the battlefield for Zachael. Steam rose from the wet earth, and fog hovered in the distance. The fog was a blessing and a curse. It gave them more cover, but it also hid their enemies.

Her boots slurped as the mud tried desperately to hold her in place as she slogged forward. Rafe panted at her side, his amber eyes constantly scanning the area for an immediate attack. The wind whipped through the chilly air, and she shivered as it moved right through her. Stars above, she hated the bloody cold.

The former rebellion leader cast a quick glance in her direction. "We need to turn back."

"No, we've gained ground."

"Only because the warlord is letting us." Rafe tensed. "Incoming."

Sage hefted her sword higher, her damp fingers slipping on the pommel for one second. That wasn't good. Her stomach bottomed out as *six* Scythian warriors materialized through the mist.

Swamp apples. "Retreat," she breathed.

Rafe sprang into action. "You in front of me."

She didn't second-guess him as they bolted back the way they came. Where had all their bloody soldiers gone? They couldn't have disappeared. The hair rose along her arms. This was all a trap. A damned trap.

She yelped as her boot sank deep into the mud. Sage slammed her hands to her knees, her extremities screaming in pain. Twisting to the side, she desperately yanked at her foot, but the suction from the mud made it almost impossible to move.

"Come on, damn you," she muttered as the Scythian warriors closed in.

Rafe stepped in front of her and drew a second sword from the sheath at his hip. "Work your toes back and forth. Once you break free, you run."

"I'm not leaving you behind." Her teeth chattered as the rain fell harder, obscuring her vision some.

"You can and you will, little one."

Sage clenched her teeth and jerked her foot as hard as she could. "I won't."

"You have no choice." He threw his shoulders back. "I'll draw them away."

Her left foot popped free followed by the right and she lunged forward, only missing his cloak by a hair as he sprinted toward the soldiers.

"No!" Sage scrambled to her feet, mud and muck smeared across her body. She took one step forward before the voice from her nightmares slithered over her spine.

"Hello, consort."

Every muscle in her body froze, and Sage stared helplessly as Rafe engaged the warlord's men, refusing to acknowledge the hulking nightmare nearing her.

"Will you not look at me?"

She closed her eyes and inhaled deeply before spinning around.

The warlord stood a measly fifteen paces from her. He smiled softly and cocked his head, his gaze perusing her form. "You've lost weight."

Spots dotted her vision, and the world dipped. Oh god, she was going to pass out. Sage dug her nails into her palms and bit the insides of her cheeks until she tasted blood, the pain keeping her from blacking out. Self-loathing and shame crashed into her as she continued to stare at the monster that haunted her dreams.

"Are you eating?" he asked, like it was a perfectly rational question while on the battlefield.

Part of her numbness melted away at his asinine question. It wasn't like they were friends catching up over bloody tea. Anger boiled in her veins. "War has hardened me."

His smile grew. "I can see that. Battle becomes you."

She tensed when he took two steps closer, his movements like a leren on the hunt. Sage lifted her blade and stared him down. "Come any closer and I'll kill you."

"So much fire," he crooned. "How I've missed it."

Her stomach rolled. Oh, wicked hell, she was going to be sick.

"Are you ready to come home yet?"

"Home? With you?" she murmured, dumbfounded. *Attack him, do something.*

He arched an onyx brow and shook his head, reminding her of something her father did when he was trying to reason with one of her unruly brothers. Her gaze darted over his shoulder and then back to him. Where was Rafe? Was he hurt?

"Yes, of course."

"I'm not going anywhere with you," she mumbled. Sage would turn her own sword on herself before she ended back in his clutches. The warlord tsked, moving closer. She countered his moves and circled, her sword held up defensively.

Sighing, he paused and pulled his sword free from his scabbard. "You'll only tire yourself out. As much as I love a good fight, you could just come willingly."

"Never," she hissed, her fingers tightening on the pommel of her muddy sword.

A smirk touched his lips. "So be it, fiery one."

Sage jerked at the pet name as a flood of memories assaulted her. The warlord feinted several times, but she could see he never intended to strike. Yet. The scar at her neck burned at the reminder of his cruelty. He was trying to draw Sage into an attack, but she wasn't that stupid. He was older and more experienced, but she could outwait him if she had to.

"Don't be shy," the warlord whispered. "It's been so long since we've been able to come together."

He attacked, and Sage blocked his swing and dodged to the side, wincing when the handle of her sword jerked against her sore hands. She needed to be careful—her stiffness, the cold, and the raw skin of her palms might get her captured or killed if she wasn't.

The warlord pursued the attack, trying to use up her energy. Sage attempted to dodge more and block less in order to spare herself, but he was just too damn quick. His sword slammed into hers, and it reverberated throughout her entire body, her teeth clacking together.

Damn it. She growled and bared her teeth at him.

He grinned. "I love this side of you. I can't tell you how much I've missed this."

Pain wormed its way up her right arm and into her shoulder as he disengaged. Her palms stung, and warm liquid heated the pommel of her sword. Without looking down, Sage knew she was bleeding.

She blinked, trying to get rid of the moisture in her eyes. Had the warlord switched his sword to his left hand, or was he carrying two swords? If she'd believed in magic, Sage would have sworn he was using some sort of illusion. Weariness must have been the culprit. She shook her head, trying to clear her vision.

Don't give up now. Think of the children. Think of Lilja.

Her lip curled, unbridled rage unfurling in her chest.

"That's it," he murmured. "Let me have all of that anger."

He lunged at her, and Sage blocked his sword and thrust back, coming body-to-body with the warlord. But that was a damn mistake. The huge monster used his strength to force her slowly to her knees.

Stupid. She knew better than to go toe to toe with someone so much bigger than herself. Sage wheezed and broke away from him, dropping to the mud and rolling away. The warlord struck, cutting her shoulder as Sage rose to her feet, dripping rain and mud. She dodged back, cursing angrily.

He paused and began circling once again. Sage spared a quick glance at her shoulder, noting how the blood and rainwater mixed together and dripped down her soaking linen sleeve. It wasn't that bad, but it still burned.

"You cut me."

"As did you when you left me." His expression darkened before it cleared, a manic look of glee replacing it. "It's not deep, but it'll make a nice scar of our first duel." He switched his sword to the other hand. "Prepare yourself, love.

The times for games are over."

She met his attack, and was barely able to follow his movements as he changed his sword from one hand to the other. Irritatingly, she was forced to admire his perfect technique—one her father had tried to drill into her over the years. And while she was an excellent swordsman, the warlord was something else. It was too damn bad he was such a demon. A pity for such talent to be wasted.

Her steps faltered, and her arms began to tremble. They were swiftly coming to the time in a battle where the lesser swordsman began to gasp for air, tremble, and make horrible mistakes. She refused to be that person today.

Dig deep for the strength you know you have.

She snarled as he switched swords, and she seized the brief moment by lunging in. Sage slashed his left arm. The warlord grunted as she cut through muscle. He jerked back and examined his wound. His fingers touched the bloody gash. Slowly, the monster lifted his head and drew his fingers across each of his cheeks, scarlet cuts marring his perfect set of cheekbones.

"And that is why you are my consort," he said softly. "You're the only one I'll bleed for."

Horror churned in her belly as he darted forward. She got in two good slashes before he knocked her feet from beneath her. Sage gasped as she hit the ground. Screaming, she ripped the dagger from her hip and sank it into his thigh, just as he stepped onto her right hand, forcing her to release her sword.

He hissed but otherwise didn't say anything as he knelt, his boot grinding her wrist into the mud. She cried out and attempted to twist the blade deeper. The warlord tore her hand from the blade and grabbed her by her braid, pinning her in place. He yanked hard on her hair, forcing her head backward, the vulnerable arch of her neck on display.

The warlord leaned close, his weight pressing her farther into the mud. His black gaze ran over her face. He leaned closer, and she did the only thing she could think of. She spit on him. He froze, and something scary crossed his face that had her quaking in her boots, but she didn't cower. He'd never see her cower again.

"I hate you."

"You think you do, but hate is easily turned into other things."

"Death is preferable to you."

Instead of her words making him visibly angry, he smiled. He released a soft chuckle. "All this time I thought I needed to steal you back." His smile grew. "How I was wrong." He pressed closer, his nose running along her jawline, and his lips rested on the shell of her ear. "You've been brainwashed. I'll not let you play the martyr." He slowly pulled back and placed a tender kiss on her cheek. "You'll come to me in good time."

He stepped back, and Sage immediately hunted for her sword. Her fingers found the pommel, and she jerked forward on her knees, slicing toward his calf. The warlord jumped out of the way and carefully pulled her dagger from his thigh. He held it up and then clasped it to his chest like a treasured gift.

"I'll be seeing you soon, consort." He backed into the fog as she got to her feet. "Don't keep me waiting too long. Every death from now on will rest on your head."

Sage screamed and charged him, but he was swallowed up by the mist. Squinting, she spun in a circle as his sensual laugher echoed around her.

"I'll be waiting."

EIGHTEEN

THE WARLORD

—◦⌒⌒◦—

HIS BODY WAS OVERHEATING.

He barely felt the winter elements as he marched into camp. Warriors parted for him as he emotionlessly passed them. Blood dripped from the wound on his leg, but he didn't feel it either. All he could see were her fiery, green eyes and sinful lips.

Blair approached from the left, a jagged cut across his left pectoral. Very close to the heart. Was his commander losing his touch?

"Come too close to an Aermian blade today?" he asked softly, striding toward his tent.

His commander, ever stoic, didn't even flinch at the question.

He's too bold, too well trained. He wants our throne. We must watch him, the voices whispered.

He couldn't agree more. That was the problem with giving men power. When they held a position for too long, they eventually turned their greedy gazes on the Scythian throne. Zane had seen it time after time, and Blair was no different. It was only a matter of time until the commander made a grab for power.

"Would you like me to send for a healer?" Blair asked.

And let their incompetent hands touch him? Zane thought not. He waved a hand as they arrived at his tent. "Make sure no one disturbs me."

With that, he entered the enormous tent. Inside, it was divided into three parts: a war room of sorts, the washing area, and his sleeping quarters. The braziers were well-stoked and heated the canvas rooms to an almost balmy heat. Sweat beaded on his brow as he pushed into his bedroom. It was simple. Warm furs created the flooring. A large bed rested near the brazier, and his desk sat to the right of the entrance.

Zane moved to his desk and sat slowly, his gaze trained on the stab wound on his thigh. He leaned down and pulled a hand-sized notebook from his boot. To anyone else, the book would look insignificant enough, but to him, it meant everything. He tugged the desk's top drawer open and fished out a quill and ink. With care, he opened the notebook to his last entry and scratched out the date on the next open page.

He focused on his wound and studied the way it bled sluggishly. It wasn't a cause for concern, but... His lips pressed together. It wasn't healing as well as it should. Perhaps he needed to change his dosage?

Maybe the fools at your lab have made a mistake, the voices hissed.

His lip curled. Fools indeed. No matter how well he trained the next alchemists, they continually made mistakes, or they were intentionally trying to kill him. A wicked smile touched his lips. The last alchemist to try that had drowned in his own poison. There was poetic justice in that. Dying by one's own creation.

He unlatched the key from the chain at his neck and opened the bottom left drawer, the sound of tinkling glass filling the air. Zane sighed. There was something about the bell-like chime of glass bottles knocking together that calmed him. He lifted a purple bottle and examined the marks on the side, the liquid matching its marker perfectly. He cast a glance at his door and listened. He heard no one but the two guards at the entrance of his tent. Although, he knew no one dared to enter without his permission, there were still those who would like to see him dead.

Carefully, he inventoried his draughts and measured out his correct dosages, noting he was low on two. He'd have to send a message to Maeve. She was the only one he trusted with his tinctures. With precise movements, he made notes in the notebook on his wound and the dosage for the day. He also scratched out a coded message for his sister.

A wave of nostalgia washed over him. It had been her idea as children to create a code for themselves. He'd only warmed to the idea as the years passed.

He flushed out his wound and didn't bother to stitch it. It would seal itself shut by the next evening.

Zane leaned back in the chair and laced his hands behind his head, his armpits sweating. He hated sweating. While he understood the necessity, the uncleanliness of it bothered him immensely. It got particularly worse when wounded. The body ran a high fever as it tried to repair itself. But there were worse lots in life.

His gaze wandered to his bed and the trunk that rested at the bottom. A silky feminine article of clothing peeked out from beneath his bow in the open chest, taunting him. In preparation of retrieving his consort, he'd taken the liberty of having a few things created for her.

So close. In our clutches. You let her go. Weak. Weak. Weak, the voices taunted.

Not weak—smart.

He smiled as he remembered the fight earlier tonight. She'd looked wild, unhinged, and absolutely stunning. War became her. When she'd stabbed him, he'd never wanted to kiss her more. In truth, the voices had been screaming for him to take her, right there in the mud amongst the blood and war. But he didn't. He'd fought through the battle-lust and really examined her. While she'd changed for the better, his consort hadn't been ready to submit to him. That's what he craved the most.

Her capitulation.

It would be all the sweeter when she broke and came to him.

And she *would*.

While he didn't *want* to hurt his consort, he knew some types of pain shaped a person into something better, something great.

Something extraordinary. Someone worth the Scythian throne.

Zane rolled his neck and stared off into space as he went over the next parts in his plan. It may have pained him to leave her there on the battlefield today, but it was worth it.

The clock was ticking.

The two of them coming together was inevitable. He calculated that she'd come running to him in less than a fortnight.

His gaze wandered back to the blue silk.

She'd be home.

NİNETEEN

SAGE

———◦∘⟨⟨⟩⟩∘◦———

SAGE SCOWLED AT THE ABUSED leather pants covering her knees. The fingers of her right hand tightened against the bottle of whiskey she was nursing. The pinch and tug of the thread and needle usually made her want to puke, but not today. All she could think about was the warlord.

He'd let her go. He could have dragged her through the mud by her hair, and yet, he'd left her. Why?

Are you ready to come home?

Her heart accelerated, and she lifted the bottle of spirits to her lips, barely tasting the whiskey as she swallowed. She relished the burn of the alcohol and how it heated her belly. Since arriving back at camp, she couldn't get bloody warm. Whether it was from the rain or her chilling experience with the Scythian warrior, she didn't know.

"You'll have to tell him," Rafe said, making sure to stay out of the healer's way. "And the war council."

She lifted her eyes and hid her flinch at his appearance. The man was a bloody mess. Sage swallowed hard. His entire face was practically an enormous bruise, not to mention all the cuts, a stab wound, and his two broken ribs. The stars only knew what would have happened if she hadn't shown up. Rafe was a beast in his own right, but if the warlord hadn't retreated when he had, Rafe would have died. Because of her.

Guilt settled on her shoulders. She was so tired of feeling guilty, but what was one more thing settled onto the chip she already lugged around?

"I know," she muttered. The war council didn't frighten her in the least, but after the rocky few days she'd had with Tehl, this was something she didn't want to talk about. He'd lose his ever-logical mind. "This changes things."

"It changes nothing."

"How can you say that?" Sage grimaced as the healer pierced the needle through her skin once more. Stars, she hated that.

"Our goals stay the same. We continue as we have been."

"I disagree." Her stomach knotted. "I have a feeling that things are going to be worse. Scythia's motives have changed."

Rafe snorted and then clutched at his ribs. "He still wants world domination. That's nothing new."

She couldn't put her finger on it but... "Something wasn't right." It was the way he dealt with her. It felt off.

"How so?"

"I don't know," Sage admitted. "I stabbed him in the thigh, and he didn't even cry out. It was like he didn't feel the pain at all." The memory of him swiping blood across his cheeks caused her belly to cramp and bile to burn the back of her throat. "He's changing."

"Into what?" Rafe asked.

That was the question. Was the warlord riding a berserker so high that he didn't feel the pain? Or was he dosing himself with some sort of draught? Either way, it made her uneasy. She rubbed her thumb along the glass bottle. "I can't shake the feeling that he's backing us into a corner we can't get out of."

Sage startled when Rafe lay his hand over her own. He pulled her left hand away and laced their fingers together.

"I'm sorry for today."

Her brows furrowed in confusion as she looked up. "What do you mean?"

"I should have protected you." His gaze darted to her wounded shoulder. "He could have taken you."

"But he didn't." She squeezed his fingers. "You almost got yourself killed out there protecting me. You did your best."

Rafe glanced away, his jaw clenching. "Not good enough."

"It *was* good enough. We are both alive. That's a victory in and of itself."

They fell into silence as the healer finished caring for and dressing Sage's wound.

Sage's shoulders slumped as they were left alone. This was something she loved about Rafe. They could just be in each other's company. There was no need to make conversations. It was enough that they loved and supported each other. Love. It wasn't something she said very often, but she'd promised herself that she'd work on it.

"You know I love you, right?"

Rafe jerked and scrutinized her. "You're not going to do something stupid, are you?"

Sage puffed out a laugh. "No." She chuckled but sobered quickly as she studied her dear friend. "We've been through many hardships together in the last few years. Never doubt that I truly care for you."

He smiled softly and leaned forward to her cheek. "I consider you my flesh and blood." Rafe pulled back. "While things didn't go as I expected them to, I still count myself lucky to love and have the love of such a fierce female."

She smiled. "It's funny how life surprises us, isn't it?" Her gaze moved past him to Blaise, who was currently sleeping. "Do you believe there is only one destined mate for a person?"

"No."

"I agree." Her smile turned wistful. "We could have been happy together before the Crown captured me. And though we may have been blissfully happy, I now can't imagine my life without Tehl."

"He is a strong mate for you, better than I."

Her brows raised. "Such humble words."

"I believe there are many potential mates for every person, and while you could make each pairing work, some just suit better." Rafe shrugged. "We would have made a powerful coupling, but you and Tehl complement each other in a way we never did." He smiled. "You were always a queen."

Sage rolled her eyes. "Such pretty words." Her smile turned smug as she caught him glancing in Blaise's direction. He'd been sniffing in the Scythian woman's direction for some time. "Something tells me your married future isn't far off."

"What makes you so sure?" Rafe asked, never taking his eyes off Blaise.

"Maybe it's the way you stare," she said bluntly. It felt good to talk about something light.

"She hates me."

"I hated the crown prince. Look where we are now."

Rafe smirked. "Soon, I'll be welcoming your fat, green-eyed babes into the world." He chuckled. "You should see the look on your face."

"Not anytime soon, I hope."

"There's only one way to control that…"

Sage blushed. "Enough," she said gruffly. "Are you ready to go?"

He stood slowly. "I've been waiting on you."

She untangled the fingers of her left hand from his and shook her head. "You always want the last word."

"And I don't know anyone like that at all," he retorted.

Sage threw her head back and laughed. It felt damn good. For a few minutes, her spirit was lightened. Darkness may have surrounded her, but, when one looked closely enough, there were always glimmers of light.

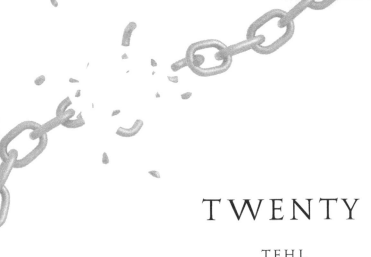

TWENTY

TEHL

"FALL BACK!" TEHL BELLOWED.

His battalion of men sprinted away from the burning war machine as Scythian warriors gave chase. Tehl's arms pumped by his sides, and he changed direction when he realized a flaming stone was incoming. It slammed to the earth a mere three paces ahead of him.

Veering right, the Aermian soldiers flanked him, keeping pace as they pushed back toward their line. His breaths seemed abnormally loud in his own ears as his heart raced. Not too far to go until they made it back to safety.

The soldier on his left crashed to the ground. A spear stuck out from his back. Tehl broke stride for one second before picking up his speed. As much as it galled him to leave the man behind, there wasn't any choice. It was war. He shut his feelings away and focused on the task. The gray clouds darkened. That wasn't good. Either rain or snow. Neither was ideal.

"They're gaining on us. Move!" Gav yelled, his command spurring the small group of soldiers to move faster.

No one wanted to be caught by the enemy. While they'd managed to figure out how to take down warriors without as many deaths, the Scythians had the unfair advantages of speed, strength, and heightened senses. Damn them.

The smoke wavered, and Tehl narrowed his eyes. Did he see movement ahead? He studied the terrain. Did the hill ahead conceal the enemy? No time to turn back now or even find cover.

"Arms up," he shouted. "Be prepared." No sooner had he given the command when enemy warriors sprung from their hiding places. Tehl raised his sword and charged forward. The wicked devils had hidden themselves in the mud. They looked like bloody swamp monsters.

Tehl's sword crashed against an enemy sword with a clang that made his teeth rattle. He tore his dagger from his chest sheath and slashed at the Scythian's chest. He knew there were only a few moments to get one of the monsters down before they killed him. His knife drew a bloody gash down the man's chest. But the Scythian didn't even blink.

Wicked hell. The warrior was already deep into the berserker rage. Tehl danced back, and the Scythian lunged, his sword high. The crown prince danced out of the way and cursed when burning pain sliced across his shoulder. He clenched his jaw and ignored the pain. The cut was minor. If it had been deep, the pain would have knocked him to his knees.

Raziel rushed in from behind and chopped at the Scythian's bare, mud-covered back. The warriors were an arrogant lot. It was stupid to show that much skin in a battle. They were proud and it would be the end of them, he vowed. The Methian prince darted under the enemy warrior's guard and cut him across the ribs. Tehl blinked and circled the warrior while his attention was on Raziel. So, he planned on riling the enemy.

The Methian took one step toward the Scythian when he turned to face Tehl, snarling. Tehl lunged back and then forward, his right foot connecting solidly with the warrior's chest. It was like kicking a stone wall.

The Scythian stumbled but didn't fall.

"Weakling," the warrior spat. "I'll enjoy your death."

Tehl kept his gaze fixed on the warrior. He hadn't kicked the enemy to knock him down. The purpose had been to rile his anger, so that he forgot that death was stalking him from behind. Raziel struck without a sound. The warrior stiffened and choked, blood dripping down his chin. Tehl nodded to the Methian prince and turned from the gruesome scene.

He knew it to be ghastly, and yet he felt nothing. No nausea, remorse, or shame. Slowly, he was becoming desensitized to it all.

Tehl waded into the fray, hardly hearing anything around him. The world surrounding the crown prince faded, and all he could focus on was the next opponent, the perfect strike point, and the safest route for escape.

His sword bit into the flesh of his newest foe and he watched, completely unfazed, as life drained from the man's gaze. He released the warrior and lifted his own head, once again scanning his battalion, searching for who needed help.

The hair at the nape of his neck rose as he caught sight of Gavriel battling a warrior who looked to be twice his size. For the first time all day, he felt something.

Terror.

His cousin was sweating and fighting with everything he had. Tehl dug his toes into the ground and pushed forward, racing toward the duel. Gav couldn't see it, but the Scythian was toying with him. Tehl cut through the swathe, his heart pounding. Only a little farther. If he could reach them, then it would be a fair fight.

Snow fell from the sky, big heavy flakes like someone had cut a feather pillow and dumped it from above. The Scythian swept Gav's feet out from under him, and a cry stuck in Tehl's throat. The enemy slammed his boot down on Gavriel's ankle and then stabbed his spear into his left thigh. His cousin screamed in pain but never dropped his sword. The Scythian pulled a short blade from his waist and leaned closer to finish the job.

Tehl's focus homed in on the enemy who'd wounded his cousin. Gav wildly slashed his sword at the enemy, managing to hit the warrior in the chest. The man bellowed and lifted his blade, his attention locked in on Gavriel.

The crown prince smiled darkly, sprinting the last few steps. The warrior spun in time to see his death coming. Tehl drove his sword into the Scythian's chest. The warrior teetered for a moment and then crashed backward, taking Tehl with him. The crown prince rolled away and held out his dagger in case the warrior wasn't truly gone. He'd seen some of the warriors stabbed over ten times and still they kept fighting until they died of blood loss. It was like something out of a horror story.

This time, the Scythian didn't rise.

Tehl retrieved his blade quickly and turned to his cousin, dropping to his knees. Gav panted, his face creased with pain.

"How bad is it?" Gavriel gasped.

Tehl knelt and eyed Gav's wound. He carefully slipped his left hand under his cousin's leg and gritted his teeth. The warrior had stabbed him clean through the leg, pinning him to the ground.

Bloody hell.

"That bad?" Gav wheezed, sweat dripping down his brow and cheek.

Tehl didn't want to tell him. He unbuckled his cousin's belt and yanked it out from beneath him, not daring to look Gav in the eye as he formed a tourniquet around the top part of his left thigh.

"Just tell me. I already know my ankle is broken."

Tehl cinched the belt to stop the blood flow and met Gavriel's purple gaze, his heart in his throat. "The spear went clear through and into the earth. He pinned you."

Emotions raced across Gav's face too fast for Tehl to read before his expression melted into determination. "You must leave me."

No.

Raziel appeared on his right side, and a loose ring of soldiers formed around Gavriel.

"How bad is it?" the Methian prince barked.

"He's stuck."

Raziel cursed and dropped to his knees. He inspected the damage and probed the wound from below. "I think we can get the spear out of the ground, but we can't remove it here." *Or he'll die,* was the implication.

Tehl eyed the six-foot-long spear. They'd need to cut the staff down to mobilize him. His gaze darted to Gav's pale face. "We'll need to cut the spear before we move you as well. Prepare yourself," he muttered grimly.

A soldier to the right stepped closer and held out part of his shirt that he'd ripped away. "Bandages for our commander."

Tehl nodded gratefully as another handed him his belt. Wordlessly, he placed the leather strip between Gav's teeth. He stared at his cousin and touched his forehead to Gavriel's.

"You have a little girl at home. Don't you die on her. Hold on to Isa."

Gav nodded, and Tehl forced himself to place both of his hands on the spear. Raziel pulled a serrated blade from the sheath at his thigh and solemnly asked, "Are you ready?"

Tehl nodded, holding the spear steady. When Gavriel's purple gaze focused on the Methian prince, Tehl pulled with all his might. Gav's body arched, and he screamed once, before passing out as he pulled the spear from the ground. The crown prince released the spear and pressed the linen against the bleeding wound. Raziel knelt and began sawing the shaft of the spear off.

"It's a blessing he's unconscious for this."

"Let's pray that it stays that way," Tehl murmured.

They had a long way to go to get back to camp. Anything could go wrong in that time.

TWENTY-ONE

SAGE

SAGE BURST INTO THE INFIRMARY tent, startling two healers. "Where is Gavriel Ramses?"

"The rear room, my lady," the older healer rasped.

She brushed by them without thanks, her legs shaking with adrenaline. News had spread fast through camp when their commander had returned hurt. *How bad was it?*

"Hold him down!" Queen Osir commanded Rafe and Raziel.

Sage rushed through the tent flap and into the commotion. People scurried about the room everywhere, but she ignored all of them when she spotted Gavriel. He lay on his right side with a spear pierced through his thigh. Tehl stood at the foot of the bed, cutting Gav's leather boot from his now-very-swollen ankle.

Stars above. Queasiness rolled through her, and she pressed a clammy hand to her forehead. Blood had never bothered her in the past, but the longer she was exposed to grisly scenes, the worse it got.

Get yourself together. This is Gav.

Swallowing her saliva, she pressed forward. Gav's glassy, purple eyes wildly searched the room. She stepped into his line of sight and smiled warmly at him. He froze and held out a trembling hand.

"It's okay," Sage crooned and dropped to her knees, both hands wrapping around his remarkably cool one. "You'll be all right."

"Hurtzzzz," he slurred through cracked lips.

"I know." She brushed her fingers along his heated brow and drew patterns on his cheeks. Her gaze caught the flash of Mira pulling scalpels from boiling water, and her belly flipped. Gav tried to look over his shoulder, but she released his hand and cupped the back of his neck. Scooting a little closer, she leaned her cheek against the cot and stroked his damp, dirty black locks.

"I'm not going to make it," he croaked.

"Don't talk like that." She mustered up the most reassuring smile she could. Not many would survive a wound such as this, but if anyone could do it, it would be Gavriel. "Soon this will all be over."

"Isa..."

"Isa will be so happy to see you when you're recovered. Just think how impressed she will be with your scars. I bet she'll ask you to show it to all the ladies in court."

"How scandalized they'll be when I start to unbuckle my pants," he gasped.

Sage laughed at the little spark of deviousness she spotted in his eyes. "They've been pining after you for years. I bet they'll take it as an invitation."

He nodded, but his gaze dimmed.

No, no, no, no. That wasn't good.

"Don't let him fall asleep!" Mira barked.

Sage removed her hand from behind Gavriel's head and pressed her fingertips into the hollows of his cheeks and pulled back. She shook him roughly. "None of that, my friend."

His head lolled, but his attention was once more focused on her face. She tipped her head to the side and shrugged her shoulder so the linen shirt slipped away from her neck, revealing the ropy scar around her neck. "Do you remember when Isa saw this for the first time?"

"She asked if a leviathan hurt you," he whispered.

"She did. Thankfully, Lilja was in the room."

Gav wheezed out a short laugh. "She really got a close view of a leviathan bite."

"We're ready," Queen Osir announced. "Anyone who is not assisting, get out!"

Sage watched the soldiers file out, and then turned her attention back to Gav. A familiar hand settled on her shoulder. She glanced up at Tehl, and her heart ached for the fear and pain naked on his face. He was covered in blood and muck. It was like he'd bathed in it.

"Are you assisting?" she asked.

He nodded and squeezed her shoulder. "Thank you, wife, for sitting with him."

She smiled and turned back to Gavriel, who watched them.

"I miss that," Gav murmured.

What was left of her heart shattered into a million pieces at his confession. "We love you, Gav. You're not alone."

Sage brushed an inky strand from his cheek.

Raziel and Rafe moved to the bottom of the bed as Zachael and Tehl moved to the top. When had Zachael arrived?

"The pain will soon be over." She leaned closer and made sure her face was all he could see. "I know you miss your wife, but your death won't bring her back. You have a little girl waiting for you to come home. This will be your hardest fight yet. I need you to give it your all. Can you do that for Isa?"

Gav nodded.

She squeezed his right hand as Tehl wrapped his hands around Gav's bicep and placed a knee on the cot to hold his cousin in place. Zachael helped pin Gav to the cot from the other side. Mira stepped around Gavriel and placed a thick strip of leather against his lips. He let her work the leather between his top and bottom teeth.

Strong lye soap and heated metal teased Sage's nose. She swallowed thickly and prayed that she wouldn't puke or pass out.

"You can squeeze my hand as hard as you need to."

Gav nodded, his fingers tightening a fraction.

"On the count of three. One, two…"

They never made it to three, because Queen Osir grabbed the head of the spear and yanked.

Sage leaned her forehead against her knees and closed her eyes. It felt like weights had been attached to her lashes. Sweat collected uncomfortably beneath her half corset, and her hair stuck to her neck and face. She rolled her neck and rested her cheek on her kneecap, watching as Mira stoked the woodstove in the corner of the canvas tent. More bloody heat. While she understood Gav needed to stay warm, she desperately wanted to cut a hole in the tent and let in some of the cold night air.

"How is your hand?" Mira asked, adding another infernal log to the fire.

Sage held up her red hand and wiggled her fingers. They ached but it wasn't horrible. "They're fine." Her hand would be bruised by the next day. In his pain, Gavriel had almost broken her fingers. She shuddered and swore she could still hear his inhuman screams echoing in her ears.

And the blood...

She nearly gagged and inhaled deeply, trying to keep herself from puking. Removing the spear from Gav's leg was a disgusting and messy business. In the end, it had taken two more soldiers to hold him down.

"You don't have to be here," Mira said softly, brushing her left hand against her apron. "He won't wake up for some time."

"*If* he makes it through the night," Sage muttered dully. The hole in his leg was a brutal mess. It would take a bloody miracle for him not to die. Heat built behind her eyes, but she forced the tears not to fall. Gav wasn't dead yet. She refused to mourn him now. He *would* get better. He had to.

She jerked when Mira touched her forearm and knelt in front of her. When had the healer moved? Sage hadn't even heard her. So much for being a paragon of observation.

"He won't even know you've gone," the healer said gently. "I've dosed him with enough herbs to keep him asleep for the night. Get your rest and then come back before he wakes."

It was a practical suggestion, but it didn't sit right with Sage. No one should recover by themselves. "I won't leave him."

She and Tehl were of the same mind. He would have stayed himself if he'd not been pulled into a war council meeting. He'd asked her to stay in his place.

Mira stood and held out her good hand. "Let's find you a better place to rest then, shall we?"

Sage stared apprehensively at her friend's hand. Stars, could she even lift her own arm? Everything hurt, and her ass had gone numb hours ago. She slapped her hand into Mira's and clambered to her feet, pins and needles running up and down her legs. Groaning, she rubbed her lower back and turned to stare at the cot Gav slept in. He looked so much like Tehl with his eyes closed. You'd have to be blind not to see the royalty in him.

"He'll be okay," Mira whispered.

"You have to say that," Sage said thickly. "It's your job as a healer."

The healer slipped her arm through Sage's and leaned her cheek against her shoulder. "No. It's my job to save lives. I promise you I will do everything in my power to help him."

"I know you will." Sage tipped her head against Mira's and soaked in the comfort of her friend. When was the last time she'd spent time with another female like this? A long time ago. She stifled a sarcastic laugh. It took Gav being stabbed.

"Come on," Mira said, pulling away.

She tugged on Sage's arm and led her to the cot at the far end of the room, nearest the exit. A cool breeze drifted through the crack of the flap, and she sighed. Sage slumped onto the cot and frowned when Mira placed the back of her hand against Sage's forehead.

"What are you doing?"

"You're flushed."

Sage arched a brow and gestured to the room. "The room is practically boiling." She squinted. "You're flushed, too."

Mira rolled her eyes and pulled her hand away. "Forgive me for worrying about your health." She sobered. "You look like a walking corpse."

Sage leaned against the outer tent post and tipped her head back, her eyes closing. "I forgot how flattering you are."

"I do my best, my lady."

Snorting, she shook her head. "Imp."

"Cretin."

"Since you're so fond of giving health advice, why don't you sit down for a little while?" Sage said, patting the cot she sat upon. "Gav isn't going anywhere." Hopefully.

The healer sat down and sighed. "My feet are killing me."

Sage leaned her head against Mira's slim shoulder and yawned. "Tell me something good. Something happy." After today, she needed to hear something light. Maybe it would keep the nightmares away. The least it would do was buoy her spirits before sleep claimed her.

"I'm... I'm being..."

Sage peeked up at her friend. Mira never hesitated. "What?"

The healer licked her lips. "I'm being courted." A pause. "I think."

What the devil? Sage kept her composure, even though she felt wide awake. "You think?"

"He spoke of his intentions a few days ago. Before that, I thought he was just a harmless flirt. Even now, I have a hard time believing that he's even interested in me."

That bothered Sage. "And why wouldn't he be?" she demanded. "You're a wonderful woman. Any man would be lucky to have you as a wife. Who is the man anyway?"

Mira's throat worked as she swallowed thickly. "Raziel."

Blinking slowly, Sage kept her mouth firmly shut, despite how she wanted to gape. It wasn't like Mira wasn't worthy of a royal husband... it was the fact that Sage hadn't the slightest clue he'd been interested in her friend. Her brows furrowed. Why hadn't Mira said anything before?

Probably because you've been too busy slaying the enemy.

Another stone to add to her mountain crafted from guilt.

"You don't sound excited," Sage said softly. "Does he make you happy?"

Mira shrugged her arm, her shoulder digging into Sage's cheek. "I don't know him very well. He's spent a lot of time in the infirmary, helping the wounded. He makes me laugh and is kind to those around him. I haven't heard him talk down to those who would be considered lesser. I find that appealing."

There was something in Mira's tone that bothered Sage. "But?"

The healer sighed. "But I've only just met him. It's been a month since we first met, and while we've spent hours in each other's company, I don't think that's enough time to decide one's future."

"Very wise."

"He said he wanted me for his mate."

Sage's eyes widened. "Bold."

"Everything about him is bold." Mira fiddled with the fabric of her apron. "I never thought I'd make a very good match with anyone."

"Why in the blazes would you ever think that?"

"I'm an orphan, Sage, and I work in a male profession. You know what has been said about me in the court. I'd planned on honing my skills and serving as a palace healer as an old maid. Raziel is... he is..."

"Scary," Sage supplied.

"Scary because he is the unknown. I've trained most of my life to become a healer, not a..." Mira huffed. "It feels ridiculous saying it out loud. I'm not a princess."

"Welcome to the club," Sage muttered wryly.

"I don't know what to do."

"That's the great thing about courtship. You have time to figure out what you want. Only time will tell if you are both suited for each other." Sage paused. "For what it's worth, Raziel is a good man. War can make beasts out of men. He's kept true to his honor." She reached out and held Mira's hand. "You're an excellent healer, but I think you'd make a marvelous princess, too." Sage chuckled. "I'm sure you'd do a better job of it than me."

"I don't know if I could do it."

"If you like him, court Raziel. Don't say no because you're afraid of change."

"Is that an order, my lady?" Mira said with a smile.

Another jaw-cracking yawn seized Sage. "Like you'd listen to me anyway."

Mira shook with suppressed laughter. "You know me all too well."

"Mmmhmmm." Sage's eyes closed, the siren song of sleep calling for her. She barely noticed when Mira helped her lay down on the cot and covered her with a light blanket. Slumber claimed her almost immediately.

TWENTY-TWO⊙

TEHL

"MORE HAVE ARRIVED," ZACHAEL SAID grimly.

Tehl hung his head. "Take me to them." His legs felt like lead as he followed the weapons master, accompanied by five Elite, Rafe, and Hayjen. He flicked a glance in Rafe's direction. The former rebellion leader looked like hell. They all did. There were some things that no person should ever see.

Their group reached the outskirts of the camp, snow still falling softly to the ground. Two men stood next to something covered with a horse blanket. It might have been cowardly, but Tehl wanted to turn around and never look under the blanket at the inevitable horrors awaiting him. He forced himself onward, their group silent except for the squelch of mud and snow beneath their boots as they reached the two men.

The taller man held the lantern higher, casting light over his sharp cheekbones and dark eyes. Blair. The Scythian commander. If he'd taken the risk to meet with them, circumstances must be dire.

Tehl halted when they reached Blair and William. William's face glowed a sickly pale yellow in the light. He looked the old man in the eyes, and his stomach dropped. William was holding back tears. Whatever the warlord had done, it had wrecked the older man. He'd never seen the general cry. Ever.

Hayjen stepped from the group and clasped forearms with Blair. "Well-met."

Blair nodded. "You might not say that when this is all through."

"What has happened?" Tehl asked, eyeing the pile, his stomach rolling.

"The warlord has prepared another gift," Zachael spat.

"Will you not say what he's done?" Tehl murmured.

The weapons master began to speak, but his voice cracked. He clamped his mouth shut and shook his head.

Tehl glanced around the silent group. No one could speak. He steeled himself and took the final step to whatever terror lay hidden. His fingers trembled when he dropped to his haunches and clasped the sodden edge of the blanket, pulling it back.

At first, nothing made sense. The shapes were wrong. They couldn't be bodies... Tehl froze when he spotted a familiar face. Bile burned the back of his throat, and he placed a hand over his nose and mouth. Benjamin's face stared up at him through sightless eyes. He was just a boy. A child. The sound of retching filled his ears, but he couldn't look away. He reached out and brushed a thumb along the dead boy's cheek. A lone tear dripped down his cheek, cooling in the winter wind. No one deserved a death like this.

Tehl forced himself to look at the others. The bodies were unidentifiable, but from their statures, it was apparent they were all young ones. Chills rippled up and down his arms as he looked at each unmarked face. Trembling, he shot to his feet and stalked away, his chest heaving with labored breaths. How could someone do such a thing? Acute pain, so piercing, stabbed him in the heart. Tehl screamed as if it would somehow release the emotions that were trying to drown him. He placed his head in his hands and stared at the white, snow-covered ground, tears rushing down his cheeks.

A hand touched his shoulder, and he shrugged it off. He couldn't bear the comfort. It should have been him, not the boys. It was *wrong*, so wrong. Angrily, he scrubbed the tears from his cheeks and pressed his palms to his eyes as if it would stop him from seeing their little faces again. This couldn't go on. Every time he thought he understood the depravity of the warlord, the devil stooped to a new, disgusting low.

His stomach revolted, and he vomited.

Little ones.

His mind could not comprehend that sort of cruelty. Children were to be protected, not desecrated. He heaved again. Tears and snot mingled on his face. Only someone truly evil could commit such a crime. He straightened and wiped his forearm across his face, turning to his men. They all looked as haunted and destroyed as he was. Old William was openly crying, his big grey beard collecting tears.

"Was this..." Tehl cleared his throat. "Was this where they were found?"

Zachael shook his head. "No. They were found on our side."

Tehl swallowed as more bile pooled in his mouth. "Did you retrieve all of them?"

"What we could, there were parts..." William paused, swallowing hard. "We did the best we could."

Tehl's gaze turned to Blair, who looked as disturbed as the rest of them. "Why would he do this?"

Blair's mournful dark eyes met his. "These are the consequences for Sage's perceived disobedience."

Sage. Oh god. It would kill her when she heard of this. The prior killings this week had torn her apart. What would these killings drive her to do? For a moment, he considered swearing everyone to silence. But he knew that would never work. They couldn't cover up something this heinous, and the boys deserved to be honored and have a proper burial.

"I don't want to tell her," he said to no one in particular.

"We can't keep this from her," Hayjen said gruffly.

"I know," Tehl bit out. His wife wouldn't forgive him if he hid something like this from her. They didn't lie to each other. He needed to trust that she wouldn't do something stupid. Or at least, not without him being part of the plan. "We need to identify all the boys and then notify their families."

"I will take care of that," William said. The old man broke from the group, pulling an Elite with him.

Tehl turned his gaze on Rafe. "We need blankets for each of their bodies and more soldiers to carry them."

"Done," Rafe said, his tone brusque. He jogged after William.

Tehl turned his attention to Blair. "We need to prepare these little ones for burial, but I need to speak with you. Can you risk staying for a while?"

Blair nodded. "I will see this through."

Tehl nodded absently, his hands jittery at his sides. He felt like he needed to be doing something. Part of him wanted to cradle Benjamin to offer comfort to the youth. The other part of him felt like it would be disrespectful to disturb the body further.

On wooden legs, he approached the line of children and pulled the rug up and over their corpses, protecting them from the elements.

"I'm so sorry," he whispered.

He didn't know how long he stood there, staring at the blanket. The snow fell harder and slowly covered the material, camouflaging what was hidden beneath it. For some reason, it made him angry. A crime like this shouldn't be covered up or forgotten.

Flames of vengeance lit in his chest. Tehl lifted his head and stared across the whitewashed battlefield. He was tired of being one step behind. Right there, he made a vow: he would sacrifice whatever it took to avenge the boys.

His soul had already been damaged.

Tonight, what was left of it burned to ash.

"Can you tell us what his movements will be?" Raziel asked.

Blair frowned and pointed to the map on the center of the table. "I only have a piece of his plan. I've told you all I can."

William scoffed. "You're his commander. Surely, he shares with you more of his plans than what you've told us?"

Blair grimaced, his white teeth a stark contrast to his swarthy skin. "That madman trusts no one. Least of all, me."

"Why is that?" Rafe asked softly from his perch in the corner.

"He distrusts anyone who holds any sort of power in his court. He gives us each a piece of the puzzle and keeps us all suspicious of each other. That way, we'll be so divided, we'll never rise up against him."

"That's brilliant," Zachael muttered, and Hayjen shot him an irate look. "I didn't mean I condone it, but it's an intelligent move. Strategically, it makes sense. Crazy, he is. Stupid, he is not."

A heavy silence settled over the group. Blair's intel helped, but it wouldn't win them the war.

"We appreciate what you've given us," Tehl said. "But it's not enough." He stared the Scythian down. "We need more information. It's key to the warlord's downfall."

Blair gazed back evenly. "I can't risk exposure. Many people will die if he suspects me more than he already does."

"People are already dying. Children are dying," Tehl said softly.

Blair flinched, but his expression blanked almost immediately. Clearly, he wasn't as impervious to death as he pretended to be.

Tehl continued on, "Every day, he pushes us farther back. Soon, our troops will be trapped against the mountains. If that happens, we lose. He'll massacre us. We need to take a hard stand now."

"My people aren't ready," Blair responded. "Even if I could, by some miracle, gain more information, it would do you no good. You don't have the manpower to implement such a plan without my troops. There are too many working parts to rush in. We wait."

"How soon will your men be ready?" Zachael asked.

Blair's lips thinned. "One to two weeks, at least. Moving undetected through the forests of Scythia is no easy task."

"Who's leading your warriors?" Rafe probed.

Tehl nodded. He wanted to know as well.

Blair's expression became unreadable. "Someone I trust."

"You're sure they won't betray you?" Hayjen muttered. "Scythians aren't known for their trustworthiness."

"I've entrusted them with my wife and daughters."

Interesting. In Tehl's experience, a man didn't leave the protection of his family to someone who didn't deserve that trust. If Blair trusted this person, that was enough for Tehl. For now.

He turned his attention back to the map, scowling at how the Scythian markers on the map stood too close to the Aermian troop line. "So, our lots are cast." They had no choice but to hang on and wait. There would be consequences. The children were at the forefront of his mind. "What happened tonight will not happen again."

"What happened?" his wife asked, her voice sleepy.

Dread filled his gut as he turned to the entrance of the tent. Sage stepped fully inside, her clothing rumpled. She even had a blanket crease across her cheek. She looked wholly appealing in that moment. All he wanted to do was carry her off to bed and hold her tight. He swallowed hard, sickened at the news he had to give her.

"There was another attack."

Her sleepiness visibly sloughed off, and she joined the group, circling the war table. "How bad is it?"

"Bad," Zachael muttered.

Her emerald gaze studied the group before settling heavily on Tehl. "Don't sugarcoat it. Just tell me."

He nodded and forced the ugly truth from his mouth. "Bodies were found along the troop line." He swallowed hard but continued. "Little bodies."

Sage stiffened, her eyes darting to each of the grave expressions on the men's faces.

"Children?" she asked raggedly.

Tehl nodded curtly. "The warlord targeted the young boys helping around camp, and those flying our banners."

Sage staggered against the table and leaned on it for support. "How many?"

"More than ten is what we gather," William whispered hoarsely. "Their bodies... It was difficult to guess."

A tear dropped down his wife's cheek. "He said this would happen."

Chills ran down his spine. "The warlord?"

She nodded and dashed away a tear, just for another one to replace it. "He warned me."

Tehl held his breath as he watched Sage wrestle with her feelings. She bowed her head and sniffled loudly. Hayjen placed a hand on the back of her neck, and Tehl looked at him gratefully. A good friend was hard to come by. He was appreciative that they had such support.

Sage drew in a deep breath and lifted her head, her jewel-like gaze meeting his own. "Where do we go from here?"

"Our first priority is to hit another ballista and hold on until Blair's troops can arrive," Tehl replied. "We may have a hard time pressing forward, but we won't allow him any more ground."

"How long until your troops arrive, commander?" his wife asked.

Blair answered, "A minimum of one to two weeks."

"The warlord knew it would come to this." Sage placed her elbows on the table and held her head. "Why am I surprised? We only have one choice." She chuckled darkly and lifted her gaze.

Tehl narrowed his eyes. What was she going on about?

Sage smiled sharply. "It's time I handed myself over to the warlord."

TWENTY-THREE

SAGE

SAGE CRADLED HER CHIN IN her palms and watched emotionlessly as chaos and shouting erupted around her. All the while, she remained strangely calm. Once the words left her mouth, peace had settled over her. She wasn't afraid, only resigned. Deep down, she knew it would come to this.

Her attention narrowed to the only two people not arguing or shouting. Tehl and Blair.

She stared down her husband as he glared daggers at her. He may not shout and scream, but his icy anger affected her all the same. Sage didn't dare look away. He'd fight her on this, it was clear.

Blair was a different story. He didn't react, but she could see the calculation gleaming in his eyes. He understood the warlord better than anyone in the room. If he deemed it a valid idea, things would go much smoother in convincing the others.

"You will not sacrifice yourself to that monster," snarled Rafe.

Sage arched a brow. He did not get a say in this. "Really? As much as I love you, don't you think that's a little like the pot calling the kettle black? How many times did *you* sacrifice *me* for the greater good?" She crossed her arms, and his mouth snapped shut. "I can see you plotting, commander."

Blair cocked his head, his dark braids falling into his face. "And what exactly do you see?"

"A way to defeat the warlord once and for all."

"And how do you suppose we do that? You're skilled, but have you forgotten about the last time you dueled? You lost. How do you expect to win?" Zachael asked frankly.

She pulled the long chain from her shirt and held up the poison ring. She grinned at an unsmiling Hayjen. "I have it on good authority that this can take down a Scythian warrior, even one in a berserker rage."

Her uncle's face turned purple. "That's for the average Scythian. That demon is not normal."

"True, but it would slow him down. Perhaps enough to dispatch him." Her gaze flickered to her silent husband doing his best imitation of stone. Tehl was *not* happy.

"You would risk your life for a maybe?" Rafe demanded.

"I would risk *everything* if it meant a real chance to rid our world of him." Her statement seemed to sober the group, dousing some of their fire. She once again focused on Blair. "I have a sneaking suspicion that even if this poison did not work, a concoction better suited to destroy the warlord would make itself available." Sage hadn't forgotten about the poison ring Maeve had gifted her when she escaped Scythia. She'd bet the warlord's sister had more things up her sleeve than anyone knew about.

Blair arched a brow in return. "I have no such skills, if that's what you're referring to."

"I'm sure. Your skills lie in combat. We both know a person with exceptional skills for deception, and a hatred that encompasses both our own."

"All of you, get out," Tehl said softly, his tone so wintery it brought goosebumps to her arms. "I need to speak with my wife privately."

She held his gaze evenly as the council glanced between them, before silently filing out. She waited thirty seconds before speaking. "My plan is valid."

He said nothing.

"I know you don't like this." She took a deep breath.

"You know nothing of how I feel," he said, his voice whisper-soft. "If you did, you'd never have suggested such an idiotic, haphazard plan."

"It hasn't been rounded out yet," she admitted. "But it's the only chance we have left."

"How can you say that?" He pointed toward the wall. "There's an army fighting for us, and they have reinforcements on the way. There are choices."

"And how long can they keep up?"

"We're doing our best!" He placed his palms on the table, his attention locked on the positions of the two armies.

"I know," she said calmly. "But it's not enough."

Tehl sucked in a sharp breath.

Sage edged around the table and laid her right hand on top of his. "I know you can see it. We've had our triumphs, but they are not enough. Soon, they'll pin us against the mountains if we don't do something."

"If only we could destroy the last three war machines," he growled.

"That would be a miracle." Sage reached out gently and touched his chin. He faced her, his expression grave. "Your men have succeeded at wrecking two ballistae, but at what cost? You never said how bad it was the first time, but I saw the haunted look on your face. You almost died out there." Tehl didn't deny it. "The second time, we almost lost Gav." They still could, but she couldn't think about that.

"Part of the Methian army is useless because of those war machines." He looked away from her, his jaw working. "We need to get them into the air."

"I can help."

Her husband shook his head. "By handing yourself over to the warlord?"

Her stomach flipped, but she tamped it down. "The only reason you're so angry is because you know I'm right." Tehl glanced at her sharply. Sage popped up onto her toes and cupped his cheeks. She smiled and ran her thumbs along his cheekbones. "Even if I can't kill him, my arrival would be enough of a distraction for your men to reach the other catapults."

He stared at her for a long time, his deep blue eyes serious. "I hate this."

"I know," she whispered, her smile trembling.

"How can I possibly allow you to go back?" he rasped. "It's not right. Everything inside me is screaming to snatch you up and run in the opposite direction. You're not safe there."

"True." She wouldn't lie to him. "But I'm not safe now. Every day that I march onto the battlefield could be my last. Life is not guaranteed."

"He's a different kind of danger."

That was an understatement. "I won't be alone. Blair will look out for me."

Tehl scoffed. "As much as he did in Scythia? You returned a mess."

Sage traced his cheekbone and ignored the need to be defensive. Her husband was worried for her. "I would have suffered at the hand of other monsters as well if he hadn't stepped in. I know where he stands. Things won't be easy, but he won't let me die."

He cocked his head and brushed a lock of hair from her face. Sage kissed his palm and gazed up at him, soaking in the love and anguish that was shining through the cracks in his mask.

"How are you so calm about this?" he asked quietly.

That was something she didn't even understand. "I don't know. When you told me what happened, it was as if everything quieted around me. It makes it easier to focus on what needs to be done." She pressed her lips together. "What happened tonight can't happen again."

Tehl nodded. "My chest hurts when I think of it."

"I know, love." Sage pulled him into a hug and wrapped her arms around his wide chest. Tehl squeezed her and rested his cheek on the top of her head. "That's why I need to go. I'm the only person who can give you a chance to destroy all three of the machines." She shrugged as her gaze went distant. "Maybe I'll be able to cut him down in one fell swoop."

His arms tightened. "Will you sneak away in the night if I forbid you from doing this?"

Sage mulled it over. "I wouldn't, but you and I both know you forbidding me from doing this would be the wrong choice. Look past your emotions. Strategically, you know this is the right move." She pulled back and peered up into his face. "I want your support. I can't do this without you."

"Are you sure you can go back?"

No, but it was what needed to be done. "I imagine it will be the most difficult thing I have ever done." She paused. "But if it saves our people and others from a fate similar to mine, I'll pay whatever price. I can do it."

"You shouldn't have to."

"You know better than I, that with privilege comes responsibility. I chose to marry you. I meant my vows when I said I would fight for the good of Aermia and sacrifice whatever was needed. If you were in the same position, we both know the decision would already be made."

"I can't ask this of you."

"You're not asking me. I'm volunteering. I would feel better going into this if I knew I had you on my side."

Tehl leaned down and rested his forehead against hers. "I am *always* on your side."

Her bottom lip trembled at the passionate declaration. "I love you."

"As I love you."

She laced her right hand with his and pulled him toward their chambers. "All the details don't need to be set in stone tonight. Come to bed and hold me."

Sage squeaked when he lunged and swept her into his arms. Her eyes widened when he stooped low and kissed her heatedly. Her tongue tangled with his as he pushed through the tent flap.

"If you must go," he growled. "I want the taste of you on my lips."

TWENTY-FOUR

MER

MER HURTLED THROUGH THE WATER toward the human body sliding through the current. She grabbed Sam beneath the arms and hauled him to the surface, gasping as the painful change overtook her. Her body expelled sea water, and her lungs inflated as a sharp spray of water hit her face, stinging her eyes and cheeks.

She kicked her legs to keep them both afloat, her eyes darting to Sam's pale face. How long had he been under? "Come on, Sam. Hold on!"

His ship released a heavy groan and creaked under the stress of the howling wind. Punishing waves tossed them about the sea, but she kept his face above the waves. Just barely. Fatigue threatened to overtake her, but Mer kept pushing on. He would not die.

The spymaster in her arms coughed and threw up the seawater he'd swallowed as he tried to fill his lungs with air.

"That's it," she murmured. "Breathe. We're almost there."

Mer held his arm, keeping his head above the water as she shifted in front of him, his body pressed against her back. Another wave crashed over them, but she managed to swim back to the surface. She pulled his trembling arms around her neck.

"Don't let go," she shouted over the roar of the winds.

Sam mumbled something incoherent, but his grip tightened on her as another rolling wave tried to tear them apart. From the surface, the sea looked black; the only shocks of color were the foaming white tips of the dangerous waves trying to suck them down.

"Damn it," Sam bit out. His nails scratched her collarbone as he clutched her shoulders tighter.

Mer kicked her legs back and forth to keep the two of them afloat and scanned the turbulent ocean, spotting their ships. "We're close." She caught the sight of a few fiilee in the sky battling the winds. "Wicked hell." Mer said a quick little prayer for the survival of their riders

She made certain Sam's arms were secured around her before she swam toward the ship. It seemed to take ages. When her fingers curled around the ladder soaked with saltwater that hung from the side of the ship, she sighed. They'd made it.

Hand over hand, Mer hauled herself and Sam up the ladder, her muscles bunched and flexed, the burn heating her blood. Her foot slipped, but she gritted her teeth and found her balance, Sam's limbs wrapped around her. Finally, they reached the top of the ship. Mer sucked in lungfuls of air, and Sam rolled from her back, eyes glazed over.

The Lure.

"It's a good thing you're too weak to chase me," she wheezed.

Mer wiggled away from him and called out to the crew, who were shouting and rushing about on the deck. Her melodious voice cut through the wind and rain like a magic spell, just enough to be heard. A young sailor boy caught sight of her and rushed forward. She held her hands out to keep him away. If he caught a whiff of her Lure, he'd be no use to Sam.

An older man grabbed the boy by the back of the shirt and yanked him backward. "Don't be dumb, boy. Remember the Lure."

Mer inched farther away from Sam, so his men could pull him from the edge of the ship without having to worry about her scent snaring them. The ship groaned, and the waves slammed against the sides. She wrapped her arms and legs around the bars of the guardrail while she caught her breath. Her gut twisted as Sam's fellow sailors and Elite dragged their spymaster somewhere safe. Shouts of gratitude were lost in the winds, and she waved them away. Hopefully, he'd recover well. When he'd been pitched from the ship, she'd sworn her heart had stopped.

It was a lucky thing she'd found him when she had.

Her heart slowed, and her breathing evened out. She wanted to crawl into a hole and sleep to regain her strength, but every moment she dallied was another life lost. Mer was preparing to throw herself back into the water when a fiilee dove from the sky. The feline landed on the nearest Aermian ship, its rider sliding from its wet back in one smooth movement.

The Methian prince Raziel.

She'd know his wine-colored hair anywhere. Her lips parted. She'd heard of the handsome Methian prince, and had even caught glimpses of him in the last several weeks as he launched aerial attacks on the Scythian fleet, but she'd never been this close to him. Her gaze narrowed when the fiilee flared its wings and knocked two Scythian warriors from the ship. Raziel launched an attack, and she cursed, noting that the ship wasn't just fighting the storm, but Scythians. How had the bastards boarded it in this weather? She'd barely managed it.

Lightning lit up the night sky, as if the storm wanted Mer to have a better look at the hulking prince. Raziel. His clothing was soaking wet, clinging to his body, and the sharp lines of his face twisted with effort as he fought with a dark figure. They turned, and she got a good look at his adversary.

Ream.

The chill of the wind and the spray of icy water disappeared, and Mer forgot where she was and what was happening. All she could do was stare at the familiar shock of white, braided hair filled with pearls and shells she'd given him on their bonding day. Her brain couldn't make sense of what was happening. Why was Raziel attacking Ream? Ream was on their side!

The thunder rumbled, and lightning illuminated the sky above the maudlin scene. She blinked in confusion, and her breath caught as she realized the Methian prince carried a sword, the side broader than her arm and nearly as long as her legs. Mer lurched to her feet, her fingers digging into the wet handrail.

"Stop!" she yelled. What the bloody hell was happening?

Raziel hefted the sword and swung. Mer screamed, her sound of fear and anguish lost to the storm. Ream managed to roll out of the way and launched toward the Methian prince, sinking his blade into Raziel's back.

"No!" she whispered.

A heavy creak preceded a fresh burst of shouts as the mast on the other ship gave way. Raziel whipped his sword and jabbed backward, stumbling toward the ship's side. Ream's mouth opened in a silent shout before the two men pitched over the edge of the ship into the waiting arms of the sea.

Horror rose inside her. Not Ream!

Her mind screamed at her to move, to do something, but she couldn't. She was frozen. The air seemed to be cut off from her lungs. Shivers began to wrack her body.

Raziel had attacked her husband.

"Move!" Sam's familiar voice bellowed.

She glanced over her shoulder as the blond prince stormed toward her, his steps surprisingly even as the ship rolled on the waves.

"Mer!" he barked. "Bring him back."

Still, she didn't move. Ream had stabbed the Methian prince. It didn't make sense.

Sam seized her by both arms and shook her, his blue eyes dark. "I need you to bring him back."

"Ream?" she whispered.

"Raziel."

"Mer." Another shake. "You have to work through this. We can't lose him. He's too important."

She nodded, not really feeling anything. Sam always had a plan. Ream couldn't be gone. He was a Sirenidae. The water was his home.

Lurching toward the end of the ship, Mer jumped, twisting in the air to land in a perfect dive. She sliced through the water, her movements mechanical. Her lungs seized as she forced herself to inhale water, and her gills opened. She scanned the current for the men. Raziel floated with the water, his dark-red hair looking more like tendrils of black blood. Her heart pounded as the scent of blood hit her full-force. Water rushed past her ears, and panic sharpened her senses. Where was Ream?

He's a Sirenidae. He'll be okay. Focus on the Methian.

Mer fought the water and debris until she reached Raziel. She'd always known he was a large man, but it didn't prepare her for his actual size. She didn't even try to wrap her arms around his chest. Even if she could have gotten a grip around his broad shoulders and torso, his clothes and armor would have made it impossible. Quickly, she used the blade from her waist to cut off his chest plate and armor. Once that was done, she grabbed one of his wrists and hauled him toward the surface. As she fought for his life, Mer realized her eyes burned. Shock radiated through her system. She was crying. They weren't going to make it. It had been too long.

Don't give up.

Mer dug deep and swam with everything she had. Chunks of debris sliced at her skin, but she didn't stop until they reached the surface. She broke the waves with a jagged cry. Her body seized, and she spewed sea water from her lungs, her gills sealing. Mer thrashed around to get Raziel's head above water. She doggedly worked toward Sam's ship, the drag of Raziel's body slowing her. Mer grunted and fought against his weight.

Snakes of blood spread from the Methian's head. She clutched him closer in desperation. Leviathans were around. She needed to move fast. Adrenaline rushed through her veins, and Mer found the strength to reach the ship. She latched onto the ladder.

"Help!" she screamed. There was no way she could get his huge body up the side of the ship.

Sam popped his head over the side and tossed a rope down. "Cinch the loop beneath his armpits!"

She struggled to keep Raziel's face above the surface as she slid the rope under his arms and secured it. "Done!"

"Pull!" Sam shouted.

The line went taught, and Raziel's limp form began to lift from the sea. Mer tiredly clung to the ladder as the Methian prince disappeared over the edge. She'd done her job and saved his royal arse. Waves crashed over her from all sides as she released the rope, sinking into the inky water. The change painfully overtook her once more.

Mer stared up at the turbulent surface as she drifted deeper into the depths of the sea.

Move. Find Ream. Figure out what the hell happened.

With the last bit of strength she possessed, she glided through the salty water. The saltwater was tainted with blood—human, animal, and Sirenidae. Her stomach dropped as she followed the scent of Sirenidae blood. It grew stronger.

It can't be him. It just can't!

Her eyes scoured the darkness until she spotted him.

Ream lay on the sand, his hands on a massive gut wound, blood leaking through his fingers. Too much blood.

Mer burst into action. Her knees caught some coral, but she didn't pay it any attention as she met his shiny gaze. Her fingers fluttered over his.

"What do I do?" she croaked. She scanned the ocean floor. There weren't any sea herbs nearby.

Ream placed a hand on her own, pulling her attention back to him. "I'm sorry," he said, more blood leaking from his mouth.

Mer's bottom lip trembled. "It's not your fault."

"I didn't have a choice. They had my daughter."

She blinked slowly, her heart thundering in her ears. Ream's daughter had died years before. "It's okay," she crooned. "No one has your daughter, love. Just hold on."

He shook his head. "They have her. I had to do as he commanded to keep her safe." His eyes seemed to plead with her. "I didn't have a choice. I'm so sorry."

Mer stilled. "What have you done?"

"What was necessary to protect my only child." He winced. "They know Aermia's movements and there are other Sirenidae helping the Scythians. Beware who you trust."

No. "Tell me you're lying," she rasped.

"I'm so sorry." He seized her hand, blood clouding the water around them.

Her throat clogged. "We'll figure something out."

"There's nothing to be done."

"Shhhh," she whispered. "Everything will be okay." Nothing would be okay.

Ream squeezed her fingers. "Listen carefully to me. A woman is being held on one of the Scythia ships. She's pregnant."

Mer's head spun. *Jasmine.* "How long have you known where she's been?" They'd been looking for her for weeks.

"Long enough." His magenta eyes were full of pain. "Look for the ship with the black leren painted on the side. You'll find her there." He gave her a tender smile. "I've always loved you, Mer. I'm sorry for hurting you. Just know that."

His body seized, and the life from her husband's eyes faded.

"Ream? Ream!" Mer screamed, her hands shaking as she clasped each side of his face. "Please don't leave me."

He didn't answer.

"No, no, no! This isn't how it's supposed to go," she cried, lifting his torso onto her legs, and cradling his face to her chest. "Forever, remember?" Even knowing what he'd done, it didn't diminish her love for him.

Time ceased to exist as she rocked her dead husband. Sobs wracked her body as she mourned the boy who'd been her best friend her entire childhood. The boy who had grown into a man she loved with her whole heart. The man who married another, only to have his wife and child die in an accident after five years of marriage. The man she'd nursed back to life. The man who supported her rebellion against her grandfather in order to fight for what was right. The person she planned on having a family with.

The man who'd betrayed her.

Unbidden, a mourning song flowed out of her. Leviathans drew close, forming a circle, their haunting hums adding to her song. They mourned with her. When the last note passed her lips, the beasts receded into the deep, leaving Mer with the soul she'd loved her whole life.

"I will love you as long as the moon shines in the night sky," she whispered.

TWENTY-FIVE

TEHL

MORNING ARRIVED WITH A BITTER chill.

He turned onto his side and watched his wife sleep. It was something that he knew was probably improper, if not a little eerie, but he couldn't stop. It was addictive to see her without her armor, so unjaded. Free.

Unable to help himself, he scooted closer and kissed her bare shoulder.

This might be the last time you kiss her.

He froze, his lips pressed to her olive skin. Slowly, he pulled back and tried to imprint her form into his mind. He was a wretch of a man to agree to such a plan. What sort of worthless rubbish would agree to send his wife back to her abuser? He hated the idea. What he hated more was that he could see the logic in it.

Damned logic.

When Sage succeeded, and she would, it would change the tide of the war.

But at what price?

Would Sage go back to being the ghost she was after escaping Scythia? His gaze focused on her once again. It would be so easy to knock her out and drag her away to some place safe, away from this mess. Away from the madness of this plan.

You promised a partnership.

Tehl squeezed his eyes shut and pinched the bridge of his nose. His wife was the fiercest person he knew. While he loathed every bit of the plan they'd formed last night, he knew he couldn't throw her in a tower somewhere. She was a warrior, through and through. They were equals, partners.

At least in this, they took the risk together. They'd be working as a team. He smiled darkly. The warlord wouldn't be prepared for that. He dropped another kiss to her skin and rolled out of bed. It was early, but he needed to check on Gav. Mira had said the first night would be the most dangerous. While Tehl would have loved to wake up his wife with his incessant need for her, she was right about one thing: with privilege came responsibility. Gavriel was more than a responsibility. He was family, and he deserved someone looking out for him.

He pulled his cold, leather trousers up his legs and hissed at the frigid temperature. Next, Tehl tossed on his shirt and clasped his cloak before jamming his feet into his boots.

He paused at the end of the bed and soaked in the sight of his wife one last time before he left. Stars, she was beautiful. He spun on his heel and moved into the war room area of the tent. Tehl spared a glance at the map but moved on.

Freezing air nipped at his ears, causing him to pull the hood of his cloak over his head. Two Elite silently followed him while two others took their place to guard the royal tent. They ghosted through the camp, the dark of the early morning only broken by a low fire here and there. Frost and icy snow crunched beneath their boots, as they made their way to the infirmary nestled in the trees.

He quietly entered the tent, followed closely by the Elite. The sight of the burned and injured men made him want to scream as they passed row after row. Upon reaching the back, he paused and took a fortifying breath before entering the room holding Gav. Sweltering heat slammed into him, and perspiration dampened the back of his neck immediately. He glanced around the room as his men took up silent posts on either side of the entrance.

Mira sat on the floor, her cheek leaned against the cot's edge, her fingers resting on the pulse at Gav's wrist.

"Mira?" he whispered. She didn't stir. Tehl approached her carefully and knelt beside the healer. "Mira?" he said a little louder.

She cracked an eye open and lifted her head. "He is all right, my lord. His pulse is steady for the time being."

Tehl's shoulders drooped in relief. "A fever?"

Mira straightened and placed the back of her hand on his cousin's brow. "Lower than it was. It spiked high a few hours ago. I brewed some special tea for him to reduce the fever."

"An infection?" Tehl asked, eyeing Gav's pallid complexion. Mira hesitated. "Be straight with me."

"Very well, my lord. Yes, likely."

He sighed. "We're long past you calling me by my title."

Mira grimaced. "It's hard to break a habit that was beaten into me." She brushed a sweaty strand from Gav's face. "It's normal for the body to run a fever when it's trying to repair itself. I did my best flushing out the wound, but there is a high chance there is infection. It's common with this sort of injury."

"Will he survive?" Tehl asked, the words bitter on his tongue.

"I can't say," Mira whispered. "I can promise you that I'll do my best to care for him."

"I know you will." He placed a hand on her slim shoulder. She'd lost weight. "Why don't you go get some food first and break your fast?"

"It's morning already?"

"More or less. Go."

"Is that a royal order?"

Tehl cracked a half smile. "If it needs to be. Get on with you."

Mira smiled in return and clambered to her feet. She stretched and groaned. "If you need me, I won't be far."

He watched her leave, passing the silent Elite, before he turned back to his friend. Gav was too still. Too pale. What he wouldn't do to have him healthy and whole.

"I wish you were well, my friend." Tehl settled himself on the faded rug, next to the cot. "Living in a world where you aren't alive and well is unthinkable. Plus, I could use your guidance." He stared down at his hands. "A decision was made last night to send Sage back to the warlord. It *feels* wrong, but I can see how it will benefit us. She'll give us a fair chance at destroying the ballistae. I wanted to talk her out of it, but her mind is set. I know she's putting on a brave face. I can see it in her eyes that she's scared." His fingers curled into fists. "What kind of man sends his wife into a den of monsters?"

Gav didn't reply.

"That's not even the worst of it." Tehl lifted his head and gazed at his cousin's profile. "I keep imagining what you went through after Emma died. You barely survived. You've never been the same. I don't know how I could bear it. What I feel for Sage…" He paused and tipped his head back. "It's too much, too big. She is my partner, but I don't want to treat her that way. I want to lock her away. Barbaric, isn't it?"

Still no answer.

He glanced at Gav, checking to make sure he was still breathing. "Part of me wishes I could go back to the time I considered Sage a traitor and spy. Shameful, I know. It was easier then. Things were black and white. If she dies," Tehl whispered, "I don't know if I can live with the knowledge that I let her go."

He felt sick even saying the words.

"When we were growing up, war was glamorized. It seemed like a heroic thing. Now, all I can see are the lives lost and the blood on my hands. Too many sacrifices have been made, and more will come. I will shoulder them to the best of my ability, as is my duty." A pale, sightless face entered his mind, the dead boy from the night prior.

He shook his head, trying to dispel the image. "I've spoken too much about myself. Sage tells me that I need to look on the positive side more often, and I realized that your attack, while horrible, has a silver lining. Last night, I experienced a soul-crushing blow from Scythia. I am thankful you were not there to witness the atrocity."

Tehl shifted around, so he could prop his back against the cot. "I'll stop speaking and let you rest. Heal quickly. You are missed."

TWENTY-SIX

MIRA

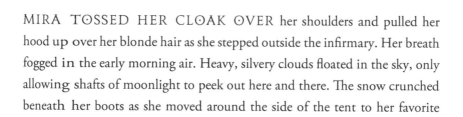

MIRA TOSSED HER CLOAK OVER her shoulders and pulled her hood up over her blonde hair as she stepped outside the infirmary. Her breath fogged in the early morning air. Heavy, silvery clouds floated in the sky, only allowing shafts of moonlight to peek out here and there. The snow crunched beneath her boots as she moved around the side of the tent to her favorite spot to sit and gather her thoughts.

Just beneath the bow of frosted evergreens lay a fallen tree trunk. Mira pulled her cloak tighter around her body and sat. The snow and frost coated every leaf, branch, and tree as far as she could see. The clouds shifted, and a shaft of moonlight pierced the inky darkness, flooding the tiny glen with moonlight. It was so idyllic, like something from a fairy story. The world looked like it had been dripped in diamonds. An icy breeze bit at her cheeks, but she didn't care. Nothing could move her from that spot. Mira held her breath as if the smallest sound would shatter the magic around her.

Jacob had taught her to appreciate the little moments. Life as a healer wasn't an easy path. More often than not, you gave yourself to the job until you felt there was nothing left to give. Still, you pressed onward. From the moment Jacob had adopted her, Mira knew she wanted to be a healer like her papa. He'd readily taken her in, despite the reservations of others. A soft smile touched her chapped lips. Jacob never let anyone tell him what to do.

A brilliant mind and willing spirit were enough for him. It never mattered that she was female.

Soft footsteps alerted her to the approach of another. She turned toward the sound. Raziel smiled at her, weaving his way through the trees, a steaming cup in each hand. He stepped over the fallen log and wordlessly handed her a mug. The heat warmed her cold fingers and seeped through the bandages of her wounded hand.

"Thank you," she murmured, lifting the earthen mug to her nose. Garlic, oregano, and pepper teased her senses. Mira glanced at the prince in surprise. "Soup?"

He shrugged his shoulders. "I figured you might be hungry."

"I am." She took a cautious sip, and the hot brew warmed her throat before heating her belly. Mira hummed in appreciation. "This is delicious."

"I'm glad you like it. It's one of my favorite recipes."

She lowered the cup and eyed him over the rim. "A family recipe?"

"One of my mother's. She made sure we all knew how to prepare it."

Mira's brows raised. "Did you cook this?"

"Surprised?" he asked with a smile, his golden eyes twinkling.

"Frankly, yes."

"Just because I am royalty?"

Mira snorted and took another sip of the delicious broth before answering. "More like because you are a man."

Raziel swiveled to face her, tossing a leg over the tree trunk. "Cooking is a skill every person should possess. I wouldn't want to get stuck in a snowstorm and not know how to prepare a meal to keep myself warm while it passes."

At the mention of snow, she shivered. While Mira loved the snow, she hadn't spent much time this far north before. Her only experience with snow was as a child, and it had melted in a day. It had seemed magical. She cast a glance around. She had a sneaking suspicion that the marvel of snow would wear off when it didn't melt away.

"What's it like, a snowstorm?"

"Cold. White. Dangerous. Beautiful."

Even talking about it made her colder. Mira took another long sip and watched the play of moonlight against the ice crystals. *Beautiful, indeed.*

Raziel shifted and his face creased in pain. He stretched his right shoulder. Her brows furrowed. "Have you been injured?"

"Nothing that won't heal. I was on the coast and someone got the drop on me."

"Has someone looked at it?"

"Yes. My mother helped bandage me up, dearest. I'll be back to prime shape in no time."

Mira eyed him skeptically. Men were so damned prideful. She'd bet the wound was worse than he was letting on, but she let it go. Queen Osir was an incredible healer and she'd seen to her son. No need to worry.

They fell into a comfortable silence. A prickling feeling started on her left side, and she peeked at Raziel from the corner of her eye. His intense gaze was locked on her. She swallowed and tried to ignore him. It didn't work.

"You know it's rude to stare at a woman? Especially while she's eating?"

"I enjoy watching you eat."

Mira cut him an incredulous look. "Well, stop. It makes me uncomfortable."

"Why should I? Is it wrong for me to take pleasure in your enjoyment of the meal I prepared for you?"

He prepared the meal *for* her?

Mira twisted to face him fully. "You jest," she chided.

The Methian prince reached out and ran the tip of his finger along her cheekbone. "Why should I not cook for the woman I am courting? It is only right that I show her that I can provide for her as well as care for her well-being."

A damned blush began to heat her cheeks. The man was too smooth for his own good. "I can care for myself."

Raziel nodded, a deep wine-colored lock falling across his right eye. "You are more than capable. But just because you can accomplish a task, it doesn't mean you have to shoulder the burden all yourself. You deserve to be cared for."

Her jaw sagged. Who spoke like that? *A man raised right.* Those were few and far between. She'd seen the best the male population had to offer and also the worst. She'd given salve to women who sported too many bruises far too often and were worked to the bone.

Mira snapped her mouth shut. "Not many share your sentiment."

"Then they don't deserve to have a mate."

His vehement statement caused her to jerk, and she almost spilled her soup. She clutched the mug tighter. A sense of true camaraderie settled over Mira. She'd taken an instant liking to him when he'd begun to help the wounded. He always had a kind word or a way of drawing laughter from even the staunchest soldier. But to hear him speak about his own sex the way he did, it made her trust him. Trust wasn't something she gave often.

She finished her soup, relishing the herbs that had settled in the bottom—a final burst of flavor. "I like you," she admitted.

"It was the soup, wasn't it?"

Mira gave him a silly smile. "Most definitely." Her mirth waned, and she eyed him. "I think I trust you as well."

Raziel's smile faded. Intent and heat filled his expression, and his posture became languid, and yet predatory. She knew what that meant. Many a young girl had fallen for such a look and found themselves in a compromised position. While she trusted the prince not to take advantage of her, Mira didn't trust herself when he was looking at her like that.

She got to her feet slowly, so he wouldn't think she was running away. Mira stepped closer, her skirts and cloak brushing his left leg. He was so tall that sitting on the log they were eye to eye. She held out the mug.

"Thank you for breakfast and the wonderful company."

He pulled the cup from her fingers but held one of her hands. Her heart skipped a beat as he laid a kiss on the back of her fingers, his gaze never leaving hers.

"The pleasure is all mine, Mira."

She snatched her hand back. "You're not courting me," she blurted.

Raziel gave her a lazy smile. "Dearest, there's no deterring me."

Mira blinked at him. "It would never work. I'm a healer, and you're a prince."

"Blood is blood. You won't change my mind."

"And if I told you there was someone else?"

The Methian prince stilled, and his eyes narrowed. "Is there?" he asked softly.

"No," she admitted. Mira wouldn't lie to him. "But I'd like to know your answer all the same."

"If I knew you'd be well cared for, you were happy, and he was a good man, I would concede."

"Just like that?"

He smiled. "If you're looking for faults within me, I'm happy to share them. There are many. What you won't find is a jealous brute who will drag you off by your hair and ravish you."

Her pulse picked up. "I thought women enjoyed a good ravishing, every now and again."

Heat filled his gaze again. "Your wish is my command, my lady. Say the word."

"You're a rake," she accused, but with a smile. He was absolutely incorrigible. Sam would probably adore him. Mira waved a hand at him and strode toward the infirmary.

"Mira?" Raziel called softly.

She glanced over her shoulder. "Yeah?"

"The more you forget to eat, the more I'll arrive with food."

"Is that a promise?"

He stood from the log. "Care for yourself, or I will take it upon myself."

It kind of sounded like a threat, but she thought he meant it as a promise. Mira shook her head at his antics but couldn't keep the silly smile off of her face.

Princes. They were way too charming for their own good.

TWENTY-SEVEN

TEHL

———⊷◦⟨⟩◦⊶———

IT WAS ALL SET.

He wanted to break something.

Tehl paced outside their tent, his gaze darting toward the entrance every time he made another agitated pass. Night had fallen and, with it, a snowstorm. He scowled at the heavy snowfall. While it would make for the perfect cover, it also meant his time with his wife was up. She needed to make her move tonight.

He passed the entrance again. This shouldn't be the only way. No matter how many times he tried to come up with a better plan, there was nothing. Tehl trusted Sage. He didn't trust their enemy. The warlord corrupted everything he touched. The image of the warlord's hands on Sage's skin popped into his mind unbidden. His lip curled, and he kicked a stone that he'd uncovered with his pacing.

You're being a coward. Get inside and help her prepare.

Female voices murmured inside the tent, too faint for him to pick out.

Tehl paused and stared at the tent flap, ignoring the Methian warriors watching him. He rolled his neck and pushed through the entrance. The war room was empty. Most likely, all who were on the council were finishing up their last-minute tasks before they attacked tonight.

Stars help them be successful.

Pushing the flap back to his and Sage's quarters, he halted at the sight that greeted him. Sage stood with her back to him, wearing dyed cream leather and white fur, the Methian queen quietly speaking with her. She looked like an angelic warrior, sent to collect souls. He'd have given his soul to her in that moment if she'd asked for it.

Queen Osir glanced between them and pressed a kiss to his wife's cheek. "You're unbreakable. Good luck." She moved past Tehl and squeezed his arm once before leaving the room.

Sage slowly faced him, her green eyes dark in the low lamp light. Would this be the last time he ever saw her?

"Don't look at me like that," she whispered. "Or else I won't be able to do what I must."

"How am I looking at you?"

Her chin quivered. "Like you can't bear to part. Like you're as scared as I am."

In two steps, he had her in his arms. Sage melted against him, her cheek pressed to his chest. He licked his lips. "What if we were to run away?"

She chuckled. "What a wonderful fairy story. Where would we go?"

Tehl ran his hand down the thick plait of her braid, trying to memorize the feel of her. "To the desert, to explore for treasures and lost secrets. Then, we'd bathe in the sea and make love until the stars were envious of us."

"What pretty words, husband. Who knew you were such a poet?"

He smiled at her teasing. "I can become anything for my lady."

Sage pulled back slightly and tipped her head back. "You are and always will be my lodestone."

Cupping her cheeks, he slid his calloused fingers along her silky skin. "If you've changed your mind…"

"I haven't." Her smile was bittersweet. "It's the right decision."

It was the wrong decision, but the only chance they had. Waiting on Blair's troops wasn't a *real* option. "When this is over, we're taking a proper honeymoon."

The love of his life grinned. "Will it involve secrets, treasure, and naked, writhing bodies?"

Tehl hid his smile at her cheekiness. "If it pleases you."

416

"Rest would please me. I'm bloody tired. I would settle for a full night of sleep with you next to me."

Wasn't that the truth? "We'll not leave bed for a fortnight when this is through. Rest and play."

Her breath hitched, and he gave her a smile Sam would have been proud of. Anything to lighten the heaviness that threatened to drown them. He didn't want to say goodbye. Her cheeks flushed a pretty shade of pink when he pulled her tighter against him.

Tehl brushed an errant strand of her hair behind her ear. The lovely locks were always escaping their confinements. He pressed his nose into the crook of her neck and engulfed her in the tightest hug he could muster. She squeaked and threw her arms around his neck. Inhaling deeply, he drew her cinnamon scent into his senses. She smelled like home, like pure, unadulterated ambrosia.

Gritting his teeth, he fought the urge to tumble her back onto the bed one last time. To imprint her into his memory, to erase any fear she was hiding from him. She tipped her head to the side, baring her neck. Tehl surrendered to the urge to rub his cheek along her neck. Her fingers dug into the back of his scalp as he pressed a hot kiss to the skin, roughened by his whiskers.

Playing his lips over hers in the barest hint of a kiss, he pulled back just enough to whisper, "I love you."

Sage grabbed his head and laced her fingers in his waves. With a small cry, she crushed her mouth to his. He let out a muffled sound of surprise and slid his lips against her velvety ones, desperate to taste her. A whimper escaped her throat, and his brain ceased to care about anything around them. His only focus was the fiery woman in his arms. His tongue slid past her lips, delving into her mouth to dance over her teeth and duel with her tongue. Sage melted into him, letting him take want he wanted.

After too short a time, Tehl gentled the kiss and left butterfly-soft caresses over every bit of her face. His wife sighed and owlishly blinked up at him. A sense of smug masculine pride filled him at the well-loved expression on Sage's face.

"It's time, love."

Sage nodded, her happiness sloughing off, steel and determination replacing it. "Don't do anything foolish while I am gone."

"I'll do my best."

She slipped her hand into his and gazed around their small chamber. "I'll miss sleeping beside you."

He nodded. "Do you have everything you need?" Tehl frowned when he didn't spot the poison ring hanging from the chain at her neck. "Where is the ring?"

A devious look crossed her face. She turned her back to him and lifted the heavy fall of her hair. Plaited into the underside of her braid was the ring. Sage dropped her hair and faced him once again.

"I'll be stripped of all my weapons immediately. This is the safest place for it."

"He won't touch…" Tehl glanced away, his jaw working. He loved playing with her hair, and the image of the warlord doing the same made him sick.

Sage brushed her fingertips along his jawline. "He won't be laying hands on me, my love. Not unless he wants another wound to go with the one I gave him last week."

He shoved his anger and jealousy down deep. "If he touches you, cut off his hand."

She flashed him a bloodthirsty smile. "It is my deepest hope that he tries."

Voices neared their tent, and he knew their time for goodbyes was up. Tehl placed one last lingering kiss on her lips. "To the end, love?"

"To the end."

TWENTY-EIGHT

JASMINE

—◦⟨⟩◦—

"YOU CAN'T GO ON LIKE this!" Mekhl growled.

Jasmine didn't spare him a glance, just kept staring out the window at the sea. The waters churned, just like her mind. Out of the three Scythian warriors she'd been forced to live with, he was the hothead. It was best not to engage him when he was in one of his moods. A self-deprecating smile tugged at her lips. Time away from Scythia had not made her forget what they were like. Even if she wanted to.

"Phoenix, will you reason with her?" Mekhl demanded.

"Leave her alone," Phoenix rumbled.

Mekhl cursed, and a door slammed.

"Are you done torturing us?"

Jasmine snorted. "You're the ones holding me captive."

"We mean you no harm, as we've said over and over."

That got under her skin. She turned toward the largest of the Scythian warriors. His cinnamon gaze held her blue gaze.

"No harm?" Her words were a whispered accusation. He didn't flinch or look sorry in the least. "You know what you've done." Movement fluttered in her belly, and her hands dropped to her stomach. Phoenix's attention lowered to her abdomen, and his stern expression softened. "No," she hissed, stabbing a finger in his direction. "You do not get to look at me like that."

"You're a miracle."

It wasn't the first time Jas had heard the sentiment. It still changed nothing.

She turned away from him and stared out the window, her emotions on a thread. For the first few weeks, she'd screamed and fought against them. Once they'd gotten her on the ship, there was nowhere to go. While she prided herself on being a great swimmer, there was no way she could get past the leviathans that circled constantly. The sky was heavy with black, grey, and green clouds. A storm was brewing.

Her stomach lurched. Jasmine inhaled deeply through her nose. Her nausea was so much worse on the ship. The babe rolled again. She'd been doing that more often. Her fingers drifted over the big bump. At this point, Jasmine thought she would explode if the babe got any bigger. She'd been trying to put it from her mind, but her birthing time wasn't too far away. Would the babe be born here? Stars above, she hoped not.

"I don't wish to fight with you," Phoenix murmured.

"Then don't. Release me."

"I can't do that. Do you understand what that babe means to us?"

"Enough that you raped an unconscious woman," she snapped, facing Phoenix, her skirts swishing around her ankles. Phoenix's jaw clenched, but that was the only sign that she'd gotten to him.

"I don't think you understand how much danger you were in."

"Danger from you, you mean?" she retorted.

Phoenix stiffened and took one step toward her, pushing away from the bookcase. "I'm done tiptoeing around you. Orion is too soft, to tell you the truth, and you rile Mekhl up too much for him to think clearly, so I'll be the one to come out with it: you were given to us, as a war prize, as a gift for our service." His lip curled. "But that gift had strings."

"That's disgusting," Jasmine spat. "Depraved."

"You're not wrong."

She blinked. That was not what she expected him to say. "That does not excuse——"

"I'm not finished," he cut in. "You've screamed abuses at us for weeks, and, not once, have you thought to hear what we needed to say. You will now. The only reason the warlord kept you alive was because you were a means to an end."

Jasmine felt off-kilter. He wasn't telling her anything she didn't already know. She placed her right hand on the back of a wingback chair to steady herself.

"You were just another way to control his consort and to control us."

"Control you?"

He nodded. "On one of your ventures, Orion made a mistake. He trusted the wrong person, and I was summoned." His jaw flexed. "If we didn't follow the law, you would have been given to brutal, heinous warriors. The warlord would have torn you away. You would have died in Scythia with no one the wiser. I couldn't allow that to happen."

"So you drugged me and stole my innocence?" God, she was going to be sick.

"We protected you when no one else would have."

"Protection?" Tears flooded her eyes. "You're despicable. There's no excuse for what you've done. You stole something that I can't ever get back!"

"I'm sorry."

"You're sorry?" Tears dripped down her cheeks. "That changes nothing."

"There wasn't any pleasure in it. I had to drink herbs just to accomplish the task."

"That's supposed to comfort me? That you didn't take pleasure in my unconscious body?" she scoffed. "Why didn't you just ask me?"

Phoenix held her gaze. "Would you have said yes?"

She wouldn't have.

He nodded. "That's what I thought. What we did was wrong, and we can't ever take it back. I wish things hadn't happened like they did. All I've ever wanted was a wife and children, but the warlord tainted that."

"I'm not your wife."

"No, but you are the mother of my child, and I intend to protect you until my dying breath. Keep on believing I am evil, I can bear that for my follies and sins. But I can't change the past, and I don't regret that you're safe and unhurt, out of that demon's grasp. We're all a product of his brutality and madness."

"Those are traitorous words, if I've ever heard them," she whispered. "Better be careful or you might be executed."

"I take the risk so you know my true feelings. Orion, Mekhl, and I were raised with women from the Pit who were taken as consorts. They suffered at the hands of our fathers. We never desired that for any woman. It's wrong. It needs to change."

"And yet you fight for him."

"For now."

Her eyes widened. What did that mean? "A few good acts don't negate the vile ones you've committed."

"True, but it doesn't mean nothing either." He blew out a breath and threw his shoulders back. "I'm getting off track. Your pain is ours. There are no words to express how sorry I am for the state of things. I wanted to let you know that Orion, Mekhl, and I have vowed to never touch you again. You need not fear us."

"How magnanimous of you." She rubbed at her temples, just moments from breaking down. "Get out."

"As you wish."

Jasmine turned toward the window, and the door closed with a rough click. She bowed her head and began to cry. How could an act she couldn't remember hurt so much? Why did she understand his logic? What was wrong with her?

She sank to the floor and wrapped her arms around herself. She wanted Sam. Even if he was with another woman. Damn her.

She was broken.

Jasmine fell out of bed.

She yelped as the floor tilted, and she slid toward the bookcases. Her nails scrabbled at the ground as she fought to find a grip somewhere. She managed to grab the edges of the bookshelves, only to cause tomes to rain down around her. She curled into a ball, protecting her belly. The floor leveled out some, and she untangled the robe from her legs and squinted in the darkness, trying to get her bearings. What the bloody hell?

Lightning flashed outside, the wind howling. She forced herself to her feet and stumbled over to the window. Dread filled her as another streak of lightning lit up the night sky. The largest wave she'd ever seen raced toward them.

"Swamp apples." Jasmine dropped to her knees and crawled under the table that was bolted to the floor and wrapped herself around its legs. She grunted and clung to the table as the wave slammed into the ship. The wood groaned and the floor buckled, causing her stomach to lurch. She puked. All over herself and the floor. Her gaze darted to the window, and all she could see was black water.

Full-on panic seized her. She would not drown in this room. She and her baby would get out of here. She couldn't leave Ethan and Jade without a mum again. Jasmine pushed through her panic and waited for the right moment. The bow of the ship dipped forward, tilting the cabin at an angle toward her bed. She forced herself to let go of the table and squeaked as she slid down the floor to the door. It was too damn heavy to open.

Jasmine glanced out the window and steeled herself. She had to wait for the next wave to hit. It wasn't long. Her breath whooshed out of her as she released the latch, and the door barreled inward.

"Wicked hell." She gritted her teeth, using the arch of the doorway to pull herself into the hallway. The ship rolled again, and the swinging door switched directions. Jasmine let go of the doorframe right before the door would've slammed shut on her fingers. Her feet slipped against the wet floor. Her gaze locked on the stairway that led to the deck. Waves splashed down the stairs, spraying her with icy water.

Jasmine latched onto a nearby doorknob and planted her arse on the ground, shivering. How in the bloody hell was she supposed to get up the stairs? If she took a fall… She glanced at her belly. If she didn't get out, they'd both drown. She just knew it. Maybe if she slipped her robe tie around each of the planked stairs and crawled up on her hands and knees, she'd make it.

Releasing the doorknob would be one of the hardest things she'd ever done. *It's now or never.*

She yanked the soggy tie from her waist and slid it around the fourth plank up, then wound each end around her hands. She only managed to get up five stairs when the next wave hit her. The breath was knocked from her as the icy water doused her. She gritted her teeth, quickly moved the tie up two more stairs and laboriously worked her way up. By the time she reached the deck, Jasmine was soaked all the way through and her knees were scraped and raw.

What she saw made her want to crawl back to her room.

Lightning cracked across the night sky, bathing the gruesome scene in stark light. Phantom-like fins sliced through the black water, as the creatures preyed on those unfortunate to be swept into the sea's dark embrace. Scythian warriors strained with ropes, shouting at each other.

Jasmine ducked her head and pressed as close as she could to the stairs, her fingers turning white against the red sash of her robe as the water rose over the edge and soaked her shivering form. She panted as water crashed over her head. Her skin was covered in goosebumps, and she gasped for breath as seawater dripped into her eyes, stinging.

She blinked as a dark figure strode her way, his steps sure despite the weather. Mekhl grunted when he spotted her, his expression grim.

"What *are* you doing?"

"I don't want to drown," she yelled.

He hauled her up and maneuvered her so they were behind another set of stairs on the deck. She watched through the gaps in the stairs, as the ship rolled to the side and bobbed back in the other direction. She vomited again. On Mekhl. He didn't say a word but tied a rope around his waist.

"Lift your arms," he commanded. She didn't hesitate. He secured the rope around her chest. "Listen to me. We're moving toward the coast. There's a lifeboat. We need to get to it."

She nodded, shaking from head to toe. Mekhl surprised her and brushed a wet, lank piece of hair from her cheek.

"Stop looking so grim. You're not dying today." A wry smile. "Although, you might get your wish. I might not make it." He paused, scanning the waves. "Move!"

Jasmine scrambled after him, her bare feet sliding all over the deck. It was absolute chaos.

"Damn it!" Mekhl changed direction and pressed her against the mast. He wrapped his arms in the rope and gritted his teeth. "Hold on!"

She managed to get a look at the oncoming wave and screamed. A wall of seawater crashed into them from above. She coughed and spewed. Mekhl groaned.

"Are you all right?" she yelled over the screeching wind.

"Fine."

Her eyes widened when he pulled his arms from the ropes. Blood leaked from cuts they'd made.

He caught her glance. "It's nothing."

Once again, they slipped and slid across the deck to where the lifeboat was secured. It looked tiny.

"Are you sure that will hold us?"

Mekhl spun, his wet braids slapping against his bare chest. "The beach is just right there. We can make it."

He tossed her into the boat, and her breathing grew shallow as the ship leaned to the side, the life raft almost touching the water. She'd sworn she'd seen a fin. "Please don't let me get eaten," she whispered. "*Please.*"

The warrior jumped into the raft and cut the ties. She shrieked when they were airborne for a moment, but then they hit the water.

"Lie in the bottom and scoot under the seat."

She did as she was told and gaped when the mast on the ship cracked and splintered as another wave struck. Their raft bobbed uncontrollably, but she couldn't take her eyes from the Scythian warship. It was as if a massive hand had punched a hole in the rear of the ship.

Where her quarters had been.

"Oh god," she cried out as another wave rushed toward them.

"We'll make it," Mekhl shouted.

They weren't going to make it.

The wave hit them and tumbled the boat over. The rope pulled taught around her upper body. She screamed, water filling her mouth. The salt water stung her eyes. She couldn't see anything until a shape moved beneath her. Mekhl's face entered her vision. With strength she didn't know anyone could possess, he maneuvered the little boat with frantic movements. Water sluiced from her as the boat was tipped back over.

Jasmine coughed and sobs wracked her chest. Was this her life? To escape one hell, only to journey into another one? She wiped at her eyes and reached for Mekhl's hand to help him into the boat. Her eyes widened when movement caught her attention.

Leviathans.

"Get in the boat," she shouted. He tried but his wounded arm failed. She pulled with all her might, her eyes not leaving the fin that streaked toward them. "Come on, come on, come on," she sobbed.

Mekhl gave her a tender look and cut the rope between them. "I'm sorry."

The monster struck, and Mekhl disappeared beneath the waves.

"No, no, no, no!" She couldn't believe her eyes. "Mekhl!"

The black water made it impossible to see anything. Another wave barreled toward her, and she ducked down into the bottom of the piddly boat, holding on for dear life.

Her screams were lost to the wind as the wild seas threw her about. The bottom of the boat hit something solid and cracked. She lifted her head. The small raft was lodged between two huge rocks.

Another wave hit. And another. And another.

The boat didn't move.

Jasmine found a rhythm. Breathe, breathe, wave.

At some point, she stopped feeling cold.

She stared at the roiling sky and screamed until she was hoarse.

She was Jasmine bloody Ramses.

Nothing and no one would be taking her from her babies.

Her stomach cramped, pain rendering her breathless. This could not be happening.

Labor was upon her.

TWENTY-NINE

SAGE

SAGE DIDN'T KNOW WHAT DISTURBED her the most.

The empty maw of nothingness that numbed her, or the morose expressions on the soldiers' faces as she neared the edge of camp. Tehl's hand warmed her as he led her to their inner circle. Zachael, Rafe, Raziel, Hayjen, Blaise, and Domin stood or sat waiting, snow falling heavily around them.

Sage released Tehl's hand and strode to Blaise, who sat on a stump. She eyed her friend's splinted leg and dropped to her haunches. "How in the blazes did you get Mira to let you out of the infirmary?"

The Scythian woman cracked a smile. "I promised not to put any weight on it, and to use the burly one as a pack horse." She flicked a finger toward Rafe. "But, in all honesty, he's not a stallion, more like a jackass."

Sage sniggered. "How very accurate."

Blaise's smile melted, and her expression turned serious. "Are you prepared for what lies ahead?"

She wasn't. Who could possibly plan to face such a thing? "To the best of my ability."

Her friend seized her hands and pulled her closer. "Do you remember what I told you before we marched to meet the warlord?"

"How could I ever forget?" Sage sighed, her breath a puff of frosted air.

Blaise released Sage's hands and pulled a tiny jar from her cloak. She pulled the lid off and dipped her fingers into the onyx Tia warpaint. "Lean toward me and tell me who you are."

Sage closed her eyes. The paint was cold on her skin, but Blaise's movements were comforting as she swirled the paint across her cheeks and eyelids. "I am Sage Ramses. Warrior princess of Aermia. I am not the warlord's pawn. I am not his consort. I am his demise."

"Very good. Open your eyes."

Sage lifted her lashes and met Blaise's dark gaze. The Scythian woman drew a line over her lips, down her chin to her throat. "Who are you?"

"I am his judgement, his enemy, and his ultimate destruction."

Blaise smiled, but it wasn't nice. "You are his death." She kissed both of Sage's cheeks and then whispered, "You are not alone. Sisters in arms, yeah?"

Sage hugged her. "Always."

"I will see you soon."

She nodded and stood, her cloak disturbing the snow as she turned to face the rest of the group. Her hands opened and closed as she stared at some of her most cherished friends. What was she supposed to say?

Zachael approached first. He pulled her into a bear hug and dropped a kiss on the top of her hooded head. "Fight hard, Sage."

She nodded and gave him a squeeze before he moved on. Rafe stepped up next and clasped both of her cheeks. They stared at each other for a long time. She could almost read his mind, just from the look in his eyes.

"Don't make me hunt for you," he said gruffly.

"I won't."

He brushed his nose against hers before retreating so Hayjen could take his spot. Her uncle pulled her into a bone-crushing hug.

"Don't be stupid," he said. "Don't let your emotions get the best of you." He pulled back, his arctic eyes pinning her in place. "Find your nothing space and stay there. It will be your protection, *ma fille*."

Her heart twanged at the use of Lilja's pet name. "I promise."

She let out a sound of surprise when Raziel pulled her into a quick hug. "I have no words of advice for you." He flashed her a smile. "You're the strongest of us all. I'll see you soon, Sage."

Sage nodded at Domin, who was also wearing white, and turned to face her silent husband. His expression was completely blank, and, for once, she was so thankful she couldn't get a read on him. If she'd seen even the tiniest bit of fear, she didn't think she'd be able to go.

"To the end, my love?"

Tehl breached the space between them and pushed her hood from her head. "And back, my love." He kissed her softly in an uncharacteristic public show of affection and then brushed his nose against hers. "I'll be seeing you soon, wife."

Her smile trembled. This man. Tehl pulled her hood back up into place and stepped back, his arms crossed. She took one last glance at him and turned her back on him, facing the desolate stretch of battlefield ahead of them.

Lastly, she dropped to her knees and held her arms out. "Come here, Nali."

The leren slunk from the darkness and butted her in the chest with her head. Sage threw her arms around the feline and hugged Nali close. "I wish you could come with me," she whispered. Pulling back, she scratched the leren's ears affectionately. "You need to stay here and protect him." Nali's golden eyes blinked at her like she understood Sage's words. She gave the feline one last hug before standing.

"Domin?" she asked, turning to her Methian guard.

"Ready, my lady."

Sage inhaled deeply, and ignored the panic that was trying to creep up and freeze her in place. The time for fear was over.

She took her first step onto the battlefield and didn't look back.

THİRTY

TEHL

WATCHING HER WALK AWAY ALMOST killed him. She never looked back.

Tehl stared until she blended in with the storm and disappeared from view. Even then, he didn't move.

Hayjen clasped his shoulder, and Tehl met the man's gaze.

"She will come back," Hayjen said.

An absurd statement. No one could promise that.

"He won't harm her," Blaise said, her smoky voice like black velvet.

Tehl looked to her. The Scythian woman pulled her cloak tighter around herself but met his gaze full on.

"My uncle won't kill her."

"And what makes you so sure?" he rumbled, hating that there was a little hope unfurling in his chest. He smashed it down, ruthlessly. To survive what was coming, he had to put her out of his mind.

"He's too obsessed with her to let her escape him, even in death. His demons wouldn't allow it."

"Blaise," Rafe chastised.

She glared at the former rebellion leader. "I am being honest." Her attention turned back to Tehl. "You can be thankful for that, at least."

A small favor—if he didn't think about what else the warlord would be doing with *his* wife. Tehl closed his eyes and sank into the quiet, calm place in his mind and counted to thirty. When he opened his eyes, everything was calm. He scanned the group.

"She's probably halfway there. We move now."

THÌRTY-ONE

SAGE

THE STORM SWALLOWED SAGE WHOLE, and time ceased to exist. They could have been traveling for minutes or hours. She didn't know.

Her cloak whipped around her as she moved stealthily across the battlefield with Domin. Thank the stars he was with her or she would have gotten lost. She pinned her eyes to Domin's cloak and stumbled as she stepped on something too soft to be the ground. Her stomach rose, but she kept plowing on. The snow blanketed the earth in a white shroud, and, while that was a blessing, it was also a curse. One never knew if it was a natural mound or a forsaken body.

Shadows in the distance appeared.

Domin darted behind a boulder, and Sage followed him. They crouched and stared at each other.

"The camp is three hundred paces past this stone. We've managed to skirt by the patrol but..."

She understood. Sage laid a hand on his arm. "You need to go back. I'll go on from here by myself."

The Methian shook his head. "You're my lady. I go where you go."

"I will not be the cause of your death. You know the plan is for me to go in by myself."

His eyes narrowed. "Plans change when put into action."

"Not in this." She squeezed his arm. "You will long for death when he's finished with you. You will also be another way he will try to control me. We give him nothing," she said fiercely.

Domin slowly nodded. "May the wind be with you."

"And may the stars shine down on you," she whispered back in the Methian way.

Sage released his arm and peeked around the boulder. She didn't see any movement, but that meant nothing. The snow protected her, but it also obscured her enemy. She glanced over her shoulder at Domin. He was gone. What she wouldn't give for skills like that. He was almost as silent as Rafe.

She blew out a breath and crept around the boulder. Sage moved carefully across the open space. Her skin prickled at being so exposed. Her senses screamed at her to run, but she forced herself to maintain the slow pace. Her clothing aided in camouflaging her approach, but it didn't conceal her completely. A slow-moving object would attract much less attention.

The first tent appeared almost out of nowhere, and her heart thundered. Damn snow. What if it had been the enemy? She eyed the tent. Was there someone inside? If there was, would the snow dampen the sound of her approach? She didn't know.

Sage slowed down even further, making sure her steps were very careful. She slunk past tents at the south side of the Scythian camp without seeing even a hint of a Scythian. She chewed her lip. It didn't seem right. It was too easy. Every step she took, Sage waited for someone to shout the alarm.

She eyed one of the quiet tents and then her stark, white outfit. While it had helped her hide on the battlefield, she would stick out like a sore thumb among the warriors. She needed a cloak. Sage crept toward the nearest tent and listened. Not a sound.

Ever so carefully, she lifted the tent flap and peeked inside. Empty, as far as she could see. Sage slipped inside and hovered at the entrance. The tent held four pallets, a chamber pot in the corner, and a few articles of clothing. She grinned when she spotted a discarded cloak.

Quickly, she tossed the huge cloak over her outfit and pulled the hood over her head. It dragged on the ground and wouldn't stand up to close inspection, but it was better than what she had before. She blew out a breath and clenched her jaw, so her teeth didn't chatter, just as they were prone to do when adrenaline flooded her body. Sage took one last glance at the tent. It was funny how four walls brought a source of comfort. It was only canvas and wood. Easily burned or cut through, and yet she felt safer inside than she did wandering through the camp. Safe, at least, until the tent's inhabitants came back to rest in their beds. Staying in the tent wasn't an option, long-term.

Sage peeked through the slit of the entrance. The coast was clear. She crept from the tent, her filched cloak trailing behind her. Sage wove to the left of a tent when three Scythian warriors materialized ahead of her and blocked her path. Where the hell had they come from?

"What do we have here?" asked the Scythian to her left. He reminded her of a leren, all dark and feline-like. Contempt seemed to radiate from his person. "Did you think Scythians are so stupid they wouldn't notice a stranger prowling around in their camp?"

She kept silent. Let them have their words. They hadn't attacked yet.

"Do you know what we do to spies?" demanded the one in the middle, his sharp features making him appear hawkish.

Torture them.

"If you're looking to die, we're happy to oblige," the biggest warrior on the right crooned. "But we have a few questions we'd like to ask of you."

Sage crossed her arms slowly, so as not to spook the warriors into violence, the movement hiding how she was freeing the blades at her wrists. The Scythians all seemed to vibrate with anger, and she knew how easy it was to set them off. She needed to time it perfectly.

"Actually, I need to speak with your warlord. He and I have some business to discuss," she said cheerfully. "If you'd be so kind as to escort me to his tent."

The warriors frowned as her very female voice surprised them.

Gotcha.

Sage lunged left, clearing the far side of her attackers' line. She paused and waited on the balls of her feet. Sage jerked her head, and the hood slid to her shoulders. No reason to have it block her vision when the ruse was up. The soldiers moved in sync, hardly batting an eye at her prior burst of speed. They knew she was slower than they were. They were going to toy with her now. Sage held up one blade in front of her and one behind her, keeping her gaze on the trio that now circled her.

"What a pretty little thing," the big man taunted. He eyed her stolen cloak. "I'm sure my lord doesn't invite thieves to dine with him. I say we take care of this right here. What do you think, men?"

The others laughed, and the hair along her arms rose a moment, before the hawkish man came at her. He tossed a large knife from one hand to the other. A surge of relief rushed through her. Clearly, this one was still young. Any warrior worth his salt knew a soldier never let go of his blade.

Sage darted beneath his guard and knocked his knife from his hands. He swung at her, and she jammed one of her blades into his ribs. He bellowed and grabbed for her. She barely managed to duck in time and caught his eyes flicking right.

Damn it.

She cut the clasp at her throat and lunged forward, spinning to see the biggest man clutching the dark Scythian cloak she'd stolen. The feline man attacked from her right, and she snapped out a side kick, nailing him in the knee. A sickly snap sounded. He screamed and yet managed to grab her boot. He yanked, pulling her off her feet. Sage dropped to her back and twisted, dislodging her foot from his grasp.

A snick on metal caught her attention. She rolled, just as a blade plunged into the ground where she had been lying. Sage surged to her feet, knocked the biggest warrior's feet out from under him, and dumped him onto his back.

Her attention focused on the hawkish man who moved slowly, each step graceful and calculated. The biggest one was the loudest, but this man was the most dangerous.

Sage danced backward as he pursued her.

"Pretty little show," the man said simply.

She shrugged. "I do what I can. Take me to the warlord, and I will make sure he spares you." A lie.

He cocked his head but never stopped moving. "What makes you so special?"

"Nothing and everything."

"Playing with words." His lip curled. "Just like an Aermian."

Her muscles tensed, and he *blurred*. Sage didn't have time to prepare herself for the blow. The warrior hit her so hard, he slammed the breath from her own lungs. She sailed backward and remembered just in time to tuck and roll. Her left shoulder took the brunt of her weight. That would bruise. Sage popped to her feet and wheezed.

He hadn't used his blades. The warrior caught her glance and smiled. "Blades are too easy. It's more personal to kill someone with my bare hands."

Another psychopath. Delightful. "Your warlord won't be pleased if you don't take me to him."

The hawkish warrior studied her and held a hand up when the other two clambered to their feet and made like they were going to join in. "She's mine."

Sage sank further into a battle-ready stance. This wasn't going to be fun.

He took one gliding step toward her when a spear struck the ground between them, quivering, planted in the snow-covered earth. Another figure appeared from behind the hawkish warrior, his long braids just visible.

Blair. She wanted to sag in relief, but she didn't. She watched as the warrior looked back, to find the commander prowling toward them. The youngest warrior with the rib wound bowed his head and grimaced.

The hawkish man didn't bow but stood tall when Blair stepped into his space. "Do you know what you've done?"

"Protected our camp from an intruder, sir."

"You've attacked our liege's consort." Blair cracked a smile that was anything but friendly. All three warriors stiffened.

Sage kept her expression blank at her title, even though it made her skin crawl.

"We had no way of knowing," the youngest began to say.

"Enough," the hawkish warrior barked. "We will accept the punishment for our actions."

"Indeed, you will," the commander murmured. He moved around the warrior and took a couple of smooth steps in Sage's direction before halting. "Consort."

"Commander," she murmured. They gazed at each other, snow falling around them.

"I will escort you to our warlord."

She swallowed hard and tried to tamp down the fear growing in her belly. There was no turning back now. Sage rose from her fighting stance, her blades still in each hand. On wooden legs, she passed the biggest warrior and the youngest one, as they both stared at her in fascination. Sage paused next to Blair, eyeing the hawkish warrior. His eyes narrowed as he scanned her from foot to toe. She arched a brow.

"She's tiny," he muttered.

"True. Doesn't stop her from fighting a good fight, does it?" Blair pointed out.

The warrior nodded in agreement.

Blair looked down at her, his amusement draining away as fast as it had come. "Put those blades away, consort, unless you intend to challenge me."

Sage worked her jaw, but returned her blades to their places. She felt utterly naked without her weapons in her hands. At least he hadn't taken them from her. Yet.

"Very good. Now follow me. He's been eagerly awaiting your arrival."

Dread filled her.

There was no going back.

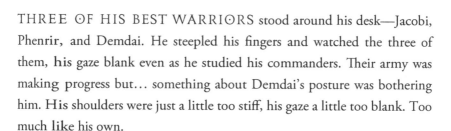

THIRTY-TWO

THE WARLORD

THREE OF HIS BEST WARRIORS stood around his desk—Jacobi, Phenrir, and Demdai. He steepled his fingers and watched the three of them, his gaze blank even as he studied his commanders. Their army was making progress but... something about Demdai's posture was bothering him. His shoulders were just a little too stiff, his gaze a little too blank. Too much like his own.

What was his warrior hiding?

"Winter is setting in, my liege," Jacobi explained.

The warlord's lips twitched, and the overly tall warrior blanched. Satisfaction warmed him at the reaction. Jacobi wouldn't be rebelling against him any time soon. While the commander excelled at following commands, he was hardly a plotter.

"True," he murmured conversationally and waved a hand in dismissal. Only a fool wouldn't have a plan. Zane's expression hardened a touch. He was not a fool. The years of bloodshed, rebellion, and death had trained him well.

Jacobi swallowed, his Adam's apple bobbing, but gathered his composure. "Of course, my lord."

Zane smiled at the man. He liked that about the towering warrior. A devious strategist the man was not, but he served in a more practical function of passing unbiased information among the warriors. A commander that followed his orders to the letter was difficult to come by.

His gaze slid over the other two warriors.

As for Demdai and Phenrir, both had their own agendas. Phenrir would never take the throne, but he had a son around Blaise's age. He wished for a union between them. That would never happen.

Traitor, the voices hissed in disdain.

His lips thinned. His niece had made a grave mistake in crossing him. She'd taken his consort from him. That wasn't forgivable.

Kill, kill, kill!

Her betrayal would not go unpunished, but not to the point of death. Zane steepled his fingers as he dropped his gaze back to the intricate map on his desk, his shuddered gaze hiding his glee from his men.

He had plans for the wayward girl. While he couldn't outright kill the only heir to his throne at the moment, the suffering and shame she'd experience when she was captured would be enough to have her fall in line. His lips twitched the tiniest bit at the remembrance of how his men hunted her down each time she set a foot on the battlefield.

Her woes were only beginning.

The warlord's eyes flicked to the haughty Phenrir. The warrior had too many ambitions—both he and his son—there would be no marriage between their families. He'd never let a sniveling wimp on his throne.

However, he did know of a warrior who might bring Blaise to heel...

"My lord?" Jacobi said.

"Continue," he said, waving his hand. Their reports to him each night were an exercise in humility. The warlord knew exactly what was happening on the battlefield and in his camp. Any good leader did. But it amused him to watch his commanders shift uneasily in his presence.

Jacobi opened his mouth to speak when Blair's deep voice sounded from outside his tent.

"Entrance, my lord?"

"Permitted," Zane answered.

His last commander pushed through the tent flap and hovered at the entrance, snow clinging to his dark braids.

"May I approach?" Blair asked respectfully.

The warlord's gaze sharpened. Here was a man who knew how to play the game properly. Blair *never* stepped out of line. That in and of itself was suspicious.

"You may," he drawled.

His commander approached the desk, not sparing a glance at the other three men staring at him with slightly veiled dislike. Another reason why he kept Blair around. His dutiful commander stirred the pot too much. They hated how many privileges Zane had given Blair. In all honesty, he hated Blair most days. The man was efficient, though, and the warlord couldn't find a reason to kill him. There were numerous fraudulent charges he could have heaped upon the good commander's head if he'd really wanted him dead. But Zane had learned not to be wasteful throughout his years.

He eyed the hostile glances being thrown from his other commanders. If his leading men hated each other, they would never unite against him.

Blair bowed deeply and straightened, locking eyes with him. "There has been a development. We have discovered a spy in our camp."

A spy? The hair at the back of his neck rose. There was only one so brazen to enter his camp. Slowly, he rose from his chair. "A spy?"

Blair nodded. "She's here."

The world slipped into silence; not even the voices whispered. His skin tingled. She was here. Sage. It was as if her name unlocked the chaos he kept tightly leashed inside himself.

Ours. Mine. Die. Possess. Pain. Ours, the voices roared.

Pain pulsed in his temples, and he glared at his men.

"Get out," he uttered softly. His warriors filed out, not one hesitating.

The warlord squeezed his eyes shut and grabbed the sides of his desk to ground himself. The wood groaned beneath his palms.

Ours. Ours. Punish. Ours.

"Mine," he growled out loud. *His.* She was his to possess and punish. His.

The warlord opened his eyes and inhaled deeply, barely holding on to the threads of his sanity.

Sage was here.

His vision dipped, and Zane bared his teeth through the howls echoing in his mind.

She was home.

The wood cracked and bit into his palms. The pain helped him focus. Slowly, he counted his breaths and released the edge of his desk, leaving smears of crimson behind.

The warlord rolled his neck and tipped his head back to stare at the ceiling of his tent.

She returned.

For once, he allowed himself a full smile.

He'd won.

She was his.

THIRTY-THREE

SAGE

THE NIGHT AIR SEEMED TO thicken, as four hulking warriors exited the large canvas tent, Blair bringing up the rear. She kept her expression neutral, as one of the warriors approached from her right side. He halted an arms-breadth away and scanned her from head to toe. His lip curled. From his expression, he clearly didn't care for her.

"So, the consort returns," he sneered from his great height.

Consort. Sage hid her flinch at the title. *Get yourself under control. If you can't handle him, how do you expect to handle the warlord?*

He leaned into her space as if to intimidate her. Her initial wariness burned away while irritation and anger took its place. She'd danced with the devil and sat by his side in hell. He didn't know what *real* fear was. This man was just a giant bully. She could sense it.

The man gave her a terrifying smile and whispered, "I hope he rips your bloody throat out for what you've done."

She lazily arched a brow at him, goading him the tiniest bit. "Where would the fun be in that?" she murmured back softly, knowing that all the warriors were listening in despite her low tone. "Methinks you don't know your lord as well as you profess to." She scanned him from head to toe as he'd done to her. "If I was a betting woman, I'd say you're only a glorified bitch for the lord to kick around."

The warrior's face turned red at the insult. "You little whore!"

How unoriginal.

"If you don't watch yourself, you might be the one with his throat cut." Sage tsked. She slanted a glance to the tent and back to the warrior's expression, which had now drained of its fire but held bitterness. "I would watch what sort of labels you throw around in mixed company. I'm told all Scythians have an excellent sense of hearing. I'm sure the warlord more than most."

The warrior's jaw set, and he hissed into her face. Her heart pounded a little harder.

"Enough, Phenrir," Blair said, a clear command.

Sage didn't fail to notice the rage that ignited the warrior's eyes before he shuttered his expression and moved out of her space, his steps almost silent as he stormed away into the camp. So the haughty Phenrir didn't like Blair ordering him around. Good to know. Sage filed that information away for later.

Her shoulders slumped the smallest bit, and she felt like she could breathe again once he'd moved away from her, hovering to her far right. While Phenrir wasn't the warlord, he still wasn't someone she wanted to be close to. Sage dismissed him and focused back on the tent entrance.

He still hadn't arrived. Her stomach quivered. On one hand, it gave her time to think, but on the other hand, it ratcheted up her nerves. Nervousness did not do her any good.

A fat snowflake dropped onto her nose, causing Sage to blink and to focus on the frigid feathers descending from the night sky. Snow fell around them, flurries dancing in a gentle breeze. She focused on one, and counted her heartbeats until the snowflake joined its brethren among the white shroud blanketing the ground.

The silence held a sinister edge to it. She studied the warriors stationed around her from beneath her lashes. They stood around her like stone sentinels, their dark gazes frozen to her. The only sign that they were alive were the warm puffs of breath that steamed into the chilly night air. How did they stand so still? Sage opened and closed her hands, keeping her fingers from stiffening up. Weren't they cold? Her toes had already begun to go numb in her boots as the snow piled up around her feet. How long did the warlord plan on leaving her out here?

Do you really want to see him so badly?

The temptation to fiddle with her shirt niggled at her, but she squashed the notion. She wouldn't give the men around her any indication that she was nervous. She readjusted her stance, and ignored the eyes that were watching her. The back of her neck prickled, but she didn't look behind her. Damn nerves.

You're more than nervous. She was on the brink of losing it.

Internally, she winced. Her mind had shut off during the journey across the battlefield. Her singular thought was to stay hidden. Now that the adrenaline was fading from her veins, her confidence seemed to wane as well. Sage surveyed her silent entourage. How was this the only option? What was she doing here? She'd asked herself that a million times already.

You're giving the people a chance.

At least, that was what she was telling herself. The pit of rage that rolled in her belly said something else.

She wanted revenge.

The hair along her arms rose at the sound of canvas flapping. The warrior to her left straightened just a touch—the first movement they'd made since arriving.

A shiver of awareness ran down her spine, and time seemed to slow, the snow halting midair. What sort of deviltry was this?

Her gaze sharpened, and the air in her lungs froze, as the tent flap lifted higher.

Out stepped her personal demon.

His dark eyes that she once believed were warm, met hers. His inky hair hung around his angular face, brushing his shoulders. He was beautiful. He was monstrous. He was pain and temptation.

"Consort."

His voice rolled over her, like thunder in a storm, all power.

She shuddered and released a slow breath. Everything about him called to her, from the straight, proud line of his nose to the stubborn chin and almond-shaped eyes. But it was more than his features; it was how he wore them. He was still the most stunning man she'd ever laid eyes upon.

And the vilest.

Time sped up, and Sage blinked once, the snow falling softly around them. Had she just imagined that? Surely, he didn't hold power over the elements?

Get yourself together.

Ice trickled through her veins, along with the blessed numbness that had been plaguing her for the last week. *Thank the stars.* Numbness would help her survive whatever he threw at her. Sage sank into it and tipped her chin up, still holding her monster's gaze. She wouldn't cower before him. Not here, not ever.

"My lord," she murmured through chapped lips.

He cocked his head and slowly perused her from head to toe. The temptation to tug her cloak tightly around her body to hide herself from his gaze almost overwhelmed her, but Sage held on. She wouldn't let him make her feel self-conscious.

"What a pleasant surprise. We've missed you while you've been visiting Aermia."

A smile lifted the left side of his mouth, making him appear boyish. Her spine stiffened and she forced herself not to look away. He was the furthest thing from a boy. Innocent, he was not. Her fingers twitched at the thought of slapping the smile off his face. She hadn't been visiting, and everyone in the silent circle knew it.

He lies. The warlord twists words. He killed Lilja, tortured you, and slaughtered wee ones. Don't let him manipulate you into giving anything away. Fight for those who have been lost.

The knot beneath her collarbone tightened at the reminder of his crimes. Sage tamped down her icy rage and sorrow and held her arms out, palms up as if she were surrendering. "I am here as you requested."

He studied her. "Has she been searched?" he asked without looking away from her.

"No," Blair answered. "Do you want me to strip her?"

Sage kept from blanching. She knew it was going to be brutal. There was no dignity in war.

The warlord teetered his head back and forth and then shook it. "No. Search her here. I'll strip her later."

Her pulse began to beat harder, and she wanted to shrink away from him as the unbidden memory of the warlord pressing her against the wall entered her mind. Her body screaming at the pain of being chained to the wall, his lips begging hers to play with his. The warlord's expression warmed, and something sensual flashed through his eyes like he was remembering it, too. It was enough to make her want to vomit.

Blair approached her and unclasped the white cloak from her neck. The wool fell to the ground, exposing her to the elements. The wind and cold cut through her linen shirt and leather pants, causing goosebumps to erupt on her skin. She'd never experienced the winter elements like this before.

"Hold your arms higher and spread your legs."

Sage did as he asked, her body heat slowly leaching from her clothing.

Blair impersonally ran his hands along her arms and down her sides. He relieved her of the daggers sheathed at her hips and one at her right thigh. It was the first time someone had touched her in that fashion, other than Tehl since her time in Scythia. While his hands never lingered, it brought back too many unwanted memories. Her mask never cracked, even as his hands traveled up the insides of her thighs and beneath her breasts.

"Boots."

Carefully, she pulled off each boot, her stocking feet immediately sinking into the snow. Sage staved off another shiver, and kept her head held high when Blair removed the last two daggers from her boots. She'd known that she'd be stripped of her weapons, but it was still unnerving. Sage hated to be without her blades.

The commander handed her back her boots, which she woodenly put on, her wet socks squelching as she adjusted her stance. Blair circled her and ran his hands along the back of her thighs, over her bum, and across her back. Sage forced herself to keep the bland, neutral expression on her face as he dug his fingers into her braid. The poison ring seemed to burn at the base of her skull. Regulating her breathing was a challenge as his fingers brushed over the cool metal. This was the true test of Blair's loyalty. Would he give her away? She hadn't doubted him, but in that moment, everything hung in the balance. One could really never tell who was the enemy these days.

"She's clean, my lord."

Relief washed over her, but she kept it tucked away.

Blair picked up her discarded cloak and examined the inside, including all the hems. He handed over her pale cloak, and she swung the material over her shoulders, clasping the garment at her throat, immediately thankful to have something to block the wind. A little fissure of delight wormed its way into her heart that Blair hadn't discovered the thin razor she'd stashed away in the lining.

Sage pulled her hood over her head, watching the commander when his gaze flickered. It was all the warning she received before a hand touched her chin. Sage startled and jerked back, but the warlord's calloused fingertips tightened and tipped her head back. He examined her face and leaned so close, his breath heated her own lips.

How she longed to spit in his face.

"This is just the beginning," he murmured.

The warlord's cool lips wandered across her right cheekbone. Sage's fingers clenched at her sides, desperate to be holding a weapon of any sort. It would be so satisfying to stab him in the chest.

"Consort, we have much to work through. I'm sure you'll soon earn my forgiveness." He gently pushed her hood back and pulled her thick braid over her shoulder, his fingers running along the silky plaited strands.

Bile burned the back of her throat. Him forgive *her*? After everything he'd done? He was clearly delusional.

"I am here," she said simply, praying that the three little words didn't give away how very much she wished she wasn't.

"An excellent first step, consort." His gaze sharpened, then he released her. "Sweep the camp. They wouldn't have sent her alone."

Terror filled her, but she kept her calm mask in place. The warlord wasn't stupid. Blair and three other warriors followed his command, silently prowling into the darkness.

Her monster turned his back on her, moved to the tent, and lifted the flap, warm light spilling onto the snow. "Come."

Everything inside her rebelled at the command, but she placed one foot ahead of the other, steeling herself for what the future held. Sage offered a final prayer as she crossed the threshold of the demon's lair.

Warmth immediately curled around her, and the tent flap closed. She stepped to the left to make room for the creature watching her like prey. Even though she'd moved, he still brushed against her.

The warlord moved farther into the room and paused at another tent flap. He slowly spun to face her. "Are you not coming in?"

What was she supposed to say to that? Best to go with honesty. "I don't know what to expect."

"Did you think I was going to throw you in a prison?"

"It wouldn't be the first time, my lord." Sage winced but didn't apologize for her comment. He needed her to be real. As much as she hated to admit it, he knew her. If she lied right now, he would know it.

"Things have not always been easy betw—"

An explosion rocked the earth and Sage stumbled a step. She gasped when hands curled around her biceps and yanked her from the door. Her teeth ground together as the warlord hauled her toward the second room faster than what should have been possible. Damn it. She forgot how fast he moved.

Her breath caught, as his midnight eyes caught hers and held fast. Another series of explosions went off, followed by shouts and screaming. His fingers tightened— almost to the point of painful—around her arms and he pressed even closer.

"Was this your doing, wild one?" he whispered.

Sage prepared herself for what came next. She released the breath trapped in her lungs, and let loose the evil smile she had been hiding. Tehl and their men had succeeded.

"Just a little present like the ones you gave me," she murmured.

Any other demon would have punished her.

Her monster didn't rage. He didn't curse. He *smiled.*

"There she is," the warlord breathed. "I was wondering when my vicious Sage would come out to play. I was worried there for a moment that an ice queen had taken your place." He lifted his left hand and brushed her bottom lip.

She snapped her teeth at him. He was *not* allowed to touch her like that. *Ever.*

"So much fire," he whispered. "Welcome home, consort. Our war has only just begun."

THIRTY-FOUR

SAGE

THE WARLORD COULD NOT BE as calm as he was projecting. He dismissed her, turning to move farther into the room, his steps fluid and graceful. Sage gave the space a cursory glance, noting a large desk to the left of the room, only a map and lantern sitting on its worn surface. A wood stove sat in the rear left corner, and a massive low-sitting bed dominated the right rear corner.

Sage quickly glanced away from the bed and focused on the predator in the room. The warlord moved behind his desk and plucked a sword from behind the furniture. He ignored her as he belted it to his trim waist, and then pulled a black cloak from the back of the wooden chair that sat directly behind the desk.

"I hate to leave you so soon, but duty calls," he murmured, swinging the cloak over his broad shoulders and clasping it at the throat. The warlord glided around the desk, and her muscles tensed as he paused on her right side.

"Yes?" she asked.

His dark eyes narrowed. "Normally, it would go without saying, but our communication hasn't always been the best in the past—"

"That's because you're a liar." Sage snapped her mouth shut. She wouldn't win his trust by acting like a hostile shrew, but who knew? The monster liked confrontation and pain. It might just be what he wanted.

"Like calls to like," he responded, his expression softening a touch. "We have much to speak of. Now is not the time. Don't do anything we both might regret."

She swallowed. He had a way of making a warning sound like a threat. The warlord waited for her affirmation. Sage nodded slowly, her mind whirling.

"Be safe."

She eyed his lack of protection. "No armor?"

He smiled smugly. "I don't need any." With those parting words, he pushed through the tent flap and disappeared from view.

Her lips split into a grin as she stared blankly at the rear of the tent. His arrogance would get him killed. All the better.

A shiver wracked her body. Now that the immediate threat had disappeared, she became very aware that her feet were soaking wet. Stars, she hated the cold. Sage rubbed her arms, trying to create some warmth, and eyed the wooden stove. It would be nice to heat up.

She crept toward the tent flap and pushed it open. The war room was empty but for the giant table they'd passed. Her brows furrowed. No warriors. Odd. Unless he really didn't like anyone in his space. Sage dropped the flap, strode back to the fire, and held her hands out, the hearth warming her palms. Once her fingers had warmed enough, she stripped her boots and socks from her feet and set them near the brazier to dry. She turned her back to the heat and wiggled her frozen toes, all the while studying the space.

From first glance, there wasn't much in the room—a desk, chair, bed, and a chest sitting at the foot of the bed. Not much to make a weapon with. Sure, she could cut the bedding to create a rope to strangle him with, but that wouldn't do her much good. He was too strong. She eyed the chair. It would be easy enough to break it and create a shiv, but that was too noticeable. Sage craned her neck and examined the metal lanterns that hung high in the air. One of those could do nicely if she could reach them. Maybe if she stacked the chair on top of the desk, it would be possible to reach one of them. Then, there was always good old-fashioned burning. Scorching coals could do much damage.

Her heart slowed, and Sage sighed. She was never weaponless, nor powerless. If she kept calm and collected, her plan would work. Gain his trust, get close, and poison him. Plain and simple. Completely warmed, she quietly moved to the desk. Time to snoop.

Three drawers ran down each side and one sat in the middle. Gently, she tried all seven. It didn't surprise her that they were all locked. The monster was suspicious of everything.

Including you.

Sage crouched and ran her right hand along the bottom of the middle drawer, searching for any little catches or hidden spaces. Nothing. Sage raised her head and squinted at the edge of the desk. Two spots along the edges were cracked. She stood and inspected the damage. What caused those? They almost looked like... Holding her hands out, she placed a palm over each spot. A wicked smile curled her lips despite how chills ran up her arms at his strength.

He isn't as calm and unaffected as he pretends to be.

The drawers called to her, but it wasn't worth taking a chance. Even if she could, by some miracle, find something to pick the locks, there'd be evidence.

Sage sidestepped the bed, shying away from the memories it would surely provoke. She knelt beside the chest, her white cloak puddling around her, so she could keep an eye on the entrance, and tried the lock. Much to her surprise, the lock slid open. He obviously wanted her to find what was inside. Sage paused, her fingertips hovering over the lid of the trunk. Did she truly want to open it? Something truly horrendous could be inside. But on the other hand, she could not waste the opportunity to find something that could be used as a true weapon. A woman could never have too many tools in her arsenal.

Gathering her courage, she opened the trunk. Gorgeous fabrics were folded in neat stacks, every color of the imagination. It was as if the trunk held a rainbow. Sage ran her fingers over a luscious red silk. Was this his dressing trunk? She lifted the fabric and shook it out. A gasp exploded from her. It wasn't *his*; it was for *her*. The garment was more scandalous than anything she'd ever seen a woman of night wear. She tossed the garment back into the trunk and scrambled away, her heart pounding in her chest. Why in the wicked hell did he have those?

Don't be stupid.

Sage squeezed her eyes closed and inhaled a calming breath. Despite his beliefs, she was not his and if he tried to force her to wear one of those, she'd burn them all in the woodstove when he left her alone. In fact—her gaze darted to the fire—she could do it now, but that didn't strike her as wise. Clearly, it was a gift of some sort.

Sage approached the trunk of clothing like it held poisonous snakes and pulled each garment out, one by one, trying to discover if there was anything useful. Once it was empty, she ran her hands along the inside of the trunk. Her finger caught on a raised nail in the corner.

Perfect.

She wedged her thumb beneath the nail and tried to wiggle it. Not much movement. And while there wasn't any appearance of guards inside the tent, she wasn't a fool to believe the warlord was not having her watched. Sage began softly singing, praying that it covered up the sounds of her efforts. It took longer than she liked, and she was a sweaty mess, but the nail came free.

Quickly, she lifted the edge of the rug, still humming, and pressed the nail into the earth. With that finished, she put the garments back into the chest, changing the order of how they were folded. True, she could have put everything back in place like Rafe had taught her, but the warlord would already suspect her of searching the room. No need to pretend that he didn't know.

She carefully closed the box and turned, yelping as she came face to face with a leren. Her butt hit the ground as she scrambled back. The feline looked at her with golden eyes.

"Bloody hell," she breathed, placing her hand over her pounding heart. "Why did you sneak up on me, Nege?"

The leren just stared at her. She cocked her head and held out a hand. The beast released a low growl.

Sage snatched back her arm and slowly scooted to her right. "Understood," she whispered. "No touching. I can do that." Careful not to move too quickly, she rose from the ground, her bare toes sinking into the carpet. Nege eyed her but made no move to attack. "That's a good boy," she crooned, edging around him and putting the desk between them. Not that it would be much of a deterrent if he decided he wanted to eat her.

"I'll just stay here," she said conversationally as she skirted around the brazier. If there was anything that could keep the beast back, it would be the fire. He paced once and then lowered himself in front of the flap entrance. "You stay there."

He huffed and laid his head on his paws, as if to say he was laying down because he wanted to, not because she told him to.

Exhaustion seemed to slam into her from nowhere, and she scowled at Nege. She hadn't planned on sleeping in the first place, but with the prickly leren there, it was definitely not possible now. He closed both of his eyes. That was something.

She sighed and Nege cracked one eye. Sage scowled at him. "Excuse me if my sigh bothered you." A sharp longing rose in her chest for Nali. How similar the leren looked, but their temperaments were so different. Again, he huffed, and closed his eye, dismissing her. "You're just as bad as Nali," Sage muttered.

Nege's eyes sprung open, and he pushed to his feet, his tail flicking back and forth. She glanced around in confusion. Was someone coming? "What is it?"

The leren slunk closer, watching her. What had she done to catch his attention? *Nali.* "Do you remember Nali?"

Nege's ears pricked at that. Her breath seized when he halted no more than a handbreadth from her, his face level with her navel. She hissed when he butted his massive head into her stomach, causing her to stumble into the canvas wall. He released a deep purr and sniffed heavily.

Sage held up her hands. "Can you smell her on me? She's okay, Nege. I take care of her, I promise." To some it might seem odd to speak to an animal, but living with Nali had taught her that leren were far more intelligent than people gave them credit for. He arched his back and pressed harder against her, just begging for attention. Her heart squeezed when she noticed new scars marring his gorgeous coat. "Oh, handsome boy. I'm so sorry."

With care, she ran a hand along his spine and was rewarded with another rumbling purr. He twisted and bumped her so hard, Sage lost her balance and ended up kneeling, face to face with Nege.

"Don't eat me."

He blinked at her and then bashed his face into hers, purring loudly. Sage smiled and began to massage the feline, enjoying the experience, and yet... her gaze was glued to the entrance to the room, guilt tainting the moment.

It seemed her greatest weapon had fallen into her lap.

And possessed teeth longer than her palm.

Sage jerked upright, her eyes blurry and her heart in her throat. How in the blazes did she fall asleep, and what woke her?

Nege rumbled softly, his attention honed on the entrance. The warlord slipped inside silently and paused, pulling off his cloak. That was a nifty leren trick. She ran a hand over the feline's head that rested in her lap. Even if she couldn't detect when the warlord was lurking around, her furry companion could. Every muscle in the feline's body was tight, on edge.

So, we're of the same mind. She and Nege both knew who the predator in the room was.

Her focus moved back to the monster. The warlord was splashed with crimson, looking like a nightmarish creature that had crawled from the pits of hell. He tossed his cloak over his desk and placed his hands on his hips, his head hanging, raven hair hiding his features. Sage took the moment to study him. He looked *tired.*

"Judging me already, consort?" he asked, not looking in her direction.

She pursed her lips. "You can't judge something you care nothing about."

He chuckled. "So venomous with words. I'm surprised you weren't born from serpents."

Sage let the slight go and just shrugged. "I am who I am." Her gaze was once again drawn to the blood. Who had he slaughtered or wounded? Was it Tehl? Hayjen? Rafe? Her stomach clenched.

Don't think like that. You need to focus. If it were someone close to you, he would be gloating already.

The thought relieved and sickened her that she could know his mind so well.

"You've changed," he murmured, lifting his head and locking eyes with Sage.

"War does that to a person." She attempted to keep her tone even, but bitterness seeped through. There had been too many casualties.

"It also sharpens them and forges strength."

While he wasn't exactly wrong, there were other ways to go about it.

He moved to the desk and leaned his hip against the furniture, and crossed his arms. "It's not like you to hold back."

She blinked at him, his words filtering through. Her attention hadn't been on his words, but how he'd casually drawn closer. Sage shifted to get her legs beneath her. It was uncomfortable to have the warlord tower over her. It made her feel like a cornered animal. Nege growled softly at being disrupted.

Sighing, the warlord ran a bloody hand through his dark hair. "You're going to be difficult, aren't you?"

"I'm here as you asked, my lord." How was that for sidestepping the question? Sam would be proud.

"Zane."

Every fiber of her being rebelled at the name. Zane didn't exist. He was just a part the warlord played when he needed to. Her jaw clenched. In no way, shape, or form would she ever call him by his given name. Monster? Yes. Demon? Every inch of him. Bastard? Absolutely. But never, *never* Zane.

He must have read the mutiny on her face. He sighed again and then blurred toward her. She screamed and leapt to her feet as he lifted his hand and blew a purple powder into her face. Sage stumbled away from him and screeched as she landed on the bed, her eyes watering. Her fingers clawed at the silk bedspread as she scrambled across the mattress and over the trunk, cracking her knee against the wood.

Lethargy seeped into her muscles as she crawled over to the edge of the rug, desperate to get to the nail, but her body wasn't responding. Arms like steel wrapped around her waist and lifted her into the air. She weakly clawed at his arms and kicked his shin with her heels, wishing she had her boots on. Her head bobbed, seeming too heavy to hold up.

"What did you give me?"

"Something to help you sleep."

True terror filled her, and she released a wail of horror.

"Shhhh, wild one. I promise you'll feel better in the morning."

She wouldn't. "Why do you keep drugging me?" she slurred, her body slumping against his.

The warlord pressed his face into the crook of her neck and inhaled. Stars, it was disturbing. Her skin crawled, goosebumps rippling across her skin.

"It's better than chains, is it not?"

It wasn't. "Chains."

He released a huff of laughter against her shoulder. "You'd make too much noise. I need my sleep tonight. I can't worry about you trying to kill me in my sleep, and from the bags beneath your eyes, you need a decent night of sleep as well."

Sage rolled her eyes. As if he truly cared for her well-being. He was just playing another game. It was always a game. The world blurred a little more and darkness crouched at the edge of her vision.

"I hate you," she mumbled through lips she couldn't feel.

He nuzzled his face into the hair behind her ear. "As I hate you, consort. Yet, neither is whole without the other. Sleep well, my love. We can fight in the morning."

Her eyelids slid shut despite how hard she tried to keep them open. His haunting words echoing in her ears—words she knew not to be true. Then why were they ringing with truth?

THİRTY-FİVE

MIRA

———⟶∘⟨⟨∘⟩⟩∘⟵———

ALL HELL HAD BROKEN LOOSE tonight. The Scythians attacked without warning again. During a snowstorm. They were bloody insane—monsters whose only goal was to spill more blood.

Mira pulled the shard of metal out just before the wound began spurting blood.

"Wicked hell, no." She dropped the knife, pressed her hands against his stomach, into the blood, and threw her full weight onto the wound. Biting her lip, Mira pressed harder still, desperate to stop the bleeding as he began to thrash.

Damn it. "I need help," she hollered. Several soldiers rushed to her side. "Hold him still."

The men gathered around the cot and held down the wounded man's arms and legs, all of them wide-eyed and red-faced as they tried to keep him from rolling off the makeshift bed. The rickety cot beneath her wounded patient creaked and complained at the added weight, as the infirmary filled with the sound of their grunts and the man's groans of pain.

Mira lifted her head and scanned the room, searching for the queen. Nowhere in sight. Double damn. She was probably attending more soldiers as they arrived. She was stuck with untrained foot soldiers.

Blood bubbled up between her fingers, warm and thick. The metallic smell was strong and settled in her mouth. There was something wrong with the smell, but she was too busy to really focus on it. "Bandages," she commanded.

One of the men, a banged-up looking fellow, snatched a wad of fresh bandages from a nearby table and waved it in front of her eyes. Mira snatched it from his sausage fingers and crammed it into the wound, pressing down.

She had to get the bleeding to stop. The bandage turned crimson within a matter of seconds. Mira hissed out a distressed breath and refused to lift up when the wounded man screamed and thrashed hard, attempting to get away from the pain.

"I'm so sorry. Just a little while longer and the pain will go away. I promise," she soothed.

It didn't help.

The shortest soldier lost his hold on the patient's arms. Mira caught a glimpse of a flying arm before she saw stars. Her vision blurred for a few moments as her head rocked back with the blow. "Swamp apples," she choked out. "That one hurt." She'd have an ugly bruise across her cheek in the morning.

A blonde lock of hair slipped from her braid and fell into the blood that coated her hands. The soldier cursed, and wrestled the wounded man's arm back to the cot.

"Sorry, Mira," he gritted out.

"Hold him tighter," she bit out. Her voice was too sharp. Was she losing her touch? She'd never had a harsh word for anyone working with her. They weren't trained healers, and they were doing their best. Her gaze flicked to the burly soldier to her left whose face was pale and bloodless. He looked like he was one second away from vomiting. Bloody hell. Hopefully he would puke on the ground, not the wound.

Her shoulders and biceps tightened as she tried to increase the pressure. If she didn't staunch the blood, he'd bleed out. Where was the queen? She needed another experienced healer. Hell, she'd take some of the other inexperienced healers.

"I need help here," Mira yelled, not caring if she roused any of the other wounded.

"Mira? What's happened?" the queen's calm, strong voice asked from behind her.

Osir. Thank the stars.

The wounded soldier surged up again with a burst of strength he shouldn't have possessed, and the cot groaned in protest. If they weren't careful, the rickety thing would break.

"How is it possible that he's still fighting?" the burly soldier to her left gritted out.

"Battle rage." Something was triggered when men fought. It was as if they gained unearthly strength for a short period of time.

The soldier nodded, and leaned more weight onto the wounded man to keep him still. He yelled and then sagged back as the battle rage left him.

The queen muscled in and eyed the situation, her eagle-like eyes assessing. "What happened?"

"The shard came out clean, but he's bleeding," she answered breathlessly. Was there something still stuck inside? Mira hadn't seen anything else.

The queen grunted in a very unqueenly manner, and then leaned closer to the bloody mess. She pulled a deep breath in through her nose and pursed her lips. The man jerked again, and Mira gritted her teeth. While she loved the Methian woman, she also hated how she'd taken to giving Mira lessons during life and death situations.

"Do you know what's wrong?"

The queen made a noncommittal sound. "What will you do once the bleeding stops?" Her voice was quiet. "Mira."

She didn't dare look at the queen.

"Mira, darling. You know what you must do."

The scent of waste in his blood was apparent. She closed her eyes for a moment and tried not to cry. Mira hadn't detected it at first, but she could now. It was a smell she'd become too familiar with. A strangled sob escaped her, and she released the pressure on the wound. The soldiers looked at her like she was crazy.

"What are you doing?" demanded the shorter soldier, his ginger hair sticking up in patches.

Mira gazed at him with sorrow. "I'm sorry."

He gaped at her, and then his lips thinned. "No."

The queen moved to his side and guided him away. The other soldiers released the wounded man's arms and legs and walked away. All but the burly soldier to her left. She ignored him as she moved to a washbasin. Meticulously, she washed the blood from her hands, the water in the bowl turning pink. Mira dried her hands and prepared herself for what came next.

She faced the cot and smiled gently at the last remaining soldier who'd procured a stool for each of them to sit on. Mira sat on the wounded man's left and the burly soldier on his right. Mira picked up the patient's hand and noted how his skin had cooled.

"Why did you stop?" the solider asked.

"Belly wounds that stink of waste mean a slow and horrid death. Sometimes, letting a person go is a kindness. Death isn't always the enemy." While her words were true, they still tasted bitter upon her tongue. There were so many limits to healing—to her abilities—she hated letting go. It felt as if she was failing. Giving up.

The soldier nodded.

"How do you know him?" Mira asked.

"I don't."

That surprised her. "And yet you're here by his side?"

The soldier shrugged. "War can be a cold and lonely thing. No one else is here for him. A man shouldn't die alone. The soldier needs someone to stand by his side when he leaves this world."

"Very noble," she murmured.

Her skin prickled as she stared down at the blood covering the front of her apron. Mira placed the wounded man's hand on the cot, and stood on trembling legs. She took a moment to yank off her soiled apron and rinse her dress of the worst of the blood, not that it would help things. The garment was stained to a point it should have been tossed in the fire. Since she'd arrived, she didn't possess a piece a clothing that wasn't covered in bloodstains.

Woodenly, she slipped a clean apron over her soiled garment and ran a cool, wet cloth over the heated skin of her neck. Stars, it felt good. Mira tossed the cloth in the basket of dirty clothes, and picked up a fresh bowl of water and a clean cloth before turning back to the dying man.

Carefully, she set the bowl on the ground and dipped the washcloth in the cool water before bathing the man's face. Her gaze darted to his belly wound.

The bleeding had turned sluggish. Her heart squeezed. It wouldn't be long now.

The wounded soldier sighed, his muscles relaxing, and he pressed his cheek more firmly in her palm. This was always the hardest for her. When they gave up and accepted death, even before their mind fully comprehended what was happening.

Her father had taught her so many skills as she grew up to prepare her for this profession, but the one thing he couldn't train out of her was her soft heart. Each death pained her, and while she couldn't save him, she'd do everything in her power to offer him comfort in his last hour.

The soldier sighed again, and his breathing slowed. The water seemed to ease some of his suffering. Mira put down the cloth and steadied herself. Mechanically, she forced herself to rinse her bloody hands in the water, focusing on getting the blood from beneath her nails. The same pesky lock of hair fell from her shoulder, crimson tipped. Her lips tightened and she took a moment to scrub the blood from her blonde hair. With jerky movements, she pinned her hair back into place. While her papa loved her long locks, she longed to chop them off. They were always in the way, no matter what she did.

She was already considered a fool among those in the court, despite her training and family name. A woman doing a man's job. How scandalous. A hint of humor lightened her temporarily at the thought of chopping her hair off. They would positively lose their minds if she cut off her hair more in the fashion of a man's, like it somehow made her more male than female.

People were absurd.

Mira glanced around the quiet infirmary. Most of those healing had fallen back to sleep. Luscious rugs were strewn across the floor, decorative lamps hung from the ceiling, and every table was covered with jars and bowls of ointments and remedies. It was a blessing that the queen had given up her own tent to help care for the men. In truth, most of them probably hadn't ever stayed somewhere so opulent. Mira had fully expected the queen to take her trinkets and luxuries with her, but she hadn't. When she'd asked the queen why, the woman had patted her on the hand and told her it boosted morale. She eyed the bright colors. It certainly was a cheery house of death.

A small noise drew her attention back to her patient. His eyes fluttered open, his gaze glassy. Mira once again began to lave his face. As she worked, his gaze focused on her face, a question in his pained blue eyes.

She smiled, brushing the cloth along his dark red beard. "You are in the infirmary. You took a wound. Rest, please."

He licked his cracked lips, and his brows furrowed. "A spear to the gut. The tip broke off…"

She nodded, keeping all despair from her expression. She was here for his comfort. No need to speak. He knew.

He closed his eyes, then opened them again and for the first time, he seemed to really look at her. "Your father is a great healer. I am honored to have his daughter care for me," he wheezed as if the effort caused him pain.

She paused. There were very few who knew her father personally. The only way he would know her father is if he were one of the Elite. "How long have you been with the Elite?"

He didn't seem to hear her or notice the soldier to his left. "He was always a gentle sort of man, but tough as nails, your father. I've never seen one look so frail and yet act the part of a dragon."

Mira smiled at his description. Her papa did resemble a dragon when his patients didn't listen to him. "I assume you were a stubborn one?"

One corner of his mouth turned up. "What soldier isn't?"

"So true."

His arm trembled as he tried to lift his hand. Mira caught it and held it between hers. "Tell him goodbye for me, and that I won't miss him sewing me up anymore."

"I will make sure to pass that along," she said softly. "Is there anyone else you want me to speak to?"

The soldier slowly shook his head. "Family is all gone."

Mira swallowed, and her smile felt like it was frozen on her face. "What is your name?"

"Micah."

"I promise I won't forget your message, Micah." Mira squeezed his hand for emphasis. A hand that was much too cold.

A wave of pain crossed his face. "Thank you, fair lady." He seemed to gather strength somehow, and he squeezed her hand and gave a slight tug. Mira lowered her hand to his mouth. The soldier pressed a kiss to the back of her hand, a roguish smile touching his mouth. "No better way to go than with the taste of a woman upon the lips."

The soldier sitting to his left chuckled. "Amen to that, brother."

Her patient winked at her and sighed. "I think I'll take a little nap."

Mira held back her tears and smoothed the hair from his face. "I think that's wise. Rest for a while."

He smiled and embraced death, even as his hand slipped from hers.

She blinked down at him, her body flashing cold and then hot. "He's gone," she heard herself mumble. "Please retrieve some men to help move him."

Her legs quivered as she stood and walked away, her steps jerky. Heat filled her eyes, and Mira held tears back, quickening her pace. She burst from the infirmary and rushed into the nearby darkened wood. Moonlight briefly peeked from between the dark clouds and spilled over her favorite spot, but she hardly noticed its usual beauty as the torrent of tears broke free. Salty droplets rolled down her cheeks, and she tipped her head back, trying to keep the sobs at bay.

Her papa loved her, but he always said she was too soft at heart. Sure, she could cut open a man and not blink an eye, but not being able to save a human being? It tore her apart. Her chest shook with silent sobs, and Mira wrapped her arms around her waist. The past few weeks had been brutal. So much death. It was despicable. What was it all for? Logically, she knew they needed to protect their land from the warlord, but he'd only played games with them. Had Tehl been able to destroy the war machines? Was Sage safe?

Mira halted in that line of thought. She could not go down that road. Her friend could take care of herself and if Mira thought too much about what Sage was going through... well, it would be easy to become distracted with worry and make a mistake while she was healing a patient. She needed to focus on her job and trust her friend to do the same.

You know what the warlord did to her. In what state will you find her this time? If you ever see her again?

Mira shoved that thought deep down, locked it in a box, and then tossed it into a bottomless pit in her mind. Her heart stalled for a second when the moonlight disappeared, a creature soaring above. A fiilee. Mira wiped at her wet cheeks as the flying feline circled closer and landed in her little glen. The feline stretched his wings, and his rider slipped from his back.

Raziel and Skye.

Frozen to the spot, she watched as Raziel murmured softly to Skye, who stared straight at her, his white whiskers twitching. Mira admired the way the Methian prince cared for his beast. He didn't look upset. If anything, he looked invigorated and proud with a smile on his face. That meant they succeeded.

She swallowed the lump in her throat, pushed her own problems aside, and stood. Raziel twisted, and their eyes clashed. His smile slipped from his face, and he darted underneath Skye's midnight wing. Mira held a hand up. If he asked her any questions, she might break down again.

He paused and cocked his head, his brows furrowed. "What's wrong?"

Giving him a wobbly smile, all she could do was shrug.

His frown deepened. "Was it bad tonight?"

Her bottom lip quivered, and she bit the betraying flesh.

Sorrow crossed his face. "Oh, Mira. I'm so sorry, sweetness. What happened?"

"I can't," she croaked, shaking her head.

"Can I hug you?" he asked.

No. That would just make it worse. If he wrapped his arms around her, she'd break.

Mira shook her head. "Sorry."

"Don't be sorry," he murmured, concern lacing his tone. "I understand that some things are just too raw to speak about." The prince shifted and glanced back at Skye. "You know, Skye has been working hard tonight. I'm sure he would love some attention, or a hug or two."

Her gaze moved to the winged feline. Skye crouched and released a loud rumble, as if he knew what was being discussed. Before she made a conscious decision, her feet were already moving through the crisp snow, her steps crunching as she flew toward Skye. The fiilee crouched and tucked his wings back, ruffling her hair. Mira threw her arms around his thick neck and sank her fingers into his luscious, silky fur. Skye released a loud purr and leaned into her, as if hugging her back.

That was the last straw.

Tears pricked her eyes. She pressed her face into the feline's fur and cried, her shoulders shaking. What was wrong with her? Why couldn't she be more like her papa? Why did she have to feel *everything*?

Skye tilted his head and rubbed his cheek against her arm as heat suffused her back and strong arms wrapped around her waist. Raziel rested his chin on top of her head and just held her. He didn't say anything, for which she was grateful. He let her have her cry until there were no more tears.

Exhaustion washed over her, and Mira turned her head to the side. She watched as more snow drifted from the clouds that had covered the moon. It was there one moment and gone the next. Fleeting, just like life. Combing her fingers through Skye's fur, she soaked in the comfort.

"Better?" the Methian prince asked.

"Better," she whispered. Sometimes, a woman needed a good cry to be able to move on, and it was only appropriate for her to mourn the soldier. He had no other family. "I won't forget you." Her words were only a shadowy whisper in the night.

Raziel shifted, making her very aware of the man holding her. Mira scowled when a little blush heated her cheeks. She tamped down the urge to twist out of his grasp and focused on petting Skye's black and white spotted fur.

"How did it go tonight?"

"Well."

It was almost as if she could hear the smile in his voice. He lifted his head when she glanced over her shoulder. "How well?"

He smiled, his white teeth a flash of brightness against his swarthy skin. "The war machines have been destroyed."

Mira sagged in relief. With the infernal death contraptions gone, hopefully the war would end sooner. "That's the best news I've had all day. Did everyone make it out safely?"

The Methian prince released her, so she could fully face him. His expression said everything.

"Tehl?" she rasped. *Please let it not be him.*

"He's okay. We lost a few, including William."

She placed a hand over her mouth and shook her head, a sense of numbness creeping through her veins. William was one of her father's oldest friends. It didn't make sense that he was gone. "He can't be."

Once again, Raziel said nothing, but pulled her trembling form into his arms and held her close.

"How will I tell my father?" Her tremors grew worse, and she finally began to feel the cold. "I'm so cold."

Raz cursed and yanked off his cloak before tossing it over her shoulders and sweeping her into his arms. "When is the last time you slept? Or ate?"

Mira didn't know. All she could do was blink up at him.

"Damn, woman. You're going to get yourself killed. How will you help others if that happens?"

She didn't answer, her teeth were clacking together too hard.

THIRTY-SIX

THE WARLORD

―――――⟴o⟴――――――

HER BODY LOST ALL TENSION and Sage sagged against him, her head lolling forward. He adjusted his grip on her and swung her fully into his arms. Her head was cradled against his chest, her braid dangling over his arm. In sleep, she was beautiful, but she was absolutely breathtaking in the heat of battle.

Fierce. Lovely. Ours.

He hitched her closer to his body and slowly moved toward the bed, the one she'd darted across like it was hot coals. The wrinkles on the bed bothered him. Chaos wasn't solely bad, but he didn't like it in his space. His attention moved back to his consort. She was proof that he liked a little chaos.

Nege hissed as he drew closer, and he slanted a glare at the feline. The leren lowered its head repentantly and backed away. Zane watched the feline slink toward his desk before using the toe of his boot to push the blankets back. What was it with this woman that inspired such devotion? Nege hadn't acted out like that in a very long time. It seemed the feline forgot who was dominant in the relationship. He must need some punishment.

The warlord lowered Sage into the bed and unclasped the cloak still secured around her neck. He scanned her head to toe. Despite the gifts he'd given her, she hadn't changed. His jaw twitched at the slight. It would be so easy to redress her while she was sleeping.

Touch. Kiss. Taste, the voices crooned.

He ran a finger along her delicate collarbone and stopped at the laces of her shirt, her breasts rising with each breath she took. Saliva flooded his mouth at the thought of tasting her skin once again. It had been too long since the last time.

His fingers tangled with her laces, and he began to pull one loose, his blood heating with excitement.

Claim, the voices urged.

The warlord froze, his body stiffening. What was he doing? How long had he waited for this woman? Was he really going to ruin everything by being weak and giving in to the voices?

His hand shook as he pulled away, breathing hard. Zane stared at his hand like it had betrayed him. Something wasn't right. He needed to take his draught and check his levels. Leaving her side was harder than it should have been. Rage at his lack of control triggered his berserker rage.

He stormed from his chambers and through the war room. The frigid night air did nothing to cool his skin. He glanced at Jacobi who stood to the left of the tent entrance. "The prisoner?"

His commander didn't bat a lash at the warlord's snarl. "The forest."

He smiled and, this time, Jacobi did flinch the tiniest bit. "Let no one inside, or everyone you hold dear will suffer in ways you've never experienced before." His tone was light, but his commander understood the gravity of the situation.

Nodding, the warlord set off for the forest.

Spilling a little bit more blood might just take the edge off.

THİRTY-SEVEN

SAGE

SAGE SLOWLY WOKE UP AND blurrily stared at the canvas wall of the tent. The air was cool. Not frigid, but cold enough that her nose was frozen. She snuggled deeper into the covers and pushed herself against Tehl to soak up his heat, her mind in a morning fog. When was the last time they'd stayed in bed? It was utterly glorious. She yawned, her jaw cracking in the process.

"Good morning, consort," the warlord whispered.

Her body stiffened, and all grogginess fled as reality set in. She was not in her bed. It was not her husband pressed against her with his arm around her waist, his hand resting dangerously close to her left breast. Sage tossed the covers back and tried to spring from the bed, but her body didn't comply. The room spun, and she found herself on her back with the warlord hovering over her, looking rumpled, his dark eyes staring at her with concern.

"Take it easy," he crooned. His thumb ran along her ribs, and she shuddered at the sensation. It was just a little thing, but it disturbed her immensely. "It will take time for the powder to wear off."

"What did you give me?" she demanded, her mind flipping through the memories of the prior night. The nail. Nege. The blood. The drugs. Her mind returned to the nail. She needed it. Her hands brushed her body, and relief filled her. She was still in her same clothes as the night before. Nothing had happened. Unless he redressed her, which was always in the realm of possibilities when dealing with the deceitful demon.

"Just a little something to make our first night back together easier." He touched the skin just beneath her right eye, causing Sage to flinch back. "You needed rest."

Rage flared in her gut. How. Dare. He. "Don't *ever* do that again," she hissed. If only she could get to the damn nail.

The warlord smiled. "It was for your own good, wild one."

Sage wriggled away from him and put as much space between their bodies as possible. She attempted to control her breathing and school her reaction, but she failed utterly. "You have no idea what is best for me. How could you take my freedom like that?" It was a dumb question to ask, but fear and anger caused the words to pop out anyway.

He sighed. "Freedom is overrated. Sometimes freedom must be taken away, because it can cause so much harm."

"So says the man with all the power," she retorted, fingers clenching and unclenching. "How would you feel if someone rendered *you* completely helpless?"

"I know the feeling well," he replied calmly. Leaning closer, he forced her to meet his gaze squarely. A powerful emotion that she refused to acknowledge passed across the warlord's expression. "You have completely undone me."

Her skin crawled, and all she could think of was getting away, if only her body would cooperate. Part of her wondered why she wasn't losing her damned mind. He was the monster that plagued her nightmares. Unconsciously, her weak hand lifted to her throat, and the warlord's gaze followed the movement. His lip curled, and fear flashed through her. This was the terror she'd been looking for. She shied away as he brushed a gentle finger along the twisted scars around the base of her neck.

"I can fix this," he murmured.

What an odd thing to say. Unbidden heat filled her eyes, but Sage blinked it back. This demon did not deserve her tears. She'd made peace with the scar, and she now wore it as a badge of survival.

"I have a balm that will—"

"No!" The vehemence in her voice surprised her.

"No?"

470

"No. I want no more of your potions. I want *nothing* from you."

But his death. The ring dug into the back of her head as she tried to relax. Could she possibly retrieve it and stab him now? No. Too risky.

His expression shifted. "You presume to dictate to me?"

Sage lifted her chin proudly, refusing to be cowed by the darkness shadowing his expression. He may have drugged her, but he was not in control of her. She'd never give him that power again. "It's my body." That was supposed to be the end of her argument, but more stupid words flooded from her mouth. "And you deserve to look at these scars. You can't erase your crimes and pretend they didn't happen. I will wear your cruelty and depravity around my neck for all my days, to serve as a reminder that not all things can be fixed. You're not all-powerful." His eyes flashed, and his hand tightened around her neck, a snarl twisting his lips. He pressed his weight along her side and leaned so close that all she could see was the pain he promised in his expression, and the madness glinting in his eyes. Her heart galloped, and her lungs screamed for air. Sage clumsily lifted her arms and yanked at his fingers. Her left hand moved to the back of her neck where his fingers overlapped. This was not how it ended. He was the one who would die. If only she could get to the ring.

Her fingers brushed the silver ring as the warlord cursed and rolled from the bed. He stormed to the desk, and pulled a key from a pocket inside his shirt. The warlord yanked open the bottom drawer from his desk and pulled a bottle from it. He turned his back to her. Sage gasped for air, her throat already aching.

What in the bloody hell was that? She was not sticking around to find out. Sage forced her muscles to work and clawed her way out of the bed. Her hands and knees crashed onto the cold floor, but she barely felt it. With her gaze on her predator, she pulled the nail from the dirt and stood on wobbly legs, determined to get out.

He slowly faced her and cocked his head. "Where do you think you're going, consort? Come back to bed."

No way in hell. "I will never be biddable."

"I never wanted you to be."

Sage snorted and edged toward the entrance to the room. "You and I both know that's not true. You can't help yourself. You want everyone to bow to you, to obey you. I will not."

He took one gliding step toward her and sighed, his bare chest rising. "I'd hoped we would have enjoyed a nice lunch together before we arrived at this part of our journey."

Her palms began to sweat. There wasn't a chance she could outrun him, but when he pursued her—and he would—it would give her the perfect opportunity to stab him and escape.

"Things will get better. You just need to let go of the past. It's not healthy."

"The past?" she whispered. "Which part am I supposed to let go? The torture? The pain? The loss of my friend and family?" She swallowed and stared him down. "I know what you did in the northern village of Aermia."

He blinked slowly, not giving anything away.

"You slaughtered them." Her throat constricted at the memory of little toes. "They were children. Children, Zane!" Her voice rose, and she stumbled back a step when his name flew from her lips, a name she swore she would never use again. "How could you?"

"I was not there."

Lies. She shook her head. "And the children outside my camp?"

He arched a brow. "They were soldiers."

"They were *children*, and you know it. What happened to your lofty principles of protecting women and children?" she yelled. "Is every word you utter a lie, a twist of truth?"

"Do you remember what I told you when we were at the Nagali palace?" he rumbled.

"You said many things."

"I gave you my word that I would not hurt you and yours as long as they did not hurt me." His jaw clenched. "You *left*. You betrayed *us*. You struck first."

Us? Unease slithered through her belly. "Do you hear yourself? Look at my neck. You chained me like an animal. From the moment I was kidnapped and taken into your kingdom, I was mistreated and manipulated. Don't you dare lay your crimes at my feet. There's only one monster in this room." Her back touched the tent flap. So close.

The warlord nodded, his expression thoughtful. "So, you hate me?"

"Hate is too weak of a word to describe what I feel for you. I am disgusted and destroyed by what you've done. You can't come back from that."

"True. But why would I when it's led me to everything I've ever desired?" He gave her a small, soft smile that confused her. It was the only warning she got before the warlord moved.

Sage spun and sprinted forward into the outer room. She made it only four steps when he caught her. Terror exploded in her chest, but she fought it back. This was part of the plan. She screamed and fought, thrashing in his arms as he lifted her from the ground.

"We love a good fight," he murmured in her left ear. "Please keep struggling, we'd love to punish you. It's what you deserve, after all."

Chills ran down her arms at the use of *we*. Sage swung her right arm across her chest, her sweat-slicked fingers holding tighter to the nail and slammed it into his neck once, twice, three times. The warlord grunted, and his arms loosened. Sage darted from his grasp and spun to face him. He blinked at her and growled while pulling the nail free. He held it in the air and squinted at the weapon.

"You're always a surprise," he rasped, smiling like a maniac. Dropping to his knees, he clutched at his neck, crimson liquid spurting from between his fingers.

Sage blinked at the liquid. It was red. It disturbed her. In her mind, she imagined him to have black blood running through his veins. Blood bubbled on his lips, and she stood there numbly watching.

Everything faded. There wasn't anger, triumph, relief, or joy. Just numbness.

He gurgled, and the haunting sound pulled her back to reality. She needed to get out of there now. Sage ran around the table and darted back into the bedroom area of the tent and tugged on her boots and then her cloak. Where was Nege? There wasn't time to find him. Hopefully, with the warlord gone, he'd find a better way to live.

She eyed the entrance to the rest of the tent, terrified she'd find the warlord standing on the other side of it. It was too risky to take any chances. Sage yanked at her braid and pulled the ring out. She pushed it onto her finger and steeled her nerves as she lifted the tent flap. He was now lying on the floor, eyes closed. Her escape was so close, but she couldn't leave without accomplishing her task. With strength she didn't know she possessed, she approached her fallen monster and slapped him on the side of the neck, her ring pricking him. How long should she wait? Her gaze darted to the exit of the tent. Every moment that passed was another she could be caught.

A whisper of sound pulled her attention back to the warlord. His pitch-black eyes stared up at her, that insane smile still on his face. Sage blanched and scrambled back, her boots slipping in the blood and her fingers tightening against the ring. She fell against the wall as he tracked her movements. How was he still alive? He'd lost so much blood. Wicked hell, she needed to get out of there.

Just as he began to rise to his knees, she backed up to the exit and another pair of hands encircled her biceps. Sage growled and kicked at the hateful commander who'd snuck up on her.

"Going somewhere?" the warlord whispered through blood covered lips. His grin grew, baring scarlet-stained teeth. "Remember, you attacked first, consort. I promise you that I won't enjoy this next part, and it will hurt me more than you. Just pray you can take the pain your people will suffer. Retribution will rain from the sky."

THİRTY-EİGHT

MIRA

—⋄∘⟨⟨⟩∘⋄—

MIRA PULLED THE BANDAGE FROM Gav's leg. It wasn't looking good. The wound had festered, and pus oozed out. Angry red lines fanned out from the wound across the skin like an insidious spiderweb. Poisoning of the blood. It was starting.

"You need to take it," a masculine voice said from behind her.

She glanced over her shoulder at the newcomer. Virdan, the Methian healer. He was only a handful of years older than her, but he acted like she was just a child. "Keep your voice down," Mira commanded softly. Gav hadn't been sleeping well, and she'd be damned if she let that haughty healer wake him.

Turning back to her friend, she plucked the rag from the bowl of water sitting next to her left foot. Gently, she dabbed the wet cloth across his forehead. Immediately, Gav's brow smoothed. At least there was something she could do to soothe his discomfort. She focused back on the airing wound.

"It needs to be done," Virdan said, rounding Gavriel's bed. The Methian healer brushed his dark hair out of his eyes that were more silver than grey.

She ignored him. His leg didn't need to be amputated.

"Don't ignore me. It has to be done, and you know it."

Mira glared up at him, hating that he was towering over her. She stood and rounded the cot, her skirts swishing with her jerky movements. "I won't do it."

He crossed his arms. "It's your job to do it."

"We're not to that point yet," she reasoned, trying to keep her temper in check. Virdan was already getting on her nerves, and he'd only been working with her for three days.

"Look at the lines, Mira. He's worsened."

"You've been here for only a short while. Don't presume to tell me what to do with my patient."

His silver eyes pinned her to the spot, his lips thinning. "If we don't amputate, he'll die."

"You don't know that," she argued. "And do you know how many survive such a surgery? Not even a fifth of the wounded survive. *A fifth*. I cannot take that risk."

Virdan's eyes narrowed, and he studied her in a way that made her feel naked. "Is he your mate?"

She blinked slowly. "No." Why in the blazes would he ask something so preposterous?

"You're emotionally attached to him."

"He's a friend."

"So, let me do this."

"No."

He shook his head. "You're going to kill him."

Mira's spine snapped straight. She'd never felt like slapping a man more than in this moment. "How dare you," she hissed. "Get out!"

"When you get yourself under control, let me know." Virdan stalked out of the small room.

What a pompous, arrogant, self-righteous bastard. What he was suggesting was dangerous for a healthy man, let alone Gavriel, who was full of infection. What was that brute thinking? Amputation rarely worked. Most times, the patient died, or—she swallowed hard—they just gave up. Life was not kind to someone who was viewed by some as broken. They were shunned, made fun of, or accused of the worst crimes just because of the way they looked. Mira would spare him that sort of prejudice and pain by keeping the leg as long as possible. People could be so small minded. A disability didn't make one incomplete.

A hand seized her skirt, startling her. Her gaze flew to Gav. His lavender, bloodshot eyes held wildness. "Don't let them take my leg."

Mira dropped to her knees and pressed his heated hand between her two palms. "I won't."

"Promise me!" he demanded, sweat dripping down his neck.

She swallowed hard and lied. "I promise." While now was not the time to take the limb, if there came a point where it was either his life or the leg, she knew what she'd have to do. Stars help her if it came to that.

Gav closed his eyes and sank back into a restless sleep. Mira pulled away, collected her cleansed scalpel, and called for help. Two burly soldiers entered.

"Wash up and then hold him down. We need to cut out the infected flesh."

They did as she bid, and Mira gently placed a piece of leather between Gavriel's teeth before picking up a wickedly sharp blade. She ran it through the fire in the corner and then approached the bed.

"Don't let him move." She knelt by his ear and whispered, "Don't fight us. If you want to keep your leg, you need to let me cut out the dead flesh." Mira moved to his thigh and placed the tip of the dagger on the edge of his jagged wound. "Ready? One, two, three!"

"Damn it, Gav. It's been a day. You have to fight!" Mira said harshly, her head in her hands. "I'm not taking your leg. I'm not doing it!"

She pushed dirty hair from her face and lifted her head. Gavriel thrashed on his bed, murmuring something incoherent. She leaned her cheek on the mattress, making sure not to put pressure on her black eye, and stared at the brazier burning in the corner. When she'd lanced his wound the day prior, he'd come out swinging. He was lucky she'd pulled the blade away swiftly enough when he'd backhanded her across the face, or she could have caused more damage to his leg. Mira wiggled her jaw. It hurt. Even her gums and teeth seemed to ache. The man knew how to throw a punch.

She frowned and wrapped her fingers around his wrist, his hot skin heating hers as she checked his pulse. His fever had skyrocketed in the last day. None of her efforts had done anything. The fever had just climbed and climbed. Today, the wound didn't seem worse, but his fever worried her. Had the infection spread? Was Virdan right? What use did she have if she couldn't heal him? How many had she lost already?

Mira squeezed her eyes shut and inhaled a shallow breath. *You can't allow yourself to think that way.*

Logically, she understood that no one could save everyone, but of late, it seemed like everyone she laid her hands upon died. A lone tear dripped down her cheek. Gav couldn't die. Although they hadn't been best friends growing up, he was still her friend. They'd practically been raised together, running around the palace and stables as young children. His wife Emma had been one of her few close friends before she died. It still killed Mira that Gav had sent Isa back to his estate when Emma died. Mira hadn't even recognized Isa when she'd come to her for healing a few months back. If Gav died, who did that little girl have?

"Mmmm..." Gav mumbled.

Quickly, she sat up and scanned his pallid face. "Gavriel?" His eyes moved beneath his lids, but he didn't wake. She pulled a waterskin from the small table sitting to her left and dripped a little liquid between his parched lips. He gurgled but then swallowed the water. As she pulled her right hand away, his hand snapped up, his fingers curling around her wrist.

She froze, staring down at him. "Gav?"

He mumbled, and his calloused thumb stroked the delicate skin of the underside of her wrist. Mira jolted at the soft touch.

"Need more," he murmured.

"More water? I can do that." She stood and lifted the waterskin back to his lips, but he didn't drink. "What do you need—"

He jerked on her arm, causing her to tumble onto him. Mira cursed and tried to backpedal, her knee bumping his leg.

"No," he moaned, sinking his other hand into her hair.

She gasped and tried to pull back, but she was effectively trapped. "Wake up!" Sweat broke out across her skin as she struggled to get up without hurting him.

"Don't leave me," he whispered.

Her gaze flew to his face at the quiet plea, just as he leaned in. Mira shook her head, but Gav's hand buried in her hair kept her immobile. Hard lips captured hers, brutal and ravenous. A kiss of possession. What in the bloody hell was happening?

She opened her mouth to protest, but he took the opening she'd unintentionally given him. His silky tongue slipped into her mouth, all heat. A tremble worked through her at the sensation, his taste of mint and lemon on her tongue. Mira struggled against him, managing to turn her head to the side to suck in a breath. Gavriel's roughened cheek rasped against her throat.

"You need to let me go," she commanded, panting. Her heart pounded like a drum when he released her wrist but slid his arm around her, bringing her into a powerful embrace.

"I'll never let you go, Emma," he murmured.

Mira's heart shattered for him. She clasped his cheeks between her palms. "It's a dream, Gav. It's Mira, not Emma. Open your eyes. You need to let me go so I don't hurt your leg further."

He didn't open his eyes. Instead, his hand slid up her back, locking her into place as he hauled her closer and ran his tongue down her neck toward her cleavage and nipped her tender skin.

That was not happening.

She grabbed fistfuls of his hair and yanked his head back. "That is enough of that! Wake up!"

Gav groaned and blinked his eyes slowly. He stared at her face, his pupils blown wide. Mira looked down at him, her breath rushing in and out of her lungs. For a moment, time was suspended as they both watched each other. Slowly, reality started to creep in, and with it, his awareness filtered in. His brows slashed together in a confused frown.

"What are you doing on top of me?" he asked, his tone holding suspicion.

Mira flushed and gritted her teeth. As if she'd assault a sick, unsuspecting man. "You asked for water, and I was helping when you tugged me onto your bed."

His scowl deepened, and it felt like he was accusing her of something.

She glared down at him. "You were dreaming."

"Dreaming?"

"Yes," she said sharply. "Now release me."

He still did not. "I don't understand."

Mira blew out a breath and winced when she realized she'd have to give him more. "You were mumbling Emma's name. Now, please remove your hands from my person. I need to check your wound."

His expression flattened at the mention of Emma's name, and his fingers flexed. She squeaked when she realized the hand that used to be on her back was cupping her bum. "Kindly take your hand from my arse, Gav."

He jerked and tore his hands away from her. Mira hissed and scrambled off him, conscious of his wound. The blanket covering his nude body had shifted, and she pointedly looked away while he re-covered himself, panting with the effort.

"How's the pain?" she forced out, a little breathless. *Get yourself together.*

He didn't answer, only stared at the ceiling of the tent. Mira shook out her dress and moved around the bed, back to her stool. "I need to check the wound again," she said as she sat.

Gavriel's jaw clenched, but he didn't answer.

She forced her mind away from what had happened and checked his leg. It didn't look worse. Lowering the blanket, she wiped her hands on her apron and stood. "I'm going to brew some tea to help with the fever. I'll be right back."

He still didn't look at her, his gaze shuttered.

She bustled toward the exit, her skin feeling tight and itchy.

"Mira."

She paused and stared at the tent flap.

"I would never have done that if I was in my right mind."

Mira flinched but nodded. "Understood. No offense is taken." Her first kiss, and he admitted that, in his right mind, he would never have looked in her direction. That hurt. She didn't even care for him that way, but it still hurt.

She bustled from the room, catching the queen's eyes as she moved through the infirmary. "He's awake and needs some willow bark tea. I need to take a break." Mira lengthened her stride and exited the infirmary, the winter air biting her flushed skin. Tipping her head back, she counted to one hundred and focused on slowing her galloping heart.

Her first kiss.

And he'd ruined it.

Bastard.

THİRTY-NİNE

THE WARLORD

⟶∘☙∘⟵

SAGE HAD STABBED HİM.

The iron taste of his blood still lingered in his mouth.

While he'd known that she'd make her move, he hadn't believed it would have been in the fashion it was. Liquid dripped down his throat, and he spat blood and saliva onto the pristine snow, ignoring the fearful looks being tossed his way.

They were not worried for him, but for the punishment that would come.

Punishment, the voices crooned softly.

For once, he agreed with them. Sage had shown that his expectations of forging her into a proper consort were futile until she learned her place. She had to know her actions would have consequences.

He glanced at her from the corner of his eye. She begrudgingly padded next to him, her movements stiff as she took in his camp—or what he was allowing her to see. Cuffs circled her wrists, and the chains clinked together in the silence. While she portrayed a calm demeanor, he knew better. Power and rage boiled just beneath the surface. A satisfied smile crossed his face.

From the first moment he'd laid eyes on her, Zane had seen her potential. He'd molded her slowly over time—now all that was left was to put her into the flames of the forge to truly transform her into something remarkable. As they moved to the back of the camp, his warriors stopped what they were doing and joined the entourage.

His consort ignored them all and held her head high. Pride swelled in his chest. She was a work of art. She ignited something inside him. Jacobi pressed closer from the right, and Sage jerked away from his commander almost stumbling into Zane.

Mine, the voices snarled.

As if he too heard the voices, Zane's commander glanced in his direction. Horror flashed across Jacobi's face, and he put space between himself and Sage.

That was better.

No one touched what was his.

As if drawn by a lodestone, Zane glanced at his consort's stony expression. She wouldn't enjoy what was coming, but *he* would.

His enemies always got what they deserved.

FORTY

DOR

⟶∘⟜⟝∘⟵

THREE DAYS HAD PASSED SINCE Dor visited Illya.

Seventy-two hours since Maeve had exposed the truth of who Dorcus really was.

It felt like a lifetime had come and gone.

Tomorrow, the Scythian rebellion marched on the warlord. Maeve wanted Dor to speak to the people of the Pit, to convince them to join them. She didn't know how to do that. In the three days that had passed, not once had she been able to speak to her mother about what she had learned.

Her foot scuffed against the smooth marble floor. She wiggled her toes, her feet a stark contrast against the pale stone. After spending years not wearing footwear, she couldn't bear to wear shoes above the surface. It made her unbalanced.

Dorcus brushed off the thought and nodded to the two guards stationed outside her family's room. She pushed the heavy wooden door inward. Another bizarre detail that made her feel even more off kilter. Her entire life consisted of open spaces, damp stone, and curtain entrance coverings. No one was truly shut away from each other. It led to a certain sense of community. Here, everyone shut themselves off from each other. Just another divide between people and other cultures.

Her mum sat in the corner of the room, rocking in the rocking chair. Her softly sung lullaby loosened the fist that squeezed around Dor's lungs. At least this was familiar. She gazed at the precious bundle in her mum's arms, and then to the wealth of shocking red hair that her mum boasted. How different she and her mum were, and yet the same.

Dor leaned against the wall. "You didn't tell me."

Her mum pulled her attention from the babe in her arms, her fingers running around his black downy hair. Her green eyes met Dor's, very solemn. She said nothing.

Her mum had always been an honest woman. Hell, she had raised Dor to be honest, and yet she'd kept one of the biggest secrets one could keep from her daughter. Even now, it was hard for Dorcus to even fathom what Maeve had revealed to her in the dragon's lair.

Dragons spoke.

Dragon Songs could understand them.

The heir to the Nagali throne still lived.

And she was both the heir and a Dragon Song.

"You raised me. My whole life you kept my heritage from me. Why didn't you tell me?" she asked quietly so as not to wake the babe. Dor already had her suspicions of why, but she needed to hear it from her mum.

Her mother sighed and shifted in the rocking chair. Dorcus's little brother murmured softly in his sleep before snuggling back against his mother's chest.

"Love, it was better if you didn't know. The secrecy was to protect you."

She nodded slowly. Her mum was right, of course. A rueful smile touched Dor's mouth. She'd always been a hellion growing up. The knowledge of her bloodline would have made her more reckless. Recklessness in the Pit meant death. While she could understand why her parents had kept the secret, it still hurt. It was as if they'd robbed a part of her. She didn't know who she was any more.

"I don't know what to do," she whispered and held her hands out. It was too much. Maeve wanted her to help with the remaining dragons and to unite the people of the Pit. Her people demanded freedom, but where would they go? Nagali was just ruins and fables. Then there was the war. Aermia was weakening according to Maeve. If a stand wasn't made soon, the warlord would sweep through the remaining kingdoms like a plague of locusts, devouring everything in its path. Where would that leave the people of the Pit?

Still enslaved.

There was truly only one option.

To fight.

"Take it one day at a time, precious," her mum murmured. "I know you will do well."

Dor snorted and ran a hand down her face. "I'm so lost. I don't have a place. I'm neither Scythian nor Nagali, slave nor master, commoner nor royal. I'm lost somewhere in between." Her breath stuttered out and she shook her head. "I don't know who I am."

"That is part of life. No person is ever only one thing, love. We're transient beings. Hold on to your morals and conscience. Let them guide you. You've been trained well. Trust in that." Her mum smiled. "You've grown into a strong woman. You have more skills to accomplish on the hard road ahead of you than you know, but you're not alone."

It felt like she was. The room took on a more stifling air, and she turned to pull open the door. "I need to think." And she wasn't ready to have the royal conversation with her mum yet. What did it even mean for her?

Her mum nodded and gave her an encouraging smile. "It is a lot to take in, love. When you're ready, I'll be waiting to answer all of your questions. This conversation is well overdue."

Dorcus nodded and slipped from the room. Two Scythian guards materialized on either side of her, their steps quiet as the group moved down the silent hallway. The back of her shoulders prickled, and she glanced over her shoulders. It felt like someone was watching her, but it was only the two guards. Spending time with Maeve was clearly getting to her. That woman was suspicious of everyone.

She focused on the high, arching ceilings and the clean, white, smooth lines. At first, the Scythian palace had inspired awe. Now, it made her uneasy. It was the opposite of everything she'd been raised with. The Pit was dark, wet, porous. Here, it was too bright. Dor felt exposed. Then there was the lack of sound. One would think with all the soaring hallways that echoes would be common, and, yet, there was nothing.

It was as if everyone was skulking around, and with the way Maeve had been executing dissenters, skulking was a high possibility.

Dor's pace picked up, and she arrived at the immense circular entrance that led to the pit. Six warriors—three on each side—guarded it. All formidable. Her lip curled as she caught sight of Darius on the end. The meddlesome warrior. He grated on her nerves more than she could express.

"I need to pass," she said sternly.

"Do you think that's wise?" Darius asked.

She glared at him and pointed at the entrance. "Behind this wood is my home. I've lived there my whole life and never feared the people. The only thing we had to fear was *you*."

Darius scowled, his lips curling slightly. Even angry, the warrior was attractive. She scowled at the thought.

"If you wish, but you won't go in alone."

"These men will die if you send them in with me. They stay here."

His jaw clenched. "Then I will go in with you."

Dor barely kept from rolling her eyes and nodded once. It would be easy to lose him along the interwoven hallways, and Darius knew how to take care of himself. If he got into mischief, she wouldn't feel the least bit guilty.

He removed a key from his throat and unlocked the door, the metal groaning as he pulled it open just enough so he could slip through.

"It's safe," his deep voice murmured. He popped his head back in and handed the key to the next warrior before beckoning her forward. She slipped quietly through and crept down the wet tunnel, ignoring the Scythian at her side. The tension in her shoulders loosened as she inhaled the familiar scent of wet stone, crushed plants, and mold. She was home.

Dorcus ghosted through the maze of hallways by memory, with one destination in mind. Jadim's home. Her heart squeezed at what he must think of her. She'd gone missing weeks prior and never sent him a word of what she was doing. In honesty, she'd been so wrapped up in the insanity around her, and just trying to survive, that she hadn't had time to think of her best friend and almost bond-mate. Her steps slowed. What would he say when he saw her? Their circumstances had changed. She wasn't required to produce a child so there wasn't any reason for them to marry. Their lives were going in opposite directions now. Her heart squeezed. The thought hurt.

"Something wrong?" Darius asked softly.

She jerked at the gently asked question, realizing she'd stopped in the hallway. "I need some privacy."

The Scythian warrior was already shaking his head. "I cannot allow it."

Her temper boiled over. Dor stalked up to him and planted a finger against his chest. "Until three weeks ago, my future consisted of being given to a warrior to be bred and then abandoned. The man who was supposed to be my bond-mate has been trapped in the Pit without any news from me or what our future holds. We need to speak about our changing circumstances." Her voice cracked. Damn it. "I need to do this *alone*. I owe it to him, to our friendship."

Darius scanned her face, and, to Dor's surprise, he pulled her hand from his chest and squeezed it once. "I understand. I will make sure you're safe and then disappear."

She snatched back her hand and nodded. It wasn't exactly what she wanted, but the compromise wasn't horrible. "His home is just around the corner."

Her mind spun as she led him to Jadim's home. She hesitated at the curtain that covered the entrance to his cave. Darius laid a hand on her shoulder in another surprising display of apparent understanding and entered before her. She followed. The home was similar to her own. A medium-sized room with a table and two chairs to the right and a bed in the far left corner. An arched entryway led to a small section that held another bed.

Dor stood in the middle of the room as her Scythian protector searched the room before nodding.

"It's safe. I will leave you in peace. Just scream if you need me."

He moved to leave.

"Thank you," she murmured.

"You're welcome," he rumbled and then disappeared outside.

Idly, she moved around the room, running her fingertips over the trinkets Jadim had collected. Her hand hovered over the cover of a faded book she'd given him when they were children. They'd been friends for as long as she could remember.

Voices interrupted her revelry and drew closer. Dor darted to the small bedroom and hovered in the dark. The voices grew louder, and the rustle of fabric alerted her to the fact that they'd entered Jadim's home.

"The people have spoken," a gruff male voice said.

"Our people are divided. They don't know what they need or want," a sharp female voice retorted. "They don't understand the cost of what will happen."

Dor's brows furrowed as she listened.

"We need to fight," the male voice growled.

"We would only die," the woman cut in. "Do you think we could really win against the Scythian army? Our population consists of weaker people."

Something crashed, causing Dor to flinch.

"We are not weaker or inferior!"

"That is not the way I meant it, and you know it, you old coot. They have taken everything from us. Do you want to put the women and children in danger?"

"We are not speaking of war," Jadim's calm voice interrupted. Dor flinched at his familiar chastising tone. "We're speaking of peace and freedom. The princess has guaranteed that—"

"You think we can trust that monster? She's worse than the warlord," boomed a new, deeper male voice. "She's playing all sides."

"There can be no peace with those who use us as slaves. They need to be eradicated from this planet," the first man rumbled.

Chills ran up and down Dor's arms at that sentiment. She hadn't been invited to be part of the conversation, but she wouldn't sit by and listen to such ridiculous talk.

She stepped into the doorway, arms loose at her side. "And that hate is what will ruin us."

Five people stood in the room. Two men, two women, and Jadim. She spared him a glace. He watched her with a serious expression, his eyes shuttered. He was angry. He only ever hid how he felt when he was about to lose his temper.

And rightfully so. You deserve it.

Dor fully entered the common room when no one interrupted her. "What you speak of is exactly what the Scythians did to the Nagali people all those years ago. Do you truly want to walk in their footsteps? If we choose that path, we will become what we're seeking freedom from. How would that make us better than them?" Silence followed her question. "Not all Scythians are bad."

The shorter woman with dark curly hair snorted and crossed her caramel-colored arms. "The scars on my body prove otherwise and so do the children that they took from me." The woman's sharp tone broke. She coughed and quickly wiped the tear that escaped her right eye.

Compassion filled Dorcus. "I cannot comprehend the pain and suffering you've gone through. I'm so sorry." She remembered well how much her mother agonized over what would happen to each of her children. "I'm not saying as a whole they're good or without blame, but I will not condemn them all. My father is a good man."

"Agreed," the gruff, older man said. "He's fighting for us. We need to fight."

"He is fighting for us, but he is also working with the warlord's handmaiden."

"We can't trust her," the other woman interjected, shaking her head, her thin ginger hair floating around her pixie face. "She's like a serpent. When you think you've got ahold of her, she wiggles from your grasp."

"True, but I've spent time in her presence since the first revolt. She hates the warlord as much as we do. She is on our side."

"For the time-being," muttered the short, skinny man whose deep voice was almost shocking. He could almost pass for a small boy.

"Change is upon us." Dor took in a deep breath and eyed the group.

The curly-haired woman dipped her chin and cocked her head. "Did they tell you who you are?"

Her words seemed to hang in the air.

Dorcus swallowed hard but kept her head held high. "They did, and I'm prepared to do what I must. I've been gone long enough. I need to know what is happening. Time is short, and we must decide which path we choose."

The woman dipped her chin, her dark, springy curls bouncing with the movement. "Our people have been waiting for this moment for a long time. My family has helped protect your bloodline for over five hundred years."

"Thank you," Dorcus said. The words felt insignificant. She glanced around the group. None of them seemed to be confused. They all knew she was the Nagali heir. Her attention snagged on Jadim. His lips turned downward, but he didn't avoid eye contact.

"How long have you known?" she asked.

"Since the beginning."

Dor stiffened. For their entire friendship, he'd known what she was and he'd never said a bloody word. Was he really her friend or had he been planted to keep an eye on her, to guard her? Her jaw clenched as another thought slammed into her.

The bonding.

"Did you *want* to bond with me?" It was an absurd question to ask at the moment, but she needed to know the answer. Had he been another line of protection or had he cared for her?

"You have always been, and will always be, my best friend," he said softly. It was only half an answer.

It was as if someone had kicked her in the ribs. Her parents had always been a suspicious and protective pair. Had they orchestrated this? Her stomach clenched. Jadim never had a choice to bond. He was just doing his duty.

Dor swallowed down the bitter truth and turned her attention back to the rest of the group. Personal feelings would have to be dealt with later. "I need to speak with our people. They deserve a right to voice their opinions on their future."

"*Our* future," the woman with ginger hair whispered. "It's surreal to say that."

"Maeve's men are going to move against the warlord tomorrow." Dor scanned the group. "Before I speak with the people of the Pit, you need to know that I've made up my mind and I will be fighting with them. The warlord must be stopped for the good of all."

"The good of all," Jadim repeated. "Will you ask if our people will fight with you?"

Dorcus nodded.

"They won't. There's too much bad blood." Jadim crossed his arms.

"Maybe," Dor said. "I know prejudice and hurt won't fade in the blink of an eye, but I won't stand by and perpetuate it. It's time we started fighting our wars together."

"As the monarch commands," the curly-haired woman said, standing tall.

"Your name?"

"Terra."

Dorcus smiled. "Well, Terra. Are you ready to change the world?"

Terra smiled, flashing crooked, white teeth. "I was born ready."

FORTY-ONE

SAGE

IT WAS DONE.

She had stabbed him.

Yet, he still lived.

It should have been impossible. A normal man would have died from the nail alone, let alone the poison ring—yet the warlord now strode next to her side, impossibly tall, his expression hard. If it wasn't for the dried blood staining his clothing, one would never have known he'd been drowning in a pool of scarlet ten minutes prior. The skin on her arms prickled at the reminder.

What sort of creature was he? Had he truly come from the pits of hell?

The snow lessened as they worked their way into the forest where the towering trees acted as a tent above them. Her breathing sounded harsh to her own ears, her steps overly loud. For one second, she thought about taking off into the forest. She'd accomplished her task. The war machines had been destroyed and her monster poisoned. But even as she formulated a plan, reality stared her in the face. The forest crawled with the warlord's warriors. She'd have to wait to escape.

Which meant facing her punishment.

As much as she tried to hide it, fear swirled in her belly. What horror awaited her?

A familiar lanky, black feline crept through the forest to her left.

Nege.

Even though he wasn't quite her friend, the leren made her feel less alone.

The trees stopped abruptly, which was anything but natural. The manmade meadow was covered in snow and opposite her, the ground rose up to form the mouth of a cave, a gaping maw of darkness. Her pulse leapt as a memory slammed into her.

"Where does that lead?" she asked. No one answered. Wherever it was, it was not somewhere she wanted to be.

One by one, they entered the black hole and disappeared. A calloused hand wrapped around her bicep. She winced at the tight hold and leaned away from its owner.

"Don't cause trouble or you'll regret it," Rhys threatened.

Her skin prickled at his proximity, and her heart galloped. He was unhinged; it was boiling right under the surface. Sage dipped her head in what she hoped was a respectful way, and wished he would release her throbbing arm.

"Good."

Sage blinked back into the present. Was it an entrance to another city? Surely, there couldn't be one so close to the Aermian border? One thing was for sure, she wasn't going inside. Her gut told her that if she entered that cave, she'd never leave it.

The warlord cut her off and moved toward a platform she hadn't noticed. Obediently, she followed him, searching the area for any clues as to what was going on. Her lips thinned as she spotted a pole standing in the ring with chains. Did they plan to beat her in sight of all the men? She squared her shoulders. What were a few more scars to replace the ones that had already disappeared?

Her boots thumped up three slick, wooden stairs onto the dais, ice crunching beneath her feet. The warlord moved to a black, stone throne with a dragon carved at the top. He attached her chains to the bottom of the throne and wordlessly faced her.

Sage froze and stared back at him. This was where their battle truly began.

He wanted to break her. Sage refused to be broken. She would bend, but she wouldn't break. Not for him. Not for anyone.

The warlord sat in his throne, his dark gaze pinned to her. He pointed to his lap "Sit.".

Her jaw tightened. Sage took slow steps in his direction and halted next to the stone monstrosity, then sank to her knees, head bowed. The chill from the snow seeped through her pants. From the outside, it looked like she was humbly serving the sovereign. In truth, it was a battle of wills. He was a proud demon. It was only smart to push him so far, especially with his men looking on.

Sage flinched when his hand touched the top of her head. His fingers caressed her ear, then ran along the edge of her jaw. He put gentle pressure on her chin, and she tipped her head back. The warlord leaned closer, his hair falling around his face, creating a curtain of sorts, so all she could see was his proud, ethereal face.

"Do you know why we are here?"

"Because I attacked you."

"No."

"No?" she echoed, surprised.

"It's been some time since we spent time with each other. I need you to understand the gravity of your actions. I want to protect you from mistakes that will make our lives difficult."

She slowly blinked at the use of the word *our*. There was no *our*, but she kept that thought to herself.

He released her chin and nodded at someone over her head.

"Get your filthy hands off me!" growled a familiar male voice.

No.

She glanced over her shoulder and bit back her denial. William. The old general looked like hell. The Scythians dragged him through the circle and chained him to the post. He cursed at the warriors and leaned heavily on his right leg. Every inch of his exposed skin was covered in cuts and bruises, both his eyes were black, and his lip had been split.

"William will suffer for your actions," the warlord murmured.

Sage briefly closed her eyes and sucked in a sharp breath. Why did it have to be her friends? She faced the warlord and lifted her hands to his knee. "Please," she begged. "Take me instead."

He caressed her cheek, looking at her tenderly. "This pains me as much as it pains you. I'm sorry, but I must do what is best for you. You must learn your place." He straightened and stared over her head. "Watch, or I will be forced to drag it out."

Bile burned the back of her throat, and she almost puked right there. With strength she didn't know she possessed, she pivoted on her knees and faced her friend. William shouted slurs and insults until he caught sight of her.

Aermia's commander lost some of his color. "No."

Tears blurred her eyes. "I'm sorry."

William shook his head, his eyes sad. "Nothing for it." He gave her a small smile. "Don't stop fighting."

Sage swallowed down her tears.

"Enough," the warlord said, his hand landing on her left shoulder.

William's gaze narrowed. "In my country, touching another man's wife can be a death penalty."

"You know nothing," the warlord said simply. "Call it."

It?

A warrior pulled a horn from his belt and blew. A haunting sound echoed around them. Nothing happened for several moments until two warriors on each side of the clearing pressed heavy levers. The snow began to move, and two enormous chains emerged from the earth. Sage's pulse ratcheted up a notch as a groan came from the ground and the chains began to be pulled in their direction, disappearing into the ground. A coiling mechanism? All thought fled when a hiss came from the cave. The hair at the nape of her neck rose.

Green reflective eyes appeared in the darkness of the cave right before an emerald, scaled beast moved into the light.

A dragon.

It looked nothing like the one she'd come across when fleeing Scythia. This poor beast was covered in scars so deep that his scales looked like they'd cracked. Her heart squeezed when the base of his wings flared slightly. His wings had been completely hacked off, just leaving bony stumps at the base of the beast's sinuous neck. An immense collar circled his neck as he crept from his cage, his hostile gaze darting around the meadow. Warriors edged the clearing with crossbows and wicked-looking spears.

Sage looked over her shoulder. The warlord stood from his throne, his thigh brushing her shoulder. "William of Aermia, you have been accused of murder, espionage, and are deemed a traitor to the Scythian throne."

William didn't blink but instead laughed, pulling the dragon's attention to his chained body. The older man shook his head, then glared defiantly at the warlord. "*You're* the traitor. You'll never rule the kingdoms. There will always be those who fight against your tyranny." He dismissed the warlord and met Sage's stare. "Be strong, love. Don't look."

It was like his words released a dam inside her. Sage lurched to her feet and jerked forward, the cuffs biting into her skin. An inhuman scream came from her throat when William turned to face the dragon that was now right behind him.

"No," she wailed, fighting to get loose. Her friend couldn't die. She couldn't sit here and do nothing. The dragon and man studied each other for several seconds before the obviously starving beast lunged. The rushing of waves filled her ears, and her skin flashed hot then cold.

"No," she whispered. "No."

Sage dropped to her knees, tears falling down her cheeks.

Just like that, William was gone forever.

She bowed her head, her body shaking with silent sobs. He'd been one of the first to accept her into the council when Tehl had proposed she join them. William had always supported her. He was her friend.

The dragon hissed.

Lifting her head, Sage watched as the Scythian warriors corralled the starving, scarred dragon back into the cave. For once, she let every ounce of hatred show in her expression, not for the beast, but for the men. They were the reason the animal had been reduced to these dire circumstances. The dragon hadn't killed her friend. The warlord had.

The dragon roared when a spear struck its underbelly.

Nausea swamped over her. Sage bent forward and placed a hand on the icy dais to catch her breath as saliva flooded her mouth. The cruelty was disgusting.

The beast released another pained, mournful cry that tugged on her soul.

Without meaning to, Sage began to hum her mother's lullaby softly while she got herself under control. When she lifted her head, the dragon had stopped struggling and was focused on her.

His emerald eyes clashed and held her own. She felt a kindred spirit with the dragon. *We are both scarred but not broken. He will never break us. I will free you.*

Sage pulled herself to her feet and turned away from the dragon, refusing to look at the warlord as he unclasped her chains from the throne. She moved to the edge of the platform without a word. Sage paused at the top, the chains tightening between them.

The warlord peered up at her, a brow lifted. "Something on your mind?"

She smiled at him. "I was thinking you look good dressed in blood."

He returned her smile. "I forgot how amusing you are."

She wouldn't be so amusing when she danced on his grave.

FORTY-TWO

SAGE

SAGE'S MOMENT OF RAGE HAD passed and grief had replaced it.

Silent tears had turned to full-on sobs as the warlord led her through the forest, back toward the camp. The warriors kept casting glances in her direction, but she didn't care. Shame had no place here. William deserved to be mourned. Another ugly sob wracked her body, and she halted, not able to move another step. She turned in the direction of the meadow.

I'm sorry.

How she wished she could have done something more.

"Leave us," the warlord commanded softly.

She was acutely aware of how the men melted into the forest, not one sound betraying their movements. Strong arms wrapped around Sage from behind and gently pulled her against a wide chest. Sage trembled with banked rage but didn't attack. She had to choose her moment.

"He's gone, and there's nothing to be done about it," the warlord whispered. "It will be okay." His words did nothing to soothe her, and her stomach rolled when he ran his hand along her tangled mass of hair. "I'm so sorry."

That was the final straw. He didn't get to hold her and pretend he cared. He was the murderer, the monster. She lifted her hands and raked her nails down his forearms.

The warlord hissed and released her. Sage scrambled forward, determined to put space between their bodies. The monster jerked her chains, sending her sprawling to the ground. Sage squeaked as she landed on her belly.

Bastard.

Her fingers dusted the ground and curled around a rock just as he bridged the gap between them. Sage rose to her knees and swung, but he caught her manacled wrist easily, his thumb digging into the tender underside of her wrist.

"Let the stone go."

Sage gritted her teeth, refusing to release the stone. She'd never willingly give him anything he wanted ever again.

The warlord sighed and brutally squeezed her wrist.

Pain ricocheted through her fingers, and she dropped the rock. He hauled her from the ground and looped the excess chain around her arms. Sage cursed and struggled to get away as he pulled her close.

"He's gone, wild one."

"Because of you," she spat, leaning so far back that her spine cracked.

"He was an old man. It was only a matter of time before he departed this earth," he reasoned, like death by a starved animal was a natural course of life. "He died a warrior's death. There's honor in that. I wanted to give you that much."

Her jaw sagged, and she shook her head, hardly believing what she was hearing. The warlord looked at her with sympathy that she wanted to destroy. The sudden silence became stifling, so much so that she felt as if she were going to drown in it.

"You need to let me go," she murmured, bile flooding her mouth. His calloused hands on her skin made her nauseated. He released her just as she pitched forward and vomited onto spiny plants to her right. Tears rushed down her cheeks and dropped onto the dirt as she heaved.

How many more would die by his hand? How could someone survive the wounds she'd given him? Why hadn't the poison worked? Would she be stuck here forever? Sage heaved again at the thought.

The warlord's hand touched her shoulder, but she shrugged it away with a whimper. William told her to fight. She was trying her best, but every time she stood up to him, the monster knocked her down again. Her stomach lurched again, and she emptied the last of its contents onto the forest floor.

Tears and snot ran down her face.

The warlord squatted beside her and brushed her hair out of her face. Sage refused to look at him.

"If only you had listened to me," he lamented, his voice filled with sadness and regret. "I hate that you're in so much pain, but you left me no choice. This hurts me as much as it hurts you. Do you think I wanted things to go this way? You brought this on us, on that man. If only you had been obedient, you could have spared him."

His words sucked the air from her lungs, and all the guilt she'd buried, from everyone she'd lost, rose to the surface with acute anguish. She slapped him as hard as she could, her chains rattling.

The warlord hissed and slowly lifted a hand to his cheek. "You're in pain, so I'll forgive you for that today. Don't ever strike me again, or you won't like what happens next."

His softly whispered words caused chills to run up and down her spine. Sage's chest heaved in and out when he removed his hand and she got a good look at the nail marks on his right cheek. She'd marked him just as he'd done to her. The scars around her neck pulsed in memory of the pain he had bestowed upon her.

"You deserved it," she said. He cocked his head, but she ignored him, wiping her mouth. She leaned onto her heels. "There's nothing in you that is good, is there?"

His dark eyes leveled on hers. "Disobedience cannot be tolerated." A pause. "No matter how much I love you, I can't let this go. His life is the price you paid for your rebellion."

Love?

Tears squeezed from the corners of her eyes. "Love? This is how you treat the ones you love?" Even *speaking* about love with this *creature* made her nausea return tenfold. "You know nothing of love!" She forced her legs to stand.

The warlord stood, towering over her. He tipped his head and leaned closer. "I've been through this before. You will work through it. You made a mistake, but I forgive you. We will right all the wrongs in the world. Together."

He was utterly delusional. "Do you really believe all wrongs can be reversed?" she asked. "How can you say such a thing? There's so much blood on your hands that you leave rivers of poison in your wake. You speak of love, and, yet, death trails you. I will never forgive you. *Never.*"

Her monster walked closer and touched her chin. Sage jerked her face away and took two hasty steps backward.

"I forget how young you are." He shook his head and sighed. "It is you who knows nothing of love. Love has a price, and it requires sacrifice. It's not easy. Love is *pain*."

Rage flashed through Sage, and her arms began to tremble. Losing any lingering fear, she stepped closer to him and tipped her head back so she could stare defiantly into his eyes. "I would never intentionally hurt those I love."

"That's the funny thing about intentions. They change over time."

"Is that how it started with you?"

"You know nothing." His expression hardened a touch. "Time changes one's perspective."

She refused to be cowed. "I know enough to promise that I will always fight for my friends and family. I will protect them and my people until my dying breath."

"On that we can agree, consort." He studied her face. "You're angry now, but it will abate. It will slowly fade into a distant memory. I promise you."

Sage held his gaze, sickened. "I can promise you it won't and that I *will* kill you." Her words seemed to hang in the air.

The warlord smiled, and she shrank back at the tender, knowing gleam in his gaze.

"Hate is a strong word, full of passion. You care for me, even if you won't let yourself admit it." He pushed past her, the chains slithering on the ground. "It will be as easy as breathing to slip into our future. We are on the right path, wild one."

There was only one path: the path of destruction.

FORTY-THREE

SAGE

SAGE PULLED HER CLOAK CLOSER around her body and numbly walked into the warlord's tent. The sun had set, but the war drums kept on going. Her heart gave a pathetic thump. Were her people okay? Tehl? She shut down that line of thought. She couldn't think about him. If she did, she'd break.

The room was just as she'd left it in her mad dash to get away. The chest lay open, emerald green silk draping over the edge. The dragon's tortured green gaze flashed through her mind, along with William's final smile. Her stomach cramped, and she bent over, dry-heaving. Everything was such a mess.

Sage straightened and glanced at the entrance. The monster had disappeared once a healer had seen to the lacerations around her wrists from the cuffs. Without his shrewd gaze on her, it was easier to study the camp around her. The rear of the camp that butted up against the forest wasn't well protected. Her lips turned down. The warlord's tent was a different matter. Every two paces a Scythian warrior stood guard. At least she gained some useful information as to the layout of the camp.

Feeling cold, she drifted toward the woodstove. She lifted the bottom of her cloak and fingered the wide hem. Her rusty nail was gone, but at least she still had her hidden blade.

Not that it will do you much good.

Prickles of uneasiness ran across her skin at the thought. If she stabbed him in the heart, would he die? The nail and poison had only slowed him down. She frowned. In fact, the wound to his thigh that she had given him only days earlier wasn't affecting him. Any normal man would be limping.

He's not normal.

As if her thoughts would conjure him, she glanced back at the entrance. Whatever type of monster he was, he shouldn't be walking among them. The bloodstain in the other room was proof of that.

Unnatural. A demon.

Chills plagued Sage, and she moved closer to the heat. Exhaustion crashed down on her as the fire warmed her. She needed to figure out how to get out, but her mind was muddled. The bed hovered on the edge of her vision, like a siren call, but she ignored it. There was nothing that would entice her to sleep on the mattress. While she believed the warlord wouldn't outright violate her, a lot had changed since she'd been in Scythia. It wasn't worth the risk.

With a curse, she yanked a pillow and blanket from the perfectly made bed and curled up between the woodstove and battered wooden desk on the floor. Plopping the pillow over her lap, she leaned her head against the tent post and closed her eyes.

Just a little sleep.

Her eyes sprang open at the sound of movement. Her tension drained away when Nege peeked his head around the desk and crept toward her. He bumped her left shoulder with his nose and released a chest-rattling purr.

"Hello," she whispered, running her fingers between his ears.

The feline maneuvered himself and plopped down, curling around her like a half moon, becoming a wall of man-eater between herself and the warlord whenever he decided to sneak up on her.

Sage stroked Nege's silky coat and spine. Her heart clenched at the scars her fingers passed over. Even with the abuse he'd suffered, Nege still offered her protection and comfort. Gratitude flooded her.

"Thank you."

He rumbled softly and laid his head on his paw, his golden eyes closing. She may not be able to hear the warlord coming, but Nege would warn her of the demon's arrival.

Sage closed her eyes. Just a little sleep, and then she would figure out where to go from there.

The rattling of glass yanked her out of her deep sleep. Sage's eyes flew open, and she peered through the fringe of hair that had fallen into her face. The warlord muttered something unintelligible. His hair was in disarray, like he'd been running his fingers through it. The bloody shirt had been replaced with a black one that was open at the throat, revealing burnished skin and a leather necklace that disappeared under his clothing. Sage focused on the little crease between his brows. Was something wrong?

Again, he mumbled something to himself, and then pulled a small leather book from inside his shirt. He sat heavily in his chair and leaned over his desk, scratching something into it with a feathered pen. Her curiosity deepened when he removed the necklace from his neck, and she saw a key attached to its end. The warlord opened the bottom desk drawer.

Interesting. He kept the key on his body. What was so special he kept locked away?

The warlord drew out a golden tincture and tossed its contents back, his profile only visible. His face slackened and his eyes closed. Sage shifted uncomfortably with the debauched image he portrayed. He seemed too comfortable.

"Spying on me is never a good idea," he mumbled, licking his lips as he opened his eyes. He shot a glance over his shoulder at her.

Sage abandoned her pretense of sleeping, and watched him as he put the empty glass back into the drawer. Carefully, he shut it, locked it, and put the necklace over his head, once again hiding the key.

"What was that?" she asked softly.

Silence met her question.

The fire crackled in the brazier, and he scratched something down in his little book before closing it and tucking it inside his shirt.

The warlord swiveled to face her and braced his elbows on his knees. He set his chin on his left palm and watched her, rubbing his fingers across his mouth as if deep in thought. "Something for healing."

Her brows rose in surprise. She hadn't expected him to answer her question. His gaze roved to the bed and back to her.

"You know that the bed is for you? I had it made for you."

She shook her head, uncomfortable. There was no way she was getting in that bed.

He nodded absentmindedly and then stood. Her whole body went on alert. Would he force her? Before she could do anything, he plopped down on the other side of the tent support, Nege's bottom separating them. The warlord propped his left foot against the floor and sighed. Her tongue stuck to the roof of her mouth. In that moment, he looked like a lounging dark god.

Sage twitched and hated that she allowed herself to think such a thing. He rolled his head to the side and looked at her with a tired gaze. It hadn't been noticeable before, but dark smudges shadowed the skin beneath his eyes and faint lines bracketed his mouth. He'd lost weight. He looked sick.

A fissure of hope burst in her chest. Was the poison working?

He huffed and then tipped his head back once again to stare at the low burning lanterns above. "You understand that hurts me, too, when I have to punish you?" His voice was soft and almost apologetic.

"How?" she asked.

"I don't like seeing you in pain."

She swallowed hard and had to look away. It was bloody unfair that he looked boyish, sad, and vulnerable. The warlord was none of those things. He was a killer. He'd hurt her in more ways than she could count. She needed to keep that in mind. The pretty shell wasn't distracting enough to make her forget about the ugliness it concealed.

Sage settled with, "I don't know what you want me to say. Is it forgiveness you seek?"

"I don't want your forgiveness. I want your acceptance."

She jerked. "My acceptance? How can I accept a monster?"

"A beauty and a monster. Poetic, wouldn't you say?"

A moment of silence lapsed between them before he turned to fully face her. Sage still avoided his gaze and stared at the desk, her hand absentmindedly running across Nege's back.

"I want peace," he said finally.

"Peace?" she questioned. "How could there ever be peace between us?"

"I could give you anything and everything. The world would be yours."

"Mine," she mumbled. "Do you really believe that?"

"Scythia has many gifts to give. We can change the world for the better."

"If you truly believed that, you would've already helped make positive changes. Yet, all you have done is cause misery and pain. You have hurt people. You have hurt *me*." The words tasted like ash on her tongue, but she said them anyway.

"Pain is a part of life." He sighed. "But I am sorry for the pain you've suffered."

Everything in his tone suggested he was sincere, but Sage didn't believe him for one second. Intrigued with the line of conversation, she carried on. "How can you do it?"

He examined his hands, uncharacteristically quiet. "Because I must."

"That's not an answer."

"You're young, wild one. You were blessed with a good family. I was raised by monsters. You call me a monster? It is an apt description since that's who created me. *I* have the power to eradicate people like that from the start. Could you imagine a world with perfect families? Children who never suffered abuse?"

Sage swallowed, feeling sick to her stomach. "And the children of the northern Aermian village?" The horrors of that place would haunt her until her last day.

"Those women and children would've died a long, painful death. I gave them a clean death. I gave them peace."

Not able to hear another word of his lies, Sage shot to her feet, startling Nege. She stepped over the disgruntled feline and spun to face the master manipulator.

"A clean death?" she hissed. "They suffocated."

The warlord slowly rose from his position on the floor, his boyish impression sloughing off as the predator took its place. This was the monster she knew. She could fight him.

"The village was deep into poverty. They were all starving to death. The children were undersized and the men weak. Even if I had given them any of my tinctures, it was too late for them. What was *your* king doing for them? His people are dying. How could I leave that village, those babes, to perish in such a barbaric way? I may be a monster, but I don't lie about what I am. I spared them pain."

Like a child, Sage wanted to put her hands over her ears to block out his web of lies. It was just deranged enough that he could delude her into believing his muddled logic.

"Do you even hear yourself, Zane?" The use of his real name startled her so much that she stumbled back a step.

Don't you dare go there, Sage. Don't let him reel you in.

The warlord moved around the leren and ran his finger along the corner of his desk, before leaning a hip against the old piece of furniture. "You know, I never wanted someone like you."

"Then why do you keep coming after me?" she cried desperately. "Just let me go!"

"I cannot." He shrugged a shoulder and gave her a wry smile. "They demand we keep you, and I have become attached to you."

"They?" Who was he speaking about?

"Things will get better," he said, ignoring her question.

"They will." *When he is dead.*

"Why do I get the feeling there was more to that thought?" She didn't answer. The warlord smiled and shook his head. "The pain of the past will fade."

"I don't think it'll be so easy," she retorted.

"You will be surprised how time passes. It'll be easier than you think to accept your fate. Our future is bright, consort, which is why I am going to share a secret with you. Today was not easy on either of us. I'm not completely cold, and I know how important family is, which is why I have a gift for you." He straightened and held his hand out. "Come with me."

Inside, she'd frozen over. *Family?* "What have you done?"

"It's what I *haven't* done. Take my hand, consort."

Sage didn't believe she had a choice, so she placed her fingers in his and let him lead her away.

FORTY-FOUR

SAGE

TREPIDATION FILLED HER AS THEY trekked farther from their tent. Sage's lip curled. From *the* tent. The horrors of the day and using his given name had thrown her for a loop. Snow crunched under her boots, and the bitter chill of winter bit at her cheeks. She glanced around the moonlit darkness, trying to take in as much of the camp as she could.

The warlord squeezed her fingers and tugged gently on her arm. Disgust wormed its way into her belly as she stared at their clasped hands. Why was she doing this? Every time she gave in, things became more muddled. His rough calluses rubbed against her own. She couldn't stand it anymore. Sage tugged her hand from his, avoiding his gaze as he scrutinized her despite the darkness cloaking them.

Her teeth ground together as his attention lingered on her face, his black gaze seeming to note every micro expression that she tried to hide. They continued their quiet trek, Sage following the warlord. Some might have mistaken her for being meek as she held her head down and stayed close to his side, but really, she was cataloguing information. Escape was imminent, and, when she left, she'd take a wealth of information back to her people.

Disquiet settled over her when they moved into the forest. Her skin crawled, and the back of her neck prickled. She was being watched. Her anxiety went up a notch when they rounded a thick tree trunk and a lone tent came into view. What was it doing out here?

The warlord didn't acknowledge the two warriors stationed outside the tent they approached. He paused and pushed back the first tent flap for her. Sage squared her shoulders and didn't hesitate as she strode inside, not knowing what to expect.

The room was similar to the warlord's. There were a few chairs scattered around, a thick rug across the floor, and two lanterns hanging from the ceiling. Nothing special. Her attention zeroed in on the additional warriors hovering near the next flap.

Her stomach dropped. Why was there another set of warriors when there was a pair stationed outside?

The warriors straightened and bowed. The one to the right lifted the second tent flap at their approach, revealing only part of the inner room. Her pulse began to hammer in her neck. What was he hiding?

The warlord leaned close. "You first, wild one."

Sage forced her legs forward and she ducked into the next room of the tent. Her breath caught. To the right, two tables held an assortment of sharp, deadly-looking tools and weapons, but that didn't shock her the most. She blinked several times, not believing her eyes. "I'm dreaming."

"You're not," the warlord murmured.

In the far left corner were two huge stakes buried in the ground. Chains hung from the tops of them and attached to the wrists of a crumpled figure on the ground.

Lilja.

Sage rushed forward and crashed to her knees beside her aunt. She fluttered her hands over Lilja's bruised body. "Lilja?" she whispered hoarsely.

Her aunt didn't open her eyes.

She placed her fingers on Lilja's neck and leaned closer, listening for breaths as she tried to detect a pulse. Her aunt wheezed softly.

Lilja was alive.

Tears blurred Sage's eyes, and she shuddered with soft sobs. "How is this possible?"

The fall of his boots alerted her to his approach. The warlord stood by her side, placing a hand on her shoulder. "I know how important family is to you.

I didn't want you to lose her, so I kept your aunt safe for you."

"Safe?" Emotion clogged in Sage's throat. Lilja was a bloody mess, but she was alive. Sage didn't know how to work through her thoughts and emotions. Part of her was so thankful that her aunt lived, but the other part was horrified. The bruises and cuts across her aunt's body couldn't have been from when Sage saw her last. They were fresh. She'd been beaten and tortured.

Sage brushed a limp lock of silver hair from Lilja's bruised cheek, her fingers ghosting over the damaged skin. What sort of horrors had her aunt suffered?

Losing Lilja had broken Sage's heart, but there was peace in death. She could make peace with it, because she knew her aunt wasn't suffering, but the idea that she'd been at the mercy of the warlord and his men for over a month was too much.

Sage put a hand over her mouth, feeling like she'd throw up. This was worse than death. How was she supposed to get them both out? Especially with the condition her aunt was in?

"She needs medicine," Sage croaked.

"The Sirenidae will get what she needs now that you are here. You will be her savior. Her life rests in your hands."

To someone else, his words might have sounded reassuring and pretty.

All she could hear was the threat: if she learned her place, Lilja would be safe. If Sage acted out, her aunt would be harmed.

"She's been a thorn in my side. Sedating her has been the only option several times. I'm sure since you're here, she'll be better behaved as well."

Sage closed her eyes. Lilja wouldn't want Sage hurt, and Sage didn't want her aunt assaulted. The warlord had played them both.

Sage chuckled, the sound rusty and dark. When would his depravity and cunning manner cease to amaze her? He would go to any lengths to control and manipulate those around him. How was he always one step ahead?

"I have to give it to you. You surprised me." Her words were hollow.

Her monster reached for her hand and pulled her to her feet. "It's late. Time to go."

Sage shook her head. "I don't want to leave her."

"I can understand your reluctance, but today has been trying for both of us. There are things we need to discuss." He reached out and traced her cheekbone, liquid heat filling his gaze. "Come along, wild one."

She froze. She knew what that look spelled.

Her head spun as she tried to see a way out of the situation. It wouldn't do anyone any good if she fought right now. It was about picking her battles.

Sage nodded, kissed her aunt on the cheek, stood, and strode out of the tent.

I'll be back. I promise.

Angrily, she wiped the remaining tears from her cheeks. The warlord's hand curled around her bicep, stopping her.

He stepped close. "Consort," he crooned. "It's time. We've patiently waited long enough."

We?

Sage's jaw set, and she glanced away, staring at the darkened forest, her breath frosting the air. "You wish to speak of sex after I lost my friend today and you exposed me to my abused aunt? I will not give you one more thing."

His finger crept under her chin and forced her to look up at him. "Not sex, but love." He smiled, his expression soft like a lover's. "It's been a long time coming, and we shouldn't wait any longer. Time is so short."

"Short for what?" she asked. "I thought you said we had all the time in the world?"

His smile turned smug. "I wish to go into battle tomorrow with the taste of you on my tongue. It will make Scythia's victory all the sweeter."

Victory? Her body flashed hot and cold. "What are you planning?"

"It matters not." He pressed into her space, his breath heating her lips. "I don't wish to be apart from you any longer."

An eternity seemed to pass as she stared up at her monster. He truly believed that she would give herself to him. Tehl's face flashed through her mind. There was only one person who got to see that side of her, and it wasn't the demon before her.

Deep satisfaction rolled through her, and a smile lifted her lips as vile, ugly words rose to her tongue. Sage released the full force of her utter disgust, loathing, and hatred. "You will *never* have that part of me," she said resolutely.

He cocked his head, a small indulgent smile on his face like he was amused by her outburst.

"You kissed me in Scythia and in the Nagali palace," he murmured, his voice dripping sin. "I didn't imagine the affection you held for me, nor the way your body curved against mine any time we were in bed. Let go of what holds you back. Your body already belongs to me. Give me your heart, too."

Sage laughed without humor. "You think you can take everything around you? You presume that you are the lord of all, but you are not."

Some of his smugness leached away. His fingers tightened on her chin. "I can take whatever I want, and I know you'll give in. You're young, and I've practiced seduction for longer than you can imagine. Admit it. You're *mine*."

She stepped closer to him, her head tipped back so she could meet his dark gaze. "It brings me pleasure to say this to you, but you will never have that part of me. I am not yours. I gave myself away freely," she paused, "*eagerly*, a long time ago to someone who is capable of love." Her chest lifted and fell with her heavy breaths.

The warlord stilled at her declaration. It was as if his body was made of stone. The fingers around her chin dropped away and wrapped around her throat. Terror flooded her, but it didn't take away the satisfaction of watching the warlord start to unravel.

His grip tightened, and he leaned into her face. "You would not do such a thing."

Sage's smile widened. "I was never yours. I belong to myself, but I gave my husband a part of me that you will never claim."

The warlord's gaze snapped shut. "You didn't," he whispered, pained.

His hand spasmed, and she wheezed for a breath.

"I know," he snarled, talking to someone Sage couldn't see. His eyes closed. "She's ours."

She grabbed his wrist when the pressure increased and his eyes opened, insanity shining through.

"You gave it to that mutt," he said harshly. He bared his teeth. "If you're so free with your body, you shouldn't have any problem sharing it with me." The warlord slammed her against the tree trunk, pressing his body against hers as she scrambled against his hold. "I'll remove his stain from your body, from your soul, if I have to. You're *mine*! You're ours!"

The back of her head cracked against the tree, and she lifted her blurry gaze to the edge of the forest. Escape was so close. The war drums marched with the beat of her heart as the demon tore at her cape and shirt. Buttons popped and scattered across the forest floor.

Sage turned her gaze to the sky and blinked slowly. The moonlight cut out, and a flying figure formed. Her brows furrowed even as her monster pressed his cold hands against the warm skin of her bare back. The shadow was too large to be a fiilee. Her breath caught.

A dragon. A *free* dragon.

Its wings flared, and Sage smiled.

If the dragon had escaped the warlord, so could she.

She cocked her head to the side and latched onto his ear, biting as hard as she could while simultaneously slamming her knee into his crotch. The warlord gasped, and his grip on her faltered. Sage wiggled away as the warlord grunted. Dots crossed her vision. She fell to her knees and grabbed her cloak and a rock.

Get off the ground. You're too vulnerable.

She stood and staggered as the warlord reached for her. Sage swung the rock with all her might against his skull, and he stumbled as she reached for the hem of her cloak. He grabbed her by the braid.

Sage screamed as he wrenched her body against him, her back against his front.

"Don't worry, consort. We consider bloodshed part of foreplay."

She didn't think, just reached back and grabbed his crotch and squeezed. He yelled and flung her forward. She crashed to the ground, striking her head on something hard. The world tilted, and she curled into herself, her shaking fingers groping for the hidden blade in the hem of her cloak.

The breeze kicked up, blowing snow into her face. Sage squinted as the dragon landed, wings outspread before the opening of the forest.

A feminine figure slid off its back and down its wing, landing in a crouching pose. The woman lifted her head and smiled.

"Hello, brother."

Maeve.

FORTY-FIVE

TEHL

"I REFUSE TO LEAVE HER for one more moment!" Tehl growled. He glanced at the men and women surrounding the war table. "It's been long enough. The war machines are no longer a threat." A pause. "Raziel."

The Methian prince pulled his attention from the map on the table. "Yes?"

"Have all your fiilee been pulled from the coast and are ready to be deployed?"

"They are," Raziel murmured.

"Good."

"Do you think it's wise to push forward without a signal from Sage or Blair?" Queen Osir asked.

"We can't wait any longer. It's been three days." Tehl hadn't slept since his wife disappeared into the storm. He stared stonily at the table. Something had gone wrong. He could feel it in his bones.

Hayjen pushed in through the tent flap, his icy blue eyes bright. "I have news. Blair's warriors have arrived and are in position." He rubbed his hands together. "It's time."

Tehl sagged in relief. A turn of luck. Finally. He glanced around the table, his heart heavy. It was too empty. Sage, Gav, Lilja, William, Blaise, and Garreth were all missing. This could be the last time he stood with what currently remained of the war council.

He smiled at them all. "Thank you," Tehl said softly. "Your dedication, sacrifice, and hard work will not be forgotten."

"It's no more than you have done," Rafe said gruffly.

"This is our last stand. Be safe and give them hell. I'll see you on the battlefield." Tehl locked eyes with each person before they filed out of the tent.

All except Hayjen.

Sage's uncle moved closer to the crown prince's right side.

"Are you ready to go get our girl?" Hayjen rumbled.

Tehl lifted his head and wiped a hand over his mouth. "I am."

"But?"

"I'm not ready for this next leg of bloodshed."

"Lilja and I have been fighting for a long time." Hayjen paused, his face creasing in pain. "We *fought* for a long time. Many lives had already been lost before you or I were even born. This fight isn't just about our people now, but for the ones who didn't get justice in their time. Today, we serve that justice."

Tehl nodded. "May vengeance be served."

"May the warlord die a horrid death," Hayjen snarled.

The men shared a smile.

The end was upon them.

FORTY-SIX

MIRA

MIRA SAT WEARILY BESIDE GAV'S cot. His fever had spiked once again, but it wasn't as terrible as it had been a few days prior. She pulled back his bandage and hummed. It didn't look better, but it looked no worse.

"Gav, I think we're through the worst of it," she mumbled. Her friend didn't answer her, likely too lost to his fever dreams. Her mind flashed back to the kiss. Mira blushed and then scowled. "Leave it to you to steal my very first kiss and think I'm someone else."

She rewrapped his wound and pulled the blanket back over his bare leg. While Mira had managed to keep his leg, Gav would never walk normally. He would walk, but with a limp.

Laying her arms on the cot, Mira pillowed her cheeks against her hands. Stars, she hoped he didn't blame her. At least he was alive. The war had already claimed so many lives. War was a brutal, ugly thing.

Her eyelids began to droop, but then a hand settled on her left shoulder, startling her. She glanced up, meeting Raziel's eyes, concern plain on his face.

Mira smiled at him and patted his hand. "I'm all right," she whispered.

He nodded and absentmindedly ran a hand over his face, uncharacteristically serious.

"What's wrong?" she asked. Had something happened to one of his family members? One of his friends? Mira gasped. "Is it Sage?"

Raziel shook his head. "Nothing like that, love." He held his hand out. Mira took his hand and stood, her body complaining. She groaned and stretched. No good deed went unpunished.

"Tonight, we attack," he said softly, pulling her toward the piping-hot woodstove at the rear of the tent.

Mira shivered, despite the heat. More men would be entering the infirmary. Raziel brushed a damp curl from her cheek, his fingertips lingering on her jawline. He scanned her face.

"I may not come back," he said bluntly.

She blinked slowly, and a fist seemed to tighten around her lungs, making it difficult for her to breathe. Mira shook her head. "Don't talk like that. You've made it so far, and there's no one stronger than you are."

A half smile curved his mouth. "What an extraordinary creature you are."

Mira slipped her hands into his. "The feeling is mutual. Be safe tonight."

The Methian prince nodded, his smile fading away too quickly. "Do you remember what I said?"

She gave him a silly smile. "That you'll force feed me if I forget to eat?" It didn't lighten the mood. He moved in closer.

"I already spoke of my intentions before. They have not changed. Goodness and kindness radiate from your soul and touch the lives of those around you. I admire and respect you."

Mira swallowed at his sentiment and tipped her head back to stare into his eyes. "I care for you, too."

He paused, tenderness playing across his expression. "I *like* you, and it will be easy to love you." Raziel released her fingers and slid his hand behind her neck, cupping the back of her head. His fingers tangled in the soft, tiny hairs at the nape of her neck. He leaned closer. "If you'll let me."

Her heart thundered as he breached the tiny gap between them. Warm lips brushed her own. Her breath shuddered, and the world stilled as Raz kissed her. It was so light, a ghost of a touch, the whisper of silk against her skin. Mira's lips parted on a gasp, and, as if that was all the permission he needed, his hands cupped her face and mouth covered hers.

The prince kissed her slowly, as if they had all the time in the world, like she was everything he needed and wanted. The first brush of his tongue caused

Mira to shiver. Her hands rose to his chest, hesitating. What sort of madness was this? She never felt like this—all hot, shivery, and weak.

"Please kiss me," he whispered against her lips.

His plea destroyed any hesitation inside her. Mira seized the front of his shirt and kissed him back, brushing her own tongue with his, tempting him to play. She jerked when he groaned, her eyes flying open.

"Did I hurt you?" she squeaked. He was the first man she'd ever kissed, other than Gav, and that didn't count, because she hadn't kissed him back. Had she done it wrong?

Raziel smiled lazily and brushed his nose across hers, then pressed a kiss to her temple. "No, love. It was perfect."

Her embarrassment disappeared at his praise, and she sank into his embrace, enjoying the wonderful hug. He felt... safe.

"I need to go," he said.

She squeezed him tightly once more. "Please be careful." Mira pulled back reluctantly.

Raz touched her cheek and gave her a charming smile. "I'll be back to annoy you before you know it, Mira. I'll see you soon. We can talk then."

It was more difficult than it should have been to watch him walk away. She lifted her hand over her mouth, her lips tingling from his kisses. He'd become her unlikely friend and suitor. And while she did like him, there was no future for them; he was a prince, and she was a healer.

Tears misted her eyes. She should have told him the truth. Babies weren't in the cards for her. A crown prince required an heir, and Mira couldn't give him one.

She'd tell him when he returned.

If he returned.

A lone tear ran down her cheek, and she closed her eyes.

Please, please stay safe.

FORTY-SEVEN

SAGE

THE WORLD TILTED AND SPUN.

Maeve strode forward, her expression as serious as ever. The warlord's boots entered Sage's vision, and she shied away. Who knew what he'd do to her in this state? She angled her head to get a better view.

He straightened his rumpled clothes and brushed his black hair away from his angular face. He cast a glance down to her, his gaze calculating. "Don't move."

She shivered as he moved away and held his arms out, moving to meet his sister.

"You finally arrive at last. Do you have what I asked for?"

"I oversaw the fermenting myself." Maeve smiled and pulled a small glass bottle from her pocket. "I came as soon as I could." She approached him, all lethal grace and power. Sage blinked. Their features weren't too similar, but their mannerisms were, so much so, it was eerie.

Sage lay on the ground, trying to make the earth stop moving. She pulled her cloak closer to her body and tried to crawl to the nearest tree. The warlord embraced his sister, and Maeve looked over his shoulder, locking eyes with Sage. An eternity seemed to pass between them. Sage owed the woman so much for getting her out of Scythia.

Maeve nodded subtly and, in the space of a second, she released a hidden blade from her sleeve and stabbed her brother in the neck. The warlord bellowed.

Sage's jaw dropped as the warlord's sister jerked the blade forward. His shout turned to a gurgle. He yanked his own weapon from his thigh, and stabbed Maeve between the ribs. Maeve jerked but never lost eye contact with Sage.

"Run," she mouthed.

Sage stumbled to her feet. The world rolled and lurched. She touched the lump on the back of her head and used the tree to catch her balance. She glanced toward the dragon—toward her best chance of freedom—then back to the tent in the distance. Leaving Lilja wasn't an option.

She crashed toward the tent, well aware that there were four Scythian guards. Time to come up with a plan quickly. Surely, they'd heard his scream? Sage exaggerated her limp and let her sobs break free when she rounded the last tree.

"They attacked," she sobbed, and purposefully tripped over her own feet. "Please help him."

Warriors emerged from the tent, and all four entered the forest silently.

I'm sorry, Maeve. Please be safe.

Sage waited until she heard shouts from Maeve's direction and rushed into the tent. She panted as she pocketed as many sharp tools and weapons as possible, shoving them into every available opening.

A small blade made its way into her hands, and she set to work on unlocking the cuffs encircling her aunt's wrists. It was tedious, and every sound Sage made ratcheted up her nerves. Sweat dripped between her breasts when the first cuff released. She moved to the second one. It was stubborn.

Each second felt like a year. "Please work," she whispered. The final lock clicked, releasing the cuff around Lilja's right wrist.

A hand seized her by the hair and yanked her back. Sage screamed and dropped her blade, clutching at the hand.

"Did you think you could run off that easily?" the warlord spat. "We will always be able to find you. You belong to us. There's no escape."

Sage released his arm and pulled a dagger from her pocket. Twisting, she slammed it into the inside of this thigh. He grunted and tossed her to the ground. Her head collided with the floor, and her vision danced. The air in her lungs fled as he threw himself on top of her, pinning her to the floor.

Revulsion struck her, as blood dripped onto her from the ghastly wound at his throat.

"Look at me," he roared, his spittle and blood spraying her face.

Her gaze snapped to his face, and Sage swore she was looking into the pits of hell itself. This was it. The end. Her monster bared his teeth. "I will not let you ruin everything. Why can't you accept me?" he demanded, his tone changing. Something vulnerable fluttered across his face. "Does no one care for me?"

She flinched as if struck. All she could see was him telling her about his past. About the monsters his parents were.

Don't let him fool you.

"You've brought this on yourself," she whispered. "You have had many chances to love, but you've chosen power, hate, and violence over and over. How can anyone love a monster?" she spat.

He leaned closer and ran his lips along her cheekbone. "'Til the bitter end, you defy me. Why do I still want you?"

"Because you're sick."

The warlord lifted his head as Maeve burst through the door. He sprung up just as his sister slammed a rock over the back of his head. He dropped to the ground, moaning. Sage scrambled back on her hands and knees as his arms clawed at the dirt. How was he still moving?

Maeve let the rock fall to the ground, and tugged another bottle from her trousers. She jogged to Lilja's side and pinched her cheeks, forcing her mouth open. Quickly, Maeve uncorked the bottle and poured the liquid into Lilja's mouth.

"You need to get her out."

Sage shook from head to toe and nodded. Her eyes widened when Lilja's lashes fluttered and her gorgeous eyes opened up. The warlord's sister cupped Lilja's cheeks as her eyes opened and locked on Maeve's.

"Old friend, it is time that you go," Maeve said. "I know you're hurting, but you need to gather your strength. I've given you something. Leave with your niece."

Lilja nodded, her pupils blown wide. "Ruuuunn," she slurred.

Sage forced herself to her feet, her gaze darting to the warlord who was trying to stand. Sage and Maeve each took one of Lilja's arms and stumbled to the first tent flap.

Maeve released Lilja and met Sage's gaze. "Go. I will stay."

Sage swallowed. Determination was clear on Maeve's face. She didn't plan on surviving the encounter. "Thank you," she choked out, knowing it wasn't good enough to express how thankful she was.

"Traitor," the warlord hissed.

That was her cue.

It took everything she had to leave Maeve in the tent, but the slither of the warlord's voice made her flee. Sage and Lilja stumbled down the path, her aunt dragging at her side. Sage gritted her teeth as she tried to balance both of them. She didn't examine the carnage of the dead warriors they passed. Silently, they moved toward the immense dragon twenty paces away.

Sage hesitated and eyed the surrounding forest. It was thick. There was no way she'd get Lilja through that to get around the winged beast.

"It's just a dragon," Sage mumbled. He was Maeve's friend. He wouldn't hurt them. Hopefully.

Lilja rolled her neck and crooned softly, a series of clicks and hums. The dragon clicked back, lowering his head so his silvery eyes were level with them. His hot breath washed over them. Sage had only experienced something like this once, with the leviathan.

"He cannot leave this place yet, but he can give us shelter under his wing."

"You speak to dragons?"

Lilja smiled sloppily. "Pirates can do anything."

The dragon lifted his leathery wing. Sage glanced around, sure that the warlord would appear behind them. There was no one.

They stumbled toward the dragon and lurched beneath his wing. He lowered his wing, cocooning them against his side. Sage paused, her eyes widening as she caught sight of another refugee barely visible. Another girl leaned against the dragon, her raven eyes watching them. She lurched away from her spot and grabbed Lilja's other arm.

"Thanks," Sage wheezed, her ribs and head pulsing with pain. Together, they gingerly lowered her aunt to the ground. Lilja slumped against the dragon, his breathing moving her body.

"So warm," Lilja murmured. She stroked a hand down his side. "Thank you."

The girl glanced from the dragon to Lilja and then to Sage. "She speaks to dragons?"

Sage shrugged. "She does a lot of things I can't explain."

"What happened to her?" the girl asked, pushing a braid over her gorgeous midnight skin.

"The warlord," Sage whispered. She still hadn't had time to process that Lilja was alive. It still seemed unreal, like a dream. "Thank you for your help," she murmured, turning back to the girl. "Who are you?"

The girl smiled, her white teeth bright in the darkness. "Dor."

"Dor," Sage repeated and then held her hand out. "I'm Sage."

The girl's expression melted into one of recognition. "I've heard of you. The consort."

Sage flinched and then gave the girl a hard stare. "I am *nothing* to the warlord. Nothing."

Dor nodded. "My mistake. I apologize."

Remorse flooded Sage. "I'm sorry, my—"

The sounds around them changed. The forest quieted. Sage's brows furrowed. Something wasn't right. She held her finger to her lips and then pointed to her ear. Hopefully, Dor understood to be quiet. The Scythians had uncanny hearing. One word could destroy them.

The dragon clicked.

Lilja's eyes fluttered open, and a true smile flashed across her face. "They fly," she whispered.

Sage stiffened. "Who?"

"The fiilee and the Dragon Songs. The tide changes tonight."

FORTY-EIGHT

MER

THE SHIP WITH THE BLACK leren was nowhere to be found.

Until Mer dove to the bottom of the sea.

She swallowed hard and darted toward the submerged ship. She prayed that she wouldn't find Jasmine in the wreckage.

Mer squeezed through the jagged, broken window at the rear of the ship. Bed linens floated in the water like specters, but no bodies. A rattle hovered above the floor, and her heart seized. Had there been children aboard? She steeled her nerves as she approached the door and yanked.

No bodies, just a hallway that was lined with doors and led to a set of stairs. Laboriously, she checked every room. Nothing but abandoned belongings and weapons.

She made quick work of the rest of the ship, thankfully empty. While she was relieved she hadn't found Sam's wife in the ship, she couldn't shake the sense of urgency that plagued her. Her gaze flew up to the tempestuous surface, dotted with bobbing debris and bodies. Dark shapes glided above silently.

More leviathans. Damn.

Stars, she hoped Jasmine wasn't in the water or bleeding.

Cautiously, she drifted toward the surface, humming a tune so that the leviathans wouldn't mistake her for the enemy, but recognize her as an ally. She broke the waves, careful to keep her gills in the seawater. Her stomach clenched when the fingers of a corpse touched her arm. Mer shied away, her senses screaming at her to leave the watery graveyard. She soldiered on.

Time slipped by as she meticulously searched through the debris. A Scythian moaned, and clung tighter to a piece of driftwood as a wave crashed into him.

Mer caught his eye. "The Aermian vessel will be here to collect any survivors within the hour."

His lip curled. "They won't find me."

She nodded to one of the dorsal fins that disappeared beneath the water not twenty paces from them. "You're right. If you keep kicking like that, they won't find you." The warrior paled and froze. "Movement draws them. Keep still, and you might survive." Then, Mer moved on. She passed three more warriors in similar situations—all of whom were not happy to see her.

The wind howled, and the waves turned rougher. Mer dove into the water, still searching. Her heart stopped when gauzy fabric caught her eye. She kicked harder and brushed the fabric away from the body it concealed.

It was a girl, but it was not Jasmine.

Mer gazed at the unseeing eyes of the young woman who couldn't be older than herself. What a waste of life. How did she end up here? Had the Scythians captured her while raiding Sanee? Or was she a slave? She touched the girl's cheek, then guiltily continued on. The young woman didn't deserve to be lost at sea.

Mer swam to the surface again and eyed the floating fragments of the ship. No Jasmine.

"Help," a hoarse voice called.

Mer twisted in the water, her hair floating around her. She locked eyes with a huge Scythian warrior who clung to a barrel. His entire face was one big bruise. A gash over his left eye bled profusely. Other than that, he looked fine. She made sure to keep a bit of distance between them. No sense in courting danger, and this warrior screamed danger.

"The Aermian vessel will be here soon to collect any of the survivors."

"Not for myself," he whispered. "There's a woman. She's pregnant."

Mer's anger ignited, and she darted forward with a snarl, grabbing the warrior's face and digging her nails into his cheeks. "Where is she?"

He didn't fight back or pull away, just held her gaze, sorrow lurking in his dark eyes. "They managed to escape into a life raft. Their destination was the cove. I don't think they made it."

She released him, her attention moving to the far-off lagoon. The weather only hours ago would have made it nearly impossible to reach the bay. Mer kicked forward, already dismissing the warrior.

"Please find her," the warrior pleaded.

The desperation in his tone had her glancing over her shoulder at the man once more. There was something in his eyes. He didn't harbor a hatred for her, nor was there any malevolence in his gaze.

She nodded once and dove.

FORTY-NINE

THE WARLORD

SAGE HAD ATTACKED HIM. TWICE.

He rose from the floor and stared at his sister, his chest aching. Maeve held her hand to her side where he'd stabbed her, blood seeping between her fingers.

"Why?" he demanded.

She met his gaze, no remorse. "You know why."

"Because I killed your dragon?" His lip curled. "He was turning you against me. You know he had to go."

His sister shook her head. "You committed genocide."

"I was protecting the world," he spat, blood running down his neck. Why wasn't he healing faster? The serum wasn't working as well as it should have been. Suspicion pricked him.

We've been betrayed, the voices hissed.

He pulled a sword from the table and examined it. "It's been you this entire time." Maeve didn't deny it. "You would betray me, your brother, your one true protector, over a handful of imperfect slaves?"

"My brother died the moment he slaughtered innocent people. *Children.*" Her voice hardened. "You know what our childhood was like, and yet you committed the most heinous crime. All children deserve to be protected, you told me that."

527

"They were tainted by association. Do you truly believe we could have taken them in? The children would have grown into adults who revolted." He ran his finger along the edge of the cutlass. "I trusted you."

"You shouldn't have."

He faced her. "It was you and I against the world."

"No, Zane," she whispered. "It was you trying to *destroy* the world. It stops here. I won't let you hurt anyone else."

"So, this is the end?"

End her, the voices howled.

Maeve pulled a short sword from the sheath crossing her back. "For you, it is."

Then, she attacked.

He walked slowly from the tent, his sister's body swaying in his arms. Her blood seeped through his shirt and ran down his body. A lone tear dripped down his cheek. It had been years since he'd cried.

Zane glanced down at her pale face, her eyes closed in death. They'd spent close to a millennium together. It was unreal to think he'd never see her glare at him or utter something sarcastic. Even in her last gasping moments, she'd spared no affection for him.

"It is only a matter of time before you join me," she'd said. "There isn't enough suffering for you to endure to make up for what you've done." Maeve had smiled. "I was the one who let Sage go." With that final statement, the life had faded from her eyes.

He lifted his head and dropped to his knees in the forest. The betrayal cut too deep. The warlord placed his traitorous sister on the ground, threw his head back, and screamed. It didn't release his anguish or rage.

His hands shook when he tightened the bandage around his neck. The war drums beat an incessant march, and the sounds of battle filtered to his ears. Aermia had made its move.

He caressed his sister's face once, then stood. He strode toward the dragon and smiled.

Pain, death, triumph.

"Indeed." He tossed his head back and laughed before shouting, "I will find you, consort!"

She couldn't be far away.

Neither could Scythia's victory.

FIFTY

SAGE

"I WILL FIND YOU, CONSORT!"

The warlord's voice cut right through, and, without realizing it, Sage seized Dor's hand. Sage widened her eyes and shook her head. They barely breathed as the warlord strode past the dragon, sputtering madness and curses. The hairs prickled along her arms, and her pulse thundered in her ears.

Sage turned her neck and stared at the dragon's wing. Was the warlord waiting just on the other side? A shiver ran down her spine.

Enough of this.

With difficulty, she battled back the fear. If her monster was lurking outside, he would have already been taunting her.

"We need to get out of here," she whispered. "It's not safe."

Dor nodded. "How do you plan on getting her out?" She pointed to Lilja.

Sage eyed her aunt who had passed out again. She grimaced. Getting them both through the camp would be nearly impossible with the warlord hunting them. Although the chaos in the camp might be enough to conceal their escape, it wasn't going to be easy.

"Unless you plan on coming with us?" Sage asked.

The young woman shifted her dark eyes back to Lilja. "I cannot go with you. I must get Illya into the skies. Someone is bound to come back to harness him. I can take your kin with me." Dor turned back to her. "You can come

530

as well. Illya can take us all away from this place."

Freedom.

It was so temtping, but she had to see this through. The warlord could not be allowed to continue his tyranny. While it would be so easy to fly away on the dragon, it would be cowardly. She couldn't run away.

"I can't," she said with regret. "I must fight with my people."

Dor squeezed her fingers and released her hand. "That, I understand. I will take the Sirenidae somewhere safe and return. I will be watching over you from the skies." She clicked softly, and the dragon clicked back. "It's clear. I'll get your kin onto Illya, and you get as far from this place as possible."

"I can do that."

The women crawled to each side of Lilja and threw her arms over their shoulders. Sage gritted her teeth, as pain ricocheted through her ribs when they lifted her aunt. It was uncoordinated, and Sage kept looking over her shoulder when they crept from beneath the dragon's wing. They managed to get Lilja settled behind Illya's haunches, with Dor right behind her.

Sage tried to climb down from the dragon gently, but ended up sliding down his leathery wing. She landed in a crouch and smiled at Illya. "Thank you."

The beast blinked its silvery eye once, and she took that as an acknowledgment. "Be safe," she whispered and stepped back. The child in her wanted to stay and watch the dragon take flight, but she knew that would be a mistake.

Sage jogged to the nearest tent and peeked inside. No one. She slipped inside and scanned the room. It was a disaster: weapons, armor, and clothing lay everywhere. Once again, she stole one of the cloaks and tossed it over her own soiled ensemble, the filched weapons clinking in her pockets.

Shouts ruptured the air, and she froze. With silent steps, she lifted the tent flap slightly. The dragon had opened his wings and sprung from the ground. A grin curled her lips. Lilja and Illya were out of the warlord's grasp. That felt *good.*

She let the canvas flap close and tiptoed to the rear of the tent. Carefully slipping her blade into the canvas, she cut a slit and peeked out. Sounds came from every direction, but it didn't seem like danger was heading specifically for her. Sage crept away and slunk through the sea of Scythian tents.

531

More snow began to fall, and she shivered, pausing when warriors jogged toward her from the right. Sage pressed herself against the nearest tent, and prayed it was enough to conceal her. Her enemies bypassed her without so much as looking toward her shadowed spot.

Releasing her breath, she tipped her head back. Her eyes rounded, and her mouth gaped. Fire lit up the *sky*. It seemed like liquid flames poured from the belly of a dragon. What the bloody hell? None of the dragons she'd read about as a child could accomplish something of that magnitude. Fire and ice battled with each other, along with the shrieks of man and beast.

The sounds of pain, death, victory.

Sage caught her breath, keeping a steady eye on her surroundings as she slipped from her hiding place. She stealthily wove through the camp, observing the Aermian force pushing the Scythians deeper into their camp. Smoke filled the air, and her eyes began to water. Her people were right there. She could join them.

You can't let the monster escape.

She panted. Even though he was evil, she still didn't want his death on her hands. It would be just one more nightmare to haunt her for the rest of her days. It was a selfish thought.

Finish this.

"Consort!" the warlord's voice roared.

Sage shuddered and stiffened. It was as if he could sense that she was thinking of him. He couldn't know where she was. Her feet were rooted to the ground, as if his voice held complete power over her.

"You cannot run from your destiny. This is our legacy. You cannot run from me! I will always find you!"

That was her worst fear. No matter what she did, he always seemed to come back.

Don't let fear cripple you. He is just a man.

Her hands trembled as an idea formed in her mind. He needed to be drawn out, and she was the key to that. The Aermian line wasn't far, and the warlord was weakened and unstable. A well-placed swing could end his life.

"I'm crazy," she muttered.

Sage eyed the area around her, trying to muster up the courage to reveal her position. Once she did, he'd be onto her. She'd only have moments to get to where she needed to be.

The war drumbeat synchronized with her heart, and she barely paid any mind to the Scythian soldiers that ran past as orange flames danced along the tops of tents in the distance. The time for stealth was over. It was time to fight.

"I've never been yours!" she shouted, her legs already in motion as she sprinted through the tents toward the battlefront. Even with the noise, she knew he'd hear her.

One heartbeat.

Two.

Three.

Sage put on a burst of speed and bolted toward the thickest fighting. She almost stumbled when she ran past the last line of tents. The earth and sky were teeming with motion—not only that, but the Scythian resistance had arrived.

"That is enough," a deep voice rumbled.

Sage skidded to a stop, and yanked two daggers from her pockets as she spun and faced the monster. The battle seemed to freeze in a watercolor painting as she faced her most bitter enemy.

Ten paces separated them.

It wasn't enough.

The warlord panted hard, his body almost swollen, like he was too big for his own skin. His obsidian eyes had now lost any pretense of civility, holding only rage and hunger.

"What are you?" she murmured.

He smiled. "Everything and nothing."

He held his hand out. She noticed how it trembled. Was he on the edge of losing himself to the berserker rage? The scars at her throat throbbed in phantom pain. Time to tread carefully.

"You cannot leave. You know your place is here." He tipped his chin toward the battle. "We can stop this bloodshed once and for all. This is our future." He held his hand out farther, bidding her to come closer and join him. "Come."

Once again, Sage was at a crossroads. The last time he'd offered his hand, she'd almost taken it, nearly believing his lies. The only thing she felt this time was disgust.

Sage squared off and shifted into a defensive position. She couldn't allow him to get to her. He was too far gone. If the warlord got his hands on her, he'd kill her.

"Fighting me until the bitter end." He chuckled. "How like you, wild one. I will enjoy breaking you more than I should. Just know you brought the pain upon yourself and those around you."

She snorted. He was the only demon here.

"I only wanted what was best for you," he whispered. For a moment, he looked like a lost little boy. It threw her off-kilter.

Then, he *blurred*.

She threw both her blades at his heart and yanked two more from her pockets when he halted two steps from her. Her mouth bobbed as she stared at one of her daggers buried in his chest, along with five arrows. He took another step toward her, and more arrows hit him.

Sage ducked, and bile burned her throat as his pained gaze met hers.

"From the moment I saw you, I knew you'd be my downfall," he wheezed.

Rooted to the spot, she flinched as he brushed his bloody fingers along her left cheek. This couldn't be real.

He stumbled forward and dropped to his knees before her. The warlord reached for her, and it broke her from the mental ice that had kept her captive. Sage skittered back several steps, and stared as blood leaked from the corner of his mouth.

What the bloody hell had happened? Where had those arrows come from? Her hands shook, and she dropped the daggers. Was this really how his reign of terror ended?

"Please," he gurgled. "Don't leave me."

A last plea.

A final time, he held his hand out, looking completely vulnerable. Heat pressed at the back of her eyes and tears spilled down her cheeks. All she could see was the abused little boy that he used to be.

Sage dashed away the tears and hardened her resolve. He didn't deserve anything from her. Abuse did not excuse the vile choices he'd made. If any other criminal had made the same last request, she would have granted it, but not him.

"You deserve to die alone," she whispered harshly.

Sage backed away, making sure he couldn't come after her. He toppled onto his side, his mouth forming words she didn't want to see. She turned her back on him and walked into battle. Blair and Hayjen stalked toward her, both wielding bows. She touched her uncle's side as he passed her, but she kept moving toward battle.

The warlord would never take anything from anyone again. He would never hurt her again. Her conscience nagged at her to look over her shoulder, but Sage didn't. She kept her attention straight ahead.

He's gone.

Even in death, she wouldn't give him one more second of her time.

Scanning the battlefield, she numbly watched as the war raged on, all the warlord's soldiers completely ignorant to the death of their leader.

It was fitting that the monster who had terrorized the world for so long had disappeared from the earth without a sound.

She pulled two more wicked-looking daggers with serrated edges from her pockets. A warrior caught her eye and charged.

Sage smiled—more of a dark slash of her lips, baring teeth—before diving into the fray.

No rest for the wicked.

FÍFTY-ONE

TEHL

TEHL SHOULDN'T FIND DEATH SO beautiful.

He stumbled to a stop as he caught sight of the most stunning thing he'd ever laid his eyes upon. His wife fought two warriors, her complete focus on the enemy. Each moment was almost too fluid and fast for him to track.

Hell's handmaiden.

Rafe appeared to his left, panting. He took one look at Tehl's expression and followed his gaze. "Finally."

"So, what's the plan?" a deep female voice asked.

Tehl glared at Blaise. "What the blazes are you doing on the battlefield?"

The Scythian woman gave him a gleeful smile. "Fighting."

"And your leg?" Rafe eyed said leg, which was weeping blood. His lips thinned.

"Nothing some herbs and rest can't heal. Both of which I can get when this is over."

Tehl pressed his lips together so as not to smile. Blaise was one of the fiercest people he'd ever met. "We'll come around back. We can't afford to distract her."

Blaise scanned the fray. "Where is he?"

"That was my question," Rafe muttered. "I can't see the warlord."

"Where Sage is, he's not far behind," Tehl murmured. "Keep an eye out.

Let's move."

In tandem, they began working their way toward Sage. But with every enemy they felled, another took his place. He spun, thrusting his sword backward into a warrior as Sage caught Tehl's eye. His heart stopped, and everything went silent around him. She didn't smile. There was no expression on her face.

What happened to you?

Years seemed to pass as they watched each other. Like the sun thawing ice, her expression melted into a gorgeous smile. Covered in mud, snow, and blood, she was his picture of perfection.

They crashed together, and he couldn't help himself. Tehl captured her lips in a quick, rough kiss. "Are you okay?"

"He's gone," she whispered.

He couldn't have heard that right. Before he had a chance to ask her more, they were swept into battle once again.

A battle cry tore through the air. Tehl frowned. Where the devil had that come from? Almost as soon as the thought went through his head, soldiers burst from the Scythian camp and *attacked* their own warriors.

Blair's rebels.

He smiled.

It was a beautiful conglomerate of mankind fighting against evil.

And they were going to win.

FİFTY-TWO

MIRA

GAV'S FEVER BROKE.

And she wept. Like a baby.

Once again, she placed the back of her hand over his brow, just to check. It was a normal temperature. She sighed and pulled her hand back. The morning light warmed the east side of the tent, and she stretched.

Her brows furrowed when Gav's breathing became louder. Her attention snapped to his chest. He wasn't breathing any differently. What the hell?

Then it dawned on her.

He wasn't breathing louder. It was *silent* outside. The war drums were silent.

She'd become so accustomed to the incessant beat of the Scythian war drums that she couldn't remember a time without them. Her hands shook, and she took one of Gav's hands in her own as hope unfurled in her chest.

"They've done it, Gav. They've done it," she whispered.

"Done what?" his deep, rusty voice rumbled.

Mira's lips parted in surprise as his eyes opened, his purple gems locked on hers.

"They've defeated Scythia," she murmured, beyond happy to see him awake. Her breath caught as he gave her a huge smile and squeezed her hand.

Today, miracles did happen.

FİFTY-THREE

JASMINE

JASMINE PULLED HER ARMS CLOSE to her torso, her whole body shivering. She tipped her head back and wheezed out a breath, staring at the dark skies that were beginning to lighten. The worst of the storm had passed, but the sea was still angry.

Another wave crashed over Jasmine, dousing her with icy water. The little boat groaned, but held. How much longer, she didn't know. She eyed the two rocks that pinned the boat in place. Thank the stars for the rocks. If it hadn't been for them, she was sure she'd have died hours prior.

It was still a possibility.

There was still so much distance between herself and the shore, not to mention it was littered with sharp rocks and coral. One wrong wave, and she'd be dashed to pieces against the stones. She had to do something. The labor pains were coming faster now, and she was already so exhausted.

Jasmine ran a shaking hand over the swell of her belly. "It's okay, little one," she said, her teeth chattering. "I will make sure you're all right."

The sea swelled and pulled back toward the open ocean. *That wasn't good.*

Jasmine glanced over her shoulder, her eyes widening as another huge wave rushed toward her.

Bloody hell.

She managed to curl in on herself as the wave crashed into her. The little boat cracked and splintered apart. Jasmine tumbled forward, her side scraping against the rock. Water rushed into her ears, and her hair caught on some coral and was torn from her scalp. She clawed at the water, and her head broke the surface. She sputtered and managed two breaths before another wave hit, once again shoving her beneath the water.

Something sharp sliced into her leg, and she cried out, water flooding her mouth. Jasmine kicked as hard as she could, her lungs desperate for air, and she managed to make it to the surface again. She gasped and tried to tread water. She didn't have much of a choice now. It was sink or swim.

Despite the fatigue saturating her limbs, she managed four strokes before her belly contracted again. She glanced to the left, just catching a fin as it sank beneath the waves, and she turned in that direction, while trying to breathe through the pain. Jasmine gritted her teeth and fought to stay as still as possible. The pain passed after a minute, but she didn't actively move from her spot. She just treaded water. Panic and fear held her in place. She didn't want to do anything to attract the leviathan's attention.

He already knows you're here. Just move slowly. You can't stay here.

She released a small whimper and kicked her legs. Exhaustion pressed down on her, and her limbs faltered. She made it only a few paces when the next contraction slammed into her. She grunted at the immense pain and crossed her legs. She lost all coordination and wrapped her arms around her belly, sinking beneath the surface. The agony seemed to go on forever.

Tiredly, she fought her way back to the fresh air, and she cried softly. The shore was too far away, and the closest rock looked impossible to climb.

She hissed when she felt the contractions coming again. A short scream flew from her parted lips as she tried to stay afloat, but she just didn't have the energy.

Jasmine began to sink again. She tipped her head back, trying to get as much air as possible, just as hands wrapped beneath her armpits. She let out a loud sob when the person maneuvered her so her back was against their chest, keeping her afloat. She moaned through the rest of the pain, hands fisting in her torn robe and nightgown. Her body sagged when it was over.

"That's it," crooned a deep, sensual female voice. There was only one group of people Jasmine knew with a voice like that. A Sirenidae. "You're doing amazing."

She leaned her cheek against the Sirenidae's chest and breathed in her amazing scent. "God, you smell good."

The woman chuckled. "I've been told that before."

Jasmine wheezed a laugh that turned into more sobs. "I can't do this."

"Yes, you can. You're so strong."

She didn't feel strong. Her eyelids lowered. "I'm so tired."

"I know, *ma fille*. Just take a little rest. I'll keep you and the babe safe."

Tears of gratitude rushed down Jasmine's cheeks. "I can't. The pains are too close."

"Just focus on your breathing," the Sirenidae crooned.

Jasmine nodded and tried to regulate her breathing. Her belly contracted again, and she squeezed her eyes shut. Her breath was completely robbed from her when the pain became so acute she thought she'd surely pass out. She opened her eyes and screamed when she caught sight of two dorsal fins that were too close.

"Peace," the Sirenidae said. "They are welcoming the child you bring into the world. The beasts are sensitive to such things and usually observe our births beneath the seas. It's an honor." She began to hum a soft melody that vibrated through Jasmine's shoulders.

It didn't feel very honoring, more like terrifying. But the agony was too intense for her to focus on the leviathans.

"That's it," the woman crooned. "You're so brave. Just breathe."

The pain receded but still crouched low in her abdomen. That could only mean one thing. Her eyes widened. "How close are we to the shore?"

"We've just entered the cove."

Jasmine gazed around, just realizing the waves had gentled to a soft lap against her wet skin. "The babe is going to drown," she cried.

"No. I've seen such things in the past. Giving birth is natural. The babe won't even realize she's parted from your womb."

"Except for the frigid water."

"Don't worry. There's a place just ahead."

Another pain hit Jasmine.

Then another.

And another.

She hardly noticed as the cove narrowed, and the water warmed significantly.

Jasmine shook, and she blinked dazedly around when her feet touched the sand beneath the water. She sighed, enjoying the brief moment of reprieve. "Thank you," she whispered as heat began to enter her limbs again. "The water is warm."

"A natural spring," the Sirenidae explained. She rotated Jasmine until she carried her like a bride. Jas blinked at the woman. She looked like the woman Sam had been kissing. She shook her head. Her luck couldn't be that bad.

She doubled over when the next wave of pain hit her. "I think it's time, and I don't know what I'm doing."

"You're doing great. Birth is natural. Your body knows what it's doing."

"But it's too soon," Jasmine cried, clinging to the woman.

"Everything will be okay." She settled Jasmine with her back against a log that had fallen at the edge of the water, then moved to kneel between Jasmine's floating legs. "When the next one comes, you push."

Jas nodded and bore down with a grunt.

"Wonderful," the Sirenidae crooned. "A few more like that and your babe will be here."

Another contraction and more pain, burning. Jasmine grabbed the log and squeezed it, her teeth gritted.

"The head is crowning. You're doing amazing, Jasmine. Just a little more."

Jasmine pushed and yelled, her voice echoing around them.

"The head is out. Just the shoulders."

The pain retreated and Jasmine sucked in ragged breaths. "I'm so tired."

"I know, *ma fille*. Your babe is almost here. Now push!"

Jas tipped her chin down and pushed with everything she had. One moment, she was in agony, and the next, there was relief. Her jaw dropped as the Sirenidae caught her babe.

"It's a girl!"

The woman lifted the infant from the water, rolled her onto her belly and thumped her on the back. The infant coughed up liquid and then released a piercing cry. Jasmine smiled, tears running down her cheeks as the Sirenidae handed the babe to her.

A daughter.

The infant nuzzled into her chest, and Jasmine pulled the cloth away so they were skin to skin. Her daughter was so tiny, petite rosebud lips puckered. All she could feel was love.

"You did it."

Jasmine tore her gaze from her daughter and held her other arm out to the Sirenidae. "Thank you so much."

The woman wiped tears from her own cheeks and then held her hand, moving closer. "She's beautiful."

Beautiful was too pale of a word.

"What will you name her?"

Jasmine stared at her daughter's closed eyes. "I don't know." Her brows furrowed. "What's your name?"

"Mer."

"Mer," Jas murmured. "That's pretty—a sea name. I think she needs a sea name, don't you?"

"I think a sea name would be fitting for your little warrior."

She smiled, brushing a finger across the infant's black hair. "I don't know any."

"What about Lana? It means calm as still waters," Mer whispered.

"Lana." She tested the word on her tongue. She liked it. "Is Lana your name?" she crooned to the baby. Her daughter sighed and cuddled closer. "I think she likes it."

Jasmine's own eyelids began to lower, and her body sagged. She was so tired. Mer wrapped an arm around her back and wedged herself between the log and Jasmine, so her long legs bracketed Jasmine's. Mer enfolded her arms around Jasmine and Lana.

"Rest for a little while. I'll watch over you."

That was the last thing Jasmine heard before her body gave out.

FIFTY-FOUR

MER

"MER."

She opened her eyes and turned toward the familiar voice.

Her grandfather stood waist-deep in the spring, his long silver hair hanging in wet ropes. She eyed him, trying to get a read on his mood. His magenta eyes so similar to her own, gave nothing away.

"My lord," she replied, overly respectful. It never hurt to be respectful, especially when one had committed treason.

"You went against my wishes," he said softly.

She swallowed around the lump in her throat. Even though his words were softly spoken, it felt like a slap. Growing up, he'd never raised his voice, but the disappointed tone he used seemed worse than physical punishment. She'd let him down. But even knowing that, Mer wouldn't go back. Going behind his back had been wrong, but so had his choice to leave the kingdoms at a disadvantage to the Scythians. Mer lifted her chin the smallest bit and refused to cower. Whatever punishment she received, she'd take it with her head held high.

Jasmine moaned and stirred in her arms but didn't wake. The poor thing was exhausted. Mer's heart beat a little faster when she thought about what could have happened to Sam's wife if she hadn't discovered Jasmine in time. The babe sighed and snuggled closer to Jasmine's chest, pulling her grandfather's attention. His expression softened, and he drew closer, water rippling around them.

"How was it?" he asked.

Mer smiled. "While the babe had a hard time coming, Jasmine fought. They both are worn out but healthy. Aren't they beautiful?"

Her grandfather gently drew a large, damp finger across the infant's downy little head of dark hair. "Children are a blessing."

She couldn't agree more. Mer gazed down at the pair with wonder. A new life was an absolute miracle. What Jasmine had accomplished was nothing short of extraordinary.

"Her name?"

"Lana," Mer whispered, resituating both babe and mother more comfortably in her arms.

"That's a good name," her grandfather murmured, his musical voice sweet in her ears. He pulled away and both fell into silence as the morning sun broke the patchy clouds. "You know I cannot let this go without punishment."

Mer's lips thinned, and she nodded.

"Many Sirenidae lost their lives. There must be justice for those souls." His heavy hand landed on her shoulder and squeezed. "I love you, but tough decisions will be made in the future. Ones that will hurt me as much as they will hurt you."

Had that statement come from anyone else, she wouldn't have believed them, but her grandfather loved her, and he meant what he said. Going against her grandfather's wishes would ultimately lead to her banishment from the sea—from her parents—from her people. Her heart squeezed painfully, but she knew she'd done the right thing.

"I'm sorry I hurt you." That much, she was very sorry for.

"I know, *ma fille*. As am I, as am I."

The resignation in his tone caused her eyes to burn. He was telling her goodbye. The next time they met, he'd be exiling her.

"This is the Spymaster's wife," she said softly, changing the subject. "I cannot leave her alone. Would you please let him know where we are? He's aboard the *Dauntless*."

"It will be done."

He leaned close and kissed her forehead. Mer closed her eyes, her tears trying to break free. This was their final moment before everything changed.

"I love you," she croaked.

He pulled away and smiled tenderly at her. "I love you far more than you could ever know." Then, he turned his back and disappeared silently into the water—ripples the only proof he'd ever been there.

Mer tipped her head back and peered up at the sky, just as soft morning light began to peek over the trees and cascade over the spring. Her heart hurt, but at least she knew she wouldn't be alone. While Lilja was gone, she still had her uncle, Sam, and... her gaze dropped down to Jasmine and Lana.

A family. Even if part of hers was gone.

Ream had died and Lana was here.

One life extinguished, one lit.

In that moment, she let herself cry for everything lost, and for everything gained. A wobbly smile touched her lips as tears coursed down her cheeks, mouth, and chin. No matter where she was, she'd find family.

FIFTY-FIVE

SAGE

SAM PULLED ON THE REINS. His horse slowed to a stop and he
swung his leg over his mount and landed on the ground with knees bent. He
briskly strode through the foliage, not taking his normal care to silence his
steps. All he cared about was getting to his wife.

His heart raced in his chest, and the air seemed to be thinner. After the
hellish night before, he'd only expected more bad news when the Sirenidae
king had appeared on his ship, morose and wet. When the king revealed the
news about Jasmine, it was almost impossible to believe. Sam hadn't given up
looking for her; he just hadn't expected the information of her whereabouts
to drop into his lap.

It had taken him ten seconds to board a rowboat and head toward shore. As
soon as his feet touched sand, he'd hit the ground running, grabbing the first
mount he came across. Technically, he was a thief, but he'd pay the family
handsomely and return the horse once he retrieved his wife.

And child.

Sam swallowed hard. The king hadn't revealed much other than Jasmine had
borne a child, and Mer was protecting her in the cove with the warm spring.

The babe had arrived early.

His anxiety ratcheted up and his strides lengthened. Was Jasmine all right?
Was the babe healthy? He'd seen when infants were born before their time.

They weren't always whole. His lips thinned. Even if the child wasn't what his world considered normal, he'd love the babe all the same.

The sound of water lapping at the shore reached his ears, as he pushed through the last vestiges of thick shrubbery and trees. Sunlight danced over the gently rippling water that kissed the white sandy edges. It was utter paradise. But that was not what stole his breath.

Mer sat waist-deep in the water, leaning against a log with her arms wrapped around Jasmine and the small bundle in her arms. Sam was rooted to the spot as he soaked in the sight of his sleeping wife. Her dark lashes rested against her cheeks, paler than normal. She was covered in bruises and scratches, but nothing serious-looking. His attention dropped to the infant nestled in her arms, cuddled against her bare chest, wrapped in Mer's sealskin.

"You can come closer," Mer's melodious voice whispered.

Sam jerked out of his stupor and yanked his boots and socks off before wading into the warm water. He was careful to move slowly so as not to create more ripples in the spring. Heat pressed at the back of his eyes when he caught sight of the tiny babe sleeping in his wife's arms. He'd never forget this moment. Ever.

"Come meet your daughter, Sam."

A daughter.

He sank to his knees, white sand mixing with the water around them. Sam reached out and hesitated only a moment before running one fingertip across the dark fuzzy hair that covered the infant's head. So soft.

A tantalizing scent caught his attention, but he ignored it the best he could. Just the Lure. "How did you find them?" Mer didn't answer. He pulled his attention from his family and studied Mer's profile. She gazed blankly ahead. "Mer?"

"I found her floundering in the waves with the Leviathan circling her." Although the words were softly spoken, they struck fear into his heart. "It was a lucky thing that I came upon her when I did."

His gaze dropped back to his daughter and wife. He had been so close to losing them, and he hadn't even known. "How did you know where to look?" he rasped. "Or did you come upon them in your patrol?"

"A Scythian survivor pleaded with me to find her. I knew it was Jasmine as soon as he spoke about her pregnancy."

While her words rang true, Sam couldn't help but feel like there was something she left out. "The warrior?"

"Probably being picked up by one of the patrols now."

His lip curled. Probably one of her abductors. "They will regret—" His growled words disturbed his daughter. The babe squirmed and released a small squall.

Jasmine roused and cuddled the infant closer, crooning softly, "It's okay, precious." Her stormy gaze wandered to his, and his heart began to race once again. Stars, she was stunning. "Are you really here?" Her voice was scratchy, like she'd screamed herself hoarse.

Sam's lips trembled as he smiled at her. "I am, Jas."

One tear coursed down her cheek as she stared at him with huge, tired eyes. Sam leaned forward and cupped her wet cheek. She sighed and pressed her face into his palm.

"I can't believe you're here," she cried, bottom lip wobbling. "You found me. You finally found me."

Sam swallowed the lump in his throat. "We made a deal, remember? We stick together."

"The twins?" she asked.

"Missing you, but healthy and safe."

More tears coursed down his wife's face faster than he could wipe them away. Jasmine adjusted his daughter in her arms, water rippling around them. The babe blinked her tiny eyes, revealing blue orbs just like her mum.

"She's stunning, love," Sam whispered in awe, and a lone tear escaped the corner of his eye as the babe's gaze latched onto his own. It was as if she knew who he was. Extraordinary. He gently ran his thumb over his daughter's tiny ear. She was so small and perfect.

"I know we hadn't settled on a name," Jasmine said softly. She glanced over her shoulder at Mer and then back to Sam. "But it seems fitting to give her a sea name because of how she was born. What do you think of Lana?"

"Lana," Sam whispered. "What does it mean?"

"Calm as still waters."

His daughter still hadn't looked away from him, placid as a lake. "I think it suits her." He touched her little fingers. "Hello, Lana. I'm your papa. I'm sorry I wasn't here to welcome you into the world, but I promise to be here every moment from now on."

"Sam," Mer said.

He forced himself to break his stare off with his daughter, and for the first time noticed how haggard and broken his friend looked. "What's wrong?"

"Nothing." Mer tried to smile, but it didn't fool him. "We need to get Jasmine and Lana back to the castle. She needs to see a proper healer. If you take Lana, I can carry Jas."

Jasmine held out the bundle, and he gingerly took Lana from her arms. She was even littler in his arms. Mer stood and helped Jasmine to her feet, water dripping down their bodies. His friend swept Jas into her arms, and Sam shook his head. He always forgot how strong the Sirenidae were.

"You have a cloak?" Mer asked, flowing toward the opposite shore.

"I do," he mumbled, preoccupied with taking slow, cautious steps so as not to jostle his daughter.

They moved back to the stolen horse, and Mer sat Jasmine gently on the ground before wrapping his cloak around his shivering wife. Jas looked one second from passing out. Mer held her hands out, and he reluctantly released his daughter into her care. He bent down and smiled at Jasmine, quickly stealing a kiss.

"You're amazing," he breathed as he lifted her onto the horse. She groaned. "Are you okay?"

Jasmine winced. "I have to be."

He frowned and wished he had a coach or something. Sam mounted behind her and gazed down at Mer, who was singing softly to Lana.

"Be good for your mum, *ma fille*. I'll see you soon." The Sirenidae carefully handed Lana up to Jasmine. His wife tucked Lana inside of the cloak, crooning softly at the fussing infant.

"Thank you," Sam murmured. The words were too plain for what he felt. If Mer hadn't found his wife, Jasmine and Lana wouldn't be here. "I owe you more than I can express. Whatever you need, if it is within my power, I will give it."

Mer nodded, her expression grave. "I may need a place to sleep in the future."

"Done," he said. "You will always have a place with us."

She smiled. "Goodbye."

Sam guided the horse around and set a gentle pace toward Sanee.

"Are we going home?" Jas rasped.

"Yes, we're going home."

Where they belonged. Together.

FĪFTY-SĪX

SAGE

BLAIR STOOD TO SAGE'S LEFT, and Tehl to her right.

It had taken only two days to secure the rest of the Scythian army.

Now, Blair's men brought three chained Scythian commanders before them and forced the warriors to their knees. She stared at their handsome faces, unaffected. Beauty often hid the ugliest qualities of a person.

From the corner of her eye, she caught sight of mud-caked boots. Sage forced herself not to look in his direction. The warlord's body was a garish sight after the rebels had gotten ahold of him.

Blair stepped forward. "Jacobi, Demdai, and Phenrir. Your warlord has fallen, and Scythia is now under the command of Aermia."

"You traitor," Phenrir spat. "I always said the way you treated your *gift* was unnatural. You would sacrifice your kingdom for a half-blood wife and her spawn?"

The commander didn't react to the taunt, even though Sage wanted to slap him across the face for such a remark. She glanced down the line to where Dor stood, her dragon a hulking, silent threat. Sage wouldn't be insulting a woman with a dragon if she was him. Illya was looking at Phenrir like he'd be a great snack.

She focused back on the Scythian commanders kneeling in the dark slush.

"Are we to be executed?" Jacobi asked mildly.

His tone surprised Sage. Almost every Scythian she'd met, who supported the warlord, wore an air of superiority. This man, however, did not. Interesting.

"This is not an execution," Blair said sternly. "We are not without mercy. Living under the warlord and his laws was not an easy life. That being said, you can fall into line or go to prison for the crimes you've committed against your people as well as the kingdoms of Aermia, Methia, Sirenidae, and Nagali."

It was still bizarre to hear the name Nagali. It boggled her mind that the warlord had been able to keep a remnant of the Nagali people hidden for hundreds of years. While she was thankful, it also broke her heart for what they must have suffered.

"While I appreciate your words, it's not you I would like to hear them from." Jacobi turned his coffee-colored gaze on Sage. "With the warlord dead, you are now our ruler. What are your orders?"

Sage blinked slowly. "I am married to the crown prince of Aermia."

Jacobi nodded. "That being said, the warlord declared you his consort, and in the event of his death or his inability to rule, leadership of our kingdom shifts to you."

That couldn't be true. She looked to Blair, who winced. Sage smoothed her expression as her mind scrambled.

"You expect me to bow down to the warlord's Aermian consort?" Demdai finally spoke up. "She's a foreigner. I could tolerate him tumbling her, but ruling our kingdom? She'll be killed before the week is over."

"Is that a threat?" Tehl murmured.

Demdai glared at Tehl. "Not a threat but a fact."

"Enough," Blair said softly. He held his hand out to Sage, his gaze steady, seemingly asking her to trust him. "Consort."

She prided herself on the fact that her expression didn't change and that her fingers didn't tremble when she took his hand. "Commander."

"Today, you are charged with the care of the Scythian people."

"Mark my words, the people will rebel. *I'll* rebel," Phenrir snarled.

Sage glared at the insolent warrior, putting on her best scary face. These men had only ever known fear and manipulation. Maybe it was the only thing they understood.

"You don't have much of a choice," she hissed. Sage pointed a finger at the warlord's body. "I'm sure death doesn't scare a big warrior like you." She smiled. "But what if your family lost all its wealth, and your sons were taken into Aermian captivity indefinitely?"

The man paled slightly even as he glared daggers at her. Not her best negotiation, but it got him in line.

"Your camp will be disbanded, and anyone hostile will be taken prisoner or killed." She straightened and stared at them. "This week, a treaty will be drafted, which I will sign, and then I will appoint a capable regent." Sage paused, making sure she had the attention of all three warriors. "If you think to take advantage of my generosity by not executing you on the spot, or you get it into your head to rebel or break the treaty, the power of the united kingdoms will invade Scythia, and you'll never recover. Do you understand me?"

"Yes, my lady," the men muttered.

She nodded and turned her back on them, barely able to stand. What had just happened?

"Long live the lady warlord!" shouted Jacobi.

Sage snarled. By the time she was done, there would be no warlords left.

FÍFTY-SEVEN

HAYJEN

HE COULDN'T TAKE HIS EYES off her for one moment.

Hayjen held her warm hand between his own, and tried to imprint every detail of her face into his mind. In the time since he believed her dead, his memory had distorted her face slightly. Nothing too serious, but enough to surprise him for such a short time.

Lilja sighed and opened her eyes, revealing the magenta orbs that had struck him speechless the first time he'd seen her. She smiled at him, her whole expression lighting up, robbing him of his breath. Tears gathered in the corners of his eyes, and her expression softened.

"Hey, handsome," she crooned. Lilja cupped his left cheek with her other hand, her own eyes filling with tears. "I missed you."

He slid from his stool, landing on his knees, and scooped her body against his, burying his face in her silver hair. "I thought you were gone," he choked out. His shoulders began to shake with silent sobs, his tears wetting her hair. Lilja stroked a hand through his hair, murmuring lyrical nonsense.

What had he done to get so lucky? They'd received a second chance. "Don't ever leave me again. I can't bear it."

"Never," she whispered. "Never again."

"Where you go, I go." He lifted his head, wiped his face with the back of his arm, and stared down into her beautiful face. "Promise me."

She studied him, her own face damp. "Where you go, I go. That's the way it's always been, yeah?"

"Always."

"Is it really over? Is he gone?" Lilja asked.

"He's gone," Hayjen said gruffly, not wanting to spare a moment of thought for the demon that had taken his wife from him.

She closed her eyes. "He can't hurt anyone else."

"That's right, love."

"We've been fighting so long to rid him from the world, it's almost surreal." Lilja sucked in a deep breath. "You're sure he's gone?"

A dark emotion that he didn't want to acknowledge slid through his chest at the remembrance of putting three arrows into the warlord's back. "He's gone. We left his body to rot on the battlefield. Soldiers have been guarding the corpse to make sure no one tries to give him a proper burial, that the monster doesn't deserve."

"May I enter?" a deep voice called from outside.

Hayjen turned toward the entrance as Blair pushed into the tent. His attention zeroed in on Lilja, and he grinned, love clear on his face. At one time, Hayjen had been jealous of Blair and Lilja's relationship. It took several years for him to understand the depth of their connection. While they loved each other deeply, they were never *in* love with each other. Their experiences had bonded them.

Blair moved deeper into the room, knelt by Hayjen's side, and pulled him into a brief hug before caressing Lilja's cheek. "How are you feeling, Lil?"

She grimaced. "Better and worse. I need to get to the sea."

Blair nodded and pulled his hand away. "I figured as much. Are you—"

"I'll survive." Lilja smiled at her oldest friend and then turned her attention back to Hayjen. "He'll take good care of me." She flicked a glance toward the entrance. "I met your daughter."

"So she told me," Blair said.

"A Dragon Song," Hayjen whispered. He couldn't believe it. Lil had spoken of such things as being real, but hearing about it and seeing it in person was another thing. "We owe her much."

"It is nothing among family," Blair murmured.

"What are you going to do?" Hayjen asked.

"Do?"

"She's the heir to the Nagali throne, is she not?"

Their oldest friend sighed, looking years older. He hung his head and rubbed his forehead. "She has her own path to forge. I have done my best to train and raise her, but I worry for her. Restoring Nagali will not happen in a day."

"Will you not go with her?" Lilja asked.

"Not immediately. Scythia still needs me, but the Nagali people need her."

Hayjen mulled that over. Dorcus would need guidance and protection. He slowly focused on Lilja, who was already staring at him. Words didn't need to be said. He could almost read her mind. She wanted to go with Dor—to protect Blair's daughter. She was ready for a new adventure, and… his gaze wandered to the entrance again. Sage was settled, more or less. His niece had come into her own and didn't *need* them anymore.

"We will accompany Dor to Nagali," he said.

Blair blinked slowly, relief coloring his expression. "It would put my mind at ease to know both of you were looking out for Dorcus and counseling her."

"We will care for her as if she were our own," Lilja rasped. "It would give me nothing but pleasure to get to know your daughter."

Their oldest friend nodded, his gaze suspiciously shiny, and pressed a quick kiss onto her forehead. "You were always a blessing."

"I love you," Lilja uttered.

"And I you."

The two friends shared a look of understanding before Blair clasped Hayjen on the shoulder one last time and stood. "There's to be a meeting of the kingdom rulers. I will pass this information on to them. Is there anything you wish for them to know?"

"Just that she's awake," Hayjen said. Sage would want to know.

"It will be done."

He hardly noticed as Blair disappeared, his whole focus on his wife. "Are you really ready to throw yourself into another scheme? Don't you need time to heal and relax?"

"Resting is for the old and decrepit. I'm not quite there yet. There's exploring to do."

"A wanderer's heart," Hayjen teased.

A glimmer of mischief entered her eyes. "A pirate's heart."

His smile grew. "Well, you did steal my heart…"

Lilja released a throaty chuckle. "Nineteen years of marriage and you're still a charmer."

"I aim to please," Hayjen whispered before brushing his lips against hers.

Life had never been so sweet.

FÍFTY-EÍGHT

TEHL

"WHAT THE BLOODY HELL?" TEHL growled, glaring at Blair. "A little notice would've been nice."

He flicked a glance toward his wife. Sage stood near the round war table, scowling at the map at the figurines that represent the armies and their leaders. She snatched up the leather bag from the surface, and one by one put the pieces away until all that was left was the warlord's leren piece. She stared at the feline figurine as the rest of their council filed in. Her jaw clenched, and she snatched the warlord's piece off the surface, then tossed all of them into the woodstove.

So, she wasn't as composed as she was pretending.

Sage moved back to his side, her expression placid. Other than their initial reunion, they hadn't spoken much in the last two days. He still had no clue what she'd experienced, or what went on in the Scythian camp. But she was too quiet. It was unlike her, and it bothered him. A lot.

"There wasn't much time to give you any warning," Blair responded. He ran a dirty hand over his haggard face. "In all honesty, it slipped my mind until Jacobi mentioned it. I'm sorry for not giving any warning."

The girl with onyx skin moved closer to Blair's side. Tehl scrutinized Dorcus. She looked nothing like her father Blair, except for the high cheekbones and the slope of her nose. He kept reminding himself not to stare. It was like he was in a fairy story. A Nagalian princess was standing in his tent—her dragon just outside. He glanced at the tent flap at the thought. He was still a little uneasy having the beast so close. It wasn't because Tehl was afraid, necessarily, but the way Illya had looked at him… it held true intelligence and understanding.

"She cannot rule in Scythia," Queen Osir said softly, both her sons flanking her. Zachael stood just to her right, nodding.

"I agree," Tehl said, glancing once more in his wife's direction.

"They would not accept me even if I was keen on ruling Scythia. I would be assassinated by the end of the week." Sage flashed a sharp smile, a bitter twist of her lips. "The Scythian commanders weren't wrong." She scanned the group of leaders in the tent, her gaze resting on Rafe and then finally focusing on Tehl. He jolted at the weary look in her emerald eyes. She was barely holding on by a thread. "The only choice we have is to appoint a regent in my stead," Sage continued. "Aermia still needs to have a presence in Scythia, but we cannot rule the kingdom."

"You're right," Tehl acknowledged. "If we tried such a thing, there would be rebellion and more bloodshed. That's the last thing we need." Too many lives had been lost already on both sides. Healing of their kingdoms needed to begin. As far as a regent…

Tehl examined the people in the room. Most of the occupants were monarchs of their own kingdoms or heirs. His mind turned to Gav. If his cousin was healthy, he would have suggested him, but Scythia was too dangerous for a wounded foreign man and his small daughter. There was only one true choice. He paused on the figure sitting in the corner.

Blaise.

She stared at the floor, idly picking at one of her nails, not meeting anyone's gaze.

"Blaise," he rumbled softly.

She lifted her head, her dark eyes meeting his. Blaise grimaced, shaking her head. "It won't work."

"You are the solution," he murmured.

Sage nodded and eyed the Scythian woman. "You know he's right."

Blaise shook her head. "I've not been trained to rule, and I have no *desire* to rule over Scythia." She rose to her feet and glanced around the room, holding her hands up. "This is a bad idea. What makes you think they will accept me? I've been working with their enemies. I'm a traitor."

"That's exactly why you should be ruling," Queen Osir cut in. "You fought for the rebels. You fought for the freedom of *all*. Those who supported the rebellion will welcome you with open arms."

"And those who supported the warlord?" Blaise asked.

"They will begrudgingly accept you because of the blood flowing through your veins," Rafe answered. "Scythia is in disarray. Even the staunch supporters of your uncle will not want civil war. You are the medium."

"Blair has more experience than I do," Blaise pointed out, crossing her arms. "He should be the one to rule."

The man in question shook his head. "I am the real traitor. They wouldn't tolerate me on the throne, any more than they would accept one of the warlord's former commanders. Then there is the matter of bloodline. I'm not royal. It has to be you." He dipped his chin. "But I will stand at your side and protect you with my life. You will not be alone."

Blaise ran a shaking hand through her hair, tears glossing her eyes. She blinked them away. "This would be so much easier if my mother was still here," she rasped.

Tehl's heart squeezed. He knew what it was like to lose a mother. "We will all support you in this. You're family."

The Scythian woman swallowed hard.

"You'll not go in alone," Sage murmured softly. "Not only will you have Blair, but we'll also send in someone to counsel you and keep an eye on your back."

Tehl hid his amusement as Rafe stilled, his attention completely focused on Sage. The Methian prince was a little too focused on the conversation—on Blaise. Intriguing.

His wife nodded to the group. "Aermia isn't the only one to have a stake in what happens in Scythia. I think it wise to have someone who isn't Aermian to stand by her side." Sage arched a brow as she held Rafe's gaze. The two seemed to share a private conversation. Her lip curled slightly. "I nominate Rafe."

He stood a little taller and turned to Blaise. Her face blanched but she quickly schooled her expression, not quickly enough that Rafe didn't catch her reaction. Poor bastard.

His expression didn't reveal anything as he respectfully dipped his chin in deference. "If that is what everyone wishes. I will happily go to Scythia."

Queen Osir smiled. "Go with my blessing."

"If no one opposes the appointment, let's move on," Tehl said. He stared at Blaise, giving her the option to request someone else. She didn't. "So, it's settled. Blaise will rule Scythia as regent, with Rafe as a mediator and counselor until a time when Scythia is stabilized." He turned toward the silent Dorcus. "You have many decisions ahead of you. Do you have a plan?"

The Nagali princess looked at her father and then focused on Tehl. "We refuse to go back to the way things were before."

Blaise limped from her corner and bowed deeply to Dor. "I know it will never be enough, but you have my most heartfelt apologies for the atrocities committed by the Scythian people." She straightened, holding her chin high. "I promise things will be different, and that you are no longer beholden to Scythia. You never should have been in the first place. Every culture should be treated with equality and respect."

"Something we agree upon," Dor said softly.

"Know Methi will support you in your ventures. Do you plan to stay in Scythia?" Queen Osir added.

"I'm not sure," Dorcus answered. "Many just desire their freedom. Scythia, however, is the only home they've ever known. While there will be many who will want to return to Nagali and begin restoring our homeland, I know there will be some who wish to stay behind as citizens."

"Consider it done," Blaise cut in. "Any who choose to stay in Scythia will be granted full citizenship."

"I don't want to be the bearer of bad will, but many of the warlord's supporters will not like this." Raziel held his hands up. "Slavery is a vile, evil practice that should never have been instituted. What I am saying is that there will be those who accuse you of crippling your kingdom. It is something you'll need to address."

"We will figure it out," Rafe cut in, side-eyeing his brother. "They may not like it, but it's the way it's going to be."

Blaise chuckled darkly and pushed the loose braids from her cheek. "For once, the high court will have to do their own work like the rest of the world has been doing for generations."

Rafe shared a shark-like smile with Blaise, and Tehl hid his satisfaction. While the two might irritate each other, they would be a force to be reckoned with when they united against a common enemy.

Tehl turned his attention back to Blair and Dorcus. "If you do not wish to stay in Scythia until your people are ready to make the expedition back into the Nagali homelands, you may find refuge in Aermia."

"Thank you," Dor said, her cocoa-colored eyes warm.

He glanced at her father, brows furrowing. Blair had said he would stay with Blaise in Scythia. If that was the case, who would go with his daughter to Nagali? "You would leave Dorcus without your guidance?"

"Tehl," Sage admonished.

He shrugged a shoulder. Better to be blunt than to have miscommunications.

"I appreciate your concern for my daughter. She will not be going on this journey alone. I've spoken with Hayjen and Lilja. They have agreed to accompany Dorcus and those who wish to go with her to Nagali." Blair smiled. "There's no one I trust more than those two with what is precious to me."

"She's awake?" Sage breathed.

Blair's smile widened. "Yes."

"Thank the stars," Sage whispered.

Tehl brushed his fingers against the back of her hand, and she flashed him a relieved smile.

"If that is all," Queen Osir said, "then I will fetch a scribe and have him draft a treaty to include all that was agreed upon today. You will be able to proof it tomorrow morning. For the time being, rest and enjoy your respite before the real work begins tomorrow—the cleanup."

FIFTY-NINE

SAGE

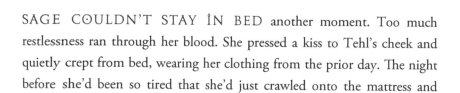

SAGE COULDN'T STAY IN BED another moment. Too much restlessness ran through her blood. She pressed a kiss to Tehl's cheek and quietly crept from bed, wearing her clothing from the prior day. The night before she'd been so tired that she'd just crawled onto the mattress and passed out.

She grabbed her cloak and daggers from the chair, and slipped her boots on before sneaking from the tent. Snow crunched beneath her boots and the cold air stung her lungs, but it felt good. For the first time in months, it was as if she could pull in a full breath. Domin sat in a chair to the left of the entrance. He arched a brow in silent question.

"I'm fine," she mumbled as she belted the daggers around her waist. "I couldn't sleep any longer. Did you get any rest?"

"I did. Thank you, my lady. My shift just began."

Her nerves settled some once her weapons were in place. Sage swept the cloak closer to her body to ward off the chill of the early morning. She peered toward the east, the sky just starting to lighten. A new day.

The tent flap whispered, and Sage turned her head toward the sound. Tehl silently stepped out, his inky hair mussed in a way that caused her heart to flutter. He pressed against her back and wrapped his cloak about the both of them, his chin resting on the top of her head. Her husband curled one arm around her waist, securing her against his body, and laced his fingers with hers, his callouses catching against her own. Sage sighed and settled into his warmth. He wasn't the kind of man she ever expected to marry. Blunt. Quiet. Awkward. But he also offered comfort and love in a gentle way she'd never experienced before. He made her feel cherished. Whole.

"You've been quiet," he rumbled, his voice deeper than normal.

She shrugged. "I'm tired."

He huffed a silent laugh against her hair. "Understatement of the year." A pause. "Are you almost ready for that break we spoke about?"

"Almost," she murmured, playing with his fingers. "There are a few more things I need to tie up."

"Oh?"

"I need to go back to the forest today." She turned in his arms and gazed up at him. "Would you come with me?"

He scanned her face, his deep-blue gaze fathomless. "Are you ready now?"

She'd been ready during the middle of the night, but that hadn't seemed prudent. Sage nodded.

Tehl gently tugged on her hand and began leading her through the quiet camp, Domin and three Elite quietly following behind them. They arrived at the corral, and she whistled softly. Peg parted from the herd and trotted to the fence, immediately pressing her nose to Sage's pocket.

"Hello, sweet girl," she crooned, running her hand down the mare's silky nose. "I don't have any apples." Peg nickered as Sage climbed over the fence. "I promise a bucketful of oats when we return."

She used the fence to mount the mare just as Tehl cantered to their side atop Wraith, his black warhorse. Their men circled them, and their group exited the corral and wound their way through the sleepy camp. A fiilee on the edge of camp stretched, flexing its wings. Skye—Raziel's flying feline.

"Raziel?" she called softly.

The Methian prince in question stood from the ground and approached, carrying a mug of steaming liquid that smelled nutty. "Going somewhere, Sage?"

"I need to return to the forest."

He scanned their entourage. "Expecting issues?"

"No, we just need some muscle. Would you be willing to come and possibly bring Rafe if you can find him?"

Raz chuckled. "My brother is always lurking about somewhere. I'm sure if you spin around three times and call his name, he'll appear."

Her lips twitched. Brothers. Stars, she missed hers. "We're heading out. I'm sure you'll catch up."

He downed the rest of his brew and nodded. "We'll be right behind you."

Sage urged Peg forward and directed her toward the huge dark lump that rested near the evergreen trees at the edge of camp. Her mare tossed her head and sidestepped as they approached Illya.

"It's okay," Sage soothed, not moving any closer. The dragon opened one silver eye that reflected the fire burning in the small camp set up near his side. Blair rose from the log he was sitting on and Dorcus followed. Apparently, no one was sleeping when they should have been.

Sage smiled. "If you're willing, we have a rescue mission this morning. Would you be willing to lend us your translation skills, Dorcus?"

Dor's brown eyes grew round. "You have knowledge of another dragon?"

Sage winced. "I do, but he's in bad shape. I promised him I would release him, but I want to make sure there are no casualties when I do so."

The Nagali heir turned to Illya, who clicked softly. "We'll do it," she said, turning back to them. "I'm new to this Dragon Song thing, so I'm not sure if I'll be able to understand him."

Her humility and humor caused Sage's smile to widen. She liked Dor. "We're meeting on the outskirts of the forest."

Tehl wheeled his mount toward the battlefield and they pressed on. Passing over the battlefield was a quiet affair. The ground seemed to be stained red. She had no doubt that the earth would be painted with blood—both ally and foe—for quite some time.

The sky lightened, and she smiled as she caught sight of Raziel and Skye soaring above, Illya following behind. Dragons and flying felines.

"It's seems unreal, doesn't it?" Tehl asked.

"I can hardly believe it."

"So, a dragon?

Sage glanced at him as they skirted the former Scythian camp and moved into the forest, forming a single line. It still was so bizarre to see snow meet forest.

Minutes passed before Peg grew frisky and tossed her head. They were close. "We leave the horses here," Sage commanded.

All dismounted, and Sage felt unsteady on her feet. Being surrounded by trees caused goosebumps to break out across her skin. The last time she had been here, she'd been running for her life. She placed a hand on the nearest tree and steadied herself.

Tehl's hand ran down her braid. "Do you need a moment?"

"I'm okay," she huffed. Sage shook off the memories and pointed in the direction they were going. "Straight ahead, gentlemen. Don't enter the ring," she warned as Raziel and Rafe caught up, leaving Skye in a small meadow. Three Elite took up the front while Rafe, Raz, and Domin brought up the rear.

"Blasted ferns," Raz grumbled. "Always in the way."

His blasé comment loosened some of the tightness in her chest. What they were doing was something good; happy, even. "Dorcus?" she asked.

"She's soaring through the sky with her dragon. Her father instructed her on where to meet us," Rafe supplied.

The trees thinned, the meadow just visible.

"What the bloody hell is this?" Raziel asked when they'd exited the tree line.

"Looks like an execution ring," Rafe growled.

Sage didn't look at either brother as she stared up at the dais and stone throne. She seethed inside. It needed to be torn down. *One thing at a time.* From the corner of her eye, she caught Tehl studying her. She could almost see the questions running through his mind, but he uttered none of them. And she was thankful for it.

Her stomach dropped as her gaze skittered over the post where William had been murdered. The pulse at her neck began hammering, and sweat beaded at the back of her neck. Sage pointed to the levers on the north and south sides with a shaking finger. "Three men on each side. Pull the lever toward the west and stay out of the ring."

Silently, the men followed her command and Tehl stepped closer to her right side when Dor and Illya soared above them before landing on the south side of the dais. The Nagali princess slid from her dragon's back and moved to flank Sage's left side.

"Pull the levers," Sage said.

The ground groaned before the taut chains began moving toward them and disappearing into the ground on either side of the circle. An emerald scaled snout was the first thing to exit the cave on the east side of the meadow. The dragon hissed, its hostile green eyes darting around the circle.

Dor sucked in a sharp breath when he was fully emerged. "His wings," she choked out. "So many scars."

Sage watched as the dragon homed in on Illya and seemed to swell in size. She took three steps forward, pulling the hostile dragon's attention. Gasps erupted around her, but she didn't pay them any mind as she locked eyes with the beast.

"That's far enough," Tehl murmured softly.

She paused and slowly unbuckled the daggers at her waist before tossing them behind her. The dragon was angry, but she could see his intelligence. Sage held her hands out and knelt, making herself as nonthreatening as possible.

"I made you a promise the last time I was here." She paused and then touched the scars at her throat. "He is gone. He can't hurt you any longer." The dragon's gem-like eyes glittered. "I plan to release you. Please don't eat anyone here. We're friends, not enemies."

Dorcus clicked, and the dragon hissed, his gaze focused on the girl. The dragon released a series of terrifying growls, hums, and clicks.

"What does he say?" Sage asked.

"She hates eating humans, so she won't bother with your men unless they attack her."

A female dragon. It would explain the size difference between the emerald dragon and the massive Illya.

Sage smiled. "It's a pleasure to meet such a fierce dragoness. I'm sure you wish to be gone from this place. Nagali is uninhabited; if you wish to be undisturbed, you should settle there. Although, you will be welcomed in any of the kingdoms."

The dragon clicked again, seeming more agitated.

"She won't leave this meadow. It's her territory," Dor translated. "Also, Illya says her wings are too damaged for travel."

Sympathy swamped Sage. It was a cruel thing to mutilate such a stunning creature. "If you'll allow it, we'll relieve you of the chains. We don't have the equipment to rid you of the collar today."

Dorcus, Illya, and the new dragon spoke in a way that reminded Sage of rough song. She eyed the chains. "Can Illya rip the chains from the ground?"

"I think so. He's much larger than the female."

The dragoness hissed.

"No disrespect intended," Dor murmured. "Give Illya room!"

Sage retreated to the edge of the forest, along with the men, when Illya scooped the chain into his mouth and crunched down. Her eyes widened as metal squealed and snapped like a child breaking a small stick.

"Wicked hell," Tehl breathed.

Illya lumbered to the other side of the meadow and repeated the action. The female dragon held her head high and reluctantly tipped her chin upward so that Illya could repeat the process on either side of the collar. As soon as the deed was done, she scuttled backward, and spines along the ridge of her back flared.

That wasn't good.

"It's okay," Dor whispered. "She's just defending her territory."

Illya held his ground but retreated eventually.

The emerald dragon scanned the tree line, and her eyes seemed to pin Sage in place. She clicked and then waited. Sage glanced at Dor, who blinked slowly.

"She says you're foolish and should leave."

For some reason, that made Sage chuckle. Staring down a dragon was on the tame end of foolish things she'd done in her lifetime.

"As you wish," she called and turned to leave.

The dragon clicked.

Dor quirked a smile, her brown eyes glittering. "Her name is Dia, and she says the little fool can visit sometime."

Sage smiled over her shoulder. A fool she was, because she'd be back.

"I'll see you soon, Dia."

SIXTY

MIRA

"I NEED TO BE THERE," Gav bit out.

Mira shook her head, dipping into her well of patience that she reserved for especially troublesome soldiers. "And I said no. You need to be on bedrest for weeks to come."

His purple eyes flashed in anger. "I cannot miss it."

"And you can't afford to lose your leg," she retorted. Mira inhaled sharply. What happened to biting her tongue and controlling her anger? In the three days since the fever had broken, Gavriel had been an utter nuisance. The charming prince was nowhere to be found, and in his place was an absolute troll. She placed her hands on her hips and met his glare. "If you attempt to leave this cot one more time, I'll tie you to it myself."

His lip curled. "Do you really want to threaten a prince?"

That got to her. Mira leaned down into his space, her loose hair pooling on his chest. "I don't see any princes in this room. Only a grouchy, defiant patient who is making my work harder." She straightened and calmly walked toward the exit. She'd already wasted fifteen minutes arguing with him, and she'd be damned if she humored him any longer.

"Don't let him get up," she mumbled to one of the soldiers standing by the tent flap. The soldier nodded once and glanced quickly over her shoulder. Mira scowled. "Don't you be looking at him. He's not in charge in this room.

My credentials trump his in this situation."

Mira tossed her head and sent Gav one last glare over her shoulder. "Don't cause any more issues or I'll sic Osir on you. She's not nearly as nice as me."

"Anyone would be better than you," he mumbled.

She gritted her teeth and kept her stride, even as she moved through the infirmary, grabbed her cloak, and exited. Her breath came a little easier as she inhaled the crisp, clean air. The midmorning sun cascaded light across the ground, the ice sparkling like a thousand diamonds. Beautiful.

Tucking her cloak closer around her body, she turned, lifted her eyes, and locked gazes with Raziel as he rounded a tent. His stride lengthened at the sight of her. Mira's heart fell. She did not want to have this conversation now.

She turned on her heel, and fled toward the glen she frequented for quiet time. Part of her hoped he wouldn't follow, but the practical part knew he would. At least no one else would learn of her shame.

"Why do I have the feeling that you're running from me, dearest?"

Mira gathered her misplaced anger and spun to face him, her plain cloak flaring around her boots. She flung her hands out and pointed a finger at him. "I am *not* your dearest." Her soul withered from the hateful words spilling from her lips.

Raz slowed to a stop and an awkward silence began to stretch between them. He scanned her face, his expression revealing nothing of his feelings. His brows furrowed, and then determination filled his face like he'd come to a decision. He stormed toward her, and Mira braced for what he would say. A squeak escaped her when he pulled her into a bear hug, her body held tightly against his.

"What is going on?" he asked softly.

Mira held herself stiffly. She began counting, and only made it to thirty before she gave in and sagged against him. After being berated by the creature that had inhabited Gav's body for the last three days, it was nice to be held. Her face pressed against his cloak, and she soaked in the comfort he was offering, even though she shouldn't be. It wasn't right for him to be holding her. They couldn't be anything to each other but friends.

Raz petted her wild hair, his fingers sinking into her tangled locks, pulling a few baby hairs at her nape. The pain helped her clarify a few things.

"I can't do this," she mumbled into his chest.

He tipped her head back and stared down at her face. "Can't do what?"

Heat filled her eyes, but she battled the tears back. "This." A rueful smile touched his mouth as she waved her hand between their chests. "It won't work."

"Give me one good reason."

"I'll give you five." She held up her first finger. "For one, I'm not royalty."

He shook his head, looking slightly amused. "I know you aren't, but it doesn't matter. We've already spoken about this. Who sired you doesn't matter in my culture, and—" another handsome smile "—I've asked around and discovered the laws in Aermia require someone who is of royal blood to marry someone of common blood. So, by your own laws and mine, we're just fine."

"You're not taking this seriously," she accused. That wiped the smile from his face.

"You're wrong. I take everything seriously when it comes to you." He gazed down at her soberly. "Tell me what is really wrong. You're skirting around the issue."

Mira pushed out of his arms and walked two steps away to gather her thoughts. Once again, she faced him, and her stomach rolled. Why couldn't he just let it go?

"I can't marry you," she whispered.

"You know what I think?" Raziel murmured. "I think you're looking for excuses not to be happy. You keep saying you *can't*, but I say that you *won't*." His lips pursed. "Did I read the signs wrong? Do you not like me?"

"Of course, I like you. You're funny, and you care for those around you with such compassion and love. You're an amazing friend."

"More than just a friend, surely?"

"More than a friend," she admitted, a sneaky tear leaking from her left eye. There was no way around it. She needed to lay it all out there for him. "I can't give you children," she said bluntly.

Raz stiffened and blinked once, slowly. "What do you mean?"

She huffed out a breath. "Exactly what I said. I cannot have children," she choked out. "So, no heirs for Methi if you were to take up with me. Your wife needs to be able to give you children, and I can't—" Her voice broke.

The Methian prince rushed forward and once again pulled her into his arms. His kindness unleashed the torrent of tears lurking just beneath the surface. Mira clung to him and cried, releasing all her pain and anguish. It had been some years since her father had told her the brutal truth, but it was only just now hitting her hard.

"I'm so sorry, dearest," he crooned, rocking her back and forth.

"An accident right when I was on the bloom of womanhood stole my future." She hiccupped. "Papa said I would never have children." Mira's chin trembled as she tipped her head back and forced herself to meet Raziel's gaze. "You understand why it's impossible for us to marry."

He dropped a small kiss onto the tip of her nose. "I don't need to have children of my own."

Her eyes flew wide, and she tried to pull away, but he didn't let her. "You don't know what you are saying."

"This war has robbed many children of mothers and fathers. Regardless of if I sire my own children, I plan to adopt those that I can care for. You needn't bear me children."

Mira was so shocked her mouth dropped open. She didn't know what to say. Having an heir was important to secure the throne. "Does your family have the same values?" she rasped.

"We will make our own family." He didn't answer her question, so a resounding *no*.

"I can't let you do that," she said finally.

"Will you rob me of my own choice?"

Mira, although saddened, smiled at the prince. He really was the best. "You don't know what you're saying. Right now, it may be easy to say you don't want your own children, but what about down the road? We've known each other a short period of time. I don't want you to regret having chosen me, and more importantly, I don't want you to lose out on having your own child. It's a miracle. I would not have you suffer loss." Mira cupped his whiskered cheek. "I care for you, and you've become one of my closest friends."

"More than that," he interrupted.

"You're right, and it's because I care for you that I'm saying no. Also, the selfish part of me couldn't handle it if you eventually looked upon me with disappointment. I want you to have every happiness in the world, Raz."

"This was not how I imagined today going." He huffed. "I had hoped to formally announce our engagement. You really won't consent to marry me?"

Stars, this is hard. "I won't." She pulled her hand away from his cheek and hugged him. "Aermia needs me. I've been trained my whole life to become the next Royal Healer." Her thoughts turned to her papa. "And I cannot leave my father."

Raziel pulled her closer and they stood quietly in the glen. "I feel like this is goodbye," he muttered. "I don't want it to be goodbye."

"We've been good friends this entire time," Mira said. "Do you think we could carry on as we did before?"

"Maybe not immediately, but I think we can be friends. The best of friends."

She smiled and squeezed him. "The best."

Things didn't always go according to plan, but sometimes even when they were bitter, they were sweet.

SIXTY-ONE

SAGE

————————⋙∘⟪⟫∘⋘————————

IT WAS DONE.

She stared at the signed document once again.

"We did it," Tehl murmured.

They did. It was surreal. The warlord was gone, the Scythian army subdued, and a real peace treaty signed between all the kingdoms.

She traced her finger over the Nagali princess's signature. A culture they all had thought lost was reborn like a phoenix. It was hardly believable.

"I have some other good news," her husband said, moving around the table to face her.

Sage smiled at him. "I don't know if I can bear anything else. I might just implode."

Tehl gave her a devastating smile. "You'll welcome this. Sam sent news. Jasmine has been found."

She stilled. *Finally.* "Is she okay? Where was she found? And the babe?"

He held up a hand. "She's in good health, and so is their daughter!"

"Daughter?" she whispered, her eyes growing damp. *A daughter.*

"You're an aunt, my love. Little Lana was born four days ago."

"Lana," Sage murmured before promptly bursting into noisy tears. Jasmine had been on her mind for days. She'd feared the worst. It killed her not to be able to search for her friend. Tehl pulled Sage from the chair and hugged her.

"I wasn't expecting this reaction."

She wiped at her face. "Women cry for all sorts of reasons."

"This is a happy cry?"

"Yeah," she croaked.

"That doesn't make any sense," Tehl mused. "The body is a bizarre machine."

Sage laughed. He wasn't wrong. She pulled away and wiped at her face. "I'm okay. Go get into the bath."

His eyes heated. "Get in with me?"

"Perhaps." She nodded toward their room of the tent. "I'll give you a few minutes."

Tehl dropped a kiss on her temple and moved through the tent flap to their room. She turned back to the bare table, holding a copy of the treaty. Once again, she gently ran her fingers over the document. In the beginning, she'd set out only to make a difference in Aermia. She'd never anticipated the far-reaching effects of her actions. While change had been brought about... a fist squeezed her lungs, making it harder to breathe... It had come with the cost of so much blood.

Never again would she see William smile or experience his gruff hugs.

Nor would Maeve's eyes twinkle with a well-thought-out plan, or train with her daughter.

Nor anyone hear one of Garreth's raunchy jokes that always inspired laughter.

No one had been left untouched by the war. Everyone was scarred in some way. Her fingers brushed the scars along her throat. Hers were more visible than others, but no person was alone in their pain and loss. *Stop being ashamed. Wear them like a badge of honor.*

She'd survived and come out stronger. They all had.

"Bloody hell!" Tehl yelled.

Sage sprang from her chair and launched into their room, daggers in hand, her reflexes taking over. She skidded to a stop at the foot of the bed and blinked, then shook her head to make sure she was seeing things clearly.

Tehl stood naked in the tub—a blade in one hand—his attention locked on the leren on the bed. A feline that *wasn't* Nali. *Damn cat.*

She slipped her weapons back into their sheaths and placed her hands on her hips in exasperation. "What are you doing, Nege?"

The feline in question growled and plopped his butt on their bed like he owned it.

"When did you acquire a new leren, love?" Tehl said through gritted teeth.

"I didn't, but I was wondering when he'd show up." Sage scowled at Nege and pointed to the rug. "Get off the bed."

He eyed her and then stretched out, gazing at her with challenge in his golden eyes. She narrowed her eyes at the beast. "Now you've done it. You are marking Nali's territory. Don't come to me whimpering when she boxes your ears."

Sage shot a glance at Tehl, and heat filled her cheeks. Bloody hell, he was a handsome man. Sage hid her smile when he didn't immediately sit back in the bath, his attention locked on the maneater. The man sure didn't like surprises. "You can sit down now."

He curled his lip and slowly sank into the water, covering all his glorious muscles. "Could have told me there was another one."

She hid her smile. "He's just a big ol' kitty cat," Sage said. "He won't hurt you, will ya, Nege?"

The feline huffed and turned his back on them, kneading the bedding with his front paws, the fibers catching on his claws. *Rotten bastard.*

"Some kitty cat," Tehl growled. "One that could eat me."

Sage moved around the end of the bed and stood beside the tub, smiling at Tehl, who still hadn't taken his gaze off the leren. "You just going to stare at him all day?"

"Don't trust him," her husband muttered.

Gently, she pulled his dagger from his wet hand and tossed it onto the chair before kicking off her boots. Tehl's attention focused on her, and she preened when his gaze sharpened as she untucked her shirt. Carefully, she leaned over the edge of the tub and kissed him gently. "Make room for me?"

"Always."

Sage grinned against his lips. "You love me?"

"Always."

She pulled back. "Is that the only word you know?"

Tehl's dark-blue eyes creased at the corners as he full-out smiled, leaving her breathless, her heart racing. "No."

"No?" she asked, wiggling out of her leather pants.

"I know two more. Come here."

"Your wish is my command, my lord."

"If only," he muttered.

Sage tossed her head back and laughed. Despite her heavy heart and the weight of loss, there was good in life. She planned on seizing it with both hands.

EPILOGUE

MER

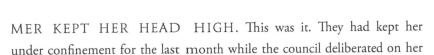

MER KEPT HER HEAD HIGH. This was it. They had kept her under confinement for the last month while the council deliberated on her punishment. She'd been informed that this was just a preliminary hearing.

"You're exiled for a duration of thirty days until the council comes to a unanimous agreement," the Sirenidae king announced. Gone was her loving grandfather, in his place the powerful sea monarch. "Then your ultimate punishment will be decided."

They hadn't outright banished her. Her brows rose in surprise. She hadn't expected that, or the emotion that came with the initial judgement. Since Ream's death and her imprisonment, Mer hadn't felt much of anything.

"You will leave our territory immediately until you are summoned to return from your final hearing. If you are caught in our kingdom, you will be put to death. Do you understand?"

"I do." Mer bowed low. It was done. For now.

Her gaze flicked to her parents once before she swam from the throne room, the judging gazes of the court scouring her skin. Guilt pricked her, but the ever-present numbness swallowed it up as she departed the city and swam toward Aermia.

Her mind wandered while she made the lonely trek from the deep sea. Mer blinked slowly when the sandy ground began to angle toward the surface. She glanced over her shoulder in the direction of her former home.

There was no going back.

Everything had changed.

SAGE

SAGE SOAKED IN THE WARMTH; the winter day uncommonly warm. A light breeze stirred her cloak as she walked along the beach with Jas, Mira, Isa, and the twins.

"That's far enough, Ethan!" Jasmine shouted.

"You too, Isa," Mira called from Sage's right.

Sage hid her smile when Ethan halted and then took one more step, the two other children looking from him to Jas. He'd been testing her boundaries since Lana's arrival.

Jasmine growled and shot Sage a glare. "Don't think that I can't see you smiling. Just wait until it's your turn."

"It will be a while before that happens."

Mira snorted. "If you say so. I'm not even married, and I have the responsibility of a parent." She paused, looking thoughtful. "Not that I don't enjoy spending time with Isa. I didn't mean it that way."

Sage placed a hand on her friend's arm. "No one could ever doubt how much you love that little girl."

"I do." Her lips pursed. "Even when she's pushing me... like now." Isa edged closer to the surf, her red curls waving in the wind. "I just can't keep her out of the water," Mira grumbled. She sped up, leaving Jas and Sage behind. "That is close enough, Isa Ramses! How many times have I told you that it is too cold to be in the water? You'll catch your death!"

Jasmine sniggered as Mira attempted to round up all the children but ended up following them to a tide pool. "Glad I'm not the only one with disobedient children."

"They're all good kids." Sage scrutinized the black bags beneath Jasmine's eyes. "How are you doing? Getting enough sleep?"

"Sleep?" Jas chuckled. "I don't know what sleep is anymore."

"You know I'd take the children whenever you need a break," Sage offered.

She loved the wee beasties. Being an aunt was the best.

"I know. Sam keeps telling me to pick a governess, but I don't like the idea of someone else raising my children."

Sage nodded. "I can understand that. Does Sam have Lana right now?"

"Yeah." A goofy smile touched Jasmine's mouth. "He passed out with Lana sleeping on his chest. They didn't even move when we left."

"He loves that baby," Sage remarked, scanning the sand for any shells to add to her collection. She'd never seen a man dote on his children as much as Sam did. Gone was the rake and seducer. Well... she wouldn't go that far. Sam would always be Sam; mischief maker, lover of women, Spymaster. Speaking of which, Sage needed to talk to him about their partnership. Now that she'd returned to the castle and war was no longer on the horizon, it was time she stepped up her involvement with his spies. She'd never wanted to be a soldier. Spymistress suited her much better.

"Mer!" Jade screeched. The little girl raced to meet the Sirenidae. Mer rushed from the waves and dropped to her knees in the wet sand, catching Jade in a hug.

"She's beautiful," Jas murmured.

Something in her friend's tone pulled Sage's attention back to Jasmine. She looked defeated. "What's going on?"

Jas shrugged and pasted on a fake smile. "Nothing. Let's go say hello."

What the bloody hell?

JASMINE

SHE PLOWED THROUGH THE SAND toward the Sirenidae, determined to be civil, despite her heart feeling like it was going to break into a million pieces at the sight of her. Over the past month, Sam had been so attentive and loving, but that didn't mean he was in love with her. Her husband loved all women, and she couldn't get the image of him and Mer wrapped up in each other from her mind. Every time he disappeared, Jas wondered if he was with her.

The hardest part was that Jas couldn't find it in herself to hate the woman. She was stunning, kind, and funny, and Jasmine owed Mer her life as well as Lana's. It was time to say thank you. She hadn't seen Mer since Lana's birth.

Jasmine steeled herself and strode right up to Mer as she put Jade down. Jas threw her arms around the Sirenidae and hugged her tight. "Thank you so much for what you've done. There aren't words sufficient enough to express how thankful I am." She pulled in a deep breath to continue and frowned when the most delicious scent she'd ever smelled washed over her. "What *is* that?" Jas pressed her nose against Mer's shoulder and inhaled, heat blistering her cheeks. What in the bloody hell was she doing? "I'm so sorry," she muttered, but she sniffed the Sirenidae again. She couldn't help it.

Mer chuckled and gently pulled back, holding Jasmine at arm's length. Her magenta eyes twinkled. "It's just the Lure."

Jasmine's brows furrowed. "The Lure?" Stars above, her mouth was watering. It was like chocolate, pears, and something exotic that she couldn't put her finger on. "I could just lick you," she blurted. Mortification slammed into her as Sage sniggered behind her.

Mer smiled. "The Lure. When our skin is in contact with seawater, we release a pheromone of sorts. It's something all Sirenidae have; a protection, if you will."

"Pheromones?" Her jaw dropped.

"Don't feel bad. You're not the first or the last to invade my personal space. In fact, Sam has accosted me a few times, though he's stronger than most to resist the Lure." Mer's smile widened. "Although, I'd welcome a hug from you anytime."

Jasmine stilled, and she bit her bottom lip to keep it from trembling. Her eyes grew glassy. "You... and Sam... you're not?"

Sage's laughter cut off abruptly.

"No!" Mer said fervently.

Tears spilled from Jasmine's eyes. All this time, she'd thought he'd been...

"I would never, *never* do that! I love Sam but he's like my brother, and you, family by extension." Mer yanked her into a hug, her lovely scent curling around Jas once more. "He loves you, only you."

"I'm such an idiot," Jasmine moaned.

"Maybe you should go take a nap, too..." Sage murmured. Jas pulled away and glanced at her friend. Sage arched a brow and jerked her head toward the castle. "I'll keep the wee ones. Their uncle wanted time with them anyway."

"You're a lifesaver." Jas jogged to Ethan and Jade, kissing them both on the top of their heads. "Be good for your auntie. I'll see you a little later."

"Speaking of time," Mira said softly, "I need to get back to the infirmary." She held Isa's hand. "You ready to go, little lady?"

"I wanna stay with Jade," Isa whined.

"I can take her, too," Sage offered.

Jas didn't hear anything else as she practically sprinted for the palace. All she could think of was getting to Sam.

They were still in the same position as she'd left them.

Jasmine closed the door softly and padded across the luxurious rug, then skirted around the massive bed. She unclasped her cloak, tossing it on the striped chair in the corner before kicking off her boots. Carefully, she climbed onto the bed and lay beside Sam, her cheek pillowed on her hands as she stared at his profile.

"Are you really going to stare at me?" he whispered, not opening his eyes.

Jas rolled her eyes. The man was impossible to sneak up on. "Did you get some sleep?"

"A bit." He turned his head and opened his gorgeous blue eyes, a sleepy smile on his face. "Did you have a nice time?"

"The best," she murmured, and her eyes dropped to his lips, then shifted back to his eyes.

The sleepy look in his gaze disappeared and something hot filled them, causing her to shiver. Her knees weakened, and Jas was thankful she wasn't standing. He was too attractive for his own good. She licked her lips, and he followed the movement. A thrill ran through her and she shifted closer, so they were practically sharing the same breath.

"I discovered something," she mumbled.

"Oh, yeah?" he asked, brushing his nose against hers.

"I love you, and I have for quite some time."

Sam blinked, and a blinding smile lit up his face. "Finally."

"Excuse me?" That was not the reaction she was expecting.

"Just been waiting on you, sweetheart." Sam adjusted Lana on his chest, making sure the blanket covered the sleeping infant before focusing back on Jasmine. "Didn't want to push."

"What are you saying?" Her heart pounded in her chest.

"That I've loved you for a while. I was just waiting for you to catch up."

This man. Jasmine closed the distance, her lips crashing against his. Sam's right hand wrapped around the back of her neck and adjusted the angle of her head. He kissed her with gentle bites and nips, as if he wanted to savor her mouth. Jas pressed herself against his side as he devoured her.

Lana mewled, and they both froze.

Jasmine opened her eyes slowly, her breath as ragged as Sam's. He smiled and released her neck, rubbing a gentle hand down their daughter's back. "Duty calls. I'll have to ravish you later."

She grinned. "Maybe *I'll* ravish *you*."

Sam smirked. "Promise?"

SAGE

"HELP ME!" TEHL CALLED. "I'M being attacked!"

Sage grinned as Ethan, Jade, and Isa climbed all over Tehl.

"One more time!" Ethan cried.

Tehl groaned but smiled and hauled himself to his hands and knees again. "Once more, and then this horsey is going to the stable."

The three children crawled onto his back as he did his best impression of a wild horse. Mira leaned over and bumped her shoulder against Sage's, smiling at the silliness. "Thanks for keeping Isa. I didn't want her to have to spend another afternoon in the infirmary."

"How is he doing?" Sage asked.

Mira's nose wrinkled. "Still being a stubborn ass."

"Still giving you grief, huh?"

"Some days, I swear he hates me." Mira's jaw clenched and she looked away. "I know it's part of the process. The pain and loss he is dealing with is extreme. It's just... difficult when it's someone you know."

Sage pulled her friend into a side hug as Tehl bucked the children off his back and tickled them. "I'm so sorry. Even if he's not appreciative now, he will be. You saved his life and his leg."

"For now he just thinks I'm the witch hellbent on making him suffer." Mira squeezed Sage's back. "But if it means him walking and riding again with his daughter, I'll play that role." She pulled away and clapped her hands, moving for the entrance. "Okay, beasties. It is time for dinner. You hungry?" Mira opened the door. "Mer is here."

"Yay!" they chorused.

Ethan popped to his feet first, followed by Isa, and then Jade. All three children ran for the exit of the study. Jade switched directions last minute. She quickly hugged Tehl and then Sage.

"I'll see you tomorrow." Sage ruffled her niece's hair and then gestured to the books lining the walls. "We'll read one of your favorite stories."

"'Kay!"

Jade disappeared out the door, the children's happy chirps fading as they moved away.

Tehl groaned as he stood, rubbing his knees. "I'm getting too old for that."

Sage rolled her eyes. "If your father can do it, you can do it too."

"I heard from Raziel," he said conversationally as he began to stalk her. Sage quickly maneuvered herself, so the desk was between them.

"Oh?"

"Methi has been in contact with the Sirenidae."

"Interesting." She moved around the desk as he slowly took another prowling pace. "Blaise wrote to me. She wants Rafe gone already."

"Knew that was going to happen. They'll work it out."

"How do you know?" she asked, watching her husband like a hawk. It was the quiet ones you had to look out for.

"We did." Two little words that meant everything. "If we could work it out and be incredibly happy, then they can too."

Warmth unfurled in her chest. "Such sweet words. I still won't go easy on you."

"Do you really think you can escape me?" he asked, a challenging glint in his gaze.

She smirked. "Catch me if you can!"

She feinted to her left, then darted to the right and was out the door. Tehl cursed, and she released a peal of laughter, putting on a burst of speed, rounding a corner to her left. That was where their strengths lay. He could catch her on a straight path, but she was nimbler when it came to obstacles. Sage took the servants' stairs and arrived at their room. No sign of Tehl.

Sage slipped into their chambers and scanned the room. There weren't many places to hide. She heard running footsteps, then ran around the bed and dove underneath it. Her heart raced, and she covered her mouth with her hand to hide her breathing. The door slammed open, and Tehl strode inside. Her heart skipped a beat when he closed the door and locked it.

No escape now. Not that she wanted to.

She shivered and watched as he checked the bathing room and then the closet. His booted feet paused at the end of the bed. She held completely still. A smile played about her mouth when he moved onto the balcony. He hadn't found her yet.

Suddenly, his hands closed around her ankles and yanked her from beneath the bed. Sage stared up at him with shock. She didn't even hear him move.

"Found you," he murmured, sapphire gaze glimmering.

She grinned. She loved Tehl's playful side. Not many got to see it. "What do you claim as your prize?" she asked breathlessly.

He hauled her into his arms and stood, as she wrapped her legs around his waist. "Don't need anything," he said simply. "I have everything I need in my arms."

Sweet man. Sage playfully narrowed her eyes at him. "You, good sir, are a liar. You said you weren't good with words."

Tehl tugged the collar of her shirt aside so he could kiss the curve of her shoulder. "Telling the truth is easy," he murmured against her skin. "What isn't is getting these leathers off you."

She tossed her head back and laughed. Life wasn't easy. It was gritty, dark, and sometimes painful. But sometimes, it offered priceless gems; like a partner who woke you from nightmares and soothed you back to sleep, a friend who sacrificed herself to keep you safe, or a future you weren't sure you deserved.

Sage kissed both of Tehl's cheeks. Despite everything, she counted herself lucky.

"You love me?" he asked, sitting her on their bed.

"Always."

THE END

COMING 2021

———◦⟫⟨◦———

THE AERMIAN FEUDS:
BANISHED QUEEN

ABOUT THE AUTHOR

Thank you for reading *Reign of Blood and Poison*. I hope you enjoyed it!

If you'd like to know more about me, my books, or to connect with me online, you can visit my webpage WWW.FROSTKAY.NET or join my facebook group FROST FIENDS!

From bookworm to bookworm: reviews are important. Reviews can help readers find books, and I am grateful for all honest reviews. Thank you for taking the time to let others know what you've read, and what you thought. Just remember, they don't have to be long or epic, just honest.